Praise for *The Magic of Recluce:*

"An intriguing fantasy in a fascinating world"

Robert Jordan

"Fascinating! A big, exciting novel of the battle between good and evil, and the path between"

Gordon R. Dickson

"Extremely interesting ... unique ... a refreshing use of the traditional fantasy elements"

Andre Norton

"In this coming-of-age heroic fantasy, Modesitt has created an exceptionally vivid secondary world, so concretely visualized as to give the impression that Modesitt must himself have dwelt there"

L. Sprague de Camp

"Adorned with a finely drawn, down-to-earth yet dangerous world, and an intriguingly ambiguous view of how good and evil interact"

Carole Nelson Douglas

THE MAGIC ENGINEER

L. E. MODESITT, Jr.

ORBIT

An *Orbit* Book

First published in the United States by Tor Books in 1994
First published in Great Britain by Orbit in 1995

A CIP catalogue record for this book
is available from the British Library.

ISBN 1 85723 272 0

Printed and bound in Great Britain by
Clays Ltd, St Ives plc

Orbit
A Division of
Little, Brown and Company (UK)
Brettenham House
Lancaster Place
London WC2E 7EN

To and for

Carol Ann

I.

SEEKER

I

THE BOY LOOKS at the iron, cherry-red in the tongs.

The wiry man—small and compact, unlike the traditional smith—holds the tongs higher as he glances toward the boy. "That's hot enough to bind storms and wizards, boy. Strong enough to hold giants, just like Nylan bound the demons of light for Ryba..." Sweat pours from his forehead despite the breezes channeled through the smithy by the very nature of the building. "Iron... iron runs through the center of Recluce. That's what makes Recluce a refuge of order."

"That story about Nylan isn't true. The demons of light were gone by then," states the child in a clear, but low voice. His narrow solemn face remains unsmiling. "And there aren't any giants."

"So there aren't," agrees the smith. "If'n there were, though, iron's the stuff to hold 'em." He returns to his work. "And black iron—that'll hold the worst of the White Wizards. Been true since the time of Nylan."

"The strongest of the White Wizards? They weren't as strong as the founder."

"No," says the smith. "But that was back then. They're a-breedin' new demons in Fairhaven these days. You wait and see." He lifts the hammer. "Then the Black Brothers'll need black steel... even if I need an order-master to help me forge it..."

Clung... clung. The hammer falls upon the metal that the tongs have positioned on the anvil, and the ringing impacts drown out the last of his words.

The solemn-faced boy, his hair redder than the cooling metal, nods, frowns.

"Dorrin, I'm done. Where are you?" A girl's voice, strong and firm, perhaps even a shout outside the smithy, barely penetrates between the hammer blows rippling through the heat and faint mist of worked metal.

"Good day, ser," says the redhead politely, before dashing from the smithy into the sunlight.

... clung ...

The smith shakes his head, but his hands are sure upon the hammer and the metal.

II

THE RED-HEADED YOUTH leafs through the pages of the heavy book, his eyes flicking from line to line, from page to page, oblivious to the scrutiny from beyond the archway.

"What are you reading?"

"Nothing." His thoughts burn at the evasion. "Just one of the natural philosophies," he adds quickly.

"It wouldn't be the one on mechanical devices, would it?" asks the tall man.

"Yes, father," Dorrin responds with a sigh, waiting for the lecture.

Instead, his father responds with a deep breath. "Put it back on the shelf. Let's get on with your studies."

As he reshelves the heavy book and turns toward the tall, thin man, Dorrin asks, "Why don't we build some of the machines in the books?"

"Such as?" The tall man in black steps around his son and proceeds toward the covered porch beyond the library.

Dorrin turns and follows. "What about the heated water engine?"

"Heated water is steam." The Black wizard shakes his head. "What would happen if chaos energy were loosed in the cold water?" The wizard sits down on the high stool with the short back.

"It wouldn't work. But—"

"That's enough, Dorrin. There are reasons why we don't use those machines. Some can be easily disrupted by chaos. Some actually require the constant attention of a chaos wizard, and you can understand why that's not practical here on Recluce, I trust?"

Dorrin nods quietly, as he sits on the backless stool across from his father. He has heard the lecture before.

"We work with nature, Dorrin, not against it. That is the basis of order, and the foundation of Recluce." The wizard pauses. "Now, tell me what the winds are like off Land's End."

Dorrin closes his eyes and concentrates for a time. Finally, he speaks. "They're light, like a cold mist seeping from the north."

"What about the higher winds, the ones that direct the weather?"

Dorrin closes his eyes again.

"You should have felt them all. You have to be able to feel the air, Dorrin, feel it at all levels, not just the low easy parts," explains the tall man in black. He looks from the sky above the Eastern Ocean back to the red-headed youngster.

"What good is feeling something if you can't do anything with it?" The boy's voice is both solemn and curious.

"Just knowing what the air and the weather are doing is important." Despite his tall, thin build, the man's voice is resonant and authoritative. "I have told you before. The farmers and the sailors need to know."

"Yes, ser," acknowledges the redhead. "But I can't

help the plants, and I cannot even call the slightest of breezes."

"I'm sure that will come, Dorrin. In time, and with more work." The man in black sighs softly, turning his eyes from the black stone railing to the other covered porch where a shaded table set for four awaits. "Think about it."

"I have thought about it, father. I would rather be a smith or a woodworker. They make real things. Even a healer helps people. You can see what happens. I don't want to spend my life watching things. I want to do things and to create things."

"Sometimes, watching things saves many lives. Remember the big storm last year . . ."

"Father . . .? The legends say that Creslin could direct the storms. Why can't—"

"We've talked about that before, Dorrin. If we direct the storms, it will change the weather all over the world, and Recluce could become a desert once again. Even more people would die. When the Founders changed the world, thousands upon thousands died, and they almost died as well. Now, it would be worse. Much worse. Even if a Black as great as Creslin appeared, and that is not likely. Not with the Balance."

"But why?"

"I told you why. Because there are more people. Because everything relates to everything else. And because there is more order in the world today."

Dorrin looks at his father's earnest face, purses his lips, and falls silent.

"I'm going to help your mother with dinner. Do you know where Kyl is?"

"Down on the beach."

"Would you get him, please?"

"Yes, ser." Dorrin inclines his head and stands. As he crosses the close-grown lawn, his steps are deliberate, carrying him along the knife-edged stone walk with the precision that characterizes his speech and dress.

After a last look at his son, the wizard turns to wend his way through the library and toward the kitchen.

III

"UNTIL YOU CAN prove you are the man with the white sword—that's how long before you could count on being the High Wizard, Jeslek."

"I suppose I would have to raise mountains along the Analerian highlands? Is that what you're saying, Sterol?"

"It wouldn't hurt," quips the man in white with the amulet around his neck.

"It could be done, you know. Especially with all the increased order created over the past generations by Recluce." The sun in Jeslek's eyes bathes the room.

"The day you do that, I'll hand you the amulet." Sterol laughs, and the sound is colder than the wind that swirls across the winter skies above Fairhaven.

"I mean it. It's not a question of pure force, you know. It's a question of releasing order bounds deep within the earth."

"There is one condition, however."

"Oh?"

"You must preserve the great road, *and* stand amidst your mountains as you raise them."

Jeslek chuckles. "Getting more cautious, I see."

"Merely prudent. One would not wish a High Wizard who could not control the chaos he released. That was the example of Jenred."

"Spare me that lecture."

"Of course. You young ones do not need the ancient

tales and parables because they do not apply in a changing world."

Jeslek frowns, but bows. "By your leave?"

"Of course, dear Jeslek. Do let me know when you plan to raise mountains."

"I certainly will. I would not wish you to miss anything."

IV

"DAMN IT, DORRIN!" The smith takes the short length of metal, already bearing a blackish sheen, even while it retains a straw brown color, and uses the tongs to set it on the brick hearth beside the anvil.

The youth flushes, the red from the forge combining with the red of chagrin climbing up from his neck. "I'm sorry, Hegl."

"Bein' sorry don't count a whole lot. Now, I got a chunk of black-ordered steel that's useless. Don't fit nothing, and nothing but a wizard's hearth gets hot enough to melt that. Darkness, you dump so much order in things, Nylan himself couldn't have forged it." Hegl snorts. "Not much call for black steel, anyway, but you don't order it until it's finished. What were you thinking of?"

"How it would look when you were done."

The smith shakes his head. "Go on. Let me finish. I'll send Kadara for you when it's time."

Dorrin swallows and turns, walking toward the open double doors designed to funnel the cool air through the smithy. Behind him, the smith extracts another rod of iron from the bin and lifts it toward the furnace.

The redhead holds his narrow lips so tightly they almost turn white. He has persuaded his father to let him spend time with Hegl, and if Hegl will not have him . . .

He steps through the open doors and out toward the washstones, where he pauses and splashes his face with the cool water, letting it carry away the heat of the smithy and the embarrassment. After pumping a drink from the spout, he leans toward the garden fed by the runoff from the washstones. Neatly edged in fitted gray stone, the different colored leaves of the herbs, and the few purple-flowered brinn plants, have formed almost mathematically precise rectangles.

Dorrin lets his senses touch the herbs, feeling the beginning of root rot in the winterspice, always a problem, according to his mother, because Recluce was far warmer than the climes of Nordla. With the practice borne of training, his senses enfold the winterspice, adding the strength the bluish-green-leaved spice needs to resist the dark fungal growths.

Out of habit, he checks the others, even the rosemary in the drier upper stone garden. With a shake of his head that displaces not a strand of his tight-curled and wiry red hair, he straightens.

"I wondered why my spices have grown so true this year." A gray-haired and stocky woman stands by the washstones.

"Your pardon," offers Dorrin.

"My gain, you mean, if you have even a fraction of the skill of your mother." She smiles. "Why are you out here?"

"Wandering thoughts," confesses the youth. "I thought about the wrong thing and turned an unfinished ingot into black steel. Hegl was less than pleased."

"He would not be," affirms the smith's wife. "But he will find some use for it, if only to demonstrate the strength of his work."

Dorrin shakes his head.

"Kadara will not be back from the Temple until later . . . she has afternoon classes."

"I know. I'm going home until Hegl needs me." The red-haired youth turns and walks down the flagged path toward the stone paved street.

Behind him, the smith's wife shakes her head for an instant before looking at the herb garden. She smiles as she studies the plants.

Dorrin's steps carry him past two of the stone-walled and split-stone shingled homes of Extina before he turns and walks up the stone drive slightly wider than the drives of the neighboring dwellings. A set of prints in the faint dust that has settled on the short wiry grass indicates where his mother's light steps have trod as she has inspected her own garden and trees.

V

THE MAN IN black looks up, preoccupied, almost as if he does not see the youth on the covered terrace as he walks slowly up the stone walk.

Looking out beyond his father, Dorrin can see the Black Holding, where the Council on which his father serves meets. No one has lived there in the three centuries since the deaths of the Founders. Slightly to the left of the Black Holding begins the High Road, which stretches to the southeastern tip of Recluce. Much of the southern part of the isle remains forested and uninhabited, except for the few crafthalls and the rich Feyn River plains, where most of the isle's grains are grown.

As his eyes flick back to the black buildings on the highest point of the cliffs, Dorrin frowns, absently wondering how true the tales are about Creslin and

Megaera. How could they have died at the same exact instant—just as the sun rose? Or is that just another bit of superstition he is supposed to swallow? At least his models do not rely on belief. He frowns. Or do they?

"Dorrin . . ." calls the thin-faced man. "We need to talk. Get your brother. The kitchen is fine."

"Yes, ser." He turns and walks down the rear steps from the terrace. Kyl is weeding his own private herb garden, as a result of their mother's threat to withhold sweets until both youths' gardens are presentable and orderly. Dorrin smiles. The order of Dorrin's garden has never been a problem. On the other hand, Kyl—his dark-haired younger brother—prefers fishing or crabbing or just staring at the Eastern Ocean to any sort of gardening.

The stocky boy is not weeding. Instead, he sits disconsolately beside a small pile of wilted weeds. "I hate gardening. Why can't I go off with Brice, like I wanted?"

"I suppose," begins Dorrin, kneeling down beside Kyl and immediately removing small unwanted sprouts as he talks, "because father is a black wizard of the air and mother is a healer. If they were fisherfolk, like Brice's parents, then they wouldn't want us to be wizards or healers . . ."

"I hate gardening."

Dorrin continues to weed, his hands quick and precise among the plants. As he weeds, his fingers stroke the herbs, infusing them with order. "I know."

"You don't like learning about the air, do you?"

Dorrin shrugs. "I don't mind learning anything. I like to know about things. I want to make things—not like Hegl, but machines that do things and help people. I'll never shift the winds or control the storms."

"Father can only do little things with the winds. He said so himself."

Dorrin shakes his head. "He only does little things, because he fears the effect on the Balance. What good is it to have a power you can't use? I'd rather do something useful."

"Fishing is useful," Kyl observes. His eyes stray to Dorrin's hands. "You make weeding look so easy."

Dorrin shakes dirt off his fingers and stands, brushing off his gray trousers before straightening up. "Father sent me after you. He has some news."

"About what?"

Dorrin shrugs again before he turns back toward the house. "I don't think it's good. He was walking slowly and thinking about something."

"Like the time when you ruined Hegl's iron?"

Dorrin flushes, but does not turn to let his younger brother see the reaction. "Come on."

"I didn't mean that . . ."

Dorrin keeps walking.

" . . . and thanks for the help with the weeding."

"That's all right."

The weather wizard stands by the kitchen table that seats but four. Both youths incline their heads slightly as they step into the room from the covered porch where they all dine together in weather better than the raw overcast outside. Their mother is sitting in the chair by the window.

"Sit down," suggests their father.

They sit, one on each side of Rebekah. Sitting on the remaining chair, the tall wizard clears his throat.

" . . . not another lecture . . ." mumbles Kyl under his breath.

"Yes . . . another lecture," affirms their father. "This is a lecture that you have heard and forgotten. And it's very important, because a time of change is upon us." The wizard sips from the cup he has carried to the table. "Among the White Wizards of Fairhaven there is a chaos wizard whose like has not been seen for centuries. They call him Jeslek. He has even begun to raise mountains in the high plains between Gallos and Kyphros."

Rebekah shivers. "Not even the Founders . . ."

Oran takes another sip from his cup before speaking. "Something is going to happen, and we have to be prepared. Chaos could crop up just about anywhere."

"Anywhere? That's silly," comments Kyl.

"You think that Recluce is immune to chaos?" snorts the tall man. "You think that the order with which we live just happened?"

"No," answers Dorrin heavily, wishing his father would get to the point. "This has something to do with me, doesn't it?"

His mother looks out the window. Kyl looks at the tile of the floor, then at his brother.

"Dorrin, now is not the time for your games with machines and models." Oran draws out the words.

"Now, Oran," temporizes the red-haired woman. "He's still young."

"Young he may be, but order doesn't flow right when he's around. Have you talked to Hegl? Poor man's afraid to work iron when Dorrin's nearby. I can't sense the storms when he gets worried. Crellor— Never mind! And with the Fairhaven wizards talking about fleets and pressuring the Nordlans to stop trading with us, things are getting too serious to have order disrupted." The air wizard frowns, then coughs. "Too serious," he repeats.

"What do you want me to do? Disappear?"

Oran shakes his head, pulls at his chin, then purses his lips. "Nothing is ever that simple. Never that simple."

Dorrin picks up the heavy tumbler and sips the lukewarm redberry.

Kyl winks at his older brother, and Rebekah glares

at her younger son. Kyl shrugs when her glance shifts to Oran.

Finally, Oran looks at Dorrin. "We've talked about this all before, about how you insist on making your models and thinking about machines. And I asked you to think about it." The tall wizard pauses. "It's clear that you haven't taken my words seriously enough."

"I have thought about it," Dorrin says slowly. "I would rather be a smith or a woodworker. They make real things. Even a healer helps people. You can see what happens. I don't want to spend my life watching things. I want to do things and to create things."

"Sometimes, watching things saves many lives. Remember the big storm last year . . ."

"Father . . .? The legends say that Creslin could direct the storms. Why can't—"

"We've talked about that before, Dorrin. If we direct the storms, it will change the world's weather, make a desert of Recluce again, and kill thousands everywhere. You're just going to have to concentrate on what you're supposed to be doing. And I can't make you. I'm sending you to study with Lortren."

"Is that wise?" asks Rebekah.

"What else can I do? He doesn't listen to me."

"Father?"

"Yes, Dorrin."

The redhead takes a deep breath. "I do listen to you. I can't do what you want me to do, and I don't want to. You are a great air wizard. I never will be. Can't you just let me be what I am?"

"Dorrin, machines and chaos were what brought down the Angels. Now, admittedly, you couldn't handle chaos if your life depended on it, which, thankfully, it doesn't. But this obsession with building machines is unnatural. What good will they bring? Will they make people healthier, the way healers do? Or will we tear up the earth in search of metals? Will we poison the rivers refining them? And part of the order of Recluce is supported by the core of cold iron ore that runs down the hills above the Feyn. Would you throw that away for machines that would run and wither away?"

Dorrin looks down for a moment, then turns to his father. "It doesn't have to be that way. Hegl doesn't make a mess. Everything there is reused."

"Hegl doesn't need stones' and stones' worth of metals. Machines do." Oran shakes his head. "Perhaps Lortren can make you two understand."

"What did I do?" protests Kyl.

"Nothing," answers the air wizard.

"But . . .?"

"Oh . . . I was referring to Dorrin's friend Kadara. She thinks that strength and skill are the answer to everything. She refuses to listen to her mother, only to Hegl, because she only respects physical strength."

"Kadara's going to the Academy, too?" Dorrin looks from his brother toward his father.

Oran nods. "I am not exactly pleased with the idea. Nor is Hegl, but the Brotherhood is even less pleased about the thought of either one of you continuing essentially unsupervised, especially as friends. Lortren should be able to teach you a thing or two."

"What if he can't?" asks Kyl fearfully.

Both parents look at the younger son.

"Well, what if he can't?" demands the dark-haired boy.

"We'll face that later," answers the air wizard. "And Lortren is a woman. She is equally adept with a short-sword and the manipulation of order."

Kyl's eyes dart from his father to his older brother and back.

Oran takes another sip from his tumbler.

Rebekah stands. "Dinner will be ready in just a moment. Kyl?"

She inclines her head toward the pantry. Kyl scurries for the tableware.

"I need to check something," the air wizard comments, setting the tumbler on the top of the pie safe before walking toward the study.

Dorrin looks toward his mother, who slices scallions into a skillet. After a moment, he walks toward the porch to think before dinner.

VI

"THERE ARE NO great weather-wizards on Recluce now. Not like Creslin."

A thin man in white shakes his head. "Was he as great as the records say? Destroying an entire Hamorian fleet?"

"That was before he really got going," snaps a heavier man in the first row. "Check the older histories. Especially about the weather."

"Don't play games with the youngster," croaks another voice. "Just tell him."

"You tell him, Fiedner."

"It is so simple, young master wizard," croaks the dried-out wizard called Fiedner. "So simple, and so complex. Three centuries past, the Council included Blacks. Not many, to be sure, for the Whites looked down upon the Blacks. And the magic of order is more complex and less directly powerful than that of chaos. Or so everyone thought until Creslin walked off the Roof of the World."

"He was real?"

"Aye, that he was. Real enough to change a White witch into an order-master near as great as he. Real enough to destroy scores of ships sent against him.

Real enough to turn Kyphros into the hot desert it is today, and northern Spidlar into a cold and snowy wilderness. Real enough to turn Recluce from a desert into a garden island."

The young man shakes his head. "Folk tales! Nonsense!" Fire flares from his fingers—not just red-tinged white, but a flame like a blade that saws a chunk out of one of the granite columns bordering the chamber. *Clunk* . . .

"Folk tales, they are. But you're here today because Creslin lived then."

"Explain," demands the slim young man with the sunlike eyes and white hair.

"The Balance is real. Aye, real, and you disregard it at your peril. Jenred the Traitor never believed in the Balance, and we have paid and paid for that ignorance. In Creslin's time, chaos dominated, and the Balance was forced to find a focus. The Blacks manipulated the focus into creating Creslin, and they had him trained outside of Fairhaven."

"Westwind? That much is verifiable."

"It is what is not verifiable that concerns you, Jeslek. Creslin was order-bound, but trained as a Westwind senior guard. That meant more then. Along the way, even before he attained his powers, he killed an entire bandit troop singlehandedly, and three or four squads of White Road Guards. Oh, and he could sing almost as well as the legendary Werlynn."

"What does that have to do with me?"

"It saved his ass when magic wasn't enough. You had better learn the same," cackles the old voice.

"Bah!" The voice cuts nearly as deeply as the chaos fire of the speaker. "Not even the Blacks of Kyphros could stop me."

"They are not the Blacks of Recluce."

The words hang for a time in the air.

"Who said that?"

But no voice owns the statement, and in time Jeslek sheathes his fires and steps into the twilight outside the chamber, walking along the never-dark, white-lit streets of Fairhaven toward the old city center.

VII

THE TALL MAN tethers the horse and locks the brake on the two-seated wagon. The two redheads reach for their belongings. Shortly, four figures traverse the stone lane that leads gently uphill from the coastal road. The two redheads bear packs on their shoulders. The two men walk as though they bear heavier and unseen burdens.

The paved and time-smoothed walk of black stone stretches toward half a dozen black stone buildings roofed with a gray slate nearly as black as the stone walls. Even the wide windows in the buildings are framed with dark wood. The grass between the walks and walls and buildings is dark green, thick, wiry, and short.

The four pass a diamond-shaped garden of blue and silver flowers—set within low walls of the same black stones. The leaves rustle in the cool fall breeze. In the deep green-blue sky, white puffy clouds scud westward.

"Where are we going?" asks the sole female, too old to be a girl, too young to be a woman.

"To the black building on the right," responds the tallest figure.

"All the buildings are black."

"Kadara," warns the shorter of the two men.

"This whole place is black."

Dorrin glances from Kadara, who has had the nerve to voice his own feelings, to his father. "Why is it called the Academy?" He has heard the answer, but knows that Kadara has not, and does not want Hegl or his father to be critical of her.

Oran's lips quirk before he responds. "Originally, it had no name. It started years ago when a former Westwind Guard tutored some younger Blacks in self-defense. They paid for the tutoring by teaching logic and the science of order to what was then the remnant of the Westwind Guard detachment." Oran pauses, gestures at the building. "The side door, there." He steps forward. "Someone supposedly called the place the Academy of Useless and Violent Knowledge. It became the Academy."

They walk up two wide stone steps onto a small covered porch. Kadara tightens her lips, and her eyes rake over both her father and Oran before coming to rest on Dorrin. Hegl shifts his weight as he stops.

"Perhaps they can teach me about using a blade," she says mildly.

Oran opens the dark oak door and holds it for the others. The three others remain on the wide stones of the porch without moving. Finally, Dorrin shrugs and steps inside. A white-haired and muscular woman a shade shorter than Dorrin appears in the doorway on the far side of a foyer that measures perhaps seven cubits on a side.

"Greetings." Her voice is more musical than her stern and ageless face.

Dorrin nods. "Greetings."

"Greetings, magistra," offers Oran.

"I'm still Lortren, you pompous ass," returns the black-clad woman. "You know what I think about titles between adults."

Oran inclines his head slightly. "This is my son Dorrin, and this is Kadara, the daughter of Hegl, here."

"Let's go into the study." Lortren turns and steps through the doorway.

Hegl looks quizzically at Oran, who follows Lortren. Dorrin and Kadara follow their parents.

"I might like her," mouths Kadara.

"Maybe." As they step into the next room, Dorrin notes the stacks of freestanding shelves filled with books—thousands, from what he can tell as they walk down a narrow passageway to the right of the shelves. Perhaps thirty cubits from the door, the shelves end, and the room opens onto a space filled with three tables. The corner table, set between two windows, contains two covered pots seeping steam and a tray filled with plain rolls. Six chairs are pulled up to the table.

Dorrin's stomach growls, not loudly enough, he hopes, for the sound to be heard. It has been a while since the noon meal.

"Sit down anywhere," offers the magistra.

Dorrin waits until his father and Hegl move toward seats, then glances at Kadara and offers her the chair he holds. She shakes her head and sits on the other side of her father. Dorrin sits beside his father, leaving the empty chair between himself and the smith.

Lortren nods toward the pots. "Hot cider or tea. Help yourself."

As Oran lifts the teapot, Lortren clears her throat softly. "Some people have called this the Academy of Useless Knowledge and Unnecessary Violence ... or the School for Sophistry and Swords. For most people who live on Recluce, the description is probably correct. We try to teach the understanding behind knowledge and the use of weapons for those who learn that understanding. Both tend to be necessary." Her eyes turn on Dorrin. "Do you know why?"

"No, magistra."

"I won't force an answer from you. That comes

later. The simple answer is that once you learn why things work, you generally upset people, particularly in places like Nordla and Candar. People who are upset often want to take it out on those who upset them. It helps if you can protect yourself." The black eyes twinkle for a moment.

"You mention travel to Candar . . ." asks Hegl hesitantly.

"Most of those who learn here end up spending time in Candar or Nordla. Some even go to Afrit—Hamor, usually."

"Why?" asks Oran casually, as if he knows the answer.

"Because instruction is never enough for those who have difficulty accepting things as they are."

Hegl swallows and nods. Kadara nods, and Dorrin frowns, wondering if the Academy is nothing more than a way to educate troublemakers for exile. He keeps his words to himself, since saying anything will change nothing.

"You speak as though your . . . students . . . are almost troublemakers," offers Kadara, her voice brittle.

"All of you are. I was once, also. It usually takes not only training and theory, but a healthy dose of reality to turn chaotic trouble-making into something useful."

Dorrin sips the hot tea and munches on a roll.

Hegl glances from the white-haired magistra with the unlined face and melodic voice to his daughter, then toward the air wizard. "I wonder . . ."

"You wonder if entrusting your daughter to me is a good idea? I would too. It's not a good idea. The only problem is that the alternatives are worse." The melodic voice turns hard. "What happens to chaosmongers?"

"They get exiled," responds Hegl.

"What generally leads to chaos-mongering?"

The smith shrugs.

"Discontent, unhappiness with life," answers the air wizard.

"That's your real choice," affirms the magistra.

"Because I'm not happy with the way you all have arranged my life, I have to learn all this nonsense and even study in Candar?" Kadara asks.

"No. You will learn enough so that you can live and survive in Candar or Nordla. Then you will decide whether you can accept what Recluce offers. And you are one of the lucky ones—whose parents can purchase the training. The others often just get a lecture and a boat ride."

Dorrin shivers. This is something he has not heard before. His eyes and Kadara's cross. Then they look at their parents, but neither man will meet his offspring's question.

Lortren stands. "That's about it. You two can go, and I'll show these two youngsters to their rooms."

While the words are polite enough, Dorrin understands that Lortren controls his future and perhaps even his life.

"How . . . where . . . ?" the smith stammers.

Lortren smiles, faintly. "If you want to see where your daughter will live, come along. It's just a small plain single room."

Hegl steps after his daughter. Dorrin looks at his father and shakes his head. Although he will never be the wizard his father is, he can sense enough to know that Lortren tells the truth.

"You'd rather I didn't?"

"I'd rather you didn't," Dorrin confirms. "Besides, you know what the rooms look like. Hegl doesn't."

"Quiet, but sharp, isn't he, Oran?" observes Lortren.

"Too sharp for his own good, I fear."

"Good-bye," Dorrin says, shouldering his pack. Oran remains by the table as the four leave.

Lortren leads them down a corridor through another dark oak door and onto another covered porch. "Over to that building." She points to a two-storied, slate-roofed structure perhaps two hundred cubits uphill with narrow windows.

Dorrin counts the windows—ten on each level. If his estimate of the width of the roof line is correct and there are rooms on both sides, the building will hold forty students. "Is that the only place where students live?"

"Not the only one, but most students live there. There's no absolute requirement for it, but it's a long walk from either Land's End or Extina, and you will be kept rather busy." Lortren hurries down the steps and along the stone-paved path toward the student housing. She walks almost at a slow run.

Dorrin stretches his own stride out to catch up. "How long will our instruction take? Here, I mean."

Lortren laughs, a short laugh that is half musical, half bark. "Probably about half a year, but that depends on you."

"How often do you start groups—"

"Are there others—"

Both Kadara and Dorrin break off in mid-question, but keep moving to stay abreast of the black-clad magistra.

"We allow new groups to start about every five or six eight-days. We usually have three or four groups at different stages."

Dorrin is certainly not the only one questioning the order or meaning of Recluce—not if Lortren is training nearly eighty young people a year.

The only sound is that of breathing, of booted feet upon stone, of the wind through the trees in their orderly spacing throughout the grounds, and of the intermittent and distant *shhhhsss* of the Eastern Ocean breaking upon the white sands under the cliffs to the east of the Coastal Highway that fronts the Academy.

Lortren pauses at the top of the uncovered stone stoop before yet another black oak door—this one to the student quarters. "Kadara, you can wait here or follow us upstairs. Dorrin, your room is upstairs on the far end."

She opens the door, and Dorrin follows. After a moment, so does Kadara. Hegl trails them up the stone steps and down the dim hallway to the last doorway on the left. The magistra opens the door. "No locks. There's a small privacy bolt." She points to the metal fastening and steps aside to let Dorrin enter.

Dorrin's room is not large, measuring no more than seven cubits long and a little more than five wide and containing only a wardrobe, a narrow desk with a single drawer, a chair for the desk, and a single bed not much more than a thin pallet upon a wooden frame. The polished stone floor is bare.

"Very plain, but adequate."

On the foot of the bed is a folded sheet and a heavy brown blanket.

"At the fourth bell—that's also the announcement for dinner—meet me in the library, and we'll go over the rest of the rules and your schedules. By then, most of the others should have arrived. There are three others here so far. Feel free to walk anywhere on the grounds. You may enter any room with an open doorway, although I would suggest knocking first." She pauses. "Any questions?"

"What would happen if I just left?"

"Nothing."

"And if I go where I'm not supposed to?"

Lortren snorts. "You can go anywhere you demon-well want to. If you interrupt a class or someone's work, they'll naturally be upset. But that's your problem. You could hurt yourself if you get careless in the armory, but that's also your problem. There's nothing secret about this place. I just don't want to explain all the rules ten separate times. That's why we'll get together before dinner and do it all at once."

The black-clad magistra turns to Kadara, who stands in the doorway. "Now . . . let's get you to your room."

As the sound of steps fades away, Dorrin stands alone in the small room.

Snifff . . .

The redhead wrinkles his nose at the faint mustiness, then glances at the desk which sits beneath the window. He has to lean across the wooden writing top in order to slide the window open. As he straightens up, his head brushes the oil lamp in the bracket affixed to the edge of the window casement.

Standing behind the desk, he looks through the open window toward the east. While the trees on the far side of the coastal road block his view, he knows that the Eastern Ocean is there, the breakers foaming on the kays of soft white sand that stretch toward Land's End.

He looks at the pack, then back out the window.

Finally, he lifts the pack and begins to remove the clothing, first the lighter shirts and the underclothing, before beginning to place them in the wardrobe.

VIII

"I SUPPOSE I owe this to you." Kadara does not look at Dorrin as they step onto the uncovered porch.

"Me?"

Kadara steps onto the stone walk to the library. "If

you hadn't been so interested in smithing, then my father wouldn't have gotten to know your father."

"Maybe . . ." How can neighbors not come to know each other?

The stiff eastern breeze carries the tang of salt as it whips Kadara's long red hair almost into Dorrin's face.

"Do you mind if I join you?" The voice is mellow, deep, and youthfully enthusiastic.

Dorrin looks over his shoulder and up at the tall blond figure with broad shoulders. "We're going to a meeting—"

"I know. I'm new, too. That's why I thought you wouldn't mind. I'm Brede." Brede wears gray trousers and a blue, long-sleeved farmer's shirt.

"Dorrin." He continues to match strides with Kadara.

"Kadara."

"I'm from Lydkler, in the hills above the Feyn Valley. It's so small no one—almost no one, anyway—has ever heard of it. Where are you two from? Are you related?" Brede's words tumble out and are followed by a broad and open smile. A gust of wind sprays fine blond hair around his face, and a hand twice the size of Dorrin's absently brushes it back.

"We're from Extina," admits Dorrin.

"Brother and sister?"

"Hardly," snaps Kadara.

"Oh . . . the red hair . . . I just thought . . ."

"It's just coincidence—the red hair, I mean."

A long shadow falls across the walk as a high puffy cloud scuds toward the western horizon and blocks the low sun.

"Oh . . . well . . . isn't Extina close to Land's End? It's not far from here at all. I saw a road marker just before we got here . . ."

Kadara's lips remain closed as she marches up under the covered porch and reaches for the dark steel handle of the black oak door. Sunlight returns to the Academy grounds.

"No," admits Dorrin. "It's only about ten kays north."

Clunk . . . The black oak door thuds shut in Dorrin's face.

"She's a little unhappy, isn't she?" observes Brede.

Dorrin opens the door.

"You're both unhappy," reflects the young giant.

"Neither one of us is exactly thrilled to be here." Dorrin pushed through the doorway. Kadara opens the next door—the one to the library.

"She isn't. That's for certain," adds Brede, an amused edge to the deep-toned voice. "It won't change anything, though."

Dorrin grins, warming to the big young man in spite of Brede's forwardness. "Somehow, I don't think it will." He pauses to note the two silver-bordered cork boards, one on each side of the foyer. Both contain grids with times at the left, and boxes filled with a few words each. The grids look similar to the appointment sheets kept by his father. Dorrin crosses the foyer and continues along the short corridor toward the library.

After stepping into the library, Dorrin scans the tables, counting three female and four male figures seated around two tables. No one is seated around the window table. With a deep breath, he edges around the table to the far left and sits next to Kadara. On his immediate left is the wall. Brede settles in the last seat at the other table, grinning briefly as Dorrin looks across the perhaps ten cubits that separate them.

On the other side of Kadara sits a solid young woman, wearing a bright orange-red blouse that does not suit her dark brown hair and pale freckled face. Beside her sits a gangly youth with shoulder-length black hair wearing a one-piece shapeless brown garment.

"Greetings."

Dorrin's study of the other students is interrupted by Lortren's entrance. The white-haired and well-muscled woman stands beside the vacant window table. The black eyes slash across the ten seated youngsters. "I am Lortren. For better or worse, I will be working with you over the next half-year to help you find out who and what you really are."

A brief smile flashes across her face. "You only think you know who you are. If you really knew, you wouldn't be here. You all have talent, of one sort or another, although we don't have any out-and-out chaos wielders here."

The dark eyes sweep the group again, and Dorrin shifts his weight in the hard and unyielding wooden chair.

"I won't bother introducing you to each other. You can work that out among yourselves at dinner, or whenever. You are the red group. Your schedule for the eight-day is posted on the board that says, clearly enough, 'Red Group.' The board is in the south foyer. That's at the end of the corridor behind me.

"No one will remind you where you are to be, or when. Getting there is your responsibility. Finding out where rooms and buildings are is also your responsibility. There is a small map in the foyer next to each board."

"What if—" begins a broad young man with white-blond hair.

"If you make an honest effort and have trouble in the beginning, Loric, no one will say anything. If you continue to show a lack of interest, you'll be asked to leave. Most people who leave here without finishing the course end up somewhere in Nordla or Candar, depending on the available shipping."

" . . . that's exile . . ." The whispered words are clear in the stillness.

"That's correct," affirms Lortren. "For those of you who have not figured it out, the Academy is all that stands between you and exile. In even clearer terms, the Academy prepares you for a controlled exile from which you can return—if you survive and if you choose."

Dorrin senses the indrawn breaths and slow exhalations.

"What kinds of things will we be doing?" Brede's overloud voice crashes through the silence.

"Your studies will concentrate on three things the study of order and chaos; the basic history and cultures of Candor, Nordla, Afrit, and Recluce; and physical training. What is expected of you will be covered in greater detail in your first meeting tomorrow morning." Lortren smiles grimly. "Most of you will discover how little you really know." She pauses. "Are there any other questions?"

Dorrin frowns. Lortren will not answer more than she wants to, and she has said all she plans to say.

"Dinner is waiting. This one time, I'll show you the way. The meal times are also on your schedule board." The black-clad magistra is leaving by the time Dorrin stands.

"Kadara . . . ?" he begins, but she too has moved out of earshot of his soft inquiry. He hastens after the others, ending up behind the girl in the red-orange shirt, so close that his left boot catches her sandal.

"I'm sorry."

She turns with her hand on the door, revealing deep blue eyes that twinkle for a moment. "That's all right. I'm Jyll. Who are you?"

"Ah . . . Dorrin . . ."

She steps through the doorway, and Dorrin follows. Kadara is already leaving the foyer. Several others, including Brede, stand by the schedule board and puzzle over the schedule printed there. Jyll and Dorrin join them.

"Is 'Order' fundamentals?"

" . . . how much physical training . . ."

Looking over the shoulder of the short and broad blond youth whose question was cut short by Lortren, Dorrin scans the schedule, his eyes drifting to a small map in the corner. He finds the dark oblong labeled "Dining," then steps away. Jyll steps away with him.

Outside he checks the walkways and starts uphill, north of the student quarters, where two other figures are entering. "I think that's where we're supposed to go."

"I'm sure someone will tell us if it's not." Jyll tilts her head, and her fine, dark brown hair, cut squarely at chin level, fluffs in the late afternoon breeze, then settles back.

Halfway to the dining building, Dorrin asks, "Where are you from?"

"Land's End, like most of us."

"Brede's from the Feyn area."

"Brede?"

"The big blond fellow with the deep voice."

"He looks like a farmer or a Nordlan warrior."

"He could probably be either, but he's sharper than he looks."

Jyll smiles. "Why did they send you here?"

"I kept telling my father that I wanted to build machines."

"That's scarcely grounds for exile." She purses her lips. "Unless you really just wanted to build them for yourself."

Dorrin flushes, but steps under the overhanging porch roof of the dining building and opens the door for Jyll.

"Thank you."

Dorrin also holds the second door. The room contains six large circular wooden tables. At the far end of the room are two open doorways through which Dorrin can see the kitchen. A long serving table is set perhaps two cubits from the wall holding the doorways. Several of the other students from the introductory meetings are loading plates from the serving table.

Lortren sits at one of the tables, along with a thin older man, two other older students, Kadara, and the thin and gangly black-haired youth.

"You know her?" asks Jyll, her eyes focused on Kadara.

"Kadara? She is ... was ... my neighbor." Dorrin forces a chuckle. "Right now, she thinks it's my fault she's here."

"Oh?" Jyll steps toward the serving table.

Dorrin follows, his voice low. "I wanted to learn how to be a smith, like her father, but I messed up some of his iron by turning it into black steel. So he got to know my father better. When Hegl had trouble with her, he asked my father what to do."

"All right." The dark-haired girl grins. "I just thought I'd ask. Do you like her?"

Dorrin blushes again, caught off-guard by the question.

"Never mind. I think you answered the question."

Dorrin follows Jyll's example and picks up one of the heavy gray plates. From the serving platters, he takes two slices of heavy dark bread, some white cheese, a mostly ripe pearapple, and a large helping of a stew that probably has too much pepper in it. He passes by the platter of mixed greens, and pours himself a glass of redberry.

Jyll, on the other hand, takes only the smallest helping of stew and piles on the greens, sprinkling them with an apple vinegar. She sits at one of the two empty tables, and Dorrin, after glancing at Lortren's table, where the gangly youth is leaning toward Kadara, sits beside Jyll.

He takes a sip of the redberry, warmer than he prefers. "If it's not intruding . . . what's your family like?"

She finishes crunching a mixture of celery and sliced fennel before answering. "My father is a trader in wools. My mother was a singer from Suthya. I don't have any brothers or sisters, yet."

Dorrin frowns. The words imply that her mother is dead, and that her father has another wife who may yet have children. "I take it that was a little difficult."

"It was fun growing up, even if I only had a nurse. Father took me on his trips to Freetown. I had my own horses, and he even let me learn blades from one of the retired Guards. What about you?"

"My life was much less adventuresome. My father is an air wizard, and my mother is a healer. I've never been much farther from home than here, at least in person." Dorrin takes a spoonful of the hot stew, followed by a mouthful of the black bread.

"In person?"

" . . . mmmhhh . . ." He waves a hand and swallows. "When you follow the winds, you send your mind out. Not that I'm very good at it. That's the problem. Father wants me to work at being an air wizard, when I'm probably a better healer or a smith than an air wizard." Dorrin sees Kadara's eyes flicker from him to Jyll. The redhead's face is impassive. Why should Kadara be upset? She was the one who marched off and left him.

"Do you mind if we join you?" asks a petite strawberry-blond girl with pale green eyes. With her stand two others, plates in hand—a brown-haired youth as tall as Brede and a slender black-haired girl taller than Kadara.

"No . . . please do . . ." offers Dorrin.

"We should get to know each other. I'm Jyll."

"Dorrin."

"I'm Alys," responds the strawberry blond.

"Shendr," adds the brown-haired big youth.

"Lisabet." The tall girl looks away from Dorrin's direct appraisal and sets down her plate with a *clunk*.

"This isn't much better than peasant fare." Alys slides her chair up to the table.

"But there's plenty," mumbles Shendr with a full mouth.

Lisabet eats slowly from a plate filled, like Jyll's, mainly with greens, cheese, and fruits. Her big hazel-green eyes seem unfocused.

Dorrin looks away from the tall girl and takes another spoonful of stew.

" . . . really can't belief that they can get away with this . . . You think a thought of your own, and they want to throw you off the island . . ." Alys continues talking to Shendr as Shendr continues shoveling in his meal.

Dorrin munches on the not-quite-ripe pearapple.

"You never finished telling why your father sent you here," prompts Jyll.

"I guess because he feels that all machines are linked to chaos. I think that you can blend order and machines, but everyone thinks that will lead to chaos. I know it won't, but they don't listen."

Dorrin wonders what part her father's new wife played in Jyll's departure. "I take it your father found another woman?"

"Father? Let's say that she found him. She's also a singer, of sorts, and very devoted to him." Jyll takes the last bite of greens.

Dorrin munches through the last of the black bread.

"Where are you from?" asks Shendr, from above a plate that is so clean the gray glaze of the earthenware almost glistens. "I've met Jyll before."

"Extina," offers Dorrin.

"I haven't met her," says Alys, adding quickly, "I'm from Alaren."

"I've spent most of my time on Recluce in Land's End," answers Jyll.

"That's a strange way of putting it. Have you traveled a lot?"

"I've been to Freetown and Hydolar and Tyrhavven," explains Jyll.

Lisabet continues to chew slowly on the remaining greens before her.

Dorrin wonders at the odd grouping of the so-called students. Alys and Jyll both seem from a somewhat indulged background, yet Brede and Shendr seem almost common in background. Not dull, but common. And Kadara is bright and willful, but neither indulged nor privileged. Finally, he speaks. "Lisabet, why do you think you are here?"

The tall girl finishes her mouthful of greens, then takes a sip of redberry from her mug. "I would suspect that all of us are present because in our inner selves we do not accept the way things are on Recluce."

"Rebels? I'm certainly no rebel," asserts Alys. "I wouldn't want to live anywhere else. I mean, in Hamor, they lock you up after you're married . . ."

Lisabet continues with the greens on her plate while Alys expounds on the oppression of women in the Hamorian Empire. Dorrin takes another mouthful of stew.

IX

THE WALLED CITY that serves as the key to the West-horns shall not fall nor sleep so long as her ruler holds fast to the Great Keep, and that keep remains girded in three layers of stone.

The fields of Gallos, the groves of Kyphros, and the highlands of Analeria shall support the same great ruler; they shall support that ruler until they are sundered by the mountains of fire.

A man with a sword of white shall lift hills from the earth; he shall set a road of stone down their spine, yet none shall see that road, nor ride it, save the servants of chaos.

From the blackness of the stars shall come one like an ancient angel, building unto himself tools such as those forged by Nylan that first vanquished the reborn masters of light, and he shall be rejected by chaos and by order; neither shall give him refuge.

He shall make a city of black stone in a place where none dwell, north of the sun and east of chaos; and the hand of every power shall be against him; his tools shall prevail and shall anchor the course of order.

Yet chaos will prevail west of the black city, north and south of the sun; and those in white shall serve light and travel the hidden highways; they shall attain richness and every favor for their pleasure.

Those of the black city and in that place where it dwells shall remain girded; their ships shall travel the oceans great and small, and they shall prosper so long as they remain in their land.

For in time, the double sun will wax in the high sky and sunder the servants of light; their towers shall melt like wax upon a forge; and their highways shall be lost; men and women will revile their names, even as seekers quest for the knowledge of light.

Never shall darkness nor light prevail, for one must balance the other; yet many of light will seek to banish darkness, and a multitude shall seek to cloak the light; but the balance will destroy all who seek the full ends of darkness and light.

Then shall a woman rule the parched fields and dry groves of the reformed Kyphros and the highlands of Analeria and the enchanted hills; and all matters of wonders shall come to pass . . .

> *The Book of Ryba*
> Canto DL [The Last]
> Original Text

X

THE SECOND BELLS still ring as Dorrin steps inside the classroom for the introductory session of the red group. Only Edil is missing, but then Dorrin has just seen the gangly youth hastily putting away his guitar. Lortren stands at the window, her back to the eight students on the pillows.

Dorrin takes his place on one of the three remaining

pillows, the one next to Lisabet. As he does, Edil, a sheepish look on his long thin face, tumbles through the doorway. Edil scrambles for the nearest pillow, nearly throwing himself into place beside Kadara.

Lortren turns. Her face is composed. "I will begin with a warning." She smiles wryly. "No . . . the warning is strictly for your benefit. I would suggest that what you learn here be shared only with others who have a similar background and understanding. This is only a suggestion, but it could make things a little less troublesome.

"Second, there are no tests. You may learn as you please. If you choose not to learn, at some point you will be exiled. If you work hard and it takes longer for you than others, then you may have that time, at least until it becomes apparent that you have learned what you can.

"Third, if you have questions, ask them. Otherwise, I and the others will assume that you understand what you have been taught.

"And last . . . any violence, except as instructed in physical training, any theft, or any other form of personal, physical, or intellectual dishonesty will result in immediate exile."

Dorrin looks at Lortren. "Could you define intellectual dishonesty, magistra? That seems awfully vague."

The magistra grins briefly. "It is vague. We do not have time or resources to deal with lying. What that amounts to is a requirement for complete and honest answers to any questions you are asked by staff members. It also means doing the best you can to learn. As a matter of principle, I would also suggest the same honesty between yourselves. There is a difference between honesty and tact." Her eyes range across the group. "If you look like the demon-dawn, don't ask someone here how good you look." A few smiles greet her sardonic comment.

"Any other questions? No? Then, I will begin with a slightly different version of the history of Recluce, highlighting a few points which bear on why you are here."

Dorrin shifts his weight on the heavy brown pillow.

" . . . common notion is that the Founders were wise, loving, and gentle people, that Creslin was a gentleman among gentlemen, a wizard who only used his power for good, and totally devoted to Megaera. Likewise, the stories say that Megaera was beautiful, talented, nearly as good with a blade as a Westwind Guard, utterly devoted to and in love with Creslin, and possessed of one of the greatest understandings of order ever seen. In a way, these are all true—but more important, they are all false."

A low hum crosses the room.

"Creslin was perhaps one of the greatest blades of his generation, and his trail from Westwind to Recluce did not drip blood—it gushed blood. At first, every problem he tried to solve with a blade. He even killed a soldier in cold blood because the man threatened Megaera—who was well able to take care of herself. He was strong enough to be able to use order to kill— and he did. More than several thousand died under the storms he called. Of course, after his feats of destruction he was violently ill, often puking all over his own men."

The silence of the ten young people is absolute. "As for Megaera, the sweet angel of light—she first was a chaos wielder who threatened her sister's rule of Sarronnyn and who killed a good score with the fire of chaos before renouncing chaos for order. She did not renounce chaos willingly, either, but fought it the entire way, submitting to the rule of order only to save her life. She took up the blade with the sole aim of besting Creslin and proving that she could kill as effectively as he could.

"And our revered founders—what of their harmonious life together? They squabbled and fought the whole way from Montgren to Recluce. They refused to share bedrooms until well beyond a year after they were married, and the lightnings and storms of their final fight were seen from dozens of kays away. Admittedly, they seemed to have settled into a less conflicting relationship thereafter, but I can guarantee it was scarcely one of sweetness and light portrayed by your teachers or conveyed by the Brotherhood."

Lortren jabs a finger at Edil. "What does this tale tell you?"

" . . . Ah . . . that things are not always what they seem . . ."

"You can do better than that." The magistra fixes her eyes upon Jyll. "You, merchant princess, what does the story tell you?"

"I think you are out to shock us with the truth—"

"Be very careful when you use the word 'truth,' child. Facts and truth are not exactly the same." Lortren looks at Dorrin. "You, toymaker. What do you think the purpose of my story is?"

Dorrin tries to gather his scattered thoughts. "Besides trying to shock us, you're trying to show that you, and I'd guess the world as well, doesn't care very much who or where we came from, and that we have lived a very . . . sheltered life."

Lortren smiles, coldly. "That's not too bad, for a start. All of that is correct. I am also trying to make you think. To reason, if you will."

Dorrin thinks about how cool and detached Lortren appears, and wonders whether his father has seen this side of the magistra. Then he recalls how carefully the weather wizard had addressed Lortren.

"Remember this. There are two sides to reality. There is what is, and there is what people believe. Seldom are they exactly the same. Why not?" This time the magistra's eyes fix on Tyren, the shaggy and brown-haired young poet who had attempted to charm Jyll the night before after dinner.

"Is it . . . because . . . people find what is . . . real . . . I mean, what is . . . I mean, is it too hard for them to believe in it?"

"That is correct." Lortren's voice softens. "All of us find some aspect of reality too hard to see as it is— even when we know better. That usually isn't a problem when it remains personal, but it can be a problem when a village or a duchy all accepts unreality."

Dorrin's eyes flicker to the window and to the deep green-blue and fast-moving white clouds. His thoughts move to the question of machines and the unthinking belief by his father and Lortren that such devices are of chaos.

"You do not agree, Dorrin?"

"No . . . I mean, yes. I agree, but I was thinking that even people on Recluce might have beliefs like that."

"I just gave you some, didn't I? About the Founders?"

Dorrin nods.

"You look doubtful. Did you have something else in mind?"

"That's different," Dorrin stumbles, realizing he does not want to state the machine argument, but he is unable to find another.

"What about the rest of you?" Lortren's eyes sweep the others.

Finally, the tall dark-haired girl—Lisabet—clears her throat, then begins in a voice so quiet that Dorrin leans toward her. "Maybe Dorrin is saying that what we believe about the past and what we believe about today are two different kinds of beliefs."

"Huhhh . . ." The involuntary grunt comes from Shendr.

"I'm not sure it matters," answers Lortren. "Whatever the cause, people have trouble accepting certain actions, events, or behaviors. Part of what I hope to teach you is to learn your own weaknesses and to guard against them."

Dorrin tries not to frown. He is more interested in learning how to get other people to change their minds about their weaknesses than in learning about any more of his own weaknesses.

"Now," continues Lortren, "why is the difference between what we have heard about the Founders and the sort of people they actually were important?"

Dorrin isn't sure he cares. People are people, and others believe what they want to. Still, he watches the magistra and listens.

XI

"WHAT IS THE social basis for the Legend?"

The social basis for the Legend? What does the Legend have to do with understanding anything? Dorrin looks around the small room. The Academy of Useless Knowledge and Unnecessary Violence indeed—but it is better than the alternative of immediate exile.

Kadara twirls a short strand of red hair around the index finger of her right hand, her forehead faintly creased. Brede shifts his weight on the battered leather cushion that serves as his seat. Arcol swallows and glances toward the half-open window and the morning fog outside.

"Come now, Mergan." Lortren's low voice carries an edge. "What is the Legend?"

"Well . . . it says that the women Angels fled and

came to the Roof of the World. They founded Westwind and the Guard and the western kingdoms..."
The pudgy girl looks at the polished graystone floor
tiles.

The magistra clears her throat. "You come from
Recluce, not from Hamor or Nordla. You should certainly know the Legend. We'll try... Dorrin, what was
unique about the Angels who fled to earth—to our
world, if you will?'

Dorrin licks his lips. "Unique? Well... they fled
from Heaven, rather than fight a meaningless war with
the Demons of Light."

"That's spelled out in the Legend. But..." She
draws out the word. "What was supposedly unique
about those particular fallen Angels?"

Kadara lifts a hand.

"Yes, Kadara."

"Weren't they all women?"

"That is indeed what the Legend says. Why is that
patently incorrect?"

"Incorrect?" stumbles the normally silent Arcol.

"Ah, yes... incorrect. Why?" repeats Lortren.

As the silence draws out, Dorrin answers. "Because
they had children, I suppose, but..."

"You were going to say something else, Dorrin?"

"No, magistra."

"You were thinking something else."

"Yes," he admits, wishing he had not.

"And?"

Dorrin sighs. "According to the Legend, the Angels
had weapons that could shatter suns and whole worlds.
Why couldn't they have had machines that allowed
women to have children without men?"

"Perhaps they did have such machines in Heaven,
Dorrin... but... if they had such machines, where are
they? Even more important, how did these powerful
Angels, who had the supposed ability to shatter worlds,

end up in a simple stone hold on a mountaintop with no weapons beyond the shortsword?"

"They renounced machines as the mark of chaos," asserts Arcol, the round face and pug nose somehow incongruous with the dogged belief in the Legend.

"Ah, yes, the answer of the true believer."

Arcol flushes, but his chin squares. "Destruction is the mark of chaos, and the Angels fled to avoid becoming the tools of chaos."

"Shall we consider that?" asks Lortren.

Why bother? Even Dorrin knows that machines do not last forever, and that anything built long centuries ago would have broken or been reused for the metals or made into simpler artifacts—or even lost under the snows and ice of the Roof of the World.

"What's the point of it all, magistra?" The voice is Brede's, the deep mellow tones more appropriate to a graybeard than to a fresh-faced and muscular youth with hazel eyes. "I mean, some women wrote down that they escaped from a bunch of crazy men. They built a kingdom on a mountain top. They used their blades to chop up anyone who got in their way and claimed that the reason was that men were all weak and silly."

"Blasphemer . . ." mutters Arcol.

Kadara's mouth quirks as if she suppresses a grin.

Lortren does in fact grin, but the expression is more the look on the face of a hill cat who has discovered a meal than a look of amusement. "Brede, you raise an interesting question. Do, by chance, you happen to know the only country in Candar that had the same government and the same power from its inception until its destruction at the hands of the White Wizards?"

"That has to be Westwind, or you wouldn't have asked the question."

Dorrin wishes that he could think as quickly as

Brede, or handle a blade as deftly, or . . . He catches his thoughts. Wishing will do no good.

"And what is the only country in the world that truly followed the Legend?" Lortren pursues.

"Westwind." Brede is matter-of-fact. "That only proves the Legend held together a country based on female might of arms. It doesn't prove the truth or untruth of the Legend. And, in the end, the white magic won out."

"Where did Creslin come from? And why do you enjoy freedom from chaos?"

"Westwind. But he was rebelling against the Legend."

Lortren smiles, faintly. "Brede is correct in his reasoning—so far as it goes. We will deal with that later, however. Back to the question of the moment— why is the Legend patently untrue on its face?" The black eyes scan the room. "Kadara?"

The redhead with the clean profile and clear skin nods momentarily. "Unless they had special wizardry or special machines, they couldn't have had children. If they had chaos wizardry, that doesn't fit, and the Legend doesn't mention machines or men . . ."

"So you are saying, in effect, that the Legend lies by omission?"

Kadara nods.

"For now, that is enough about the truth of the Legend. We've avoided the Legend's social basis, although Brede spelled it out rather bluntly."

The blond youth looks at the floor, as if displeased at the attention.

Kadara smiles. Dorrin swallows as he watches her eyes light on Brede.

"Why is the Legend effective?" Lortren points at Mergan.

Mergan glances helplessly at the floor, at the

window, and finally back at the white-haired magistra before mumbling, "I don't know, magistra."

"Think about it," suggests Lortren. "Arcol is sitting there ready to strangle Brede, nearly twice his size, because Brede doubts the truth of the Legend. Westwind was the longest single continuing stable government in Candar, or in the world, and the only one which was guided since its beginning by the Legend. The next most stable and long-running is that of Recluce, founded by someone raised in the Legend. What do those things tell you?"

"I don't know." Mergan looks at the stones in front of her leather pillow-seat.

"Dorrin?"

"Is that because people believe in it?"

"Correct. Any government supported by a deep and widely-held belief will remain effective and stable so long as that doctrine remains widely believed. Why did Westwind hold to the Legend, despite the clear factual inaccuracies?"

"Because the Legend worked for Westwind." Brede's polite words are almost sardonic, but not quite.

Dorrin shakes his head. Beliefs! Machines and tools are much more solid than all the talk about governments and cultures. Even weapons are more solid than beliefs. He wishes he were back in his room, where he could work on the drawings of the new engine. His eyes turn toward the red-headed young woman, whose eyes, in turn, are upon the athletic and poised Brede.

" . . . then why are the Whites so successful . . . ?"

Dorrin purses his lips. Lortren doesn't understand, either, though she knows more than his father. Beliefs and blades are not all that can move the world, yet how can he prove that?

" . . . most people in Fairhaven are pleased with their lives. Why? Tell me why that might be, Arcol?"

Dorrin looks toward Arcol, whose mouth is open like a dying fish. He ignores the glimmer in Kadara's eyes as she watches Brede, who, in turn, disregards that warmth bestowed upon him.

XII

"Why do I have to study weapons?" protests the wiry youth.

"First, we live in an uncertain world," says the muscular white-haired woman. "Second, because the skills will improve your physical condition and mental processes. And third, because you will need them in Candar."

"What? I'm not going to Candar. It's dangerous there."

The white-haired woman smiles, and her eyes twinkle. "You're not going today, but you will go—along with a few others, like your friend Kadara."

"Why is Kadara going?"

"For the same reason you are."

"Because we don't understand what a wonderful place we live in?"

"Not exactly. Because you don't understand *why* it is a wonderful place."

"But I do."

"Then why do you use every free minute to sketch machines or build models of things that do not fit into our world?"

"But they could. The ones I think about are the ones you could use with order. I mean, you could forge them with black steel—"

"Dorrin . . . listen to what you're saying. You're admitting that there is no place for them. Who could build these machines? What smith could handle that much black iron? And who could use them?"

"You could," Dorrin states.

"But why? Our fields are more bountiful than any in the world. Our healers keep us healthy and happy. Our stone and timber homes are solid and warm and proof against all elements. Our crafts are becoming known as the finest on the Eastern Ocean. And chaos is excluded."

"But things could be so much better."

"Better in what way? Would your machines make people happier or healthier? Would they make the crops stronger? The trees straighter or taller? Or would they require ripping open the mountains for more iron? Or digging through fertile fields for the coal that lies beneath?"

"But it doesn't have to be that way."

"Listen to your own words, Dorrin. Each time that I have said something, you have said 'but.' Doesn't that say that you believe my words, but feel that the machines are worth more than the pain they will create?"

Dorrin cannot dispute her, yet something is missing, something he cannot exactly name or place. "It isn't that way at all, but I cannot tell you why."

Lortren shrugs. "You may be right. Darkness knows that you've taught me a thing or two. But—and it's my turn to admit things—you cannot object to what is. You must find the understanding within you not just to build your machines, but to ensure that they improve our way of life. You will never gain that understanding here on Recluce."

Dorrin looks helplessly at the desk in the corner of the study, with the row of texts. The faintest of breezes

bearing the tang of the Eastern Ocean cools the dampness on his forehead.

"Now ... off to the practice hall. You need to start
on your weapons training."

Dorrin's steps are slow as he leaves, Lortren's eyes
hard upon his back. Even more deliberate are his steps
into the room to which Lortren's words have directed
him.

"You're Dorrin?" asks the guard. She stands next
to a small table and chair, and her dark eyes pin
Dorrin to a spot just inside the dark oak door.

The redhead nods, his eyes going past her to the
racks of weapons that line the space, which is less than
twenty cubits square.

"Well ... the first thing is to wander around and
pick a weapon that feels right." The guard offers a
lopsided smile that may conceal humor.

"I'm not particularly fond of weapons."

"If you're serious about traveling in Candar, you're
going to have to learn something about how to defend
yourself," says the thin woman in black. She gestures
toward a rack of weapons on the armory wall. "We
can give you some basic training in any of those."

Dorrin steps toward the arrayed bows, blades, and
other assorted tools to deliver force upon other individuals.

"Try a blade first."

Dorrin takes another step. He recognizes the shortsword that many of the Brotherhood prefer, especially
the women, perhaps because of the traditions estab-
lished from their Westwind heritage. Or perhaps
because the blade works.

His left hand grasps a plain hilt, and he lifts the
blade. Somehow, the coldness of the metal, the feel of
the edge—whatever the reason, the blade feels oily,
almost unclean. He studies the weapon for a time, not
only with his eyes, but with his senses, as a healer

might study a sick person. Shivering, he sets it in the rack. Farther along he sees a battle axe. His eyes pass over the double-bladed weapon, as well as the broadsword, and the other bladed weapons, for his senses register the same uncleanliness.

At the end is a long staff, the wood polished smooth, although worn in places. His finger tips touch the wood, then grasp it. He nods as he picks up the staff.

"You a healer?" asks the guard. "Should have told me. Most healers have trouble with the edged weapons."

Dorrin wants to protest that he is not a healer, but stops. He is nothing in particular, but a healer comes closest. That, or less than an apprentice smith. At least, that is what he thinks, and thinking so does not give him the throbbing in his skull that misstatements and evasions do.

"That's as close as anything, but that's the problem."

"Oh . . . one of those . . ." nods the guard sagely, as if she has seen his kind before.

Dorrin finds himself flushing.

She gives an embarrassed grin in return. "I didn't mean it badly. Besides, a staff is a better weapon for most travelers."

"Why would that be?" He recalls the deadly feel of the blades.

"Most people don't think of it as a real weapon, for one thing. For another, you can generally hold off two blades if you know what you're doing. In time, a good blade can get you, though."

"Then you must be a very good blade to know so much."

The guard flushes. "You start here at the second morning bell."

"That's all I do today?"

"That's all. You'll make up for it on the days to come."

XIII

THE CHILL BREEZE riffles through the youth's hair, and, to the east, when the wind dies, he can hear the winter waves crashing on the eastern shore. In his left hand is a small length of spruce, in his right, a knife.

Whiicckk, whiccckk . . .

The low clouds seethe, grayness moving within and around grayness, but no rain has fallen since they rolled over the Academy after the second bell.

"Hello . . ."

At the sound of the bright voice, he looks up.

Kadara, wearing the faded blue of her heavy exercise clothes, stands by the black stone wall where he sits. "Carving again?"

"I don't have a forge, and I get tired of reading all these theoretical arguments about the basis of order and the inherent conflict between . . ." He flicks off another bit of wood. "I still don't believe that machines and metals are the tools of chaos . . ."

Kadara grins. "They aren't. A sword is a tool, and they teach us bladework. Woodcrafters use saws and chisels." She brushes a wisp of the short hair back over her right ear.

Dorrin looks into the blue eyes of the redheaded girl he has known ever since he can remember. "It's just the complex ones, anything that might use something besides water or muscles to operate." He opens his hand. "See?"

Kadara frowns at the object which resembles three carved triangles joined at one end. "What is that?"

"This? It's a fan, a mechanical one. I got the idea from a drawing showing the Imperial Court at Hamor.

This is just the blade, but if you put a handle here, and ran it through something like an axle hoop, you could turn it with your hand. If you put a simple gear here . . ."

"Dorrin . . ."

"Sorry. I know—you half-believe that garbage about machines." He lowers the carving.

"I'm going to the practice hall. Do you want to come? Gelisel says—"

"I know. I need more practice. A beggarman does better with a staff, and I make a one-armed, white-haired bandit look like a master blade."

Kadara shrugs her broad shoulders. "Practice would help, Dorrin."

"I know." He sheathes the knife, tucking the length of spruce into the pack lying on the stone beside him. "I know."

"What are you working on?"

"Just an idea."

"I won't tell anyone."

"Even Brede?"

"Dorrin." The lilt leaves her voice.

"Sorry . . . but Brede . . ."

"Brede is a good person. He'd never say anything. It's not as though I'd tell him anyway. He feels everyone should do what they want as long as no one gets hurt." Her stride lengthens as the paved stone walk steepens. "But don't ask me to keep things from him."

"I'm sorry." Dorrin takes a deep breath. "It's just that Lortren . . . well, she's not very happy about my toys."

"Toys?"

"That's what she calls them."

"Hmmmm . . . I hadn't thought of that."

Dorrin has to stretch his legs to keep up with Kadara, though she is only slightly taller than he is. "Thought of what?"

"Why don't you just make toys?"

"I don't want to make toys."

Kadara stops. "You're not only stubborn, Dorrin. You're slow. You make models of machines. What's the difference between toys and models except the name?"

"But that's not honest."

"Your toys, models, machines—even I know they're not chaotic or evil. So call them something else if it will make Lortren happy."

"I suppose you're right." Dorrin purses his lips.

"I promised Brede I'd spar with him. You want to join us?"

"All right. It probably won't be much of a challenge, though. You're both a lot better."

"Maybe we'll try staffs. Gelisel has started us with them."

"Why?"

"She says that you should learn something about all the other weapons."

"Kadara!"

Both Dorrin and Kadara look up at the sound of Brede's voice.

XIV

JESLEK WALKS ALONG the edge of the hot springs, wrinkling his nose at the faint odor of sulfur. Finally, he brushes the snow from a small boulder and seats himself less than a dozen cubits from the springs.

The White Wizard frowns as he sends his perceptions into the water, tracing the warmth and the fire of chaos that feeds the springs. His thoughts flow ever deeper into the rock and heat beneath.

From under a pine that has been twisted and buffeted by the mountain winds until only the limbs on the southern side have retained needles, two White guards survey the cloudy afternoon.

The gray-bearded one glances from the rocky hillside behind the ice- and snow-strewn expanse back along the road leading down to the plains of Gallos. "This one's a great one, light take him!" His voice is barely above a whisper.

The woman, her hair under the cold cap shorter than the man's, smiles. "You don't like the great wizards much, do you?"

"Demon's flame, no. They do great deeds, and most everyone else gets scorched. We're still paying for the great deeds of Creslin and Jenred the Traitor."

As if to underscore his words, the ground trembles.

Both guards look toward Jeslek, who stands beside the boulder. Steam rises from the spring, yet the heat wells away from the figure in white, circling upward into a funnel that spreads into a white cloud.

Jeslek smiles, and his eyes flash.

The two guards exchange glances. The man takes a deep breath and shrugs; the woman smiles a smile of resignation.

XV

"THERE'S THE RYESSA," announces Gelisel, her long legs slowing.

The harbor spreads out beneath them—the stone piers, the round-sided ship, and the dark green swells beyond the breakwater, swells that surge over the rough stones with alarming frequency. The ship seems toylike against the unending expanse of the ocean beyond the northern tip of Recluce.

While he has certainly been to Land's End before, even eaten in the old tavern reputedly built by the Founders, he had not come before with the idea that he would be leaving Recluce. "It's rather small."

"Nonsense," snaps the arms-master. "You should see the paintings of the old Montgren sloops the Founders used. Or what the Hydlen free-traders use."

Brede pulls at his longish chin.

Kadara looks from her tall and muscular blond companion to the shorter and wiry redhead. "They do this all the time?"

"As regularly as a sand glass is changed. In the summer they trade the northern ports, and in the winter they alternate between Lydiar and Esalia." Gelisel clears her throat. "Come on. They're expecting you, but there's no sense in lagging."

"Will Edil and Jyll and the others take a ship like this?" asks Dorrin.

"The next group is bound for Brysta. No—they'll probably be on a Nordlan brig. That's a bigger ship, but then, they'll have to cross the entire Eastern Ocean." Gelisel strides down the last kays of the northern terminus of the High Road. The fitted stones of the road stretch nearly six hundred kays from Land's End in the northeast to the black cliffs at the southwest tip of the island continent of Recluce.

Dorrin again thinks of the Founders' insistence on the High Road, even when southern Recluce had been a worthless desert before the rains came. He is willing to think about anything except the trip ahead.

"Come on, Dorrin." The red-headed girl's right hand touches the hilt of her blade, but she does not look back. Brede's steps are easy, not even hurried as he matches the long strides of the arms-master.

Dorrin, on the other hand, has been forcing his

shorter legs the entire walk from the coach stop at Alaren. The next wagon to the harbor would not have been until noon, and Gelisel had insisted that the five-kay walk wasn't that far, especially considering the traveling the three have before them.

On each side of the inclined road that angles toward the old keep rise two- and three-story black stone dwellings, mainly of merchants and traders serving the spice and wool trade. The dark slate roofs appear silver in the bright but cool midmorning spring sun.

" . . . nyah, nyah, nyahhhh . . . Ferly is a White . . . Ferly is a White . . ."

Dorrin winces at the children's taunting that drifts over the courtyard walls they pass, wondering who Ferly is and what the poor child has done.

" . . . nyah, nyah . . . Ferly is a White . . ."

" . . . am not . . . AM NOT!"

Dorrin hurries to catch up again.

. . . clickedy . . . click . . .

He steps to the left for a Brotherhood courier on a black mare. The young woman flashes a smile at Dorrin as she continues uphill. Dorrin smiles in return, although the dark-haired rider is already ten cubits behind him on her way toward Extina or Reflin or any number of towns on the High Road.

The four reverse direction as the port road swings through a wide descending turn away from the old black keep on the hillside and back toward the main pier of the harbor. The old keep still flies a replica of the Founders' original ensign—the crossed rose and blade—rather than the current banner—the starker black ryall on a white background.

Dorrin's nose twitches at the scent of winterspice and brinn from the narrow stone warehouses. For generations, Land's End has smelled of spices, for only the master healers of Recluce can use their talents to grow all the world's spices in one country, spices both to preserve food and to preserve health and life itself.

The calls of a few children, the conversations between older residents on the small hillside square below the wide turn in the road, and the muffled sounds from within shops and warehouses are carried on the spring breeze.

" . . . won't see a port this clean again . . ."

Dorrin misses some of Gelisel's comments as his eyes take in the statue of the Founders in the square downhill from the road.

"Why?" asks Kadara.

"Only Fairhaven is this clean. Even Lydiar has garbage and slop in the back alleys."

Brede shakes his uncovered head, his blond hair streaming in the breeze.

"This way . . ."

The road straightens and heads straight north, arrowing toward the main pier of the harbor. A hundred cubits or so later, they walk past an inn—The Founders' Inn, according to the sign. Dorrin has eaten there once before, with his father and his brother Kyl.

"There's the Founders' Inn," announces Gelisel. "The food's not bad, but the prices are damned high."

"Hmmm . . ." offers Brede.

Kadara keeps her eyes fixed on the harbor ahead.

Dorrin follows the other three over the time-polished stones toward the only ship on the pier. His eyes drop to the dark green water, then rise to the plank gangway, where a single sailor, wearing a short blade, lounges in an imitation of guard duty. As the man sees Gelisel's black tunic, he scrambles to attention, waiting as the four travelers approach.

"Magistra . . . you are expected."

"Thank you." Gelisel starts up the gangway.

Dorrin pauses, again studying the rounded sides of the coaster, his eyes catching the name plate under the bowsprit—*Ryessa*. The name is familiar, although he cannot say why it is.

"Come on. You need to meet the ship's master."

As Dorrin follows the other three up the wooden plank and onto the smooth planks of the deck, the ship seems to rise slightly with the swells that the breakwater cannot totally damp.

XVI

BREDE IS STILL snoring when Dorrin pries his eyes open. In the top bunk, Kadara's breathing is far softer, unheard against the background of the ship's noises.

The wiry redhead eases himself out of the bunk and into his heavy brown trousers and boots. The shirt follows. As quietly as possible, he leaves the closet-sized stateroom and clambers up the ladder and onto the rain-splashed deck. Although the rain no longer falls, the spring day is dismal under rolling gray clouds and a brisk wind. He shivers as he passes various members of the crew who are already working—adjusting various lines and cables, coiling a rope, and disassembling a winch.

With the hope that his stomach will remain settled, Dorrin ducks into the deck-level cabin that is the *Ryessa*'s mess and eases onto one of the oak benches at the empty table. One of the ship's officers sits alone at the other table, a heavy brown mug in his hand.

Dorrin slides onto the bench at the empty table. On one platter before him are hard rolls and a wedge of cheese. On the other are dried fruits—apples, red currants, peaches. A pitcher sits inside the bracket fastened to the tabletop. Dorrin looks again, realizing that the platters are similarly constrained and that the heavy brown earthenware has raised edges, presumably to keep the food from sliding off. The two tables are attached to the floor, as are the backless benches.

The redhead takes a cup from the rack and pours the tea into it. Even with a healthy dollop of honey, he winces, both at the lukewarm temperature and the bitter taste. He dips a roll into the tea, hoping that it will at least soften the stale and hard crust.

He forces himself to eat slowly. The *Ryessa*'s mate never meets his eyes. Clearly, the crew has eaten earlier, much earlier. Just as Dorrin finishes his second biscuit and some dried peaches and is thinking about leaving, Kadara arrives, with Brede a step behind.

"You were up early," she observes.

"I couldn't sleep any longer."

"Hmmphhh . . ." grumbles Brede.

Kadara sits heavily, but not quite so heavily as Brede, and then pours the dark tea into two brown earthenware mugs. "Honey?" she asks.

Brede shakes his head. "No."

Dorrin downs the last of his mug, looking around for a place to leave it.

"Don't leave just yet, Dorrin."

"It's not as though I have anywhere to go." Dorrin looks at the heavy planks of the deck. Finally, he sets his mug down and refills it, following the tea with an enormous dollop of honey from the server, an earth-brown squat pitcher that matches neither the mugs nor the teapot.

"You're something," begins Kadara, her voice rising. "You stay on deck until we're asleep. Then you come in and wake us up, and then you get up with the sun and do the same thing."

Brede sips his tea and looks blankly at the table before him.

Kadara takes a deep swallow of the tea and pulls a

pile of mixed fruit off one platter—mostly dried apples. She replaces most of the apples and picks some peaches and pearapples. Next come some of the hard rolls that it would take the force of Hegl's hammer to dent.

At the moment, Dorrin misses the smith more than he appreciates Hegl's daughter across the table from him. Dorrin takes a sip of his tea, bitter even with the large glob of honey.

Brede crunches through a hard roll, oblivious to the sounds or the force he has exerted. He follows the destruction with a gulp of tea that drains the mug. A huge hand reaches for the pitcher and refills the mug.

Finally, as the silence drags out, Dorrin puts his half-empty cup in one of the slots in the center of the table and stands, glancing from Kadara to Brede and back. Kadara looks up. "We'll join you on deck later."

Brede just keeps eating, slowly and methodically, his eyes on the smooth brown wood of the table as he shovels in the heaping pile of fruit, cheese, and hard rolls.

Outside on the main deck, the wind has dropped into a gentle breeze, and patches of blue appear in the clouds to the west. Dorrin stands on the left side of the *Ryessa*, watching the wind carry spray from the crests of the dark green waves. The *Ryessa* does not exactly cut through the sea, her motion more closely approximating a lumber.

Dorrin wipes the spray off his forehead. How can he even decide what he wants to do? Lortren, Gelisel, and his father have all been telling him that everything is obvious, that machines are the tools of chaos. But are they? A still small voice within Dorrin protests that classification.

The *Ryessa* surges through another heavy swell, and the spray from the impact cascades over Dorrin.

"May I join you?"

Dorrin jumps.

Kadara stands almost beside him.

"Where's Brede?" Dorrin asks.

"You're as direct as ever," she says. "He's still eating, but I imagine he'll be here shortly."

"Wonderful."

"Dorrin . . ." Kadara's voice is soft, but carries an exasperated edge.

Dorrin holds a sigh. Does he really want to talk to her? "Sorry."

"Brede can't help it if he's good with a blade."

Or with you, Dorrin thinks. Instead, he answers, "I suppose not."

"You know I owe this to you?" Kadara does not look at Dorrin as they stand by the railing.

"You've said so more than once."

The stiff western breeze carries the tang of salt as it whips the short red hairs around Kadara's face.

"Do you mind if I join you?"

Dorrin looks over his shoulder and up at the tall blond figure with broad shoulders. "Feeling better, Brede?"

"I was hungry." The blond man smiles, a warm and winning smile. He wears gray trousers and a bright blue, long-sleeved shirt. Without the long sword he usually wears across his back, he looks far more like the Feyn Valley farmer's son he is than the well-practiced blade he has become in the two seasons the three have spent at the Academy under Lortren.

"How long before we get to Tyrhavven?" asks Kadara.

"Another day or so, at least," answers Brede.

Dorrin shrugs, looking back at the bow of the *Ryessa* just in time to catch another faceful of stinging salt spray.

A gust of wind sprays fine blond hair around Brede's face, and a hand twice the size of Dorrin's absently brushes it back.

"That's a long way from Land's End," muses Kadara.

Silence and the swishing of the sea are preferable to a dubious discussion. Instead, Dorrin watches the water. Brede frowns, then straightens and heads toward the stern. Another spray almost touches the edge of the deck.

"You don't make conversation easy, you know." Kadara's voice is quiet.

Dorrin barely hears her above the waves, the whisper of the wind, and the creaking of the ship. "What is there to say?"

"That's it. You never talk to me anymore. It's as if we're strangers, yet we grew up next door to each other."

You have Brede, Dorrin wants to snap at her. Instead, he shrugs.

The *Ryessa* lurches, and a sheet of water sprays past Dorrin, leaving him with wet legs and a tighter grip on the railing.

When he looks up again, later, Kadara is gone.

XVII

DORRIN WALKS THE deck, studying how the ship is constructed. He probes at the underlying patterns, the forces, the stresses—and especially he looks at the simple machines.

Flappppp . . . thwipp . . .

Aloft, some of the crew are resetting sails. Not all of them, but the mainsails. A line of dark gray and brown stretches southward off the port side. Dorrin looks up where a huge Suthyan flag flies atop the aft mast. The clouds that had splashed the ship with rain in the early morning have lifted, but the skies are still gray.

The *Ryessa* continues to make surprising speed into the wind, angling toward a break in the low dark hills. Behind the coastal hills is another set of low clouds. Dorrin looks again, this time with his senses, before realizing they are not clouds at all, but a second line of snow-covered hills. While spring may have come to Recluce and to Tyrhavven, it has not yet reached the higher hills that lie south of the Sligan port.

He heads back toward the cabin. There Kadara and Brede have finished replacing their gear in their packs—long enough ago so that the two step apart as Dorrin opens the door.

"We should be landing in a little while," he notes curtly, ignoring the flushed looks. He grasps the pack he has prepared earlier from his bunk.

"We'll be up in a little bit," offers Kadara.

"It takes a while to tie up," adds Brede.

Neither moves away from each other or toward their packed gear. Brede does not wear his shoulder harness or sword, nor does Kadara.

"Fine." Pack in hand, the wiry young man grasps the staff and turns back toward the door. He does not shut the door as he leaves.

As the *Ryessa* eases shoreward, Dorrin studies the harbor town. His pack and quilted leather jacket and staff now rest by his feet. Tyrhavven is scarcely inspiring. Only two short piers, smaller than those of Land's End, comprise the harbor facilities, and the stone breakwater is half the length of its counterpart on Recluce. The two piers are of heavy weathered and unpainted gray timbers, except where a brown line shows the replacement of an older plank by a newer one.

"I told you it would take some time." Kadara, wearing dark gray, appears with her pack. At her belt are two blades, both gray-hilted; the one on the left is a Westwind shortsword.

Brede towers behind her, his single blade heavier than either of Kadara's, strapped in place in his shoulder harness. His open gray jacket shows his heavy blue shirt.

The wind seems to pick up as the ship wallows toward the pier.

" . . . sails!" Commands issue from the bridge. ". . . hard port . . ."

With his broad shoulders and long-chinned but square face, Brede grins. "Ready for an adventure?"

Dorrin is neither ready for an adventure, nor enthusiastic about the relationship between Brede and Kadara. But what can he do?

"Neither am I," admits Kadara.

"Well . . . like it or not, we're going to have one, and we stand a better chance together than separately."

Brede makes sense, and Dorrin would be foolish indeed to spurn the assistance of the bigger and quicker man's blade and disarmingly cheerful manner. Dorrin takes a deep and slow breath, nodding slowly.

"Why so reluctant, Dorrin?" Brede's voice is warm and friendly.

"Dorrin would be happier if they had just let him play with his machines," observes Kadara.

"They never will," Dorrin adds. "So . . . I'm off on an adventure."

In the short time the three have talked, the *Ryessa* has jockeyed up to the empty pier. Perhaps half a dozen figures stand waiting; two wearing white surcoats are armed.

"White guards . . ." Brede moves up to the railing.

Dorrin turns to see the captain motioning. "He wants us off the ship."

"That's not surprising," Brede snorts. "Fairhaven hasn't ever liked the coasters' being involved with

Recluce." He swings his pack on his shoulder, readjusting the harness to ensure that he can still reach the blade quickly, and marches toward the gangway.

The gangplank is barely in place as the three line up.

"Thank you for a smooth trip, Captain." Brede's voice is deep and mellow.

"Yes." Kadara offers a flash of the smile that Dorrin wishes were directed at him.

"My pleasure, lady," answers the captain. "My pleasure."

Dorrin nods politely to the ship's master, but only mumbles a low "Thank you."

The captain inclines his head in return.

A pair of seamen are still tying lines to the bollards on the pier as Dorrin steps onto the weathered planks.

A long-faced functionary with a white circular patch on the shoulder of his heavy quilted leather jacket waits just shoreward of the gangplank. He carries a thin leather folder. Behind him stand the two White guards, while off to one side loiter three travelers, all with grips or packs, presumably waiting to embark upon the coaster. Each guard wears a sword, but their hands are empty as they wait with bored looks upon their faces.

In the chill sunlight of midmorning, more like late winter than the spring that the calendar indicates, Dorrin wants to shiver. Instead, he stands straight behind Brede and Kadara, tightening his grasp on the staff.

"Travelers?" squeaks the long-faced man in a high and thin voice. Because he is not even as tall as Dorrin, his eyes must look up to Brede, who overtops everyone on the pier by at least half a head. "The entry fee is half a silver a person."

Brede presents a single coin. So does Kadara. Dorrin fumbles forth five coppers.

The functionary places the coins in a purse and makes three marks on a parchment sheet. "Do you have any weapons beyond what you show?"

"Nothing except a brace of knives . . ."

"Knives . . ."

"A knife," finishes Dorrin.

"Noted. You are free to travel the domains of Candar." The functionary jerks his head at the guards. "The cargo and the manifest . . ."

Dorrin glances back at the *Ryessa*. Only a regular crewman remains by the railing looking at the pier. The man grins at Dorrin, then lets his face turn impassive as the captain walks past him to the top of the gangplank to greet the long-faced man with the folder.

Dorrin follows Brede and Kadara up the pier toward Tyrhavven. The wind from the hills behind the city ruffles his hair, but not even a gale would loosen those tight curls. His ears tingle in the chill that seems more like winter than spring.

Of the bollards on both piers, only three sets are used. The *Ryessa* is moored on the eastern pier. Two smaller fishing boats rest at the western pier.

Dorrin lengthens his stride to catch up to Kadara. Her steps are still quick, and she does not even look at the shorter man as the three step off the pier and onto the stone pavement in front of what appears to be a warehouse.

"Where now?" asks Dorrin.

"Who knows?" snaps Kadara.

"We need to see about mounts," interjects Brede quickly. "We can't just walk across Candar."

"What about provisions?" asks Dorrin.

"That, too."

The buildings behind the warehouse—timbered and weathered—scarcely resemble the neat and polished stone frontages of Land's End. He swallows, wondering if he will see Land's End again.

XVIII

DORRIN TRIES TO match the map in his head, with its neat drawings, to the weathered, almost abandoned-looking buildings, the muddy street, and the ragged and disreputable figures lounging by the end of the pier. Tyrhavven is all too real, especially as the harbor town smells of salt and rotten fish and seaweed, over-laid with wood smoke. Finally, Dorrin looks southward up the gentle slope of a half-cobbled street that seems to lead toward a row of two-storied buildings. From the chimney of one building rises a thin gray plume.

"Come on." Kadara's voice is gently insistent. "The chandlery has to be this way."

"But chandleries are for ships," protests Dorrin.

"Here they sell everything," adds Brede, over his shoulder.

"But shouldn't we get horses first?"

"The chandlery is next to the stable."

"How do you know?"

Dorrin adjusts his pack and scrambles to follow the two taller exiles as they stride away up the uneven pavement.

" . . . haa . . . haaa . . ."

The redhead with the wiry hair ignores the cackling laugh of the old man sitting against the seawall, but he moves even faster to catch up.

" . . . haaa . . . haa . . ."

The three turn left at the first cross street. While the brown cobblestones are worn and often cracked, the street does contain virtually all its paving stones. Only a few small puddles offer a reminder of the morning rain, although the clouds remain dark and threatening. A single horse, swaybacked, is tethered before the store Brede points out as a chandlery. The sign that swings from the protruding crossbeam has no name, just a crude black outline of two crossed candles on a white background. Much of the white has flaked away, showing weathered gray wood beneath.

Brede's feet, half again as big as Dorrin's, whisper on the wide plank steps, as do Kadara's. Dorrin's boots thump as though he were the heaviest.

The interior of the store smells faintly of oil, varnish, rope, and candles. Those are the scents which Dorrin can distinguish. A dozen steps inside the doorway stands a squat iron stove, radiating a gentle heat. On the right hand wall is a row of barrels. Each barrel is topped with a circular wooden cover. Across from the barrels is a counter running the remaining depth of the store. Another counter runs across the back of the store.

Beside the stove lies a thin dog on a tattered blanket folded into a rough bed. One eye opens as Dorrin closes the door with a *thunkkkk* . . .

"Is there anything special you need?" The flat voice comes from a man with thinning sandy and silver hair and a drooping handlebar mustache. His leather jacket bears a range of leather patches that do not match the original, and he sits on a stool behind the counter almost opposite the stove.

"We're looking for some travel goods," explains Kadara politely.

"Suit yourself."

Brede studies the counter, while Kadara starts with the barrels.

. . . *hhhnnnnn* . . .

Dorrin looks at the dog again and swallows, sensing the animal's pain. Then he looks at Brede and Kadara, efficiently determining their needs. He steps toward the counter.

. . . hhhnnnn . . .

With a sigh, he edges toward the stove and squats next to the hot iron and the dog. "You hurt, lady?" His voice is low.

"She's just old." The storekeeper's voice remains flat.

"All right if I pet her?"

"Suit yourself. She's a touch cranky."

Dorrin extends his senses toward the dog, feeling the infection and the age within the body.

. . . hhhhnnnn . . . thump . . . The dog's tail flicks against the plank floor.

His hands, as gently as he knows how, scratch the shaggy brown coat between her ears, even as he tries to help the ailing animal. Certainly, a little order cannot hurt.

. . . slurrppp . . . A damp tongue runs across his wrist.

"Easy, lady, easy . . ."

. . . thump . . . thump . . .

Dorrin scratches the dog's head again before standing up. "You'll feel better in a while, lady," he says quietly, bending and patting her head.

Both eyes are open, watching as the wiry redhead walks to the counter.

"Like dogs, boy?"

Dorrin looks toward the flat-voiced shopkeeper. "I never had one," he admits, "but I do like them. She seems nice."

"Best bird-dog I ever had. Just got too old." The man shifts on his stool, but does not rise.

There is another silence while Dorrin studies the small rectangles of dried travel food wrapped in paper and dipped in some sort of wax.

"The trail cheeses are in the cooler at the end."

Behind him, Dorrin can hear Brede and Kadara quietly talking about cooking sets. "What about horses, ser? Is the stable across the way . . ."

"Hope so." A snort follows. "My sister's man runs the place for Rystel."

Dorrin smiles faintly. "Do you have any saddlebags? Perhaps an older set?"

"Halfway down the counter. Some sets there, a few others on the bottom."

Dorrin follows the instructions. One set is practically new, huge, and made of heavy stiff leather. He sets the bags aside, and picks up the second set, setting it down quickly as he feels the whitish red that signifies chaos. Although he has only felt chaos as a part of healing, there is no doubt that the bags have been associated with chaos. The third set is serviceable.

Finally, he drags out a dusty pair from underneath the counter. Although the leather is stained, and the bronze fittings are pitted in places, Dorrin nods, more to himself than anything.

"Good eye there. Cheap, too. A silver for you."

"How much are the heavy ones?" Dorrin asks idly.

"Those? You'd need a draft horse to carry them. Half a gold."

Dorrin purses his lips. While he has enough coins for the cheaper saddlebags, he does not know about the trail food, and he really needs a waterproof of some sort. He also does not like purchasing goods before he even has a mount to carry them. Unlike Brede, he worries about such details. "I need some sort of waterproof."

"Hmmmm . . ."

A moment later a square of dark fabric appears on the battered wood of the counter top. "Nothing fancy. Just a good cloth dipped in the waterproof stuff. Probably a little small for the likes of your friend there." The shopkeeper drops a shoulder toward Brede, who stands before a barrel from which he is extracting small pouches of something. "So I couldn't ask that much for it. Say . . . half a silver."

Dorrin nods. From what he has seen of Candar, he will need it.

"Shopkeeper?" asks Brede in his deep and polite voice.

"I'll put these over here," suggests the man to Dorrin. "Yes, young ser?" His voice flattens again as he addresses the tall blond man.

Dorrin drifts over to Kadara. "How are we doing trail food?"

"I thought we'd split the cost for meals. Anything extra you buy yourself. I told Brede that, too." She smiles. "He did agree."

"I don't have that much," Dorrin says.

"With your father, I can believe it." Kadara looks back at the barrel.

Shrugging, Dorrin goes back to the other counter, avoiding Brede and the shopkeeper.

. . . hhhhnnnnn . . .

With a grin, he walks back over and pets the dog, adding another touch of order and reassurance.

. . . thump . . . thump . . .

Perhaps it is his imagination, but her eyes look brighter. "Good girl," he adds, before returning to pick out two oblong packages from the cooler, with the words *yellow cheese* scratched into amber wax.

What else does he need? He has his heavy jacket, a bedroll, gloves, extra boots, what clothes he dares carry, a small pouch of healing goods, and now he has a waterproof and saddlebags. His only weapon is the staff. While he has a belt knife and the carving knife, of course, they are tools, not weapons. He could not carry a sword in any case, not with the conflict an edged weapon creates.

More compressed food, perhaps, he decides, in case he is separated from the others. He adds several blocks from the counter to the cheeses and places them beside the waterproof and saddlebags.

Brede examines the large bags Dorrin has rejected, and the shopkeeper slips along the counter back to Dorrin.

"All together, that's two silvers and two."

Dorrin fumbles in his wallet, still not used to the hardened leather outer case, and comes up with two silvers and a half. He hands the three coins across.

"You want this stuff in the saddlebags?"

"That would be fine." Dorrin glances back at the dog, who has lifted her head. She struggles upright, then sits and looks back at him.

"Boy, how did you do that?"

"Do what?"

"Stella. Poor bitch couldn't move."

Dorrin flushes.

"Recluce kid?"

Finding he cannot lie, Dorrin nods.

"Don't tell anyone. You aren't wanted."

Dorrin waits.

"Boy?"

Dorrin looks up. "Here's your change." The shopkeeper counts out the coppers into Dorrin's palm. Then he adds a wooden token. "Give that to Gerin. He's at the stable. Tell him I sent you. Hertor ... that's me." He lifts the partly full bags across the counter.

Dorrin nods as he takes the leather bags. "Thank you. I hope she"—he nods toward the stove—"is a little better. Maybe the warmth by the stove will help."

"Best bird-dog I ever had," repeats the older man in a low voice. "Tell Gerin. Now don't you stand on pride, young fellow."

"I won't, ser." Dorrin nods politely and steps back.

At the end of the counter, Brede is holding up the heavy saddlebags.

Dorrin turns to Kadara, who is looking at the dog, as if she has overheard the low-voiced conversation with the shopkeeper. "I'm going over to the stable."

"I'll need some coin from you."

"How much?" Dorrin fumbles in his wallet again.

"I'd guess around five coppers."

He hands her the coins. "If it's more, let me know."

"Those will be two silvers, young sir." The man's voice is flat again as he addresses Brede.

Dorrin says nothing as he steps into the chill breeze and closes the heavy oak door behind him. He pauses at the top of the wooden steps. Is it wise to leave the others?

A woman, bundled in a worn leather coat, ungloved hands red from the cold, walks away from him, downhill toward the port, where three wagons creak toward the *Ryessa.* Across the mud and cobblestones from where Dorrin stands, an older man, heavy and bald, strains to roll a barrel toward a side door.

With a deep breath, the young man shrugs his pack into place, steadies the saddlebags that he carries on one shoulder, and, staff in hand, heads down the steps and to the right, toward the stable.

Thweeeeett . . . The sound of a whistle drifts uphill from the harbor. Dorrin studies the storefronts he passes until his eyes and nose agree. Despite the chill, the stable smells like a stable, and Dorrin looks as much for where to put his feet as where to find Gerin, wherever the man may be.

Gerin is wrestling round bales of hay from a stack at the back of the stable onto a flat cart.

"I beg your pardon . . ." begins Dorrin.

"You want something . . . give a hand," grouses the thin sweating figure.

Brede and Kadara are not around.

"Are you just going to stand there?"

Dorrin sets his gear on a half wall to an empty stall and hoists a heavy bale onto the cart. "Here all right?"

"Fine. Put the next one crossways."

Dorrin lifts two more bales into place.

"That's fine. If you want it, the job's yours."

Dorrin shakes his head.

"What do you mean? You don't want it? You work good, but jobs aren't that easy to find."

"I'm sorry, ser. But I was really looking for a horse. Hertor sent me. Are you Gerin?" Dorrin flushes at the misunderstanding.

"And you hoisted hay?"

"You looked like you needed help," Dorrin admits.

The thin man shakes his head. "Takes all kinds." His face stiffens. "Lots of people say Hertor sends them."

Dorrin fumbles and finally produces the wooden disc.

Gerin shakes his head again. "You're too young to be buying a horse."

"I really don't have that much choice." Dorrin reclaims his pack, staff, and saddlebags.

"And too damned young to be traveling alone."

"I have two friends. They'll need mounts, too. They're still at Hertor's, getting some supplies."

"Stupid . . . should get the mounts first. How are they going to carry all that crap?"

Dorrin has no answer.

"Come on. I'll show you what's here. You ride much?"

"I can stay on a horse. That's about it," Dorrin says, feeling very inadequate at having to admit shortcoming after shortcoming.

"Hmmmmph . . ." The thin man heads back toward the front of the stable, ducking around a stall door that has fallen off its pins and dug into the packed clay floor.

Dorrin follows Gerin, wondering what is he doing alone in a strange country in a strange stable with a scarcely friendly liveryman. Still . . . what choice does he have? Lortren hadn't said much, only that Dorrin can't return until at least the following summer, and not until he has visited Fairhaven and until he knows why he had to leave Recluce. Dorrin takes another deep breath, and wishes he had not as they pass an open drain.

"Watch your step there."

Watching his step is all he has been doing, it seems, but he steps even more carefully in skirting the sloppy mess around the hole in the clay floor.

"Here. Two golds is the best I can do, even for Hertor."

Dorrin follows the man's hand to the horse that stands in the stall—black with what appears to be a white patch on the forehead.

Wheeee . . . eee . . .

The horse tries to nip, but Dorrin casts his senses at the beast, attempting to calm it, and discovers that she is a mare. She settles down and lets him stroke her neck—the little he can reach over the stall door.

"Thought you didn't know horses."

"I don't."

"Why did Hertor give you a token?"

"I'm not sure."

"He gave up a token, and you don't know why?"

"His dog," Dorrin admits.

"Stella?"

"I don't know her name. She was by the stove."

"And?"

"I helped her a little, I think."

"She's still alive?"

"She was sitting up when I left."

Gerin shakes his head. "You a healer?"

"Just an apprentice."

"That explains it."

Dorrin remains bewildered. What is so strange about being a healer? Surely, there are healers in Candar.

"Maybe I could go a gold and a half, but I'd have to take the other for a saddle and blanket."

"And a bridle?" Dorrin asks tentatively.

"That, too."

Dorrin is saddling the black mare, under the eyes of Gerin, when Brede and Kadara march in.

"Those are my friends."

"I don't know as I have much that will carry a young giant." Gerin's voice is hard again, though the words are polite, as he steps over to address Brede. The horse dealer's glance takes in the long and heavy sword.

"I am not as heavy as I look," Brede answers softly.

"Anything you could do would be helpful," adds Kadara, and her voice is gentle. Not manipulating, just gentle.

Gerin looks from Dorrin, who looks spindly even beside the broad-shouldered Kadara, to Brede and back to the apprentice healer. Finally, he adds, "I have a big gelding. Strong, but not too bright, and another mare."

XIX

"Ooooo . . ." AS HE dismounts, Dorrin winces. He will never be able to sit on a hard surface again. He slowly fumbles with the straps on his pack.

Brede vaults off his gelding in a fluid motion, ties his mount, and begins to unstrap the packs.

Whheeeee . . .

"Sorry." Dorrin apologizes to the mare.

Kadara has already unloaded, tied her horse to the post at the south end of the way station, carried her packs to the hearth inside the windowless square building, and returned. "You should have spent more time with exercises and horses, instead of carving machines that will never be made."

Dorrin clamps his lips together, then continues to unstrap his pack, laying it beside Brede's and following the taller man's example by leading the mare down the stone-walled ramp to the stream.

With the sun behind the hills, the temperature has dropped. Despite the heavy wool-lined jacket, Dorrin shivers, and his legs seem to alternate between the hot aches from riding and the chill of the late afternoon.

"How much farther?" He stops beside Brede and lets the mare drink the chill water.

"We've just started, Dorrin. It's at least another five days at this pace just to Vergren."

"I still don't understand why we have to go to Fairhaven."

"Because," answers Brede," Lortren said Kadara and I did. I don't know what she said to you." He halts the gelding's greedy slurping. "Don't let your mare drink too much at once." The tall man steps back, leading the gelding up the ramp and across the chopped ground that is beginning to refreeze.

Lortren had only told Dorrin he must visit Fairhaven and find himself, whatever that meant.

It takes Dorrin an effort to pull the mare away from the icy stream that gurgles across rocks long since worn smooth. Clearly, the watering space has been man-made, since the stream banks above the watering spot are steep and rocky, while the space where Dorrin and the mare stand slopes gently into the stream and is flanked by rough stone walls on all sides—except for the ramp itself, which rises through the walls to the higher ground by the way station.

As Dorrin struggles back up the ramp, his eyes lift to the southern horizon and trace out the outline of the hilltops. He stops on the uneven ground above the ramp and sniffs the air, but it seems only chill and damp, with the faintest odor of wet leaves and decaying matter. His senses go out toward the hills.

Whheeee ... eeeee ... The mare protests.

Dorrin's brow furrows as he struggles to focus what he feels. Finally, he walks to the way station, part of his mind still in the low hills above the road.

"Dorrin, can you find some brush, small sticks for fuel? All they have here is logs." Kadara gestures toward the pile of wood by the simple open hearth. The stew pot she had bought in Tyrhavyen is before her.

Dorrin smiles faintly. Certainly, he never would have thought of bringing a stew pot, strapping it on a mount.

"Dorrin? I asked about fire starters ..."

"Sorry ... We have problems."

"Problems?" asks Brede, sounding, for the first time, somewhat dense.

"There are three bandits on the hill. They're watching us. I don't think they have bows, but they're waiting to catch us unaware."

"How do you know—" begins Brede.

Kadara motions for silence. "What are they doing now? Right now?"

Dorrin squints, struggles in his efforts to sense the brigands. "They're beginning to move downhill, I think, toward the horses. Just three of them."

"Do they have horses?"

"I didn't feel any."

"Let's go out and check the horses, Brede. That's what they want."

"But ..." protests Dorrin.

"You stay a little behind. Let us know if they have anything besides blades. Or if more show up." Kadara straps on both blades and looks at Brede, whose hands reach for the big sword, as if to make sure it is still in place.

By the time they reach the horses, three figures are

emerging from the leafless trees across the frozen clay strip that is the road to Vergren. Brede continues toward the three, Kadara at his shoulder. Dorrin grips his staff and follows. Brede stops.

"No trouble, travelers," rasps the center figure, a brown-bearded man almost as tall as Brede and easily two stones heavier, with a protruding gut. "You just let us have the horses, and we'll let you alone. Even the lady, and that's making things easy for you." His sword gestures toward the horses.

Kadara snorts softly. "Why don't you just set down those tooth-picks and get out of here?"

"Oh . . . maybe we won't leave you alone. Women with spirit are rare . . . these days." He leers, showing blackened teeth.

The two smaller men, also bearded, one with matted blond hair, and the other with greasy black hair, raise their swords.

Snick . . .

Brede's big blade glitters in the fading light. Equally quickly, if silently, Kadara's blade has left its scabbard.

"You really don't want to do that, youngsters. You Recluce types just can't kill when it gets right down to it." The big bandit laughs harshly.

Dorrin, standing three steps behind Brede and Kadara, holds his staff, wishing that he had practiced more with it. But how could he have known that so many people actually enjoyed killing? For a long moment, the cleared area before the way station is quiet, except for the raspy breathing of the black-haired bandit.

"So . . . you really aren't going to give in." The big bandit shrugs, half-turns. "Well, it was worth a try."

Whhstttt . . .

The heavy man swings through the turn and thrusts toward Kadara.

Brede slashes, not toward the big man, but toward

the smallest, the blond man in the tattered blue surcoat. In two strokes, Dorrin marvels, the blond bandit is dead, and Brede is pressing the black-haired brigand. The big sword flashes as if it were only a toothpick.

Dorrin's mouth opens, for the sword has dropped from the heavy bandit's hand, and he sways in the twilight, like a rotten oak, before pitching onto the ground.

Kadara swings toward the black-haired man, who has circled away from Brede and is now closer to Dorrin than either Kadara or Brede.

Dorrin regrips the staff, waiting, swallowing, knowing what is about to happen, and hoping that it will not.

" . . . healer!" The bandit ducks and lunges toward Dorrin.

" . . . ooohhhh . . ." A line of fire lances across Dorrin's shoulder even as the staff drops the bandit onto the frozen ground. Dorrin looks stupidly as Kadara's blade flashes once again. Three bodies lie strewn around them.

"You'd better practice with that staff some more, Dorrin," observes Brede.

Kadara glances at the big man, and Brede closes his mouth. "Are you all right?" she asks.

Dorrin looks at the slash in his sleeve, and the red line. "It's just a surface cut, but the jacket won't be the same."

"The leather and quilting probably saved your arm."

Dorrin rests against his staff, still wondering at how quickly things happened. Kadara is kneeling by the black-haired man, examining the body.

"Not much here. A gold necklace, silvers, and a few coppers."

Brede has already stripped the valuables from the other two, including the swords.

Dorrin squints. Looting the bodies makes sense, although, somehow, the thought burns a line across his brain. He rubs his forehead, but the throbbing remains.

"The blades aren't much, but we can sell them—or teach Dorrin how to use one."

"The staff . . . just need to get better . . ." Dorrin straightens. "What about the bodies? The ground's frozen."

Brede smiles crookedly. "I'll dump them up in the woods. The big cats are probably hungry."

Kadara gives Brede another sideways glance as she cleans her blade on the tattered blue surcoat before replacing it in the scabbard. "Dorrin? Could you see if anyone else is lurking in the woods?"

The healer takes a deep breath, but he sees the wisdom of her request and sends his senses beyond the road and the nearby trees. With the headache, mild as it is, the effort brings tears to his eyes. He sways as he returns to himself. "Nothing . . . nothing nearby."

Brede and Kadara nod and walk in different directions.

By the time Dorrin has gathered his wits and senses into his own skull and cleaned the gash in his arm, Brede is carrying the second body up the gentle hill across the road from the way station, and Kadara has a fire started in the ancient-looking hearth. The sun has completely dropped behind the lower hills to the west when Dorrin straggles into the station with an armload of finger-width wood.

"Thanks. I can use that later, or in the morning. You might water the horses again. Just a little." The redhead does not look up from her preparations with the stew pot.

With all the time it takes him, and the stubbornness of the mounts, the stew is ready when he stumbles back into the way station. Brede sits on one end of the stone bench.

. . . tu . . . whuuuu . . .

Dorrin jerks his head up.

"Just an owl," Brede says quietly. "They hunt earlier here in the cold weather, I think. It's probably too cold for the rodents late at night."

"Here." Kadara hands Dorrin a tin cup filled with something hot and brown. Then she hands a second cup to Brede.

"Thank you." Brede's voice is appropriately grateful.

"Thank you," echoes Dorrin, conscious of sounding like an echo.

"You're both welcome. Just eat it." Kadara fills her own cup.

For a time, there is silence except for the chewing of hard travel bread and the muffled slurping of the stew.

Dorrin sets down his cup and takes out the carving knife and a small piece of wood. In several deft strokes, he fashions a crude needle. Then he strips off the quilted winter jacket and uses the point of the knife to work a series of evenly spaced holes in the outer leather. After more stew, he uses the wooden needle to thread a thin thong he has worked down as finely as he can through the holes.

"Clever . . ." mumbles Brede through another mouthful of stew and travel bread. He is finishing his third cup of the spicy brown stuff.

"Had to do something," Dorrin replies, as he redons the jacket, leaving the front unbuttoned, for the fire leaves the way station passably warm. He slowly finishes the cup and edges toward the pot for seconds, filling the cup perhaps halfway. Then he cuts a small slice of the travel bread, realizing that the headache has begun to fade.

"You're a healer. Why can't you heal yourself?"

asks Brede after a large mouthful that finishes his fourth cup of the brown stew.

Dorrin shrugs, ignoring the twinge in his arm. The cut is not infected, but it will take a little while to heal. "It's not that simple. It doesn't take much to strengthen your body so a cut doesn't fester, especially if you clean it. But knitting the muscle, or knitting bone especially, takes a lot of energy. There are stories about unwise healers who saved mortally wounded patients—and died. The patients lived."

"Then what's the point of healing?" Brede's brow furrows.

"I'm not a great healer. But most battle deaths are from infections, and a good healer can stop a lot of those." He grins crookedly. "You can't fight again in that battle, but you get to fight a lot more battles."

The blond man nods. "I guess that makes sense."

"Also, sometimes healing makes a difference. Enough effort to exhaust a healer, but not kill him or her, might save someone just on the edge."

Brede nods again as he finishes his second thin slice of travel bread.

"You think it will be like this all the way to Vergren?" Kadara's eyes flicker toward the darkness outside.

Brede shakes his head. "Not likely. The higher hills are too sparse for highwaymen." Then he shrugs his broad shoulders. "Still, you can't really tell. I can't. Glad Dorrin can, though."

... *tu* ... *whuuuu* ...

"So am I," admits Kadara.

Dorrin, pleased to be of some use to his more athletic and weapon-skilled companions, looks down at the coals of the fire, their red-white of honest destruction almost, but not quite, the white-red of chaos. As almost an afterthought, he pulls over the saddlebags and opens them, checking the contents. A glint of coin catches his eye, and his hand follows. In the bottom of the left bag is a silver ... and another wooden token. He shakes his head, even as he replaces the silver in his wallet. After a moment, he puts the token there as well.

"What was that?"

"Wooden token," Dorrin admits.

Kadara's eyes narrow. "How did you work it, Dorrin?"

"Work what?"

"The horses?"

"I wondered about that," Brede adds. "Nobody was really interested in selling to us, not until you started talking to that shopkeeper."

"Hertor," Dorrin says absently, musing about the silver and the token.

"Well ..." Kadara shifts her weight, and the hazel eyes fix upon his.

Dorrin shrugs. "His dog."

"What about the dog?" Kadara's voice bears an exasperated tone.

"The poor thing was old and in pain. It had some sort of infection. I could sense how much she hurt. So I healed her a little."

"I thought you said you couldn't heal that much." Brede's voice is accusing.

Dorrin sighs. "It's not that simple ..."

"You said that before."

"Dogs are smaller than people. It didn't take very much for her, and she hurt a lot."

Kadara shakes her head, slowly. "For that, he gave you a token? I saw you slip it to the horse dealer."

"I didn't know what it meant," Dorrin says sheepishly. "I thought it might help, but I didn't want to mention it in case it wasn't anything."

"Well," Brede laughs easily, "it certainly helped get

us the mounts. Who would have thought a dog meant so much?"

Dorrin frowns, recalling the tone in Hertor's voice when the man had said, "Best bird-dog I ever had." But he says nothing as he sets aside the saddlebags.

"Let's get these cleaned up." The firmness in Kadara's voice indicates her words are not a suggestion at all. "We have a long ride tomorrow."

XX

DORRIN SQUIRMS UNEASILY in the saddle. His legs are nearly raw, and his buttocks bruised. Would it have been better to walk? Ahead of him, Kadara sits easily in the saddle of the larger chestnut mare, practicing blade exercises as the three horses trudge the cold hard clay.

Dorrin wonders whether he should do the same with the staff that sits in the lance holder, but another twinge from his overstressed legs discourages him. With his lack of skill, practicing on horseback would probably result in damage to Meriwhen or himself. Why he has named the mare Meriwhen is unclear, even to himself, but, for whatever reason, she needs a name. He cannot just say "horse" or "mare." Why does the mare even need a name?

He looks at the staff. Can he afford to put off practicing? To have Kadara and Brede defending him and looking down at his ineptitude? One encounter with brigands and his shoulder is still healing, while Kadara and Brede dispatched the three bandits as if they had no skills whatsoever.

He glances at the structure ahead. "That can't be the keep of the old Dukes of Montgren." The small white stone keep is scarcely fifty cubits square with walls no more than fifteen cubits high. Yet it sits on the flattened top of a ridge that extends hundreds of cubits on each side of the small keep. The ridge is covered only in grass, long and often matted by wind and weather, but grass nonetheless. Below the ridge, in the valley, lies Vergren, low stone walls age-streaked, but apparently intact. High white clouds dot the midafternoon sky, and the sun's warmth on his back is more than welcome.

"What's the problem?" Brede circles his gelding back toward Dorrin. Kadara rides beside Brede, her short red hair fluttering in the breeze.

"Nobody ever mentioned . . ." Even as Dorrin gestures, his thoughts are calculating, wondering at the force it took to level the old citadel.

"Well, there's the keep, and someone's home. Let's pay them a visit." Brede's cheerful voice echoes across the ridge line. His big gloved hand gestures toward the red-edged white banner flying from the tower.

"I'll pass, thank you," Dorrin says. "I'd rather just head into the town itself.

"Do you really think we intended to ride up to a White Wizard's keep?" asks Kadara.

Dorrin flushes. Why does he always take Brede so seriously? Because the big young man always sounds so sincere? Dorrin chucks the reins, suppressing a groan as the mare starts forward and his thighs remind him that he was never cut out to be a horseman. He steadies the staff in the lanceholder, and does not look back, fearing that Kadara is laughing at him again. Why does he always fall for Brede's outrageous statements? Why is it so hard for him to laugh? He tightens his lips against his own questions and against the throbbing in his legs.

The three ease their horses to the right along the road downhill toward Vergren itself.

"Wonder . . . what happened to the old keep of the Duke . . ." Dorrin mumbles to himself as the three ride abreast.

"What?" asks Brede politely.

"Well . . ." Dorrin explains. "The Founders' accounts all mention the keep of the Duke, but it's clear that the White Wizards leveled it after his death. The Prefect of Gallos still rules Gallos, and the Duke of Hydlen still holds Hydolar. All of Hydlen, I mean. It's all rather confusing."

Brede looks at Kadara, then back at Dorrin. "Lortren explained that."

"Dorrin was probably thinking about machines," opined Kadara.

The wiry redhead flushes.

"It's a matter of practical politics," Brede explains. "Fairhaven took over Montgren because it was so close. The wizards don't really rule the other duchies. They just have treaties or understandings. And they get paid for maintaining the roads."

"Stupid," mutters Dorrin. "Who wants to travel that much anyway?"

"It's not stupid," snaps Kadara. "Recluce has the Eastern Ocean. That's nothing more than a highway."

Dorrin knows she is right, and that his anger is at being on a road that isn't even a highway. His legs and thighs hurt, and Kadara and Brede have each other. As the timbered gates of Vergren appear, Dorrin reins in Meriwhen and lets the two blades lead the way.

Although the timbered city gates are heavy, and the oiled iron hinges twice the size of Brede's forearms, the gates have been fastened back against the gray stone. They have not been closed in years, except to work the hinges. Only a single guard is present, and she sits behind an overhead crenellation, surveying the three horses and their riders. A sense of whiteness surrounds the guard, but her expression does not change as the three pass underneath. Meriwhen's hoofs click on the stones.

"Where to?"

"We'll start at the central square," Brede replies. "All towns have them."

On the right side of the narrow street walk two women in boots, trousers, and heavy shapeless shirts. Each carries a large basket of damp laundry, but neither looks or speaks as the horses edge by.

Dorrin glances down an alley, but, unlike the alleys in Tyrhavven, there is no rubbish, no mud, only hard clay with a few weeds growing next to the rough plastered back walls of the buildings. He grins at a pile of horse droppings, even as a youth appears with a shovel to remove them. The boy keeps his eyes from the horses and darts back into a doorway.

"It's quiet." Kadara's soft comment is the only sound besides the clicking of hoofs.

As if to disprove the assertion, a horse and wagon lurch out of an alley before them. The wagon bed is of oiled but unpainted oak, as are the high spoked and iron-banded wheels.

"Gee-ahh!"

In the wagon are covered baskets, neatly lined up. The driver wears the same shapeless trousers and shirt that the laundry women wore. Brede reins up, as do Kadara and Dorrin, while the wagon driver eases his way into the narrow main street.

Whuuu ... uffffff ...

Dorrin pats Meriwhen on the neck. "Easy, girl. Easy." Extending his senses, he touches the baskets, then nods—potatoes. They follow the wagon southward toward an opening in the stone and plaster buildings.

In the center of the square is a flat stone platform, ringed on three sides by a low brick wall topped with a slate capstone. Dull red bricks pave the area around the platform, running perhaps two dozen cubits to the stone curbs that form an approximate square.

On the north side, facing the square, cluster three buildings which appear to be a drygoods, a butcher, and a cooper. The southern side boasts a long narrow building without description or visible activity. On the western side is an inn. A recently painted sign, in green letters, proclaims *The Golden Ram*. Under the old Temple letters is a stylized golden ram.

Brede studies the green and white awning shading the varnished and shining double oak doors. "Too expensive."

"Obviously," adds Kadara.

A heavy-set man, wearing leathers, and a double-bladed sword in a shoulder harness, stands by an older brown gelding.

Brede reins up. "I beg your pardon . . ."

"Speak up, big boy."

"Lodgings? Somewhere less expensive than . . .?" Brede gestures toward the Golden Ram.

"Take the corner street there. Bunch of places down a ways." The mercenary points to the southeast corner of the square, swells his cheeks as if he wants to spit in the gutter, then looks toward the unmarked building and swallows.

"Thank you."

"Don't thank me," mumbles the bearded man, untying his mount.

The farm wagon creaks around the square and out of sight along the southwest corner street. Less than a dozen people walk the raised stone sidewalks that front the buildings on the square.

"Shall we?" asks Brede.

Dorrin looks at the well-painted and orderly-appearing inn, dreading where they may end up in order to keep expenses low. A good half kay down the street, after inquiries at the Gilded Cup and the Trencher's Board, finds them at the Three Chimneys.

"How much for a place to sleep?" asks Brede.

"A copper a night—that's the common room. You provide your own blankets, pallet. Darkness, you can sleep on the planks if that's all you have." The thin woman innkeeper rakes her eyes over the trio.

"And the stable?"

"That's two a night a horse, just hay and water. No grain."

"What about food?"

"Plain and good. Soup and bread. Yellow cheese. Beer or mead. Three coppers each for soup and bread. A copper more for the cheese, and two for beer or mead. One for redberry."

"Well . . . we're hungry right now."

Dorrin's stomach growls, as if to reinforce the message.

The wiry woman looks the three over.

"Sit there." Her bony finger jabs toward a corner table. "Less trouble that way. No blades out in the house. Understand?"

"We understand." Brede smiles.

The Three Chimneys cannot properly be called more than a hostelry, not with only two bunkrooms and a single common room for eating. Personally, Dorrin would have preferred paying more and feeling less out of place.

An older woman, neither heavy nor thin, with silvered hair cut short enough to reveal long ears, appears behind Kadara. Her graying apron, bearing the signs of past stains, is freshly washed. "The regular, dears?"

"Regular?" stammers Dorrin.

"Soup, bread, and beer. That's three coppers, and a lot less than anywhere else in Vergren."

"How about redberry?" the healer asks.

"That's still three, but I could make the loaf a little bigger."

"I'll have that."

"The regular, with cheese," adds Brede.

"And you'd be needing that, young fellow."

"Just the regular."

As the serving woman steps toward the kitchen, Dorrin looks around the squarish room. Less than half the tables are filled, certainly because it is well past midday, and at many of the tables sit older men, silently nursing mugs and little else.

"Wonderful place," observes Kadara.

"Not much sense in spending coins we haven't figured how to replace." Brede responds.

Dorrin rubs his nose, trying to stifle a sneeze. "Aaaachooooo . . ."

"It's not that bad." Brede grins momentarily.

"Aaa . . . choooo . . ."

"Here you be, dears."

Three chipped brown earthenware bowls land upon the table, followed by three equally chipped mugs, and three large, scraped, and bent spoons.

"And here's the bread."

True to her word, she supplies Dorrin with the largest loaf of the dark brown bread, although the smallest loaf—Kadara's—is well over two-thirds of a cubit long. The server slips a small wedge of cheese onto the table before Brede. "Be you needing anything else, dears?"

"No, thank you," Dorrin answers.

She bobs her head and is gone to pick up a mug and a copper from a fat and bald graybeard.

Brede breaks off nearly a quarter of the loaf and chews his way through it even before Dorrin has had two mouthfuls. Kadara has almost finished her section of the bread in the same time.

Dorrin uses the battered tin spoon to sample the dark substance presented as soup—lukewarm, salty, and bitter, but without anything that feels dangerous. He takes one spoonful, then another, chewing on the bread between spoonfuls.

" . . . how may I help you, your honors?"

Dorrin looks up at the forced heartiness of the hostel keeper's voice.

Three guards in white leathers stand in the doorway, two men and a woman. The men are clean-shaven, and all are hardfaced.

"The only large table I have is there," announces the wiry woman, pointing, it appears to Dorrin, right at them, rather than at the vacant adjoining table.

The three sit around the table. The older gray-haired man wears a black circle on the lapel of the white leather vest. His eyes range over the three, and he pauses for a moment, as if studying Dorrin. Dorrin meets the glance, then looks down.

The senior guard looks away and points. A fingertip of flame appears before the face of the serving woman, who turns quickly, sees the white leathers, and scurries toward the three guards. "Yes, your honors?"

"Soup and cheese, with the good beer, not the swill that Zera says is all she has," states the man.

"Same here," adds the woman.

The last guard only nods, preoccupied with cleaning his finger-nails with the point of his white-copper belt knife.

The gray-haired server retreats through the smoke to the kitchen, and the rest of those eating pointedly ignore the White guards.

Dorrin licks his lips as the woman guard looks in his direction.

"I won't eat you, sweetie. Not yet . . ." She leers at him, and the scar on her left cheek imparts a twist to the leer.

"Knock it off, Estil," snaps the leader. "He's a decade younger, and one of those pilgrim healers."

"Where was he when I needed healing?"

"Knock it off."

"All right."

Dorrin glances toward the doorway, trying to ignore the conversation about guard rotations, someone called Jeslek, and the unfriendliness of the people in Vergren.

" . . . centuries later, and you'd think we'd personally fired the old keep . . ."

A bearded man swings open the battered door and staggers out into the afternoon, where a fine and cold spring rain has begun to fall. A gust of chill damp air flows into the hostelry, cutting through the stale warmth.

Thhuummpp . . .

The serving woman is setting mugs and bowls before the White guards, efficiently and quickly.

"About time . . ."

The senior guard hands the server a coin of some sort, and she nods.

"Why do we have to eat here?"

"You know why."

"I know . . . because we have to show up everywhere, and besides it's easier on the Council's treasury if we eat cheap . . ."

The three from Recluce exchange glances. Brede pops the last of his bread into his mouth, while Kadara tilts her mug all the way back. Mechanically, Dorrin slurps the last of the soup and chews the remaining bread crust, although his stomach is more than full.

"Let's go."

Dorrin reaches for his pack.

"So long, sweetie!"

Dorrin flushes. Kadara grins, and a faint smile creases Brede's face.

"Estil . . ."

"He's sweet—not like you."

Dorrin looks away from the last exaggerated leer and stumbles into the afternoon drizzle.

"You certainly made an impression there."

Dorrin ignores Kadara's comments, and instead looks toward the rail where the horses remain tethered. "Now what should we do?"

"Check out the stable. Then we can walk over to the farm market we passed, see about supplies for going on."

Dorrin pulls his waterproof over his shoulders and wipes the rain off his forehead. "It's too quiet here. Nobody says anything. Or not much."

"We're outsiders. What do you expect?"

XXI

THE HIGH PLAINS shake.

A ball of light flares around the single figure in white who stands in the midst of that eye-searing radiance.

Whhhheeeeee . . . rrrmmmmm . . .

Smoke circles from the hills that shudder upwards around the white wizard with the glistening white hair and the eyes like points of sun.

. . . rrrmmmmm . . . thrummmbblle . . .

Still, the ground shakes.

In the distance a river shakes from its bed, and silvered waters pour southward, inundating what had been meadows. At a greater distance, buildings rock, and stone walls shiver. Some roofs collapse upon their hapless inhabitants.

The hills shudder yet higher, dwarfing even more completely the magician who has raised them, yet they do not threaten him nor the glistening strip of white stone that stretches westward.

. . . wehhhhheeeee . . . cracccckkkkkk . . . crackkkkk . . .

Across the Eastern Ocean, five men and women, garbed in black, look upon a mirror. Those who do not shake their heads frown. One man does both. He is tall and thin.

"He builds mountains to protect their road."

"Yet they do not rise to crush him."

"Is he the result of too much order in Recluce?"

"How could we have less? Already we pay a high price." The dark-haired woman looks to the thin wizard.

"He will be the next High Wizard," says the thin man.

"Getting to be High Wizard is easier than keeping the amulet," observes the woman.

In the mirror, the smoke swirls around the blinding point of whiteness.

XXII

WHAT DID HE expect from the people of Vergren? The words had worried Dorrin all through the afternoon and evening, through the eerie walk along nearly spotless streets that were tinged with unseen whiteness, through an evening supper of stew not much thicker than the soup of the midday, and through a near-sleepless night on the dusty planks of the Three Chimneys.

Sleeping on hard planks in a garret with Kadara and Brede is bad enough, but listening to the two nuzzle and coo is much worse—even though they are polite enough, or circumspect enough, not to make total love until he is asleep or after he has staggered up and out in the morning.

He scratches a flea bite under his armpit. While he can persuade the creatures to leave him while he is awake, his healing talents do not work quite so well asleep—although more accomplished magisters can erect wards that work even while they sleep.

As they ride eastward out of Vergren, the fog swirls around them, and water drips from slate roofs onto the stone. Townspeople appear—like the spirits of ancient angels—in and out of the fog, their steps silent on the stone pavement. A clinking harness echoes down the street.

"Quiet," observes Brede, and his words sound almost hollow.

"You said that yesterday," snaps Kadara.

"It was quiet yesterday."

With his senses ranging through the fog and mist, Dorrin gathers nothing beyond the unseen whiteness that oozes beneath the entire town, almost like an unvoiced grief. Are all towns ruled by the White Wizards so quiet?

Or is it the spirit of Vergren that still languishes? Because Montgren helped the Founders? Or because the people instinctively embraced order?

Dorrin shakes his head. The White Wizards must have *some* order. They cannot be totally chaotic, not if Fairhaven has successfully ruled most of Candar for the centuries since Creslin fled Candar. Yet Vergren oozes despair amidst its order.

Meriwhen whinnies and steps sideways to avoid a pile of manure.

"Dorrin?"

"... uhh... what?" The healer turns toward Kadara.

"You need to watch where you're riding. Stop thinking about machines and whatever."

"I was watching." But he straightens himself in the saddle, and pats Meriwhen on the neck.

After the walls of Vergren fade into the morning mist and disappear behind the hills, the loudest sounds along the stone road are those of hoofs and the voices of the three from Recluce. Even the sheep graze silently, like so many miniature clouds drifting across the damp hillside meadows.

Brede and Kadara converse in low voices.

" . . . Spidlarian blade is too thin, not enough metal to stand up to a hand and a half . . ."

"You wouldn't fight it that way . . . use the edges to slide . . ."

" . . . still think that the shortsword is best all around . . ."

" . . . not enough length to protect you . . ."

Dorrin yawns. He is supposed to stay awake listening to technical talk about blades? He shifts his weight in the saddle and casts his senses out toward the endless sheep. Nothing roams the hillsides but the sheep, the shaggy dogs, and an occasional fox.

" . . . shields . . ."

"Too cumbersome for mounted work . . ."

The healer yawns, wondering how long the ride will be.

Midmorning passes, and the low clouds have still not lifted. One hillside looks like another, and the sheep in each meadow could have been the same sheep that the three had passed leaving Vergren.

"How do you tell one sheep from another?" Dorrin mumbles as he reaches yet another hill crest. The narrow road drops out of the rolling hills that they have ridden up and down, up and down, ever since they left Vergren. The clay-packed thoroughfare descends before the three exiles—mostly straight—to the town ahead, where it then winds through the houses like a smooth brown river. Perhaps a handful of stores rise on the far side of the town, just short of the line of trees that may mark a true watercourse.

Dorrin peers at the stone bearing the name *Weevett* on the right-hand side of the road. "Wonder if they make wool here."

"Probably." Brede inclines his head toward the stone wall to his left, and to the sheep beyond. "They probably card and spin it everywhere around here."

"Why are we doing this?" Dorrin asks.

"Because we need to get to Fairhaven. You know that." Kadara flips the sword into the air and catches the hilt, then replaces it in the scabbard.

"Show-off. I meant why are we going to Fairhaven at all?"

"Because we have to if we ever want to get back to Recluce."

Dorrin fingers the staff in the lanceholder. "They'll never let us return, no matter what Lortren said. Did you ever run into anyone who has?"

"Lortren," offers Brede.

"Besides her?" Dorrin should have guessed. Of course, Brede and Kadara believe they will be allowed to return. They are blades, like the white-haired magistra. And perhaps they will be allowed to return— after demonstrating their repentance or whatever total acceptance of the Brotherhood's goals that may be required.

For him, it is already clear, the price is at the very least his rejection of his dreams of order machines and his acceptance of an irrational concept of true order.

"Felthar," adds Kadara.

"Another blade."

"What does that have to do with it?"

Dorrin shifts his weight in the saddle trying to stretch his legs. Meriwhen whinnies.

"What Dorrin is saying, Kadara, is that very few healers return."

"But why?"

"I don't know," Dorrin says heavily. "But it's true."

Since there is little to say beyond that, the three ride silently eastward and downhill into Weevett, past yet more sheep grazing on the rolling hillside.

XXIII

IN THE SPRING light, the road throws white glare up into the faces of the three riders. Dorrin rides with his eyes squeezed almost shut, relying more upon senses thrown to the faint breeze that smells of new-turned earth than the blurry images that dance before his eyes. His senses twist when he directs them toward the city down in the valley, and he begins to alternate between sense and vision, squirming in the saddle.

"What's the matter?"

"The glare."

"What glare? It's a bit bright, but not that bad." Kadara looks toward the midmorning sun, then back toward Dorrin.

Dorrin still squints.

In the gentle valley ahead, white structures not quite randomly placed are interspersed with white roads, green grass, and evergreens barely taller than the roofs they shade.

"Not any tall buildings." Brede glances from the whiteness of the road and from the low city ahead to his right, to the west. "You'd think the wizards would have a tall building or two."

"There might be one near the center of Fairhaven," offers Dorrin, "but there won't be many. Tall structures and chaos don't really go together."

"Why not?" Kadara also looks to the side of the road.

"Because," explains Dorrin, "chaos has the tendency

to weaken any material, and the higher you build something the more support it needs. That's why we ought to build machines."

"Huhhh ... you still worried about machines?" Brede shakes his head.

"He's always thinking about machines," Kadara adds softly.

"I mean it," Dorrin insists. "Order can hold machines together even against chaos, if they're built of good black iron. But chaos couldn't possibly use such machines."

"That's all right in theory, but if the machines are so good, why does the Brotherhood oppose them and why are you here?" Brede squints toward the city and the horse and wagon that appear to be moving out from Fairhaven and toward them. "Someone's headed this way."

"Because they're afraid of them, and they don't understand them. Machines can only do what they're built to do—"

"Dorrin ... we've heard it before," interrupts Kadara, "and we're not the ones you have to convince."

Dorrin closes his eyes. Rather than form a reply, he gropes with his senses to find the wagon. "The wagon's empty, and there's just a driver. He feels like an old man."

Creeeeaaakkk ... As if to punctuate Dorrin's observation, the sound of ill-lubricated wheels squeaks toward them.

First, against the morning brightness appears a wavering black silhouette. The silhouette creaks into the brown-boarded shape of a farm wagon pulled by a single large, if swaybacked, gray horse.

"Geee ... ahhh ..." The driver's flat, emotionless voice carries from the bench seat. The wagon trundles down the left side of the stone-paved road, squealing past Dorrin so closely that he could reach out and touch the driver's whip. He does not. Instead, his lips purse, and he swallows.

The driver looks no older than he or Brede, but feels ancient to those senses which can—sometimes—show reality more clearly than mere eyesight.

Dorrin chucks the reins to catch up to Brede and Kadara, for he has fallen behind as the wagon has passed. Before he reaches them, a messenger, dressed in white, with a red slash across his tunic, gallops past. Two more wagons pass in the other direction.

In time, the three near a pair of low and empty towers, built of whitened stone, resembling gates.

Dorrin studies the gates, then glances at the pale green leaves of the spreading trees and the trimmed bushes beyond them, then back at the whitened granite of the gatehouse and the pavement and curbs. His forehead throbs, warning him that he must try to figure out why he feels so assaulted by what is the White City, the center of all that is Candar and will be Candar for generations, if not millennia, to come.

Creaaakkk. Another wagon passes, heading westward out of the wide divided boulevard that the east-west highway has become as it enters the White City. White indeed is the city, a white more blinding than the noonday sands on the eastern beaches of Recluce. White and clean, with off-gray granite paving stones that sparkle white in the sun, and merely shine in the shade.

After following Brede and Kadara past the old and empty towers, Dorrin looks across the valley, amazed at the confluence of white and green. Green leaves cloak trees that should be taller, in some fashion. The leaves flutter in the light breeze, interposing themselves between the lines of white stone walls and boulevards that intertwine. Yet for all the grace and curved lines, the great avenues—the east-west highway and the north-south road—seem to quarter the city like two white stone swords.

They pass an invisible line inside which almost all the buildings appear white. A central strip of grass and bushes, curbed in limestone, separates two roads of the boulevard. Although it is spring, even warmer than in Tyrhavven and Vergren, he sees no flowers, no colors except the greens of shrubs and grass and the whites of the curbstones and pavement. All of the horses and carts headed into the city are using the right-hand road, while those leaving use the left road. All those on foot use the outside edge of the roads. Toward the center of the shallow valley the whiteness becomes more pronounced and the greenery less. A single stone tower rises from the center of the city.

Dorrin takes a deep breath, then casts his senses to the winds—and reels in his tracks, barely withdrawing into himself at the swirling patterns of whitish-red that seem to fill the entire valley, that seem to twist and tear at his whole being. He wipes his suddenly dripping forehead with his sleeve. White wizardry seems to permeate everything, for all the artful stonework laid by skillful masons, and the greenery of the trees and grasses.

Dorrin barely catches Kadara's words to Brede.

"Just what are we going to do here? And how can we afford to keep traveling? Everywhere we stay it costs more coins. I don't know about you, but I don't have all that much left—not if we've got to spend a year in this forsaken country." Kadara cases her mare up beside Brede.

Dorrin wipes his forehead again, then reaches for his water bottle. He takes a deep pull, almost draining it.

"It's simple enough," offers Brede. "We take jobs with a trader, or something."

"With what they pay? And the way they look at women blades?"

"Do you have a better idea? You're the one who just pointed out that we need coins."

"There must be something better."

"I can't sleep here tonight." Dorrin cuts the discussion short.

"Why not? You can't do this, and you can't do that, and all you want to do is go off someplace and build stupid machines." Kadara's voice sharpens.

"There's too much chaos." Dorrin shivers, feeling again the tentacles of whiteness that seem to creep from the road, from the buildings, like the stinging spines of jellyfish hidden just beneath an ocean's surface.

"It's a perfectly pleasant and clean-looking city, Dorrin." Kadara gestures at the well-kept grass in the median strip between the two roads. "There's no reason not to enjoy it for a while."

"Fine. You stay here. I can't. I'll meet you somewhere."

"Dorrin, that's the stupidest . . ."

"Kadara." Brede rides closer to the healer. "Can you tell us why you can't sleep here? Besides the chaos?"

"It's everywhere, like invisible jellyfish with pointed spines. It just hurts for me to ride, and it's hard to look at anything without my eyes watering and stinging. Already, sometimes I feel like I can't breathe."

Dorrin looks down at the pavement, then up at the low oaks that barely clear the house tops, their trunks somehow paler than those of the trees in the hills of Montgren. "Even the trees aren't quite right."

"Do you need to leave now, or can we talk to some traders first?"

"I *think* I'm getting the hang of it . . . but I don't think I could rest anywhere around here."

"Wonderful . . . not only does he dream up impossible machines, but he sees impossible jellyfish and strange trees."

Both Brede and Dorrin glare at Kadara.

"I happen to trust his feelings, Kadara, and if you want to sleep in Fairhaven by yourself, I'll be more than happy to ride with Dorrin."

Kadara looks down at the mare's neck. "I'm sorry. It's just . . . a little hard to believe."

Dorrin grins in spite of the stinging in his eyes. "If it didn't hurt so much, I wouldn't believe me either."

"Is that just chaos?" asks Brede.

"Just?" Dorrin's tone is wry.

Brede laughs. "Point to you, Dorrin."

"You two. Men . . ." mutters Kadara.

"We still need to find some traders," Brede says. "Do you think they'll be around the central square?"

"How would I know?"

"Well . . . we'll check the square first."

Dorrin nods. The square seems as good a place as any to begin, and it's easier to follow Brede through the hidden swirls of chaos. Another farm wagon creaks past, heading back in the direction of Montgren.

"Why don't you just ask someone? You men seem to think it's a disgrace to ask for directions. It's a lot easier to ask than to ride forever."

Brede blushes. "Fine. You ask."

"I'd be happy to." Kadara eases the mare in front of Brede's gelding and toward two men unloading a wagon before an unmarked building. "Sers . . . could you tell me where I might find the traders' area?"

A potbellied man with a shock of wispy white hair that stands on end in the breeze drops a sack of flour onto a hand cart, then looks up. "Free traders or the licensed ones?"

"The ones in the city."

"That'd be the licensed ones. Most of 'em got places around the traders' square."

"I'm new here. Is that near the main square ahead?"

"That's the wizards' square."

The second wagoner spits into the gutter, then lifts another sack, avoiding any eye contact with the three riders.

"Where is the traders' square?"

"Take the avenue here a ways past the White Tower until it forks. The right fork leads there." He shakes his head and hefts another sack, letting it rest almost upon his protruding gut.

"Thank you."

Neither wagoner acknowledges her appreciation.

As the three ride toward the wizards' square, they pass a squad of white-coated troopers, all of whom turn cold eyes upon them. Even though chaos twines around each of the white riders, Dorrin forces himself to meet the cold eyes of the leader, trying to look as open and curious as the rawest traveler. None of the White guards speaks, nor do the three from Recluce, and the loudest sound is that of hoofs.

As they near the White Wizards' square, Dorrin senses the increasing chaos—that and the lack of trees. Now only grass and low bushes comprise the greenery.

Squeakkk . . .

The healer looks down a narrow alley at the cart, which is wheeled by a man wearing little more than rags who is chained to the cart he pulls. Behind the cart are a woman wreathed in the unseen white of chaos and dressed completely in white and another raggedly dressed man. Behind them are two armed White guards on foot.

The White Wizard gestures at a pile of rubbish, and a line of fire runs from her fingers to the heap on the stones.

Whhhsttt. White ashes drift lazily down.

The second man quickly bends and sweeps the ashes into a pan which he empties into the small cart.

Squeaakkk . . . The cart rolls on.

Dorrin swallows. No wonder the streets of Fairhaven are clean. But the cleaning method also explains his dislike for the city. Years of that casual chaos-clean-up have certainly cloaked Fairhaven with white dust that bears the imprint of chaos.

"That seems like a waste of magic." Brede's voice is low.

"Probably a punishment for the wizard as well. Of course, it was a woman." Kadara glances back at the alley, although the cart is no longer visible.

"Can we ride around the square?" Dorrin asks plaintively, wincing from the forces that swirl in the white buildings ahead.

"I'd like to see it."

"I'll meet you on the far side."

"Will you be all right?" asks Brede.

"Better than if I ride through that . . . stuff." Dorrin glances at the single four-story tower rising above the square, then shivers, swaying in the saddle, at the force of the energies that surround the White Tower. He forces a smile as he senses the lines of black that contain the tower's white granite blocks. Even the chaos-masters must use some order!

"Are you sure you'll be all right?"

"If I stay away from the worst of it, I can handle it for a while." Dorrin pats Meriwhen's neck. "I think," is whispered to himself as Brede edges the brown gelding toward Kadara.

Dorrin turns right at the next cross street and angles down a narrower way. Although he feels Brede's eyes on his back, he does not look back, concentrating instead on avoiding the few pedestrians who hug the edges of the thoroughfare. None look up at him as they walk quickly along the white-granite streets, their feet lifting puffs of the fine white dust that rises, then sifts back into the narrow joints between the stones.

At the end of the first block, he turns Meriwhen to the left, along a street paralleling the main avenue. After less than a hundred cubits he reins up while a vendor maneuvers a food cart into a small narrow oblong of greenery in a wider part of the street.

Perhaps five men in shapeless gray tunics wait for the vendor to set up his grills and set forth a few already-cooked pastries. Once more, no one looks up at the healer, acting almost as if he did not exist. By the time he rejoins the avenue, Brede and Kadara are waiting for him.

"Took you a while."

"You went the more direct route. See anything interesting?"

"There really weren't many people in the square," Brede says slowly. "Would that be because they're afraid of the wizards?"

"Why? The wizards keep the city clean and free from most crime." Kadara nudges the mare into a walk. "Let's go."

"That much focus on chaos probably makes people uneasy," speculates the healer, easing Meriwhen into line behind Kadara.

More than a score of people throng the traders' square, and wagons creak in and out of the buildings that flank it.

Brede points to one of the stone buildings—almost no buildings in Fairhaven are of timber—and to a long hitching post in front. From the building, made of the same whitened granite as most of Fairhaven, projects a small sign—*Gerrish—Trader*. Under the Temple-style letters is the outline of a cart and horse in dark green paint.

To Dorrin's eyes the outline appears crude, although the lines are even and the paint relatively new.

"Shall we try this one?" asks Brede, dismounting with the fluidity that Dorrin continues to envy.

"We have to start someplace." Kadara slips off her mount with equal ease.

Dorrin clambers off Meriwhen, wincing at the continuing soreness in his thighs. By the time he has tied the mare to the fir pole suspended between two stone uprights, Kadara and Brede have brushed away the faint white dust that seems to rise from the streets of Fairhaven and straightened their harnesses and swords. Dorrin follows their example, except that he leaves the staff in the lanceholder. Carrying a staff more than four cubits long into a trader's place won't add anything.

Besides, the way things have been going, he would probably trip over it. So, empty-handed, he follows Brede and Kadara through the half-open door into a small room. A heavy-set man stands by a long table, studying a map held flat and weighed down at each corner by fist-sized stones.

"Hirl?" He pauses. "You're not Hirl. What do you want?"

Brede smiles openly. "If you're Gerrish, I heard you might be looking for help. Guards, general assistance . . ."

"Haaa . . ." The trader shakes his head. "You're big enough, but your . . . friends . . ."

"Kadara's probably better with a blade than anyone you have."

Kadara's eyes lock upon the trader, who is the first to look away. He then focuses on Dorrin, who avoids the swarthy man's stare by looking at the plain wooden timbers that frame the wall behind the trader.

Dorrin's eyes skip to the archway to the trader's right, through which he can see the open space of a warehouse and stable, including stacks of small barrels directly beyond the opening.

"Blades . . . why would I need blades?" snaps the trader.

Brede shrugs. "Perhaps my information was mistaken."

"Maybe a copper a day for you, and that's hauling cargo when necessary . . . that's all I need." The heavy man shrugs.

Brede looks down on the squat dark man. "I'm a little surprised. We ran into bandits on the way from Tyrhavven. Yet you say that you need no guards."

"Look. We don't travel the back roads. They're not patrolled by the White guards, and they're slow and twisty."

"Do the wizards' roads go everywhere?" interrupts Dorrin.

"Of course not," snorts the trader. "They only connect the major cities. But that's where the people are, and where the people are is where the coins are."

"Don't so many coins tempt bandits?" Brede persists.

"Not if they want to stay alive." He gestures. "Go on. I don't need guards, especially outlanders, and women. Besides, armed guards means using weapons, and using blades means that someone's going to get killed, and that's not good for business."

Brede steps back. "Who does trade the back roads?"

"You might ask in the alleys, friend. Nobody with brains, that's for sure."

Gerrish is not telling the whole truth, but Dorrin does not shake his head. Instead, for a moment, he looks at the figures unstacking barrels in the warehouse beyond. Then he turns his eyes back to the trader. "Do the unsanctioned traders still operate from the old grounds outside the city?"

"How would I know? Outside the city, the alleys—it's all the same to us." The trader squares his round shoulders and broad paunch, with a look toward the warehouse.

"Thank you, trader." Brede gives a half-bow.

Kadara ignores the man as she turns, her hand on the hilt of her blade.

Dorrin, although tempted to wish the man well in the name or order, just to see him squirm, merely nods as he turns away from Gerrish.

Back on the white-paved street, the three look to the horses, which wait, apparently undisturbed. Brede stops by the stone support, glancing across the street toward another sign with a trader's symbol.

"Now what do we do?" asks Kadara.

Dorrin glances around the traders' square, his eyes flickering from one white stone building to another, none more than two stories tall. The avenue beside which he stands runs straight as a spear toward the great city square of Fairhaven, where the wizards' buildings surround a well-kept park that contains even a few ancient white oaks. The vegetation in the center of the traders' square, circled by the same white paving stones that comprise every main thoroughfare in the White City, is comprised only of the short wiry grass and evenly trimmed low bushes with blue-green needles—candlebushes.

The healer recognizes that the greenery consists of plants which can withstand chaos and few, if any, true flowers in Fairhaven.

Two men and a woman, wearing the pale blue tunics of traders, enter the building which the three exiles had just left.

"Well . . . what do we do now?" repeats Kadara. "Try one of the others?"

Dorrin shakes his head, and both look at him. "You can't pay protection to two masters, and the traders here must look to the White Wizards. Maybe I'm wrong, but"—his head inclines toward the sign across the white paving stones from where they stand— "trader Alligash probably would give you exactly the same rationale."

"Do we just give up?" Kadara's hand remains on the hilt of her blade.

"We need to look outside Fairhaven," opines Dorrin.

Brede looks at the sun, now hanging just above the stone roofs on the western side of the square, and grins ruefully. "We probably ought to find somewhere to stay. This isn't a place where you can sleep in the square."

"Our coins aren't going to last forever," reminds Kadara.

"Then we need to get out of the city," suggests Dorrin.

Both Brede and Kadara glare at Dorrin.

Click ... clickedy ... click ...

" ... shit ..." Kadara reaches for her saddle, but does not attempt to mount.

Three horses move quickly into the square from the direction of the main city square. All three bear the white-clad and white-armored guards. Two guards are female, but all are hard-faced and short-haired, and their white-bronze blades glitter with the white-red of chaos.

"So where are we headed?" asks Brede, his big right hand on the reins to the gelding. He does not untie the leathers from the post.

"Out of the city. Toward the west," suggests Dorrin.

"Hold it!" The speaker is the leading guard, a rangy older man with salt-and-pepper hair and a beaked nose.

"I beg your pardon?" offers Brede, the reins to the chestnut in his hand.

"You're outlanders?" asks the White guard.

"We're not from Fairhaven—that's true," admits the tall man, his voice mellow and polite.

"Another bunch of those young Recluce pilgrim types, I'd bet." The low-voiced comment comes from the dark-haired female guard. She shifts her seat on the gelding directly behind the group leader who had spoken to Brede.

"They're more interesting than the one-god pilgrims from Kyphros," adds the third guard, a heavier blond woman.

Dorrin senses some discomfort behind the words, discomfort not exactly linked to the three from Recluce.

"Where are you headed?" demands the older guard, swinging off his horse.

"West. Through the Easthorns and beyond," Brede answers simply.

"Likely story." He half-snorts, but looks toward the trader's building, then at the dispatch case in his hand. Finally, he shrugs and looks at the blonde. "Derla, I need to talk to Gerrish. You can take care of these . . . pilgrims . . ." He ties the horse beside Brede's, and his boots click on the stones as he walks into the trader's.

"So . . . what brings you to Fairhaven?" snaps Derla. She edges her mount forward until the gelding almost separates Dorrin from Brede and Kadara.

"The usual," Brede replies. "We were sent out to learn about Candar and the world."

The woman's discomfort is almost palpable to Dorrin, and he squirms, wondering what he should do. She is, after all, a White guard and a servant of chaos.

"What do you think?" Derla looks at the younger and dark-haired guard.

"According to Zerlat, the big one's a natural blade. The redhead is a mage, but he's no Creslin. He can barely sense the winds. He is a pretty fair healer . . ."

Dorrin catches his breath, realizing that the meeting in the square has scarcely been chance. He edges toward the one called Derla, and his hand brushes her leg. Chaos or not, he must respond to the twisted knot of agony tied within her. Despite the invisible white flames that lick around her, there remains a core of order that he touches, easing the pain and strengthening her. He shivers as he steps away, pale, and takes a deep breath, shaking his head against the throbbing caused by the contact.

Kadara closes her mouth quickly, but not so quickly that Dorrin cannot sense her disapproval.

"You didn't have to do that," snaps the guard.

Silence, except for the heavy breathing of six horses, shrouds the corner of the square.

"Fair's fair." Derla eases the gelding back away from Brede, Dorrin and Kadara. "And I'm more than sick of bleeding all over the entire continent so that some stupid man can have a child someday and boost his frigging ego."

"I'm sorry." Dorrin leans away from the blonde.

"Don't apologize. You're a man. It's not your fault that you're all glands and little brain." The white-clad guard smiles politely and turns toward the other female guard. "So . . . what should we do with them?"

The dark-haired woman shakes her head. "The Council doesn't like people from the isle, and Jeslek is saying that Recluce has stolen our rain and our crops for centuries."

"Have the orders changed?"

They both grin.

"Young fellow . . . Dorrin . . . whatever your name is . . . if I were you, I'd get out of Fairhaven real quick and quietly. And take your friends with you."

Brede and Kadara look from the guards to Dorrin. Then Brede vaults into the saddle. Kadara studies the dark-haired guard for another long moment.

"You heard what I said, witch-blade. If you want to swing that toy of yours much longer, I'd get out of here." The blonde turns to her dark-haired compatriot. "Hard to believe they're descended from Creslin . . . so dull . . ."

In the process of clambering onto Meriwhen, Dorrin suppresses a grin as he senses Kadara's combined puzzlement, anger, and frustration. But, as he turns the mare, he inclines his head to the two guards. The blonde flushes, although her expression remains as cold as that of a formal marble statue.

Until they clear the square the three ride in silence.

Finally, Kadara looks over her shoulder and then back at Dorrin. "What they see . . ."

"Kadara." Brede's voice is low, but firm.

"Don't 'Kadara' me!"

Brede and Dorrin exchange glances.

"And stop looking at each other like that!"

Both men shrug, almost simultaneously.

Dorrin looks at the road ahead, leading westward.

XXIV

KADARA, BREDE, AND Dorrin ride along the white-paved highway south toward the old trader's grounds. Dorrin pats Meriwhen's neck when they pass another set of mounted White guards, but the guards only look, and turn their mounts onto a narrower road headed east. Kadara again looks at Brede.

Dorrin can stand the unspoken reproaches no longer. "Would you two stop it!"

"Stop what?" Kadara's voice is vaguely amused.

"You know what I mean."

"What do you mean?"

Dorrin swallows his anger and refuses to speak. Instead, he squirms on the hard saddle, and momentarily stands in the stirrups to stretch his legs.

Meriwhen whinnies, and he pats her neck again.

The three continue until they have passed through

the outer low gates and the curbstones have given way to a flat stone highway from which white dust rises with each descending hoof.

Dorrin sneezes. He sneezes again. Kadara and Brede exchange whispers. Although he could call their conversation to him on the breeze, he does not. Instead he sneezes again.

"Can't you do something about that?" asks Brede. "You're supposed to be the healer."

"Not . . . accchoooooo . . . that good. It's the dust, or something."

Kadara and Brede exchange another glance. Dorrin bites his lip and tries to suppress another sneeze. Intermittent sneezes punctuate the next several kays, and his legs are aching from the effort of riding and sneezing by the time his nose begins to stop itching.

The arrow in the stone guidepost directs them onto a packed clay road. Before they have climbed a kay up the gentle grade, heavy brownish dust clings to the legs of each horse. The road flattens at the crest, and less than half a kay away is a small kiosk. To the right of it are flat clay, patches of grass, and scraggly bushes. Less than half a dozen tents dot the area.

"Not exactly a thriving trading ground."

"No." Kadara brushes a strand of hair back over her ears.

"No wagon?" The guard remains seated on the stool leaned against the back wall of the kiosk. The kiosk's white paint has begun to flake away.

"We're not traders."

"Ride around the pole, then." The guard's eyes close even before Brede guides the gelding around the turnpole and through the two-cubit-wide gap.

"Not even a fence."

"The posts are close enough together to keep out any wagons."

The posts, each set about two cubits from its neighbor, enclose a space perhaps three hundred cubits on a side. The traders' grounds contain no more than a handful of tents, all pitched in the higher northwest corner.

"Wonderful idea." Kadara glances at Dorrin. "No one here could afford one guard, let alone two—or a healer."

"So . . . we ride to Jellico." Dorrin's legs are stiff, but they no longer ache—at least not much.

"And arrive penniless?"

"We can only do what we can," says Brede. "No one in Fairhaven would hire us, and staying there would have cost far too much. Besides, those guards made it clear that we needed to leave while we could. They don't like Black healers—that was clear enough."

"Sorry."

"Don't be sorry. You got us horses we probably wouldn't have and warned us about the highwaymen. This time, you're the one they don't like. Even so, that business with the White lady probably got us out of there. It evens out." Brede gives a long look to Kadara, who swallows.

"I'm sorry, Dorrin. It's just been . . . a long trip already."

"I didn't mean to cause trouble. I just thought . . . maybe at least here."

"All we can do is try." Brede guides the gelding toward the nearest tent. Beside the brown patched canvas are a wagon and two horses. Two men watch as the three ride up. One holds an already-cocked crossbow loosely.

"Who you looking for?"

Brede reins up, and Dorrin and Kadara follow his example.

"We heard that there might be some traders who could use some help," begins Brede, his voice mellow and convincing.

"Not us, young fellow. Don't need young and hungry bravos. Look somewheres else." The man with the crossbow cackles, showing blackened teeth. "Try Durnit there. In the patched tent." He cackles again, but raises the crossbow. "Get!"

"I don't think that's wise," Brede answers.

"Maybe not, young fellow . . . but I don't need you and yours. Now go bother some other bastard."

The three edge their mounts away, still watching until the trader lowers the bow. Then they turn toward the brown tent that is more patches than original fabric. A single man—whose clothes, once solid leathers and linen, approximate rags—sits in front of a low fire, turning something on a spit. Outside of the tent is tethered but a single swaybacked horse.

"Are you Durnit?"

"Maybe. What's it to you?"

"We heard you might need some help on your next run."

"Ha! Sure as I would, but I've not a copper left from the last." The trader turns the spit again. "There's my profits—one scrawny bird. They say the Suthyans'll take a trader as a factor on the Nordla run. I'll try that. Can't fight the wizards and their roads, and can't afford a road pass."

"Is there anyone around here who might need help?" Dorrin asks softly into the silence.

"You might try Liedral. Tent's over there, with the blue flag." The bearded trader's thumb gestures toward a smaller tent on the hilly rise. "Jellico type." He spits into the dirt beside the fire.

"Thank you."

"Don't thank me. Just let me finish eating. Last meal for a long time." He eases the blackened fowl off the spit with the short knife, and greasy fingers worry away a small drumstick.

Brede's hand lifts as if to reach toward the sword

in the shoulder harness before he turns in the direction pointed by the hungry trader.

Another hundred cubits westward stands the neatly squared tent, although the short blue banner hangs limply in the golden light of late afternoon. A single chestnut and a mule are tethered to iron stakes driven into the clay on the eastern side of the tent, and an iron chain links the two-wheeled cart to a third iron stake on the western side.

The figure feeding the fire from a pile of stubby split logs is broad-shouldered, beardless, dressed in faded blue leathers, and wears a broad-brimmed blue felt hat. The trader straightens and waits, appearing nearly as tall as Kadara. The three from Recluce ride slowly forward.

"Are you Liedral?" Brede begins.

"Yes." A smile follows the single word delivered in a light baritone.

"Durnit—the trader back there—he suggested you might need some help on your next run."

"We all need help." The laugh is soft.

Dorrin's senses conflict with his eyes over the trader's appearance.

"I can't pay three guards."

"They're guards," Dorrin offers. "I'm just an apprentice healer."

"Your staff indicated something like that." Liedral gestures to the fire, and the kettle suspended over one side. "You've ridden a while. You can at least rest for a bit. I can't offer much besides some spare redberry or a spice tea."

Brede and Kadara exchange glances. Dorrin dismounts. Both look at him.

"My legs are sore."

Brede shrugs and slips from the saddle with the fluid grace that Dorrin still envies. Kadara follows.

"You're all from Recluce?"

"Yes." Dorrin sees no point in dissembling.

Kadara raises an eyebrow; Brede looks for somewhere to tether his mount.

"Use the stake the wagon is chained to," suggests Liedral.

"All three?" blurts Dorrin.

"For now, it should be more than adequate." The dryness of the trader's tone brings a flush to Dorrin's freckled face.

"Why the iron?" asks Brede, as he loops the leather through the fist-sized eyelet of the stake.

"More than a few free traders have lost mounts and wagons." Liedral pours water into the kettle before swinging it out over the hotter coals with a heavy leather glove.

Kadara quickly tethers her mount.

"Is that why there's iron in the tether ropes?" asks Dorrin.

Again, Brede and Kadara exchange looks. Kadara shakes her head.

"You may need two guards just for yourself, healer." Liedral laughs softly.

Dorrin's face feels warm, but his words are firm, almost snapped out. "If you were White, I'd know, and, besides, none of the Whites would want that much iron around."

"Fair enough. Let me find some mugs." Liedral disappears into the tent.

Kadara fixes Dorrin with lowered brows. Dorrin leads Meriwhen over to the iron stake, where he follows Brede's and Kadara's example.

By the time he returns to the fire, the trader is passing out the mugs. "Spice tea or redberry?"

"Tea." Kadara takes a heavy brown mug.

"Redberry," adds Brede.

"Tea." Dorrin is left with a fluted gray mug with a chip on the rim.

The trader's deft hands pour chopped tea into a metal basket on a chain, which goes into the kettle before the top drops back in place. "Be a bit."

Dorrin concentrates on the trader, then nods, hiding the smile he feels as his senses confirm his feelings. He smothers a smile and waits.

Liedral gestures to the ground. "I can't provide any comforts, but please be seated." The trader settles onto a small padded stool.

Brede sits cross-legged, as does Kadara, before the fire and to the trader's right. Dorrin's muscles are too sore and tight for that, and he shifts his weight on the hard ground until he finds the least uncomfortable position on the trader's left.

The low *ooooo* of a dove echoes across the trading grounds from the higher grasses of the low hill to the northwest.

"Where are you headed?" Brede asks.

"A few folks might like to know that, questor." Liedral's voice carries a faint tone of amusement.

"Questor?"

"That's the more polite term for those of you from Recluce."

"The less polite terms being . . .?"

"We'll not go into that."

"We're not exactly other traders." Dorrin shifts his weight on the hard ground again.

"It's really no secret. I'm one of the few that runs the northern triangle. Most times, I don't come to Fairhaven, just to Vergren, but Freidr insisted that I come here, just to get a feel for it once." Liedral frowns. "Once is enough, and I wasted too much time. I'll leave tomorrow."

"You traveled all that alone?"

Liedral shrugs. "Bandits generally don't like the cold, and dyes and spices aren't the easiest to sell if you don't have the contacts." The trader's eyes flicker to the bow and quiver hanging by the slit in the tent.

Dorrin's eyes alight on the shortsword, nearly a match to the one worn by Kadara. "You've been taught in the Westwind style."

Liedral laughs. "You definitely need a keeper, healer."

Kadara shakes her head. Dorrin flushes.

"What about you?" pursues Brede.

The trader shrugs. "I get by. Profits don't cover hiring guards. They did once, back generations, but not now, not unless you run with the wizards."

"They control the trade through the roads?" Brede remains cross-legged.

Dorrin shifts his weight again, wondering how the bigger man can remain comfortable with his legs folded.

Liedral nods, then stands. "Tea should be ready. You first, healer."

Dorrin extends his mug.

After pouring Dorrin's and Kadara's tea, the trader replaces the kettle, swings the swivel to the side of the fire, then retrieves a flask from the tent to pour the redberry into Brede's cup. "There."

"Thank you," Dorrin says, looking straight into the hazel eyes.

"Thank you."

"Thank you."

The sounds of low voices drift from the other tents, punctuated by another *oooo* from the unseen dove.

"What is this northern triangle route you follow?" Kadara brushes a strand of red hair off her forehead, then sips from her mug.

"Usually the points of the triangle are Spidlaria, Vergren, and Tyrhavven. From Vergren I'll make Rytel, then follow the old north road through Axalt and into Kleth. Then a barge down to Spidlaria. Dastral owes me a passage back to Tyrhavven. That's where I pick up the dyes and spices. Take the river road back to Jellico. That's back through Rytel twice, but both stops are short. Spend an eight-day or so putting the old warehouse in order—Freidr always lets things get out of hand—and then start all over again."

"Why are you here?"

Liedral shakes her head. "Like I said, call it a pilgrimage. For Fairhaven, that is. There's a market for spices, even here, and they don't take that much space. But I really don't like going farther than Vergren."

Dorrin grins.

"Why is that funny?" asks Kadara.

"Oh, it's not funny, but I should have figured that out."

All three look at him.

He shrugs, embarrassed. "Chaos is hard on living things. Food comes from living things. It follows that they'd need spices, and that the White traders wouldn't do as well."

"If you say so . . ."

"He's right," observes Liedral. "I'd like to know more about why you feel that has to be."

"It just follows," mumbles Dorrin. "I mean . . . chaos is the destructive force . . . It breaks things down . . . especially living things. Spices preserve food, but they're delicate . . ."

"What do you recommend?" asks Brede, his deep voice gentle. "For us?"

The soft-voiced trader turns. "No one here will hire you. They might in places to the northwest, like Diev, or some of the other cities in Spidlar. The wizards' reach isn't that tight there—or in southern Kyphros or Southwind."

"Southwind's a trifle far." Kadara's voice is edged.

"And you can't afford a guard?" Brede finally shifts his weight, to Dorrin's relief.

"Or two guards and a healer, much as I'd like to have all three of you?" Liedral smiles. "Hardly."

"What about traveling with you?" asks Dorrin. "For some pittance ... at least."

The two others look at him.

"Well," he explains, "if we have to get to Spidlar to get paying work, we might as well see about the least costly way to do it."

"Perhaps a silver or two toward food—that's the most I could go."

"You trust us?" asks Brede thoughtfully.

"No. I trust the healer."

Kadara and Brede again exchange glances. Liedral grins at Dorrin. Dorrin looks at the fire.

XXV

THERE WAS A strange party in Fairhaven, two blades and a young healer ..." ventures the apprentice.

"That sounds like Sarronnyn," snaps the sun-eyed man.

"But the healer also could feel the winds, according to Zerlat."

"Where are they?"

The apprentice shrugs. "According to the standing orders—"

"Damn the standing orders! Does anyone know where they headed?"

The apprentice lets out a slow breath as she watches Jeslek's eyes fade into the vague look that means his senses are somewhere else.

"Where?" demands the hard voice. Not all Jeslek's senses are elsewhere.

"They headed toward the Easthorns."

"What did they look like?"

The young woman purses her lips, ignoring the distant look on her master's face. "The healer was thin, with curly red hair. One blade was a red-headed woman. She carried double swords, including a Westwind shortsword. The other blade was a man, pretty young, but big."

"And no one thought such a group was strange?" Jeslek's eyes are fully alive again. "Two blades, just to protect a poor young healer? Who knows just what that healer is? And just as we're starting to tighten the noose on Recluce. Doesn't anyone think?"

He is out the door from the tower room, and his feet echo on the stairs before the apprentice can answer his question.

The apprentice frowns, mumbling, "You're not the High Wizard yet." But she takes a deep breath and continues polishing the mirror on the table.

XXVI

DORRIN FLICKS THE reins to keep Meriwhen abreast of the cart. Kadara and Brede ride ahead. The pack horse trails, harness tied to a ring on the cart.

"Why are all the Blacks so opposed to Fairhaven?" asks Liedral.

"Wouldn't you be, after all the trouble it took to escape the Whites?" counters Dorrin. "Besides, living with chaos is rather ... painful ... if you deal with order."

"Recluce seems rather ... arbitrary ... about defining chaos."

Dorrin laughs, a short harsh sound. "They're all so concerned about maintaining the pure Black way. Any change is considered chaos." He brushes away a mosquito. "Even order changes, but they don't see it."

"What determines what is Black and what is White?" asks the trader.

"They hammer that out in lessons when you first start your schooling."

"Who gives the lessons?"

"One of the Black mages."

"Do they all teach the same lessons? What happens if one of these learned Black mages dies?"

"That doesn't happen much in Recluce. His apprentices and the others know what he knows, for the most part."

Liedral frowns. "People remember what they want to. You learn that as a trader. You know how to write, don't you?"

"Of course." Dorrin sighs. "I've been through my father's library. Recluce has books and more books. At least, my father does."

"So . . . all of the White and Black magic is written down?"

"Not the White. Not even very much of . . . Actually, there's not much at all on *why* things work, or how to do things—just the conditions." Dorrin shakes his head. "Why are you interested in all of this?"

"I'm just interested, healer. I'm a trader. The more I know, the longer I'll live."

Dorrin glances at the smooth brow under the floppy hat, then toward his compatriots as they ride toward the rolling hills ahead.

"Why do you hide—"

"Because. I'd prefer you leave it that way. Do your friends know?"

"I haven't said so, and neither have they. Kadara wouldn't bring it up, and Brede is rather sharp, but he can keep his tongue. I don't know."

"Just think of me as a trader, all right?"

"Fine. If that's the way you want it." Dorrin wonders if being a woman is so restrictive in Candar. Of course, magistra Lortren has shown how the Whites had eventually brought down Westwind because of its feminine domination. But why did either sex have to dominate? It was all too clear that people fought over beliefs, but why? The fighting never changed anyone's mind— unless you killed them. He looks toward the hills that separate them from Weevett, the small farm town that they had passed through only days before. Overhead, the sky is clear, although he feels as though a cloud masks the white-yellow sun. Looking back, he sees a black bird circling.

Then he looks forward toward Brede and Kadara, but they have also turned, as if aware of the nearing black wings. Kadara points to the bird.

"Vulcrow. The wizards watch through their eyes." Liedral raises her voice.

Dorrin extends his senses on the breeze to hear what the two blades are saying.

"The vulcrow's probably a spy for the wizards." Brede fingers the hilt of the heavy blade.

"Wonderful," snaps Kadara.

"You don't know that they're looking for us." Brede doesn't even turn from the road ahead. "Who would care about a young healer and two blades?"

"I don't know. But things happen around Dorrin. They always have."

Dorrin watches as the vulcrow's circles widen toward them. Meriwhen whinnies, takes a sidestep, before Dorrin pats her neck. "Easy . . . easy . . ."

After unstrapping the bow, Liedral sets the quiver by the seat.

"What are you doing?" asks Dorrin.

"Getting ready to shoot a vulcrow."

"But—"

"The damned wizards tell their traders. Besides, they don't like to admit they use the birds."

The dark bird flaps nearer, but the trader flicks the reins, and the cart squeals as one wheel lifts over a muddy hummock that has encroached onto the stone pavement. Liedral reins up the cart horse, extracts an arrow from the quiver, and draws the bow.

Dorrin's senses reach skyward, stretching toward the whiteness around the ungainly flapping bird. The trader nocks the arrow, and as the shaft flies, Dorrin screams. "No!!!!"

Kadara and Brede turn, their movements trapped in the syrup of white-clouded and slowed time. Liedral's mouth hangs open. The vulcrow's wings freeze on the upstroke, pinions spread.

Sun-eyes appear in the sky, except they are not there, and the unseen eyes glare down upon the travelers. "SO . . ."

The white fog that Dorrin can feel but not see descends with the speed of lightning and the force of a gale. As the chill rips at him, tears at his thoughts, he thinks, "I am me . . . Me!"

The white storm tosses his thoughts aside like a leaf in a cyclone, and another kind of blackness descends. *Whhnnnnn . . . nnnun . . .*

The sound of the mare rouses Dorrin.

"Wha . . ." His tongue thick, his head splitting, Dorrin finds his face buried in Meriwhen's neck, the fingers of his left hand locked in her mane. Feeling like an insect narrowly escaped from a giant flyswatter, he loosens his fingers from Meriwhen's mane. After straightening slowly in the saddle, he squints against the afternoon sun, barely above the clouds that cover the lower quarter of the western sky. Afternoon? Where are the others?

The cart and pack horse are less than a hundred cubits up the road, motionless. A dark figure is half-sprawled across the seat. Dorrin swallows, trying to moisten his mouth, then looks past the cart.

Several hundred cubits farther along the dusty road, Brede stands by the low stone wall, holding both horses. Kadara sprawls over the fence, retching.

Dorrin waves to Brede, points to the cart. There is nothing he can do for Kadara, and Brede is there. The trader remains motionless as Dorrin rides up to the cart and dismounts. His fingers brush her forehead, and his senses confirm that Liedral is beginning to wake. He transfers what little energy he can to her and opens his water bottle, moistening her lips.

" . . . never had that happen before." She struggles upright.

"You never traveled with questors from Recluce before, either." Dorrin offers her the water bottle.

Liedral takes a deep pull, then returns the bottle. "We need to get going. I don't like being on the road at dark, wizards' peace or not."

"If this is peace, I'd rather not see war." Dorrin replaces the bottle on the saddle, then remounts.

Liedral straps the bow and quiver back into place, checks the harness and the horse, then slips onto the cart seat. "Let's go."

"Was that your doing?" Brede reins up beside Dorrin, Kadara, still pale, following.

"No."

"Then . . . why—"

"I don't know. It was a White Wizard, and we were beneath his notice. I'd guess that he was showing how powerful he was." Dorrin twists, smacking his neck in an attempt to squash the mosquito that has drawn blood. He rubs his neck, then wipes blood and mosquito off his hand.

"Sending a message?" Brede muses. "It could be, but why us?"

Four sets of eyes exchange glances.

"Let's go," Liedral finally snaps.

XXVII

"WHAT WERE THEY?" asks the High Wizard. "You retreated . . . sought your study in haste."

Jeslek shrugs. "Youngsters from Recluce. Like the guards said. But you never know, and I wanted to make sure. Some of the prophecies in the Book have come true."

"I thought the superstitions of the Legend were beneath you."

"One must know them to disregard them."

"That's a fitting proverb for you."

"You wish to relinquish the amulet, as you promised?" asks Jeslek idly. "After all, I have demonstrated that . . ."

"I recall something about completing the job."

"As you wish. It's not something that can be done overnight, and the Book certainly doesn't state that it will happen overnight."

"It's good to see that you are cultivating patience." Sterol smiles. "What about the youngsters? Did you incinerate them or bury them under molten stone?"

"No. I'd rather have them spread the word. Two were blades. The other was barely worth calling a healer." The thin man with the yellow-sun eyes takes a sip of water from the goblet. "Since they were no danger, I'd rather save my strength for other things."

"Like the last half of the hills between Kyphros and Gallos?"

"That's one thing. There were at least some hills on

the route to the Easthorns. But the Gallosian side is too exposed."

"I am sure the guards will appreciate your concerns."

"Besides . . . we still have to think about the blockade of Recluce."

"Ah, yes. The next step on your agenda."

"You said that we needed to do something, I do recall." Jeslek smiles politely.

"So I did. I suggested something less direct, however. Still, directness has a certain . . . flair."

XXVIII

"Now THOSE ARE walls," observes Brede, inclining his head toward the massive granite blocks that rise nearly seventy cubits above the river plain on which the city of Jellico rests. The walls are a lighter and pinker gray than the clouds that shroud the sky. The wind moans and keeps blowing Dorrin's hair across this forehead. As he pushes the too curly and far too long strands out of his eyes, he wishes he had cut it.

"Why do they need them?"

"They were originally built by one of the early viscounts to hold off Fairhaven," Liedral responds dryly.

"Oh?"

"You will notice that there are no marks upon the walls, either."

Dorrin shifts in his saddle as the stone road widens into a causeway that leads to the river bridge. Even from the bridge, the eastern gates are visible, swung open, and bound in heavy iron. The grooves for anchoring the gates and the stones in which they have been chiseled are swept clean. A half squad in gray-

brown leathers, three men and three women, plus a
single White guard, wait to inspect the travelers.

"Your occupation and reason for entering Jellico?"
asks the White guard, his voice polite, emotionless.

"Liedral—I'm a trader here in Jellico. My warehouse is on the traders' street off the great square. I'm
returning from a trading journey."

Looking over the parapet crenellations on the wall
above, a crossbowman watches, his weapon resting on
the granite.

"These your people?" asks the guard.

"Yes. The guards are mine. The healer is traveling
with us for protection."

The White guard pokes at several bags, taps a jug,
frowns, and finally nods. Liedral flicks the reins, and
guides the cart through the stone archway and into
Jellico. The houses are tile-roofed, two-storied structures of fired brick with narrow fronts, pitched roofs,
and heavy, iron-bound oak doors, closed against the
cold spring wind.

The four pass less than a score of pedestrians as
Liedral wheels the cart left, and then down a narrow
street that leads toward the center of Jellico.

"There," the trader states at last. The stone-walled
building toward which Liedral points is three stories
high, the width of three houses, with a high-pitched
roof. The warehouse is a floor higher than the adjoining structures, a cooper's shop toward the square and
a silversmith's toward the city gate. Toward the square
are the grayed facades of even taller structures that
appear to predate the warehouse, perhaps by centuries.
The square is another hundred cubits down the narrow
street.

Three doors open from the warehouse—a sliding
door level with the rough stones of the street and wide
enough to admit Liedral's cart. The second door is
iron-bound and barred, and the last, closest to the

square, is a door of plain oak under a green-painted portico.

Brede swings off the gelding without an invitation and points to the sliding door. "You want me to open this one?"

"If you would. Leave it open. Freidr never airs anything out." Liedral drives the cart through the door and onto the smooth and hardpacked clay. A faint aroma of spices permeates the space. Liedral climbs off the cart.

"If you want to clean the stables and do the loading, you can sleep in the stableboy's room," Liedral offers. "Freidr doesn't keep one any longer. He claims it's my responsibility, since I've got all the horses."

"What about a place to wash up?" Dorrin is all too conscious of the grime that enfolds him.

"You can use the washroom as much as you like— so long as you pump the water and clean up any mess you make." Liedral loosens the last strap from the cart harness and leads the horse into the second stall. "You three can have the last three stalls at the end. I daresay they'll need some cleaning. But that comes after you help me unload and shift things around. The bins are probably a mess, again."

"Is Freidr . . ." asks Kadara.

"My brother. He and Midala live on the third floor. My rooms are on the second—when I'm here. He factors here in Jellico what I gather."

Brede tethers his gelding by the last stall. "What goes where?"

"The four purple jugs? That's glaze powder, and they go up on the first level, just up the staircase. There should be a picture of a pot in purple outside the right bin and a jug like these inside."

"What's cerann?" asks Dorrin.

"Take it easy with that. It's a rare oil, goes on the second level, the bin with the green leaf."

"How rare is rare?" muses Kadara, lifting a heavy sack.

"Each bottle in the case is worth a gold and a half. The sack is sweet beets. Put it in that big bin over there."

"That's rare."

Brede has returned to the cart. "What next?"

Dorrin climbs the stairs slowly, ensuring that each foot is placed firmly on each riser. He doesn't have eighteen golds to spare. That he knows, and he doubts that Liedral can easily absorb such a loss. By the time he has stored cerann oil, tublane, pottery glaze, and dozens of other small items, Dorrin understands why the trader is broad-shouldered.

Liedral leads them through a doorway at the end of the warehouse. "Here's the washroom. I need to talk to Freidr. We'll have a late supper, sometime after the twilight bell. You're invited. You might look around the great square."

"After I do some wash," Dorrin says, looking down at his travelstained browns. "Actually, I need to find a good curry brush."

Kadara grins. "The same fastidious Dorrin. In a new city, and you think about laundry and currying."

"I'm also thinking about me, and the way I smell."

Liedral pauses. "There are several curry brushes in the tack room. If you want to keep one of the older ones, that would be fine."

"Thank you. Meriwhen will like it."

"Now you've named the horse?"

Dorrin flushes.

Liedral backs away and steps through the doorway to the living quarters.

"Fine. Let me wash up first," suggests Kadara. "I'm not doing laundry. You can go curry your Meriwhen."

"Fine."

While Kadara washes, Dorrin unloads Meriwhen,

curries her, and gathers his soiled clothes. Then he pumps two tubs full of water before Brede appears. Brede is stripped to the waist and carries a small towel and a razor for his blond stubble.

"Still doing wash?" Kadara has changed into a gray tunic and trousers, with a bright green scarf that sets off her hair and eyes.

"I just started." Then Dorrin sighs. Once again, he has answered a rhetorical question. He never learns.

"I'll do mine later." With the travel grime off her face and the light tan almost covering the faint freckles, she looks almost like an etching of an ancient Westwind Guard—beautiful and deadly. "I'm going to the square to see if I can find some things."

"What things?" asks Brede from the other side of the washroom.

"Just . . . women's things."

His elbows deep in the tub, Brede splashes water across his face and looks up at Dorrin, water dripping down in a stream from his chin. Dorrin looks at Brede, and Kadara is gone.

Dorrin rinses out his travel trousers and wrings them over the waste bucket, then hangs them over a laundry table as he picks out a soapy tunic.

Brede hurriedly finishes washing and dries off, leaving Dorrin alone in the washroom. The healer finishes all his once-filthy clothes, and carries them out into the warehouse, hanging his wash in the empty fourth stall, spreading it on a rope he has found coiled in the corner of what was once a tack room.

"You don't have to be that careful, healer."

The short and squat man who accompanies Liedral nods. Despite the dark beard and cold blue eyes, he appears little older than Dorrin.

"This is my brother Freidr."

"I'm pleased to meet you. My name is Dorrin."

"Are the others around?"

"They went off to the great square. I thought I would follow their example after I wash up."

"We will see you at supper, then." Liedral points, and the two traders climb the steps. "The cerann was a good buy . . . overextended a bit . . ."

Dorrin returns to the washroom with his one dry and clean set of browns, where he washes himself thoroughly, then cleans the washroom, then dries and dresses. As an afterthought, he reclaims his staff from the stableboy's room.

As he walks toward the great square, he notes again the relatively small number of people on the streets, few indeed, even for a blustery spring afternoon under gray skies. The stones underfoot are dry.

Dorrin passes several booths selling weapons, but all have the white-bronze blades of the Whites. Nowhere does he see iron. Is Jellico totally controlled by the White Wizards?

"Dorrin!" Brede waves from fifty paces away.

The healer returns the wave and steps toward the tall blond.

"Have you seen Kadara?"

"I just got here," admits Dorrin. He pauses to look at the display to his left, at the edge of the square.

"Seeds! The best spice seeds this side of Suthya!" The man's white hair bears an unhealthy yellow tinge, and his gray garments almost flicker with white. Pouches of seeds are set on the small single-axled cart, a cart that could be drawn by a man or a dog. Neither a dog nor a pony is visible.

Dorrin edges closer to the small leather pouches, frowning at the water stains on the leather, wondering about the use of leather with seeds. If the leather has been tanned with acorn extracts or other acids, and then gotten damp, neither brinn nor astra will grow.

He extends a hand toward the nearest pouch, not touching the leather, letting his healing senses reach the seeds. Most are dead. He shakes his head. His left hand tightens on his staff.

"What's the matter?" asks Brede.

"Most of the seeds are dead," Dorrin explains.

"You're a fraud, friend," claims the peddler. "My seeds are the best, the very best."

Dorrin nods politely, and steps back, heading toward the cart with a grill from which drifts the warm dripped-fat scent of roasting fowl.

"The youngster in black said his seeds were dead . . ." mumbles an older woman in brown.

Dorrin frowns. His clothes are brown, a deep and dark brown, but brown.

"More 'n likely," sniffs another gray-haired woman in a patch-work of wools. "He's a white-back."

The three women leave the white-haired man without customers.

"I said you're a fraud!" The peddler shouts. "Thief! Thief!"

Two white-coated guards appear before Dorrin, white blades pointed toward him. "What's the problem?"

"Him and his Black quackery! He says my seeds aren't any good. That's theft!" The peddler is almost hoarse, his voice is so loud and ragged.

Bystanders step away, almost melting into the streets off the square.

"You a Black healer?" snaps the square-faced guard.

"No. I'm a questor."

"Same thing. What about what the peddler says?"

Dorrin faces the guards, his staff resting still in his left hand. "I said nothing, except to my friend. I certainly am no trader." A warning flash slides through his brain, although his words are literally true.

"Those women—they would have bought except for him!"

"What women?" asks the other guard, looking around the nearly deserted section of the great square.

The peddler looks around, then waves his arms. "He scared them away."

"Likely story." The guards lower the white blades.

The square-faced one turns to Dorrin. "You, youngster—keep your Black thoughts to yourself. You understand?"

"Yes, ser." Dorrin nods politely.

"I don't want to see you making more trouble, young fellow." The square-faced guard turns to Brede. "Nor you either, with that iron toothpick!"

Brede nods. "I will be careful, ser."

The two guards march across the square.

"Well, are you going to pay me?" snaps the peddler.

Brede looks at the peddler. "For what? False accusations? The healer couldn't tell an untruth if his life depended on it. That's more than one could say of you."

The white-haired man shrinks away from Brede's glare. "Black bastards... trouble-makers... all of them..."

Brede grins. Dorrin shrugs as they walk toward the stalls on the far side of the square. Brede's grin vanishes as he watches two men fold their tables at the approach of the two questors. Another throws a cloth over his silverwork to signify that he is closed.

"Sorry," Dorrin apologizes.

"There's not much we can do." Brede nods toward the avenue. "Might as well head back."

Dorrin feels the eyes of the White guards on their backs as they cross the square and head back up the avenue toward Liedral's building.

Kadara is hanging up her laundry when they slide open the stable area door. "You weren't gone long."

"We had a few problems."

"I had a few problems," Dorrin corrects. "A local

peddler was selling dead seeds. I remarked on it, and the authorities overheard. By the time they were through, everyone decided it was time to close."

"Oh, Dorrin." Kadara pats his shoulder.

The doorway from the quarters opens. "If you're all back, we could eat," Liedral announces. The trader wears clean dark blue trousers and a high-necked tunic, with damp and clean brown hair longer than Dorrin's but shorter than Kadara's ear-length cut.

The dining room is on the lowest level. The long red-oak table is polished, oiled, and only slightly battered along its eight-cubit length. There are wooden armchairs, not benches, for the six who gather. Four other chairs are placed in the corners and against the wall. Freidr stands by the head of the table. To his right sits a thin blond woman.

"Dorrin, Brede, and Kadara, I would like to introduce you to Midala. Midala," Liedral says smoothly, "Kadara and Brede are blades; and Dorrin is a healer."

Freidr smiles and gestures to the table. "Please be seated."

Dorrin finds himself between Midala and Liedral, who sits at the foot of the table. Brede and Kadara sit side by side with their backs to the high windows that front upon the street.

A young woman in dark blue sets a platter heaped with thin strips of meat covered in a dark brown sauce before Freidr. As he serves himself and Midala, the serving woman returns with two other deep platters, one filled with potatoes coated in cheese and another with limp and dark greenery.

Liedral takes a small helping of the potatoes and hands the platter to Dorrin, who follows her example.

"What's the greenery?"

"Chiltach. It is bitter enough that it takes some

getting used to, but it goes well with heavier meat and potato dishes."

"How have you found Candar so far?" asks Midala.

"Generally hospitable." Brede spears some meat and places it on his plate. "Somewhat colder than I thought, and"—he grins—"the size, especially of the mountains, takes some getting used to."

"You haven't seen the Westhorns yet, either." Liedral takes a moderate helping of the chiltach.

"Why does Recluce still send young people to Candar?" Midala has taken only a small nibble of the potatoes.

"The idea is that we should come to appreciate order more," volunteers Dorrin. "Especially the way the order-masters want us to."

Kadara swallows hard, almost choking on a bite of meat.

"You don't sound thrilled with the order-masters, healer." Freidr pours from the brown pitcher placed before him by the serving girl. "This is dark beer. The white pitcher has redberry."

Dorrin looks at the white pitcher, then lifts it to pour for Liedral, who nods. He fills the trader's mug, and then his own, before turning to Midala.

"Yes, please." The blond woman nods.

"Well," Dorrin temporizes, "following order most strictly can be somewhat difficult if one is young."

"I've heard it's difficult at any age." Liedral sips from the stoneware mug.

The serving girl returns with a woven basket filled with steaming golden-crusted bread sliced into wide slabs. After offering it to Liedral, who declines, Dorrin takes a slab and offers the basket to Midala. The blond woman takes the smallest slice and sets the basket before Freidr.

"What about you?" Freidr turns to Brede.

"If one is a blade, I suppose some experience helps."

"You're not told to scout an area or bring back information?"

"I rather doubt that is necessary," Dorrin says. "The air wizards can see a great deal from the winds."

"You're rather confident about that," laughs Freidr.

Dorrin flushes, and covers his embarrassment behind the mug of redberry. Then he takes two slices of meat and begins to slice them and eat quickly.

"I think that's been well known since Creslin," notes Kadara tartly. "It's not exactly a secret."

Freidr inclines his head to Kadara and smiles warmly. Midala smiles also, politely.

"I take it that trading is a family tradition." Brede's voice breaks the momentary silence.

"The tradition is somewhat strained these days." Liedral stabs a slice of the meat and lifts it from the platter to her plate.

"Oh? Why is that?"

"Politics," adds Freidr. "To travel the great white roads, one must have a license, and that means approval of the Prefect, who is advised by his White Wizard. It used to be a simple tax."

Brede nods. "It has become a loyalty test?"

"Of sorts. It appears as though everyone has a loyalty test these days, does it not?" Freidr looks at Dorrin.

Dorrin takes refuge in another sip of redberry. His eyes stray to the small and dusty guitar upon the wall.

"That? Actually, that's an heirloom. It's said that Creslin once played it. Who knows? It's an old family tale, but, these days, there's certainly no way to tell. It's seen better days." Freidr shrugs off the instrument. "Ah, yes, loyalty and legends."

"If I might ask," Kadara smiles politely at the dark-haired Freidr, "What exactly do you do while Liedral is out trading?"

"Mind the warehouse, try to factor what she's

gathered to shops in Jellico—that sort of thing. It doesn't do much good to obtain things if you don't sell them."

"Freidr's very good at factoring," Midala adds proudly.

"I can imagine," Kadara says brightly.

Dorrin eats, wishing he were in the stable or even in the great square.

"Tell me," continues Freidr, as if nothing had been said, "where you will be heading from Jellico."

"Toward the Westhorns." Brede refills Kadara's mug with the dark beer, then tops off his own. Setting the pitcher down, he sips the foam almost silently before taking a healthy swallow.

"Through Passera and Fenard?"

"That's along the wizards' highway?" asks Kadara.

"The wizards haven't finished it there. You'd have to take the old road through Gallos."

Brede and Kadara exchange glances, but avoid looking at Dorrin.

"I would think a more northward route," ventures Brede.

"That might be the wisest." Freidr inclines his head to Kadara. "If you would pass the beer?"

"Of course." Kadara smiles and hands the young factor the pitcher.

Dorrin reaches across the table and retrieves the bread, taking a slab before offering the basket to Liedral. All six eat for a time as the serving woman replaces the depleted bread basket and removes the empty meat platter.

"Faya! Some more beer!" Freidr lifts the pitcher.

When Faya returns, Freidr fills his mug and offers to pour for Kadara.

"No, thank you, ser Freidr."

Dorrin quietly refills his mug with redberry and

takes another slice of the warm bread. He looks at the remnants of the chiltach on his plate.

"It's not that bad, Dorrin."

"I think I've seen rotten seaweed that smelled better," he mumbles.

"You must have tasty seaweed then," Liedral quips.

"You eat seaweed on Recluce?" asks Midala.

"Sometimes." Again Dorrin finds himself flushing.

"Are you finished, ser?" asks Faya, standing at Dorrin's elbow.

He nods gratefully as the platter and the chiltach vanish into the kitchen. Shortly, Faya sets before each diner a small cup filled with a single golden orb—honey-brandied peaches.

"This is excellent." Brede finishes his in three bites.

Dorrin has used his knife to spray honey on his fingers and the table in attempting to cut the fruit into smaller sections. He continues to eat small sections long after Brede and Kadara have finished.

"We will not keep you, travelers," says Freidr, rising. "It has been a long day for you."

Dorrin swallows the last of the redberry in his mug and stands, following the others to their feet.

"Thank you." Kadara's soft and warm voice is echoed by Brede, and finally by Dorrin.

Then, with Brede leading, the three ease away from their chairs and file toward the warehouse, and the stableboy's room. Liedral slips behind them, but stops at the doorway from the quarters to the stable. The trader's warm fingertips touch Dorrin's shoulder, squeeze briefly, and drop away. "Try not to mind Freidr. Things aren't always easy for him."

"Because he's from a trading family, and he doesn't like trading? Or because he'd like to be on the council or whatever advises whoever rules this place, and he can't?" Dorrin licks the last of the honey off the corners of his lips after he speaks.

"He likes governing, and traders can't, especially not us."

"I see ... I think. We'll be going in the morning, I think."

"Good. So will I. We can travel to Kleth together."

"What makes you think we're going there?"

"You don't have much choice, Dorrin." Liedral smiles. "Your friends don't want to head west to Gallos. That means you either head over the hills to the south toward Hydolar or you go north to Rytel and northwest to Kleth—unless you want to go back to Tyrhavven ... or go cross-country, which I wouldn't advise." The trader steps back, half shutting the door. "So we might as well travel together."

"I don't know."

"I'll see you in the morning."

Dorrin shakes his head as he walks toward the fourth stall—empty except for laundry—where he has placed his bedroll on the straw. Sleeping near Brede and Kadara will not make for a restful night. He senses too much, and is reminded too often of the red-headed girl he once kissed in the spice garden.

"You look troubled." Kadara emerges from the second stall, brushing straw from her hands.

"The trader is coming with us tomorrow to Rytel."

"You don't like that?"

"Liedral knew, and I didn't."

"I'm sorry." Kadara's voice is soft. "We thought you understood. Freidr made it pretty clear, and after that incident in the square ..."

Dorrin waits.

"We didn't think it was a good idea to stay in Certis or head toward where the White Wizards are working ... and we wanted to get to the Westhorns."

"And that means heading toward Spidlar along the northern route?" Dorrin finishes.

"Yes. It's better for you, too. You could go the other way, if you want."

"Me? I can't even carry a blade or stand up to a White Wizard. I may not have much choice, Kadara, but I'm not stupid. Slow... but not totally stupid." He walks past her and into the stall that holds his bedroll, where he sits on the blankets and strips off his boots, ignoring Kadara until she looks down and turns away.

XXIX

THE ROAD ANGLES up and down over the low rolling hills of Certis, paralleling the Jellicor River toward Rytel. The creak of the cart and the clop of hoofs are almost lost in the whine of the spring wind. Dorrin leans toward the cart, his staff in his left hand. "Would you have left this soon if we weren't headed this way?"

Liedral shifts her weight on the cart seat. "I wasted too much time in seeing Fairhaven, and I'm not sure it was wise."

"Seeing Fairhaven or wasting time?"

"Either. Freidr's worried about the White Wizards, but he's too comfortable with Midala to go check himself. Besides, I need to get to Kleth to pick up the stuff from Jarnish. Some came from Diev."

Dorrin has heard of Kleth, but not the other names. Still, he has another question. "Your brother... he doesn't seem quite like a trader."

"A trader?" Liedral snorts. "He went to Rytel once. He lost more than if he'd dropped the whole cart in the Jellicor and watched it wash all the way down river to Tyrhavven."

"Then..."

"Politics."

"Oh." Dorrin understands. The Whites hate the Legend, or women who control anything. He considers the trader's apparel and manners before asking another question. "Who's Jarnish?"

"What about politics?" asks Brede belatedly.

"Jarnish is a factor in Kleth, but he doesn't travel."

"Where's Diev?"

"Right at the foothills of the Westhorns. It's about as far north and west as you can go without entering the mountains. Small three-season port, but not all that much there. Lumber for Spidlar, but Axalt and Sligo are better for anywhere else."

"When you talk about Spidlar," mentions Brede, who has ridden the gelding closer to the trader's cart so that he and Dorrin are on opposite sides of the trader, "all you do is talk about trade. Doesn't anything else happen there?"

"Spidlar's still an independent trading country. There's a Council of Traders that runs things. They were the only ones in eastern Candar to avoid the mess that created Recluse, and their Council tries to avoid conflict."

"No duke, or viscount?" Brede leans forward, untangling the gelding's mane.

"What about the wizards?" Dorrin straightens in the saddle and twirls the staff, happy that he can finally do the simple exercise.

"Careful with that!" snaps Kadara from behind him.

"Sorry." He replaces the staff in the lanceholder. "You did say that I needed to practice."

"Dorrin . . ."

"What about Spidlar?"

"Is that Rytel over the hills there?" interrupts Kadara, pointing toward a low wall rising out of a flat expanse of brown and green.

"What's that?"

A thread of silver winds from the south toward the walls.

"The river? That's the Jellicor. We've been following—"

"No," explains Brede. "The line of trees across there."

"That's the Estal. It meets the Jellicor on the other side of Rytel, and the Jellicor flows into the Northern Sea at Tyrhavven, not that it gets much bigger or that Tyrhavven's all that great a port. It's a lot better than Diev, though."

Liedral flicks the reins to get the cart moving again, and the four begin the downhill trek toward the still-distant town.

Dorrin slaps at his neck. The mosquitoes are out, and they seem to prefer him to the others. Unlike the fleas, the mosquitoes move too fast for him to persuade them to move elsewhere—and there seem to be clouds of them.

"Healer?"

"Dorrin," he corrects.

"Try this. Smear a little on your neck. It might help."

Dorrin takes the leather pouch and squeezes the ointment into his palm. His senses tell him it is faintly order-based, and he rubs it across the back of his neck. "Thank you."

"Sometimes, simple potions are more helpful than complicated magic."

So, Dorrin believes, are relatively simple machines—but he seems to be one of the few raised in order that thinks so. He frowns. He never did hear any more about Diev, although Liedral had been hinting at something.

XXX

DORRIN LEANS SIDEWAYS in the saddle to avoid banging his head into the rocky ledge as Meriwhen carries him around the switchback. Then he wipes his forehead, clearing an accumulation of sweat and cold rain that has splattered off the canyon walls and onto his face. Behind him the cart creaks, and the inside wheel scrapes on a boulder.

"Darkness . . ." mumbles Liedral.

Dorrin swallows as he glances at the fifty-cubit drop-off to his left.

"It's worse in the Westhorns," Liedral says cheerfully.

Ahead, Brede hums, in perfect pitch, a Temple hymn.

"Would you stop it?" snaps Kadara.

"Oooofff." Dorrin's grin is wiped away as his staff bangs the side of his face, knocked there by an ice-covered root protruding from the canyon wall—just high enough for the three to ride underneath, just low enough to catch the tip of Dorrin's staff. He pushes the staff back into place and concentrates on the narrow winding road before him.

Three more descending switchbacks bring them to a narrow canyon that seems to wind due west, although it is so narrow that the three ride in shadows, ice still filling the crevices on the left side of the road, and the light of the midday sun only apparent on the clifftops when Dorrin looks straight up. Kadara wraps her cloak about her more tightly.

"Up ahead are the guard towers. Keep your hands away from your weapons," explains the trader.

"Guard towers? We're still in the mountains," Kadara says.

"Who said a town had to be on the plains?" asks Liedral.

Shortly the canyon widens to reveal a stone wall rising nearly a hundred cubits, punctuated by an iron-bound gate. A handful of soldiers with crossbows are stationed on the ramparts, and several weapons are trained on the travelers. Outside the gate, beside a stone sentry box, stand two men in quilted gray uniforms.

Liedral reins up the cart and waits. So do the three from Recluce.

"Ah . . . Trader Liedral. Who are your companions?" The tall man with the high-pitched voice and shoulders even broader than Brede's marches over to the trader, who has climbed from the cart seat.

"Two guards and a healer." Liedral nods to Dorrin.

"Well, he does have a staff and that look about him. And they are definitely guards. And you, and your father before you, have always been truthful. Such a pity. It has been such a long time since my men were able to practice on real targets. Even the White guards do not venture down our canyons."

"They will, sooner than you think, Nerliat."

"So said your father."

"He was a little premature. They took Hydlen first, and Kyphros."

"There are no mountains to block their passage into Spidlar."

"True. We will see. May we enter the secure haven of Axalt?"

"There is the matter of the road tariff, trader."

"Ah, yes. The tariff." Liedral's hands do not move toward a purse.

"Since the guards are armed, that would be two

coppers each. A copper for you, and nothing, of course, for the healer."

"Could I claim the guards were students?"

"Liedral . . . even as students of the blade, it would be two coppers."

"Ah, well, Nerliat. Five coppers it must be, I suppose. Did you know that the great wizard of chaos is raising mountains in the high plains between Gallos and Kyphros?"

"Tales without substance," snorts the squad leader.

"I wish it were so. I have seen the new mountains, smoking lumps of black rock, burning on the horizon."

"Kyphros is far from here."

Liedral shrugs. "The Kyphrans thought Fairhaven was far, too."

"Five coppers, trader."

"As you wish." Liedral removes the coins from the purse.

Nerliat gestures, and the outer gate rumbles open to reveal an inner portcullis, which, in turn, lifts almost silently. Liedral climbs back onto the cart and flicks the reins. Dorrin follows the trader, and Kadara and Brede follow Dorrin through the fifteen-cubit-high gate.

Once through the walls, nearly forty cubits thick at the base, Dorrin looks at the third set of gates, already swung open. Behind them the portcullis drops and the outer gate closes.

"How long has that stood?" asks Dorrin. "No army could take that wall."

"Longer than my family has been trading, and the western gate is just as imposing. But it doesn't matter. How could it stand against a wizard who could raise or topple mountains?"

"I don't understand that," asks Brede. "Why would a White Wizard waste all that power raising mountains? What's the purpose?"

"Who knows?" snorts Kadara.

Dorrin frowns. "That would take a great deal of ability and power. Anyone with that much ability probably wouldn't do it frivolously."

"Perhaps it's to prove his power," suggests Liedral, turning the cart to the right and down a stone-paved and inclined road. Beneath them, still a hundred cubits lower, the town sits in the midst of a valley still covered primarily with patches of snow punctuated with gray and brown.

"It's just because he's more evil, and wants to destroy things. At least that's what your father would claim, Dorrin," suggests Kadara.

"I suppose so." Dorrin gently rubs his cheek, which aches from where his staff thumped him. Why does his father insist that the Whites are so evil? Certainly the White Wizard who tracked them is powerful—so powerful that Dorrin felt almost like a fly about to be squashed. But . . . there hadn't been an evil presence, just the white of chaos. And is chaos evil—or merely chaotic?

"So would Lortren," adds Kadara, shifting in her saddle as the four ride around another descending turn in the wide stone road that leads downward into the valley.

Only a hundred or so dwellings dot the wide valley surrounded by the steep cliffs. To the west there is a single gap in the cliffs. "This place looks like it was created by magic."

"I know!" exclaims Brede. "It makes perfect sense."

"What does?" The squeak of the cart wheels punctuates Kadara's question as Liedral guides the cart around another wide descending turn.

"The wizard. Why would a wizard want to show his power, but not use it on a town?"

"I don't know," snaps Kadara. "I'm hungry. Just answer your own question."

"If he uses it on a town, then he's destroyed the town."

"So what else is new?"

Liedral and Dorrin grin at each other.

"The White Wizards have enough problems with chaos spilling over and tearing down things. You can't run a kingdom if you have no kingdom to run. What happens if he raises mountains and shows that he can level a city—and then asks the Spidlarians or whoever to submit to Fairhaven? They still have the city and the taxes or goods or whatever."

"Hmmmmm . . ." muses Liedral. "That's fine for the Kyphrans, but the Spidlarians are pretty stiff-necked. So are the people here."

"Still—whatever battles the Whites don't fight . . ." suggests Brede.

Brede has a point. Then, Brede has always been quick to understand.

"This is mighty Axalt?" asks Kadara.

"This is Axalt," affirms Liedral, "and, believe it or not, it will only cost a few coppers for a good room at the inn—and they'll have enough rooms. They like to encourage travelers."

"What about drink?" inquires Brede wryly.

"Wine, mead, brandy—probably half silver a mug."

"That's more than the cost of the room." Dorrin flushes as he realizes he has declared the obvious.

"There had to be a catch," Brede muses. "And I suppose everyone's thirsty? What about water?"

Liedral grins, and Dorrin smiles at the trader's expression. "The water's free, and good. But neither blades nor traders are fond of water."

Liedral turns the cart through the last switchback and directs it toward the pair of two-storied buildings ahead. The one on the right side of the road bears a sign with the image of a tan mountain panther. The one on the left bears the image of a horned black mountain goat. "We'll stay at the Black Ram. It's quieter."

"Is there any real difference?" Kadara rides up alongside the trader.

"Not much—except the clientele. Even the stables are similar." She drives the cart past the stable and turns into the yard behind the Black Ram.

Two stableboys bounce out onto the clay.

"Is the front corner stall free?" The trader's light baritone is hard.

"Yes, ser."

"I'll take it, and anything near for my party's horses."

"Would you like grain, too, for the horses?"

"How much?"

"A copper a cake, ser."

"Two cakes a copper, and we'll take four cakes."

The two look at each other, then nod. "In advance, if you please."

Liedral climbs from the cart. "You bring the cakes, and I'll come up with the coppers."

The cakes appear almost as quickly as the trader speaks, even before Dorrin can dismount, although Brede and Kadara are already following the one stableboy toward the stalls.

"Saddles you can leave," advises Liedral.

Dorrin leads Meriwhen after the others, toward the stalls. He manages to get her unsaddled and the saddle and blankets racked not much after the others, just in time to gather his gear and staff up and trudge after the trader into the inn.

Inside the pine-framed doorway is a foyer ten cubits square. On one side is a counter that sits before a curtained arch, and behind the counter stands a bald man with a long face and a white pointed goatee. The goatee and white eyebrows are the only hair upon his head.

"Trader Liedral. You would like your usual room? Alas, that corner is taken, but the north corner is available."

"The north would be fine. What do you have for the healer, here, and a room for two blades?"

"Two or three rooms?"

"Two," states Brede.

Dorrin purses his lips.

"Two more I can do. Three would be hard."

"You're that crowded? Since when, Wistik?"

Wistik raises his eyebrows. "It does happen. Some Sligan shipwrights are here."

"Timber?"

"Rumor has it that Fairhaven is commissioning another fleet, perhaps two." Wistik looks at the three from Recluce, then inclines his head to Dorrin. "Your pardon, healer."

Dorrin inclines his head to Wistik. "No offense taken, innkeeper."

"In any case, trader Liedral, as you know, one must sell what one has to sell. Oh, and the room charges?" Wistik smiles politely.

"Two for each room." Liedral sets two coppers on the desk.

Dorrin adds his two, as does Brede. Wistik lifts an eyebrow, then adds, "Your party has the north side, trader."

"Thank you, Wistik."

"And I would recommend the lamb stew. The goat pies are a trace strong."

Dorrin shifts his pack and saddlebags, lowering his staff to follow Liedral through the archway to the right of the counter and up the narrow stairs. He tries to ignore the handholding between Brede and Kadara and concentrate on hanging on to his gear.

As Dorrin stumbles off the stairs, Liedral smiles

sadly for an instant at him before turning down the hall toward the north corner.

XXXI

"WHAT'S SPIDLAR LIKE?" asks Dorrin.

"A bit like everywhere else in Candar," Liedral muses. "Except their Council still hasn't knuckled under to Fairhaven. They're stiff-necked, even more so than Axalt. And they're basically orderly. That might be because they're all merchants and traders."

"I wouldn't think of merchants and traders as orderly," Dorrin says, swatting at a mosquito that whines behind his neck.

"Did you put on that lotion?"

"I forgot." Dorrin twists in the saddle in an effort to reach the right saddlebag. As he holds the front rim of the saddle with his left hand and unfastens the buckle with the right, the mosquito attacks, and Dorrin slaps it with his left, nearly falling off Meriwhen and onto the cart.

The trader's hand covers a laugh.

"Are you clowning or trying to get yourself killed?" Kadara's voice is sardonic, but Dorrin senses her concern.

"Some of each, I guess." Dorrin finally extracts the flask from the saddlebag, managing to keep Meriwhen on the narrow road. "You never answered my question about why traders are orderly."

Liedral eases the cart to the right as the road narrows, the right wheel barely clearing the rocks. Dorrin drops back until they complete the turn.

"Honest and orderly traders make more money, especially away from Fairhaven. I couldn't exactly tell you why. Probably because people trust them. Spidlarian traders have a good reputation—shrewd but honest. But they have trouble around here. The traders tied up with the White Wizards—they're mostly Certan and Lydian—have too many advantages. They can use the great roads with lower tolls, and the port at Lydiar. Belonging to the Fairhaven guild means you don't pay fees in each city; and you can sell in Fairhaven itself, and that's a big advantage."

"How come the Spidlarians don't belong?"

"The Spidlarians are mostly seafarers and don't need the great roads, and the White Wizards didn't want trouble with Analeria, Kyphros, and Spidlar at the same time."

"But Kyphros is part of Gallos," interjects Brede from behind the cart.

"Tell that to the Kyphrans," Liedral snorts.

"And Spidlar has managed to avoid knuckling under to Fairhaven."

"For nearly two centuries . . . until the Whites finished their damned road through the Easthorns. Your founder Creslin slowed that down a bit, I understand. But, with this mountain-building business, the Spidlarians are worried—or they ought to be."

"Why do they care? It sounds like all they do is buy and sell. Fairhaven would still let them do that."

"They'd have to do it Fairhaven's way, and the Spidlarians want to sell their way. They sell everything—even soldiers. Probably more Spidlarians work as mercenaries in other parts of Candar than serve in the Council's army. Somehow, it's almost a disgrace to be a professional soldier in Spidlar."

"But it's all right elsewhere?"

"I didn't say it made sense." Liedral lifts the reins, urging the cart horse onward. "Besides, they get paid more elsewhere." She glances at the thicker clouds to the west. "I'd really like to be clear of the hills before that rain comes in."

"Hmmmm . . ." Brede pulls at his chin. "That might mean the best blades are also elsewhere."

"I don't like this," offers Kadara.

"You won't like starving, either."

"What about Dorrin?"

The healer shrugs. "Most places, they need healers. I'd rather work for a smith, though."

All three look at the thin youth.

"I'm stronger than I look. Even your father said so."

The trader's eyebrows lift, even as Liedral's eyes flicker again to the clouds.

"Hegl was a smith. He taught me a lot."

"Did all three of you grow up together?"

"No," Brede says. "I met them later."

"Why are you worried about the clouds?" asks Dorrin, edging Meriwhen closer to the cart.

"There's still a lot of snow and ice in the rock." Liedral glances back toward the ice-tipped peaks of the Easthorns, back in the general direction of Axalt. "Warm rain—and that's what's coming—could melt it quick." The low ice-edged stream runs less than three cubits below the road.

"How much farther?"

"Until midday. The clouds will be here by mid-morning."

"The rain won't start melting things all at once."

"Let's hope not." Liedral flicks the reins. "We need to get out of the canyon before it rains hard."

Dorrin nudges Meriwhen.

They have covered another five kays before a fine mist begins to fall, so fine that the rock walls facing north begin to take on an icy sheen.

Liedral picks up the pace, pushing the cart horse on the straight stretches between curves. "Just a few more kays," the trader mutters as the cart wheel scrapes the canyon rocks yet again.

"Until what?" asks Brede.

"Until we're safe. From the flood, that is."

A drop of warmer water splats on Dorrin's nose. "It's raining."

"We've noticed." Kadara shifts in her saddle and closes her jacket, dropping slightly farther behind the cart. Brede eases back with her, and the hum of low voices is lost in the growing hiss of the rain and in the rushing of the small river to the left of the road.

As they plod through the rain, the river cuts deeper into the stone so that, another three kays toward the hilly plains of Spidlar, the road runs nearly thirty cubits higher than the waters.

"We're past the worst, praise darkness. And just in time." Liedral points to her right.

From the road, Dorrin follows Liedral's finger. Almost as he watches, the water begins to rise, climbing until the bottom of the canyon is filled with white froth. Occasionally, a blackened tree bounces across or emerges from the froth, only to be swirled under. The rain pelts down, seeping under his collar and oozing down his back. "How long will this go on?"

"Why don't you tell us?" asks Kadara.

Dorrin's flush is lost in the wind-swirled rain. He sends his perceptions into the storm, the way his father taught him, but can only sense the heaviness above and around them. "Too much water," he gasps.

"So it will continue for a while?" Brede asks.

"Unless it blows over. There's a lot of water in the clouds."

"There always is," Liedral points out. "Here, at least. We might as well go on. It's coming from the west."

Dorrin hunches into his jacket and follows Brede and the trader's cart, occasionally blotting his forehead. The canyon walls have begun to widen, and their slope lessens with each rod that the four travel downward. At least the rain has also carried away the mosquitoes.

XXXII

THE THREE DAYS of rain have subsided into an afternoon mist falling over Kleth, seeping down the stone walls framing the now-muddy waters of the River Jellicor. An occasional chunk of ice bobs past. Liedral finishes inspecting the ties on the cart and steps back to the dock, eyes traversing the three from Recluse, pausing slightly at Dorrin before glancing back at the riverman by the tiller. She hands two silvers each to Kadara and Brede. "I wish it could be more, but you will recall . . ."

"We enjoyed the company and the guidance," Brede says.

"Be sure to tell Jarnish that I sent you. I'd come, but the rivermen wait for no one."

Kadara's eyes go to the wide river scow tied to the pier, rubbing up and down against the worn wooden guides with the swells of the rain-swollen river.

Dorrin wishes he were as glib as Brede. He will miss Liedral, especially after seeing beneath the trader's carefully maintained exterior, but he can say nothing as the trader places two silvers in his hands.

"I hope you can find a smithy in Diev. Let Jarnish know where you can be found. I do get to Diev every once in a great while."

"Thank you, Liedral."

The trader smiles. "It was nice not to travel alone.

I'd forgotten how good it can be." The tone hardens. "But it's back to business."

"Need to cast off, trader!" calls the bearded riverman.

Liedral steps back to the scow, even as one scruffy youngster loosens the forward line and the riverman at the tiller loosens the aft one. Dorrin watches as the scow eases toward midstream.

"Dorrin, we need to get moving. It's near midday."

Kadara is right. He doesn't need to stare at a river scow drifting downstream toward Spidlaria, even though they don't have that far to go. He climbs slowly into the saddle, then takes a deep breath before nudging his heels into Meriwhen's flanks. The mare whinnies, more of a token protest, as she breaks into a trot. She slows without any urging from Dorrin when she nears the other two.

"That was more than I expected," Brede is telling Kadara.

"Of course." Kadara grins widely. "Thank Dorrin for that."

"Thank you, Dorrin." In turn, Brede grins.

Dorrin finds himself blushing. "Why?"

"You certainly captivated the trader."

"Indeed he did," Kadara adds gleefully.

"It's too bad," Brede guides the gelding off the river road.

The three turn onto the road toward the factor's establishment. A gap in the clouds allows sunlight to warm them. Beyond the mud that borders the stone thoroughfare is trampled brown grass, still dotted infrequently with patches of snow. Behind the grass stand scattered small huts, some with goat pens, some few with a tethered cow, and all with ragged thatched roofing.

Kadara nods. "That brother of hers is worthless,

and she does all the work. The Whites still fight the Legend."

"Not all men are worthless," protests Dorrin.

"That wasn't the point of the Legend. The point of the Legend was what happened when men refused to listen to women, or to allow them equal say."

"Ware horses!" screams a woman from the front of a hut on the left side of the road.

Dorrin reins up Meriwhen to keep from riding down a youngster chasing a ball across the stone paving slabs. He waits for the youngster, barefoot despite the chill and the cold clay alongside the road, to reclaim the ball.

The woman shakes a broom at him, so hard that straws fly from it. "Watch your riding, stranger!"

Dorrin continues to wait. The shaggy-haired boy grabs the mud-spattered ball, and never looking up, saunters back across the road.

"Demon-damned travelers . . ."

Dorrin nudges Meriwhen, and the mare trots to catch up with Brede and Kadara, who have slowed to wait for him.

"Slow down!" screams the woman behind him. "You're as like to kill someone!"

"Right, Dorrin. Slow down." Kadara shakes her head before turning in the saddle.

"Since when didn't women have equal say?" mutters Dorrin, his hand checking the staff to make sure it is firmly held in place.

Overhead, the clouds close, and the light dims. Behind them, the Jellicor flows north to the cold sea, and a woman in graying rags shakes a straw broom.

XXXIII

DORRIN PEERS INTO the kitchen, looking for the factor.

"Jarnish left for Hitter's. Be back in a bit. You want breakfast . . . give us a hand here." The cook gestures toward the kitchen water tank.

"How can I help?"

"Fill the tank. Here's a carry-bucket. Use the back well—the one down the outside steps here."

Dorrin takes the carry-bucket and opens the rear door.

"And wipe your feet good, boy."

He steps out into the dawn chill, wishing he had been able to sleep longer. But lying there on his bedroll on the hard attic floor, with Brede and Kadara asleep and entwined not three cubits away, had been too much.

The steps descend into a stone-walled enclosure perhaps fifty cubits square, half of which is comprised of raised garden beds that have been turned but not yet planted. White frost covers the dark garden soil, and his breath puffs away in a thin cloud as he steps up to the well.

He drops the well-bucket down the stone-sided well, holding to the rope, letting the heavy oak and iron splinter the surface ice. Then he lifts the bucket the ten or so cubits to the stone ledge where the water, like liquid ice, slops over his bare hands, as he pours the well bucket into the smaller carrying bucket. He walks toward the kitchen steps, his breath a white cloud. From the chimney above the kitchen a thin white plume drifts northward.

"Mind you now, wipe those feet."

"Yes, cook."

The flat-nosed woman continues to chop and dice an assortment of dubious vegetables. Dorrin finds himself staring at the flicking knife.

"Never seen a good stew being made, boy? Ha!"

Dorrin carries in three full buckets from the well, topping off the kitchen tank and replacing the cover.

"Took long enough," snorts the old cook. "Breakfast's on the table."

"Thank you," adds Lyssa, the wide-eyed maid.

"Don't thank him, girl. He's just another questor, and he'll be gone tomorrow or next eight-day—if the White guards don't run him in for something. Can't understand Jarnish."

Dorrin pulls out a stool and sits down. On the dented table are a loaf of black bread, a wedge of cheese, a plate of dried fruits, three battered clay mugs and a gray stoneware pitcher from which a wisp of vapor seeps.

"What about your friends?" grumbles the cook. "They intend to sleep all day?"

Dorrin looks out at the gray morning, barely beyond dawn. "I don't think so, but it's only a bit past dawn, isn't it?"

"You want to succeed in life, boy, you don't sleep past the cock's second crow."

Lyssa looks at Dorrin and grins before taking the tray and leaving.

"Tell the old Missus, if she wants more hot cider, to ring the bell twice." The flashing knife halts, and the cook sweeps the vegetables into the dark liquid in the deep stewpot.

Dorrin pours hot cider into a mug, then hacks off a chunk of bread and a slice of cheese. The bread is warm and chewy, the cheese cold and sharp. "Very good bread."

"Course it is. I don't bake any other kind. You do

something, boy, you best do it right. Otherwise you're just taking up space."

Dorrin takes another bite from the bread, followed by a sip from the cider. "Good cider."

"Didn't you hear me, boy? I'm a good cook. I don't serve bad food. If I did, I couldn't call myself a cook." She brings the knife to bear on some undetermined haunch of dark meat.

Dorrin tries one of the dried pearapples. Not surprisingly, it is also good, dried or not.

"Is this the place?" Brede's cheerful voice precedes him down the stairs from the attic.

"Place for what?" snorts the cook as Brede steps onto the wide plank floor. "You best get moving if you want to get where you're going by sunset."

"You're right." Brede pulls up a stool across from Dorrin and pours two mugs of hot cider.

"Course I'm right, but I don't need a soldier boy to tell me that."

Kadara eases onto the stool next to Brede, her hands going to the earthenware mug, cradling it in both hands under her chin and letting the steam wreath her face. "Mmmmm . . ."

"You're too pretty to be a lady blade." The cook's knife jabs toward Kadara. "Looks like yours'll slay more men than that killer blade you carried yesterday."

Dorrin almost chokes on a mouthful of cheese and bread.

Kadara swallows, following her small mouthful with the warm cider. "Don't say a word," she whispers to Brede. "Or you either," she adds to Dorrin.

Dorrin grins at Brede.

"It's not false pride to look good. But it's inviting the demons into the parlor when you deny your looks. Many's a poor wench found herself with child and worse because she said, 'Who, me? I can't be that pretty.' Ha!" The knife flashes through the last of the haunch, and the bare bone drops into another kettle.

The kitchen door opens, and Jarnish steps through.

"Good day. Did you sleep well?" The factor takes a deep breath. "Be stew for dinner, I'd say. A lovely aroma already, Jaddy." His heavy jacket comes off, and he sets it on one of the pegs on the crosstimber by the door.

"Never trust a man's tongue—not when he talks about food or love." Jaddy snorts.

"She's always got a word for everyone." Jarnish pulls a long-handled clay pipe from a brownish dish on the otherwise empty serving table and a pouch from his vest pocket. He tamps shreds of tobacco into the pipe, then lights it with his striker. Pulling the one armchair in the kitchen up to the end of the table, he sits, taking the pipe from his mouth. "You'll be off shortly, then."

"Yes, ser," Brede says quietly. "Once we get to Diev, Kadara and I will try the road guards first."

"They'll take you. Darkness, they'll be a-taking anyone who can swing a blade and stay mounted."

"You don't have the highest opinion of the Spidlarian road guards."

"Not much good except to pick up those souls too poor to know how to be a highwayman and too desperate to be otherwise." Jarnish takes another puff on the pipe and the acrid smoke drifts toward Dorrin.

"They're good at picking up tavern wenches with their tales," offers Jaddy.

"What about you, lad?"

"I'd like to apprentice to a smith, ser."

Kadara looks at Brede with the slightest of frowns.

"A smith? Aren't you a tad slender?"

"I'm stronger than I look."

"Any experience?"

"Was an apprentice for a while."

Jarnish takes the long-handled pipe from his mouth,

blowing a cloud in Dorrin's direction. Dorrin tries not to choke. No one on Recluce smokes, although he has read of the practice, especially in Hamor.

"What kind of smith, young fellow? Must be a dozen smiths in Diev, not that I know them all from here— smiths for the traders' ships, smiths that make horseshoes and not much else, smiths that make who knows what."

"The kind that makes tools and parts for wagons or sawmills—that sort of thing."

Another cloud of smoke follows before the factor speaks again. "Just two smiths like that in Diev. There's Henstaal, and he's got a place out beyond the south wall, just off the turnpike. Good solid forge. Then there's Yarrl, and he's on the north side, off the guard road."

Dorrin munches another piece of dried pearapple.

"Henstaal's got three big sons, older 'n you. Yarrl's only got a daughter. No apprentice, not the last time I heard. Rumor was he made his daughter help him." Jarnish blows another cloud of smoke down the table.

"What's the problem with Yarrl?"

"Not as there's any problem... exactly... young fellow, but they say as his woman's got the evil eye, and his daughter... well, her tongue... and they're not from here, either. He set up shop there when I wasn't much older 'n you, and never said where he was from. Never has, either. Good work, but... says what's on his mind. Can't keep apprentices. Last one lasted three days."

"All I can do is try."

The factor stands. "Can't mint coins if you don't keep hammering, nor milk if you don't water the cows."

Dorrin takes the hint and rises. "We'll be on our way as soon as we gather our packs together."

"Don't need to hurry that much. Let the lady blade finish her cider."

Brede stands. "We thank you for your hospitality."

"That'll not be a problem. I owe young Liedral, and this'll help with that debt." The factor gestures with the pipe, then sets it back in the brown dish. "I'm off to the barge landing, Jaddy. Maybe they'll have some winter trout at the market there."

"Don't take any unless they're silver. The brown ones turn bitter."

Jarnish shrugs as he pulls on his jacket.

Once the factor has stepped outside, Dorrin heads up the stairs to gather his jacket and pack, leaving Brede and Kadara to finish their breakfast. In the dusty attic, he rolls his bedding and cinches it tightly, and packs his gear into the saddlebags. He pulls on his jacket. With the bags over his right forearm, his staff in hand, and the bedroll in his left arm, he heads back down the stairs, nose wrinkling at the acrid odor of burned tobacco . . . and at the faint aroma of something else carried by Jarnish, except it is not a smell. It is almost as though a faint dusting of chaos flakes off the factor. Dorrin shrugs. Traders have to deal with all sorts.

Brede has finished the dark bread and has just set his empty mug on the table when Dorrin reenters the kitchen. Dorrin's nose itches, and he snuffles to keep from sneezing.

"Are you all right?" asks Brede.

"Fine." Dorrin eases around the table and toward the back door. Lyssa opens it for him. "Thank you."

Lyssa smiles, and Jaddy shakes her head, not pausing in measuring out flour onto her work table.

The chill air relieves the itch in Dorrin's nose. Meriwhen whuffles and tosses her head up from an empty manger as Dorrin opens the stall. "I know. You're still hungry. You're always hungry." Dorrin rummages through the feed barrels and finds the oats and a scoop. While he hasn't discussed the feed with Jarnish, a scoop or two from the large barrel shouldn't be too bad. His head throbs as he thinks the thought. Clearly, he will have to leave a coin or something for the extra feed. "You're always causing problems," he says as he empties the oats into the manger.

Meriwhen only chews the grain as Dorrin takes out the brush and begins to curry her. The headache continues after he replaces the brush in the saddle bags and starts back to the kitchen.

Brede and Kadara are leaving as he approaches.

"I forgot something," Dorrin explains.

"What? You have that guilty look." Kadara frowns.

"I need to pay for some extra oats."

"Why bother? The factor could spare a handful."

"I need to." Dorrin steps around the redhead and up the stairs.

"Such a stickler . . ."

"I doubt he has much choice, Kadara," answers Brede. "He is a healer."

Dorrin steps inside.

"What do you need now, boy?" demands Jaddy, elbow-deep in flour.

"I just wanted to leave a copper or two for some extra feed." Dorrin reaches for his purse.

"Jarnish won't be minding that."

"Probably not, but I will."

"You're order-bound, aren't you, boy?"

Dorrin nods.

"Too bad there aren't more like you. World would be a better place." She looks at the wooden bowl filled with dried pearapples and peaches. "Lyssa!"

The maid appears from the pantry.

"Wrap up a double handful of the fruits for them. Jarnish said to send 'em off proper." She grins at Dorrin. "Just leave the copper on the table there. I'll be a-telling Jarnish, don't you worry." She glances at the maid who has wrapped the fruit in a thin gray cloth. "Another handful or so. Jarnish wouldn't have these folks starving on the road."

"You didn't have to—" protests Dorrin.

"Neither did you, boy. Now take the fruit and be on your way."

"Thank you."

"Nonsense! Just be on your way. Bring me a trinket from the forge, someday."

"I will."

Jaddy looks back to her baking, and Dorrin takes the cloth filled with dried fruit and walks down the steps and out to the stable.

"What's that?"

"Dried fruits—pearapple and peaches."

Kadara shakes her head while Dorrin packs the fruit into his left saddle bag. Then he struggles with the blanket and the saddle, with the saddlebags, and finally with the hackamore.

"Are you ready?" asks Brede, leading the gelding toward the stable door. "I shoveled out the worst of the stalls."

"You two . . ." Kadara flicks the reins of the chestnut.

"You catch more redtails with honey than vinegar," observes Brede calmly.

Dorrin clambers into his saddle and follows them out to the still-frozen and rutted road. The sun has finally cleared the trees to the south of the factor's yard, and only a few thin and high white clouds break the green-blue of the sky.

"This heads toward the mountain road." Brede points westward.

"I heard the factor."

Dorrin just nods and follows, his gloved hand touching the dark wood of his staff. The three ride at an even pace westward, toward the first low rise in the road.

Uncounted hills later, Dorrin squirms uneasily in Meriwhen's saddle. His legs and his buttocks are bruised—even after all the kays. Will he ever get used to riding? Ahead of him, Kadara sits easily in the saddle of the larger chestnut, absently running through a set of blade exercises, then sheathing the larger sword.

Dorrin glances at his staff, then takes a deep breath and extracts it from the lanceholder. Slowly he begins loosening up his shoulders.

"Dorrin . . ."

The redhead turns. Brede is flat against the gelding's mane.

" . . . I don't mind if you practice, but would you look before you start? That wood is hard." Brede grins.

"Sorry. I thought you were behind me."

"What did Lortren say about assuming things?"

Dorrin flushes.

"It's not that bad, so long as you're not intending to be a blade."

"It's not that good," admits Dorrin. "It's still hard to get a feel for the wood." He looks across the hillside beside the road at the muddy trail that leads to a small stone house. A plume of white drifts from the chimney into the clear sky of late afternoon, rising above a small stone-walled barn and a wooden privy.

"Why?"

"I suppose because it's a weapon, when you get right down to it, and weapons are for destruction, and that's chaos."

Brede nods. "I'm glad I'm not that order-linked."

"So am I," adds Kadara.

"How much farther?"

Brede sighs. "That means another day after today,

maybe a day and a half to Diev, if your friend the trader's directions were accurate."

"Liedral's been right so far," Dorrin says.

Kadara doesn't turn, but Dorrin can feel that she is grinning.

"Stop it."

"Stop what? I didn't say a word." Kadara takes out the shortsword for at least the third time since morning and begins to twirl it.

Dorrin looks at his staff, then slowly resumes the exercise. He shifts in the saddle again as Meriwhen reaches the top of yet another low rise in the chain of seemingly endless rolling hills. The stone walls separating the flattened and brown meadows from the road look little different from those outside Kleth.

"There should be a way station before too long," Brede announces cheerfully. "We can take a break."

"You aren't planning on riding all night?" Dorrin asks.

Neither blade answers him, but Brede eases his gelding past Meriwhen and up beside the chestnut. A clump of mud flies past Dorrin's leg.

The next rolling hill brings no sign of the promised way station, and, with a deep breath, Dorrin shifts his weight in the saddle once again.

II.

SMITH AND HEALER

XXXIV

BREDE AND KADARA wait on the crest of the hill. Dorrin reins up beside them and looks over the shallow valley that separates them from their destination.

On the flat cliffs above the low waterfall begins Diev, divided by the River Weyel, not sprawling like the herder towns of Weevett, nor huddling within a proud wall like Jellico, nor slowly dying like Vergren under the white lash of Fairhaven. The lower section of Diev squats in the delta, a fourth-rate port behind Spidlaria and even Sligo's Tyrhavven, a port so poor that not even the near-desperate Liedral visits it often.

Diev is merely a town to serve the northwest sheep farms and the scattered mountain holdings, a town without pretensions, a town on the single road that leads from Kleth to the inhospitable north coast of Candar. That poor road peters out into a trail that eventually deadends a few kays beyond Diev, the town where the Westhorns meet the Northern Ocean. Beyond the buildings and the rising plumes of smoke that twist over the low plateau, the Westhorns loom, still a mass of white snow, heavy rock, and glittering ice that dwarfs the small efforts of the men squatting below the mountains.

"Not terribly promising," offers Brede.

"It meets the criteria, at least," Kadara says. "We've traveled through Fairhaven and the Easthorns, and we will serve—somehow—at the foot of the Westhorns ... for longer than a year."

"The longer-than-a-year phrasing still bothers me," Brede says slowly.

Dorrin frowns. Lortren never set forth any such rules for him. She only told him he must find himself.

"Well ... sitting here in the wind won't get us to Diev." Kadara flicks the chestnut's reins.

Brede follows Kadara down the road toward Diev. Dorrin watches for a moment, seeing how easily each sits in the saddle. Then he lifts Meriwhen's reins and pats her neck. "Let's go, lady. Wherever we're headed."

XXXV

DORRIN PATS MERIWHEN on the neck, surveying the smithy—the covered walkway that connects the square-chimneyed forge building to the narrow house, built of smoothed and dressed planks; the small barn; the corral with the pair of horses and the pig pen. Beyond the barn are three solid oaks, still without leaves, growing almost in a perfect triangle.

Should he have come alone? When all is said, he is alone. Brede and Kadara must fight their own battles in finding employment as blades.

"Hallo!" He reins up before the forge building. There is no answer. After tying Meriwhen to an iron ring on a square post, he steps into the faintly eye-burning mist and hot metallic smell of the smithy. Dorrin edges past the broken implements and unidentified metal parts that line one wall. Compared to Hegl's smithy, Yarrl's is a confused mess, and even the tool rack is filled with a bewildering array of hammers, tongs, and other tools. Some he recognizes, like the standard hammers, swages, fullers, and punches laid out on the hearth edge in easy reach. But he sees tongs shaped almost like serpents, and there are two large cone mandrels on huge weighted bases. Of the two slack tanks, one is divided into two parts.

Muscles on the smith's back ripple as the hammer rises and falls, as the tongs reposition the hot iron. Then the iron cools and is thrust back into the forge. The smith watches the metal heat and returns it to the anvil.

At length, the piece—a complicated and twisted brace of some sort is set on the edge of the forge to anneal. Then the hammer is set aside, and the smith turns. "Who are you, youngster?"

"My name is Dorrin. I'd like to be your apprentice. Jarnish said you might need one."

"Jarnish? What's a factor know about a smithy?"

Dorrin smiles politely.

"Scrawny fellow. You'll eat like a hog. All young fellows do." The heavy-chested man circles around Dorrin. "What makes you think you're a smith?"

"I've been an apprentice."

"So why aren't you still there?"

"I'm from Recluce."

"Oh, one of them? So why'd they throw you out?"

"I wanted to make toys, little machines. They don't have much use for them."

"I can't say as I do, either."

"I can do the work."

"You expect to take over the place in a year or two, boy?"

"No, ser. I don't ever expect to take it over."

"Not good enough for you?"

Dorrin bites his tongue. "If I become a good smith, then I'll have to leave before you're ready to give up. If I don't, you'll find someone else."

"Ha! Sharp in thinking, leastwise. What do you know about smithing?"

"A little . . . but not enough."

"You willing to handle the great bellows there? Can you make nails? A good apprentice could turn out hundreds in a morning. How good's your scarfing? Good enough to make a solid weld? Can you fuller a bar even enough so it doesn't split?"

"Usually." Dorrin can sense someone else approaching, but does not turn to see who the newcomer might be.

"Hard work. You listen. Do what I say. No lip."

"Can I ask questions?"

The smith frowns.

"You let this one go, Yarrl, and you be a damned White fool." A firm voice intrudes.

The smith looks up at the angular woman. "Smith business, Reisa."

Dorrin follows the smith's glance, forces his eyes to study Reisa casually, even as he notes that the gray-haired and broad-shouldered woman's right arm ends just below the elbow. The smith finally looks back to him.

Yarrl shrugs. "Don't pay much. Food, a bed in the smithy corner room, and a copper an eight-day until you're good enough to work your own metal. If you can't learn my needs for a striker and make good nails within an eight-day, you're no good to me."

"Fair enough. Is there a spare stall in the stable I can use—in return for cleaning it?"

Yarrl opens his mouth, closes it, and finally speaks. "You want a stall? To sleep in?"

"I have a horse, ser."

"How will you feed it? Don't expect me to pay you and feed your animal."

"No. If I'm good, I'll make enough to feed her. If I'm not, you won't keep me. I have a few coins, enough for a while."

"I don't know . . ."

"Yarrl . . ." Again, the low voice cuts off the smith.

"All right . . . you clean the stable on your time, not mine. Now, get the animal put away and get back here. Might as well see right off if you can earn your keep."

"Yes, ser."

" . . . least he's polite . . ." The smith turns and lifts the hammer.

Reisa smiles at Dorrin, with the slightest of head shakes, then adds, "I'll show him the stable."

Dorrin follows the one-armed woman to the barn, and the three stalls. A mule stares at Dorrin from the first. The second is empty, as is the third.

"Petra has the bay and the wagon at market."

"Is Petra your daughter?"

"That she is, and a good one." Reisa's voice bears an edge.

"Then you're lucky." Dorrin smiles.

"Are you really a smith apprentice?"

"I've been one. Also been a healer."

"And you want to be a smith? The work never ends, not even for Yarrl."

"Somehow . . . I need to work the metal . . ."

"I thought so . . . but you're still a healer, one of the Black ones?"

"Yes." Dorrin looks at her right arm.

"No. I know no one can do that. You do animals?"

"If it's not too bad."

"Goats?"

"I've never done one, but I could try."

"Get your horse settled and your things in your cubby. It's not much. Better than the barn, though, and, you work out, Yarrl will let you fix it up better. Then you look at my goat."

He takes the hay rake and smoothes the clay, then spreads straw over it. He unsaddles Meriwhen, racks the saddle, and quickly brushes the mare. Then he lifts the staff and saddlebags over his shoulder, and hoists his bedroll.

Reisa leads him back toward the smithy, but to a door in the rear corner that opens onto a nearly bare room with a single shuttered window without glass. The rough floor planks are dusty, and the only pieces of furniture are a straw pallet on a wide shelf built out from the wall, a four-legged stool and a wobbly table, on which rests a battered copper oil lamp.

"Not much, but it's snug."

Dorrin sets the bedroll on the table and the bags on the stool. Before he lies on the pallet he wants to use his limited order senses to persuade various vermin to move elsewhere. "The goat?"

Reisa turns, and Dorrin latches the door behind him. In a small pen by the barn is a wide-bellied goat.

"Burlow's damned ram got in here."

"Where is he now?"

"Some of him's salted; the rest was dinner."

"Oh . . ." Dorrin steps through the gate. The nanny edges away, but wobbles. His hands touch her shoulder, then her flanks. "She's carrying."

"I knew that."

"I'm no animal healer, but I'd say she's carrying too many."

"How many?"

"Three, I think."

"Can you do anything?"

Dorrin shrugs. "Maybe." He lets his senses go out to the goat, lending a sense of order to her, and to only one of the unborn kids. Perhaps that will work. Finally, he steps out of the pen, wiping his forehead, trying not to sneeze at the water-damped odor of straw.

"Well?"

"I don't know. It may take some time."

Reisa watches the goat. "She's not as unsteady."

Dorrin leans against the fence and takes a deep breath.

"Young fellow, you need to eat before you go into the smithy. Just sit on the porch and let me get you a bite. I forgot how healing's such work."

"All right."

Dorrin sits on the edge of the porch, his booted feet on the second step, listening to the muted thumps of the smith's hammer, letting the late winter sun bathe his face. Spring has not come to Diev.

"Here."

"Thank you, madame Reisa."

She flushes. "I'm no lady, youngster. Just eat, please."

On the scarred wooden platter are two thick slices of oatmeal bread, slathered with butter and topped with a dark preserve. A thin wedge of cheese sits between the bread. Reisa hands him a stoneware mug filled with cold cider. Dorrin's shakiness abates with the bread and cheese.

"You'd best get into the smithy."

Dorrin stands. "Thank you."

Once inside the smithy, he peels off his jacket and shirt, leaving only the sleeveless undershirt, and hangs both on a corner peg.

"There." Yarrl nods toward a heavy leather apron set out on a side bench. "Work the bellows. It's got a standard counterweight, and the overhead lever's angled to make it easy. Want that to stay not quite white, like the corner there."

Dorrin slips on the leather apron, hoping he will not have too many blisters before his hands toughen again.

XXXVI

"WHY DO WE even have to do anything about Recluce? All the Blacks do is sit on their island and cultivate order. Anyone who causes trouble gets thrown out—usually to our benefit."

"We're not talking about a military action now," Jeslek says mildly. "Aren't you tired of our gold going to Recluce so that the Blacks can use it to buy Bristan and Hamorian goods?"

"Their spices and wines are better and cheaper," a heavy voice rumbles from the back row.

"So is some of their cabinetry," adds another voice.

"And their wool—"

"If you can wear it, Myral!"

"So . . . what are you proposing, Jeslek?"

"Nothing major. Just a thirty percent surtax on goods from Recluce."

"Thirty percent? I'd rather drink that red swill from Kyphros," rumbles the bass voice.

"Precisely my point."

"That will increase the number of smugglers."

"We'll use some of the money to build up the fleet to stop that."

"And the rest? Does it go into your pocket, Jeslek?"

"Hardly. That's up to the Council, but I'd suggest that it be split between an increased stipend for Council members, rebuilding the square, and funding the road construction. Would anyone else like a word?"

"Won't that just funnel more golds into Spidlar?"

"What about Sarronnyn . . ."

"Southwind will love that . . ."

After stepping from the chamber, Sterol looks at

the red-headed Anya. "Very transparent. Transparent, but clever."

"They'll approve it."

"Of course. And he'll be popular, and the fleet will get larger."

"What will Recluce do?"

"Nothing. They'll trade more across the ocean and complain." Sterol smiles, faintly. "What it will do is direct even more trade from Lydiar to Spidlaria. In a year or so, we'll have to take over Spidlar if we don't want to put our own merchants out of business."

"Do you think . . .?" The red-headed wizard lets her words trail off as the High Wizard continues. Her faint smile contains a hint of irritation.

"By then, Jeslek will be High Wizard, and it will be necessary to ban all trade with Recluce. He won't say it that way, of course. The surtax will be a hundred percent, and the Black Council will worry because all of their specie will have to go for grain and flour from Hydlen, and too much spoils when it's shipped from Hamor. The Blacks will dither and moan and bitch, but their population's too great for them to risk meddling with the weather, the way Creslin did, and, more important, they don't have anyone who can."

Anya nods, her eyes flicking toward the chamber.

"The discontent will stir up disorder, leading to chaos, which will result in more exiles from Recluce, and less action—for a time."

"You sound like you believe Jeslek's plans will work."

"Being High Wizard in times of change presents certain . . . problems." Sterol laughs, softly. "We need to go back in and preside over the vote, even if it is a formality."

"Will they work—his plans, I mean?"

"They might—unless he's too successful, which he

will be." Sterol nods toward the chamber. "Come along, Anya."

Anya frowns, but follows the High Wizard into the council chamber.

XXXVII

"THAT'S ALL." YARRL lowers the hammer.

Dorrin lets the two-chambered great bellows expand, locks the overhead lever in place, and then dips the rag in leather oil and carefully dusts the outside of the bellows suspended at the east side of the square forge. Yarrl puts away the straight peen hammer and the anvil tongs.

Dorrin racks his hammer and picks up the broom. Although sweeping the hard clay is not strictly necessary every night, Dorrin feels better when the smithy is as clean and neat as he can leave it. He has already replaced the less-used implements in their racks, the ones which had gathered some dust. Those Yarrl uses regularly he has left where the smith has placed them.

After Yarrl leaves, Dorrin finishes sweeping the scraps, bits of ash, and droplets of metal too small to reclaim into the waste pit. Then he replaces the broom and scoop and closes the sliding door. He walks to the well, where he folds back the cover and draws a bucket of water, still cold despite the coming of spring and sunlight. He washes off the worst of the ash and grime, then waters the small flower garden under the porch with the last drops from the bucket.

After replacing the well cover, he walks toward his room, glancing to the north, and the clouds building up over northern ocean, and then to the west, where the sun almost touches the tips of the Westhorns, the highest peaks still glittering with ice and snow.

Lifting the latch, he steps inside. The green-dyed rush mat helps make his room seem warmer, as does the old but clean quilt Reisa has provided. Soon, he will finish the braces for the table, and then he will work on something in which to store his few clothes. With a sigh, he picks up the staff behind the door. After closing the door, he walks to the barn.

"Nnnnaaa . . ." Mora pleads.

Dorrin stops and scratches the nanny's head, adding a trace of order to the goat. One offspring is strong enough to survive, but the black flame of order is too weak for mother and even one kid. He purses his lips, realizing how much he did not learn. He scratches Mora's head again as she rubs against his hand. After a time, he steps back from the fence. "That's all, girl."

Then he opens the barn door. Once inside, he leans the staff against the wall, and hangs up the rough straw figure he uses as a target. Even after a few eight-days, he can sense a growing sureness in his hands and his staff—not that exercises are any substitute for practice with a real person. But at least he can feel what he is doing with the staff.

After the first set of exercises, he throws the rope over the beam and ties the small sandbag to it, then swings the bag out. Once he manages five successive strikes on the moving bag, each from a balanced position, but generally he has trouble with both balance and accuracy after two or three.

He is sweating again when he stops, and his knees are rubbery. Just a short period of exercise with the staff following a long day is exhausting. After storing his targets, he sets the staff aside and finds the curry brush. Meriwhen whinnies.

"Yes, I know. I should have curried you first. But I'll ride you after supper."

The mare whinnies again.

"After supper. I promise." Dorrin sneezes once, then again, before he steps into the stall and begins to groom the black mare.

XXXVIII

DORRIN TIES MERIWHEN to the iron ring on the weathered timber post outside the mill building—a shedroofed structure twenty cubits wide and fifty cubits deep with only a single sliding door. The door is ajar enough for him to enter without turning sideways. Once inside, a row of high small windows on the south side of the mill provide enough light to guide him to a single small cubicle in the southeast corner of the building, less than a dozen cubits from the idle saw blade.

Dorrin's nose itches from the sawdust raised by his steps, and he rubs it before stepping into the office where a young black-bearded man sits, slowly chewing on some cheese and bread.

"I beg your pardon. Are you Hemmil?"

"Me? Hemmil? How I wish, young fellow! I'm Pergun, just a journeyman mill hand." Pergun's eyes study Dorrin's brown clothes. "Why does a healer need Hemmil? You are a healer, aren't you, looking like that?"

"I'm partly a healer, but I'm mostly an apprentice smith for Yarrl. I didn't need Hemmil, exactly, but I was looking for some mill scraps . . ."

"No doubt wonderful scraps two or three cubits long and finely cut?" Pergun speaks with his mouth full and bits of food fly with the words.

"Darkness, no. I meant real scraps. I mean, if I found an end perhaps half a cubit or cubit..."

"All right, young fellow." Pergun laughs, then stands and walks to the doorway of the walled-off room, swallowing the last of his midday meal. "Hemmil'll be back in a bit, and we'll get back to work. Till then, you can scout up some scraps. There's also the burn bin over there. Bring what you want back here, and we'll dicker." He turns, then looks back at Dorrin. "Why does a smith want scraps, anyway?"

"Oh, Yarrl doesn't. I need them for my work." A faint headache reminds Dorrin he must provide further explanation. "I'm making some working models."

"Oh... I suppose that makes sense." Pergun's hand lifts, as if to scratch his head, then drops. "Well... bring the wood you want back here."

"I appreciate it."

"Young fellow—what's your name?"

"Oh, I'm Dorrin."

"How do you get on with Mistress Petra? Understand she's got... I mean... maybe you've heard... well..."

Dorrin grins. "She doesn't have an evil eye, if that's what you mean. Neither does Reisa. They're good people, even if they stay to themselves."

"Wondered about that. Honsard says Yarrl does good work. Did some good stuff for Hemmil, too. The new saw blade was his. Keeps its teeth better than Henstaal's, but we can't say much." The millworker jabs a thumb toward the sawdust and fragments beneath the still saw blade. "Better get moving, Dorrin."

Dorrin collects likely lengths of wood, his eyes wandering around the long mill shed as he does. The odor of cut wood is somehow soothing, even in the chill of the mill shed. He needs to hurry, for Yarrl has agreed only reluctantly to let him take a little time, and only because the mill is never open later than the smithy.

When he has what he needs, Dorrin turns back toward the entry, cradling the short lengths of red oak and the armful of mill ends, setting them on the bench outside the office where the brown-haired man is talking to Pergun.

" . . . have to charge him . . . every apprentice in Diev . . . be out here . . ."

"Yes, ser. He only wants short pieces, though."

" . . . short pieces . . . we'll see . . ."

Both men turn as if they sense Dorrin. Hemmil nods at Pergun, and the younger man walks out to the bench. Hemmil steps past the two and heads toward the saw.

"How much for these?" Dorrin asks.

"I'd give them to you, but—" Pergun nods toward the mill owner.

"I heard." Dorrin looks down at the odd-sized pile. "Perhaps a copper?" He tried to keep his voice from sounding plaintive.

"It's not as though I see any large pieces." Pergun grins, running a hand through his dark beard. "So a copper it is, but only because I'd not want ill will from any healer. Leastwise, that's what I'll tell Hemmil."

Dorrin scrabbles in his purse.

"Like as it's fine with me to give them to you, but Hemmil would fry me. It's not been that long since I was an apprentice, and I know apprentices have little enough." Pergun pauses. "You ever go to Kyril's? Some of us gather there on the eight-day ends."

"I haven't been. I don't know Diev very well, and I'm pretty tired to go off doing much exploring."

"You're too young not to explore." Pergun shakes his head. "You'll marry Mistress Petra and never go anywhere."

"Not Mistress Petra, nice as she is," Dorrin protests.

"Then come and see Diev."

"Maybe I will." Dorrin produces the copper and hands it to Pergun.

Pergun shakes his head. "Any end-day . . . and bring a few coppers. That's all it takes."

Dorrin scoops up the wood. "Probably not this end-day, but soon."

XXXIX

WITH A GROAN, Dorrin carries the staff into the open space in the middle of the barn, beginning the exercises Lortren taught him more than a year earlier—has it been so long already? Concentrating on the staff, he tries to blend the order within him, the staff, and his movements. After a time, he sets up the swinging target and launches it, then sets his stance, trying to strike from the totally balanced position.

"Offf . . ." He has stepped too close to the second stall, and the staff ricochets off a wooden brace. Trying to regain his balance, Dorrin slips on the loose straw and staggers. Incidents such as these both keep him practicing and ensure that he practices out of sight.

Finally, drenched with sweat, with odd pieces of straw and chaff clinging to his damp face and arms, he sets the staff down.

"Your moves are pretty good, but you're acting like it's an exercise." Reisa stands just inside the doorway.

Dorrin lets the end of the staff drop to the packed clay of the barn floor.

"You're not really following through, and if you had to use that, a good blade would only have to step back a bit."

"I know. Kadara kept telling me that." Dorrin

gestures toward the swinging target. "That's why I set this target up."

"Just take another step forward when you make the follow-up thrust." Reisa grins. "Actually, you're pretty good. Especially for a smith who's also a healer. What could you do with a blade?"

"Nothing."

"That because you're a healer?"

Dorrin wipes his forehead with the back of his bare forearm, then nods.

"Are your friends that good with their blades?"

"Better. Much better."

A gust of wind blows through the open barn door, whipping Reisa's trousers around her legs. "I wish . . ." The gray-haired and one-handed woman shakes her head.

"You wish you'd been born in Recluce?" Standing by Meriwhen's stall, Dorrin unties the rope for his swinging target. "Where were you trained?"

"A long ways from here." She looks over her shoulder. "Southwind."

"Do you wish you'd never left?"

"Sometimes. But you don't ever get what you wish for, only what you can make happen." Reisa pauses. "You going to be here for supper?"

"I don't think so. I'm supposed to meet Brede and Kadara at the inn."

"They're too good to be here."

Dorrin lowers the target, waiting for the smith's wife to continue.

"When you're too good for what you're doing," she reflects, her eyes focused on the past, "chaos finds you. With you, it will take longer."

"Why?" Dorrin coils the rope attached to the target.

"You haven't learned all you need to know." Reisa smiles faintly. "But don't pay too much attention to an old woman's ramblings. Have a good time with your friends." She leaves the barn as quietly as she entered.

After putting away his exercise gear, Dorrin takes out the curry brush and starts to work on Meriwhen. The mare shivers slightly and edges sideways in the stall. He pats her flank. "Lady, we need to keep you in shape."

Following the grooming, he washes up at the well and towels fully dry in his quarters, putting on his clean traveling clothes—linen shirt and brown trousers. Then he slips on the thin leather jacket and heads to the barn.

Dorrin saddles Meriwhen deliberately. Should he take his staff? He frowns but places it in the lance holder and leads the mare into the yard. Red dust puffs under his brown-booted feet.

A spray of yellow straggles from the flower bed in front of the back porch, and the purple of the sage brightens the green of the herb garden in the late afternoon sun. Taking a deep breath, he enjoys the scent of the flowers and the herbs, almost lost in the smell of the meadow behind the house.

He swings into the saddle, far more easily than he ever would have believed possible when he first climbed upon Meriwhen so laboriously. Mora bleats from the pen beside the barn, and Dorrin waves—not that the nanny understands—before turning and riding out of the yard and onto the road into Diev.

Scarcely has he turned onto the flattened clay beyond Yarrl's than he overtakes an empty wagon bearing both Honsard's emblem and the master hauler.

Dorrin inclines his head. "Good-day, master Honsard."

"'Day," grunts the hauler.

Farther along the road, after the clay turns to the stones that lead into the city, but before the low gates that are never watched, the healer passes another wagon bearing stacked bales of hay toward Diev.

White puffy clouds make a line across the western horizon, just below the afternoon sun, when Dorrin reins in Meriwhen opposite where the inn had stood. Faint smoke rises from the rubble.

Coming from the west, a trooper in the blue of Spidlar reins up in front of the leaning half-wall and the charred sign, not twenty cubits from where Dorrin has halted Meriwhen. Part of the sign is legible—the bottom of a tankard. The top third of the sign has burned away. Behind the leaning and scorched bricks lies a man-high heap of still-smoldering debris, covered with broken tiles from the roof that has collapsed.

"Demons!" mutters the trooper.

A woman holding a child sits on a stone at the edge of the still-smoking rubble. Gray rags flutter around her grimy face in the warm breeze of early summer. "A copper, ser, for my daughter and me to eat? A copper to eat?" She extends a hand to the trooper. "A copper to eat?"

The soldier pauses, then shrugs. "Would have drunk it anyway." He tosses a coin toward the woman.

The coin clinks on the pavement at her feet, and she leans forward, painfully extending one hand. Another ragged figure darts from the far side of the alley, the side not filled with rubble from the burned inn, and scoops the copper off the stone, running in the general direction of Dorrin.

"Thief!" The beggar woman's cry is half plaintive, half shriek.

Without thinking, Dorrin finds the staff in his hands, extended, quickly enough to trip the urchin.

"Bastard!" The youth, taller than Dorrin had realized, scrambles to his feet with a short blade glinting. His eyes flicker toward Meriwhen's legs.

Dorrin shifts the staff, lets it move, and the heavy

wood slams the youngster's wrists. The knife skitters onto the stones. "Toss the coin back to the woman!"

The youth looks toward the knife, then up at Dorrin. He ducks forward, then turns, and dashes across the street and into the other alleyway.

Dorrin's staff misses this time. He should have practiced the mounted exercises as well, as if there were ever enough time.

The Spidlarian trooper—watching from the saddle—guffaws as Dorrin dismounts and recovers the knife. "Never catch the little bastard, fellow."

Dorrin slips the urchin's knife—the metal ugly white and bronze to his senses—into the small pouch at the front of his saddle, where the hilt protrudes slightly. He would prefer not to carry the chaos-tinted metal, fearing that the blade will slice the leather of the pouch.

He also wonders where he should meet Brede or Kadara. They had said the Tankard, not Kyril's Red Lion. The troopers frequent the Tankard, while the townspeople tend more toward Kyril's, and call it Kyril's, not the Red Lion.

"Guess the Lion's all that's left 'round here, fellow." The trooper turns his dappled gray back up the street.

Dorrin takes a last look at the burned-out inn and lifts the reins to follow the trooper.

"My copper, ser? Would you forget me?" The woman waddles toward Dorrin. The sense of chaos—not evil, but disorder—wafts from her.

Dorrin scrambles into his pouch and finds a copper, carefully tossing it to her. "Here." Then he takes the urchin's knife between two fingers, and tosses it after the coin. "Take that, too. Maybe you can sell it."

Meriwhen skitters sideways, as if the mare responds to Dorrin's dislike of the chaos-tinged knife and the almost equally chaotic beggar, before turning up the narrow stone way, passing from the reddish light cast by the sun just above the horizon into the long shadows of the shuttered dry goods store. Dorrin blinks as the hot wind carries grit into his eyes. When he looks up, the beggar woman is gone from the street before the smoldering Tankard.

The stable at the Red Lion is filled, mostly with troopers' mounts. Dorrin dismounts and, holding the reins, peers toward the end of the narrow shed. He holds his staff in his left hand.

"Healer?" The stringy-haired stableboy looks up from the bale of hay he is dragging toward the second stall.

"Hello, Vaos. You've got quite a stableful tonight."

"Kyril'll be happy, but the troopers are a pain in the butt."

"All of them?"

"Demons, no. But you don't know which are happy drunks and which are mean. And the mean ones are *mean*."

Dorrin nods.

"Put your mare in the end stall with Kyril's gray. He'll be too busy to notice, and they're both good horses."

"You sure?"

"Trust me, healer."

Dorrin grins, and pats Vaos's shoulder. "Thanks, friend."

Vaos smiles back, but looks at the heavy hay bale.

Dorrin sets aside the staff, hands the boy the reins, and shoulders the bale. "Where do you want it?"

"Dump it in the manger in the second stall. I'll cut the cords and spread it from there."

In the second stall, a white stallion whinnies, baring his teeth as Dorrin steps up to the manger. The healer pauses, still balancing the bale on his right shoulder, and tries to send a sense of reassurance to the white. After a moment and another protest, the stallion whickers, and Dorrin eases the hay into the open manger. His fingertips brush the stallion's forehead.

"The white is hurt, somewhere."

"I didn't see him come in." Vaos leads Meriwhen toward the end stall.

Dorrin walks to the stall door. Again, the stallion protests, but eventually Dorrin's hands glide over his body, finding the whip marks. With another deep breath, he provides a small measure of healing and comfort, of healing and order—only a small measure, for the stallion is at least four cubits at the shoulder. Vaos looks at Dorrin when he leaves the stall.

"Whipped too much."

"Damned troopers." Vaos's words are not an expletive, but a statement.

Dorrin wonders if he has missed Brede's or Kadara's mounts. "Not all of them."

"I'll get some grain for your mare."

"You don't have to."

Vaos grins. "You didn't have to help the stallion."

Dorrin can't help but grinning back. "I do what I can." He reclaims his staff. Vaos is rummaging through a barrel with a battered tin cup as Dorrin steps into the twilight and walks toward the inn.

"See! I told you he'd figure it out." Kadara's voice brings him up short. She and Brede are waiting outside the door.

"What did you do with your horses?" Dorrin asks.

"Had to put them at the livery stable. What about you?"

"Oh . . ." Dorrin pauses. "Well . . . Vaos found a place for Meriwhen."

"What did you do for him?" Kadara asks, almost condescendingly.

"Nothing much. I just talk to him."

"You come here alone?"

"No. I've been a couple of times with Pergun. He works at the mill."

Brede grins broadly. "See, Kadara. Your little friend is neither little nor helpless. He just does things his own quiet way."

"He's always done things his own stubborn and quiet way."

Brede shrugs, as if to say, "I tried."

Dorrin shrugs back.

Kadara looks from one to the other. "Men . . ."

Brede claims a table vacated by two departing troopers, and Kadara commandeers an empty chair. Before the three are even seated, a heavy-armed serving woman stands there.

"What's to drink?"

"The dark beer."

"Same."

"Redberry," Dorrin adds.

"Oh, it's you, healer. What about food?"

"What is there?"

"The usual—stew, fowl pie. That's for three coppers. For another you can have chops. Don't bother. They're not worth it."

"The stew," Dorrin says.

"Same here," both Brede and Kadara say nearly simultaneously.

"And here, I thought we were rescuing you from the continual drudgery of the smithy." Kadara mock-accuses Dorrin.

"You are. I do occasionally rescue myself, and Pergun does sometimes."

"You still like working for the smith?"

"I'm still learning. Yarrl keeps telling me how much more I need to know. I think he's as good as Hegl."

"Here you be!" Three mugs come down on the table in rapid succession. "That's two for each."

Dorrin offers up his two coppers, but Kadara hands a half silver and a copper to the serving woman.

"You didn't—"

"This time it's our treat."

"Thank you."

"So . . . how is it really going?" Kadara asks again.

"All right. Yarrl lets me use the forge at night, and I've put together a few things. It takes time."

"You may have more than you thought," Kadara says in a low voice.

"Why?"

"Fairhaven's put a surtax on goods from Recluce."

Dorrin sips the redberry. His stomach growls, and he blushes.

"Don't you understand?" Kadara asks.

"I'm hungry. But doesn't that mean—" His stomach growls again.

"The man's hungry." Brede laughs. "What Kadara's saying is that she's worried. With the tax, fewer and fewer ships will travel between Candar and Recluce, and that when our time is done we won't be able to get home."

"Aren't you?" Kadara looks at her beer.

"What good will it do? Lortren won't have us back now, and in a year anything can happen." Brede takes a deep swallow from the gray stoneware mug.

"You two." Kadara looks from Dorrin to Brede. "You're too stubborn to give up your machines, and you're convinced that everything will work out."

Dorrin hopes his stomach won't rumble again, and looks toward the kitchen for the waitress and the stew and bread.

"I didn't say that," Brede says. "I don't see much point in worrying about what I can't change. I can't stop a war between Recluce and Fairhaven."

"Will it come to that?" Dorrin asks in spite of himself.

Brede nods his head. "I think so. For the first time since long before Creslin, the Whites have a truly great wizard."

"Does that mean a war?" Dorrin asks. "I mean, what would they get from it? If they destroy Recluce, they get fewer spices and wool, and they'd cost more, and they wouldn't be able to sell as much grain. And if they don't, lots of people get killed, and lots of gold is wasted."

Kadara laughs. "You're too reasonable to fight anything, Dorrin. You'll still be asking questions when the White legions march over the hills looking for you. People don't have to be reasonable. You should know that."

The smith and healer smiles wryly. "I guess so. I know my machines are only based in order, and it's logical, when you get right down to it. I mean, chaos gums up anything complex. So, for a machine to work, it has to be order-based. But no one is logical about it."

Kadara and Brede exchange glances.

"Ah . . ." Kadara finally says, "I never thought about it that way."

"Neither did I," Dorrin admits. His stomach growls. Brede laughs.

"Here you go!" The serving woman drops three heavy bowls on the table, one right after the other, all steaming. "Where's your coins?"

Brede hands her a silver. "For all three."

She hands back a copper, and a platter with a single long loaf lands in the middle, still vibrating on the uneven and battered dark wood after the server has turned to the next table. "More of the same, gents?" she asks the pair of tradesmen.

"Thank you," Dorrin says politely to Brede, even as he wonders if people will always be looking out for him. His eyes burn from the smoke and the closeness of the air. Kadara smiles at Brede, softly enough that Dorrin wishes he were the recipient.

"My pleasure, Dorrin." Brede takes a deep pull from the mug and raises it until he catches the server's eyes. She nods, and he lowers the mug.

"How long are you going to stay here?" asks Brede.

"In Diev?" Dorrin pauses for another sip of the redberry. "Until I discover who I am."

"Oh . . . Dorrin." Kadara's voice breaks, and she looks down at the table. "How cruel."

Brede's eyebrows lift.

"Lortren, she's a bitch. She knows how honest Dorrin is." Tears seep from the red-headed blade's eyes before she wipes them. "It'll be years . . ."

"I'm sure that's what she had in mind." Dorrin's voice is dry. He takes a spoonful of the heavily peppered stew, then breaks the end off the brown bread. "Let's enjoy the food."

"Might as well." Brede breaks off the other end and offers the platter to Kadara, who shakes her head, still wiping her eyes.

"Here's your refill, trooper!" The serving woman pours more beer into Brede's mug, then looks at Kadara. The redhead shakes her head.

Dorrin takes another spoonful of the stew, blinking. His eyes burn. From the smoke, he thinks, from the smoke. For a time, none of the three speak, and Dorrin finishes his stew not long after Brede. Kadara is still eating, taking small nibbles from the chunk of warm bread in her hand.

Dorrin yawns. "Tired, I guess."

"Is smithing that hard?"

"Well . . . I am doing a little healing, mostly animals, and I work on my designs sometimes at night."

"Designs?"

"It helps to draw them out before I try to make

anything. Sometimes, I carve it out in wood even. I'm working on gears."

"Gears?" This time Kadara is the questioner.

"You can't transfer power without gears. I read about them in the old books in my father's library. And, I mean, the point of a machine is to do something, and that means transferring power from something, like a waterwheel or an engine."

"But we have waterwheels on Recluce."

"And there are gears, but I want to build a steam engine."

"Oh . . . Dorrin," Kadara says once again, this time only shaking her head.

Dorrin yawns again. "I need to go." He stands up. "Thank you. I enjoyed it. Will you be around for a while, or are they sending you out?"

"Not for a while," Brede answers. "That could change tomorrow. If there are highwaymen below Kleth or Syda, our squad would be the next to go."

Dorrin pats Kadara's arm. "Good night."

"Good night, Dorrin."

Dorrin picks up his staff from behind his chair along the back wall and walks through the tables and past the soot-smoked lantern hanging outside the Red Lion. The wind chills his face. Overhead, the stars glitter coldly as he walks into the stable where Vaos snores lightly on two bales of hay pushed together.

XL

"PASS THE SQUASH," grumbles Yarrl.

Petra sets the bowl before him. "It's good, especially with the pepper."

"Pepper? Can't afford spices, can we, Reisa?"

"It came from the garden. It's early and green, but it helps."

"Oh . . . that your doing, young fellow?"

"I helped a little," Dorrin admits.

Yarrl shovels a pile of the mashed yellow squash onto the brown plate, then uses his tin spoon to take a mouthful. He chews and swallows. "Pepper helps." He takes another mouthful.

Dorrin takes an early summer peach and slices it into quarters, letting the quarters fall onto his plate beside the curried lamb. Then he alternates mouthfuls of the hot lamb and barley with slices of peach.

"You're a good healer," Petra says slowly. "That business with the piglets—we would have lost all but one. And Mora . . ."

Dorrin frowns. "I still worry about Mora—"

"Not bad for a young fellow at the forge," mumbles Yarrl. "Except he spends too much time with his toys."

"They're cute," Petra protests. "They do things."

"Still toys."

Dorrin swallows another slice of peach—a trace green, but the tart moisture cools his mouth from the heat of the spiced lamb. "They're models, really. Someday, I hope to build bigger ones."

"Need a light-blessed pile of iron," Yarrl declares. "And what would you use them for?"

"Whatever . . ." Dorrin demurs.

"I still wonder why you'd be a smith, rather than a healer," Reisa says as she ladles an additional scoop of lamb and barley onto her plate.

"I'd like to be both," admits Dorrin, "but I have to learn to be a good smith first." The drumming of the rain on the roof begins to subside as Dorrin finishes the last slice of his peach. "Looks like it might clear up."

"We needed the rain."

"Turns the roads into mud, and Bartov is supposed to deliver some ingots and coal tomorrow."

Petra covers her mouth and looks at her mother, her eyes still crinkled in a smile. Reisa shakes her head.

"Why are you shaking your head, woman?"

"Just the rain, just the rain."

"Well, pass the meat."

Dorrin lifts the heavy bowl and sets it before the smith.

"You going to work tonight, youngster?"

"Not tonight, I think. I banked the coals and tightened the vents." His stomach tightens at his evasion, but he sips the cool cider from his mug without revealing his discomfort. "Not at the forge," he finally adds.

"Good. Work too much . . . fry your brain. None of us smiths got much left."

"I doubt that." Dorrin laughs. "Brugal certainly would. He claimed you were sharper than the Prefect of Gallos."

"Hmmmm . . ." Yarrl pushes himself away from the table. "Going to see Honsard. Wants to talk."

"He wants to get you tanked on that green wine and get a better price for wagon work." Reisa's voice is tart.

"Don't go and talk, and I get no work." The smith stands and pulls a leather jacket from the peg on the wall.

Dorrin carries his plate to the wash bucket.

"I'll do that," Petra says. "You look to the spices, the sage especially."

"Sage . . . hmmphhh . . ." Yarrl opens the back door and steps onto the porch. "Clear night, leastways."

"Keep a clear head, too," advises the gray-haired woman.

Dorrin follows the smith off the covered porch and down the steps, stopping by the spice garden while the smith ambles toward the barn, and the bay he will ride to Honsard's wagonry. After surveying the spice garden, Dorrin kneels and removes a few weed sprouts, his hands brushing the pepper bushes and the sage, for the heavy rains and dampness are unsuited to either. He sees another set of weeds beyond the dill, and absently removes those, waddling around the garden, touching, sensing, and drinking in the scent and feel of the growing herbs.

Standing, he brushes the dark dirt from his hands, noting again the difference between the carefully composted soil of the garden and the clay of the yard. Creating any garden from the red clay takes time and patience. Reisa has supplied those; he has only added a touch of order.

He fingers the small carrot in his pocket as he walks toward the corner of the barn. He slips into the goat pen, and Mora butts him gently. "I know, I know, but I didn't bring much." He slips the nanny the wilted carrot, even as he touches her shoulder.

She is close to term. That he can tell, but how close? With a shrug, he leaves, checking the gate, placing his feet to avoid the worst of the puddles.

The sound of a bullfrog rumbles through the misty twilight as Dorrin walks back to his quarters. He lights the lamp. On the floor, he now has a woven grass mat, and a quilt covers his pallet bed. A crude planked wardrobe stands in one corner, and the writing table has been strengthened with iron braces. Two towels are hung on a rack he has built, and a chipped but serviceable washbowl rests on the shelf between the dowels that hold his rough cloth towels.

As he sits on the stool, he takes a sheet of paper from the wooden box and dips the quill into the ink, beginning to sketch out in greater detail the idea that has been swirling inside his head. The better his design, the less work at the forge—and that is easier on his body and his limited funds for materials. He considers it work, but would rather not mention it to Yarrl. Besides, Dorrin has promised Pergun he will go to Kyril's the following evening. He hasn't gone recently, and he knows he needs to, if only to hear what is happening in and around Diev.

In time, he stops the sketch and takes out another sheet of paper, this time slowly calculating as he places numbers at various points on the sketch. He wishes the numbers were better—or that he had paid more attention to the higher calculations at the Academy.

Finally, he sighs and puts aside the quill, and places the papers in the other wooden box—the one under his pallet with his notes on his models. Then he strips off his trousers and shirt and climbs into his bed. Thoughts of black steel and carts that move without draft horses and boats that move without wind swirl through his thoughts until darkness claims him.

"Dorrin!" His name is followed by a rapping on his door. "Dorrin!"

"Yes?" He struggles out of his bedroll and off the pallet, yanking on his trousers. "What is it?"

"It's Mora. I need some help."

"I'll be right there." He pulls on his trousers, boots, and work shirt, and unlatches the door. Reisa is half-way to the barn. Dorrin follows.

The nanny lies on a pile of straw under the slanting roof of the barn, shuddering periodically. Reisa is bent over the suffering animal, her good arm repositioning the goat's hind legs.

Dorrin squats down to help, to help with whatever Reisa will direct him to do, for he has no experience with any sort of birth.

Mora moans, and Dorrin winces at the pain. Pain follows pain, with one interlude of joy, and, after what seems an endless night, Dorrin slumps against the fence. No order remains in the twisted body of the nanny goat. Nothing he can do will change that. A single kid whimpers from Reisa's arms.

"Sorry—I tried."

"I know. I watched you visit her almost every night."

"I tried."

"Youngster, some things will be. Not all the order in the world, nor all the chaos, can change fate." She cradles the kid. "What about this one?"

Dorrin studies the still-damp kid. "If you can get some kind of milk, broth, something, I can probably keep her alive until she can eat on her own."

"But you couldn't save Mora."

"I'm not strong enough. This one's small."

"I won't call her 'this one.'"

"What will you name her?"

"Zilda, I guess. It means 'lost one' in . . . where I came from."

"Aren't we all?"

"I don't think you're lost, young Dorrin. You're solid. Where you are is where you are. Don't lose that. Yarrl laughs at your toys, but he'd give an arm to be able to make them. I'd almost give my other one to grow herbs and heal like you." Reisa pauses as a faint whimpering "baaaa . . ." escapes from her arms. "I'd think either cow's or goat's milk would do. I can trade some pepper with Werra or Ghunta. Some broth, tonight, I'd guess."

Dorrin touches Zilda again, trying to strengthen the blackness within the kid. Then he takes a deep breath and straightens. "Now what?"

"Petra can take care of Mora."

Dorrin understands, although neither will speak of it. All that can be used will be, but Reisa will not ask that of herself, or Dorrin.

Dorrin nods and turns back toward his quarters and his pallet.

XLI

JESLEK SMILES AS he looks westward at the needle peaks, still covered with the ice of the winter. Behind him, the red-headed woman, also in white, glances from the guards to the Westhorns and back to the guards. The three guards look down at the whitened granite of the road.

The wizard's senses begin to probe the chaos deep beneath the last stretch of the high grasslands of Analeria, loosening a bond here, leaving another untouched. The ground begins to tremble, and on a distant hillside, indistinct dots that are sheep collapse into the high grass as the shaking increases. Yet the road remains stable, with only the faintest hints of vibration underneath.

A faint haze spreads across the sky, and smoke begins to rise from the grasslands on each side of the white road. Slowly, ever so slowly, the road appears to sink, as if dropping below the surrounding terrain.

Anya smiles nervously, while the guards keep their eyes firmly on the granite underfoot.

Jeslek's eyes focus downward also, following his senses deep beneath the earth, opening channels of chaos, and letting the earth do its work, thrusting small mountains upward, no longer restrained by the bonds of order.

"A great one, he is," murmurs the youngest guard. "They say he's the one foretold in the Old Book."

The road shudders, strongly enough that Anya stumbles against the guard who has spoken. The guard steps back from her with a start, as though he had been burned.

XLII

DORRIN WIPES HIS forehead, then lifts the adz, driving it down into the charcoal. He lifts the adz again, wondering why Tullar delivers charcoal in such large chunks, and why the smithy burns so much—but he knows the second reason. The sound of Yarrl's hammer interweaves with the impact of the adz as Dorrin breaks the charcoal into smaller chunks. When he has a reasonable heap of broken charcoal, he sets aside the adz and shovels the charcoal into the wheelbarrow.

He sets aside the shovel and wipes his forehead, the silence from the smithy informing him that the smith has also stopped work—or moved to something quieter.

Dorrin blots his forehead once more with the back of his short-sleeved work shirt. Unlike the smith, he needs the tattered shirt, if only to keep the sweat under control.

The summer air is still, humid, so silent that he can hear the swish of the broom inside the smith's house. Petra or Reisa? Probably Petra, since he doubts that the one-armed mother would use the broom—although he has no doubts that Reisa can handle almost anything, one-handed or not.

A fly buzzes toward him, and he waves at it. The insect veers away, but he knows it will return as soon as both hands are back on the adz. He blots his forehead yet again before returning to breaking up the larger chunks before him. The fly circles, waiting for him to resume work.

An almost shadowy projection of order keeps the

vermin from his pallet. Can he do the same thing with the flying insects? He concentrates.

Hoofbeats drum through the damp and hard red clay of the yard, and two familiar horses enter the yard. Dorrin sighs and looks up. Both riders wear the dark blue of Spidlar.

Dorrin glances down. He still hasn't shoveled enough charcoal. He sets aside the adz, leaning it against the wheelbarrow.

"Dorrin!" calls Brede.

The apprentice smith nods. Kadara returns the nod. The sound of the broom ceases.

Dorrin wipes his forehead again. "You're off somewhere? Again? You just got back less than an eight-day ago."

"How could you guess?" Kadara brushes a strand of the flame hair she has cut shorter and shorter off her forehead.

"The packs, the travel uniforms, and the fact that you came to see me."

"I didn't mean . . ." Kadara shakes her head.

Dorrin flushes. Once again, he has answered a rhetorical question. Will he ever learn? He brushes back the insistent fly.

"Anyway . . . we just wanted you to know."

"Thank you." Dorrin gestures toward the charcoal. "I do keep busy."

"I still think you'd be better off as a healer." Kadara eases her mount closer to the pile.

"Not if I want to build my machines."

"Oh, Dorrin. Another year, and we can return to Recluce. If you'd ever give up such . . ."

Dorrin finds his chin stiffening.

"Kadara, could he ask you to be a hearth-holder?" Brede's mellow voice is reasonable, even.

"We're leaving in the morning," Kadara states, as if

she had never hinted at the stupidity of his desire to build machines.

"When will you be back?"

"They never tell us that." Brede laughs. "I think it's highwaymen downriver of Elparta. Who knows?"

Dorrin wipes his forehead.

"Anyway . . ." Brede says into the silence.

"All right. Good luck."

"Thank you." Kadara eases her mount back.

After the sound of hoofbeats fades, the sound of the broom resumes. Dorrin drives the adz into the largest chunk of charcoal, ignoring the light footsteps on the porch behind him. After two more swings with the adz, he sets it aside and lifts the shovel, scooping up perhaps a third of what he has broken and dropping the shovelful into the wheelbarrow.

"She's not for you."

Dorrin jumps. Reisa stands almost at his shoulder.

"I know. She only sees Brede, that . . ." He shakes his head. Brede is intelligent, caring, and talented. What can Dorrin really say?" I suppose it's natural. He's quick, strong, and intelligent. I'm just a sometime apprentice, sometime healer."

"Stop feeling sorry for yourself. You're a damned fine healer. I should know. That wasn't what I meant."

Dorrin lowers the shovel.

"You told me you grew up with your red-haired friend. And she still doesn't understand you. Doesn't that tell you something?"

"I suppose so." Dorrin looks down the road, but Brede and Kadara are well out of sight.

Reisa snorts. "Men . . ."

Dorrin waits, but Reisa has turned and walks back toward the smithy. He takes a deep breath and lifts the adz. Another few swings and he will have enough to fill the wheelbarrow. Inside the house, the sweeping continues.

A flash of white appears on the porch. "Baaaa..." The small head cocks at Dorrin. He reaches over and scratches Zilda between the ears. The kid licks his hand. He strokes the soft curling hair once more before lifting the adz, then grins as he realizes his fingers have left a faint black shadow on the kid.

XLIII

DORRIN INCREASES THE tempo of the bellows, trying to contain and direct the heat as best he can while Yarrl wrestles with the heavy wagon spring.

The tongs move, and the hammer strikes. The smith returns the spring to the forge again, then, after watching metal glow cherry red, grunts as he swings it back to the anvil. Dorrin concentrates on striking the metal exactly where Yarrl indicates, following the smith's signals.

"There!" Yarrl straightens. "Thought we'd have to do that again, but the heat held." He eases the heavy piece to the annealing shelf of the forge and sets down the tongs to wipe his steaming forehead.

"You know..." Yarrl wipes his forehead again. "Been able to do things ... since you came." He looks at the coals, dying almost unnaturally, as if robbed of energy now that the bellows has ceased its heaving. "Not sure anyone else could do 'em. All folks from the Black island like you?"

"No. I had to leave because I wanted to make things—machines like my models. They said it wasn't order-based."

The burly smith coughs and spits. "Demon-driven idiots. You put so much order in your metal that no damned White could touch it. Temmil says those shoes you did cured his old mare's limp. Didn't want to do shoes—hate it, but poor old bastard can't afford Migra. Hope we got them right."

Dorrin frowns. Could ordered iron help hold off chaos? It makes sense, even if he's never thought about it.

The door rumbles as it eases open, and a gust of damp air follows Reisa into the smithy, bringing with it the scent of cut grass from the meadow uphill. Both men turn.

"There's a trader fellow here. Claims to know young Dorrin."

"Driving a cart?" Dorrin blushes. Every trader would drive a cart or a wagon. "Not too tall, broad-brimmed hat?"

"I guess you do know the fellow."

"Liedral's probably why I'm here. Told us about Jarnish."

"Well . . . go see your friend . . . I can wind this up, and it's not like you ever slack off."

"Thank you."

"Don't thank me, Dorrin. Sometimes . . ." The smith looks at Reisa.

"Just go see the trader."

Dorrin still racks his gear before unstrapping his leather apron and hanging it up. He swallows, trying to get the odor of hot metal off his tongue and out of his throat, then walks toward the yard.

Liedral has tied the cart horse to the same iron ring Dorrin had used when he first came to Yarrl's, and she stands by the cart, the broad-brimmed hat on the seat, the short and silky hair ruffled in the warm and humid breeze that promises an evening rain. "You look very smithlike."

"I feel all too smithlike." Dorrin pauses. "I didn't think you ever came to Diev."

"I don't usually." Liedral looks up, and Dorrin turns to see Reisa walking toward them.

"Liedral, I'd like you to meet Reisa."

Reisa inclines her head with a smile. "Any friend of Dorrin's is a friend of ours. If you don't mind simple fare, you're welcome for supper."

"I couldn't do that," protests Liedral.

"Nonsense. You can trade for your dinner in tales and news, if that makes you feel better."

"I'd like to do that," the trader admits. "Inn fare or no fare gets tiring after a while."

Reisa nods, almost militarily, as if acknowledging a subordinate's sound decision. "That's settled."

As Reisa steps onto the porch and into the kitchen, Liedral shakes her head.

"What's the matter?" asks Dorrin.

"Nothing . . . do you always end up around military types or blades?"

"Reisa? She was a blade for Southwind, I think." He walks toward the well and removes the cover. "If you don't mind, I'd like to remove the smithlike appearance and odor."

Liedral looks toward the barn.

"I don't think they'd mind. You can put your horse in with Meriwhen."

"I'll take care of that while you wash up."

As Dorrin lifts another bucket of water, Zilda bleats, and the thin chain that tethers her to the porch clinks. "All right, little one." He sets aside the water and steps to the edge of the porch, ruffling the kid's fur and scratching between her eyes.

"Is she your other lady?" Petra's voice is even, standing in the doorway from the kitchen. With her gray trousers and shapeless shirt, without the frizzy hair, she would bear a general resemblance to Liedral.

"Zilda? I suppose. She thinks so." He gives the kid a last scratch.

"I meant the trader. You don't see many women traders."

"She passes as a man most places, especially near Fairhaven."

"She came to see you?"

"I don't know exactly why. She didn't say."

"Dorrin, you men are impossible." Petra sighs. "Do you like her?"

"Of course. She's been good and fair and helpful."

"Leave the poor man alone, Petra, and give me a hand." Reisa's voice is not quite stern as it carries into the dampness of the gray late afternoon.

"Just a moment, mother." Petra pats Zilda, then smiles at Dorrin. "I think I'm going to like her, Dorrin." She steps back into the kitchen.

Dorrin walks back to the well and begins to wash the worst of the grime from his arms and face. First Kadara and Brede, and now Reisa and Petra. Why had Liedral traveled five days out of her normal route? He draws another pail of water to carry to his room, looking at the barn where he can hear Liedral whistling as she curries the cart horse.

Once washed, shaved, and dried off, Dorrin pulls on his lighter-weight brown shirt and trousers, then his boots, and combs his hair. He looks around the room, which seems suddenly stark, almost empty, before opening the door and crossing the packed clay on the north side of the yard to the porch.

Liedral, Petra, and Reisa sit on stools under the overhanging eave that serves as a roof. Zilda begs from Reisa, butting at her leg, and clinking the thin chain that took Dorrin several evenings to fashion, mostly to learn the technique.

" . . . little one here always looks to him, like a father almost . . ."

" . . . too young for that." Petra laughs.

"You look less smithlike," Liedral says. She, too, has

removed the dust and dirt of travel, as well as the dark jacket, and wears a dark green shirt buttoned up almost to her neck.

"I would hope so."

"Now, he just looks like an innocent healer."

"Innocent?" asks Petra.

Dorrin blushes.

"Innocent," confirms Reisa, "but learnedlike innocence."

Liedral smiles sympathetically.

"Aaaa . . . ummmm," coughs Yarrl from the kitchen doorway.

Reisa rises from the stool and picks it up. "Time for supper."

"Was time a while ago," grouses Yarrl.

"Oh, papa. You weren't washed up, and neither was Dorrin."

"Washing up, washing down, wash, wash, wash . . . you'd think I was a stinky old goat or something."

"Well . . . not old," Petra affirms.

"Child." Yarrl cannot quite hide the smile.

As the others sit down before the wide stew plates, Petra lifts a heavy crockery dish from the oven of the coal stove whose iron and ceramic expanse gives it the look of a small forge. She sets the dish on a clay tile in the middle of the oak table. Reisa sets a basket of bread at each end. A small plate of dried fruit rests beside the stewpot.

"Go ahead, trader." Yarrl nods to Liedral.

"After you, ser," Liedral responds.

"Only because you insist." But Yarrl is pleased at the deference.

"What new is happening beyond Spidlar?" asks Reisa.

"One hardly knows where to start." Liedral pauses, then continues. "The White Wizards continue to build the mountains across the high plains of Analeria, and they say the ground shakes all the time there. Fairhaven has imposed an additional thirty percent surtax on goods from Recluce."

"The Spidlarian Council must be pleased with that." Reisa ladles a large helping of stew into Liedral's dish, and then a smaller helping into her own.

Dorrin wrinkles his nose. Even with the pepper he has coaxed from Reisa's stunted plants, the mutton odor of the stew is overpowering. Still, he is hungry.

"They ought to be worried, but they haven't seen that far ahead. The improved trade will just make Spidlaria a more attractive target for Fairhaven once the wizards finish with Kyphros. Right now, they're still pushing the Analerian nomads and their herds into the Westhorns."

"Are there any left?" Reisa asks.

"Not many. There's not much grass in the rocks, and they lose too many cattle to the cats and wolves." Liedral takes a mouthful of stew and swallows. "They say there's a new emperor in Hamor, and that the Nordlans and the Bristans are boarding each other's ships. That's why Fairhaven can tax Recluce goods. Not much is crossing the Eastern Ocean, except from Hamor, and that's even more costly."

"Hmmmm . . ." mumbles the smith.

"Sarronnyn is rebuilding the old garrison at Westwind . . . the Duke of Hydolar died of the flux, and the regent is another White Wizard, a fellow named Gorsuch. The Duke's son is only four, and that means there will be a long regency . . ."

"Like forever."

"Fairhaven has doubled its orders of timber from Sligo, and most of it is to be delivered to the shipyards in Lydiar . . . and there's a rumor that Recluce has stopped sending questors to Candar, at least eastern Candar . . ." Liedral looks at Dorrin, then away.

"How'd you get to be a questor, young fellow?" asks Yarrl.

"When I finished the Academy—that's the school for questors—they sent me here." Dorrin's head throbs at the incomplete answer.

"Didn't your parents have anything to say about it?"

Dorrin laughs. "It was my father's idea. He was offended by my wanting to build machines."

"Machines?"

"You've seen my models. I'd like to build bigger ones. Like the steam engine that I read about. There's no reason why you couldn't build one to drive a mill or a boat."

"You read about an engine that runs on steam... What does this engine do and where did you read about it? Is it some sort of magic?" asks Petra.

"Hardly. Your kettle over there: when it boils, steam comes out of the spout. When it boils too hard, if you put a plug in the spout, what would happen?"

Petra doesn't answer.

"It would blow off the top or push out the plug," answers Reisa.

"There's power in the steam. It's not magic. I want to make the steam work for me."

"A steam engine," muses Liedral. "But what fuels it?"

"Coal would be best, but you could use wood or charcoal."

The conversation lags as Petra spoons out seconds of stew. Dorrin takes a deep swallow of cold water.

"Why would your father send you away because you wanted to build this machine?" Reisa breaks a silence punctuated only by Yarrl's noisy chewing.

"Because he doesn't understand it, I think. He's afraid that it would create chaos."

"Would it?"

"No. You can't build one that's not orderly—even a little one."

"I don't understand," Petra says slowly.

"Seems simple enough." Reisa refills her mug. "People don't like change. They don't like changes or people who are different. Spidlar's as open as anywhere in Candar. More than ten years since we came, and some people still won't use your father's iron work, for all that it's twice as good as Henstaal's."

"Truth," snaps the smith. "Take the crap they know over quality stuff they don't. Isn't that so, trader?"

"I'm afraid it is," Liedral admits. "They don't like women traders, and they always need reassurance that something is either from the same person or just like that person's work."

Another silence falls upon the table.

"What about your parents? Do they even know where you are?" Petra asks.

"Not exactly. There hasn't been exactly any way to send them word."

"You could, you know," Liedral says after swallowing another mouthful of the mutton stew. "The going rate is around a half silver for an envelope. You give it to a Spidlarian shipmaster, and they'll carry it to one of the factors in whatever country, who will send it to the town you want with the next shipment. Sometimes it takes a season, but they do get there."

"Even to my parents on Recluce?"

"If you're not in a great hurry, I can help take care of that." Liedral sips the thin light beer from her mug.

"When you go to Tyrhavven? Or Spidlaria? How long will that be?"

"Spidlaria. I'm a bit late already. I really shouldn't be here, but I wanted to see how you were coming. It's two hard days from Kleth."

"Oh . . ."

"This time it worked out all right. Jarnish's nephew

found some cammabark in the marshlands, and I'll offer it to the Spidlarian Council."

"Cammabark?"

"Fire powder—they use it in skyrockets and cannons. It's best if it's mixed with black powder. Touchy stuff—if it gets too dry, it explodes."

Dorrin nods. "I expect it wouldn't be much use against the White Wizards."

"They use fire well enough," Reisa adds coldly.

Yarrl coughs once, then again.

"My background is no secret to Dorrin. He's rather observant."

"At least about some things," Petra adds.

Liedral lifts her mug, coughs, and covers her face. Reisa shakes her head as she looks at Dorrin.

"Watch the women," Yarrl mumbles through a mouthful of meat. "Watch the women. Least a few steps ahead all the time. Poor man's got no chance."

"Poor papa." Petra grins.

Dorrin takes a sip of his redberry.

Yarrl takes a final swallow of the thin beer and stands up, abruptly. "Off to see Gylert."

"He's been promising you iron work for seasons."

"He *is* the head of the local traders' council."

"Maybe he will provide work." Reisa shrugs and looks at Liedral. "What do you think?"

"I'd try a smaller trader. Good work at a lower price is more important to the smaller ones."

"Perhaps you could do both," ventures Dorrin, slowly.

"How be that?" ponders the smith.

"Thank ser Gylert for seeing you, and ask him to suggest some smaller trader who might need unique or special work. That way, he doesn't have to tell you 'no,' and he can't complain that you have ignored or avoided him."

Reisa swallows abruptly, and Liedral looks at Dorrin for a long moment.

"I'll be thinking about that." Yarrl's eyes rest on Petra. "Did you groom the bay, daughter?"

"I did, papa."

"Good." Yarrl tramps through the door, across the porch, and down the stairs toward the barn.

Dorrin finishes another chunk of the crusty bread and swallows the last of the water in his mug.

"Would you like any more, trader?" asks Reisa.

"I've had more than enough. It's far, far better than inn fare." Liedral leans back slightly in the wooden chair.

A chain clinks, and Dorrin smiles. "Any scraps for Zilda?"

"That greedy kid? A few might be managed." Reisa leaves the table and reclaims a battered dish from the porch, scraping the leavings from her dish into it.

Dorrin brings over his dish and Liedral's. The table scraps barely cover the bottom of the chipped brown stew dish. Reisa shakes her head and adds a chunk of bread. Dorrin takes the dish out and sets it in the corner away from the door where the kid can eat without being disturbed. He ruffles her fur before heading back toward the kitchen. Liedral meets him at the door.

"Just talk to your friend, Dorrin," Reisa calls.

"Can we sit here?" Liedral points to one of the stools.

He takes the other. Inside the dishes clank, as mother and daughter clean up. Outside, Dorrin studies the garden, the barn, and the low grass of the meadow beyond. Zilda's chain clanks on the chipped crockery from which the kid eats.

"What happened to your friends?"

"Kadara and Brede? They joined the Spidlarian

Guard here in Diev. They're somewhere around Elparta now, searching for highwaymen."

"Most likely inspired by Fairhaven."

"Oh?"

"That happened in Kyphros, too. Thieves appeared where there hadn't ever been any. Cattle disappeared. Fairhaven asked the Prefect to act, but the Prefect's troops never could find them. Eventually, that was one reason that the wizards gave for taking over the plains."

"You seem convinced that Fairhaven will conquer all of eastern Candar."

"I suppose so." Liedral gazes into the growing darkness. "I try not to dwell on it. There's enough else to worry about, like being a trader."

"You seem to manage."

"You've seen how well I manage, scraping by on one cart and sometimes a pack horse, rattling around in a barn of a warehouse that once was always full, letting half of what I bring in go to Freidr, just so his political friends won't look too closely."

Dorrin looks at the barn. What can he say? He has always thought of Liedral as extraordinarily competent. The faint hum of a mosquito punctuates the evening, followed by the indistinct words of a conversation from the parlor between Reisa and Petra.

"That was a good suggestion you gave Yarrl," Liedral finally says, shifting her weight on the hard oak stool. "How did you come up with that?"

"It made sense. Powerful people don't like to be asked for money or for jobs. They do like to be asked for advice, and they don't like being surprised." Dorrin disengages Zilda from his trousers before she can worry a hole in them. He scratches the kid's head. The white fur makes it easy in the dimness of early evening.

"She likes you."

"I'm not sure why." Dorrin runs a hand through his

curly hair. It needs cutting, but it seems to him like it always needs cutting. The faint whine of a mosquito warns him, and he frowns, trying to recast the sort of ward that will work to discourage the flying insects. He wishes he had read those sections of his father's library far more intently, but in concentrating on machines, he never considered the continual annoyance of hungry mosquitoes, which always seem to prefer redheads.

"I am."

The kid's chain clinks as Zilda attempts to chew on Liedral's boots.

Dorrin wipes his forehead. Has he gotten the ward correct? The sound of the mosquito seems fainter, at least.

"You're kind. Stubborn, though." After a pause, she continues. "I meant that about the letter."

"I do owe them something, I suppose." He waits, and sits quietly as Zilda bounces into his lap and curls up. A faint breeze, smelling of distant rain out of the Westhorns and sheep, caresses his smooth-shaven face. "Why did you come here?"

"You know why."

"I still have a lot to figure out," Dorrin says after another long silence. "And I want to build my machines."

"I know. But you'd better think about making golds, too."

"Why?"

"How can you afford metals, or wood, or whatever you need for materials?"

Dorrin laughs. "I guess I had better think about it. What do you suggest?"

"Me? I'm just a poor trader."

"But what kind of things sell?"

"Anything rare or well-made and functional or a necessity of some sort."

"Just the sort of things Recluce has exported for the past centuries."

"Why else would anyone buy things from the Black Wizards?"

"I'll have to think about that. I could grow spices. I'm pretty good at that. Perhaps sell some of my models as toys. They are well-made."

"You'd sell those?"

"I'm not a collector. Some of them served their purpose once I finished them. They didn't work the way I expected."

"Oh . . ."

"That's the way it works. You design it, and then you try it out. It's a lot easier to make models than to spend the effort on building something big. Of course, models still work better than the full-sized machines, but most times, if the model doesn't work, the machine won't either."

"Dorrin, do you mind?"

"That you came? No. I'm glad, but I couldn't tell you why." He grins in the darkness, knowing that she cannot see the expression. "You are a bit older, you know."

"And wiser."

"There is that."

"I'll leave it at that." She stands. "You have a letter to write, and I'm leaving early in the morning." She has entered the house even before Dorrin has managed to set Zilda on the porch. He shakes his head, then turns back toward his quarters, thankful that, with his growing sense of order, he needs no light, except for detail work like smithing or writing.

Once inside his room, he lights the lamp with a striker and takes out a sheet from the box of parchments he uses for designs. He finds a quill and the ink. Then, after turning up his lamp, Dorrin smoothes the parchment. What should he write? How should he address it? Carefully he dips the quill into the ink, then begins, leaving a space for the salutation. The dim light is more than adequate as he writes deliberate word after deliberate word.

I am well, working as an apprentice smith here in Diev. The smith is brusque, but not unkind, and I have learned much more than Hegl would have believed, and I no longer ruin good iron. I hope that Hegl is happy that his lessons have not gone to waste.

We passed through Vergren and saw the wonders of Fairhaven on the way. I found Fairhaven too rich for my blood and am much happier where I am. I now have a mare I call Meriwhen. You can tell Lortren that my riding skills have improved.

Kadara and Brede are with the Spidlarian Guard. For the past few eight-days, they've been patrolling the northwest roads.

The weather here is colder than in Extina, and even the spring ice took some getting used to, but working in a smithy is not chilly even when the snow gets knee-deep outside. It only has once, a late-spring snow that was unexpected, although the older folks talk about the times before the Black Wizards changed the world and the weather, when everything was better.

I have not found whatever it was that Lortren expected I would. If I have, I don't know that I have. I hope Kyl has found what he must find, and that this letter finds you all healthy and happy.

Dorrin.

After he rereads it, he dips the quill yet another

time and pens in the salutation, compromising with "My dear family."

Then he lays it aside. He will fold and seal it in the morning for Liedral to take.

Liedral—how can a woman seem so much like a friend, and so solid a person, and yet...? He knows he does not lust after her, as he has after Kadara, or even after the comely tavern singer, but he was glad to see her, in the way he is glad to see the dawn, or the sunlight after a cold rain. Is that friendship?

He pulls off his shirt and trousers and lies down upon the pallet, pulling the worn and somehow comforting quilt over his bare shoulders. Outside, a bullfrog's *burrruppp* ... echoes through the darkness, underscored by the sighing of the leaves in the oak trees beyond the barn.

XLIV

THE SUN HAS not fully cleared the eastern lowlands when Dorrin steps into the barn. Liedral is already harnessing the cart horse.

"Here's the letter." He hands her the letter and a half-silver. "Is that enough?"

"That should be more than enough." She holds the harness in her left hand. "Do you ever sleep? Reisa says some nights you work until midnight."

"I don't need that much sleep, and Yarrl lets me use the worst of the scraps, but they take a lot of effort. Sometimes I have to actually melt them, and that's dangerous."

Liedral frowns.

"Iron burns when you get it hot enough ... if you're not careful." He lifts the bag.

"What do you have there?" She brushes the silky hair back off her forehead. Dorrin glances at the broad-brimmed hat upon the cart seat.

"Yes. I'm headed back to be the young trader—presumably male—that no one really wants to look too closely at." She places the sealed letter inside a leather case under the seat and turns back to the horse.

Dorrin sets the bag on the cart seat as she buckles the harness. He extracts the miniature sawmill blade and wheel. The black steel blade glints in the light through the barn door, and the red oak is smooth and polished.

"It's beautifully done."

"You turn the handle and the blade turns. It won't really cut much. You think you could sell it for something?"

"I won't sell it unless I can get what it's worth."

"How much is that?"

"I don't really know, except that Palace toys for Sarronnyn go for as much as four golds. This is as good as some. Why are you giving it up?"

"It didn't work the way I wanted."

"How can you tell?"

Dorrin looks toward the door before speaking. "Once it's built, and I work with it, I can sort of sense the sticky spots, the points where the design isn't right. This one . . . it doesn't transfer the force from the handle to the blade very well. I have a new idea, using an angled gear and little iron balls. They're hard to make. Might just be easier to make them bigger."

This time, Liedral shakes her head. "You just might change the world . . . if the White Wizards don't find you first."

"Me? An apprentice smith and sometime healer?"

"You." She takes the model, a half cubit long and less than a span high, and puts it inside the case with the letter. "It does fit. Good." Then she turns back to the smith. "I don't know when I'll be back. If you need me, you know where I am. Jarnish can also get me a message."

"You're leaving now?"

"I have to make up lost time." She leads the cart horse toward the door.

Dorrin takes his leather bag and opens the door wide enough for the cart.

"Remember, Dorrin, there has to be a reason. You see that with your machines, but it's true of people and countries as well." Liedral leads the horse and cart clear of the barn.

"I suppose so." He purses his lips, not knowing what else to say.

Liedral slips up onto the cart seat. "Take care, Dorrin." She flicks the reins, and the cart lurches forward over the hardened clay.

He watches until she is on the road, but she has not looked back. He heads toward the smithy, not feeling like eating. Not on this morning.

He begins the day's work by breaking up the longer lengths of charcoal to the proper size for the forge and by bringing in what will be needed for the morning. As he completes his efforts, Yarrl appears and unbanks the forge, the coals still hot enough to smoke sawdust as he begins laying in charcoal.

"Get the heavy stock, Dorrin . . . the big bar on the top end."

Liedral's words still run through his mind. "Why are things the way they are? There has to be a reason, doesn't there?"

He fingers the length of wrought iron in his hands. What makes iron different from copper, or tin? They are different, but why? And how is cast iron different from steel or wrought iron? And why did ordering wrought iron make it stronger than steel, yet less brittle?

He looks at the metal, again, letting his senses enfold it.

"Dorrin? Is it hot enough?"

The apprentice smith lays aside the iron. "Almost . . ." He takes the overhead lever of the bellows and begins to pump, evenly. Later, he will have to make nails, a tedious job at best. Before that, though, he will certainly have to get out the files and smooth out whatever Yarrl forges.

XLV

"No SOONER DO we take action against Recluce than traitors here in Candar steal the livelihoods and the coppers from our people . . ." The words of the heavy-set and black-haired wizard garbed in white rumble across the chamber.

"Proud words, Myral . . ."

"I stand with Myral." The wizard who speaks is soft-spoken, with short brown hair, frail in appearance. "The renowned Jeslek and the noble Sterol have done their best to improve the lot of our people. Can we do any less?"

"What's in it for you, Cerryl?"

Cerryl smiles softly, letting the clamor die down before speaking. "With such imposing figures as Jeslek and our High Wizard Sterol already expressing their concern . . . how about survival?" He grins.

A patter of nervous laughter circles the chamber as he steps off the low speaking stage and edges into a corner.

"While I would not be so direct as gentle Cerryl . . ." begins the next speaker, a man with white hair, but an unlined and almost cherubic face.

Cerryl pauses next to the redhead in the corner.

"Most effective, Cerryl."

"Thank you, Anya. I presume the effect was as you and the noble Sterol wanted." He smiles softly. "Or as you wanted, should I say."

She returns the smile. "You flatter me."

"Hardly. With your ability . . ." He shrugs. "Perhaps you will someday be High Wizard."

"Being High Wizard in these times might require rather . . . unique skills."

"That is certainly true, a point which Jeslek is certainly not adverse to making—repeatedly. I would prefer your approach, I suspect."

"A woman as High Wizard?" Anya's tone is almost mocking. "You do me high honor, indeed."

"I recognize your talent, dear lady." His smile is bland.

"You are . . . sweet . . . Cerryl." She tilts her head. "Would you like to join me for a late supper—tomorrow evening?"

"Your wish is my desire."

"You are so obliging, Cerryl."

"When one is limited in sheer power of chaos, one must be of great service, Anya."

"I am so glad you understand that." She turns and steps toward a broader wizard with a squared-off beard.

Cerryl smiles faintly, nods to his colleague, and continues toward a seat on the back bench.

XLVI

DORRIN WHISTLES AS he rides. In the rain, even under the oiled leather waterproof, he is damp. On the east side of the road, he sees the golden grain bending under the water that has fallen for days. His notes are off-key, but whistling is better than complaining. Besides, so much rain has fallen that a continual sheet of water now lies around the smithy, and Yarrl is almost out of charcoal because the roads from Tullar's forests and charcoal camps are impassable to the heavy wagons.

Dorrin casts his senses into the heavy clouds in the west. He smiles as he finds that the rain will break before long. He stops smiling when Meriwhen tosses her head and sprays his face with horse-scented water droplets.

In the pouch at his belt are the three golds sent from Liedral through Jarnish and then through Willum, at the chandlery in lower Diév, for the model sawmill. His hand strays to the pouch. Three golds? For a model? Or is Liedral sending him more than she received for it?

He has several others that he could sell. Would Willum offer one for sale? Then he could get some idea of what they might be worth, although people in Spidlaria could certainly pay more. He guides Meri-when along the grassy edge of the road leading down off the main road and into Hemmil's mill.

He has barely entered the covered area when Pergun greets him.

"Ever see such crappy weather? The vintners are claiming it will ruin the grapes; the farmers can't get the grain out of the fields; we're having to slow down because no one can pick up anything because the side roads are impossible. And here you are."

"Why not? This hit just before we were due to get charcoal; and Yarrl wants to save some just in case."

"What do you want? More scraps?"

"No. A small lorkin sapling, log, about this big around." He uses his hands to indicate a diameter slightly less than a double thumb span.

"Hemmil'll want to charge you dear for that."

"I thought so. Where are they?"

"At the far end on the side toward his house." Pergun shakes his head. "I'm cleaning out the saw pit. Let me know when you find what you want."

The smith wanders down the center of the warehouse. After a time, Dorrin finally touches one of the black logs. One end is useless, with fractured heartwood, but the remaining six cubits are certainly straight and strong enough. He eases it out and walks back to the saw pit.

Pergun climbs out, covered with sweat and dampened sawdust.

"This one? How much might it be?"

"A silver, at least. Lorkin takes years to grow," explains Pergun.

Dorrin pauses, regretfully looks back toward the end of the warehouse. "Perhaps a copper I might spare ... but a silver, Pergun?"

"Half a silver, and you won't find a better bargain anywhere in Certis. Hemmil doesn't like to sell the lorkin."

"Two coppers, and that's if you trim it to my measure."

"You may know plants, Dorrin, but timber is heavier and worth more," observes the black-haired mill man, winking and nodding toward the office. "Four coppers, but only because I'd not want ill will from any healer."

Dorrin scrabbles in his purse. "I'd not do you in," he says firmly, "but three and a bit is all that I have, save a single other copper with which to eat." His head throbs slightly as he speaks, for Reisa does indeed have some of his purse.

The mill hand frowns, then shrugs. "Like as I'd rather not, but if it is all you have, it's all you have. You carry the scraps to the bins, though."

"That I can certainly do, and a few others as well, if that would help."

The dark-bearded man grins. "I should have held you to that earlier."

Dorrin laughs ruefully. Now all he has to do is trim the heavy wood—which will take days with his knife—and, once he has earned a few more coppers, spend more time at the forge. All for an idea he is not even sure will work—but ordered wood and ordered black steel should make a better staff.

XLVII

DORRIN SETS THE box on his writing table, plain enough red oak, except for the butterfly hinges that, once again, he had been forced to make twice before getting correct.

"Aye, and you can do butt hinges, but any apprentice can do that." That had been Yarrl's view. So Dorrin forged butterfly hinges. He also had to make a second set for Yarrl, in return for the iron and the screws for the hinges. Iron, that was the kicker. Dorrin had never realized, not fully, how expensive and heavy it was. A cubit-long rod as thick as his thumb weighs a stone and a half and costs nearly three pennies—more than a meal at some inns. The smith's scrap pile makes a lot more sense in that light.

Dorrin runs the oiled rag over the oak again, lightly. Inside—resting on the quilted padding Reisa and Petra contributed in return for a small iron flower—is the model spring-driven wagon. As usual, the unusual—the spring engine—had been the hardest, difficult enough that Dorrin knows that a larger machine driven by springs will not work. Still, he is learning, after his own fashion.

After slipping the box into an oversized and battered saddlebag recovered from a corner of the smithy, he walks out into the early fall haze—and sneezes from the dust of the threshing from the fields. He sneezes again, and again. His nose waters profusely by the time he reaches the stable.

It will be a long day. Yarrl's hammer rings in the background with the harvest-related repairs to mower bars, horse rakes, and wagon tires and braces. Dorrin has promised to work as long as necessary to make up for the time he takes in Diev. Unlike smiths, chandleries close before sunset.

After saddling Meriwhen and lashing the extra saddlebag in place, he leads the mare out into the warm and dusty morning. Reisa waves from the porch, where she has been checking the netting over the fruit-drying racks before reentering the kitchen. Even between sneezes and mowing dust, Dorrin can smell the pearapples and late peaches being jellied.

Once on the road, Dorrin finds himself riding up behind two hay wagons in a row. Each creaks, and the rear right wheel of the trailing wagon sways out of true. As he passes the driver, he calls. "'Ware the back wheel."

"Thanks, fellow, but tell it to Ostrum—dumb bastard. Can't wait to get this to the Guard barracks—

while the price is good. Not your problem, but thanks be to you anyway."

Dorrin urges Meriwhen past the two-horse team. The road traffic is heavy, and dusty, and Dorrin sneezes more. Ash and soot and charcoal do not bother him, but harvest time and road dust do.

The dust diminishes once he rides on the stone road into lower Diev. Passing the rebuilt Tankard, he sees the beggar woman who continues to plead for coppers. But there are no troopers there, not this early.

Willum's chandlery is a long block shy of the trading compound and the piers of lower Diev. The crossed candles of the sign have recently been repainted, and the wood has been revarnished. So have the wooden floors, and new hangings cloak the entrance to the back room of the establishment.

A single man stands behind a counter on the right side. Opposite him is a polished iron and brass stove, unneeded in the harvest heat.

"I'd like to see Master Willum, if possible." Dorrin smiles politely.

"It's always possible, but I don't know as it's likely unless you got business planned with him."

"That's what it's about."

"No charity, no begging for alms for the poor, healer?" The man looks over Dorrin's brown clothing.

"I'm also a smith, and I work for Yarrl."

"Can't be working hard if you're here now."

"I'll be working well past your supper and bedtime." He forces a smile. "But if one wants to do business with a chandler, one must do business when the chandlery's open."

"True enough, true enough, young fellow," interrupts a heartier voice from the end of the counter. "And what might you be interested in selling?" The speaker is blond, with a belly that flows over a wide brown belt and almost submerges the heavy brass buckle. His shirt is brilliant green, and his brown trousers match both belt and boots.

Dorrin walks to the end of the counter. "You might say that it's a curiosity, but you are known for having strange and unusual items . . ."

"That I am, fellow. That I am. And I travel all the northern ports to get and to sell. That's my business. So what is this curiosity?"

Dorrin sets the box on the counter.

"A box? Nice enough, especially the hinges, but Petron the cabinetmaker does better, and certainly not a curiosity."

Dorrin opens the top to show the wagon.

"Hmmmm . . . a wagon, but it has no horses."

The smith takes out the model and sets it on the flat counter, twisting the crank a half turn. The wagon rolls toward the far end.

"Magic . . ." whispers the first man from the corner.

Dorrin shakes his head. "No. Just an ingenious little spring. It's all mechanical." He tries not to smile as Willum closes his mouth.

"Who did you say you were?"

"Dorrin. I work for Yarrl."

"The foreign smith fellow—does work for Honsard and Hemmil and types like them?"

Dorrin nods.

"How come you wear healer brown?"

"I'm also a healer."

"A healer-smith. A smith-healer with a curiosity! That's worth a silver just to say I saw one." Willum's voice is hearty, but his eyes are cold.

Dorrin retrieves the model wagon and replaces it in the box, but leaves the top open for the moment.

"Curiosities draw business, young fellow, but not many people buy them. I'd buy it just to let people know the great Willum has another one. But who could I sell it to?"

"I'd suggest it to one of the Spidlarian Council members as a unique present to a son. Or perhaps as a gift to the Sarronnese court."

"Fine words."

"It's good work. Worthy of a fine trader and chandler—especially one with all the contacts that you have, Master Willum." Dorrin closes the box. "I'd rather you . . ."

"Let's not be hasty, young fellow. It might be worth five silvers."

"The last one sold in Tyrhavven for more than three golds."

"You don't bargain much," Willum says, a trace sourly.

"No, ser. I'm not a bargainer. I don't make many, and each one is different."

"Each one?"

Dorrin nods.

"I'll give you three golds for it—if the box comes with it."

Dorrin frowns. "Three golds and the box—if I also get a few cubits of fine material to line the next box."

Willum laughs. "Light! I'll give you three cubits of good material. Roald! He can have the end of that Suthyan turquoise velvet."

"I take it that the turquoise wasn't popular." Dorrin tries to keep from grinning.

"How was I to know that pale blue was the color that they said the devil witch of Recluce wore? Some biddy started the tale, and no one would buy that color. But it will look good lining a solid box, won't it, fellow . . . Dorrin, is it?"

"Dorrin." He waits as Roald appears with a small leather pouch and a bolt of fabric wrapped in ragged flour sacks.

Willum opens the pouch and counts out the three golds. Dorrin puts the coins in his purse.

"How soon before you might have another . . . curiosity . . .?"

Dorrin smiles wryly. "As your man pointed out, there's a great deal of very heavy and practical smith work to be done right now."

"That might be for the best." Willum smiles. "Good day, young Dorrin."

Dorrin inclines his head. "Good day, Master Willum."

Clouds have begun to build over the northern ocean, clouds that promise cooling later on, but little else. Dorrin fastens the empty saddlebag in place. Meriwhen whickers as he mounts, and he pats her neck. "Good girl."

In the dust just beyond the end of the stone road, a kay beyond the bridge into Diev proper, rests a tilted hay wagon, bales thrown off the road. The carter is slowly stacking the hay by the roadside as he unloads the wagon bed. The iron tire of the now-shattered rear wheel rests against the side of the wagon.

"Get that mangy team back . . ."

"You saw us coming . . ."

Two other carters, the outboard edges of their traces tangled, snarl at each other, even as the two wagons block the road.

Dorrin guides Meriwhen up onto the grass and around the confusion.

XLVIII

THE TWO TROOPERS ride van, half a kay ahead of the squad, their mounts picking their way along the rough road around the south side of the escarpment. The sun hangs low on the western horizon. Neither speaks.

Each listens for a branch cracking in the sparse firs to the north or the crackling of dry grass in the seasonal wetland to the south. Above the firs are the half-bare and twisted branches of the maples, partly cloaked in faded leaves.

The blond man reins up, nods to his left. The woman's eyes follow his gesture to the trail less than fifty cubits ahead. He removes the bow from its case, strings it easily, and opens the closed quiver. The woman loosens the straps on the long sword; the West-wind shortsword is always ready.

With the faint crackling from the lowest clump of firs, the blond spurs his gelding, and both riders charge toward the trees, low in their saddles.

An arrow barely misses the man, and he reins the horse up, nocks an arrow, and looses it, almost before his mount has stopped.

"Oooo . . ." The indrawn breath and moan are clear enough.

The blond trooper has a second arrow ready.

"Hold your shaft! Hold your shaft! I'm a-coming down."

The woman reins up farther along the trail. "Better come out, boy."

"Spidlarian bastards! Let my boy go! He didn't do nothing." A bald man with a straggly ginger beard and an arrow through his right arm lurches onto the road.

A youth, not that many years younger than the troopers, stands up, still half-concealed by the browned tall grass.

"Keep your hands up," orders the redhead.

"You're a woman." He looks past her toward his father.

"I'm a trooper." She flips the sword in the air, then catches it. "I can also throw this hard enough to put it right through you."

"Bitch . . ." the youth mumbles.

"I've been called worse. Now get up here. Where are your horses?"

"Ain't got none."

"The tracks show otherwise."

The boy looks past her, then bolts uphill. Her arm goes back, and the blade flies. The youth falls, moaning, and the trooper dismounts and reaches him before he can move.

"You killed my boy!"

"I'll kill you if you move," snaps the blond trooper. He can hear the clinking and footsteps of the squad behind.

The redhead reclaims the shortsword, yanking the youth to his feet. "The cut on your leg isn't that bad. If I'd wanted you dead, boy, you'd be dead."

He writhes, but her hands are like steel, and her shoulders are broader than his, and more heavily muscled. She whips a length of rope from her belt and binds his hands. By the time she has dragged him to the road, the rest of the squad has arrived, and Brede has bound the bald man.

" . . . hellcat got another . . ."

" . . . so'd the big fellow . . ."

" . . . you want to get in their way, Norax?"

"What you got here, Brede?"

"I'd say the two who tried to take that Certan merchant. Their horses are somewhere back up behind the grove. If you'll take over this one, I'll see if I can get them."

" . . . let him take the risk . . ."

The squad leader nods, and Brede eases his mount into the narrow trail. Kadara looks down at the youngster standing on the hard clay, then rummages in her saddlebags and takes out a short length of cloth. She dismounts again, and lifts away the ragged trousers, binding the long slash in his leg.

" . . . first human thing I seen from the she-cat . . ."

"He's just a bandit, Kadara. They'll just hang him."

"Don't hang him . . . he's just a boy," pleads the bald man.

"He helped you rob a peddler and try to take that Certan trader. That's enough to hang for." The squad leader's voice is tired, cold.

Kadara straightens and swings back into the saddle.

At the sound of hoofs, the troopers look toward the trail. Brede leads back two bony horses, both bearing packs. "Looks like some of the peddler's copper work."

"Good. Set them on their mounts. If you can call them that."

Brede dismounts, hands his reins to Kadara, heaves the older highwayman onto one horse, almost effortlessly, and then sets the youth on the second.

" . . . demon-damned ox he is . . ."

The wind, picking up as the sun touches the horizon, moans softly.

"Let's head back. We can leave them for the magistrate in Biryna. He'll hang them nice and proper." The squad leader turns the black gelding around. "Kadara, Brede, you can have the rear."

The two drop back behind the squad.

"As for you two, try to stay in your saddles. Rather have you hang than be a target for Shenz here. Not much difference in the end, I suppose."

"You damned Spidlarians! Bleed us friggin' dry." The bald man with the ginger hair twists in the saddle of his gaunt horse. Both the animal and the would-be highwayman show their ribs clearly. "You bastards and the damned wizards. The wizards burned all the sheep, and you take our last pennies for wormy grain. Can't afford shit, and—"

"Shut up," snaps the squad leader.

The younger captive looks back, in the general direction of Gallos.

"You won't see that again," mumbles a trooper with one arm in a sling.

Brede and Kadara exchange glances and slow their mounts until a wider gap opens between them and the eleven horses of the main body.

"They're starving." Brede's voice is low.

"That's what Fairhaven wants. We'll see more as the winter wears on."

"The more we hang..."

"If we don't, no one on the roads will be safe."

Brede shakes his head, and the horses carry them westward toward Biryna, toward their tents—and the magistrate.

XLIX

WHITE LIGHT FLARES from the tall slender man as he strides across the central square toward the tower.

"He's come to claim the amulet, Sterol." A red-headed woman in the white of chaos looks at the High Wizard. "So I will leave this to you."

"You don't want him to know you were here, I take it?"

"If he bothered to check, I couldn't keep it from him, but he's not concerned. He knows he's the most powerful White." Anya's tone is ironic. "And, after all, I am only a mere woman."

"A mere woman? Now, Anya ... I doubt many here would call you—"

"Unlike Jeslek, who believes himself clever and powerful."

"He is very clever, and exceedingly powerful."

"You're going to give him the amulet?" Anya steps toward the door.

"How could I keep it from him?" Sterol sighs. "I promised it to him, and he shall have it. Whether he can keep it is another question."

Anya nods, turns, and departs.

Sterol glances at the mirror on the table, thoughts not totally focused, but wondering about the next challenge posed by the forces of order. He finds a vague picture emerging from the white mists—a young redhead hammering iron. Then the image dissolves, almost simultaneously with the sound of a rap on the door of the tower room. The High Wizard purses his lips—a young man forging iron? A second rap on the door reminds him of his situation, and he turns to greet his successor.

"The mountain wall now runs complete from south of Passera all the way to the Westhorns, and the great road is protected on all sides." Jeslek steps into the room and bows, but the inclination is minimal.

"I understand that a section near the central ridge of Analeria was somewhat disturbed," Sterol murmurs mildly.

"I recall that the only stipulation was that I stand upon the road and complete the work. If the mountains were to remain stable, some minor redirections were necessary." Jeslek smiles.

"Was it necessary to incinerate all those Analerian herders?"

"I warned them. Most of them left, and those that didn't—well, accidents do happen, Sterol."

"You realize that the price of mutton will rise considerably, just as you're placing another surtax on Recluce goods?"

"I doubt there were that many sheep involved."

"Not that many, but what will the rest eat? You did turn several thousand square kays of high grassland into rather warm rock that won't support much vegetation for several years, to say the least."

"We'll pay for the extra through the surtax."

"As you wish." Sterol removes the amulet and offers it to Jeslek, who bends his head to allow Sterol to put the golden chain around his neck. "If you don't mind," Sterol continues, "I will be removing my works to the lower room. Derka will retire to Hydolar. He came from there, you may recall."

"How convenient."

"Yes. It was." Sterol smiles blandly.

L

AFTER DORRIN FINISHES currying Meriwhen, he saddles the mare, patting her neck. "Hard to believe you and I have been around Diev this long."

When he leads Meriwhen out of the barn, Petra waves from the porch. "Will you be late for supper?"

A hail of red-golden leaves flies from the oaks behind Dorrin like a momentary veil flung by the fall winds between them. "I hope not."

While he needs to meet Quiller, the toymaker, he scarcely looks forward to the encounter. He touches the staff, then nudges Meriwhen with his heels. With a soft whinny, the mare sidesteps, then carries Dorrin toward the road. They turn right, toward the Northern Ocean, which lies beyond the single line of rolling hills, and down the hard-packed clay.

The small cottage with the one-room shed off the sagging porch stands less than a hundred rods down a muddy side road from the kaystone where the stone paving begins on the north military road as it makes its last wide arc to head west into upper Diev.

Dorrin guides Meriwhen onto the brown-grassed shoulder of the side road to avoid the water and cold mud. The sign outside the shed displays a spinning top in flaking red and black paint.

Dorrin wipes his boots on the fraying rush mat before stepping into the shed. The man on the stool looks up, dull brown eyes focusing on Dorrin from under a mop of brown and gray hair. "Don't have much today." His face screws up before he continues. "Who are you? I don't know you, do I?"

"I don't think so. My name is Dorrin. I'm a smith apprentice to Yarrl."

"You're the nasty one with the fancy toys! I heard about you!" Quiller slams his knife on the workbench top, then grasps the bench to keep himself, and the stool, from toppling.

"No. I'm not a toymaker." How has Quiller heard about the models? Dorrin has only sold two.

"Why do you make those wonderful toys?" Quiller wipes his forehead, squinting. The single half-shuttered window admits little enough light, and the oil lamp on the wall is dark. "Willum just laughed at my wagon, and he showed me yours. Why did you do it?" The man's voice almost breaks.

"To solve problems, mostly," admits Dorrin. "I came to talk to you about toy-making . . ."

"I knew it! You want to steal my secrets! You want my customers!"

Dorrin takes a deep breath. "No. That's why I came."

"To take my customers? You admit it?"

"No!" protests the healer. "I don't want your customers."

"But they're good customers. Why wouldn't you want them?" Quiller reaches down and massages his ankle. Quiller's right foot is twisted, splayed somehow, larger than the left, and encased in a type of soft leather moccasin. A heavy-handled cane stands in the corner behind the toymaker.

"Because," Dorrin explains patiently, "I am not a toymaker."

"Then why do you make toys?" Quiller straightens, exhaling loudly.

"I make models of things I want to build. But I came to explain that I'm not a toymaker, and I don't want to sell anything like what you make."

Quiller rests his game leg on the rung of the stool. "Why should I care, exactly, young master Dorrin? This here's a pretty free city, and who would I be to tell you that you couldn't be a toymaker?"

"I'm not a toymaker. I do make toys, but that's just to learn how things work. But it costs me time, and I have to buy the materials." Dorrin pauses. "I know you have a family to support."

"Not a family—just a widowed sister and her boy."

"That's family." Dorrin shrugs. "I don't know how things work here." He pauses with the distractions of the older man's eyebrows and the pain from the twisted ankle. Once again, Dorrin has started trying to smooth the way for his machine-building, and he has to worry about healing again. He wipes his forehead. Quiller twitches again.

"Your foot? Has it always been like that?"

"Don't know about always. Got crushed under a wagon when I was working for Honsard, younger 'n you. Started carving, 'cause I couldn't do much else."

"Would you mind if I looked at it?"

"Looked at it? Thought we were talking toys. You're still a toymaker."

"Please . . ." Dorrin is almost pleading, so clear is the man's pain.

Rylla couldn't help, you know." Quiller's left hand squeezes his work table. "Pain still comes and goes." His face clears for a moment, although his forehead is damp. "You Yarrl's apprentice?"

"Yes."

"The one who's a healer? Why are you here? You're a smith."

"Could I look at your foot, first?"

"Don't see as why not. One quack's like to another."

Dorrin touches the ankle, frowning at the near-permanent reddish-white. As he senses the foot, he touches and somehow changes a few small patterns.

"What did you do?" asks the toymaker, squinting.

Dorrin shakes his head. "The bone's healed all wrong. I can't fix that, but most of the time, from now on, it won't hurt so much." He slumps against the table, taking a deep wracking breath, then another.

"Can't pay you," snaps Quiller.

"I didn't ask you to," Dorrin snaps back. "I didn't fix the bone, and I can't. I'm not a master healer."

Quiller rubs his forehead. "Hard to remember what it's like without the ache. But I get along."

Dorrin rubs his forehead and then the back of his neck.

"Suppose your making a few toys makes no mind . . ." muses Quiller.

"Not the kind you make," ventures Dorrin.

"There be one thing, healer."

Dorrin shifts his weight from one foot to the other and looks at the miniature wagon in front of Quiller.

"You might be thinking about joining the guild."

"The guild? Is there a healers' guild?"

"Don't know of such a thing for healers. I mean the guild. That's what they call it. The people who make the odd things—like my toys, or Thresak's coats, or Vildek the cooper. Don't know as it helps much, but it's only a few coppers a year, and the Spidlarian Council does investigate their grievances."

"Do you belong?"

"Sometimes, when I can pay the coppers. Now, times are hard, and the winter was cold. Have to pay for wood with this foot."

"I appreciate the information."

"Talk to Hasten, if you can get in a word." Quiller looks down at the block of wood that will be an ox or a horse to go with the cart. "You might as well be on your way, young master. Not much as I have to offer you."

"Good day," Dorrin says quietly, inclining his head.

"A better day than in a time. Aye, a better day." Quiller picks up the knife, and Dorrin steps out into the breezy twilight.

Meriwhen whinnies as he swings into the saddle.

LI

USING THE TONGS, Dorrin slips the first iron band into place one-third of the way down the staff, using his order skills to bleed the heat away from the lorkin. The clamps slide into place, and the iron fasteners. Sweat oozes from his forehead as he repeats the operation with the second band, and as he struggles with iron, and heat, and order.

After releasing the clamps, he eases the staff into the slack tank, bathing wood and iron in liquid and in order. With the two middle bands in place, he takes a deep draft from the mug of cold water. Then he takes the first end cap in the tongs and sets it in the forge. Once it is nearly straw-yellow, he slips it over the end of the staff and repeats the quenching.

He drinks the last of the water before setting the other end cap. When all the black iron is on the staff, he lays it at the edge of the hearth and wipes his forehead with the back of his bare forearm. The almost-completed staff radiates blackness and order. He must wait for the staff to cool before filing the

black iron, and ruining a file in the process, then
smoothing the wood. At least, he can make his own
files, if laboriously.

In the dimness beyond the forge, he senses someone,
and he turns.

Petra steps into the dim circle of light. She still
wears trousers and a heavy jacket. "What are you
doing?"

He gestures at the staff. "Making a better staff."

She looks at the staff on the forge bricks, then shivers. "It's cold, like the stars on a winter night."

Dorrin racks his tongs and the hammer. The forge
is still too hot to clean out the old ash, and that means
he will have to be up early.

"In a way, so are you, you know. People think you're
pleasant enough, but your outside is as cold as winter
compared to the forge fire deep inside. I hope your
little trader is tough enough to handle it."

"Little? Her shoulders are broader than mine, and
she's taller."

Petra studies the staff, not touching it, nor looking
at Dorrin. "You're still learning. Mother told me that,
and I didn't believe it. Not then." The jacket swings
half-open, revealing a thin shift.

Dorrin can see erect nipples under the thin material.
"Why did you come down?"

"Father told me to watch you work. I used to help
him sometimes—before you came. I had trouble sensing what he needed. He kept telling me to try to feel
the iron. I didn't know what he meant. Now I do."

"But why . . ."

"I couldn't sleep. Someone was forging the world—
that's what it felt like. Every blow of your hammer
echoed through me." She tosses the frizzy hair off her
forehead with a quick flip of her head.

Dorrin follows her eyes and looks at the staff, sees
the blackness beneath the dark wood and black iron.

"Good night, Dorrin." Petra clinches the jacket around her and turns, walking back into the darkness on her way to the house and to sleep.

Dorrin begins to sweep up. Forging the world? Absurd.

LII

"How ARE WE to deal with Spidlar?"

"Repeal the surtax," suggests an anonymous voice from the mid-benches of the Council chamber.

Jeslek swivels toward the voice. "Who suggested that?"

There is no answer.

"If you don't want the Spidlarians or the Blacks making golds, then you'll be making the Hamorians and the Nordlans rich," suggests the heavy bald man in the first row. "Or the Suthyans and the Sarronnese. Trade is like water. It has to go somewhere."

"Why can't it flow here?" demands Jeslek.

"That is easier said than done."

"Why not increase the tax on Recluce goods?" asks another White Wizard.

"Think again, Myral. The surtax is a hundred percent already."

"So? Those are spices, wines, luxury goods. Besides, who can wear their wool anyway? People will pay still more, and the Treasury will benefit, but not the Hamorians and Nordlans."

"Couldn't we use the tax to build a larger fleet?"

"We could build the ships, but why do we need any more?" asks Cerryl.

"To cut off outside trade to Recluce, of course,"

snorts Jeslek, young-looking despite the white hair and golden eyes.

"That would have worked three centuries ago, but after Creslin we had neither ships nor money. It won't work now. All Recluce is doing now is buying our grain from the Nordlans. The Nordlans pick it up in Hydolar and ship it to Recluce. Then the Blacks sell their stuff to the Nordlans in return. It costs them more, but we lose all that trade."

"That's Jeslek's point," offers Anya in the silence that follows. "Unless we cut off trade to Recluce, we lose."

"That's fine in theory," snorts the bald wizard. "But I have yet to see something that will work. Nor did any of our predecessors. Do you honestly think, Jeslek, that previous councils have approved of the growing power of Recluce? Did they lose scores of ships and thousands of troops on purpose?"

"Of course not." Jeslek frowns, then smiles. "But, remember, the Blacks cannot use the winds now—even if they had a Creslin. What if we put more wizards on our ships?"

"How many would that take?"

"Not that many. That way, we could blockade Recluce. The Nordlans won't make enough off the island to want to lose ships." Jeslek's face bears a smug look, the look of a man who has discovered a solution.

Another wizard shrugs. "That may be. Bring the council a plan."

Jeslek still smiles as the others turn their attention to the next item of discussion. So does Anya.

LIII

"WELL . . . ASK HIM . . ."

Dorrin senses the whisper, rather than hears it, even as his hammer continues to weld the upset ends of the broken wagon brace. He thrusts the brace back into the fire, noting the coolness of the iron almost as automatically as he checks the grain and the crystal sizes. As the metal reheats, he looks up to see Petra outlined in the smithy door.

"Gerrol's dying . . ." protests another feminine voice, a deeper hoarser one.

"Dorrin's a smith," Yarrl says.

"He's also a healer."

"Who will pay for his time?"

Dorrin's head throbs. Money or not, he cannot refuse what he knows will be asked. He pulls the brace from the forge and turns it on the anvil. Another series of sequenced hammer blows and the brace goes on the forge bricks to cool slowly. Then he sets the hammer in its place on his rack, followed by the cross peen hammer and the punch.

"I will, if it comes to that."

"Oh . . . daughter. You ask him."

Petra walks to the forge, followed by a young woman with straight brown hair and bloodshot eyes. Both wear loose gray trousers and gray jackets.

"Dorrin?" Petra's frizzy hair flares away from the heat of the forge, and she blinks from the heat and the tiny particles in the air.

"Yes, mistress Petra?"

"Will you help us?"

"I can but try." He continues to rack his tools, in

contrast to the ordered disorder of Yarrl's hammers and punches and swages.

"You didn't ask who or what." Petra coughs. "Sheena's little brother Gerrol is fevered and dying."

"It doesn't really matter. I am, like it or not, still a healer."

"Oh . . ." Petra's sharp face softens. "How awful. I didn't know."

"Do I have enough time to wash off quickly?"

Petra looks at his smudged and sweating figure. "It might be best. Honsard would not believe a sweating smith to be a healer."

"Fine. I'll bring my staff." Dorrin grins briefly, as he grabs a pail from the hook on the wall and heads for the well.

"Do bring that staff," Petra says quietly.

A chill northern breeze reminds him that it is near winter, despite the clear skies and a bright midafternoon sun. Dorrin quickly lifts a full bucket of water. As he straightens, his trousers are jerked.

"Oh, it's you, little demon." He scratches Zilda between the ears and ruffles the kid's neck. With a last scratch for the little goat, he carries the bucket to his quarters, where he pours some into the wash basin. Then he strips to his drawers and washes as quickly as he can using the water in the basin for his face. After drying off with a gray towel, he pulls on one of his two brown traveling outfits and takes the staff from the corner.

Petra has already saddled Meriwhen by the time he reaches the barn. He checks the cinches and mounts, following the two women, Petra on the bay, and Sheena on a gray, as they start down the north road toward Diev.

Honsard's wagonry is less than three kays downhill from the smithy. Two barns flank a two-storied yellow house with a wide covered porch. A matched team of

Rumoag draft horses pulls an empty flatbed wagon from the hauling yard. Their hoofs clop easily on the stones of the main road.

Petra reins up at the rail before the house. Dorrin dismounts, leaving his staff in the lanceholder, and follows them onto the porch.

"This your famed healer, daughter?" Honsard is square-built, with a paunch below heavy shoulders and chest. His small green eyes are set deeply under thin eyebrows. His faded blue tunic and trousers are mud-spattered.

Sheena nods.

"You're paying for him."

"No, I'm paying for him," announces Petra.

"Could I see the child, ser?" asks Dorrin.

"Help yourself, esteemed healer. Or my daughter will show you the way."

Dorrin studies the haul-master, sensing flickerings of chaos within him. Then he leaves Honsard standing on the top of the stairs to the covered porch.

The boy is dying. The thin frame shivers from a chill, despite the heat radiating from the parched forehead, despite the quilts heaped over him, and the closed and shuttered window.

Dorrin's fingers brush the child's forehead, and he concentrates. The fever alone will kill the child before too long. He straightens.

"He hasn't been cut or wounded, has he?"

"No. He fell sick two days ago, and he just kept getting hotter, and he wouldn't wake up this morning."

"Is there a tub, one you can fill with water?"

"A bath! You must be mad! Baths are the demon's invention, or the legacy of the cursed Legend," rasps Honsard from the hallway.

Dorrin's eyes harden into black steel and focus on the heavy-set man. "Do you want him to die?"

The man's eyes say yes as he shakes his head.

"The fever alone will kill him before long."

"You're a healer."

"I know my limits, ser. Without a cool bath to drop that fever, I cannot help enough to heal. Even with a bath, it will be hard. Wait longer, and no healer, not even the greatest, could save him."

"Please . . . father . . ."

"On your head, daughter! Have the man do as you will! You have already. You brought this to pass." Honsard turns. "There is a tub in the kitchen."

Dorrin looks at Petra. "Can you boil some water? Water from the well will be too cold, I think." As the two scurry for water, Dorrin again touches the fevered brow, letting his weak order senses touch what he can. He does not know what the disease is, only that flickers of an ugly whitish-red permeate the child.

In time, a tub of lukewarm water stands in the kitchen. Dorrin lifts the boy from his quilts and, with Sheena's and Petra's aid, strips off his soaked underclothes.

"He'll need a dry bedgown and bedclothes, and a towel in a bit." Dorrin lowers Gerrol, moaning and thrashing, into the tub.

"Now what?" asks Petra. "Will this stop his burning?"

Dorrin shakes his head. "Some fever is not too bad." Not from what he recalls of his mother's teaching. "But too much can kill. The water helps also if he cannot drink. At least his skin can."

He tries again to strengthen the black flames of order within the boy. Has he succeeded? He cannot really tell, except that Gerrol seems to breathe easier. He watches—how long he cannot tell—until the boy's skin begins to raise chill bumps.

"Can you get his bed ready?" he asks Sheena.

She nods, her eyes bloodshot, but not tearing.

Dorrin turns to Petra. "He's going to need several

baths like this. If he stays in the water too long, it will also raise the fever."

"Bah . . ." mumbles Honsard from the doorway. "He'll live or die, not mattering what some quack does."

"Are you telling me to let him die?" snaps Dorrin.

"That's not what I meant."

"Good," says Petra coolly.

Dorrin lifts the light figure from the water and into the towel held by Petra. She staggers under the boy's weight, and Dorrin slips an arm under Gerrol's shoulders to help.

"You're stronger than you look," Petra says wryly.

"Your father works me hard."

"Not as hard as you work yourself."

They wrap Gerrol in the quilts again, and Dorrin watches.

By the time the sun touches the horizon, Dorrin has immersed Gerrol three times, and the boy's fever has clearly dropped and stayed lower. Gerrol lies under the clean but gray sheet. A light sheen of perspiration coats the boy's forehead, and the worst of the reddish-white flickers of chaos have vanished.

"You need something to eat," Sheena says.

Dorrin's head feels light.

"Sit down."

The healer slumps into the chair, and a cup of broth is placed under his nose. He sips, and the worst of the lightheadedness departs. He eats three large slabs of bread with cheese. His head clearer, he studies the child again, the too-long lank brown hair and the narrow face so like his sister's. He touches Gerrol's forehead and lends a shade more order to the still-faint blackness within. The red-white ugliness of chaos has retreated into faint flickers of white.

"He needs some boiled water."

"Boiled?" asks the narrow-faced young woman.

"Boil the water and let it cool in a clean and covered pitcher that has not been used for milk."

"I'll take care of it," Petra promises, as she leaves for the kitchen.

Dorrin takes another slab of bread, understanding for the first time why his mother often came home white-faced and exhausted. Healing is every bit as hard as smithing.

"Why does he need boiled water?" asks the sister.

"It's easier for the sick to drink and keep in their body," Dorrin simplifies. "You want a good clean well, don't you?"

Sheena nods.

"Boiled water is cleaner than even good well water—if you store it in a clean pitcher."

"Where did you learn all this?"

"From my mother."

"Does she live near here?"

"No."

"Oh."

Petra returns. "The kettle is filled and over the coals. Is the old gray pitcher in the corner cupboard all right?"

"That's fine. Just be careful, please. It was mother's."

"I can use another."

"Use it. She'd be pleased."

Petra leaves Sheena and Dorrin on the stools, watching the sleeping boy faintly bathed in the flickering light of a single candle.

Dorrin touches Gerrol's forehead again and nods. "I think he'll be all right. Just make sure he has plenty of the boiled water and just breads for a while until his stomach settles. Then try some soup, and little bits of other things." He stands.

"Thank you." Sheena's arms go around Dorrin, and her lips—hot and dry—touch his . . . and cling, and her hips move suggestively against him." ... all I can give ..."

Dorrin gently disengages from her.

"Don't you ...?"

"You don't owe me for doing what I had to do."

"No one else could have saved him."

"I almost didn't, and it will be weeks before your brother's well."

Sheena looks at the faded carpet, her eyes focusing on a rose pattern.

"Darkness." Why hadn't he seen? "Your son?" Dorrin whispers.

Sheena does not look up, but Dorrin can see the tears.

"It is your secret." His voice is low, and his own eyes burn. "But, then, you have more than paid." His hand touches her shoulder, and he wills her what comfort he can.

Finally, she looks up, muddy tracks streaking her cheeks. "Are they all like you—the Black ones?"

"They are good, mostly, but not like me."

"They sent you away?"

Dorrin nods.

"Why couldn't they see?"

"They and I have different dreams. For them, as for most people, what is different is evil." He stands, then walks toward the door.

Honsard stands halfway down the stairs.

"He should recover," Dorrin says quietly.

"What do I owe you?" the wagon-master asks peevishly.

"Nothing." Dorrin pauses. "Unless you want to give Yarrl some more paying smithy work." He steps out into the morning chill.

Sheena stands on the porch. "I gave your mare some grain and water."

"Thank you."

Sheena is still standing on the porch when he turns onto the road back to the smithy.

LIV

"THEY'VE ADOPTED ANOTHER surtax." The tall Black wizard opens the meeting with his announcement.

"That's not as big a problem as the Whites deciding that they want the Fairhaven ships to sink all blockade runners." The slender dark-haired woman's voice is level. "The Nordlans will not unload grain at Land's End once Fairhaven threatens their ships—unless we take steps to remove the White ships."

"Why don't we?"

"Because the only real weapon we have is the winds, and even I can't bring more than one or two big storms—not without changing Recluce back into a desert ... or a swamp." The air wizard lifts his hands. "Or handing Jeslek even greater power than it took to raise mountains. We already have given him too much."

"What are we supposed to do—starve? Or forsake order just to keep a White Wizard from getting power?"

"I've given up more than you—far more! And we won't starve. We have our orchards, and the Feyn River fields produce some wheat and more than enough barley ..."

"Darkness, Oran! We haven't had to eat barley for generations. Drink it, yes. Why can't we grow more wheat, like the farmers have below Extina?"

"The ground isn't ready—not without a lot of healer work, and that just strengthens Fairhaven's side of the Balance." Oran wipes his forehead.

"You've got so many demon-driven reasons why we can't do anything . . ."

"You were the one who opposed our building warships."

"And what would we fight with? We can't use the winds—at least we haven't had an air wizard who would dare in generations. We can't use gunpowder or cammabark because the Whites would blow us apart with our own powder. We've been coasting on Creslin's reputation, and they've called our bluff. They'll burn any ships we have before we can get close enough to board. Sure, black iron shields work fine on the ground, but how do you get close enough at sea?"

Oran shrugs. "We can work with some of the healers on switching the oldest Feyn Fields."

"What about timber? We're still—"

"I know . . ."

"What will we do with the excess wool . . .?"

" . . . and what about the chaos-tinged ones we send to Candar and Nordla or Hamor?" asks the white-haired blade.

"We don't have to reach solutions right now," temporizes the air wizard.

"No," answers a quiet voice from the left corner. "But how will things be any better next year or the year after?"

Oran wipes his forehead again.

LV

DORRIN CHEWS THROUGH the last chunk of cheese he has cut and swallows it quickly, hungry as he is, for he has slept later than he should have. Healing Gerrol had been harder work than he thought it would be, far harder, and he had gone right back to the smithy. His shoulders still ache, and a dull throbbing ebbs and flows behind his eyes.

"Don't try to swallow it whole, Dorrin. Papa knows how tired you are." Petra refills the mug with warm cider. "Gerrol was so much better last night."

"Hee-yaaaa . . . hee-yaaa . . ."

All three look through the single kitchen window into the yard where a small wagon has drawn up, heavily laden enough that the tires leave narrow ruts in the yard clay.

"That's Honsard's man Wenn. Why's he here?"

Dorrin swallows the cider and bolts for the porch. The scent of the forge, dried leaves, and moldering post-harvest fields swirl past him on the light breeze. Zilda butts his leg as he hurries past the half-grown goat. He reaches the carter before the man enters the smithy. "Ser . . . might I help you? I'm Yarrl's striker."

"I got a pretty load of work for your boss, fellow. Honsard's stuff."

"I'll tell him."

The man looks at the broken parts and sections heaped in the wagon box, then at Dorrin.

"Just wait a moment, and I'll help you unload."

The carter nods. "That'd be fine."

When Dorrin walks into the smithy, Yarrl jabs the hot set he holds toward Dorrin's leather apron. "Need to get working, healing or no healing."

"Honsard's man is outside. He has a pile of work for you, and he wants to talk to you."

"Honsard? Cheap bastard said I charged too much. Said it'd be a white day in heaven 'fore he'd come here. Course, he was tanked." Yarrl lays the iron on the forge, shaking his head. "Let's see."

Dorrin follows the smith to the yard.

"This is what you and Honsard talked about last eight-day. He said he'd hold you to your price." The carter looks down at the pile of dried leaves by the porch steps, scuffing a foot in the clay.

Yarrl glances from the heaped wagon to the carter and then to Dorrin. A flutter of gray catches his eye, and he looks up on the porch, where Petra stands. She nods at her father and points to Dorrin.

"Can't do all this at once," the smith says.

"Honsard knows that. When you get some done, let him or me know. We'll get it. He'll pay as each bit's done."

"I don't say as I understand, but that's what will be done."

"I'll help unload," Dorrin volunteers.

"Demons," mutters the smith. "Seeing as I won't get back to work until it's done, might as well have everyone unload. You, too, Petra."

The carter lets his breath out as Yarrl slides the big smithy door open more than the normal two cubits.

The fall breeze flings leaves around the trousers of the four, but Zilda has only managed to clank her chain half a dozen times before the wagon is empty and the carter is on his way.

"Honsard . . . be demon-damned." The smith looks at Dorrin. "Your doing?"

"Well . . ."

"Dorrin?" Petra is smiling mischievously.

Dorrin thinks about evading the question, but the pounding behind his eyes returns. "I suppose so. Honsard asked me how much I owed him. Nothing, I told him. But I felt a little nasty. So I added that he could send you some honest smith work."

Yarrl shakes his head. "Must have scared the darkness right out of him. He's a hard man."

"Baaaa . . ." interjects Zilda.

"Not as hard as Dorrin," Petra adds.

"I'm not hard at all," protests Dorrin.

Both Petra and her father raise their eyebrows.

"Really."

The smith puts his shoulder to the door, returning it to the mostly closed position. "We got work to do, healing or no healing. Even more now, with all this stuff." He gestures to the additional items stacked up in order. "You get business, and you have to deliver."

LVI

OUTSIDE THE RED LION, a low wind whines, promising snow and chill. Inside, Dorrin sips from the battered mug, glancing toward the singer seated on the high stool beside the fire.

> I watched my love sail out to sea,
> His hand was deft; he waved to me.
> But then the waters foamed white and free
> Just as my love turned false to me.
> Oh, love is wild, and love is bold,
> The fairest flower when e'er it is new,
> But love grows old, and waxes cold
> And fades away like morning dew . . .

"Sings well." Pergun nods his head toward the thin woman in the faded blue blouse and skirt. "Wonder if she's good in bed."

"Why?"

"Most tavern singers do both. She doesn't look the type."

Dorrin sips redberry from the mug. The singer's long reddish hair slips forward over her left shoulder, and she has an open and slightly freckled face that is somehow pinched, even as her fingers glide across the strings of the guitar. "Are we all types? Pieces on the game board of chaos and order?"

"Master Dorrin... begging your pardon... but what does that have to do with whether she'd sleep with me?"

"She won't. Probably not with anyone. Not any more, at least."

"Oh. Was worth a thought." Pergun lifts his mug, then sets it down. "How'd you know? More healer wizardry?"

Dorrin nods, listening to the next song from the small woman, marveling at the depth of her voice and the honest silver of her notes.

> Cuera la dierre,
> Ne querra dune lamonte,
> Pressente da lierra
> Queira fasse la fronte...

"What's that?"

"Bristan, I think. I'd recognize any of the Temple tongues." Dorrin sips his redberry slowly. He has no desire to spend more coins, not when he has so many things he must purchase.

"Sure she won't sleep with me?" Pergun gulps the last of his dark beer and raises the mug.

"You sure you want another one?" asks the serving girl.

"Course I want another one." Pergun lays two coppers on the wood.

"It's your head."

"Whose head would it be?" argues the mill hand, but the serving woman has left. "She talking to me?"

"She likes you."

"Some liking. Won't even take my coins!"

"Pergun." The one word silences the mill hand. "Listen to the singer."

... the soldiers, they searched for many a year.
They ripped down the mountains and tore up the trees,
But never they found what they never could hear,
That dashing young man with the wind-bearing skis.

"What's that?"

"It's about Creslin."

"Who's he?"

Clunk! Another mug hits the table, and foam spills onto the wood. Pergun rubs his finger in the liquid and licks it. "Mustn't waste any."

"Your coins, fellow?"

Pergun hands her the coppers. She looks at Dorrin, and Dorrin understands that this beer is Pergun's last.

"After this one, we need to be going."

"Going? What ... I got to go for ... nothing ... cold pallet ... cold-hearted women ..."

Dorrin sips the last of his redberry, then pulls his jacket off the back of the chair. "Let's go."

" ... haven't finished ..."

"Let's go."

"Aw ... right ... no fun ..."

Dorrin retrieves the black staff from the floor along the wall and stands. The serving girl looks at him, and the staff, and steps back. Pergun fumbles into the battered sheepskin jacket and pushes himself upright. Dorrin steadies the table with his free right hand, then guides Pergun to the door.

"Wonderful ... wonderful beer ..." mumbles Pergun. He extends a hand to steady himself, but the hand fails to touch the edge of the door, and he staggers into Dorrin.

"Come ... on ..." Dorrin roughly redirects Pergun. "Where's your horse?"

"Got no horse ... me ... horse ... ha ... shank's mare ..."

One of the two torches outside Kyril's has guttered out, and the winds and the snow whip down the street. Dorrin looks toward the dark stable, gripping the staff more tightly, then forcing his fingers to relax. His boots squish through the mixture of slush and mud that covers the paving stones.

" ... got no horse ... got no mare ... got no pearls ... got no girls ..." Pergun sings, so far off-key that the notes are leaden in the night.

Dorrin supposes that Meriwhen can bear double for a short distance.

" ... got no mare ..."

As they near the stable, Dorrin can sense the man in the darkness, even before the blade appears, even before his eyes adjust to the darkness, and his hands automatically reposition the staff.

Meriwhen whuffles, skittering back away from the armed man, who holds the reins in one hand and the sword in the other.

"You just better be going on your way, fellows. Off to a nice bed or back to your master."

" ... got no horse ... got no mare ..." Pergun half mumbles, half sings, putting out a hand to a timber. " ... who are you ... who ... you ... you ... who ...?" He laughs.

Dorrin takes a step forward. His guts are cold, but he knows that he will not abandon Meriwhen to the stranger.

The mare whinnies, and the highwayman wraps the reins around a peg on which a wooden bucket hangs by its ropes.

" ... got no horse ..."

"It's a pity, young fellow ..." The blade weaves toward Dorrin.

Dorrin's hands and arms react, flicking the heavy

blade aside, then reversing the staff and thrusting straight up through the diaphragm.

"Ughhhh..." The blade clunks against the bucket and drops into the straw. The highwayman takes a half step, then sags slowly onto the dirty straw, eyes going blank.

Dorrin barely staggers to the stable door, his feet scrabbling through the pile of straw and manure to the left of the entry. White burning flares blaze through his skull.

"... shit ... no fun, Dorrin ..." mumbles Pergun.

Dorrin's fingers claw against the wood, and he squints, trying to shut out the light and the pain. Finally, he straightens up, still fighting the headache that feels as though Yarrl were fullering his brain with long heavy strokes. After looking at the black staff, he walks slowly back to Kyril's, leaving a second set of tracks in the light snow that falls like a curtain.

He closes the inn door, and the half-empty room falls silent.

"What's the matter, healer?" asks the heavy-set proprietor, running a grayish rag across the counter.

"One dead thief ... in the stable."

Kyril grabs the single-bladed axe from beneath the counter. "Just one?"

"He's dead."

"I hope so, but let's see. Forra!"

A younger man, nearly as heavy as Kyril, but with broader shoulders and less gut, sticks his head out from the back room.

"Trouble in the stable."

Torch in one hand, and a cudgel in the other, Forra leads the way to the stable, where the three find two prone figures, one face up, the other face down.

Pergun looks up sleepily. "What took so long ...? Wanna go home ..."

Forra prods the bearded highwayman with his

cudgel, then rolls the body over. The surprised
expression remains frozen on the man's face.

"Light! His chest's caved in." Forra looks at Dorrin.

"His blade's there." Dorrin gestures with the staff.

In the light of the torch, Kyril studies the dead man's
face. "You do this, young fellow?"

"I didn't mean to, but he wanted to kill us and take
Meriwhen . . ."

"Meriwhen?"

"My horse, there."

"You're that young healer who's also an apprentice
to Yarrl?"

Dorrin nods.

"Where did you learn to do this?" Kyril gestures at
the dead man.

"When . . . I was in school . . . they taught me the
staff . . . can't use an edged weapon." Dorrin's legs are
shaking, and he sags against a stall wall.

"You got some coins coming, young fellow. This
here's Niso. Council has a reward. Not much—ten
golds. He killed a trader on the piers last fall." Kyril
turns to Forra. "See why no one messes with a smith,
even a skinny one? Flesh and bone won't stand up to
someone who beats iron."

Forra, for all his bulk, looks from the dead Niso to
Dorrin and back, then wipes his forehead on his sleeve.
"Lot more of this, these days."

Kyril shakes his head, sadly, once more. "Hard
times . . . The White Wizards making it hard on everyone, and they're all coming here, thinking they can
steal from us."

Dorrin shivers as a gust of wind blows snow in his
face.

"Dorrin . . . promised . . . get me home . . ." complains Pergun. The mill worker has managed to prop
himself into a sitting position against a barrel.

Kyril shakes his head again. "You take your friend home. I'll let the Council know."

"Dorrin gets a reward ... Dorrin gets ... a reward..." Pergun singsongs.

"He'll get a reward, my drunken mill man. Believe me, he will. You think anyone wants to cross him and Yarrl?"

Dorrin represses a sigh and helps Pergun to his feet, and onto Meriwhen, where the dark-haired man sways. Dorrin puts the staff into the lanceholder.

" ... help ..."

"Just hang on." Dorrin unties the mare and leads her into the snow squalls before swinging up behind Pergun. He can feel both Kyril's and Forra's eyes on his back as Meriwhen bears him out onto the snow-covered road that leads toward Hemmil's mill.

LVII

DORRIN HOLDS THE sledge, waiting for Yarrl to bring the iron from the forge to the anvil. As the iron goes down on the fuller, Dorrin begins the routine—strike and recover while Yarrl slips the iron across the bottom fuller, strike and recover, strike and recover—until the bar stock cools and the smith reheats it. Then the fullering continues until the iron is rough-flattened to the thickness of the heavy barn hinge. Next comes the flatter, and the quick blows to smooth the fullered iron.

Even though the smithy is warm, outside the snow continues to fall. With each stroke of the sledge, Dorrin puzzles over the highwayman as he automatically responds to the smith's directions.

Petra appears at the edge of the smithy. This time

she does not wait for a break in the routine, but steps past the slack tank, ducking under the bellows cross-lever, until Yarrl sees her and sets the iron on the forge.

"Better be important, girl."

"There are two traders here. They say they're members of the Council. They want to see you and Dorrin."

"Invite them in, Petra, unless they want to meet in the kitchen."

Petra hastens back toward the doorway to the rear yard.

"What did you do, young fellow?"

"I . . . killed a highwayman. Kyril said there was a reward, but . . ."

"You thought it was more hot air?"

"I didn't know."

"Demon-damned traders. Not one thing, it's another." Yarrl eases the unfinished iron closer to the forge fire, sets down the tongs, and places the flatter on the bricks.

Two men in heavy cloaks of dark blue step past the broken wagon parts awaiting repair and into the warm area near the forge. One is white-haired and heavy, but tall, over four cubits. The other is dark-haired, almost rail-thin, and short, shorter even than Dorrin.

The heavier trader inclines his head to Yarrl. "Master Yarrl, I am Trader Fyntal and this is Trader Jasolt. We are here on behalf of the Council. Is this your striker?"

"Dorrin? 'Course he's my striker. Didn't you just see him with the sledge?"

"And his name is Dorrin?" pursues Fyntal.

"So far as I know, he's always been Dorrin."

The functionary turns to Dorrin. "You were at the Red Lion last evening?"

"Yes, ser."

"According to the innkeeper, you were attacked by

a rogue highwayman, and dispatched him with a staff. Is this true?"

"Pergun and I were leaving. He was stealing my mare. He threatened to kill us. I tried to stop him, but I didn't mean to kill him."

"You must be well regarded by the smith, to use a horse," adds the younger trader, so smoothly that his words ooze oil.

"He's a good striker," Yarrl asserts, preventing Dorrin from having to correct the misapprehension about Meriwhen's ownership.

"Well then . . . so long as that is clear. Your striker has . . . resolved . . . a matter of long-standing concern to the Council. The highwayman he . . . dispatched . . . was the notorious Niso. This Niso person was responsible for the death of Trader Sanduc, and the trader's family offered through the Council a reward." The trader lifts a leather pouch from his belt and bows, extending the pouch to Yarrl.

Yarrl takes the pouch without inclining his head, and passes the heavy leather to Dorrin. "Appreciate the honor of seeking out young Dorrin. He's a good striker, and a fine fellow."

"We're sure he is. Good day, smiths." Fyntal nods, not quite wrinkling his nose at the smithy, and turns.

Jasolt turns also, and the two walk heavily from the smithy. Jasolt has to swirl his cloak to free it from a bracket on the main slack tub. A gust of chill air blows past the smiths, then drops as the door is closed.

Reisa and Petra appear. Petra is giggling. "They're so stiff. The young one almost tripped over Zilda, his nose was so stuck up."

"Aye," Yarrl says slowly. "Stuck up they are. But honest. More than you can say for most."

"You killed a highwayman?" asks Reisa.

"He tried to take Meriwhen."

"With your staff?"

"I got very sick," Dorrin temporizes, looking sheepish.

Yarrl laughs. "A good striker and deadly with a staff, but he gets sick after killing a killer."

Reisa nods. "But he's a healer, Yarrl. Don't forget that. He's a healer."

Yarrl looks at the floor, then at the forge. "Out, women. We got work to do. Look at all that work there."

Dorrin grins as he reaches up and begins to pump the bellows. Yarrl retrieves his tongs and the iron for flattening.

LVIII

THE TROOPERS RIDE uphill. On each side of the road stretch meadows half-covered with an early snow. The right side of the road is bordered by a low stone wall. Vulcrows circle a point over the crest of the hill.

"Shit," mutters a wiry trooper in the van, wiping his forehead with a neckerchief of Spidlarian blue, despite the chill wind that blows off the ice-covered peaks to the west. "More trouble ahead."

On the right of the wiry man rides Brede. On his right rides Kadara, who is practicing with the West-wind shortsword.

" . . . all she does is play with that damned sticker . . ."

" . . . lucky doesn't use it on you . . ."

" . . . saved your neck more 'n once, Vorban . . ."

When the Spidlarian squad reaches the crest of the hill, a handful of vulcrows explodes from the carcasses and corpses on the downslope. One wagon has been driven or rolled into a stone wall on the right side of the road.

" . . . bastards . . ."

"No one here, now," announces the squad leader, as he reins up beside the wrecked wagon. "Been half a day, at least."

The body of a fat man, dressed in the dark blue of a Spidlarian trader, sprawls in the brown leaves between two patches of light snow. Dark stains have soaked through the heavy cloak, and his hands are extended, as though he had tried to pull himself toward the low dark stone wall.

Kadara studies the crumpled wagon, noting a bolt of blue silk rough-slashed. She frowns, then looks over the rest of the wagon. Another bolt of cloth is wedged under the spring seat of the wagon.

Brede follows her glance, then dismounts and hands her the reins to the gelding. He kneels at the side of the road.

"What in darkness are you doing?" demands the squad leader.

"Checking something."

"Frigging bandits . . ." mumbles Vorban.

"So, Brede, just what brilliance do you have to show us today?"

Brede looks up from the print in the clay next to the road. His face is impassive as he swings back into the saddle.

"That bad, big fellow?" asks the wiry trooper.

"Worse. That's a standard road shoe."

"Huh?" The squad leader closes his mouth abruptly.

"They weren't bandits. Probably Certan troops."

The squad leader motions, and Brede rides up beside the man. "You want to explain?"

"Kadara pointed out something. They didn't take some of the cloth—there's a bolt of silk still left in the wagon. You know how much that's worth? Then the shoe prints. They're all alike."

"Light and all the demons." The squad leader swallows. "They just want it to look like bandits."

"Exactly."

"I think we'd better head back. Giselyn needs to know this." He wheels the bay and gestures. "We're headed back." He pauses. "You can check out this mess and keep what you can find."

Only the squad leader and the two from Recluce remain mounted while the nine others paw through the three corpses and the two wagons.

" ... purses gone ... "

" ... crappy cloth ... "

" ... nice knife!"

Finally, the leader calls. "Mount up!"

"Thanks, big fellow." The wiry trooper grins from his saddle, holding up a knife and sheath. "Hot food and a soft bed. That's for me."

Brede shakes his head. "Enjoy it while you can."

"So it's the Certans. They're not worth a copper."

"I'm worried about who's paying the coppers."

The wiry man pulls on his black neckerchief. "You always have a way of spoiling things." He spurs his mount ahead and alongside Vorban.

Kadara draws her mare up next to Brede. "I don't like this."

"What can we do?"

"We can't get home. The Whites have closed off all ships to Recluce except smugglers. Right now I'm not desperate enough to take that kind of a chance."

"I'd rather not, either," admits Brede.

"These aren't traces of chaos. It's the beginning of a damned war."

"It does look that way," Brede agrees.

"Looks that way? Is that all you can say?"

"What can I say?" He sighs. "I sort of wish I were

a healer or a smith like Dorrin. I wonder how he's doing."

"Probably healing and smithing and making people think he's wonderful."

"Maybe." Brede flicks the reins to urge the gelding to close the gap between them and the rest of the squad. "I imagine he has his problems, too. It's been that kind of a year."

LIX

YARRL TURNS THE metal on the anvil. Dorrin strikes, evenly, stroke after stroke as the smith moves the flatter across the iron. Dorrin sets the light sledge down as Yarrl returns the metal to the forge.

Yarrl's tongs bring the metal back to the anvil, where he sets the drift punch in place. Dorrin gives the drift a light tap, and Yarrl flips the metal over, positioning the bulge in the metal over the hardie hole. Dorrin strikes the drift; the metal plug drops. Another strike, and Yarrl nods, returning the metal to the forge. They repeat the process with the other end.

Next comes the twisting on the spring fork, which Yarrl handles by himself. Dorrin takes the liberty of gently raking the damp charcoal at the edge of the forge toward the working coals.

Reisa steps into the smithy and waits by the bellows and the slack tanks.

The smith reheats the spring to cherry red before plunging it into the big slack tank. Once the iron is gray, he lifts it clear and returns it to the forge fire, checking as the tip of the heavy spring changes from straw to brown to light purple. Then he plunges the spring into the slack tank and swirls it through the liquid. Only when he has cooled the metal and lifted it from the tank does Reisa speak.

"There's a young fellow here for Dorrin. He says his name is Vaos."

"Know him?" Yarrl asks.

"He's the stable boy at Kyril's. Good boy, I'd say."

"Wants a job, I'd bet," grumbles Yarrl.

Reisa nods to the two and steps past the line of broken wagon parts waiting for either Yarrl's or Dorrin's attention and back into the gray light of the cloudy winter day.

"You could use him."

"Why? You planning on leaving?"

Dorrin has not planned to bring up the subject quite so soon. "Ah . . . well . . . I had thought about doing some healing, too . . ."

Yarrl spits into the corner. "Can't say as I'm surprised. When you want to leave?"

"I don't want to leave. I still want to work here. I want to spend some time working at healing, too."

"Man can't serve two crafts, Dorrin."

"I think I can. Will you let me try?"

Yarrl spits again. "Best striker I ever had. Do more in a half day than some do in an eight-day. Would you still work midday to night-fall?"

"I'd thought that. I like working here."

The smith looks down and coughs. "Well . . . let's see this boy. Going to need someone on the bellows and grindstone."

Vaos has strawberry blond hair, green eyes, and a dark bruise that covers most of his left cheek. He sits on the porch stairs, petting Zilda, who stands on the pile of frozen snow trying to nibble the ragged edges of his ripped leather boots. "Ser Dorrin . . . ser smith . . ."

"Why are you here?" Dorrin asks softly.

"The business with Niso . . . ser . . . Forra said it was my fault, that I fell asleep. I worked all day, even unloading the hay wagon and cleaning all the stalls. They took my coppers, said I'd work an extra four eight-days . . ."

"Come here," Dorrin says.

Vaos stands up and walks toward Dorrin with tentative steps. Dorrin reaches out and touches the boy's cheek. He can sense the throbbing pain, not only in the jaw, but across the youngster's back. "Did you strike back?"

"No, ser. But I ran."

Dorrin's hand drops away, leaving a sense of order in the child, and a black smudge over the bruise. "He's telling the truth. They beat him."

"Do you want a job, boy?" asks the smith. "Feed you, and you get a corner in the smithy, and a half-copper an eight-day."

Vaos swallows. Then he squares his shoulders. "I got a half-copper an eight-day at the stable, but I got a few coppers from the customers."

Dorrin tries not to grin at Vaos's spunk. Yarrl purses his lips as well.

"Say a half-copper an eight-day, but I'll spring for new boots and britches, and, if you're as good as you are spunky, an extra half-copper every other eight-day."

"Yes, ser. What do you want me to do first?"

Dorrin grins at Reisa, who has eased out onto the porch to listen. Her breath smokes in the cooler air trapped under the porch roof. Reisa reaches down and ruffles Zilda's head. Then she straightens and grins back at Dorrin, before opening the door and slipping into the kitchen.

"You can pedal the grindstone for me." Yarrl smiles faintly at Dorrin.

LX

THE BANNER SHAPED like a three-lobed leaf hangs limply in the still air outside the neat but small cottage. Dorrin ties Meriwhen to the fence, and the mare whickers softly, lifting her feet as if to protest the chill of the frozen snow underneath. He lifts the black staff from the holder.

The herb garden that flanks both sides of the gravel walkway is organized enough. Under the thin blanket of early winter snow, he can sense the astra and the stunted brinn roots on the right, and sage and dill on the left. The faintest sense of order pervades the garden.

Dorrin refrains from reaching out to the herbs. Now, that is not his business. Meriwhen remains tied to the fence, and the road back downhill toward Diev is as empty as when he rode up it. In the clear cold air, he can easily see the smoke of Yarrl's forge.

Downhill through the scattered trees to the left are an abandoned chimney and the stone-edged doorway to what may be an old root cellar. His eyes turn toward the river of ice that will be a stream in spring. The narrow wedge of ice winds through the tree-filled ravine to his right, spilling down to a level expanse of ice that covers a small pond. By midwinter the ice will be twice as wide, if it is even visible under the snow.

The red-haired youth steps up to the doorway. Someone is inside, presumably Rylla, the older of the two local healers.

Thrap . . . thrap . . .

"Coming . . ."

Dorrin shifts his weight from one foot to the other, still holding the black staff.

"Yes?" The thin and gray-haired woman stands in the half-open doorway.

"I understand that you might be open to a part-time apprentice . . ."

The healer frowns. "An odd notion that would be, young fellow. How can one be something only part of the time?" Her eyes look up toward the horse tethered by the fence.

"Might I come in and explain?"

"Might as well. You mean no harm; that's clear." She opens the door wider. "Just come in quick now, and don't let the chill in."

The front room of the three-room cottage contains a hearth, one large and two small tables, and three narrow cabinets against one wall. The plank floor is worn smooth, but swept clean. Over the low fire a kettle hangs on a hook whose design Dorrin recognizes from Yarrl's work. Steam seeps from the spout.

The woman gestures toward the wooden armchair. The other three chairs are all armless. Dorrin nods toward her, waiting for her to sit.

A wry grin greets his gesture. "Well-mannered young fellow, too. What do you really want, you young scoundrel?" Rylla takes her chair.

Dorrin flushes, then manages to return the grin. He loosens his jacket and sits in the armless chair across from her, laying the staff across his knees. "I'm working at the smithy for Yarrl, but I was trained at both healing and smith-work. I miss the plants . . ." He has to tell more of the truth. "And I need to earn more."

"Ha! You've seen my garden, and my wealth of patrons, boy."

"I might be able to help with the plants."

The gray eyes under the silver eyebrows study the redhead again. "That could be dangerous."

"Selling spices isn't that dangerous, and healers are supposed to be able to grow things."

"And you'd do the growing and the selling?"

"As I can."

"Is it a girl, young fellow?"

"I suppose so ... though more coins won't help now."

"As old Rylla knows, healing's not much for glamour, boy. And neither's being a smith. They won't get you the girl."

With a shrug, he looks at the floor. "Still ..."

"I've got a few winterspice seeds. Never tried them. Think you could grow them?"

Dorrin nods slowly. "If they're still alive ... I think so ..."

"You're one of the outcasts, then."

His eyebrows lift.

"I may be a weak healer, boy, but I can still think."

"Do you still want to take me on?"

"Why not? I always wanted to see winterspice grow. Even Elrik can't do that." Her eyes narrow on him. "Will your master let you spend time here?"

"I've worked it out. I'll spend the morning here."

"What else do you want from me?"

"Land."

"You're an honest scoundrel, boy. What do you have in mind?"

"I'd like to use the land by the pond, build some things. I'd pay you rent for it."

"You've not even shown me you can heal. Or that you have the power."

Dorrin steps to her chair, where he lays the staff across her knees.

Her fingers stroke the black wood for an instant.

"Darkness, boy! You don't need me. You the one who saved Honsard's boy? Fixed Quiller's foot?"

He nods.

"Being as I'm a foolish old lady, could ye tell me why you're asking me for a favor? It doesn't seem as you need me." She strokes the staff a last time and lifts the heavy wood to him.

"Outsiders have problems. People who live in a town don't."

"Ha! You're a sharp one, too. What's your name, boy?"

"Dorrin."

"You want to be the lumber miller's apprentice nextwise, so as you can take over his place?"

"No." A quick flash of pain strikes through Dorrin's skull. "I mean, all I really want to do is build some machines, but I need iron and wood. That means coins. And I'd like my own workroom and cottage."

"But you don't want people a-thinking you're a danger?"

"No. I'm not."

Rylla laughs softly. "Boy, soft as you speak, and polite as you are, you be the most dangerous man I've seen in a long life."

Dorrin's eyebrows lift, involuntarily.

"But that's no matter. I like you, and I'm an old fool."

LXI

DORRIN CLOSES THE barn door, his eyes going to the smithy chimney where the hot air from the forge fades into the gray cold of early winter. He looks down at the faded green cover of the book in his hand—*The*

Healer—with a wry expression on his lips. Somehow he had never expected Rylla to be literate, or to have such a volume. Every time he makes a critical judgment about someone, it seems, he is surprised.

"Willow bark—you didn't use willow bark on the boy? Waste of your energy, Dorrin. You won't always have it, you know." Dorrin represses a grin. Working with the old healer has had its benefits.

Creaakkkkk . . . As the heavy forge wagon turns off the road, Dorrin hurries to his quarters, where he leaves his jacket, his book and staff, and strips off the better shirt for his stained smithy shirt. The forge wagon has only eased into the yard, pulled by four horses each almost twice the size of Meriwhen, by the time Dorrin reaches the smithy door. On one wagon side panel is the legend *Froos & Sons.* The carter eases the wagon up to the side door of the smithy. By now, Dorrin and Yarrl stand by the door, Vaos next to them.

"He delivers iron to the shipwrights in the harbor," Vaos says quietly.

"Long run up here." Yarrl coughs as the wind shifts and whips the hazy and faintly acrid smoke from the forge chimney down into the yard.

"The iron forge is only in upper Diev." Vaos's eyebrows lift.

"Long run with fifty stone of iron bars. We're about the last on the run." Yarrl steps forward, a leather pouch in his hand.

Dorrin's eyes and senses pick up the animals' fatigue.

The carter slowly swings down from the wagon seat. Heavily muscled arms bulge under a stained brown shirt. He wears not a coat, but a sheepskin vest and heavy gloves. "The lot comes to a half gold, Yarrl."

"That's up a silver."

"Froos can't help it. The Council's buying more iron, and he had to install some more pumps."

"You start unloading. I'll be back with your cursed half-gold." The smith tucks the pouch in his belt and heads toward the steps on the porch.

"I'm not supposed to unload until I've got the coin."

Yarrl spits into the corner between the porch and the smithy. "I ever shorted you?"

The carter grins. "Seeing as it's you . . ."

Dorrin looks to Vaos. "You take the small stock, at the end, there."

"I can take the bigger stock."

Dorrin and the carter exchange grins.

"Fine, boy. Take this." The carter hands a single flat bar, a span wide and three cubits long, to Vaos.

The boy staggers under the three-stone load, going to his knees before Dorrin lifts it, saying mildly, "It's heavy."

"Striker, you're stronger than you look."

"He's good with a staff, too," Vaos interjects.

"Oh . . . you're the one." The carter looks down at the hard-packed damp clay. "Makes sense you'd be with Yarrl." Then he shakes his head. "A striker taking Niso down with a piece of wood."

Dorrin lugs the flat iron stock into the smithy, and Vaos follows with an armful of the smallest rod stock. Dorrin racks the iron. "The small rods go there."

"Yes, ser."

"I'm not the smith."

"You're almost one."

By the time they return to the wagon, Yarrl has returned and is paying the carter. "Still highway robbery."

The carter lifts some midweight rods and follows Dorrin.

"Set them there, if you would," Dorrin requests politely.

The carter eases them onto the empty edge of the workbench, then straightens. Vaos follows with the last of the small rod stock, which he racks. All three trudge back outside to repeat the process. After the last iron is off the wagon, the carter closes the tailgate and slides the locking bolts into place.

Dorrin steps up beside the wagon seat. "How much would a plate of iron be, the same thickness as the thin stock, but—could you get one four cubits by four cubits?"

"Hard to say, but the miners in Bythya get some that's five by five, and it's a silver a plate. Why do you want something that big? That's heavy."

"I'd guess fifteen, twenty stone."

"Takes a six-horse team." The carter shakes his head. "And three big men to lift those plates. Anyway, you'd have to talk to Froos." He looks toward Yarrl. "See you next time, smith."

"Just don't raise the prices again," Yarrl grumbles.

The carter shrugs. "Times are tough. They say the Whites are pushing the Analerians into south Spidlar. Dirty herders!" He spits toward the brown stalks of the frost-killed herb garden. "Damned wizards! Not much to choose between the two." He flicks the reins, and the wagon creaks, though not so loudly as when it entered the yard.

"Back to work." The smith slides the door to the smithy back to a narrow opening. "Still have to finish Blygers's chain clamps." He turns to Dorrin. "You still thinking about building that engine?"

"Yes. But I haven't figured out the pistons yet."

Yarrl frowns as if the word is unfamiliar.

"Probably be better to make two smaller ones, on each side of the shaft. If they're exactly opposite, I won't have the problem of synchronizing them."

"These pistons are round cylinders?" inquires the smith.

"They could be any shape, but they'd be stronger as a cylinder."

"Like rockets and firearms?" asks Vaos.

"Don't the pump makers build iron cylinders?"

"I wonder what one would cost," Dorrin reflects.

Yarrl lifts several iron rods, those left by the carter on the bench, into the rack. "Your friend Pergun's sister is married to a striker for Cylder. He's a pumpwright for Froos." The heavy rods slide into the timber rack. "Let's get the rest of these stored. Not only got to do Blygers's job, but we need to get back to finish that stuff of Honsard's." He turns to Vaos. "We'll need another barrow of charcoal."

"Yes, ser."

"Going to be a long winter . . ." Yarrl lifts the tongs and slides the partly forged clamp from the bricks into the fire, reaching for the mid-sized swage as he does so.

Dorrin begins to pump the bellows's lever until Vaos returns with the charcoal.

" . . . long cold winter . . ."

Vaos wheels the barrow next to the forge, and the smith begins to load the charcoal into the forge while Dorrin stores the last of the rod stock.

LXII

THE SMALL DINING table is set for two, and a bottle of wine rests in a basket on the side table. Jeslek glances around the room again when he sees the sheet of parchment on the white oak screening table. He picks up the sheet, glancing toward the bookcase, then back at the words and the numbers. The calculations show the need for another twenty wizards for the additional ten ships under construction in Sligo.

"I know just which twenty."

Still holding the sheet with the numbers in his left

hand, he frowns, thinking about the problems created by order, and by the stubbornness of the Spidlarians. Order and Spidlar—what is the connection? He looks at the mirror on the table, concentrating on the two.

The mists part for an instant, and the image of a red-headed man with a hammer and tongs in his hands appears. Jeslek does not recognize him.

The sound of a gentle rap on the door reaches him. At the sound, he straightens, letting the image vanish. Then he slips the paper into the leather folder, which he slides into the corner of the bookcase. He is careful not to touch any of the volumes, since each usage of a book shortens its life.

He opens the door, smiling at the scent of trilia that accompanies Anya. "Good evening, dear lady."

"Good evening, High Wizard." Anya's lips brush his cheek.

He closes the door behind her, but does not lock it.

"You didn't lock it." She smiles.

"Why?" Jeslek smiles, turning away from the door and toward her. "Locks scarcely stop screening, or anyone powerful enough to enter. Unlike Sterol, I am a realist." He laughs softly. "So are you. Or you would not be here."

"Oh?"

He stands by the table and pours wine into one glass and then the other, before lifting the first and extending it to her. "You are more powerful than even Sterol. But you know it is unlikely the Council will ever select a woman as High Wizard." He inclines his head.

"Yet you obviously enjoy putting yourself in a compromising position." Anya takes the glass, and her eyes flicker to the wide couch beyond the table. Then she smiles.

"Dear Anya, no one can touch either of us . . . and

not even you and Sterol are strong enough to take me on." He lifts his glass. "To you, dear lady."

Anya lifts her glass. "To the High Wizard."

They drink, each with eyes and senses on the other.

LXIII

A LOW WHINING moan shivers through the smithy building. Dorrin's breath is white in the dim light.

"Wonderful for practicing order control . . ." he mutters. While he is comfortable in the chill, even with the waist-high snow that clogs the smithy yard, even with the long icicles that hang like daggers from the eaves, he still wishes the winter in Diev were not quite so cold.

He looks again at the numbers, his fingers going toward the quill. Instead, he sets the figures aside in the covered box and pulls out the other box, the one with his scribblings in it, the one with the semi-pretentious title on the front—*Thoughts on the Basis of Order*. He glances over the last page.

> . . . a staff, or any other object, may be infused with order. Concentrating such order, if the Balance is maintained, must result in a greater amount of chaos somewhere. Therefore, the greater the effort to concentrate order within material objects, the greater the amount of free chaos within the world.

The logic is sound, but are his presumptions? He rubs his forehead. He has nothing really to add to his presumptuous commentary this night. He closes the second box.

His hands turn down the wick of the lamp slightly, and he carries it to the bracket by his bed. As usual, things are working, but not exactly as he has planned. Assuming he can even build the steam-fired engine, and that remains a question, how can he ever afford the material? Of the sixteen golds he has gathered from the reward from the Council and the sale of the two intricate models, he has a little over twelve left.

Still . . . that does include the iron that he has bought and the lorkin left from the staff and the other wood that is his. But the iron and copper alone for his engine will run nearly twenty golds. The fittings and pumps—he shakes his head. And the first engine, if experience is any guide, will not work well, if at all.

He needs more coin—more than he will receive from either Rylla or Yarrl. What can he do? Toys? He sits on the edge of the pallet bed and pulls off his boots. What kind of toys? Can he do something different from what Quiller has done? Will Willum buy somewhat less elaborate toys?

He swings his feet onto the pallet and draws the quilt around him. Then he takes out the letter and begins to reread the words on the off-white page.

Dorrin—

I had thought to swing back through Rytel and down through the road we had taken to Axalt, but the White guards have blocked the way. They claim that Axalt owes Fairhaven trade duties. This letter, if it reaches you, will have come through friends in Fenard, since apparently only the main routes are safe for one reason or another, and I cannot afford the duties to trade on the wizards' roads.

Some goods are getting harder and harder to find at any price. Spices are in short supply, as are dried or preserved fruits. If I could obtain it, green brandy from Recluce would fetch two golds a bottle. And so would a cubit-span of wound black wool yarn.

Freidr has urged me to stay close to Jellico, but how can a trader make coins if one doesn't travel? When I do get to Diev, it will probably be by coaster to Spidlaria or Diev directly, and that means it cannot be until spring when the ice has cleared the Northern Ocean.

Most kinds of cloth are now dearer, because of the need for canvas for the additional ships Fairhaven is building. Some of that is mere speculation, I would guess. That doesn't make the cloth any cheaper.

I would hope that you might consider making some more models for sale. I could have sold several at that price. I also have more questions for you when next we meet, whenever that may be. I wish you well and trust that you are accomplishing what you find necessary.

Liedral

After his eyes have digested the words yet another time, he folds the sheet and slips it into the back of *The Healer*. Then he blows out the lamp and draws the quilt around him more tightly.

Outside the wind moans and throws the snow against the wall with such force that a dusting of flakes lies under the door sill and swirls gently across the plank floor.

LXIV

ANYA OPENS THE lower tower door without knocking, enters, and closes it silently. She slides the bolt. The room is lit by an oil wall lamp and one on the side table by the closed window. The winter wind rattles the casement.

Sterol stands up from the screeing table, letting the white mists cloud the mirror. His eyes are dark. "How are you?"

"It's a strain, dealing with the great lover and chaos master."

"You don't have to, you know."

"That's easy for you to say. You know what the history of the Whites is for women?"

"Tell me anyway."

"Don't patronize me, Sterol. Every one of you is out to lay me, and to prove that, in wizardly matters, I'm no match for any man."

"You're better than most."

"And who will admit it?" Anya slumps into the chair across from the former High Wizard. "Do you have any wine left?"

"Certainly . . . certainly."

"Darkness! I told you to cut the patronizing act."

"My! Aren't we testy tonight."

"If you want me to tell Jeslek you're up to no good, you're certainly headed in the right direction."

Sterol retrieves a glass goblet from the top of the bookcase, gently blows it clean of the fine white powder that none of the Whites' buildings—even the newest—seems to be without, and pours the rest of the red into the goblet. "This is what's left. You're welcome to it." He extends the goblet.

"Thank you." She sips the wine. "He's not a very good lover."

"I wouldn't have guessed. All force and no technique—like his magic?" Sterol seats himself across the table from her, the mirror between them.

"There is a similarity. His magic has more finesse."

Sterol swallows silently before speaking. "What does he plan next?"

"He intends to subdue Spidlar, but as he has discussed, gradually. He hid something just before he answered the door, and the energy was still in his glass, and it had the faintest trace of Black to it."

"Jeslek? Calling on Black energies?"

Anya frowns, then takes another sip of wine. "This is turning already."

"I apologize. It was only brought in tonight. What about the Black energies?"

"It was more like he was studying something Black, but it wasn't that ponderous feeling you get when you study Recluce."

"That's an interesting way you have of describing it. You and Recluce?"

"Just because I'm a woman doesn't mean I haven't studied Recluce."

"So . . . he's found something or someone else that's focusing order. Hmmmm . . . I'd watch that closely."

"I intend to." Anya drains the goblet. "Do you have another bottle?"

"Actually . . . yes. I thought you might like some."

"You are thoughtful, Sterol." The redhead smiles at the former High Wizard before he rises to get the second bottle from the ice bucket.

LXV

DORRIN PULLS OUT the sheet Jarnish had delivered just before supper and slits the seal. Then he pauses. Had Jarnish come all the way to Diev just for this? Had the seal already been broken and resealed? He lets his perceptions study the hardened wax. Then he shrugs. After the vigor with which he has applied his knife to the seal, there is really no way to tell. Besides, what difference does it make whether some factor reads a letter?

Dorrin smoothes out the sheet and begins to read, pausing as he realizes that Liedral had apparently not received his letter when she wrote.

Dorrin—

I was going to travel through Passera and down river to Elparta. That is no longer possible. The road guards now will protect only those traders licensed by Fairhaven. They say that there have been more and more highway attacks and robberies. Even the licensed traders are afraid to take the roads in and out of Spidlar, although some will.

The worst of the famine in Kyphros and Gallos has abated, they say. That is because all those who were starving have died. Most of the herders are gone, and their flocks with them.

The winter snows continue to melt off the new mountains—the Little Easthorns, some call them—that now separate Gallos and Kyphros. Another trader—Dosric—told me taking the wizards' road is a frightening experience. Snow melts off the hot rocks. That makes a constant fog that you can hardly see through, and nothing grows there yet.

Trade is slow here, and everywhere, but that is true enough in winter even in good years. I hope to see you, somehow, before too long.

Liedral

Dorrin rereads the letter before refolding it and slipping it into the box in which he has her other letter. Then he retrieves the sheet that has his toy plans on it, and stands up, pushing the chair back. His breath steams in the cold room, but the cold does not bother him much anymore, at least not while he is awake. The quilt and blanket are enough for sleeping.

He takes a deep breath. The day has been long already, but he is far from finished. He ducks into the light snow outside, closing the door behind him, and follows the packed path around the smithy alongside the chest-high snow piles beside the building.

Once by the forge, Dorrin lights the single lamp with a pine splinter touched to the forge coals. After setting the charcoal he had brought in before supper around the coals, he pumps the bellows rod until the charcoal catches and the coals reach forging heat.

Dorrin looks at the sheet he has brought, then sets it on the back of his workbench, reaching up and adjusting the lamp. He pumps the bellows rod once.

"Dorrin? Need some help?" Vaos stands by the slack tank.

"I'd appreciate it, but . . . this is my work, not for any paying customer. At least not yet."

"Doesn't matter. It's cold. Petra gave me another old blanket, but it's still warmer when you have the forge going. I'm not tired." Vaos yawns. "Not too tired, anyway."

"It's been a cold winter."

"Coldest I can remember." The youngster steps up the bellows lever. "What are you doing?"

"Trying to see if I can make some toys."

Vaos pauses. "I never had any toys."

"What kind would you have liked to have?"

"I don't know." The blond boy shrugs, and the blanket slips away from his shoulders. He catches it and wraps it back in place. "I never saw any up close, just in Willum's window. I tried to use a leather knife once to make a top, but it didn't work real well. Forra beat me 'cause I dulled the knife."

"Oh . . ."

"How hot do you want the charcoal, Dorrin?"

Dorrin studies the glowing carbon, both with eyes and his senses that go beyond sight. "Slow down on the bellows—about half as fast."

"What are you going to make?"

"A small windmill with a crank to make the blades go, I think."

"Wouldn't it be easier to carve it?"

"Yes. But it's more interesting out of iron, and I can use the template to stamp out the gears."

"Could you do that with real gears?"

"Hardly. You have to cut them. They use special machines for the pump gears." He takes the other half of the template, black iron, and sets it where he can reach it quickly. "They have to fit together just right."

Dorrin takes the tongs and lifts one of the smaller rods from his own rack and eases it into the forge. "Here, for a toy, I don't have to be quite as exact, but I need to make sure the two gears mesh just right."

Vaos continues pumping. "This about right?"

Dorrin nods again, watching as the metal heats. When it is cherry red, he brings it back to the anvil and begins to fuller it into a smaller octagonal cross-section. He returns it to the forge as necessary during the fullering. When the cross-section matches the template, he sets the circular die—almost like a round-bottom swage with a square base—into the anvil's hardie hole, and places the metal in the forge once more.

Next, using glancing blows on the end of the fullered rod, he begins to upset the end that will fit into the swage die. Another reheating, and two solid blows to the unfullered end, and the small gear wheel is forged. A last blow with the hot set to cut the forged piece clean and he sets the wheel on the forge bricks to cool.

"You doing another one?" asks Vaos.

"Probably three tonight. That's half. I'll do two more like that, and then three of the end with the crank."

"That's a lot of work for toys."

"That's just the beginning. I'll have to grind the edges, file them smooth, and polish them before fitting them to the wood." Dorrin retrieves the rod stock from the forge. "A little slower on the bellows."

Vaos wipes his forehead. "Least it's warm here."

LXVI

WHEN THE COLD air strikes Meriwhen like a whip, the mare whickers and sidesteps. Zilda backs away from the cold air, looking up at Dorrin.

"I don't think you want to be out here," Dorrin says. The goat chews on a mouthful of straw.

"Easy . . . easy." Dorrin pats Meriwhen's neck, then closes the barn door. The breath from his words drifts away in a white line. He eases up into the saddle, a saddle hard from the cold even inside the barn, and turns the mare eastward, out toward Rylla's cottage.

His hands touch the staff. While he will not need it at the healer's, he may need it on the way to see Willum.

The strong plume of white from the chimney indicates that the healer has been up for a time, and the two sets of fresh footprints in the dusting of snow that covers the packed snow path to her door show that she has visitors.

Dorrin looks for a more sheltered place to tie Meriwhen before he finally leads the mare up to the south side of the cottage, where he ties the reins to an elder bush trunk. He leaves the staff in the holder—it will be more than safe there.

After stamping his boots mostly free of snow, he knocks and steps inside, closing the door quickly. "Rylla, it's Dorrin." He takes the small broom off the stand and brushes his boots clean, then opens his jacket and takes it off, so warm is the cottage.

"'Fraid I'd have to wait all morning for you, young fellow.'"

In the room before the fire are a woman and a child. The girl—although the mother looks barely beyond childhood herself—cradles her left arm with her right, and her face is tight and pinched. She wears a cutdown herder's vest, so worn that the sheep's wool is brown and the leather is lined and grimy.

"Little Frisa, here, got her arm caught in a stall door." Rylla's voice is almost flat.

"Gerhalm didn't see her in time. He really didn't," explains the mother. Her voice cracks. She wears only a worn and patched wool cloak that may have once been blue.

Dorrin can see the redness in the mother's eyes, and a different kind of pain than that of the daughter. He takes a step toward Frisa, but the little girl shrinks back against her mother's stained brown trousers. Dorrin stops, looking around until he sees that Rylla has moved the stool into the far corner, almost touching the small three-shelf bookcase that bears no more than a dozen volumes at most.

"Frisa needs her arm looked at. She's a mite skittish," Rylla adds in the same too-calm voice.

The little girl's dark eyes flicker from the older woman to Dorrin and back to the floor in front of the hearth.

After picking up the stool, Dorrin seats himself and looks at Frisa. "I don't know much about girls," he begins slowly, not looking directly at the child, even while he tries to extend a sense of reassurance to her. "I do have a mare. I suppose you'd call her a girl horse. Her name is Meriwhen."

"Silly name for a mare." Rylla's voice is gruff.

"Well, she said her name was Meriwhen. What could I say?" Dorrin shrugs, then puts his hands on his knees. "Is your name Kitten-in-the-Snow?"

Frisa continues to look at the plank floor in front of the hearth.

"Or is it Filly-Who-Runs-Too-Fast?"

Dorrin lets the silence draw out before speaking again. "I suppose Meriwhen was a filly once. She told me that she hurried too much when she was little, but I didn't know her then."

"Horses ... don't ... talk."

"Meriwhen does. When we ride a long ways, she has a lot to say. Sometimes she talks about the grass, and sometimes she complains about the horseflies, and sometimes ..." He pauses. "She's a big girl, but you'll be a big girl someday, too." Dorrin swallows at the knife of fear that strikes from the mother, forcing a smile instead, trying to reassure the child. "Meriwhen can be silly. When we're out in the meadows, sometimes she wants me to take off her saddle, and she wants to roll in the grass. She likes the smell of green grass."

"You're ... silly."

"That's what my mother said to me a long time ago. I guess I never did grow up."

Frisa looks shyly at Dorrin, but remains with her back pressed against her mother's legs.

Dorrin looks into the fire, trying to build more reassurance into the frightened girl. "Maybe that's why Meriwhen and I get along. After we look at your arm, would you like to meet Meriwhen?"

"You really have a horse?" asks the mother.

"He's not exactly an impoverished healer apprentice, Merga," Rylla says.

Dorrin grins. "Meriwhen is quite real. I did tie her to the bushes next to the house—the elders, not the peppers."

"She'd better not eat them," Rylla says.

"I fed her before we left."

"Can I pat her?" asks Frisa.

"After we fix your arm," Dorrin responds.

"It hurts."

"I know. Where does it hurt most?"

"It just hurts."

Without standing, Dorrin eases off the stool and into a sitting position before the mother and the girl. "Can I see?"

Frisa remains against her mother, but does not shrink away as Dorrin's fingers brush the arm.

"Needs a splint, I'd bet," Rylla offers.

Dorrin, sensing the break, nods. He can also feel the hunger. "Do you have a slice of bread? If she could chew that . . ."

"She might choke."

He looks at Frisa. "We want to fix the hurt. It might hurt more for a moment, but it will get better. When we finish you can have some bread."

"Can I hold it now?"

"Just an instant, child."

Rylla appears with the splint—a contraption made

of canvas and oak ribs. Her eyes question Dorrin. He nods.

"Help keep her still, Merga. Can you do that?" asks Rylla.

Merga nods.

"Oooooo . . ." Frisa moans, and tries to twist, but Rylla holds her fast as Dorrin, guided by his senses, lines up the ends of the bones, infusing the girl with order and reassurance as he does. "Ooo . . ." Her fingers crush the scrap of bread.

Rylla tightens the splint straps while Dorrin keeps the arm straight.

Dorrin touches Frisa's forehead lightly. "It's done, Frisa. If you don't run into anything, it should heal straight."

Merga looks to Rylla, then to Dorrin.

"Four to five eight-days, I'd guess," he says slowly.

"Can I see your horse?"

"I'll tell Merga what to do," Rylla says. "You show her your horse."

"Can I have some more bread?" asks the child.

"I'll get it," Dorrin says quickly, heading for the kitchen and the breadboard, and ignoring Rylla's quickly smothered frown.

Frisa grabs for the bread with her free hand when Dorrin comes back, and he scoops her up, deftly, but gently, careful not to touch the splinted arm.

"Bring her back here in two eight-days for me to look at the arm. Don't let anything hit it . . ." Rylla speaks slowly to the young mother as Dorrin opens and closes the cottage door.

"Here you are." Dorrin stops short of Meriwhen. The mare has nibbled on a small elder bush, but halted after a sampling. The healer grins. Elder bushes are bitter, very bitter. "This is Meriwhen."

Whuuuffff . . . the mare responds.

"She's . . . pretty." Frisa's breath forms a cloud around her head.

The morning air is still now, and the snow sparkles in the light, so brightly that Dorrin must squint, a cruel brightness that reminds him, absently, of Fairhaven.

Meriwhen suffers her forehead to be touched by Frisa's unhurt arm. Frisa shivers, and Dorrin turns. "We need to go."

"'Bye, horsey."

Inside, Dorrin closes the door and sets Frisa on the floor.

"He has a horsey, a black horsey."

Merga bows to Dorrin. "Thank you, great one." Tears streak from her eyes, as she takes her daughter's hand. "We must go."

Dorrin glances at Rylla, but the healer's wrinkled face is calm. He opens the door and watches as they walk across the packed snow and ice.

"Close the door, Dorrin. No sense in wasting the fire."

"What did you tell her?"

"I told her the truth. You're a great healer. A young one, but a great one."

"Darkness, I'm barely a decent smith, and not even that as a healer."

"Look, boy. You got enough order in your bones to shiver a White Wizard all the way to the tips of the Northern Ocean. I saw what you did for that girl."

"She didn't get caught in a stall door. Her father beat them both. I really want to—"

"You can't go settling people's lives for them."

"I know. I did what I could. It won't be enough."

"It will be for a little while. And in healing you do what you can. Just knowing order isn't all there is to healing." The clear blue eyes that seem oddly young in the wrinkled face survey Dorrin from head to foot. "Does just a strong arm make a good smith?"

"No."

"Does growing herbs tell you how to use them? 'Course not! You're like all the other Blacks." Rylla pauses and adds, "Maybe not as bad. Leastwise, you listen. Take a broken bone, like Frisa has. Bone's stronger when it grows at its own pace, and the bones have to be put back where they fit together. How do you keep them together?"

"You splint them, and add a touch of order."

"I can do the first, but only a Black healer can do the rest."

A knock on the door interrupts them.

"Who be there?" rasps Rylla.

"Werta . . . I still got this wart."

Rylla grins at Dorrin. "Come on in and close the door behind you."

Dorrin grins back. Warts, yet.

LXVII

THE STILLNESS HAS given way to a light wind, and the near-noon sun lights a bright blue-green sky. Dorrin unties Meriwhen from the elder bushes, swings into the saddle, checks his staff to ensure it is secure in the lanceholder, and urges Meriwhen toward Diev. In the left saddle-bag are three sample toys—a small wagon, a windmill with a hand crank, and a miniature sawmill. There are two complete sets in the other bag.

Meriwhen's feet are sure upon the road now that the rollers have pressed it into a hard surface. They pass a freight sleigh stacked with barrels, whose driver cracks his whip as his two horses struggle in toward Diev.

On the town side of the Weyel river bridge, the

rolled and packed snow gives way to an uneven jumble of packed snow, ice, and partly uncovered paving stones. Dorrin lets Meriwhen set her own pace, and he loosens the top button of his jacket, conscious that he is making some progress in learning how to let his body deal with a cold that never reaches Recluce.

All four chimneys at the Tankard are billowing white smoke, and a small stable boy is wrestling to unload a bale of hay from the farm sleigh. The beggar woman is nowhere in evidence.

The space before the chandlery is empty, but smoke also rises from Willum's chimney. Dorrin ties Meriwhen, pats her neck, and swings the saddlebags over his shoulder before taking his staff from the holder. Then he climbs the steps and opens the door to the chandler's. The warmth billowing from the cast-iron stove in the center of the store is momentarily welcome, and he is careful to close the oak door behind him.

The thin clerk behind the counter along the right wall looks through Dorrin. "Your business?"

"I'm Dorrin." He lifts the saddlebags. "I have some goods that ser Willum might be interested in."

"In late winter? Ha! Be on your way, fellow." The clerk sets something on the shelf before him. "Selling to a chandler?"

Dorrin turns to face the clerk head-on, and his eyes blaze. His voice is quiet, and his words seem to fill the store. "I am here to see Willum, and I do believe he will see me."

His face white, the clerk steps back. "I'll see . . . ser."

Dorrin frowns as the other scuttles toward the back room. Why are people so difficult? And why does insisting on simple things make them so afraid? If Willum does not want to buy the toys, he certainly doesn't have to.

The blond chandler/trader steps out into the store from behind a dark green velvet curtain. The counter does not quite conceal the heavy club he holds, a stained oak length only slightly lighter than his brown trousers and dark leather vest. "You—" Then he sees the brown shirt under the jacket and the dark staff. "You're the smith who's the toymaker, aren't you?"

"Yes, ser. I thought you might like to see some new ones."

"It's all right, Roald." Willum looks at the clerk emerging from the back room. "Sorry, fellow—is it Dortmund?"

"Dorrin."

"Dorrin. We've had some smash and grabs lately. Times are hard." He smiles politely. "Your curiosity was well received in Fenard. But"—he shrugs—"I doubt many have golds to spare now."

"So would I." Dorrin sets the leather saddlebags on the counter and opens the left one. "These are a bit simpler."

Willum looks at the three toys, finally picking up the windmill and cranking it. "Well made. I have to say that. But times are hard."

"I understand. That also means you must have trouble finding unique items to trade."

Willum grins. "You should have been a trader, young Dorrin. You haggle with the best."

"You flatter me, master chandler."

"Hardly. You seem to have some idea of their value. And what are you asking—not that I can pay much, you understand?"

"I thought you might get a half-silver, perhaps six pennies, for each of these."

"Six is stretching. I could offer a silver for all three."

Dorrin frowns. "A silver plus two, would be more like it."

"It's not worth my time to take just three."

"If I made two more sets . . . then how about three and a half silvers?"

"That would be fine, but"—Willum shrugs again—"could you have them by tomorrow? Otherwise, I could offer but a silver plus one."

Dorrin smiles, and the chandler shakes his head.

"Don't tell me you have them?"

Dorrin offers a wry smile. "I had hoped . . ." He opens the other bag and produces the other six.

Willum inspects all six, minutely. "You do good work, fellow." He coughs. "Roald—three and a half, please."

"Yes, ser." The clerk eases behind Willum's bulk and into the back room, without so much as looking at Dorrin.

The chandler purses his lips, then asks. "I might also be interested in another curiosity . . . say by early spring?"

"That might be possible." Dorrin's thoughts burn, since he has two older models for which he has no use. "Very probable, in fact." His headache subsides, but not completely. He needs someone else to do the haggling, or he will have headaches severe enough that he will not be able to think straight.

Roald reappears with the coins, which he passes to Willum. In turn, the trader puts them upon the counter. He still holds the club in his right hand, although his grip is relaxed. "There are your silvers, Dorrin."

"I thank you, master chandler. Later, might you be interested in other such toys?"

"I might, but I know where to find you, should I need them quickly. If not, see me in perhaps three or four eight-days." The chandler/trader looks toward the door, where a tall thin man enters. "Good day, Nallar."

"Terrible day, Willum. Terrible day. Need to talk about lamps."

Dorrin scoops up the coins and slips them into his purse. Then he nods, "Good day, ser Willum."

Willum nods, but says nothing as he steps along the counter to meet Nallar. Roald looks away from Dorrin's glance. Dorrin puts the empty saddlebags over his shoulder and steps around the heat of the stove, heading back out into the cold.

Outside, he pauses. Now that he is truly selling toys, should he follow Quiller's advice and join the Guild? With a sigh, he turns Meriwhen toward the harbor.

The harbor has but three piers, and the Port Council building is at the foot of the center pier of the three, a gray wooden structure two stories high. Next to the Port Council building is the smaller, shedlike building that holds the Guild. After tying Meriwhen at the far end of the rail that also holds a larger bay, Dorrin edges through the slushy snow to the building. No matter how hard the snow is packed in upper Diev, near the shore it is slushier, even when the sea is choked with ice floes. Sometimes, a brave coaster will run the ice, but it is a run for only the most experienced.

Dorrin opens the pine door, stamping his feet to remove the snow and slush, and looking around in the dim lamplight that contrasts with the cold brightness outside. Because he does not know what to expect, he carries his black staff.

"Who ye be looking for, young fellow?" A gray-haired man stands up from shoveling coal into the stove.

"I don't know. Quiller told me I should come here."

"Quiller—the crazy toymaker? Why would he do that?" The gray-haired man closes the stove and walks toward Dorrin. He wears a heavy blue sweater that matches heavy blue trousers.

"He said that if I made things, I should join the Guild."

"And who are you?"

"My name is Dorrin; I'm a striker for Yarrl."

"Yarrl never joined the Guild. You need a sponsor." The gray-haired man sighs. "Why do you think you need to join?"

"Well . . . I'm making toys and selling them."

"To whom?" The man's voice is sharper.

"So far, just to Willum, the chandler."

"Oh . . . that's all right. He belongs. Still . . ." The man frowns. "I suppose that *could* qualify as a form of sponsorship, and it's clear you're trying to do the right thing. Toys . . . probably an artisan, lower grade, I'd guess. That won't break you, young fellow. It's four coppers a year—until you sell more than ten golds. Then it's a silver for the next year."

"Is there something on parchment I sign, ser?"

"No sers, here. I'm Hasten. You can sign your name?"

"Yes. I write a little also."

"Odd . . . never thought Yarrl was the type."

"Does it matter if I'm also an apprentice healer?"

"Oh . . . dear . . . you're that one. I should have guessed from the staff. No, it certainly doesn't matter, ser. Not at all. Just a moment . . . if you do have the coppers?"

Dorrin counts out four coppers and extends them.

"Just a moment . . ." The older man fumbles across the desk with a quill and a square of parchment. "Free artisan . . . one Dorrin. Do you know how to spell that? Silly, of course you do, but would you spell it for me?"

"D-O-R-R-I-N." Dorrin tries not to frown as he still holds the coins, but the fear emanating from the trader is almost palpable.

"Here you are." Hasten hands Dorrin a parchment square. "That be your receipt of dues in good standing."

Dorrin hands him the four coppers. "Thank you, Hasten. I just wanted to do things right."

"I wish all ... all folks would. You have a good day."

Dorrin realizes he has been dismissed. "You too." He turns, opens the door, and shuts it behind him, trying not to shake his head. What has he done to make the older man so afraid? Could it have been the incident with Niso? Surely, people have killed thieves before?

Meriwhen whickers, and Dorrin shakes his head, almost to clear his thoughts. The mare does not like the chill breeze off the water. He resets the staff in the holder and remounts. Once back at Yarrl's, he will have to brush Meriwhen and get the snow and ice out of her coat, especially along her legs. Then he will have to work late to catch up on the wagon work stacked along the smithy walls.

Does he ever work less than late—one way or another?

LXVIII

A SMALL FIRE burns in the ancient and blackened hearth, warming slightly the half-circle of bedrolls in the way station. A guard sits upright by the half-shuttered single window, eyes flicking downhill and across the starlit snow and the dark line that is a stone wall beside the highway. A bow stands beside him, although it is not strung.

"Crappy, frigging duty ... hate that bastard Mortyl ... out here trying to stop farm raids ... chasing spirits ... finding burned-out huts and barns ...

freezing our asses..." The words come from the bedroll nearest the fire.

"Shut up, Vorban. You want to freeze your frigging tongue, you do it quiet."

"You couples got each other. You flaunt it, Sestal. All I got is this bitch winter, and she's frigging cold."

"Shut up." Sestal grins in the darkness at the lady blade he holds under their shared blankets.

In the far corner Brede and Kadara lie side by side. Kadara's lips are almost touching Brede's left ear. "... will we ever get home? So tired of the ice and snow."

"... don't like the cold much, either," adds the sentry, "but why complain? Doesn't help."

"I never saw so many starving people, or so many mean ones." Kadara wriggles closer to him.

"It has something to do with the White Wizards."

"Damn them. I want to go home. Lortren said a year."

"She said at least a year, but unless you want to cross the Westhorns in winter and walk to Sarronnyn or Suthya..."

"We can't take the wizards' roads. I know, but it doesn't make me any happier. I feel sometimes like I'll die here. Yes, we can return after a year, if we could find a ship. Lortren and her lies!" Kadara's voice hisses. "It's fine for Dorrin and his damned machines. He has food and a warm bed."

"It looked pretty cold and empty to me. There's not even a fireplace in his room. And he doesn't have you." Brede squeezes her shoulder.

A loud cough fills the room.

"Stop all the sweet talk. I want to sleep."

"You're just jealous, Vorban," Brede calls softly.

"Demon-damned right. I'm frigging jealous, and even more frigging cold."

"Just go to sleep, Vorban. Or take my place, and let me go to sleep," snaps the sentry.

The way station settles back into low mumbles and an occasional snore.

"Just hold me." Kadara shakes as she whispers the words to Brede, and his arms go around her. "Just hold me."

Outside, the wind brushes feather-light snow across the road and walls, and the distant screech of a snow-hawk echoes under the distant unwinking stars. The sentry shifts his weight on the bench.

LXIX

"DORRIN?" REISA STANDS by the small slack tank, next to the smaller grindstone.

Vaos continues pumping the bellows, and Dorrin holds the sledge, waiting as Yarrl turns the iron in the forge.

"Your trader friend's here to see you. It must be important." Reisa grins briefly.

Dorrin cannot keep the flush from running up his face. "It'll have to wait until we finish these pieces."

"Demon-dark right," grunts Yarrl.

"She'll be in the kitchen. It's too cold to wait outside."

Yarrl watches the iron until it reaches cherry red, then deftly turns it onto the bottom swage set in the anvil's hardie hole. He brings the top swage into place. Dorrin begins striking with the sledge. Despite the chill that lurks around the edge of the smithy, he is sweating heavily even before Yarrl returns the iron to the forge. When the iron is again ready, they resume.

How much later it is when the wagon crane frame is finished, Dorrin does not know, only that his threadbare shirt is soaked, and Vaos has stopped pumping and scurried out for another basket of charcoal.

"Light-fired awkward thing." Yarrl has set his tongs aside. The crane frame lies tempered and cooling on the forge bricks. "Makes cart loading easier, Honsard says." He coughs. "Go talk to your friend. Only need Vaos for the bolts. You can grind the edges and file it later—or tomorrow."

"Appreciate it." After wiping his face with the back of his forearm, Dorrin steps out into the cold, cloudy afternoon, his sweat almost freezing as he crosses the gap in the snow piles and takes the steps to the porch and kitchen. He cleans his boots before entering.

The large room is warmer than the smithy, since it has no drafts and since Reisa has been baking.

"Use the wash stand first," Reisa orders dryly. "I won't make you use the well."

"Thank you, mistress of the house."

"Don't forget it."

Liedral grins as Dorrin steps into the corner where the wash stand sits in the winter months. After finishing, he looks at the dark water, shaking his head. Then he walks to the door and down to the well. After breaking the ice with the heavy iron chunk on the rope, he fills two buckets and sets them on the bottom step while he ducks into his room and changes from his ragged smithy shirt into one more presentable. Then he carries the buckets up the steps into the kitchen with the empty basin.

"I think you did that to get more water," he says with a smile.

Reisa gestures to the table. "Sit down and have a slice of fresh bread. I opened some preserves. Darkness knows whether what we have will last until the trees fruit. Sure won't get much from the harbor markets." Reisa pours one bucket full of icy water into the big water kettle on the stove.

Dorrin sits across from Liedral. "How did you get here? I thought you said you'd ..ave to come by sea."

Liedral grins, but the expression only emphasizes the blackness under her eyes and her reddened face. "It took some doing. There's a coastal sled run between Quend and Spidlaria. They run the beaches. They say it's safer than running the ice floes. I brought in dried pork and a few other things."

"She brought supper—a good ham." Reisa does not turn from the ceramic and iron stove. "They're dear, now."

"Be getting dearer." Petra fastens her jacket before heading to the barn.

"Why . . . ?" Dorrin stops. Of course, with the Northern Ocean frozen north and west of Diev, Spidlar is cut off from the western trading routes. Few traders will dare the icebergs that dot the ocean between Spidlar and Sligo. He shivers, considering the pinched faces he is already seeing. It will be another season before even the early crops are ready or the coasters from Sarronnyn or Suthya will travel the Northern Ocean.

"Thought it might make more coins. You trade where people need it. Besides, I don't like staying around Freidr for too long." Liedral sips the hot spiced cider. "And even if I go back empty, I'll still be ahead. Not much, but something's better than nothing, especially in winter."

"It seems a mite risky," offers Reisa.

"All trading is risky these days, thanks to Fairhaven. You risk losing your coins or your life." Liedral takes another swallow of the cider.

Petra sets a mug in front of Dorrin. "This time I got it for you. But just this time."

"Thank you. Next time you can get the water."

"He's impossible," Petra confides to Liedral.

"He's a man," answers the trader.

Vaos hammers his way through the door and into the kitchen.

"Don't touch anything," snaps Reisa, lifting the kettle with her single hand and pouring warm water into the empty washbasin. "You need to wash up before you eat."

Petra adds some of the cold water from the bucket.

"But, Reisa, I'm starving."

"Wash."

Vaos looks at Dorrin, then steps up to the wash table.

"When's dinner?" asks Yarrl, shutting the door hard, and bending to set his boots in the corner.

"As soon as you wash up," Reisa repeats.

Vaos grins as he hurriedly wipes his hands and face on the gray towel.

"Sometimes . . . think you were a washerwoman by the river . . ." But the smith follows Reisa's instructions. "Smells good."

"The trader brought a ham."

"A real ham out of Kleth, smoked the slow way," adds Petra.

"Ought to taste real good." Yarrl washes hurriedly and sits at the table. Reisa hands him a knife, and he begins to slice the meat.

Vaos licks his lips, and Dorrin and Liedral look from the boy to each other and smile.

Reisa sets two platters on the table, one with a steaming pile of vegetables, and one heaped with roasted yams. "Help yourself."

Liedral spears two yams and takes a spoonful of beans. "Thank you."

"What's happening with the White Wizards?" asks the smith as he lays slab after slab of ham on the chipped platter.

"They're trying to cut Spidlar off without saying

that's what they're doing. They're talking about building more ships."

"Let's enjoy the ham," Reisa suggests.

Vaos's eyes remain fixed on the platter as it goes to the trader, then to Dorrin, and Petra.

"Here you go!" Petra holds the platter in front of Vaos.

"Thank you, Miss Petra," says the boy as he takes the two top slices, but his eyes linger on the platter.

"Take another, imp."

Vaos docs, and for a timc, no onc speaks.

"Good ham," Vaos says.

"Very good," Dorrin agrees.

"Personally," Liedral says with a smile, "I liked the roasted yams, and the beans. You don't get those traveling."

When Dorrin finishes his plate, he swallows the last of his cider and turns to Liedral. "Do you want to talk? I need to finish up some things in the smithy." Dorrin stands.

"With all that hammering?" asks Liedral.

"It's just filing and polishing."

"He never stops," Reisa says dryly.

"No one's ever seen him stop, anyway," adds Petra.

"Not even me," adds Vaos from the end of the table.

"Quiet, boy." Dorrin's voice is playful.

Yarrl chews the end of the loaf of bread, methodically, before speaking, his mouth full. "That's what makes a good smith. Not yammering on and on."

All three women look at the smith. Yarrl continues to chew.

Dorrin grins, standing by the door.

"Let me get on my jacket. I wasn't raised on a mountaintop."

Dorrin does not protest that Recluce is milder than even Jellico; he waits while Liedral pulls on her coat. They walk to the smithy, where he lights the lamp.

Then he takes off his shirt and puts it on a wall peg before returning to the workbench and lifting the box with the iron toy parts in it.

"Aren't you cold?"

"Not really."

He sets the box on the clay, sits on the stool, and begins pushing the foot pedal, dipping the iron piece in the polishing paste before setting it against the grindstone.

"Oooooo . . . how can you stand that?"

"I suppose you get used to it." He turns the miniature gear/power train and continues to grind and polish the dark metal.

Liedral watches as he works the metal.

When he is done, he replaces the metal parts in the box and wipes his hands on the tattered towel at one end of his bench.

"Do you have any toys that are done?" Liedral's brown eyes meet Dorrin's, then look over his shoulder at the forge as he pulls on his shirt.

"Not as simple as those. I have some like the first one. They're in my room. Would you like one?" He snuffs the lamp and steps toward the yard, waiting for her to leave the smithy before he closes the door against the winter chill.

"I can't afford one, not the way things are going, but once the ice breaks, I'm taking a wild run to Nietre, upland hills of Suthya. It's far enough from Rulyarth that most traders don't bother. Lousy roads, not wide enough even for the cart. That's fine, because it's cheaper just to take two horses on the coasters."

"Things are really bad?" He stops by the well and draws some water, pouring it over his hands, ignoring the chill.

Liedral shivers. "Isn't that cold?"

"Yes, even for me." He walks toward his room, and Liedral follows. Once inside, he dries his cold hands on his working towel. Liedral sits on the bed and shivers. He lifts the quilt and wraps it around her.

"Your hands are warm already."

"I've learned a few things already from being a healer." He settles into the hard chair that has replaced the stool.

"Your room is cold." Liedral wraps the faded quilt around her more tightly. "You must be related to mountain cats, or something else that prowls in the cold. And yes, things are bad. You don't even write me back."

"I've sent you a letter."

"How?"

"Like you told me. Through Jarnish."

"You really did?" Liedral squirms on the hard pallet.

"I did. I'll admit I only sent it an eight-day ago, but I did get around to writing you. I didn't expect to see you this soon."

"You didn't?"

"Not from your letters. You were talking spring."

"I didn't know about the beach runners."

"Neither did I." He shifts his weight, then gets up. "What about another model?"

"I can't pay you . . ."

"We can do it the same way you did last time. This one's different."

"That's probably better, if it's as good."

"You judge." Dorrin returns with an object almost a cubit long.

"What is it?"

"A boat. You wind this, and these bands tighten."

Liedral points at the stern. "What's that?"

"Oh . . . that's a screw. It's like a fan, except it pushes water instead of air."

"But what does it do?"

Dorrin grins. "When it pushes the water, it makes

the boat go in this direction. I made it to see if the idea really worked. The bands here are a rubber and string mixture. They really don't work that well. The rubber comes from Naclos. The druids don't always trade, and that makes it hard to get."

"I've heard. I've never been that far south, though."

"When I build a full-sized ship, it will have a real engine."

"Engine?"

"A machine that will turn the screw like the bands do."

Liedral takes the model. "The bands seem simpler."

"They don't work as well when you build them bigger."

Liedral looks over the boat. "Why do you want to sell it?"

"I've done better ones." He holds up his hands. "The second one has a spring, but it isn't big enough."

"You amaze me."

Dorrin looks at the rough-planked floor.

"You work like a smith. You're a healer, and you make wonderful toys—

"Models."

"Models . . . whatever . . ." She pauses. "Why did you write me?"

"Because . . . I think of you. It's different."

"Would you sit next to me? Please?"

Dorrin sits on the end of the pallet.

Liedral edges next to him. "I came to see you. Not to make coins. Not to make polite conversation."

"I know. But I feel . . . so . . . young."

Her arms are surprisingly strong as she pulls him to her, and her lips are warm on his.

After the kiss and embrace that seems timeless, he looks at her. "I missed you."

"I missed you. And I'm not that much older than you, especially in love."

"But . . ."

"Look at me, the way you do when you're healing."

Dorrin does, and sees the rightness, the essential order. "Oh . . ."

"Now, do you see?"

He nods. Knowing little of order, Liedral is still wise enough to know that she needs order in her lover. He tightens his arms around her, and her lips touch his again. Soon, not just lips touch, nor skin, nor souls.

LXX

"YOU'RE IMPOSSIBLE . . . AFTER last night . . ." Liedral's lips touch Dorrin's, and his fingers dig into her bare back.

"Last night . . . was just . . . the beginning."

There is a rap on the door. Dorrin looks up. Another rap follows.

"Yes?" Dorrin says.

"It's Reisa. If you two lovebirds aren't too tied up, you might want to bundle up and come up to the hilltop. I forgot. Tonight's Council Night."

Dorrin sighs. "Council Night?"

"They'll be starting the fireworks soon."

The two look and each other, then burst into giggles.

" . . . fireworks, indeed," Liedral mutters, pulling on her shirt.

"Couldn't we have both kinds?" Dorrin pleads.

She throws one of her boots at him, but he ducks, and it crashes into the wall. "All right."

Dorrin shrugs, then frowns.

She grins. "Don't worry about it. Let's go out into the cold and watch the fireworks."

Dorrin groans, but yanks on his shirt and boots.

After they don jackets, and Liedral pulls on a knit cap, Dorrin takes her face in both hands, then brushes her lips with his.

"Cold fireworks, first."

"All right."

Reisa and Petra stand on the hilltop, looking down on the frozen river and the harbor beyond.

"You did manage to venture out into the cold."

"Ah . . . yes," Dorrin stumbles.

The three women exchange knowing glances. Dorrin blushes and looks toward the harbor.

A skyrocket bursts, and pinwheels of light cartwheel from it, casting momentary shadows of the leafless trees against the hills to the west. The ice on the River Weyel shimmers.

"It is beautiful." Liedral's voice is barely audible as the sounds of the next skyrockets echo through the darkness. "What are they for?"

"Celebrate the founding of the Council." Reisa snorts. "Not that the Council'll last much longer unless they do something about the White Wizards."

Dorrin thinks about the skyrockets, about what powers them, and whether the black powder would or could power a machine.

Another *crummp* echoes through the velvet night as the shower of red sparks it has delivered is already fading.

"The Wizards don't move that fast," Liedral says slowly. "They're very careful, very thorough. When they do move, it's usually too late to do much."

"Wonderful." Reisa coughs in the cold.

Another rocket spews golden sparks across the black and white winter sky. Petra clears her throat.

Dorrin squeezes Liedral's hand, and she returns the pressure.

Yet another explosion of light flares over the harbor.

Reisa coughs, once, twice, and again. "Going in. Cold's too much."

The three remain, near-silent, until the last rocket flares.

Petra stamps her feet in the snow, turning back toward the house. "Stupid time for fireworks. It's winter, for darkness's sake."

Dorrin and Liedral grin at each other. Dorrin has to cover his mouth and swallow hard.

As they reach the yard, Liedral says softly. "Good night, Petra. Thank your mother for telling us about the fireworks."

"Good night, lovebirds." Petra's voice is warm, even as she closes the kitchen door.

"She's nice." Liedral squeezes Dorrin's hand again as the two cross the frozen yard to his room.

"She is. But you're special."

"Like fireworks?"

They grin again.

Once inside the room, Dorrin slides the bolt.

"I'm cold." Liedral has the quilt wrapped around her.

"You need more fireworks?"

A boot flies in his direction, and he ducks, then catches her. Their lips meet again.

"Fireworks . . ."

LXXI

DORRIN AND LIEDRAL stand outside the barn in the cold, but bright, morning light.

"Do you want to take Meriwhen?"

"Your precious mare?" She grins.

Instead of answering, he bends down and crushes

together the icy snow, then straightens and throws it at her, spraying her with icy powder.

"You . . ." She edges closer to him, tilting her lips for a kiss.

He bends forward, closing his eyes—and finds himself falling backward into the hard packed snow next to the barn. In spite of himself, he laughs, and she reaches down to help him up with gloved hands. Instead he pulls her down and into his lap. They kiss once . . . and again. In time, he struggles upright, lifting Liedral with him.

"You're much stronger than you look."

"All that smithing. Do you want Meriwhen?"

"No. I'll take the nag I bought."

"What are you doing today?"

"Being a trader. Trying to find what people will sell cheaply. I'll know it when I see it. Part of it's just feel." She shrugs. "Just like part of being a smith is feel."

He opens the barn door, and they step inside, hand in hand. Dorrin kisses her again, feeling the chill of her cheek and the warmth of her lips.

"Don't you have to go to the healer's this morning?" She breaks away.

"I should." He sighs. "More hungry children, more broken bones."

"Broken bones?"

"Always women," he explains. "They say they have accidents. They're lying, of course. When times are hard, the men beat them."

"Can't you do something?" Liedral looks for the battered saddle for the even more battered gray mare that shares the stall with Meriwhen.

"What?" Dorrin takes a deep breath. "They won't leave the men. Where would they go, especially in winter? What could they do? Most of the men won't change." He pauses. "Look at you. You dress and act like a man. Why can't you be a trader and a woman?"

"People still fear the Legend, I guess."

Dorrin hands her the worn brown saddle blanket, waits until she puts it on the gray, and swings the saddle into place, deftly cinching the girths.

"You've gotten a lot better since we first met." She grins. "At a lot of things."

He finds himself blushing.

"But you still blush the same way."

He slips the gray's bridle in place.

"I can do that. I was doing it before you knew what a horse was."

"I know you can, but I like doing things for you." He hands her the reins and begins to saddle Meriwhen. "Darkness!"

"What?"

"I forgot my staff. Have to get it on the way out." Meriwhen steps sideways as he slips the hackamore in place.

"That's a giveaway, you know?"

"What?"

"The hackamore. None of the great ones used bitted bridles, not according to my father. He said even Creslin used a hackamore."

"How did he know?"

"According to the family tales, Creslin once was a guard for a distant ancestor. That's why Freidr is so assiduous in courting the Whites in Jellico." She snorts. "Much good it does us."

Dorrin looks toward the barn door. "I suppose we ought to get moving."

She leans toward him for another kiss. He obliges.

"Later . . ." she finally says, breathless.

"That's a promise."

She smiles as he opens the door. He watches until she turns left on the main road toward Diev. Then he closes the door and leads Meriwhen across the yard, leaving her outside for the moment it takes him to reclaim his staff.

After returning and setting the staff in the holder, he mounts, and flicks the reins. "Let's go. Rylla will be complaining that I wasn't there at dawn."

LXXII

DORRIN GLANCES AROUND the barn, but Leidral's gray is nowhere to be seen. Quickly, he unsaddles Meriwhen, brushes her, and then hurries to his room, where he deposits his staff and shirt. He looks at the stains that resulted from his efforts to mix honey and spices. The shirt needs washing, but washing is a chore in the winter. With a deep breath, he pulls on the ragged shirt he wears in the smithy. He still thinks about the fireworks. Can he obtain some cammabark or black powder? Where would he store it? The old root cellar down the hill from Rylla's cottage?

Vaos looks up from the grindstone. "Good day, master Dorrin."

"Good day, Vaos."

Yarrl sets the iron rod he is working back in the forge and wipes his forehead. "Good thing you're here early."

Dorrin sets the sledge on the clay by the anvil. "Why?"

"Trader named Willum stopped by. The fellow who's a chandler." Yarrl grips the tongs and nods toward the bellows. Vaos follows the implied directions and begins to pump the bellows lever.

"He was talking about one of those little toys you

made for him," grunts the smith, withdrawing the metal from the forge.

Dorrin shifts his grip on the sledge, following Yarrl's gestures as the older smith moves the metal across the anvil's horn.

" . . . darkness good . . . smith . . . for such a young fellow . . ."

The wiry young man has never mentioned his abilities to sense the level of heat within the firebrick, or the order within the iron, nor does he intend to, not after his brief visit in Fairhaven.

The smith thrusts the metal back into the inferno. "Anyway, he's headed down to Fenard in the next day or so . . . wanted to know if you could make him a few more . . . said he'd pay half silver each . . . especially if you could do little boats of some sort. That mean anything to you?"

That Willum has stopped and asked for toys—and offered more coins—is interesting. Dorrin does not whistle, but his lips are pursed. Nearly automatically, he gestures to the bellows rod again, noting that the fire needs more air. Vaos sighs and resumes pumping.

"He likes my toys. I made a wagon, a windmill, and a sawmill. I could do a boat, but that would be harder, especially to make it float properly."

"An iron boat? Even one that's part iron?" Yarrl coughs, then swallows, wiping his forehead with the back of his bare forearm.

"An empty bucket floats, doesn't it?—and it's part iron."

Yarrl brings the metal to the anvil, and Dorrin lifts the sledge.

A half silver for his toys? He brings the sledge down, then lifts it. Yarrl shifts the iron, and Dorrin strikes as they pick up an easy rhythm.

At least twice, Dorrin looks over his shoulder,

certain that someone is there, but only the three of them are there.

LXXIII

"I DON'T WANT to go." Liedral's arms are tight around Dorrin.

"I don't want you to go."

"I've already stayed too long. You need more time . . . and so do I."

Dorrin wonders where the time has gone. Her horses—she has another pack horse, bought cheaply because feed is scarce in Spidlar now—are packed and heavily laden, and she can pick up one of the few coasters in Spidlaria, but only if she leaves soon. Finally, he reaches out and touches her, not just with his fingers, but with a touch of darkness, blackness, that is soul. They stand, locked together, for yet one more time before she breaks away.

He watches the road long after the horses have vanished into the dawn light. Then he washes and shaves in ice-cold water, and, as an afterthought, washes the stained shirt he has promised himself he will wash for almost an eight-day. He hangs it in his room and dons the lighter one, and his jacket, then takes his staff and returns to the barn to saddle Meriwhen.

At least, he will be early at Rylla's. He snorts as he closes the barn door and mounts. Meriwhen retorts with a whicker.

"I know it's early. Traders get up even earlier than healers or smiths." He whistles tunelessly as Meriwhen's hoofs crunch through the road's crusted surface. Although the nights are cold, the days are getting warm enough to melt the snow and ice. Spring will be welcome, but how much mud will arrive with it?

A feeling of melancholy brushes across him, and he straightens in the saddle, for the feeling is somehow distant, not exactly his. His eyes water. Is it from the wind? Liedral? How could he have asked her to stay? Should he have gone with her? But what could he have done to make a living? Now, at least, he is earning coins, from the extra smith work and from his toys. When Willum had showed up the afternoon before, Dorrin wished he had completed more than the half-dozen small toys. There had only been one boat, and not his best work at that. But Willum had rubbed his hands and paid on the spot.

Meriwhen skitters slightly as a hoof slips on ice. Should he have reshod her with ice shoes? It's too late in the winter for that, but something to think about next fall. There is always something else he should have done.

He turns Meriwhen off the main road into the deeper unpacked snow of the narrow way. The white smoke shows that Rylla, as usual, has a warm fire burning.

Dorrin ties Meriwhen at the post. The day will be warm—for winter. He loosens his jacket as he walks to the door and opens it. Five people are standing or huddling in the main room—three women, a boy, and Frisa, who is held in Merga's arms, whimpering.

Dorrin takes off his jacket and hangs it on the peg behind the door.

"Least you're here when you're supposed to be." The grumpiness does not hide the concern in Rylla's voice. "Kysta's got the flux; and Weldra's covered with red blotches; and . . . maybe you'd better look at little Frisa. Merga says she took a bad fall." Rylla's eyes fix on Dorrin. "I still have some brinn that might help with the flux."

"Do you have any astra?"

"It's dried. Put 'em together, you think?"

"With a herb tea. Rebekah said that it sometimes works."

"Darkness . . . why not?"

The thin and red-eyed young mother holds Frisa. "She can't walk."

"You carried her here? How far is that?"

"Down from Jisle's farm. A long two kays, master Dorrin."

Dorrin gestures toward the stool. "Can you sit by the fire, Frisa?"

A whimper answers his question.

"You remember my horse? If you're good, I'll give you a ride home."

"That not be necessary, ser," protests Merga.

"You can't carry her back all that way."

"I managed her here."

Dorrin holds his sigh as Merga eases Frisa onto the stool. The child winces. The young healer runs his fingertips along her neck, letting his senses search out the injury. Pain and bruises cover her back and legs.

The powdered willow bark will remove some of the pain, and he can instill some order, but the child has little nourishment and less spirit.

He studies the mother. Darkness on one cheek indicates a scarcely healed bruise, and he can sense others, less well-healed. He stands abruptly, glaring at the fire, his guts churning in rage. Finally, he says softly, "I'll need to get something for you, Frisa."

After walking to the kitchen and the cabinet next to the old-fashioned hearth, which also burns, though little more than coals, he takes out the jar with the willow powder and measures some into a small cup. Then he pours a dash of herb tea into the cup and swirls the mixture. The taste, he knows, is awful, but the potion does reduce pain and helps joints and bruises heal. He stuffs a chunk of stale bread into his pocket when Rylla is not looking.

" . . . drink this," orders Rylla to the older crone with the cane. "None of your nonsense, Kysta. Just drink it." The healer glances at Dorrin and looks away.

Dorrin carries the cup back to Frisa. "You need to drink this. It doesn't taste very good, but it will make you feel better."

"Don't want to."

Dorrin looks at the battered child. "Please, child." His fingers touch her wrist, and he tries to send a sense of reassurance.

"Don't . . ."

He looks into her eyes. "Please."

"If I can have a ride."

He nods and holds the cup. She gulps.

"Awful . . . ugggg . . ."

"You were a good girl." He squeezes her hand, then stands up, looking at the mother. "She can't walk yet. I'll give you both a ride."

"But . . . Gerhalm . . ." Sheer terror fills Merga's eyes.

"I intend to see Gerhalm." Dorrin's words are like ice, and, instantly, the entire cottage stills.

" . . . darkness . . ." whispers the old woman Kysta.

The room is quiet long after Dorrin carries· Frisa out to Meriwhen. He boosts Merga up and then hands her daughter to her. He hands the stale bread to the little girl. Then he begins leading the mare westward up the hill.

Jisle's farm is less than the two kays Merga promised, and Dorrin is barely puffing when he leads the two into Jisle's barnyard. Three one-room huts squat between the barn and what looks to be a fowl coop.

"That be our cot." Merga points to the one nearest the barn, her voice trembling.

Dorrin sets Frisa on the flaking brick stoop. The

door is of warped and splitting pine with obvious gaps between the frame and the door itself.

"Who you be?" A squat man emerges from the barn and barrels toward the three. He carries an axe.

Dorrin lifts the staff from the holder, letting Merga dismount as she may. "I'm Dorrin. I'm the healer that's trying to help your daughter."

"Filling her head with ideas of horses. You're the one." Gerhalm holds the axe in both hands.

"Why do you beat them?" Dorrin tries to keep the anger from his voice.

"Don't beat them. They just have ... accidents." Gerhalm's voice turns oily.

The blackness within Dorrin surges forth, and he drops his staff and grabs the heavier man with both hands, letting the blackness flow through him into the farm worker.

Gerhalm tries to wrench free, but the smith's arms are as hard as black iron. " ... darkness ... no ... no ... NOooo ..."

When Dorrin releases the man, Gerhalm sinks onto the step, the axe dropping in the dirty snow by his feet.

"You will never lift a hand to either Merga or Frisa. Ever!"

Merga backs away from Dorrin and her man, eyes flickering from the blackness that seems to enshroud the healer.

Gerhalm drops to the snow, almost groveling. "Don't ... not that ..."

"Get up," Dorrin orders.

Gerhalm backs away from the healer. "Not again, master ... not again."

Frisa sits on the stoop, still chewing on the last crust of the bread. Dorrin turns to Merga, who has sunk onto her knees.

"I didn't know," she whispers. "I'd a not done it to Gerhalm . . ."

"I didn't hurt him. He just won't beat you again."

"I didn't know . . ." The young mother refuses to look at Dorrin as he remounts Meriwhen.

"'Bye, horsey," calls Frisa.

All the ill have left Rylla's cottage by the time he returns.

The old healer shakes her head. "Darkness . . . what you did! You put a curse on Gerhalm, too?"

"Hardly." Dorrin's laugh is forced. "I couldn't curse a soul. I did put an order command on him. He can't lay an angry hand on either."

"For a man, these days, that be a terrible curse." Rylla's laugh is as harsh as his. "What will ye do when he leaves her?"

"You think he will?"

"Not in the next few eight-days, but by summer's end." She leans back in the chair, sipping her herb tea.

"I don't know." He takes a deep breath. "I'd better think about planting spices and building my own cottage. If that's all right with you."

"Be fine with me. No one'd touch an old healer with a Black master living near."

"I'm not a Black master."

"Maybe not yet. Nearest thing to one around, though." She takes another sip from the chipped mug. "Might as well be getting you back to old Yarrl."

"Might as well."

"Your mind still on your lady trader?" Rylla smiles.

Dorrin shakes his head. That kind of understanding he will never have.

The ride back is quiet, except for the splashing of Meriwhen's hoofs in the melting ice and snow. When he opens the barn door, he sees Reisa.

"You're back early." Reisa is breaking apart a bale of hay to feed the mule and the bay.

"I was helping a child who was beaten." He removes his staff from the holder and leans it in the corner.

"She'll just be beaten again. That type never changes."

"No." Dorrin's voice is flat. "He'll never beat her again."

"You didn't . . . use your staff?"

"No. I was more cruel." Dorrin is all too aware of the darkness in his eyes as Reisa steps back. "I bound him never to hit either the mother or the child."

"Darkness . . . some ways you scare a body."

"Sometimes I scare myself." Dorrin finishes loosening the saddle girths and removes the saddle, racking it carefully. He folds the blanket, then removes the hackamore. Meriwhen is happier with it, and he needs no bitted bridle. He takes the brush and begins to groom the mare. Reisa stands and watches. Zilda clinks her chain from the far corner of the barn.

"Why did you let her go?" asks Reisa when he finishes. "The trader?"

"Because she needed to go. Because I won't hold her when she needs space. Because I'm still confused."

"You're young." She frowns. "The young always make their own mistakes. By the time you learn, you're old, and the young won't listen."

Dorrin asks gently, "What are you trying to tell me?"

"Life is short, Dorrin. Too short." She lifts her handless arm. "I thought I'd always be able to match a blade with anyone. Sometimes, it only seems like yesterday. Twenty years—gone in a flash. Most of them were good years, but the good ones went with the bad."

Dorrin closes the stall door and puts the curry brush on the shelf. Meriwhen whickers softly.

"White Wizards are closing in. Hope you see her again. Next time, don't let her go, no matter what she tells you." Reisa coughs, wipes a damp eye, and then takes the curry brush. "Bay needs brushing." She opens the second stall door. "Better get into the smithy 'fore Yarrl kills himself doing too much. That way, you two come from the same cloth."

Dorrin walks slowly across the packed snow toward his room to change. Was he wrong to let Liedral go? But how could he demand she stay? He can barely support himself. His head aches as he thinks of the golds in his strongbox. No—that is not true. He can only support himself if he wants to build his machines.

His eyes burn, even as his head throbs. Things had been simpler, much simpler, before Liedral came.

LXXIV

A THIN LINE of smoke dribbles into the clear blue-green sky ahead of the column of riders. Brede hunches down in his jacket to keep his ears warmer against the wind, even as the squad plods east on the rolled and packed snow of the road to Fenard. Unlike the bare-headed Brede, Kadara wears a knit cap. Both wear heavy fleece-lined gloves.

"Damned wind . . ."

"You're always damning something, Vorban."

"Shut the frig up, Sestal."

Brede and Kadara exchange glances and head-shakes.

"Why should I? You complain too much. Least we're getting paid. You want to be some peasant farmer? Sit buried under this snow waiting for the spring to turn it all to mud?"

"Paid for what—freezing our asses off chasing thieves that aren't thieves? Pretty soon, we'll be fighting Certan regulars. Then what?"

"All right," snaps the squad leader.

Kadara's eyes fix on the smoke. "Another trader, I'd bet."

"On his way back," Brede adds.

"How do you figure that?" asks Vorban, riding behind Brede.

Brede turns in the saddle. "That way, they get his goods and coin, and Spidlar gets nothing. It doesn't hurt their traders, just ours."

"All right," repeats the squad leader.

" . . . all right . . ." mimics Vorban, in a voice low enough not to be heard beyond those around him.

The riders plod onward through the packed and crusted snow that has refrozen, melted and refrozen.

"Check your weapons."

On the opposite hillside, a fire burns, and a handful of riders trot uphill and eastward, leading three horses, and leaving behind two smoldering wagons. They wear the dull purple of Gallos.

" . . . shit . . ." mumbles Vorban.

Brede and Kadara look wordlessly at each other.

" . . . light and darkness . . . shit . . ." repeats Vorban.

LXXV

THE SLENDER MAN in white looks again at the object on the table, then at the box from which it came. His hands draw away from the darkness that surrounds both. "Where did you get this, Fydel?"

"A trader named Willum. In Fenard," replies the bearded man, also in white, although he does not wear either the gold and white starburst on his collar or an amulet around his neck.

"It feels like something from Recluce."

"With the Blacks' disdain of complex tools?" The stolid White Wizard snorts. "You aren't saying that those iron-headed conservatives would ever allow this, are you, Jeslek?"

"Hardly. But the combination of natural wood, black iron, and order—who else could produce that? Did the trader say where he got it?"

"Not at first. I pressed him a little, and he sweated, but he didn't say. Before he saw me, he was telling people that it was a miraculous toy brought from afar. Someone asked him if the Black devils made it. He just laughed and said it didn't come from that far away. I got him later—solved several problems. Before he . . . ah . . ."

"You didn't use chaos-fire, you idiot?"

"I'm not that dense. Plain torture works fine. Then we took him out onto the main road and made it look like another highway attack. The Gallosians all thought it was just that."

"You're awfully prolific with illusions. Is that wise?"

Fydel shrugs. "The burned wagons and loot were real."

"What did you find out?"

"The crafter who made it lives in Diev. His name is Dorrin. No one has heard of him."

"Where's Diev? That's somewhere near the Westhorns, isn't it?"

"It's a small seaport and mining town on the coast. It's about a hundred and fifty kays northwest of Spidlaria."

"That could be even worse," muses the taller wizard with the golden eyes.

"Oh?" The stolid wizard's eyes dart to the toy on the white oak table.

"Well . . . you pick it up and hold it, then."

"I'd rather not," Fydel says apologetically.

"What if it were a full-sized windmill? Built like this?"

"They wouldn't use that much black iron in proportion. Besides, why would they want to?"

"Fydel." Jeslek's voice is hard, and the other wizard steps back. "Say it were a ship or . . . whatever. What could you do to it?"

"I'd leave it alone—but they can't built ships like that."

Jeslek shakes his head. "Am I surrounded by idiots? They don't—not now. This proves someone can. Do you want it to be Recluce?"

"But it's not from Recluce." Fydel nods at the toy he has brought in a box to avoid touching it more than necessary. "One craftsman isn't a community."

"Look at it," snaps Jeslek. "That contains solid carving, or some sort of equivalent woodworking, worked black iron, and a small infusion of order. That means a smith, a woodcrafter or toymaker, and a healer—or someone who's all three. If this Dorrin is . . . I've never seen anyone like that."

"So . . . making toys . . . what danger is that?"

"None. Just so long as he keeps making toys. And so long as Recluce doesn't get the same idea." Jeslek studies the toy again, walking around the circular table.

The bearded wizard ducks backward, his tunic brushing the white stone wall behind him. "Maybe he was from Recluce. They probably exiled him for doing something like that."

"They can't stay that stupid forever," returns Jeslek. "They're still reliving the legends of Creslin."

"Let's just hope that they continue to do so." Jeslek turns to the other wizard. "Put out word to all the road guards and inspection points . . . and anyone else—you know what I mean. If there's anything about this Dorrin, I want to know about it. Do you understand?"

Fydel nods.

"I'll keep this ... darkness-damned thing ... for now." Jeslek looks toward the doorway, and the other wizard inclines his head.

"Good day, High Wizard."

After Fydel leaves, Jeslek ponders the toy, thinking about the young smith who has forged it. Does he know what power he possesses? Clearly not. Like all the Blacks, he sees only a fraction of what is.

He smiles as a light tap strikes his door. "Come in, Anya."

The red-headed wizard slips in, again sliding the bolt behind her.

"You don't have to lock it. Who would intrude?"

"I do prefer privacy." She smiles demurely.

Jeslek glances toward the window, and the darkness outside, lit faintly by the whiteness of Fairhaven itself.

"Your efforts against Spidlar are proving unexpectedly beneficial."

"You mean, the business with the increased chaos energy? Of course." Jeslek laughs, but his eyes do not echo the sound.

"It's effective. Spidlar requires more order to survive, and you create more chaos in Gallos and Kyphros."

"That may be." He gestures to the toy on the table. "What do you think?"

Anya makes no move to touch it. "About what."

"The toy there. Go ahead. Pick it up."

"Is this a joke?" The red-headed wizard laughs, uncertainly, but she does not touch the toy.

"I see Fydel already told you about it."

"What if he did?"

"Oh, Anya." He shakes his head sadly. "We need to crush Spidlar before this toymaker makes bigger things. And you worry and plot about whom you would make my successor, and how you would use your body to control him."

"You're impossible."

"No. Just realistic. And slow. But not totally stupid."

"Not totally." Anya settles into the chair next to the wine. "Would you mind if I poured the wine?"

"Please do."

"You don't seem terribly upset."

"Why should I be? White is White. An adder is an adder. My views won't change you, and you are lovely. So why shouldn't I accept what you offer? You're no real threat to me. To Sterol or Fydel, yes."

"You seem rather sure of yourself." She fills two goblets.

"I'm dense about these things, actually. You know that. But it doesn't matter. You know that as well, although I'm sure you haven't told Sterol that. So does he, although he hasn't told you. You both are waiting for me to overreach myself. In times of troubles, every High Wizard does, you know. I'm hoping to be the first who doesn't. You're betting I'm like all the others."

Anya takes a deep swallow. "This is . . . rather . . . amazing."

"Not at all." Jeslek steps up behind her and runs a hand under her collar and across the skin of her shoulder. "Not at all."

LXXVI

OUT OF THE black predawn sky, the rain falls like iron nails driven into the sodden snow—snow that an eight-day earlier had been waist deep in the fields and hard-packed more than knee deep in the smithy yard.

Dorrin hurries onto the porch, where he knocks slush and mud off his boots, then brushes them with the shoe broom. After that, he wipes them on the mat before stepping into the kitchen. Warmer than the cold damp outside, the kitchen is still cool and dim, lit by a single oil lamp set on the table.

Yarrl sits at the end of the table, two slices of bread, each with a wedge of cheese, before him. "Slop season."

"It wasn't like this last year, was it?"

"It was—just before you came. Only seen one spring that wasn't slop. Don't want to see another. Drought was so bad half the animals died." The smith chews through cheese and bread, his left hand on the mug of cool cider.

Dorrin cuts himself bread and cheese and looks in the cupboard for some dried fruit. "Any fruit?"

"No fruit. Damned White Wizards."

"If that's a curse, you don't need it. They were damned by better people a long time ago, and Creslin was the only one who made it stick." Reisa, wearing a heavy sweater and bulky trousers, steps into the kitchen. "There is dried fruit. Liedral left us a small cask of it. Mixed pearapples and something else. I haven't opened it."

"Woman, you haven't opened it, and it's like there isn't any." Yarrl grumbles through a mouthful of bread and cheese.

"No, it's not." Reisa slips shavings into the cold stove, uses a striker to light a candle stub set in a holder, then uses the candle to light the shavings. She waits for the shavings to catch before adding a shovelful of stove coal. "I'll make bread for dinner, and it'll still be warm for supper."

"Fat good that does me now."

Dorrin pours cool cider into a mug.

"Can't argue with women, Dorrin. They don't

answer what you ask, and answer what you never thought of asking."

"You can't argue with men, Dorrin," Reisa says evenly. "They don't listen to what you say, and they hear what they want to, not what you said."

"I guess that means you can't argue," adds Petra from the doorway. She looks at the half loaf of bread remaining on the cutting board, then takes the knife and cuts two slices, offering the first to her mother.

"Thank you." Reisa takes the bread with an eye still on the wide stove.

"Worse than White Wizards . . . have an answer for everything, and they're sneakier."

Dorrin sits at the corner of the table. "Brede and Kadara say the thieves are riding horses with Gallosian horseshoes—the kind with the funny angles on the sides of the cleats."

"If the cleats are angled, they're not properly cleats."

"Father," snaps Petra, "stop being so difficult."

"That doesn't sound good." Reisa, measuring flour into a bowl, looks up. "Oh, Petra. I'll need milk earlier today."

"It's raining an ocean out there." Petra looks into the dim dawn and the curtain of water, then closes the door.

"I still need the milk." Reisa coughs. "Before long, the Prefect will be claiming that the midlands above Elparta belong to Gallos."

"They never have," snorts Petra.

"We're going to need nails, couple of small kegs of common flatheads—longs and shorts. Werthen always wants a keg right after the mud clears." Yarrl grins. "Doesn't like Antra's or Henstaal's."

Dorrin groans. He hates making nails, even if the pattern is now easy.

"A true smith—groans at nails, but makes 'em good.

Darkness, that's why smiths got strikers—to make nails, draw scrap into rods and bars." Yarrl stands and drains the last cider from his mug. "Let's get moving. Where's that worthless scamp?" He pretends not to notice as Vaos slips into the kitchen.

Petra slices a hunk of bread for Vaos and hands him a wedge of cheese. Then she pulls a tattered oiled waterproof off one of the pegs by the door.

"Where is that worthless scamp?" asks Yarrl, still ignoring Vaos.

"Playing with Zilda, probably," Dorrin answers, winking at Vaos.

"Better not be playing with her. That's a she-goat."

"Father . . ."

Vaos gulps the cider that Reisa hands him. Reisa glances at Dorrin and shakes her head. They both know that for Yarrl work comes before politics, and discussing politics doesn't make nails or bread—or milk the cow.

Dorrin swallows the last of his hasty breakfast and heads for the smithy.

LXXVII

A LOW FIRE burns in the long barracks room, and half a dozen troopers sit on stools around the coals. Others lie on pallets away from the walls through which drafts convey the chill of the cold rain on the melting snow outside.

Brede and Kadara sit midway between the fire and the small closed room where the section commander is meeting with the squad leaders. Behind that battered red oak door, the conversation continues, a muted discussion loud enough for those outside to recognize that an argument takes place, but muffled enough so that they cannot decipher the substance.

"Someone's unhappy." Kadara leans against Brede's shoulder.

"Very unhappy." He touches her hand. "I'm glad we're not out in this slop."

"Me, too." She squeezes his hand in return. "We will be before long."

"Thank you for reminding me, dear one."

The door opens.

"Brede?"

Brede stands. "Yes, ser?"

"The regional commander would like a word with you."

Brede raises his eyebrows, shrugs, then steps toward the small room where the squad leaders meet. The other troopers look away as the tall blond man makes his way through the pallets. The oak door shuts with a heavy click.

"Trooper Brede, this is Commander Byskin."

"Yes, ser." Brede inclines his head in a gesture of respect, standing easily before the table, looking straight at the regional commander, a middle-aged soldier, still trim, if compact. The commander is half bald, and his remaining short-cut hair is half brown, half silver.

"Is it true that you come from Recluce?" asks Byskin.

"Yes, ser."

"What would happen if the White Wizards caught you?"

"I doubt that would happen, ser. They'd probably not want anyone from Recluce as a prisoner."

"Are you saying that they would execute you on the spot?"

"If they could, ser."

"Would you be interested in becoming the squad leader of a new squad?"

"That sounds interesting, but, if you wouldn't mind, ser, could you explain a bit more?"

"You're cautious, aren't you?" Byskin laughs.

" . . . and oh so polite . . ." The whisper seeps into the room.

Byskin looks in the direction of the three other squad leaders, and absolute silence fills the room. "As I was saying, I have decided that we need to do something different to stop all the raids on our traders. After the last raid, where a rather prominent trader was killed, the Council has authorized a larger expenditure to recruit a few additional blades and form another squad. This squad would operate independently, almost, if you will, waiting near the points where attacks seem to occur . . ."

Brede nods.

"In view of your background . . ."

"You are asking if I would lead this squad?"

"Yes, Brede. That is exactly what I am asking. You would receive the same pay as other squad leaders, plus risk pay when in the field. Oh . . . and, if you are agreeable, your assistant would be Trooper Kadara."

Brede smiles politely. "I see."

Byskin frowns. "Do you want the job?"

"Who do I report to?"

Byskin smiles, coldly. "To me, Squad Leader Brede. You are accountable to me for all actions."

"When do we start?"

"You'll get your first recruits within the next few days. You'll have two eight-days to get them in shape."

Brede listens as Byskin continues to describe his new duties.

" . . . not necessary to take prisoners, except in unusual circumstances . . . three eight-days out, one back ... primary emphasis on safety of Council traders ..."

When Brede steps out of the room, he wears a gold collar insignia, and the barracks room is hushed. He sits beside Kadara on a stool.

Kadara shifts her weight on the pallet, without commenting, as Brede explains. Both ignore the wide space accorded them by the other troopers.

" ... and it's all a rather nasty job."

"Why did you agree?"

"I thought the alternatives were worse. None of the squad leaders really likes having us in his squad. Also, I think we can make a difference. I'm getting tired of riding up to find dead bodies and looted wagons."

"You haven't mentioned something else."

"I didn't think I had to." He shrugs. "Until this is resolved, we can't find a ship home."

"We could cross the Westhorns this summer."

"I don't like running away."

"It's sometimes safer."

Brede shakes his head. "You just get an arrow or a sword in your back."

"If you think it's best ..."

"It's not 'best.' You know that. What else can we do?"

"I don't know. I envy Dorrin. At least, he doesn't have to go out and fight for his life all the time."

"He will." Brede's voice is soft, almost sad. "He will."

LXXVIII

"WHERE DID YOU get this?"

"From one of our traders in Spidlar," answers the square-bearded Fydel.

"This doesn't look like—"

"It's not the original. I had it copied, and then had him send it on."

"That was a good idea." Jeslek glances at the copy on the white parchment of Fairhaven.

Liedral—
  Your letter did arrive, and without much delay, given its path. I must apologize for being so late in responding, but I am not a good writer.
  I was surprised to learn that my small models have any market at all, let alone more than a single buyer. Perhaps I should go into the toy-making business. It could not be much harder than smithing, and it might pay somewhat more. Upon reflection, it might not. The winter was cold here, and hard upon the less fortunate.
  I have been working as a healer also, and it is sometimes sad. The chill is hardest upon the children and the old. In the cold, when the flux struck, the old ones often died so quickly. I could sometimes save the young ones, but there were too many to save them all. Rylla, the healer who is teaching me, tells me that I cannot heal just the needy, for a healer without coin soon needs his own healer. The water is generally better in the winter, except in the towns, but people still think I am strange when I tell them to boil it in

a kettle before drinking it. Most would rather drink beer or wine, but who among the poor can afford either?

Kadara and Brede spend much time on the road now. Even in winter, it seemed like the banditry and raids continued. It does not seem natural, given the impassibility of all roads except the main ones that are packed and rolled by the traders. Even dried fruit is hard to come by, and spice shipments are almost nonexistent. That may provide some more coins come late summer, assuming you can reach Spidlar by coaster.

In some ways, it seems as though I have known you much longer than for two short times together, and I do hope that it will not be too long before your trading brings you back.

Dorrin

"I assume you are following this to track the recipient?"

"We already know. It's a trader named Liedral—"

"That's obvious."

"—who works out of Jellico. She generally passes for a man, but does not pay dues to Fairhaven. She uses the back roads. Because she is less successful, no one has paid much attention. That's also because she comes from an old Jellico family. Her brother is active in local politics."

"How active?"

"He's on Sterol's payroll, I think."

"Oh . . . so our good friend Sterol continues his spy network?"

Fydel raises both eyebrows. "You would expect any less?"

"Not really." Jeslek grins.

"Do you want some sort of accident to occur?"

"Not yet. I need to think about this." Jeslek looks

at the glass on the table, then quickly out the window and into the rain.

"Is that all?"

Jeslek nods, but does not turn as Fydel leaves and closes the door behind him. Then he looks at the mirror and concentrates. The image of Dorrin appears in the mirror. This time the smith is working on something black and small. Abruptly, Dorrin looks up, and his eyes appear to meet Jeslek's before the mists close over the image.

"Hmmm . . ." The Black smith is getting stronger, much stronger. Still, he is young and attracted to the female trader. Jeslek paces from one side of the tower room to the other.

Then, too, there is the problem with Fydel. Delaying giving the letter to him for nearly a season—that was a bit much, almost an insult. Jeslek laughs, thinking about the ships nearing completion.

LXXIX

DORRIN STRUGGLES WITH the wedge-shaped warren, slowly turning the clayey soil to extend Rylla's garden for the winterspice and potatoes. Gardening is even harder than smith work, or so it seems, but that may be because of all the small insects that seek him out.

He brushes away a horsefly, not wanting to spend time or energy on wards. He wipes his forehead, wrinkling his nose at the pile of manure he must yet turn into the soil. While there is certainly a growing market for spices, or will be, if he can raise more, he still forgets that even wonderful ideas take work.

With a deep breath he starts on the second furrow. Halfway down the row, he wipes his forehead again, swatting at some other flying insect. He glances toward the knoll above the pond, mentally measuring. If . . . He shakes his head. Already he is aiming at another project. He has not even set the foundation stones for the cottage and smithy, and he is planning piping water.

He takes up the warren again, thinking wistfully of the steaming smithy and hammers, and even of making nails. He laughs.

By midmorning he has completed what he has set out to do. Tomorrow he will plant the seeds and cuttings. Rylla can do some of the watering.

"That's not a garden; it's a field. I suppose you expect me to water and weed it?" Rylla's voice is gruff, but there is a sparkle in her eyes.

"Only some of the time. We'll need it all."

"Have more spices than . . ." She coughs. "Can you sell them all?"

"I hope not, but I bet we will. Even the potatoes on the end."

"This something you've learned from your blade friends?"

"They made Brede a squad leader and added another squad."

"Ah . . . and the Council's never been known to be generous with its coin, or favorable to someone tinted Black."

Dorrin thinks about the need for . . . something . . . to stop the Whites. "Do you have any saltpeter?"

"Not if you're a-fooling with black powder. 'Sides, a good White will just set it off from a distance."

"I had something else in mind."

"Don't want my cottage in flames, Dorrin."

"I'll use the old root cellar."

"I'll get ye some redberry." Rylla walks slowly back into the cottage.

Dorrin hopes her comment is tacit assent. Is he

trying too much? Probably, but time is growing short. Something is happening, something beyond the White Wizards' trying to bankrupt the Spidlarian traders, or even take over Spidlar itself. The Whites are not all that good in battle, and yet they control almost all of eastern Candar. Have they accomplished it all through subversion? Greed? Bribery?

He thinks of Fairhaven itself and laughs at the irony. They have held what they hold because they have provided a basically more orderly government than what preceded—and they really do not govern. They let the old Dukes, Counts, Viscounts and Prefects govern, just leaving a White Wizard at hand in each of the old domains. Shaking his head, he turns and follows Rylla.

LXXX

DORRIN GUIDES MERIWHEN along the rain-splashed paving stones, past the Red Lion and then past the Tankard. The beggar woman and her child sit on the weathered mounting block that once served a building that no longer exists.

"A copper, master? Even a half-penny, for a widow and her child?"

Dorrin knows he is not exactly charitable, but the woman's whine gets on his nerves, and he has never seen her do anything but beg. He ignores her cries and rides toward the chandlery.

Somehow the building looks different. His eyes study the crossed candles of the sign, and he realizes that there is no name above them. He enters the store, carrying both saddlebags and staff. The potbellied stove, unneeded now that the cold weather has passed, still stands in the middle of the floor, and the oak counter runs along the right side of the room. The hangings still block the way to the back room, and Roald still stands behind the counter.

"Yes, ser?" asks Roald, eyeing the staff warily.

"The changes . . ." Dorrin offers vaguely.

"Not too many, ser. Ser Willum's son and widow have retained me to continue the business and to train young Halvor."

"I had not heard the details."

"The highwaymen, ser. The guards found his body, but his goods and profits were gone." Roald glances at the bags Dorrin carries. "You were the one with the elaborate toys?"

Dorrin nods. "Ser Willum held them in some favor."

"Perhaps we might take one or two, ser Dor . . ."

"Dorrin."

"Thank you, ser. We might take one or two, ser, but since we must rely on others for travel now . . ."

"I understand." Dorrin removes an assortment of the smaller toys. "I would presume that the smaller ones would be more appropriate."

"I would think so. Perhaps the boat, here, and the mill? For, say, a half-silver?"

Dorrin smiles politely. "Even at his best, ser Willum paid almost four apiece."

"Ah . . . but we cannot trade that much now. The best, and I would not offend, ser Dorrin, would be a half silver and a penny."

Dorrin can sense Roald's fear and concerns, and he nods to the man. "Times are difficult all over. Six it is."

Roald smiles, as much in relief as pleasure. "A moment, ser."

Dorrin packs away the others, leaving the boat and mill on the counter.

"Here you be."

"Thank you." Dorrin inclines his head. "Might there be other iron items that would be of use?"

Roald pauses, then shakes his head. "None that I can think of."

"Thank you."

As he leaves, he thinks about Roald's manners. The clerk had been too deferential to a mere toymaker or smith, not really as interested in haggling as in getting Dorrin out of the store. And Roald needs iron goods, but doesn't want to get them from Dorrin. Is Roald worried about Dorrin, or something else? For whatever reason, it's clear that he will have to find other ways to sell his toys, or other items to sell, or others to sell to. What about Jasolt or Fyntal? Or should he talk to Hasten at the Guild?

Dorrin puts the staff in the lanceholder and swings up into the saddle, turning Meriwhen toward the harbor and the small, shedlike building that holds the Guild. The rail outside the building is empty of other mounts, and the wind off the harbor carries an icy edge to it, as if winter lingers on the water a season behind the land.

Carrying his staff, Dorrin steps through the open pine door, looking for Hasten in the comparative dimness of the long room.

"Who ye be looking for?" Hasten looks up from some sort of ledger.

"I'm Dorrin, Hasten, if you might recall . . ."

"Oh . . . the artisan fellow." The gray-haired man sits back in his chair. "Sit down. Don't mind me, but the old bones haven't recovered from winter."

Dorrin sits, wondering if Hasten is the same man who had been so skittish the last time he had come to join the Guild.

"What can I do for you?"

"I was wondering if you might have some ideas—"

"Ideas? Of course, I have ideas, but the free ones are worthless, usually." The older man chuckles.

"—about who else besides Willum trades in novelties like my toys."

"Ah, yes, poor Willum. Fyntal told him it was a bad idea to go overland to Fenard, not that you can go any other way. Ha ... ha ... Traders in toys? Hmmmm? You make those fancy ones. I don't know for sure, but that young fellow, Jasolt, ships high-end goods to Suthya. And Vyrnil—he's over by the third pier—he has something going with the Hamorians. They're big on novelties. Maybe that other old fellow ... Risten ... he's got a small place by Jasolt's." Hasten shrugs. "Offhand, that'd be where I'd be starting."

"Where is Jasolt?"

"Oh ... he's at sea now, I understand, but his store is on the short street—Pearapple Place, he calls it— behind Willum's place. Is it true that his clerk Roald is running the chandlery?"

"That's what I understand." Dorrin shifts in the hard chair.

"Terrible mistake, if you ask me. No business sense at all. Good at selling to townspeople, but no sense of value."

Dorrin rises slowly. "I appreciate your advice."

"Not at all. Not at all. You won't mind me if I don't see you out, master Dorrin?"

"Darkness, no."

"Don't forget that your annual dues need to be paid before midsummer."

"I won't." Dorrin heads back into the welcome cool of the harbor breeze. Even the faint odor of decaying fish is preferable to the close Guild office.

He fastens his staff back in place and rides down to the end of the third pier. He finds the sign easily enough—Vyrnil's. There are no pictures, just the name, indicating the higher nature of the trader's clientele.

Dorrin walks inside the small building, looking at the open bins along both sides of the walls. In each are different goods, and each set of goods is neatly organized. A circle of chairs is formed around the desk in the center of the small building. The single man in the building rises and steps toward Dorrin.

"Hmmm . . . dark staff, brown clothes, red-haired and younger than the average tradesman—you wouldn't be Dorrin, would you?" asks the white-haired man with a tanned but wrinkled face. The trader wears a faded blue shirt above equally faded trousers. His boots are dark polished leather.

"Ah . . . yes. How did you know?"

"Fyntal described you at the midwinter Council meeting. He said you were dangerous, but most orderly. Then Willum told me you made ingenious toys. Willum's dead, and Roald doesn't travel. Jasolt's at sea. So"—he shrugs—"I guessed. It impresses people. What can I do for you?"

"Buy some toys," Dorrin suggests, responding as directly as the trader has opened the conversation.

"I'd be happy to, in principle. In practice, that depends on the toys and the price." The trader gestures to a small table beside the desk.

Dorrin sets out the toys.

Vyrnil studies each in turn, slowly, checking each one, walking around the table as he looks, as if he can never quite stay in one place. "You're stamping the gears here, rather than cutting them, aren't you?"

"For toys, it doesn't seem to make much difference."

"It probably doesn't. Besides, who could afford to cut gears for small toys? The stamping idea is a nice touch." He sets down the boat. "I like this best, but they'll all sell in Hamor and Nordla. I won't quibble the way Willum did. Four pennies each, rounded up to the nearest half-silver."

Dorrin lays out the ten toys he has left.

"That'd be four and a half. Let's say five, if you'll let me see the whole lot first next time."

Dorrin studies the trader.

"How did I know? I have a boy watching the competitors. Roald's sharp enough to buy some of what you offer, but won't take risks. And no one makes uneven numbers of different styles, especially someone as orderly as you."

Dorrin shakes his head and laughs. "I'm afraid you have me pegged, ser."

Vyrnil returns the laugh. "No. You have me pegged. I'm the one buying."

Dorrin shrugs, even as Vyrnil is counting out the five silvers.

"Here you go, Dorrin. I probably can't take any more until after midsummer. I hope to see you then." He walks Dorrin to the door and watches as the younger man mounts.

Dorrin tries not to frown as he turns Meriwhen back toward Yarrl's. Who is Vyrnil? Just an abnormally sharp trader? Or more? He certainly has no sense of chaos about him, and his building is orderly, even if the man is personally overwhelming.

The scent of rain builds as Meriwhen carries him past the Tankard and back uphill into upper Diev.

LXXXI

"Archers! Now!" Brede's voice booms across the hillside.

Nulta, Westun, and Clyda rise from behind the low

wall and loose their arrows, firing in succession, not in volleys. One arrow clunks on the stone wall by the first wagon. Another slices through the purple clover of early summer on the highland plains. A herd of distant black-faced sheep graze on.

"Ambush! It's an ambush!"

One purple-clad rider grasps his shoulder. Another looks toward the stone wall. " ... where are the bastards?"

The trader who has been fending off a saber with a staff uses the distraction to deliver a crashing blow to another rider. The Gallosian looks from the trader to the archers, and slashes wildly before urging his horse back along the road to Gallos. One rider clutches at his chest, tumbling off his mount, one foot tangled in the stirrup and hobbling his mount.

" ... east! Back along the road."

"Mount!" Brede's voice is low, but the response is instantaneous, and the Spidlarian squad waits for the arrival of the raiders.

Hoofbeats drum on the damp clay as the Gallosians pound down the road away from the archers and their arrows.

"Now!"

Brede's sword is like lightning—two Gallosians fall before they even understand the blond giant is among them.

" ... bastards ... "

" ... aeeii ... "

Kadara, double swords cutting through arms and necks, follows in Brede's wake. Brede wheels and starts back through the Gallosian raiders, dropping one raider, then another. The eight others do less damage, cutting down perhaps four others among themselves.

A single horseman struggles through the melee and heads uphill. Kadara wheels her mare after the man, bending low in the saddle. He looks back, sees the pursuer and spurs his horse.

Kadara smiles, but lets the mare run easily. Another kay, and she is within a rod of the flagging horse.

The Gallosian turns in the saddle, sees the single female guard, and grins, raising his saber.

The grin drops from his face as Kadara drops the reins and lifts the dagger-pointed Westwind short-sword—then hurls it into his back. She slams aside his weak saber parry with the longer sword and rips it through his throat backhandedly.

When the raider slumps over his saddle and his horse slows, Kadara catches the reins, slows, and cleans both weapons. Then she leads the horse, bearing the dead Gallosian, back toward the rest of the squad.

As she nears the site of the skirmish, she can hear the shovels. The traders, of course, are gone, hurrying back toward Elparta, recognizing the dangers of attempting to reach Gallos—at least on this day. "They'll try some other road in another eight-day . . . the idiots," murmurs Kadara.

" . . . she-cat got another one . . ."

" . . . wouldn't want her after me . . ."

She reins up beside the other woman blade. Jyrin is digging a grave. Kadara tumbles the dead raider from his mount, expertly removes perhaps two silvers in assorted coins, as well as a knife, two rings, and a pendant, and the saber and scabbard. "Want to take a rest and let me start on this one?"

Jyrin hands the shovel to Kadara. "Be my guest."

Kadara cuts through the turf and lays it aside, then begins to dig through the damp clayey soil. She does not halt as Brede rides up and surveys the two partly dug graves.

"Remember. Try not to leave too much in the way of traces." He rides on to the next group.

"Don't know as it makes much difference," opines Jyrin. "What do you think?"

Kadara brushes away a fly as she does so. "I guess the idea is to have these Gallosians disappear. How would you feel if a whole squad just vanished?"

"Don't know as I'd like that. That why you chased down the last one?"

"Yes." Kadara continues digging.

"I wondered about the shovels." Jyrin looks from the two bodies to the blond squad leader overseeing another set of graves. "You two are scary ... real scary."

Kadara brushes back the sweat from her forehead, wishing the heat of summer had held off, before continuing to deepen the unmarked grave.

LXXXII

DORRIN STUDIES THE three piles, comparing each to the fourth, the one filled with dark gray granules, letting his senses enfold one after the other.

Finally, he understands ... enough. Carefully he replaces the yellow powder in its jar, the white in its jar, and the charcoal in its container. The gray powder he carries over to the barrel in the corner, where he eases the iron-bound wooden cover off and carefully pours the powder back. After climbing up the packed clay steps, he lifts the battered door, holding on firmly while closing it against the winds that precede the thunderstorm.

His caution in dealing with the powder only during storms may be excessive, but he recalls the feelings of being watched and his father's lessons about how storms disrupt the far-seeing powers of the White Wizards.

Leaning against the near-gale, he makes his way uphill from the old root cellar, the one that has outlasted the house that once stood there, past the trees that are more than saplings and less than mature oaks, and back to Rylla's cottage. He glances toward the other knoll, the one by the stream where he will build, if he can, his own cottage. He and Liedral will need somewhere to live and to work.

He pauses by the enlarged garden as heavy rain droplets begin to fall, bending and letting his fingers caress the blue green of the winterspice sprouts and the pale, almost white brinn. If they continue to thrive, there will be enough for Vyrnil or Liedral or someone to sell. He hurries toward the cottage as the wall of rain walks down the hillside. Stopping to untie Meriwhen, he leads her under the broad side eave of the cottage.

Rylla is grinding herbs as he walks into the main room.

"The storm's about to hit."

"Like as to the demon's own," mutters the healer.

"Me or the storm?"

"Oh, the thunderstorms are like as to the White Wizards. Filled with lightning and lots of rain. When they're over, they're over. You, Dorrin . . ." She shakes her head. "You're like a deep river—all calm on the top, the kind the rivermen love and respect, and fear."

"Me?"

"You. What you're doing with your twiddles, this old woman doesn't know, but you're going to change the world if the Whites don't get you first."

"You believe that, and you let me stay here?"

"This old world needs changing, child. What do I have to lose?" Her hands hold the pestle, and she continues to grind in the deep mortar. "Don't know as I like how you did it, but you stopped that Gerhalm from killing Merga and her child. Already those sprouts in the garden are taller than any I'd plant would be by midsummer."

"Anything I can do?"

"In a moment." She empties the mixture of dried and crushed leaves into a small clay jar and corks it, then wipes the mortar clean. "You can grind some pepper."

"Just pepper?"

"You asked if you could help."

Dorrin takes the mortar.

Rylla hands him the bowl of peppercorns. "Just a thumbful or so, for soup. It's always chill after a mountain thunderstorm, and these old bones get cold."

"You're hardly that old."

"All healers are old. Even you are. And start grinding the pepper."

After the worst of the storm has passed, Dorrin reclaims Meriwhen, pleased that she has not gnawed the bushes—not that she likes the elder bushes anyway—and wipes the saddle as dry as he can. He really needs a small stable to go with the cottage he plans. Every time he plans something, it gets more complicated. Then again, perhaps that is life.

The sun shines on his damp shirt by the time he rides into the yard behind the smithy. He waves to Petra, who is raking out Zilda's pen, and receives a quick wave in return.

After he has finished a quick currying of Meriwhen, and as he is closing the stall, Reisa walks into the barn.

"That trader, the thin one from Diev, he stopped by this morning and left this for you." Reisa hands Dorrin the folded parchment. "He seemed almost relieved when I said you weren't here. He left in a hurry."

Dorrin frowns, looking at the seal, letting his senses

touch the wax. Both the hint of chaos around the seal and the wax itself tell that the letter has been opened and resealed. "He well might."

"You don't like him?"

"There's something there that bothers me," Dorrin temporizes, trying not to reveal the discomfort the evasion causes.

"It's more than a little something."

Dorrin shrugs rather than say more about Jarnish. "I need to get into my smithing clothes."

"I'll bet you read the letter first." Reisa grins.

Dorrin blushes.

"Still in love?"

He keeps blushing, even as he walks toward his room.

The room, shutters and window open, is still almost stifling as he eases open the seal and begins to read.

Dorrin—

It took a long time to get back to Jellico, since the coaster's captain didn't want to risk Tyrhavven and couldn't afford the dues at Lydiar. We ended up in Pyrdya, a sad port, if you can call it that. I rode my nags to Renklaar and took a river barge up to Hydolar. That took two eightdays against the current, but I needed to save the horses for the hills on the way home.

I did sell your toy in Hydolar, but have kept the money until someone trustworthy is headed in your direction. I hope you get this letter, but since I cannot be sure, I am not sending coin with it.

The warehouse was a mess. Freidr was upset because I wasn't there, and the Viscount had insisted on inspecting all trading houses. The supposed reason was that someone had stolen some goods belonging to the White Wizards. Of course, no one ever said exactly what those goods were. And we got such a thorough inspection that a lot of goods that were there when I left are nowhere to be found.

Spring had almost ended when I arrived home, and the heat of summer has already begun to press down upon us. There may be some coin to be made on a quiet run to Sligo northeast of Tyrhavven. I cannot leave too quickly, because the warehouse will take some more work.

I also miss you. I miss the laughter, even the snow in the face, and sitting in the cold talking. Sometimes, I think I should have stayed, but how could we have managed? I'm an impoverished trader, and you are a struggling smith. For that matter, how could Freidr have managed? But I miss you, my love.

Liedral

Dorrin purses his lips. Nothing in the letter is odd or strange. Why would a White Wizard be interested in a letter between two lovers? And what White Wizard? The one who looked over all of them on the road from Fairhaven had dismissed them casually. Is Freidr tied up with the Whites? Liedral's brother is certainly not a White himself; that Dorrin would have known even when he met the man.

He refolds the letter and places it inside the wooden box. He misses Liedral, and the broken seal on the letter nags at him.

He pulls off his brown shirt, now showing some considerable wear, and pulls on the near-ragged castoff he uses in the smithy. Nails—he will probably be making nails, or something equally stimulating.

LXXXIII

AFTER BRUSHING AWAY a fly, which buzzes towards Kadara, Brede takes a deep pull of the cold redberry. "How do you keep it cold?"

"In the well," answers Petra. "Dorrin says that the water comes from the Westhorns."

Kadara waves away the fly, looking toward the goat pen. "Is that the one you saved?"

"Zilda? The white terror?" Dorrin laughs. "She'll chew on anything. So she spends more time in the pen these days."

"Especially when company's here." Reisa brings out a chair from the kitchen and sets it in the corner nearest the smithy door.

Dorrin looks out at the long shadows and the reddish cast to the light thrown by the setting sun. He shifts his weight on the stool, happy enough just to be sitting.

"Supper was good, thank you," Kadara offers.

"Very good," adds Brede. "Especially the seasoning."

"You'll have to thank Dorrin for that. Last year he took over the spices, and we were able to dry everything from peppers to mustard to sage. This year"—she gestures toward the patch of green behind the well—"things look even better. Darkness knows how he has time."

"How are things with your squad?" asks Dorrin quickly.

"For now, they're fine," Kadara says. "But by late this year or early next year, that will change."

"Perhaps," adds Brede.

"Perhaps, cowdung! He's been so good that we've been able to cut down on the ... thieves raiding our traders."

Dorrin rubs his chin with his left hand, still holding a half a mug of redberry in his right. "If you're successful in stopping them in Spidlar, wouldn't they just wait until the traders got into Gallos or Certis?"

Kadara tries not to look at Brede.

Brede shrugs. "I imagine the White Wizards have their own ways."

"Besides," Kadara continues, "they can't very well make an agreement with the highwaymen only to rob Spidlarian traders."

"I would expect not," Reisa says from the corner. "Still, I hold with Brede. The Whites will find some way. They always do."

"By the way, Dorrin," asks Kadara, "how is Liedral? You've managed to avoid answering any questions for most of the afternoon and evening. She came during late winter, and you never mentioned that."

"She's all right, according to her last letter."

"That's not exactly ..." Kadara shakes her head. "She traveled through frozen light to get here, and you just think she's all right?"

"Kadara ..." Brede says.

"No, it's all right. I worry, but there's not a lot I can do. I probably shouldn't have let her go ... but I wasn't thinking ..."

"Oh ... now it comes out. You're actually admitting you care for the woman?"

Dorrin looks at the barn, wondering if Kadara has forgotten how many years he went next door searching for her. Or is this her way of expressing relief that he has found someone who loves him?

"You should have seen them," affirms Petra.

"Now, Petra. They did watch the Council night fireworks with us in the snow."

"Where they stood melted."

Dorrin hopes that the fading glow of twilight will hide his flush.

"Shouldn't she be all right in Jellico?" asks Brede.

"Her brother is somehow tied up with the Whites, and he knows we're from Recluce. Their warehouse was rather thoroughly inspected, and some things are missing."

"You don't think her brother would . . ."

"No. But . . ." How can Dorrin explain the feeling he has of being watched from a distance? Or letter seals that have been resealed? Or the general unease that follows him, that sometimes drives him to working to the greatest extent that his body will take?

"You don't know what the White ones will do," adds Reisa.

"We're beginning to understand," Kadara responds dryly. "But why would they be interested in Dorrin?"

"I don't know." Dorrin looks blankly southward, up the sloping hillsides toward Rylla's cottage. "They may not be."

"You don't really believe that, do you?" The voice is Yarrl's. With the older smith's comment, the conversation halts for a moment.

"Why do you say that, papa?"

"Man puts order in everything he does, even cold iron. Whites don't seem to like that kind of order. Things just sort of fall into place around young Dorrin. Were I a White, I'd be interested in what he was a-doing."

"So would I," squeaks Vaos, from the steps, where he munches on a leftover bread crust.

"You're still eating, scamp?" asks Petra.

Vaos nods as he takes another bite.

"Makes sense . . . in a way," muses Brede.

And yet, in Dorrin's mind, too much is missing. What has he done besides heal a few people, grow some spices, and make ordered models and toys? Brede has killed more than a few chaos minions. Dorrin has done nothing of the sort. Dorrin looks southward at the last hints of light on the Westhorns. After all, what more can he say?

LXXXIV

THE GRAY STONE is heavy ... too heavy. Dorrin lifts the sledge and pounds the tube into the space between the stones. Then he pours the powder down the tube until it is filled. The cap is wedged in place, and Dorrin lights the fuse—and sprints downhill and behind the rotting tree stump.

Crummmppp ...

After trudging back uphill, he surveys the hole that will be his cellar, shakes his head, and places another wooden tube. With luck, by late summer he will have his foundation in place, one way or another. Again, he lights the fuse.

This time, the results are better, and he begins to shovel clay, soil, and broken rock. Still, he is revising his plans. The cellar will be smaller, far smaller, than he has planned. He wipes his forehead and pauses, looking uphill toward the healer's cottage.

Rylla walks through the grass, bringing a pitcher of redberry and a ragged towel. Dorrin uses the towel first.

"There's an easier way, Dorrin. And ye'd have more time for healing."

"Oh?"

"Right now, some of the farmers and farm hands have slack time for a few eight-days. Not much, but some. You could pay them to dig out the rest."

Dorrin frowns. "How much?"

"A half-copper a day a man."

The healer is right; he cannot do everything. He should have asked, but it is hard for him to ask others.

"They dug the cellar for my cottage in two days. Yours would be bigger, it be true, but you have a hole for them to work from."

"How do I do it?"

She smiles. "You put stakes at the corners, and make a rod showing how deep' you want the hole. I will talk to Asavah. He was my sister's man."

Dorrin sips the redberry. He had not even known the healer had a sister. "Do you have any nieces or nephews?"

"A nephew, Rolta. He is a sailor, a mate, on ser Gylert's biggest ship."

Dorrin swallows the last of the redberry and points across the ridge toward the garden. "Now that you've solved that problem, let me go back to checking the spices, especially the winterspice. Can we get fine sand somewhere? I think the soil has too much clay."

"Asavah might have some." Rylla follows Dorrin up the slope.

"At a few half-coppers a wagon?"

"It might not be that much." The healer smiles. "The sand, even from fresh water, is free. It's the time of the men and the use of the wagon. We can get sand from the upper branch that goes into the Weyel. And don't you worry, young fellow. This old healer can afford sand. Who knows? I might even be able to work it into the garden with ye."

Dorrin opens the cottage door.

"There ye go again, treating me like a fine lady, instead of the old crone I am."

"You're more of a lady than most who claim the title."

"You'll turn my head yet, young scoundrel. I take

it the fine words mean you'll be on your way to the smithy? After not healing at all this morning?"

Dorrin blushes.

"Now ... now ... you won't even let me have a compliment without taking it away? Shame on you!" Rylla grins. "Off with you."

"What about Granny Clarabur?"

"She can do without your pretty face. Besides, all she wants is to tell everyone how terrible her health be. She'll have been doing that for near on ten years, and she isn't close to dying yet."

Dorrin bows to Rylla's superior logic. "Then I'll see you tomorrow."

"I'll see if Asavah can bring the sand, along with those strong fellows to dig your hole. You just bring the coppers, in coppers, mind ye."

Dorrin is still shaking his head as he rides back to Yarrl's.

When he arrives, he finds that Reisa has Vaos weeding the garden.

"Master Dorrin, master Dorrin, you'll be needing me in the smithy, won't you?" The imp's voice is as close to pleading as Dorrin has heard, and he lifts his mud-covered hands almost in prayer.

"Yarrl decided to deliver the wagon work to Froos," Reisa noted.

"Froos is in no hurry to collect what he commissions, I take it."

"Nor to pay," adds Petra from the barn.

"He said you'd know what to do."

"Harness work for Honsard and Bequa, and the old cooper ..."

"Milsta," Reisa finishes.

"Master Dorrin?" asks Vaos.

"I need to curry Meriwhen. It'll be a bit. You can finish there."

"Yes, ser."

Reisa grins from behind Vaos. "Just finish that row, young Vaos, and then you can wash off all the dirt."

Dorrin dismounts and leads Meriwhen into the barn, still grinning at the thought of Vaos gardening.

"You're mean." Petra leans against the hay rake.

"Why?"

"Just because you never played as a boy, you don't think anyone should." She smiles, but her words are firm.

"I played," Dorrin protests, unsaddling Meriwhen.

"At what?"

"Oh, I watched Hegl, or my mother, and sometimes I tried to build boats and sail them in the surf."

"Who was Hegl?"

"Kadara's father. He was a smith. And sometimes Kadara and I played."

"Likely story. You probably spent more time watching her father."

Dorrin pauses.

"I thought so." Petra shakes her head, then sets aside the rake and walks toward the field where the cows are tethered.

Dorrin takes out the brush and ponders. Has he ever really played—except when Liedral has come to visit? Is that why he misses her? The only reason? No . . . that is hardly the only reason. He takes up the brush. He still has too much to do, and he needs to get to the smithy.

Once changed and in the smithy, Dorrin can see a broken wagon tongue and the old harnesses that Yarrl has left out, and even a skiving knife, should he need it. Vaos almost scampers into the forge area, his hands still wet.

"The big tank is low, Vaos," Dorrin says. "I'd say we'll need two pails of water. But first bring in another barrow of charcoal. Yarrl must have left even before midmorning."

"Yes, master Dorrin, he did."

"I'm not a master, you imp. I'm a striker, and flattery won't get you out of getting the charcoal and refilling the slack tank."

After looking over the work at hand, Dorrin lays out the tools he will need, and then rebuilds the forge fire once Vaos brings in the charcoal.

"Before you get the water, keep pumping this until we get white across to here."

Vaos nods glumly.

"What's the matter?"

"It's my mum. She's talking about hooking up with Zerto. He's a mate on old Fyntal's *Dorabeau*. If'n she does . . ."

"You sleep here most of the time, anyway."

"It's not me. It's Rek. He's my little brother. He's ten."

Dorrin waits.

"She won't take him or me. She says my dad left us on her, and she's had enough. I'm settled, but Rek . . ."

"What's the problem?"

"He's got a clubfoot. So he can't run. Can't do stable work or quick errands."

"Can he stand or carry things?"

"Yes, ser. He's as strong as I am."

Dorrin realized Vaos has trapped him. "I'll take a look."

"Would you?"

"I said I would. But any decision's Yarrl's, you understand, and if you say a word, I won't even try."

"Yes, ser."

"Get the water."

"Yes, ser."

Dorrin checks the forge heat, then takes the tongs and sets the flat iron on the bricks. With the cold chisel he cuts off the old rivets and removes the broken sections, checking the iron. Finally he nods. The tongue can be welded together, but he will need new stock. He frowns, then walks along the junk pile until he comes to the assorted wagon and sleigh spars and timbers. As he vaguely remembered, there is a square oak brace that will do, with a bit of shortening.

He clamps the brace in the box vice, measures it against the original, and shortens it with the crosscut saw, then rasps and files it smooth. After loosening the vice, he removes the brace and checks it against the cracked original tongue, nodding. Finally, using the brace and bit, he drills the holes for the rivets.

Next comes the welding. First he takes the narrow bar stock and heats it, fullering it down with hammer blows across the anvil horn until it is thin enough to wrap around the cracked tongue. Then he sets the fullered bar in the forge to heat, while he takes the tongue and heats it almost to white-hot before removing it and using the hammer to scarf the contact points and upset the edges where he will wrap the bar stock. Next come several taps to remove the scale, followed by the flux. He sets the tongue back in the forge until both it and the thin iron are white-hot. Both come out, and Dorrin quickly hammers the two together, striking from the inside out with a few light strokes. He sets the welded tongue on the forge bricks to cool to forging heat before completing the shaping.

While the iron cools to cherry red, Dorrin fullers the small bar stock to rivet size, then uses the hot set to cut them, setting both on the forge while he returns to the tongue and uses the flatter to finish smoothing the tongue.

After wiping his forehead, he dips the tongue brace in the slack tank and sets it on the anvil. He heats the first rivet, then drives it through the brace until it flattens against the round-bottomed swage.

Dorrin lifts the ball peen hammer and with four quick offset strokes finishes the top of the first rivet holding the iron of the wagon tongue in place. With the tongs he lifts the second rivet from the forge and slides it into place. A quick stroke flattens the bottom side against the swage, and Dorrin follows up with another set of glancing strokes, first on the top, and then on the bottom.

After setting aside the hammer and tongs, Dorrin carries the heavy tongue out into the corner for finished work and then lugs back in the heavy leather harness, which he lays on the workbench. A heel chain clevis, and two hame line rings need replacing, and that means reworking and riveting the harness as well.

With the cold chisel, he cuts away the old rivets and measures them to get the right rod stock. He sets the stock for the replacement rivets aside, and takes the larger rod he will need to fuller down to forge the hame line rings. According to Yarrl, weight-bearing rings for carter's harnesses must always be forged fresh. That may be, reflects Dorrin, why Yarrl's work holds up better than Henstaal's.

"You're almost as quick as Yarrl." Vaos's face is flushed, and sweat runs from his hair.

"Take a break and get some water," Dorrin orders.

"Thank you, ser." Vaos does not scamper from the forge heat, but walks toward the comparative cool of the yard.

Dorrin looks at the boy's back, wondering why he has even agreed to see Vaos's younger brother. If Rek can pump the bellows, perhaps he can offer to pay part of his upkeep. Dorrin turns to the next harness.

LXXXV

As THE LAST beam falls in place, Dorrin grins.

"Why are you so cheerful?" asks Pergun. "It's only the frame for a small barn." He points toward the large foundation less than fifty cubits away, composed of neatly mortared stone. "You still haven't told me how you're going to get the frame up on that."

"The same way we did this." Behind Dorrin the rectangular frame stands, even with what will be the doorway to the hayloft squared off in beams.

"Huuhhh?"

"Look. That's why I build models. You figure it out on a small scale, and then you do it bigger. This crane will work. I can do that. That saves me coins so that I can hire others to do the things that take time—or pay for timber at Hemmil's extravagant prices."

"Why do you need a small building at all?"

"For horses."

"But that one is big enough."

"Not for a house and a small smithy and a small warehouse. The smithy doesn't have a foundation. It's on the other end—the cleared part."

Pergun spits out away from the stable.

"You want to earn your coppers? Get out that hammer. We need to frame this and get the flooring across the top before we put the roof joists up."

Pergun lifts the hammer. "For this, I'm spending a free day?"

"You're lucky you get free days."

"Does everyone from Recluce work like you do?"

"No . . . just those of us who got kicked out."

"You know . . . all the troopers are scared to death of your friends."

Dorrin opens the small keg of nails he has forged. "Here. Why?"

"Good nails. You make them?" Pergun slips a handful, more like miniature bridge spikes, into the cloth pouch on his belt.

Dorrin nods.

"Vorban told me the she-cat threw a shortsword through a highwayman."

"Through him?" Dorrin puts a plank in place, and, in three quick blows, fixes the top in position. "Even for Kadara, that's hard to believe."

"He looked over his shoulder when he said it. They still would rather follow the big guy, though. Vorban says that he knows what he's doing. Most of the officers don't." Pergun works on the other side of the door frame, framing the pine planks away from Dorrin.

Before midmorning, the small stable is framed, and Dorrin has Meriwhen and the crane lifting the pre-joined roof trusses into place.

" . . . that's it . . . a little lower . . ." Pergun wipes his forehead. "How did you think of those brackets?"

"It seemed logical." Dorrin unstraps the leather cradle before moving the crane to the other side of the building.

"Never seen anything go up this fast." Pergun walks to the other side of the floor, avoiding the square opening. "Better do a ladder here."

"Good point. Need to box off one stall, too. But the roof should come first." Dorrin resets the crane and puts the cradle around the other truss.

"First man I know who builds a stable for his horse before he builds a roof over his own head."

"It's simpler this way. Besides, I can see that I'll

need different brackets—heavier, too—for the main building."

Pergun shakes his head and waits for the truss to rise to him.

"If I designed some clamps, here," says Dorrin, half-aloud, "I could do this alone."

"Light! Don't you like people? You do everything alone, and you do it better."

"Of course, I like people. But I can't afford to pay all of them."

"There is that."

"Here it comes." Dorrin urges Meriwhen forward, and the truss is lifted up to Pergun, who guides it into the brackets. Next come the cross beams, which fit in the notches in the trusses, then the flat planks for the roof.

It is late afternoon when Pergun eases the borrowed wagon away from the framed stable and the foundation of the main building. "You ever stop working, Dorrin?"

"There's a lot to do," Dorrin replies from atop the stable where he is installing shakes. "Like you, I can't take off very often."

"You'll be here till sunset."

"Probably until the roof's done. The rest I'll do in bits—until I put up the house and smithy."

"When will that be?"

"At least a couple of eight-days. I want to get it up before harvest, though. Rylla says there's a slack time just before that, and I can get some help for not too much."

The mill hand surveys the ridge. "They'll have you on the Council in a couple of years."

"Not me."

"You make coins, and you don't have much choice." Pergun flicks the reins. "Don't get caught up there after dark."

"I'll try not to." Dorrin frowns at Pergun's last comment. Does making money limit choices? How much? He continues nailing shakes into place.

LXXXVI

"He's getting totally insufferable." Anya takes a deep swallow.

"Getting?" Sterol's fingers touch the edge of the screeing glass.

"All right. He's always been arrogant. It's just bothering me more now." Anya finishes the wine with a full swallow. "He flaunts his power. He said he'll bring down Axalt singlehandedly. But not until the spring."

Sterol represses a smile. "Do you think he can?"

She refills her glass. "Of course. Whether it's wise is another question."

Sterol walks over to the dining table, where he fills his own glass. "I take it that he's continuing to hide his plans from you."

"If he has any."

"Sarcasm that blunt doesn't become you. Jeslek has great plans."

"He's concerned—not quite worried—about something in Spidlar. Something to do with the Blacks. He's stewed about it all spring and summer."

"He's told you this?"

"Of course not. But I can sense hints of it."

"What has Fydel told you?"

"You obviously know." Anya sips from the second glass more slowly.

"Why would Jeslek worry about letters from a poor trader in Jellico? So there must be something in the ironworker that isn't obvious."

"You are so brilliant, Sterol."

"The same Jeslek who would smash a city is tiptoe-ing around a mere youngster. So who is the youngster?"

"He's from Recluce," Anya says, conceding nothing the older man does not already know.

"Does that matter, really?"

"It must, mustn't it?" She smiles crookedly.

"You know, Anya," sighs Sterol, "you aren't nearly so clever as you think. Neither is Fydel. Jeslek may be insufferable, but he's far from stupid. Neither am I. You don't want to be High Wizard because you think whoever is will fail in any confrontation with Recluce. So you want to be second behind whichever of us is in control."

"And if I do?"

"That's dangerous, too. Not so obviously." Sterol shrugs. "In any case, if Jeslek is worried about this smith . . . he bears watching."

"Are you telling me that just because this . . . ironworker . . . has powerful parents across the ocean, Jeslek is being more careful of him than . . . ?"

"Than you? That's exactly what I'm saying. If I were Jeslek, I'd try something indirect, or have the young man perish in the fall of Spidlar, but not before. Why risk getting Recluce involved earlier than necessary?"

"It's not a risk."

"Anya, dear, anything is a risk. Best you remember that." Sterol sips from his glass, before responding to the knock on the door. "I believe supper has arrived."

"It's about time."

LXXXVII

"COME ON, GIRL." Dorrin urges Meriwhen forward, and the harness tightens as the ropes thread through the pulleys and the last of the four frame sections rises into place.

Although the morning is yet cool, with the sun low in the east, his work shirt is stained with sweat, and an occasional fly buzzes toward him. With deft movements, he brushes back a horsefly, clamps the lines in place, and checks the antique-style crane before releasing the harness tension. Then he walks to the northern post and eases one of the two side stones into place in the hole, then the other. The keyed stones follow. Once the four stones are locked tight in place, he begins to shovel the clay around the outside. After several shovelfuls, he takes the heavy short limb he is using as a tamper and compacts the clay. Then he repeats the process with the other post. With this, all four posts, and the longitudinal beams holding each pair together, are held in place, but he cannot count on their continued stability until both cross beams are raised, and lowered into position.

Raising the cross beam will be tricky. First he must stand on the short triangular ladder to undo the leather cradle, then reposition the crane and fasten the cradle around the shorter beam. After loosening the leather and ropes, Dorrin readjusts his makeshift crane and Meriwhen.

"Let's go, girl."

Whufffff . . .

"I know. I know. You're for riding, not lifting and

hauling. But lifting and hauling is what we need to do."

Finally, the cross beam hangs precariously in the air, just above the brackets and notches that represent Dorrin's fusion of woodwork and ironwork. Dorrin gets back on the ladder and guides one end into the bracket, loosely tying it down so that the far end is correspondingly higher. Then he eases up on the clamps to lower the beam until it almost touches the bracket top at the far end. Again he moves the ladder and readjusts the cross beam before releasing the clamps. The cross beam locks into place. He has another six cross beams to go before he can bracket the posts between them and the foundation sills.

With a deep breath, he repositions the ladder, undoes the leather cradle, and steps down. He moves Meriwhen, the crane, and the ropes and pulleys, and their anchors to the other end of the foundation, where he sets up for the same effort. After the main cross beams, he must do the smaller frame for the smithy that will stand at the south end of the structure.

It is well after midmorning, and the thunderclouds have begun to form, before the frame is locked in place. He sits down and drinks from the pitcher of water and chews a hunk off the loaf of bread. Despite the intermittent clouds, and the breeze, he is soaked with sweat. So far, he has a foundation and the basic frame for the building that—he hopes—will house him and Liedral.

He wipes his forehead. Then he takes the wheel-barrow and the smaller casks and trundles them over to the stream, where he fills the casks. After pushing the cask-filled wheelbarrow back, he adds the water to the mortar and begins to mix. Mixing the heavy substance by hand is tedious, and he stops a number of times before the cement feels right. With the wheel-barrow he has borrowed from Yarrl, he carts one load to the northern post, and pours and shovels the mortar in between the heavy stones bracing the post. He wheels the barrow back to the battered half-barrel he uses as a mixing tub and refills the barrow.

By noon, he has cemented in place all the posts, and bracketed the sill beams in position, along with most of the posts that fit between the cross beams and sill beams. Meriwhen is tied up and grazes by her recently completed stable, presumably glad that she is not lifting beams.

Actually, raising the frame of the main structure has been the easy part. Designing, measuring, smithing, and assembling the frames and trusses has taken most of the eight-days since midsummer.

Dorrin sits on the front stoop and rests, thinking about the enormous amount of work yet to do before fall, and especially before the winter grips Diev . . . and all for a place that may be in jeopardy from the White Wizards even before it is truly finished.

Why is he doing it? Why does anyone do anything? There's always a reason not to do something. After all, he reflects as he walks toward Rylla's cottage, wiping the sweat that will not stop off his forehead, death is the result of life. So if you'll die, why bother to live? Or do anything right?

He wonders what his father or Lortren would think—Dorrin considering solid work as a necessary protest against the futility of life and chaos.

He looks back at the clear structure of order he has raised on the ridge. Then he smiles and walks quickly toward the healer's cottage and garden.

LXXXVIII

DORRIN SURVEYS THE small pool, noting the green scum around the edges. Above the pond, the water flows down the rocky ledge, clear and fresh, from the underground spring. His eyes turn from the rock face nearly twice his height down the browning hillside toward the ridge his framed house and stable share with Rylla's smaller cottage. Even with the morning shadows, he can see the silver dew across the fall grasses.

The healer has insisted on having the Guild document her sale of the land to Dorrin. "What would ye do if lightning struck me dead?" she had asked. "A dead person doesn't keep good faith."

"You won't die," Dorrin had protested.

"We all die. Now get that worthless Hasten out here and seal this."

Hasten had come, bowing and scraping the whole time.

Dorrin looks back at the near-stagnant pool and laughs softly, ruefully, thinking of how the gray-haired Guild functionary fears a mere healer and sometime smith, as if Dorrin were anything more than a toy-maker with dreams. After all, that is all he is. And his head does not ache at the thought.

Whhnnnnn . . .

He swats at the mosquito—and misses. The insects must be hungry to be so active so early in the day. A swarm of the insects gathers around him, so many that his attempts to ward them away are nearly useless. He swats another, pulping it on his neck, and getting his own blood on his fingers. He shakes his head, then takes a deep breath, still trying to wave off the hungry insects, before placing a powder-filled tube in the muddy bank over which the water flows into the winding trickle that feeds the pond below their houses.

After striking the fuse, he retreats past yellowing oak saplings and behind the flaking and crumbling stump of an oak cut for timber years earlier.

Crummmpppp . . .

The charge creates enough of a hole in the bank that the small pond begins to drain immediately. Dorrin picks up his shovel and begins scooping out the muck. Once he cleans out the area, he will divert the water while he installs the stone catch basin and the piping that will lead to his water tank. There is no reason why he cannot have running water in his kitchen, even if it will be cold, but he will have to ensure that the piping and the spring are deep enough not to freeze.

He continues to dig and swat until it is time for a late breakfast—except that it would have been the time he once ate a normal breakfast not too many years before in Extina. How things can change in such a short while!

Using the cold water from the spring, he strips to his waist and washes up as well as he can, still avoiding the mosquitoes, and carries his shovel and work shirt as he trudges through the bushes and low growth back downhill.

He wishes he could do more, but he needs to gather another assortment of spices and deliver them to Vyrnil, not to mention checking with Rylla to see if she needs him for any of those who may come for her services. Some of the early corn is already being harvested, and there are always harvest injuries.

He glances back uphill at the spring. Will he ever be able to put all the pieces together? The house and workroom are framed and roofed and even glazed, and the plasterer has finished. But outside of the forge, a stove he has built himself, and a bed, a table, and two chairs, he has no furniture.

He stops beside the stable; he has not fed Meriwhen. Setting the shovel back in the barn and draping his damp shirt over the stall wall, he fills her manger with hay. Then he levers the top off the grain barrel and uses the wooden scoop to fill the smaller section of the manger.

Whuffff . . .

"I know. I was late this morning. Better late than never." Dorrin looks at the water barrel, still a third full. He can refill that later.

He still has to gather the spices, bundle and package them and write out the labels for the trader—and get to Rylla's. He closes the stall, picks up his shirt, and heads toward the nearly empty house.

After leaving his boots on the small covered porch, he steps into the kitchen, glancing at the papers by the box on the corner of the table. He picks up the letter, frowning again at the signs of tampering. Why are the Whites so interested in Liedral's letters—and presumably his to her?

His eyes skip down the page.

> . . . run to Sligo was profitable enough, but it was lonely. I did pick up some fine black wool, almost as good as what they grow in Recluce . . . These days I seem to miss you more, even when I am busy. Jellico is quieter than when you were here, and Freidr has been encouraging me to travel more . . . especially after the Sligo trip . . .
>
> . . . word is that things have settled on the borders between Kyphros and Spidlar . . . but the word is that trade is still not safe . . . except by sea . . . and that gets expensive . . .

... perhaps after harvest I can work out something ... love you and miss you ...

His own letter—carefully set in the top of the writing box—is not finished, not with the care he must take in writing something that is clearly being read.

Why are the White Wizards so interested in a lady trader and a toymaker and smith? Even if he could make his machines, and his steam engine, he certainly cannot make very many. And even if he does, neither Fairhaven nor Recluce want them ... so who would use them besides himself?

He looks out the window toward the healer's. Wool gathering will not get the herbs gathered and bundled, or the harvest injuries treated and healed. Or the iron work waiting at Yarrl's done.

LXXXIX

THE WHITE MISTS swirl away and reveal the fall brown grasses of the upland meadows somewhere north of Fenard and south of Elparta. In the center of the mirror, a trader's wagon plods southward. A red-haired woman drives the wagon, and a thin dark man rides beside.

Over the top of the hill waits another group, wearing the dark green tunics of Certis. As the wagon nears the hill crest, the riders fan and charge toward the two traders.

Just as quickly, the redhead halts the wagon, and two men with bows throw off brown cloths, aiming their arrows at the charging raiders. A pair of swords appears in the hands of the redhead, and from behind the raiders Spidlarian guards appear, led by a blond giant who strews bodies before him.

Not a single Certan raider survives. As the shovels appear for gravedigging, Jeslek waves his hand, and the image vanishes from the mirror. "Bah . . . no magic at all. Just good tactics and cleverness. No one survives; no bodies are found, and the rumor spreads that the Spidlarians are using magic."

"It doesn't exactly help to tell that to either the Viscount or the Prefect," observes Anya from the chair by the window.

"Or to admit it took more than a season and magic to figure it out," adds Fydel. "That's hard when they claim to have lost nearly a hundred men over the last two seasons."

"Do we know who is responsible?" asks the normally quiet Cerryl. "Beyond the obvious?" He gestures toward the blank mirror.

"Our . . . sources in Spidlar would indicate that most of the damage has been caused by one squad formed for this purpose last spring. Supposedly, the squad leader and assistant are outcasts from Recluce."

"Supposedly? That's rich! They exile two people, and those two people just happen to be in the right spot to block everything. Do you really believe that, Jeslek?" asks Fydel.

Jeslek does not correct Fydel's mathematics. "I said supposedly."

"What do you plan to do?"

"Now . . . nothing." He holds up a hand to forestall objections. "I'm not playing Jenred's waiting game. But do any of you really want a winter war?"

Headshakes cross the tower room.

"Once the roads clear in spring, I will personally direct our forces in the invasion of Spidlar. Over the winter, we should step up efforts to close off as much trade as possible—and, if possible, minimize the impact of Recluce's meddling." He smiles at Fydel. "We need to make it a hard winter indeed in Spidlar."

"Spidlar isn't the real enemy; Recluce is," reminds Fydel.

"You and I know who the real enemies are." Jeslek smiles with his mouth. "And their time will come."

"So clever, and so cryptic," murmurs Anya under her breath.

Jeslek's eyes fall on her, and her lips are silent. His eyes glitter, and she shivers. Fydel swallows, and Cerryl looks out the tower window.

XC

DORRIN TURNS ON the pallet. He should get up. The forge at his own smithy must be finished, and he needs to find someone else to buy his toys, and harvest is approaching, and Yarrl will need help . . .

"Ooooo . . ." He is hot, so hot. But he cannot seem to move.

"Easy, Dorrin. You need to rest."

Something cold presses his forehead, easing the fever, and he drops into darkness. When he wakes, his forehead is hot, but dry. Someone is talking.

"He was up there in the hills, setting up that fancy water system, and the mosquitoes got him. There'd be too many even for our smith mage to ward off, I'd say. Oh . . . you're waking, are ye?" Rylla leans over and sponges off his forehead. The coolness is welcome, more than welcome. "Drink this." She thrusts a mug at his lips.

"What . . . is . . . it?"

"Cider with willow bark and astra. It tastes terrible, but you need it."

Dorrin drinks, very slowly, trying to ignore the bitterness. He finishes the concoction, and leans back, marveling at the effort merely to drink.

He is not aware of exactly when he falls asleep or even when he wakes, except the sky outside is gray, and rain patters lightly on the roof.

This time Vaos sits on the stool by the bed. "You awake?"

"Sort of . . ."

"I'll be right back." The boy scampers from the room, but returns after a time, slightly damp, with Rylla.

The healer studies the smith, touches his forehead. "You'll heal. Wasn't totally sure about that before, but you're built like your forge inside." She turns to Vaos. "About half of them that get the hill fever die in the first couple of days. The rest live."

"Wonderful," groans Dorrin.

"Have some more of this," orders Rylla.

"Ugghhh . . ." But Dorrin drinks another mug of the bitter mixture.

"Keep him drinking the clean water, boy," she addresses Vaos. "And don't let him do anything but rest. Reisa will get me home now. He'll get well by himself. Just be quiet." The healer nods to Dorrin and leaves.

The smith rests, and sleeps, and wakes.

Vaos is not there when Dorrin wakes, but a mug filled with cool water is on the table beside the narrow bed. Dorrin's hand shakes, but he manages to get the mug. He is sipping the water when Vaos peers into the room.

The youngster slips onto the stool. "Vyrnil came by. I said you were away. He wants something new. He left a sketch of it—says it's something he saw on a Hamorian ship."

"Why don't you get the sketch?"

"The old healer said you weren't supposed to do *anything*."

"I can think," Dorrin snorts, ignoring the blurriness the gesture creates. "Go on. I won't move." That is true enough. He is scarcely in any shape to move anywhere, thanks to whatever fever the mosquitoes carried.

Before Dorrin has even thought much about moving, the strawberry-haired youngster has returned with the sketch.

"This is it."

Dorrin squints. The drawing does not seem to make much sense at first. "Turn it the other way."

Vaos complies, but the lines still make little sense to Dorrin.

"He said that it's a better way to sight the sun. Does that mean anything to you?"

Dorrin frowns, a glint of understanding trying to emerge from his still-fevered brain. "Perhaps it will." He closes his eyes for a moment. When he opens them, Vaos has set down the sketch.

"Why can't you heal yourself?" Vaos sits on the stool.

"Can you lift yourself off that stool?" growls Dorrin.

"Sure." Vaos hops from the stool.

"No," says Dorrin slowly. "Sit down."

Vaos's eyebrows lift, but he sits.

"Put your hands on your belt, and lift."

"Nothing happens."

"If I were well, could I lift you by your belt?"

"Ah . . . yes."

"Healing's the same way. You can only do it to others. Mostly," Dorrin adds.

"But why?"

"I don't know, and I'm too tired to think about it now." Dorrin leans back on the pillows and closes his eyes.

XCI

DORRIN RUBS HIS forehead, trying to reduce the throbbing in his head. Why has it taken so long to heal from a fever? All he has been able to do is move his few things into the new house—not even much in the way of light smithing—and the moving wouldn't have been possible without Vaos. He wants to slam his fist into the wobbly wooden table.

Instead, he sips the bitter mixture from the battered mug beside his writing box. He sets the mug down, picks up the sheet, and reads silently.

Liedral—

I am sorry it has taken a while to answer your latest letter, but I have been ill with a mosquito fever. I hope that, by the time you receive this, I will be fully back at work.

The house is finished. It should not take too much more work to finish the forge itself. The anvil was the expensive part! Do you know how much eleven stone of solid iron weighs? I also need more tools. Some of the hammers, like the straight and cross peen ones, I have already made for myself, and I have three sets of tongs. I also have some hot sets and some forks and swages and fullers—but not nearly enough. Most of what I have made from the toys and other devices has been spent. Being sick has not helped at all.

The house seems empty, even with Vaos living in the room off the smithy. I look forward to your coming when you can, and trust you will find the storage arrangements suitable for all that you might desire. Yarrl and Reisa have made a number of observations about the now-unused space, and Meriwhen is lonely. They often ask when you will be coming.

I recall when you saw the bird, and I had to catch the cart on the road to Jellico. That bird is still out there, flying around, I am certain, but we are not together.

Dorrin rubs his forehead again. What else can he say that will warn Liedral and not tell the readers of his letter that he knows it is being read? He takes another sip of the medicinal potion. He is stronger—that he can tell—but not strong enough to lift hammers for long. He dips the quill and resumes writing.

Thrap . . .

He looks up at the sound, glimpsing a figure through the small window that opens onto his too-small porch.

"Coming." He rises slowly, letting bare feet carry him to the door.

"At least you're up." Kadara's face is smudged, and her blue uniform is soiled. Beside her, Brede appears equally travel-stained.

"Come on in."

"You look like something the light fried." Kadara sits on one end of the crude bench on the other side of the table.

Brede closes the door and takes the other end of the bench.

"Thank you," Dorrin says.

"For what?"

"You came right after you arrived, didn't you? You both look like you've been riding for a long time."

"We have," Brede admits.

"Success is worse than failure." Kadara's voice is hard. "The better we get, the more they give us to do."

"I've got some cider." Dorrin walks toward the cooling tank in the corner of the kitchen and pulls the jug from the icy water. "It's cold."

"You put running water in here?"

"Such as it is. That's what got me sick. There were too many mosquitoes up in the hills when I put in the catch basin and piping." Dorrin pours cider into two crude glass tumblers, handing one to Kadara and the other to Brede.

"Why did you bother? Spidlar will be gone in a year, and we'll be on the run." Kadara pours down half a glass. "Darkness, that's good."

"Hmmmm," adds Brede.

Dorrin waits and refills both glasses. Then he sits down, trying not to wipe his forehead. "The Council won't give in to the Whites."

"They won't have much choice. They've posted notice of spring levies in Certis, Kyphros, Montgren, and Gallos."

"Has the Council recalled Spidlarian mercenaries from other duchies?"

Brede and Kadara exchange glances.

"They have, but the Whites are making it hard for them to return?"

Brede nods. "We'll get some back, but some have no desire to get ground down under the levies in the spring."

"Levies aren't as good as fully trained troops," Dorrin points out.

"No, but there are a lot more of the levies."

"And we can't even get the darkness out of here," snaps Kadara. The cider splashes onto the table when she sets down the tumbler. "There aren't any ships to Recluce, and Suthya and Sarronnyn have refused to allow anyone from Recluce to land there."

"Why?" Dorrin raises his eyebrows.

"Fairhaven is paying top golds for grain, but the ban

is part of the agreement. We tried to book passage to Rulyarth."

"It's going to be a long and cold winter," Dorrin says.

"And a bloody spring."

"Can you stop them?"

Brede shrugs. "Do you have any machines that would help?"

"No. Nothing I can make would help."

"What good—" Kadara breaks off as Brede's eyes catch hers. "I'm sorry."

"Let me think about it." He finishes his medicine and refills his mug with cider. "Darkness... I can't even make a sword, you know?" Dorrin holds up his hands helplessly. "Maybe I can think of something else."

"Well..." Kadara says, "we heard you were sick."

Dorrin raises his eyebrows.

Brede coughs. "It was... sort of a joke..."

"I see. The wonderful healer can't even heal himself?"

Brede looks down.

"That's all right. My own helper asked me the same question. It sounds stupid, but that's the way it works."

Brede stands up. "We really need to get back to the barracks. We're only here to get back up to strength and to resupply."

"How long?"

"An eight-day, if we're lucky." Brede steps toward the door.

"Dreamer," mumbles Kadara. "We'll be out again in three days." She drains the last of the cider. "Damned good cider." Then she too stands and heads for the door.

"Take care," Dorrin says. What else can he say? It is as though they are slipping away from him.

"You, too, Dorrin."

He watches from the door as they ride through the cold misting rain. Mud streaks both their horses and their trousers and boots. His eyes flicker to the muddy streaks on the once-clean plank floor. After he rests, then he will mop it again. And after he finishes the letter to Liedral.

A long cold winter, and a bloody spring—wonderful.

XCII

THE COLD RAIN that seems more like early winter than autumn continues to pour down. Except near the forge, the air in the smithy is damp. Vaos pushes the wheelbarrow inside, stops to close the door, and then wheels the load of charcoal up the forge. Rek pulls the bellows lever. Yarrl turns the iron on the anvil, and Dorrin strikes the cherry-red metal.

Yarrl returns the iron to the forge. Dorrin sets down the sledge and wipes his forehead. Usually, the heat doesn't get to him so much, but his weakness may be from his hill fever.

"So when are you going to open your own smithy and take work from me? You got your house about done." Yarrl's attempt at humor does not hide his concern. "Keep pumping, Rek." The smith turns the iron in the tongs.

Dorrin wipes his forehead again. "I'm wearing out poor Meriwhen riding back and forth." He wants to add some humor, but his words sound flat.

"It's a nice house. You do good work. The lady trader will like it."

"I hope so, but I haven't asked her." Dorrin coughs. "But I won't be taking work from you. Vyrnil is asking for more of my toys, more intricate ones, and Jasolt wants something different. He wants me to duplicate some navigation device used by the Hamorians. He sent me a picture, or something." Dorrin pauses as the older smith takes the iron from the forge and lays it upon the bottom fuller. Then Dorrin lifts the light sledge.

Clunnngggg... clunnggg...

When Yarrl returns the iron to the coals, Dorrin continues. "I wouldn't take work from you."

"Vaos will want to go with you."

"He's your helper."

A smile creases the smith's sweating face. "He followed you to begin with. Rek's my helper. Rek's a good boy. Likes the forge. Vaos likes you." Yarrl shakes his head as he brings the iron back to the anvil.

Dorrin again lifts the sledge.

"When would be best for you?" Dorrin asks later, after the base of the cart crane goes into the long special slack tank that they have built for it.

"You have to do what you need to, young fellow."

"I can still come here and help with the heavy work."

"You would, I think." Yarrl lifts the crane base, his shoulders straining, and sets it on the back of the forge. "If I need you, I'll let you know. You take care of that little trader woman before she gets in trouble the way Reisa did." Yarrl looks into the dimness behind his workbench.

Dorrin waits, rubbing his forehead. Somehow, he feels flushed. He wishes that the aftereffects of the fever would pass more quickly. He is sleeping more, and working less, and getting impatient in the process.

"The world doesn't like strong women, Dorrin. Especially the Whites—they don't at all. I wanted to protect her, but she wouldn't have me then. Then she said a one-armed woman was no good as a wife. Bunch of cowdung... take her armless... but don't you tell her that." Yarrl looks back at the bench. "Need to do that arm now. Check the fire, would you?"

Dorrin smiles. Yarrl has never asked him to check the fire, and the request is a tacit acknowledgment that he is a smith in his own right. Perhaps a lowly one, but Yarrl is a good smith, and Dorrin values the request, and the approval it conveys.

XCIII

AS HE WALKS by the bookcase, the White Wizard tucks the folded parchment back into the folder that sits in the top shelf. He pauses by the window, enjoying the temporary warmth of a sunny day in early winter as it flows into the tower room.

"What was that?" Anya stretches in the white oak chair, somehow making the movement more than just a stretch.

"Nothing."

"Nothing?"

"A letter." Jeslek's eyes straying to the mirror on the table.

"Don't tell me you're getting love letters?"

"I don't appreciate the levity." Fire appears on Jeslek's fingertips. "It has to do with the trouble in Spidlar."

"Trouble? The great Jeslek admits there is indeed trouble in Spidlar?"

Jeslek's lips tighten. "Sometimes, Anya. Sometimes . . ."

"You are so serious, dear wizard. You really need to unbend." She eases out of the chair in a sinuous movement and steps up behind him, close enough that she blows gently on his neck, then kisses it, slowly, warmly.

A faint smile plays across his mouth as Anya's lips warm his neck, and as her hands reach for his white belt.

XCIV

THE CREAK OF the wagon as it jolts over the frozen ruts in the yard rides over the even blows of Dorrin's hammer, as he deftly maneuvers the hot set to cut the iron into the fish-shaped pieces necessary for the compasses for Jasolt. Cutting the iron is easy, and arranging it to be magnetic is no harder than forging black iron.

He nods to Vaos, and the boy pumps the bellows lever.

For Dorrin, the hard parts of the compass are ensuring the water-tightness of the copper casing—although the seeking arrow floats in oil and not water—and not bending the copper rivets on which the needles turn.

He brings the hammer down on the fullered iron, and the hot set cuts through the iron that is almost parchment thin. While he could use shears, the cut is cleaner with the hammer, and his shears twist thin iron. He needs to remake them, but he has not yet had time.

Another creak reminds him of the wagon outside. With a sigh, Dorrin sets the iron on the forge bricks. He walks to the smithy door, and Vaos follows.

The cold air is refreshing, and Dorrin wonders if he did indeed make the smithy a shade too snug. Still, at least Vaos doesn't freeze in the cooler weather.

Petra and Reisa sit side by side on the wagon seat.

Both are smiling, but wind carries the white steam of their breathing toward the stable.

Vaos looks up at Dorrin. The smith steps toward the two women.

"You'll need this sooner than later, we figure," Reisa announces, vaulting off the wagon one-handedly. Her boots thump as she lands on the clay that is nearly as hard-packed as that in Yarrl's yard—but only because it is frozen.

"Need what?" Dorrin walks forward to help Petra down, but she already has set the wagon brake and is walking briskly to the tailgate.

"A decent bed, of course." Reisa grins.

Dorrin blushes.

"This one Yarrl got years ago from Hesoll's widow, and it's been in a corner ever since. It might need some new fittings in a couple of places, but that's something you can certainly handle." Reisa uses her hand and other arm to open the tailgate.

Petra lowers the gate to reveal the cargo. The high headboard is carved red oak, with matching scrolls on each side. A footboard mirrors the design on a smaller scale.

"Wow . . ." murmurs Vaos. Then he looks at Dorrin. "Maybe I could have your old bed?" He grins.

"Scamp!" Dorrin looks from Reisa to Petra. "All of you . . . but why?"

Reisa shakes her head. "You know why. You still give a great deal, beyond the ironwork. We all felt that you—and your little trader lady—would need this."

"Liedral?"

"She'll be here sooner or later," affirms Petra. "You don't even look at your red-headed friend anymore."

"He writes the trader when no one is looking," volunteers Vaos.

Dorrin glares at the strawberry-haired imp.

"It won't be long," Petra says. "Not if he's writing love letters."

"Let's get this bed inside," suggests Reisa, "before we all freeze."

"Where do we put Dorrin's bed?" asks Vaos. "Don't we have to move it out first?"

"All right, all right," Dorrin concedes. "You can put it in your room."

The youth bounces onto the porch. "Does that make me a striker?"

"Vaos! Don't push it."

"Yes, ser. I'll take care of the old bed." The youngster scampers into the house.

"You have your hands full with that one," says Reisa dryly. "Somehow, I imagine you were like that."

"No . . ."

"You would have been if you hadn't been raised on Recluce."

As they speak, Vaos bears out the pallet section of Dorrin's narrow bed. "This is great—a real bed."

Petra stamps a booted foot on the hard ground. "This ground is hard. We'd better not drop Dorrin's bed."

"Yes, daughter." Reisa grins.

Dorrin turns toward the wagon and takes one side of the massive headboard.

XCV

THE RAIN, WHICH began as snow, has turned back into snow by the time Dorrin has finished his latest toy forgings and banked the forge. He pauses at the door to Vaos's small room, but can hear only a faint snoring.

Then he walks to the outside door, still ajar because

the smithy stays too warm in the early winter. From there, he looks across the ridge toward Rylla's cottage, but all the windows are dark. He closes the door and makes sure the latch catches. His steps drag as he walks through the snow to the porch and the kitchen door.

Although he can see objects well enough in the dark—most born of Black families can—he has trouble with finer details, like writing. He lights the small oil lamp on the wall, opens the cover on the cooling tank, barely above freezing with the water from the high spring, and pulls out the jug of cider. So far his design of the tank as a continuous flowing system that carries the water to the pond below has kept the water from freezing and limited the well in the yard to quench water for his slack tanks.

After pouring a tumbler of cider, he takes down the thicker box filled with manuscript pages, followed by the quill and inkwell, and glances idly through his efforts at describing order, starting with the almost presumptuous title page—*Thoughts on the Basis of Order*.

> All physical items—unlike fire or *pure* chaos—must have some structure, or they would not exist . . .
> Because all wrought iron has a grain created from the forging of its crystals, the strength of the iron lies in the alignment and length of the grain. Using order to reinforce that grain is the basis for creating black iron . . . Its strength lies in the ordering of unbruised or unstrained grains along the length of the metal . . .

He nods and begins to pen the words he considered earlier. Now, when he forges most items, he can also—sometimes—think of other things.

If order or chaos be without limits, then common sense would indicate that each should have triumphed when the great ones of each discipline have arisen. Yet neither has so triumphed, despite men and women of power, intelligence, and ambition. Therefore, the scope of either order or chaos is in fact limited, and the belief in the balance of forces demonstrated . . .

Dorrin pauses. Does the fact that no triumph has occurred show that—or merely that no one of great enough power to do so has yet arisen? He takes another sip of the cider. There is so much he does not know.

XCVI

"You never come here much, anymore." Pergun looks into the half-full mug of dark beer.

"I was sick for a while, you know." Dorrin sips redberry from his mug.

"That was eight-days ago. You still work too hard. What are you doing now that you have your own place? Just the toys?"

"No. I still help Yarrl with heavy pieces, and he passes off some work when he gets too busy. I did a few copies of that Hamorian sextant for Jasolt." Dorrin pauses. "Hardest things I ever did. Had to do even brackets for mirrors, and adjusting screws. And I had to do all of the pieces in polished black iron so it wouldn't rust. It might have been easier to do in copper or bronze, but trying to learn another metal . . . The compass casings were a nightmare. Maybe I'll learn copper some other time."

Pergun drains his mug and looks across the half-full room toward the serving girl. "I can't believe that Kyril's asking four coppers for a mug. Four coppers for dark beer."

"Everything's gotten dear."

"Damned Wizards! Begging your pardon, master Dorrin."

"I'm as damned as the rest of them."

"Not you." Pergun finally raises his hand toward the serving girl.

"Can you pay for it, big fellow?" asks the woman.

Pergun opens his hand, showing the four coppers.

"How about you, master Dorrin?"

"No, thank you." Dorrin smiles at the woman, but she has already headed for the kitchen.

"Master Dorrin?" The painfully thin and dark-haired Jasolt stands at the edge of the table.

Dorrin rises. "I'm honored, trader."

Pergun looks to leave, but Jasolt raises a hand. "Please stay, and do sit down, Dorrin." Jasolt pulls up a chair and perches on the edge. "The sextants work well, or so Rydlar tells me."

"Make sure he keeps them as dry as he can. They really should be made of brass or bronze."

"I told him, and he will." Jasolt looks down at the table, finally turning his dark eyes on Dorrin. "What do you think?"

"About what?"

"I overheard your friend here talking about the higher prices for beer. It's like that everywhere, you know. I'm just glad you're here . . . still."

Dorrin's throat is dry. "I have as little choice as you, trader. Right now, at least," he adds. "Is it that bad?"

"You may have noticed there were no fireworks this winter to celebrate the founding of the Council."

"I must admit I didn't."

"Also, Certis has posted notices for spring troop levies."

"The false highway thefts didn't work," Dorrin says flatly.

"Was that Recluce's doing?" Jasolt's voice is even lower.

"I doubt that it was by intention."

"You don't think the great ones of Recluce care?"

"No." Dorrin does not want to elaborate.

"What are you going to do?" Jasolt asks.

"I built a new house, you know," Dorrin says conversationally. "I'm hoping to live in it for a while."

"Can you forge something that will help the Council guards? Something . . . based on order?"

Dorrin looks into his mug. Jasolt is asking the same questions that Brede and Kadara have kept raising— and people are looking to him for an answer. But what answer can he provide? He feels uncomfortable trying to forge such items as knives—let alone swords.

"Here's your beer, big fellow," interrupts the serving girl, setting the mug before Pergun. "Where's the coin?"

Pergun extends the coppers. "Light of a price for a single beer."

"Everything's dear, big fellow."

Pergun watches her sway toward the next table.

"Anything . . .?" prompts Jasolt.

"I don't know. I'll have to think about it. There might be something. But being an ordered-smith poses a lot of restrictions."

Jasolt frowns.

"It's hard for me even to pick up an edged weapon, let alone forge one. That's why I use a staff."

"The way you use it you scarcely need a blade." Jasolt's voice is wry.

"I don't know," Dorrin repeats helplessly. "I'll have to think about it."

"That's all we can ask." Jasolt looks straight at Dorrin. "You might think about joining the Council."

"Me? I'm scarcely in that category."

"I doubt that it will be long. I did observe your new dwelling has ample . . . storage . . ."

Dorrin does not want to mention that the space is for Liedral, not with the Whites already reading their letters. "It's . . . easier to build it that way to begin with. I don't have any plans to be a trader." His last phrase is certainly true. He has no real desire to be a trader.

"Whatever . . ." Jasolt smiles politely and stands. "We hope you can help. Cold winter . . . First time I've ever hoped it's long, and spring comes late. Sad thing when a man has to hope for a long, cold winter. Good evening, ser Dorrin." He inclines his head and turns.

"Light . . ." murmurs Pergun, setting down his mug after a long pull. "That dandy treated you like you . . . like you were a fancier trader than he is. Just what are you, Dorrin?"

"I'm me. Sometimes I'm a smith, sometimes a healer, and sometimes I'm not quite sure."

Pergun sips the beer. "Need to make this last."

Dorrin looks at the mug, and the few drops of juice in the bottom. He finishes his redberry with a last swig. "I need to go. Do you mind?"

"I think I'll stay," Pergun says. "Got nothing to go back to. Hemmil keeps the place colder than lake ice." He jerks his finger toward a ginger-bearded man dicing in the corner. "Gerba has a wagon. He'll drop me off."

"Are you sure?"

"Asked him 'fore you got here."

"I'll see you later."

Pergun nods and picks up his mug, heading toward the corner game.

A boy Dorrin does not know is holding Meriwhen by the time Dorrin reaches the stable.

"Your horse, ser Dorrin."

Dorrin parts with a copper. "Your name, boy?"

"Alstar, ser." The youth looks down.

"Thank you for taking care of Meriwhen."

"A pleasure, ser." The child still does not meet Dorrin's eyes, and Dorrin leads the mare out into the night.

Only a single lantern lights the front of the Red Lion. As Meriwhen plods through the slush toward the bridge, Dorrin surveys the houses they pass. Most are dark, and those few not dark show only faint glows that might come from single candles or lamps. Yet it is early. Despite the bitter air, few plumes of smoke rise from the chimneys of Diev.

The price of dark beer has doubled. It is cold, but few fires are lit, and few candles or lamps. Yet Jasolt prays for a long, long winter.

He pats Meriwhen's neck. "Easy, girl."

Once he has ridden across the bridge, Meriwhen's hoofs drum against hard-packed snow and ice, and the snow heaped on each side of the road reaches nearly waist high. He turns in the saddle, but sees few lights or fires.

He shivers as he faces the uphill ride to his empty house. A long, cold winter will kill all too many in Spidlar, and yet . . . so will an early spring.

XCVII

After feeding Meriwhen, Dorrin closes the stable door and walks along the path he has worn in the snow between his house and Rylla's. The snows have reached knee-high, and the morning wind swirls the night's dusting of powder across the packed surfaces.

The gray clouds overhead are cold, but do not promise more snow—not immediately.

A thin gray plume of smoke twists from Rylla's chimney, carried by the wind toward the Northern Ocean. He looks back at the smithy, where Vaos is supposed to be building a tool rack. The faintest of white lines rises from the forge chimney, indicating the heat in the banked fire.

Dorrin stamps his boots on the porch, knocking off the snow, and wipes them on the worn rush mat before opening the door and easing inside.

A heavy older woman coughs . . . and coughs—deep wracking coughs. Her face is mottled, almost purple, and between coughs, she wheezes like an ill-constructed bellows. Rylla holds a cup, waiting for the coughing to subside.

Hunched beside the hearth of the main room is a man, twisted, bent, who shivers, despite the heat from the low fire, and despite the layers of ragged blankets that cover him.

Dorrin sees the thin woman and the child in the corner, even before Frisa asks, "Can I see your horsey?" She steps toward him, but her hand does not let go of her mother's faded gray trousers. Merga—her thin face sad—has on a herder's jacket, a larger and more tattered version of what Frisa wears.

There are no obvious physical injuries to either mother or child. The farm woman looks at the plank floor, her eyes avoiding Dorrin's. The heavy woman's coughs ease, and she takes a wheezing breath.

"Drink this," orders Rylla.

"It smells awful."

"Do you want to cough your lungs out, Erlanna?"

Erlanna takes the cup, and Rylla walks over to Dorrin. Her eyes flick to Merga and Frisa. "Gerhalm walked away into the last snow. Asavah found his body yesterday."

"Why? He walked into the storm because he couldn't beat his woman?" Dorrin tries to keep his voice low.

Rylla nods toward the kitchen, and the two walk to the far corner, by the back doorway that overlooks the ice and snow covered pond.

"Gerhalm worked when he was told, did what he was told, and was paid whatever Jisle thought was fair. When the crops were good, so were times. When the weather was bad, so were times . . ."

"You're saying that the man had no control over his life, and that the only things he had control over were his woman and his child, and when I took that away, when times got bad, he couldn't take it anymore?"

Rylla nods. "Merga has no place to go. She's not strong enough to work the fields for Jisle."

"Darkness . . ." Now what will he do? The two will likely starve or . . .

"She can cook, I'm told, and she could be a serving maid. She was when Gerhalm got her pregnant."

"I don't really . . ." Dorrin sighs. "I'll work something out, I suppose."

A heavy knock, repeated twice, thunders on the door. Dorrin looks up, glances at Rylla. The older healer walks to the door and opens it, admitting a heavy man in a long, blue woolen cloak. He sweeps off his hat with dark leather gloves. "Is this where I might find ser Dorrin, the healer?"

Rylla points toward Dorrin. "There he be."

The man's eyes fix on Dorrin, avoiding Erlanna and Merga. "Ser Dorrin?"

"I'm Dorrin."

"I'm Fanken, and I work for Trader Fyntal. His lady is quite ill, with something of a fever and a flux, and the trader would request your immediate attention." The words are polite, but stiff, as if the man has been instructed to be polite.

Behind Fanken's back, Rylla nods, pointing to the purse at her belt.

"I will need a moment to finish here," Dorrin responds, "and to gather a few items that may be of help to the lady. You can wait here, or . . ."

"I will wait by the door."

Dorrin turns to Merga and Frisa.

"Can I see the horsey?"

Dorrin swallows, his mouth dry. "I heard that . . . hard times . . . have fallen on you . . . I am . . . truly . . . sorry . . ."

"You did as you saw best, master Dorrin. The summer was good, and we hoped . . ." Merga chokes back tears, and shakes her head.

"I . . . could use a cook and serving maid . . . Not much more than room and board . . . I'm not . . . that well-off."

Merga's red eyes catch Dorrin's. "I'd not accept such charity . . . save . . ." She looks at the dark-eyed child who watches.

"It need not be charity in time. This is sooner than . . . I had planned."

The silence stretches out. Fanken coughs. So does Erlanna.

"She can stay here for a while, Dorrin," offers Rylla. "You need to go with Fyntal's man." She bends over and whispers in his ear. "Healers have few opportunities for real golds."

"There is that." He looks toward the door and the dour Fanken. "But if Merga could stay here until I can rough out another room in the storage area, that might be better." Dorrin shakes his head. He has only a few golds left, and even pine timbers and planks will not be cheap. Perhaps nothing serious is wrong with Lady Fyntal. He nods toward Merga and walks back toward the herb shelves in the kitchen.

"I told you," Rylla says gently. "You be putting curses 'pon people, and they come back."

"It wasn't a curse. How can keeping a man from beating a woman be a curse?"

Fanken leans forward, his face stiff, as if to catch every word.

"You can take the little bag there," Rylla suggests. "Brinn, astra, willow bark . . ."

The younger healer nods and begins to pack. He adds in pinches of several other herbs, tied in twisted squares of cloth, and a small stoppered bottle of liquid willow bark.

"Remember," Rylla notes in a low voice as he picks up the bag, "traders can pay in gold."

Dorrin recalls that he has committed to taking on a servant he does not need—all because he stopped a beating. As he passes Erlanna, the woman coughs again, and his perceptions brush her. Like so many, she has not eaten well, despite her weight, and the sickness preys upon her weakness. How many will die of diseases simply because they have lost the strength to fight them? Too long a winter, and Fairhaven may not have much of a fight.

Outside the healer's cottage, Fanken walks toward a thin gray. The trader's man looks from the thin horse to Dorrin.

"I'll be with you in a moment. I need to saddle my horse." Dorrin points toward the barn, then continues in the direction he has pointed.

Fanken grunts.

The wind is sharper than earlier in the morning, and the clouds overhead are darker. Without really trying, Dorrin can sense the heavy oncoming snow, and he stops by his house to grab his heavy jacket before going to the stable. Still, he saddles Meriwhen quickly and rides to join Fanken.

"Nice horse."

"She's been good to me." Dorrin turns Meriwhen downhill on the main road, toward the bridge. "Where is Trader Fyntal's house?"

"On the ridge west of the harbor. Past the third pier and up the road."

"Do you know how long Lady Fyntal has been ill?"

"No."

"Did the trader say any more about her illness?"

"No."

Clearly, Fanken does not like his role as messenger. "Are you from Diev?"

"No. Quend. Came here as a boy."

"Ever take the sled runs on the beaches?"

"No. Damned fools who do."

Dorrin asks no more questions, but concentrates on riding. Lower Diev is warmer than upper Diev, but not that much warmer. Few fires burn despite the chill wind, and the streets are empty except for one mounted trooper bearing dispatch cases and riding out toward the Kleth road.

All three piers are empty, except for a single small fishing boat tied at the first. Beyond the breakwater, the sea is more white than blue, and Dorrin can even see two ice floes tossing amidst the white-caps.

"Too rough even for the Bristans." Fanken directs his horse up the sloping road toward the ridge top where two solid dwellings of gray stone and timber survey the harbor. Unlike so many houses in Diev, both houses sport healthy plumes of smoke from their many chimneys.

Fyntal's house is the one closest to the Northern Ocean, slightly smaller, and with a view of both harbor and sea. Fanken rides past the covered porch and around to the stable where a stable boy darts out.

"Just stable the healer's mount."

"Yes, ser." The boy looks away from Fanken, though his lowered eyes glance sideways toward Dorrin.

"Easy, girl." Dorrin dismounts, and pats Meriwhen on the neck. "Just treat her gently."

"Yes, master healer."

Fanken hands the reins of the gray to the boy. "Be back in a bit." He turns and marches across the rolled and packed snow of the yard.

Dorrin smiles at the blond stable boy.

A heavy white-haired man opens the door even before Dorrin reaches it. He looks down from his four-cubit height at the healer, his bag, and the black staff. "Master Dorrin, I apprcciatc your coming on such short notice." His eyes turn to Fanken. "And I do appreciate your getting the healer for us, Fanken. You may go, if you would like."

"Thank you, ser. I'll be at the warehouse." Fanken nods and turns.

Dorrin follows the older man into the foyer, placing his jacket on the old branched cloak tree, and setting his staff in the corner behind the tree. The foyer is paneled in dark-stained oak, and a leaf-patterned Hamorian carpet is centered on the stained and varnished oak floor that reflects the light of the two gleaming brass oil lamps in matching sconces.

"Leretia is upstairs. She had the flux—all of us did. I think it was some bad fowl. But she just got worse and worse. Wine didn't help. Neither did warm baths. Don't believe in healers much, but Honsard's girl told Noriah how you healed her brothcr. I thought it couldn't hurt."

"How long has she been ill?"

"More than an eight-day. She just lies there." Fyntal's voice quavers almost imperceptibly, and he coughs softly and starts up the stairs.

Dorrin picks up the herb bag and climbs after Fyntal, whose booted feet barely whisper on the carpeted steps, so lightly does the heavy man move.

Dorrin feels like his feet shake the stairs.

Leretia lies on a wide bed, pale, thin-faced, and radiating heat. The coverlet, rimmed in Suthyan lace, has been thrown back to her waist, exposing a cotton nightgown also trimmed in lace. On a stool in the corner sits a blond younger woman, eyes dark-rimmed and red, wearing a soft blue blouse and matching trousers.

"So ... hot ..." murmurs the woman on the bed, but her eyes do not seem to take in either Dorrin or Fyntal, or the younger woman.

"Our daughter, Noriah," explains Fyntal in a whisper.

Dorrin nods briefly to the younger woman, sets down the bag, and steps to the bed, letting his fingers brush, first her wrist, and then her forehead. He tries not to frown at the knot of white chaos centered below her stomach, nor at the lines of sullen white fire that entwine her.

If he could but cut out that small diseased organ ... He wants to laugh. Even if he knew how, he has neither tools nor the skill to cut so deeply. What else can he do? He steps back.

"So sick ... am I going to die?"

Dorrin forces a smile. "Not if I can help it, lady."

"No 'lady' ... just Lera ... so hot ..." Her eyes glaze as she looks nowhere, and her chest heaves.

Noriah sits up straight in the chair.

"Will you not do something?" pleads Fyntal.

"I could do much, but I would prefer doing the right thing." Dorrin looks at the older man, who steps back. Noriah opens her mouth, but closes it without saying a word.

The chaos-pulsed section of Leretia's abdomen is clearly the problem. Dorrin takes a deep breath and begins to weave a shield of order around the small organ—but the chaos/infection fights back. He wipes his forehead, then lets his perceptions examine her body again. There may be a way.

He turns to Fyntal. "I will need some additional materials. We can discuss them." He walks into the hallway and waits for the trader.

Fyntal closes the door.

"You did not summon me first, did you?"

"No. Sustro... he said she would die. He said I should seek miracles. I thought of... you."

"She may still die. I am going to try something."

"You aren't going to cut her open?" Fyntal's voice rises from a whisper to a hoarse rasp. "That would kill her."

"My skills do not lie in those areas. I will need a large basket of clean soft cloths. I will also need a bottle of something like clear brandy."

"That sounds like a surgeon's stuff," protests Fyntal.

"I will not touch her with an edged item," snaps Dorrin. "I cannot. Do you want me to try for your miracle, or...?"

"I will get the cloths." Fyntal sighs.

Dorrin opens the door and steps back into the bedroom where Leretia moans. Her eyes open momentarily, then close.

"Easy..." he says, his fingers touching her wrists, as he begins building his walls of order, including the curved tube that runs from the heart of chaos to the surface of her skin. He pauses and turns to the younger woman, Leretia's daughter. "Would you help me?"

She steps to the bed. "What do you want?"

Dorrin sketches out a square area above the mother's stomach. "We need her gown away from that area, so that it is clear to the air."

Noriah frowns. "You aren't going to..."

"No cutting. I can't. But there is an infection beneath that, if I am successful, will burst forth here.

I can contain it, but it will be much easier if the ... corrupt material does not become fouled in the gown."

"I'll take care of mother. Would you ..."

Dorrin turns and glances toward the window, through which he can see the white-tipped waves of the Northern Ocean. His eyes touch on the matched oil lamps, evenly set on each side of the window, and the polished glass mantles.

"Ooooo ... hurts ... so hot ..."

"Easy, mother ... you'll be better soon."

The door opens. Fyntal brings in a basket of soft, folded cloths. A short man behind him carries a corked bottle. Dorrin takes the bottle and extracts the cork, then lifts one of the cloths from the basket Fyntal has set beside the bed.

"Will this do?" asks the blonde.

Dorrin turns. "Yes." He pours some of the brandy onto the cloth and gently wipes the bare skin. Then he wipes his own fingers. The liquor leaves them sticky, but he wipes off the stickiness with a dry part of the cloth.

He stands over Leretia and continues to build his walls of order, using the pressure of order to constrain the chaos to a tighter and tighter focus, driving it into a tighter and tighter line.

His eyes burn as the sweat drips into them, and he shifts his weight from one foot to the other.

"Would a chair help?" asks Fyntal.

"Yes." Dorrin does not look away from the patient, even as he sits beside her, even as he reaches for the top cloth and lays it gently on the bare skin.

"Oh ... like a knife ... darkness ... hurts ..."

Dorrin places one hand on her forehead, offering some sense of reassurance. "It will hurt for a little, but we're all here."

"Fyntal ..."

The trader stands on the other side of the bed, and

Dorrin senses the tears that flow down the craggy face. Fyntal says nothing, but holds Leretia's hand as though it were the most precious of gems.

Dorrin continues to press the chaos back into the diseased organ but the white fire begins to gnaw its way along the order tube toward her skin.

"Burns . . . oh . . . burns . . ."

Dorrin touches her forehead, willing her to sleep, wishing he had recalled that option earlier.

"What did you do?" asks Noriah.

"Let her sleep," Dorrin answers, absently. "Should have thought of it earlier."

How long it is before the corruption gnaws through the smooth skin of her belly Dorrin does not know. But he continues to sponge it away with the cloths, discarding them in turn, ignoring the greenish cast on the trader's face or Noriah's stumbled retreat from the room and her chastened return.

The lamps have been lit, and they cast shadows from the room when he cleans Leretia's skin for a last time and sprinkles the wound, which looks more like a circular burn, with crushed astra.

"I . . . feel better . . ." murmurs the older woman.

"Don't move," Dorrin says. "Not much, anyway."

"What did you do?" asks the trader from another chair in the corner. "It looks like you did surgery."

Dorrin squints, then holds on to the chair. He cannot talk. Then he cannot see, either.

"Catch him . . ."

When Dorrin wakes, lying upon a strange bed, he finds the stable boy sitting on a stool. "Hello."

"Hello, master." The boy's eyes avoid Dorrin's. "Let me get the mistress." He darts out the door.

Dorrin sits up. His head aches, and he rubs his neck. This kind of healing is worse than smithing. Since the lamps are not lit, it must be the next day. He hopes it has only been a day. He was supposed to help Yarrl with a cart crane. He finds his boots next to the bed and pulls them on.

"You're awake." The blonde, now wearing a soft green blouse and trousers, steps into the room.

"I take it your mother is better."

"She's better. But she's still hot."

"She probably will be for days." Dorrin stands. "I need to see her."

"I think you need to eat. You're as white as the snow."

Dorrin considers the wobbliness in his knees. He grins sheepishly. "You're probably right." He follows her down the back stairs to the kitchen, where dried fruit, cheese, and fresh-baked bread are laid out on the table.

After he has eaten, feeling somewhat refreshed, he climbs the front stairs to the main bedroom. Noriah follows. Fyntal, sitting by the bed, looks up. Leretia's eyes follow the trader's.

"Good morning," Dorrin offers.

"Good morning, master healer," Fyntal says dryly.

"Thank you," whispers Leretia.

"I still need to look at that wound," Dorrin says.

"Just a moment . . ."

The healer looks out the window, noting that the Northern Ocean is calmer, that only a few whitecaps dot the dark blue waters.

"Here . . ."

Dorrin lifts the dressing, as gently as he can.

"Ooooo . . ."

"I know." He lets his senses check the wound. Small traces of chaos still flicker around the opening and within. He concentrates.

"Ohhhh . . ."

"Oh . . . I should have warned you." He looks for the brandy and some more cloths. Noriah hands him the bottle and a cloth. He continues to concentrate until a small amount of greenish pus oozes forth. Then he cleans Leretia's skin again, and sprinkles the wound with the astringent astra, and replaces the dressing.

"This could ooze for a few days. Keep it clean with the brandy, and change the pad daily, or if it gets sticky. If you get very hot again, don't wait. Send someone for me immediately." Dorrin takes a deep breath.

"You don't do this often, do you?" asks Fyntal.

"No. No healer can."

"I can see why," observes Noriah.

"Why did you do it for us?" whispers Leretia.

Dorrin tries not to blush. Then he swallows. "There were two reasons. First, I came because I needed the coin. Second, I stayed because everyone loves you."

"Pretty speech," says the trader dryly.

"I'm being honest." Dorrin looks at the trader, who looks away.

"Honesty doesn't always impress people." Noriah's voice is gentle.

"No."

"Could anyone else you know have saved me?" asks Leretia, pulling the bedclothes back up to her chest.

Dorrin hesitates.

"Be honest."

"No. I wasn't sure I could."

"You sound like there's no doubt now."

"If the wound doesn't get infected, you should be fine within several eight-days, perhaps sooner." Dorrin sits down on the single vacant chair. His knees are still somewhat rubbery.

"It's clear your kind of healing is exhausting." Noriah's voice is almost impish. "Or you are not used to exercise."

"I'm mostly a smith." The words come out before Dorrin can consider the impact.

"And a healer?" asks Leretia.

"I said it had to be exhausting," points out Noriah.

"Enough," says Fyntal. "I expect my lady needs some rest, and master Dorrin has another life as well."

"All right," concedes Noriah, standing.

Dorrin rises slowly, nods to the woman in the bed.

"No. Thank you," says Leretia.

Dorrin blushes, but recovers, before he turns and steps into the hallway.

"I will meet you in the foyer, master Dorrin," Fyntal says firmly when he closes the bedroom door.

Dorrin nods and heads down the stairs. Noriah watches from the landing as Dorrin recovers his heavy jacket and his black staff.

Fyntal appears at the back of the foyer, apparently having taken the back stairs. He hands Dorrin a heavy leather pouch.

"But . . ."

"You said you needed the coin," Fyntal states with a smile. "And I am more than willing to pay for a miracle. Unlike some, I appreciate second chances. I can't say I have need of your smith work, but should I need an honest smith, I'll find you."

"Thank you." Dorrin inclines his head to the young woman on the landing and to the trader. "Remember to watch her fever. I don't think it should come back, but get me if it does."

"I will—never fear." A grin creases the craggy face.

Dorrin steps into the bright chill of winter, realizing that the warmth of the trader's house had made him forget the season. He slips the heavy pouch inside his jacket, then one-handedly fastens the jacket as he steps toward the stable.

The same stable boy has Meriwhen saddled and waiting. Dorrin takes a moment to check the girths and hackamore, but both are firm. "Thank you," he says, fumbling in his purse and offering a copper.

"I couldn't, ser."

"Yes, you can. You were good to Meriwhen."

"I did feed her the grain mash, and she let me curry her."

Dorrin grins. "Good." He puts his staff in the holder.

"But you healed the lady, and everyone said she would die, and she's too good to die."

"Too many good people die," Dorrin says slowly. "This time . . . I could help." He has already wondered how many good people, like Erlanna, are poor and dying. He takes a deep breath and swings up into the saddle.

The boy waves as Dorrin rides into the yard. Fyntal still stands in the open doorway watching until the healer rides down the drive and out onto the road.

Dorrin does not need to open the pouch to know that it bears a dozen golds. A dozen golds. He is glad he could heal Leretia, and he needs the coin. But how many others will lose lovers and mothers for lack of such healing? And, even if they could find him, how could he heal all of them? His knees and legs are still weak.

He rides slowly past the empty piers, past the chimneys that do not waft smoke into the clear winter sky, past the empty yards of the Tankard and the Red Lion, and over the bridge and up the packed snow of the road to his house.

XCVIII

CRACKKKKK! THE WHITE guard continues to lash the figure strapped facedown on the long table, and a line of red slashes across the legs.

The White Wizard's hands move, fighting back the white mist that threatens to appear in the mirror on the table in the corner of the cell. Perspiration appears on his forehead as he maintains the image in the midst of the mists. A red-headed young man stands in the center of the white mists. At one edge of the scene stands a woman with short brown hair.

Crack! The lash cuts across the bare shoulders.

" . . . hnnnn . . ." The prisoner whimpers.

The wizard frowns and the face of the man in the mirror distorts—showing pointed teeth, blood dripping from the corners of his mouth, and he lifts a jagged blade toward the woman. She backs away, and he lunges.

Crack!

The image vanishes into the white mists.

"Try it again," suggests Anya.

"I've done it four times," he snaps.

"You want the effect deep."

Instead of responding, Jeslek takes a sip from the tumbler. Then he concentrates once more. This time the red-headed man is moving slowly toward the woman in the mirror. The woman has a knife in her hand. Jeslek nods to the guard, and the whip snaps across the woman's bare back.

"Oooo . . ."

This time the image of the red-headed man lunges, growling, and the woman plunges the knife full into his chest. The man vanishes in a welter of black smoke.

"Again . . ." insists Anya.

Jeslek wipes his forehead, and nods to the guard.

Crack!

The images re-form in the glass, with the red-headed man attacking and being stabbed.

Anya smiles. "That should do it."

"Ohhhhh . . ." The scream of the woman on the table dies away as she faints.

"Was that necessary?" asks Jeslek.

"As necessary as anything you do, dear High Wizard."

Jeslek gestures to the other wizard. "You know what to do, Fydel. We might as well make a lesson in Jellico as well. Black sympathizers ... bah ..."

The guard unstraps the unconscious woman and lifts her over his shoulders like a sack. He follows Fydel from the lower Tower room.

As the door closes, Anya slides in front of Jeslek, moistening her lips, letting her hands reach up his back and drawing his body close to hers. "We have a little time ..."

Her lips burn on his.

XCIX

OUTSIDE, THE SNOW continues to pour down, coating the packed yard with another soft white blanket. Dorrin worries about the ride home.

Rek brings in another barrow of charcoal and wheels it next to the forge. Then he wipes the water from his forehead.

Dorrin raises the hammer and strikes, his thoughts more on the carpentry that Pergun has done to turn another corner of the storage area into a room for Merga and Frisa than upon the heavy bar before him. Pergun can use the coppers, and, thanks to Fyntal, Dorrin has more coins than time. And Dorrin cannot complain that someone else is cooking—except that he has now had to worry about buying food—when it is in short enough supply, and dear.

A soundless scream whimpers in the distance. Dorrin shudders, barely keeping the sledge on target. The impact on the flatter sounds dull, weak.

"Careful there," admonishes Yarrl. "Got a problem?"

Dorrin sets the sledge on the hard clay. Another shudder takes him, with a wave of distant pain and whiteness. Slowly, he walks out of the smithy and into the storm.

"Dorrin. Darkness damned. Need to finish this strap."

Yarrl's words are lost as he looks into the heavy gray snow clouds over the Westhorns. Liedral? But what? Another wave of white horror and pain washes over him, and he puts a hand on the ice on the stones of the well ledge.

For a time, with the hazy winter light fighting through the clouds, he stands next to the well, enduring the waves of pain that are not his, until they subside. Then, mechanically, he opens the well cover and drops the bucket. Just as mechanically he hoists it back up. Was Reisa right? Should he have made Liedral stay? But what has happened?

" . . . just shuddered and dropped his sledge . . . like as he's not here, daughter . . . Look at him."

The cold water on his sweating face helps—the colder the better. Finally, he swallows some of the water. That helps also.

"Crazy . . . cold water on his face in midwinter . . ."

Something tugs at his leg. He looks down at Zilda, at the end of the chain held by Petra. The goat is yanking at his trousers.

"Sorry . . ." he says.

Reisa and Yarrl stand by the porch steps. Yarrl spits into the corner.

"What happened?" Reisa smiles sadly.

"Something with Liedral. It's stopped . . . now, but she's been hurt."

"Do you know where she is?"

He shakes his head.

"Wizards' business . . . no good to come of it," mumbles Yarrl.

"Can you do anything?" Reisa pursues.

"Not yet . . . not yet." He takes a deep breath. "Might as well finish the big straps—while I can."

"You sure?" asks Yarrl.

"I'll let you know when I'm not." Dorrin wipes his face and walks back toward the smithy.

Behind him, Reisa and Yarrl look at each other. Finally, Yarrl follows the younger smith back to the forge.

C

FAT SNOWFLAKES FLOW past Dorrin's face as he rides uphill from Yarrl's in the darkness of early evening. What has happened to Liedral? Why did he feel the pain? Where is she?

Somehow, in some way, it is connected to the White Wizards. Still, none of it makes much sense. Dorrin has made little progress in building the machines he has designed, even the simple steam engine. He cannot make weapons, at least not the conventional ones, and he cannot return to Recluce. He is a good journeyman smith, and, in some ways, a good healer.

Liedral is a woman and a trader who can barely make ends meet.

Unless he can do something, or unless Brede and Kadara are far more successful than Dorrin, within a year or perhaps two, Spidlar will be under the heels of the White Wizards, and there is a good chance he will be in a work camp building roads, or dead. Yet the White Wizards are worried.

He nudges Meriwhen off the road and up the drive

past Rylla's cottage. The smoke from the kitchen chimney, the one serving the stove, shows that Merga has been busy with something. He hopes it is better than his own cooking. He dismounts outside the small stable. As he slides off Meriwhen, he hears footsteps.

"Can I feed the horsey?" asks Frisa, still struggling into the too-big herder's jacket, snow coating her short black hair.

"Her name is Meriwhen," Dorrin explains again, opening the stable door and leading Meriwhen inside.

"Can I feed Meriwhen?"

Dorrin hands the girl the bucket, and opens the barrel. "Put three big handfuls in the bucket and let me see it."

While Frisa scrambles with the barrel and bucket in the dimness of the stable, Dorrin loosens Meriwhen's saddle and racks it.

"It's dark."

"We won't be here long." Dorrin winces as the distant pain sears through him. Somehow that agony is closer. But why? Can he find Liedral? How?

"Is this enough?"

"What?"

Frisa thrusts the bucket at him.

"Three more handfuls," Dorrin decides. Her hands are much smaller than his. He leads Meriwhen into her stall and takes out the brush. "This is going to be quick, old girl."

"Horsey's not old."

"Meriwhen."

"She's not old."

"You're right." Dorrin continues brushing.

"Is this enough?"

Dorrin turns and looks at the bucket that Frisa holds, moving the child back away from the mare's legs—not that he believes Meriwhen would kick, but not all horses are Meriwhens. "That's fine. We'll put it here." He lifts Frisa up to the level of the manger. "Pour it all out."

"Good Meriwhen."

Frisa stands outside the stall while Dorrin finishes grooming Meriwhen. He picks up his staff and steps into the snow, waiting for Frisa to follow before closing the stable door.

Frisa darts ahead and is stamping her small feet on the porch even before Dorrin's boots touch the steps. He cleans his own boots as Frisa ducks into the house.

"Good evening, ser." Merga inclines her head at Dorrin's entrance. "Seeing it was wet and then snowing, and seeing as you're growing young fellows"—she jabs a long wooden spoon at Vaos, who stands in the corner by the stove—"I made a stew."

Dorrin sniffs the welcome scent of stew. Vaos grins at the smith.

The kitchen is dim with only the two oil lamps lit, but Dorrin only has the two lamps—yet another shortcoming in his household supplies. He also only has a single large jug of lamp oil. Building the house was only the beginning of his expenses. Even the golds from Fyntal may not last long. Dorrin turns from absently studying the lamp in the wall sconce to Merga.

"Frisa and me, we set some snares near the pond, and we got two fine hares. You had plenty of potatoes in the cellar, even some roots."

"You snared some rabbits?"

"Yes, ser. I had plenty of practice, and Jisle didn't mind. He said that they only ate the crops."

Dorrin tried not to smile as he sinks into the chair at the table.

"But ser, for a proper pantry, you be needing more staples. A barrel of flour, more potatoes, some yams . . ."

"Probably, Merga, I'll need all that and more. But could I afford it?"

"Even these days, you could get a barrel of flour for a silver, and you'd get a couple of coppers back for the barrel when you emptied it. Potatoes are cheap, if you go to Asavah."

Dorrin takes a deep breath. "We'll talk about what we need in the morning. It's been a long day, and I am hungry."

"Frisa, you can take this." Merga hands a worn basket to the child who carries it across the room and sets it before Dorrin. The aroma of fresh-baked bread fills his nostrils. "I got some yeast mix from Rylla. She says it will do until your lady brings her own."

Dorrin coughs, then rises and heads for the cooling tank and the cider. He fills four mugs and sets them around the table.

Merga sets the heavy pot on the wooden trivet in the middle of the table. "If you'd serve, master Dorrin."

The smith understands. Only the master or the mistress of a house should distribute the food. But he serves Frisa first, then Vaos and Merga. There is still plenty left.

He takes a spoonful, then breaks off an end of the bread and hands the basket to Vaos.

"Begging your pardon, master Dorrin," Vaos says, "but this is better than bread and cheese and fruit."

"So? I'm not a cook."

"The master is a healer," asserts Frisa.

"He's a smith," counters Vaos. "A good smith."

"I do both. Now, eat!"

Vaos crunches through his large chunk of bread.

"Yes, master," agrees Frisa. "Would Meriwhen like stew?"

"I don't think so." Instead of shaking his head, Dorrin bites into the bread, still warm and crusty.

After several mouthfuls of stew and bread, he looks up to see the other three eating equally ravenously.

"Can you ride a horse, Merga? Or drive a wagon?" he asks later.

"Yes, ser. I used to drive the teams for Gerhalm, when he wasn't a-feeling well. Jisle, he looked the other way."

There is a knock, and Dorrin's eyes flash to the door. He stands, bumping the table, and has to steady his mug before he answers the knock.

"Pergun? What are you doing here?"

"Well . . . ser . . . I was just a-thinking . . . it was looking like snow . . . and I wanted to make sure the work I did . . ." The mill hand looks up sheepishly.

"Come on in. Have you had supper?"

"I ate a little."

"Do we have another bowl?" asks Dorrin.

"I've finished," Merga says quickly. "I can wash mine out." She stands and offers her place on the bench.

Not only does he need more crockery, but he needs more chairs and a longer table. Dorrin takes another mouthful of the stew, watching Merga smile at Pergun as she puts a bowl full of her stew in front of him. The mill hand looks back at her.

"Did you walk here?" Dorrin asks.

"It's not that far," Pergun mumbles through a mouthful of stew.

"Hmmmm . . ." Dorrin almost feels like smashing things with his biggest hammers. The more he does, the more out of control he feels. Everything seems to lead to something bigger, and each time he manages to accomplish something that he thinks will help him build his steam engine, his efforts result in more problems than solutions. He wanted space to work in; instead, he must support a growing household. He didn't want to worry about a wife; now he worries about Liedral.

Abruptly, he stands up. Everyone in the small kitchen stops and looks at him. "I'm tired. You all enjoy yourselves. I need to lie down and think."

He walks slowly to the back bedroom and closes the door. Not all the rooms have doors yet, but his does. Nor does he bother with the lamp as he pulls off his boots and trousers.

Lying under the coverlet on the wide bed meant for two, Dorrin tries to cast his thoughts out—the same way he was taught so long ago by his father, the air wizard. This time he is not seeking natural storms, but chaos.

Sparkles of white fire flicker from the countryside, a sullen white different from the snow, but Dorrin is too tired to cast his thoughts even to Kleth. While Kleth is nearer than that distant agony of Liedral's, he cannot yet tell in which direction she lies—assuming that the pain is hers. But to whom else could it belong?

So he tosses and turns in the night.

CI

VAOS GESTURES AS Dorrin finishes the hammer stroke on the cherry-red iron he is fullering into thinner strips for hinges. Somehow, between everything, people always need things like hinges and nails. He holds his stroke. "Yes?"

"The big guard, the blond one, him and the red-headed one . . . they're here to see you."

Dorrin lifts the iron and sets it on the bricks before placing his hammer in the rack. "Have Merga warm up some cider and see if there's some bread. Then bring in some more charcoal, and sweep up the place."

"But . . . ser . . ."

"Vaos."

"Yes, ser."

Dorrin still worries about Liedral, but his senses only tell him she is closer than before, closer and in pain. And now Brede and Kadara will bring more worries. He walks to the smithy door. Both an icy wind and the glitter of the frozen white snow strike the smith as he steps into the yard. The tracks of the two riders cross his own earlier prints out to the stable.

Brede and Kadara tie their mounts to the railing. Brede wears a ragged beard, a fresh scar across one cheek, and his eyes are set in dark holes. Kadara's face is an angular caricature, with deep circles around her eyes.

Dorrin gestures toward the kitchen. "Can you have something to eat?"

Brede nods tiredly. Kadara says nothing as she tromps up the steps.

"You can stable them if you want."

"Can't stay all that long," Brede grunts.

"This is a lot warmer than where we've been."

Both troopers knock the snow off their boots before stepping into the kitchen and slumping into chairs. Merga looks up. "The cider's not quite warm, ser. But I can set out some bread, and cheese, and there's a little dried fruit."

Dorrin takes off his leather apron and hangs it on a peg by the door.

"That sounds wonderful," says Kadara.

Brede just unfastens his jacket.

Dorrin looks at Merga. "Why don't you and Frisa go see how Rylla's doing? I'll take care of the cider."

"Yes, ser. Might be as she could use some help with the heavy snow. Frisa's in the room. I'll be going."

Merga grabs for her herder's jacket and scuttles out onto the porch.

"Building a domestic empire, Dorrin?" Kadara's chuckle is hard, forced.

"No. I ended up with them... because I tried to keep her and her daughter from getting beaten. The man committed suicide, and..." He rises to get the pot in which Merga poured the cider and spices. Without spilling much on the table, he fills both mugs.

"Thank you." Brede holds the cup to his face, inhaling the steam. "It's been a long winter."

Kadara sips silently.

"You need something," Dorrin suggests into the silence.

"Yes, we do," Brede answers. "The problem is that I don't know what I need. Come spring—and winter cannot last forever—the Certan levies will pour down the roads toward Elparta. They could use the rivers."

"I can't make edged weapons. I could make some black iron shields."

"They're heavy," Kadara says slowly.

"They're what Recluce uses against the fireballs of the White Wizards. I could make them pretty thin."

"That might help—if we had one or two for emergencies." Brede nods. "That won't be enough. We need something that will stop them on the roads. Do you have some magic knives that slice up troops from a distance?" Brede's laugh is harsh and cynical.

"I never... besides..."

"I know. You get ill even thinking about edged weapons, let alone forging them."

"I can't do it." Dorrin sits in the chair across from her.

"How convenient," Kadara says.

Dorrin looks at her. "Every day I try to heal people who are dying because their bodies don't have enough food to resist flux or consumption or fever. Half the people in Diev are slowly freezing because they can't afford wood and don't have the strength to get into the hills to cut it and bring it back. I feel guilty because we have food. Even being a trader has become a high-risk occupation—you know that. What do you want, Kadara?"

"I'm sorry, Dorrin. But I'm not. We're getting old and tired, and you're getting wealthy and successful. You have a house. You have a clean bed every night, and people look up to you. Everyone looks away when we ride by. Death sticks to us like a leech."

Dorrin looks down at the table.

"This isn't going to help," Brede says tiredly.

"Let me think . . . I said that in the fall, didn't I?" Dorrin looks at the table. Knives—what cuts like a knife that isn't a knife or a sword? Can he do anything with the gunpowder? "Will they have White Wizards with them—the Certans, I mean?"

"Probably. Some detachments will."

"How is your squad doing?"

"It's Kadara's now."

Dorrin looks at the two, realizing they both wear braid.

"Brede's a strike leader, with three squads under him."

"Oh . . ." Dorrin tried to think. "Do they always use the roads?"

Brede snorts. "We all use the roads. How else can you move troops through the hills at any speed? Everything else turns to dust and mud."

"Hmmmm . . ."

"If it will help, good coin-oriented smith, the Council has authorized me to buy up to two golds' worth of weapons . . ." Brede's tone is ironic.

"Use the coins for supplies," snaps Dorrin.

This time Brede looks at the table. Kadara breaks off an end of the loaf and chews on it.

"I'll develop something—darkness knows what—but something . . . and you'll get a couple of shields." Dorrin stands and walks back to the stove to refill their mugs. First, though, he pours himself a mug.

"You've worked hard," Brede says slowly. "Maybe not as hard as a trooper, but your eyes are tired, and there are new lines on your face."

"I've been trying," Dorrin admits, "but everything takes more than I thought. If I want to build an engine, I need coin for metal and tools. To get that means working hard . . ." He steps back to the table and refills the mugs.

"Dorrin, just what are you going to do with such an engine? What will you use it for?" Kadara asks.

"I could use it to run a sawmill or a ship or a grain mill. The ship makes the most sense, because the ocean has more order within it."

"You'd better build it quickly," Brede says, "unless you can find a way to stop Fairhaven and its captive levies."

"Have you seen your trader friend lately?" asks Kadara.

"No." Dorrin sits. "She's been hurt, somehow, but I can't locate her."

"And you're just sitting here?" Kadara sets her mug back on the table.

"Where do you suggest I go?" Dorrin asks.

"Sometimes, it pays to wait," Brede says. "And that is often the hardest thing to learn." He breaks off a piece of bread and chews it.

"Stop being so old and wise and philosophical." Kadara smiles faintly.

Dorrin lets his breath out slowly.

"Isn't that better than being young and rash and stupid?" Brede laughs.

"Not a great deal. How about being young and happy once in a while?"

"That was in another country, wench. But I will try."

Dorrin takes a bite of the dried pearapples, then sips his cider, thinking about shields and invisible knives and roads ... and the nearing agony that is Liedral.

CII

THE RAIN SLASHES his face as Dorrin urges Meriwhen down from the ridge road and along the muddy flat and toward the trees south of Jarnish's yard.

Liedral has to be at the factor's, or somewhere near. He had left Diev once his senses indicated she was getting nearer. In Kleth, at least, he will be closer to anywhere else in Spidlar—between the roads and the river.

The wind moans in his ears as he sees Jarnish's small warehouse. Meriwhen's hoofs squish through the thin mud that overlies the stones of the road. Kleth is noticeably warmer than Diev, and the snow has begun to melt off, leaving the fields with a blotchy appearance.

As he guides Meriwhen into the factor's yard, he recognizes the cart tilted upward by the stable. Both the burning in his guts and the fear in his heart are sharp—sharp enough to cut. And lying over the entire yard is a sense of diffuse whiteness, a vague fog of chaos.

Even before he dismounts, Jarnish is rushing from the kitchen.

"I was going to send a message ... but no one was going to Diev ..." The chaos Dorrin sensed clings to the factor.

Dorrin swings down, and immediately brings the black staff into his hand.

Jarnish is bowing, almost groveling in the mud. "I did what I could, master Dorrin . . . I got the trader here . . . I did."

"Where is she?"

"She? Liedral . . . that's the one I mean."

Dorrin swallows. Jarnish does not know? "Where is Liedral?"

"Couldn't put him in the house . . ." Jarnish's eyes edge to the stable.

Dorrin, staff in hand, marches into the stable.

The agony welling from the beaten and whipped figure lying on the pallet in the corner of the stable grasps at him, and for a moment, he cannot see, so blinding is the pain in and behind his eyes.

"I owe the trader . . . but not enough for the Whites . . . See what they did . . . Brother they fired in his warehouse. Thought you could help." Jarnish pulls at his beard. "Can you move . . . Don't want . . ."

"I'll take care of . . . the trader . . . but I can't move . . . not now . . ." Dorrin's forehead beads with sweat, despite the chill of the stall.

Liedral? Why? Just because she hasn't paid road duties or joined the traders' association? Or because she carried his toys? Or because the Whites are after him?

"You'll move the trader as soon as you can?"

His eyes burn as he turns on Jarnish. "The Whites aren't anywhere close, not the ones you fear. I'm the one you need to fear." He lifts the staff. "You wouldn't even put her in the house, you gutless bastard."

Jarnish backs away.

"Get me some boiling water, clean cloths, and some blankets."

Jarnish looks at the healer, blankly.

"You want us out of here? Then get me boiling water, clean cloths, and blankets."

As Jarnish stumbles from the stable, Dorrin wipes his eyes. Then he takes a deep breath, and his hands touch the surprisingly small wrists.

Blood is everywhere, crusted across her back, down her legs, matted into her skull, yet none of the wounds is deep, as if they were designed for pain, and more pain. Even worse is the feel of chaos that coats her, although it mostly dusts her—unlike the factor, who seems infused with the whiteness.

His fingers brush her arms, sensing the infections beginning on her back and thighs. At least the pallet and sheet on which she lies are clean. Offering some directed order to Liedral before returning to Meri-when, he leads the mare into the stable and ties her in a corner, then unloads the saddlebags with the herbs he has brought.

Lyssa, the maid, struggles into the stable with a basket of rags, which she carefully lowers onto the straw next to the stall door. "Jaddy says it will be a bit for the boiling water."

"Could you get me a bucket of clean well-water?"

Lyssa does not meet his eyes. "Yes, ser."

"And, when you have a moment, a clean shift."

"A shift?"

"The trader is a woman. She hid it to avoid something like this." Dorrin's words are calculated.

"They beat her . . . for being a woman?"

"The Whites don't exactly favor the Legend," Dorrin snaps. "Could I have some water?"

Putting Liedral in the stable, of all things. Clearly, Jarnish is under the Whites' influence, and there is a terrible reason for the beating. The Whites seldom engage in unnecessary cruelty, and with that thought his fists clench momentarily. If only he had insisted she stay in Diev... but he had not, and he cannot change that.

Lyssa struggles back in with a bucket of icy water.

"Thank you." Dorrin tries to soften his voice, but he reaches for a rag and wets it.

"I have an old shift. It's soft, and it's clean."

"Thank you," he repeats softly, using one hand to brush back the tears. He begins to clean away the dirt and the blood. How had Liedral made it this far? Or did the Whites ensure that she did? Why? He pushes away the questions as he works.

The dark pulse of order finally beats strongly in Liedral's weakened frame. Darkness has closed over the stable when Dorrin curls up on the straw in one of the two blankets Jarnish has so reluctantly furnished. The dark staff rests beside his fingertips, and he hopes that it will alert him to any danger.

Outside, the darkness remains when he wakes, grasping for the staff.

"... no... not that..." Liedral mutters, and each mutter brings a turn on the pallet, and a fresh surge of agony.

Dorrin touches her forehead.

"... oh..."

"Just rest easy..."

"Dorrin... where...? So thirsty... Why did you hurt me? Why?"

Half of her words dwell on his hurting her—why? As he questions, he eases the slightest trace of water between her lips, and uses his senses to slide her back into a deeper and healing sleep.

Whether he will sleep after glimpsing the horror in her thoughts is another question. His fingers clench around the staff, and he wishes he were a blade like Kadara and Brede. But how can he forge destruction out of order? And if he can... should he?

But ... Creslin did. The Founders did, and they survived.

What kind of machine? What kind of magic knives, as Brede put it? He does not know, but he will heal Liedral, and he will repay the Whites. Somehow.

CIII

LIEDRAL IS PROBABLY not well enough to travel, but Dorrin will risk it, muddy roads and all, before staying longer so close to the chaos that has grown up around Jarnish.

He continues to pack the two sacks of assorted knickknacks that were in the cart bed into sacks he has retrieved from the corners of Jarnish's stable. He places a layer of clean straw covered with some rags on the cart bed. The thin pallet will go over that.

Next comes saddling Meriwhen and harnessing the cart horse. He is thankful he has watched Liedral, although his smithing work has given him some greater idea of how harnesses work.

After readying the horses, he pauses, rubbing his stubbly face, realizing that worrying about shaving is stupid. Time enough to shave when he gets back to Diev. What else does he need? Food—of course, since the trip will take at least three days, and perhaps four. He should have thought of provisions earlier. He sighs, then glances at Liedral, whose eyes find his. He walks over to the pallet.

"Dorrin ... terrible ... you hurt me ..."

She has used the same words over and over. He places his hand on her forehead, trying to reassure her. "I'm here; everything will be all right."

" ... thirsty ..."

He eases more water into her parched throat, but some dribbles onto the pallet because she has trouble drinking. Yet she cannot lie on her back or sides, not with the terrible welts there.

In a few moments, she sleeps again, almost as if to escape thinking about the terrors she has endured. He loads the trade bags on Meriwhen, and, with a look at the sleeping Liedral, heads toward the factor's kitchen.

After knocking the water and mud off his boots, he steps inside, carrying the empty saddlebags.

"How's the young trader? Terrible thing, that," says the cook. "And a fearsome bunch are those White Wizards."

"The trader's better. Could I buy a few provisions for the trip back?"

"Sure and you won't travel the roads in this weather. The mud would stop anyone."

"It's a hard-packed road to Diev, and I made it here. Besides, we cannot stay." Dorrin glances at the door to the rest of the house.

"Sad thing it is when you must drag a wounded soul across all Spidlar. And after such a long and frightful winter, too."

"About the provisions?"

"We've some, but not as many as we'd like. Yet how could I not refuse a healer's coin?" Jaddy begins to rummage through the small barrels. "Some dried apples and pearapples . . . and brick cheese. Here are some road biscuits, hard but still good . . ."

Dorrin smiles at the running commentary and at the small pile of food that appears on the cutting table.

" . . . and the poor trader will need something that can be softened. Just moisten the travel bread with water or cider. Moisten it; don't soak it." The cook looks at Dorrin. "You understand, young fellow, healer or not?"

"Yes, I understand."

"Well, don't just stand there. Pack it all up in your bags. Why else did I get it out?"

Dorrin can't help grinning momentarily. As he begins to pack, he asks, "What might I—"

"We're not so poor here that a little food can't be spared, even if you are daft to take to the roads now."

Dorrin is still shaking his head as he loads the food under the cart seat. The half-smile vanishes as Jarnish slides into the stable. Dorrin turns and meets him.

"Ye owe me—"

"I asked your cook . . ."

"No. Pox on the food. Ye owe me, healer, for taking in yer lady trader." Jarnish's voice is hard, but his eyes are fixed on the muddy clay of the yard. "It were a big risk for me."

Dorrin's hands reach to the staff he is about to place in the makeshift holder beside the cart seat, where he can easily reach it in this time of trouble. The fingers of his right hand tighten about the dark wood. "It was little risk."

"Ye owe me," Jarnish insists, his voice even harder, and Dorrin can sense the prodding of chaos behind the trader's words.

"Then I will repay you in like coin." Dorrin releases the staff.

Jarnish looks up, and Dorrin's eyes catch the other man's, and the smith's hands, hard and unyielding like the iron he fashions, seize Jarnish's hands by the wrists.

"I will repay you in order." Dorrin laughs, a harsh almost crying sound, as he weaves order around the factor. "You will no longer be able to tolerate chaos in the slightest of matters, and your skin will itch, and crawl when it nears you." His eyes flare, and darkness falls from them over Jarnish, who tries to break from the iron grasp.

The trader has shivered, whimpered once, and ceased his struggle long before Dorrin releases him.

"You've killed me," the older man sobs. His hands rip at his clothes, then he turns and shambles from the stable scratching his neck, and pulling at his garments.

Dorrin does not watch, instead returning to the stall and lifting the pallet, Liedral and all, into the cart. Then he leads the cart horse and Meriwhen out of the stable.

Jarnish is standing in his underdrawers beside the well, pouring a bucket of cold water over himself. "Another one . . . another one."

Jaddy scurries through the mud toward Dorrin.

He waits. At least he owes her that.

"A terrible curse you put upon him! No good will come from that, and I thought you were a nice young fellow."

Dorrin smiles sadly. "I only blessed him with a desire for order."

"Oh . . . that be an even more terrible curse! How could ye be so cruel?"

Dorrin looks pointedly toward the cart bed.

"You'll be thinking he beat her . . . I know he didn't."

"Had he beaten her," Dorrin says slowly, "he would not stand. Ever."

"A just man you are, and that makes you all the more terrible." Jaddy looks back toward Jarnish, who shivers under another rush of cold water. "No one could curse you more than you already are. For all those around you will suffer, and suffer."

"They already are," Dorrin admits. "They already are." He climbs onto the cart seat and flicks the reins.

The cook watches as the cart lurches through the mud of the yard and out to the road.

CIV

CREAAKKK... DORRIN GUIDES the cart around the uphill turn and back onto the straight. Behind the cart, Meriwhen whickers, still complaining about the packs she carries. Liedral, lying on blankets and between two pillows, sleeps in the small space behind the cart scat.

Driving the cart is worse than learning to ride had been. The seat is hard, and the roads a mess of mud and slush. And Liedral still moans, sleeping or half-awake.

"Holloa, the cart!"

Two ragged figures sit on the fallen tree beside the road. Dorrin's heart beats faster, and his perceptions fly toward the men. There are only two of them, and neither carries a bow. Still, he reaches down with his left hand and eases the staff into a position where he can grab it easily.

He might as well continue up the gentle slope and through the trees too far apart to be a forest, since he cannot turn the cart quickly enough to escape—and because he needs to get back to Diev.

The two men amble into the road. Each carries a sword.

"Holloa. We'd like to collect the tolls." The dark-bearded man stands a half-head taller than Dorrin and waves a battered sword.

"I wasn't aware that there were any tolls on this road."

"There are now, my peddler friend."

"Aye, and they're steep, too," growls the shorter man, who holds his sword more like a bludgeon.

Dorrin bends and brings the staff up with a one-handed fluid motion.

"Ah . . . the peddler has a toothpick."

Dorrin reins the cart to a halt and drops to the muddy road, sliding as he does.

"Poor peddler . . . Aye, and he can't even stand." Both men come around the left side of the cart horse toward Dorrin.

Dorrin wiggles his boots, trying to get a firmer footing in the muddy road, then squares the staff and waits.

The taller man stops. "Now. Let's have the purse."

"No." Dorrin doesn't care that much about the purse, but he has no illusions that providing the purse will allow their escape.

"Poor peddler . . . poor dumb peddler . . ." The tall man swings the sword.

Before the blade even reaches forward, the black staff has thrust, then cracked across the man's wrists. The sword lies in the mud, but the would-be bandit lifts a knife and lunges. This time Dorrin is even quicker, and one body lies in the road mud.

The smaller, ginger-bearded man's sword sweeps toward Dorrin before he can recover fully with the staff, and he ducks, but the blade tip rakes across his forehead.

Dorrin's feet slide on the muddy road, but he manages to lurch into position with the staff before the remaining bandit can bring the sword back. He waits for the clumsy swing with the old blade, parries it, and then slams the end of the staff into the bandit's diaphragm. Even as the man falls, Dorrin automatically follows up with a second blow.

Then, as the white agony sears through his brain, he leans on the side of the wagon, barely able to hang on.

After the pain subsides to hammers banging through

his skull, he checks the wagon, but Liedral still moans in her sleep, and Meriwhen whickers when he touches her neck. Then he drags the bodies into the melting snow beside the road, and, attempting to be practical, checks the robbers' purses. He finds one silver and four coppers, plus a gold ring, all of which he slips into his own purse. He leaves the battered swords next to the bodies, which he does not even attempt to bury. The winter has also been hard for the scavengers.

Dorrin has no illusions about his prowess. Neither man was a real highwayman, and his work with the staff was clumsy at best. He uses one of the clean rags he brought from Jarnish's to clean and blot the cut across his forehead, trying to sprinkle it with some crushed astra, which burns as he applies it.

After climbing back onto the cart, he flicks the reins. Is this the sort of desperation Brede and Kadara deal with all the time? What can a mere smith do? He shivers, even as his free hand brushes Liedral's fevered forehead, trying to instill yet more order and reassurance.

The cart slides over the hill crest, and Dorrin can see the haze of Diev in the distance, reinforced by the kaystone on the curve at the bottom of the hill.

"Thirsty . . ."

With one eye on the road, he fumbles with the water bottle, dribbling some on Liedral's cheeks, but getting most of it into her mouth.

" . . . Dorrin . . .'

"I'm here."

Creakkkk . . . The cart hub scrapes the kaystone as Dorrin tries to guide it around the curve while still reassuring Liedral. The wheels barely have purchase on the slush that remains of the rolled and packed snows of winter.

"I'm here," he repeats, glancing toward the West-horns beyond Diev, and the gray clouds that promise another cold rain, even more miserable with the pounding that surges through his skull. He hopes they will make it to his holding before the rain does. "I'm here."

CV

DORRIN LOOKS AT the plate on the anvil. He has never done much cold-working, but armor, even shields, requires cold hammer work. Yet black iron cannot be hammered.

He sets the larger plate aside and takes a smaller chunk of iron, scrap from a strap, and uses the tongs to ease it into the forge. As he watches the color of the metal, Vaos wheels in another load of charcoal in the iron-tired wheelbarrow. The front wheel drips mud all over the smooth clay floor.

"Vaos, after you . . . Just clean up the mud."

"But, ser, the floor is just clay, and I'll get more mud on it when I go out again. It's pouring."

"The mud bothers me. It may be unreasonable, but I need it cleaned up."

"Yes, ser." Vaos trudges toward the broom.

"Brush it off the wheel, too, if you would."

"Yes, ser."

Dorrin brings the iron to the anvil, strikes the metal to thin it down to the thickness of armor, slowly infusing order to turn it into black iron. When he is done, he sets the fullered and ordered iron on the back edge of the forge to anneal, and searches for another chunk of scrap.

The second chunk he fullers down to plate thickness and then turns into black iron, placing it in turn on the back of the forge.

Next he gets out the charcoal and tries to calculate on the smoothed plank he uses for his smithy figures. If the shield is roughly a twentieth of a span in thickness . . . He checks the figures. Just the metal surface of a shield one and a half cubits across will weigh more than a stone.

"Darkness!" The braces and frame straps will add more than a half stone. What if he thins the metal further? Will it withstand a White Wizard's firebolt? He wishes he knew more. Even Brede would not want to carry a shield weighing a stone and a half. If he decreases the size of the shield, and thins the metal . . .

Dorrin sighs and refigures again, and again.

While the metal anneals, he goes back to work on a hand-cranked, metal-bladed fan—a novelty item for Jasolt—wishing that he had an answer for Brede, besides the small shields for wizard fire.

Hammering out the curved blades and setting them in the circular centerpiece that connects to the two gears takes most of the afternoon, but that is the hardest work left, since the gears are already forged and cut on his makeshift cutter.

Vaos has to bring in charcoal—and sweep out the mud—twice more before Dorrin nods that he is done with what he will do on the fan.

Then he picks up the chunk of black iron forged to plate thickness and lays it on the anvil. He takes the half-stone hammer and strikes. The shock nearly paralyzes his arm. There is the faintest of scuffs on the metal. No, black iron cannot be forged cold.

Setting aside the plate-thickness chunk, he retrieves the piece fullered to the proposed thickness of his shield and sets it on the anvil's cutting edge. Positioning the cold chisel, he lifts the hammer.

The same shock runs through his arm, and the iron holds.

At least, he can hot-forge the shields, since he

doubts that any sword wielded by a trooper can bring any more force to bear than his chisel under the power of the heavy hammer. He lifts the roughly cubit-square sheet of plate into the forge and motions to Vaos.

"The light sledge."

"You're going to let me strike it?"

"I don't have a lot of choice if we're going to get this done. Strike just one blow on each point where I show you, and make sure the face of the sledge is even."

"I know. I watched you and Yarrl."

As he watches the youth lift the sledge, Dorrin wonders how Hegl ever stood it with him. On the third blow, Vaos is off center, and Dorrin dances aside as the hot iron sails toward his legs.

"Vaos!"

"Sorry, ser."

"Don't be sorry. Just bring it down straight. We can make some extra time. We can't make extra arms or legs."

"Yes, ser."

The hammer strikes are slower, but more careful from that point on.

Finally, when the iron, still iron, is roughly the thickness Dorrin wants, he calls a halt. "That's enough for tonight. I need to do the frame tomorrow, and then I'll use the bench shears to cut it before turning the edges to accept the frame."

"But I was just getting the hang of it."

"You were also getting ready to hit my legs again with the plate. Now, get this place swept up again, while I bank the forge."

Vaos sets down the sledge. His arms shake. "Yes, ser. But I could have done more."

Dorrin grins. "You will. Don't worry about that." He turns to attend to the forge. When he is done and has racked his tools, he looks at Vaos, still sweeping the clay. "Don't forget to rack your tools." He takes off his leather apron and hangs it on the peg beside his tool rack.

"Yes, ser."

After leaving his boots on the mat inside the door, Dorrin washes in the kitchen, trying to avoid Merga's efforts with the mutton and potatoes, before heading to the bedroom to check on Liedral.

"Will your lady—"

"She's not my lady, at least not yet."

"Will the lady be joining us for dinner, master Dorrin?"

"I would doubt it, but let me talk to her and check." He steps into the short hall and walks to the end, easing through the doorway.

Liedral is lying on her stomach, looking at the healers' book Dorrin has borrowed from Rylla.

"This is interesting."

He touches her shoulder, and she winces. "Sorry."

"It's not that . . . I don't know. Something's not quite right."

"You kept saying that I hurt you . . . but I didn't. I couldn't even find where you were. And I came as soon as I could."

"I know." She eases into a sitting position on the bed. "This is a lovely bed, and you've been wonderful . . . and dear. Everyone has been. Reisa, she came today in this rain, and she was so nice." Her face crumples, and a tear oozes from her right eye.

Dorrin wants to touch her, to hold her, but senses that it would be wrong. He is frustrated, because he can sense no permanent injury, no lingering chaos, no compulsions laid upon her. Yet something is definitely wrong. How could a whipping change everything between them? Yet it has.

"Are you hungry?" he asks softly.

"Yes! I'm starving, and I'm tired of lying around. I can wear one of your shirts over this."

"Are you strong enough—"

"Of course, I'm strong enough to eat with everyone in the kitchen. Just let me get something on besides this shift."

"Are you sure?"

"Dorrin."

He shrugs and grins.

"Shoo. Let a woman have some privacy." She gestures toward the door, and he closes it behind him.

Dorrin looks into the small room next to the main bedroom, empty except for the table he uses as a writing desk, a stool, and the pallet he is using as a bed. He wishes that Liedral were better. It would also be nice to sleep in a more comfortable bed. Right now, even Vaos and Merga have more comfortable sleeping arrangements than he does.

With another deep breath, he steps into the kitchen.

"Master Dorrin," asks Merga, "would you carve the mutton while I finish the biscuits?"

Dorrin is reluctant to cut the mutton, but he is the head of the household, such as it is. He takes the knife and begins to carve, awkwardly, aware that Vaos sits at the table, leaning forward, staring intently at the slab of meat. "Stop drooling, Vaos. You won't get fed any sooner."

"I'm hungry, and we don't get slabs of meat that often."

"Thank Liedral for that. Reisa was so glad she came that she brought over the mutton leg for us."

"Thank me for what?" Liedral stands in the doorway.

Dorrin, carving knife in hand, looks up and turns. "For the—"

"NOOOOOOOOoooooooooo . . ." Even as the blood

flows from her whitened face, Liedral is crumpling to the floor.

Dorrin drops the knife on the table and stumbles to Liedral, touching her wrists. Merga's biscuits spew across the floor.

Frisa, sitting on the stool next to Vaos, lets out a small shriek.

Dorrin can feel the pounding of Liedral's heart, but there is no resurgence of chaos, no renewed illness or infection.

"What happened?" asks Merga, looking over the two of them.

"I don't know."

"She looked at us, and she screamed."

Vaos and Frisa stare from the table.

"You can heal the nice woman," Frisa insists.

Dorrin gently lifts her limp form, trying to keep his hands off the welts and wounds on her back, and carries her back to bed. He lays her gently on her stomach on the double bed.

"Don't just leave her there like a sack of grain." Merga fusses at the unconscious woman, gently turning her head, and making sure Dorrin's shirt does not bind against her back.

"Oh ... the knife ..." Liedral shudders. "Why did you hurt me?"

Dorrin and Merga exchange glances.

"Daft ... out of her mind ... You couldn't hurt a soul, her especially."

"She thinks so," Dorrin whispers. "I'm here. I didn't hurt you, and I never will."

"But ... it hurt ... so much ... so much ... and you did so often."

The White Wizards—what did they do? How did they link the torture to him?

"She'll still need something to eat," Dorrin whispers.

"I'll bring a plate."

"I'm here," he says helplessly as he sits on the stool. "I'm here."

Liedral struggles up slowly, easing up until she sits on the edge of the bed, her feet dangling. "What happened?"

Dorrin frowns. "I was carving the mutton. You came in and looked at me. Then you screamed, and began muttering about how much I hurt you."

She blots her face with her sleeve. "It's stupid! I know you won't hurt me, but I'm so scared. I hate not being in control of myself. I hate it!"

Merga steps back at the violence of Liedral's words.

"And I'm not going to eat in here. I'm not a baby." Liedral pauses. "Have you finished carving the mutton?"

"Merga can finish it."

"That I can. I'll just put your plate on the table, lady."

"I'm Liedral."

But Merga has gone back to the kitchen.

Dorrin extends a hand to Liedral. Shivering, she still takes it, but lets go once she is on her feet. They walk quietly to the kitchen.

CVI

"WHY AREN'T YOU working?" Liedral stands in the doorway to the kitchen.

"I came in to see about you. I keep worrying."

She shakes her head. "What about your projects for Brede and Kadara, or your engine? You always used to talk about your engine."

"This business . . . between us . . . your fears that I'll

hurt you, that I have—makes it hard. I hate the damned White Wizards."

"So do I. But you tell me that you can't do anything to heal me."

"I've tried everything." Dorrin clenches his fists. "Rylla has no ideas, either. We know what they did. Somehow, they linked the torture to images of me. But I don't know why."

"Darkness! Standing around won't solve either our problems, or anyone else's." She walks to the table and looks at the wedge of cheese, then at the knife. Almost without thinking her hands reach for the hilt, and her fingers curl around it.

Dorrin turns toward the table, frowning slightly. What can he do to remove the distance between them? He rubs his head and turns.

Liedral's eyes are blank as she shifts her grip on the knife and steps toward Dorrin. The knife rises, as if she does not really see the blade.

Dorrin's eyes widen, and he steps back.

"Liedral."

She continues to lift the knife, then draws back her arm.

"Liedral."

He backs up. She steps forward, both hands now going around the hilt, the tip pointed toward his heart. Dorrin eases backward, noting the blankness in her eyes, and gently, oh, so gently, tries to project some sense of order, reassurance toward Liedral.

She steps forward.

Dorrin concentrates, and steps backward, but Liedral, eyes white, lunges forward, the knife slamming like a firebolt toward his chest.

He twists sideways, his hands grasping for her wrists, but she turns. Powered by muscles knotted like iron wire, her wrists wrench clear of his fingers, and the knife slashes toward him again.

Dorrin stumbles as he backs away, and the edge of the table digs into his hip as he tries to twist clear of the knife. His hands clamp around Liedral's wrists, but the knife continues to move toward him—Liedral's arms are like iron bars pressing down on him.

"Oh . . ." Merga stands in the doorway, eyes wide and mouth open.

One of the benches crashes to the floor, and Dorrin staggers back, losing his grip on Liedral's right wrist.

The knife slashes. Dorrin twists frantically, and pulls Liedral toward him, instead of resisting.

A line of fire rips across his chest and shoulder, but he manages to grab both her wrists and twist.

The knife thuds dully on the floor.

Dorrin gathers—too late—what little order-sense remains, and thrusts it upon Liedral, but she has collapsed like a sack of milled grain, and he staggers again, trying to hold her upright, even as the fire continues to burn across his right shoulder.

"Master Dorrin . . . master Dorrin . . . what be—" Merga's words stop by themselves.

Dorrin shifts his grip, trying to hold on to Liedral. How deep is the slash across his shoulder? It does not feel deep, but how would he know? He has never been stabbed before.

"Why . . . why did you hurt me?" Liedral's eyes flutter, and her voice is almost childlike as she half rests, half lies in Dorrin's arms. Blood oozes across the slashed edges of his shirt.

"Hurt you?" Dorrin blurts. "You took a knife to me." He tries not to wince as he sets Liedral in a chair and quickly kicks the knife across the floor toward Merga. "Take care of that, please."

"Yes, master Dorrin."

"But you hurt me . . . you whipped me. Didn't you?" Liedral's voice is less childlike. "You whipped me. It hurt."

"I never touched you. How could I?" Dorrin lets his senses examine the long, shallow wound—more than a scrape, but not deep enough to cut into the muscle. It already stings. He winces as he thinks of the crushed astra compress he needs.

"Indeed . . . how could he?" repeats Merga as she scoops up the knife and wipes it clean, her eyes flicking from the bloody slash across Dorrin's shirt to the woman at the table.

Liedral's eyes open wide, and she shudders. "I tried to kill you. I . . . tried . . . to kill . . . you . . ." Her hands touch the table, and she bends forward, her body convulsing in heavy, wracking sobs.

Merga points silently to Dorrin's shoulder, then steps toward the table. "We all do things we shouldn't . . ."

Dorrin opens the door to the storeroom, and to the herbs and dressings within. He hurries as he fumbles out what he needs, listening to Merga.

" . . . that man of yours . . . he wouldn't hurt anyone . . ."

Dorrin's jaw sets. There are some he will hurt.

CVII

DORRIN LIGHTS THE lamp on the table in the predawn darkness of the kitchen. His hand strays to the dressing that covers the shallow gash across his right shoulder, then drops as he hears steps.

Liedral stands by the doorway from the hall, a blanket wrapped around her shift.

"Are you all right? I didn't want to wake you." He adjusts the wick and straightens up.

"Yes . . . No . . . What am I supposed to say?

Darkness! They wanted me to kill you... to kill you..." Liedral shivers, one hand on the wall.

Dorrin extends a hand.

"No ... I'm sorry. I can't help it." She shivers again. "I love you, and I can't touch you! Darkness! I hate them."

Dorrin pulls out the chair. "At least you can sit down."

Liedral leans forward with her arms on the table. " ... hate them ..."

After a time, Liedral sits up. "What did you do to them? Why are they so afraid of you, or us?"

The smith shrugs. "I don't know. They've been reading your letters to me, and mine to you, I think."

"You didn't tell me?"

"How?" Dorrin asks dryly.

Liedral laughs. The sound is harsh, bitter, short.

"You need something to eat. You're pale. I'll get you some cheese to go with the bread." Dorrin's head turns toward the cutting table; he sees the knife that Merga has left and frowns.

"I'm still hungry, if that's what you mean." She looks at the knife, so like the knife that she used on Dorrin, and shivers. "Where are the things that were in my cart?"

"They're in the racks in your storeroom. Why? What does that have to do with cheese?"

"My storeroom?"

"I built it for you."

Liedral sighs. "Why didn't you ask me to stay last time?"

"Because I was young and stupid." Dorrin looks at the plank floor. "What do you want from the storeroom?"

"I can get it. I'm not made of glass."

Dorrin grins and points to the solid door at the far end of the room. "I thought it should be easy to get to." He picks a lamp from the sconce and uses his striker before heading to the door. "It has an outside door too."

"You need more lamps."

"I need more of a lot of things." He opens the door. "All your goods are in those racks. Some of them ... I don't know what they are."

"That's why I could still make coins." Liedral's slippered feet whisper across the packed, cold clay floor.

Dorrin follows her with the lamp as she rummages through the shelves.

"Here we are. A cheese cutter."

Dorrin raises his eyebrows. "How does it cut cheese? There's no blade."

"You'll see. I thought it might be useful for people like you." Liedral shuffles back to the door, then steps up into the warmth of the kitchen.

"How about you?" Dorrin follows her back to the cutting table, snuffing the lamp and replacing it as he passes the sconce.

"It might have been better if I had an aversion to knives."

"You didn't want to use it." Dorrin touches her shoulder ever so lightly.

"No. But I did. It wasn't like I did, but I still did it." She looks to the window, and the drizzle outside. "Would you put the knife away?"

Dorrin bends and takes the knife, putting it back into the cutlery box.

Liedral adjusts the cutter and applies it to the cheese, ignoring what Dorrin is doing. "See ... The wire cuts just like a blade, maybe neater." Liedral slices off three thin wafers of cheese, one after the other, and drops them onto the battered plate.

"Wire ... You wouldn't think ..." Dorrin's mouth drops open. "Wire ... black iron wire, or black steel wire ... Magic knives, and I'll bet they couldn't even see it. Need to build a drawing wheel, and special dies—but it should work." He reaches out to squeeze her shoulder, and she shivers and backs away.

"I'm sorry . . . I can't help it." Liedral eases away from the smith.

Dorrin looks at her. "I'll talk to you later." He turns and walks out the kitchen door, heading through the drizzle to the smithy.

"What are we working on this morning?" asks Vaos, pumping the bellows to bring up the fire.

"Wire drawing."

"I haven't done that."

"We'll be doing a lot of it, I think." While he still doesn't know exactly how he will make his magic wire knives, Dorrin knows they will work—and the White Wizards deserve whatever havoc they cause.

"Go get some breakfast." He nods toward Vaos.

"Yes, ser."

Magic knives—the White Wizards deserve those and more. His fingers whisper across the iron bars.

CVIII

DORRIN REINS UP outside the barracks. He wipes the mixed sweat and water from his eyes, wondering if the continuing rain will wash Spidlar away and save the White Wizards the problem.

Where will he find Brede or Kadara? He finally dismounts, tying Meriwhen to the only rail he can find outside the long one-story building. A single trooper lounges outside the door. As Dorrin approaches, the man sits up.

"I'm looking for a strike leader named Brede," Dorrin says.

"Who are you?" The trooper, hand on blade hilt, eyes the staff, the saddlebags, and the flat and leather-covered object that Dorrin carries.

"Dorrin. I'm a smith."

The trooper straightens. "Wait here, master Dorrin. I'll be right back."

Dorrin waits in the cold drizzle, but not for long.

The door opens, held by the trooper, who beckons Dorrin inside. Dorrin shifts his grip on his things and turns sideways to get past the soldier.

"Dorrin. It's good to see you. Kadara has her squad on a local patrol. She'll be sorry to have missed you." Brede is clean-shaven. His leathers and blue tunic are clean, and his boots polished. But the circles under his eyes remain, and his face is so thin as to be gaunt.

Several troopers watch from the space before the hearth, which contains only dying embers.

"It's not a pleasure call."

"Before we get to that . . ." Brede clears his throat. "We have a mystery. Dorrin, didn't you just bring Liedral back from Kleth? She was sick, Kadara tells me."

"She was tortured and beaten," Dorrin says sharply.

"At least she's alive. With you, she should get better." Brede coughs. "Did anything strange happen to you on the way back?"

"Was it that obvious?"

Brede chuckles, almost harshly. "Two dead bandits with all their clothes. One has a broken neck, and the other's chest is caved in with a single blow. Their blades are lying by the bodies, and there are cart tracks in the mud."

"Yes, I had some trouble. Liedral was fevered, and I wasn't sure she was going to make it."

"Why did you travel with her, then?"

Dorrin sighs. It gets so complicated. "Because Jarnish is tied up with the Whites, and she was there."

Brede stares. "You didn't do anything? When we're in a war for our lives?"

"I didn't say that," Dorrin snaps. "The last time I saw Jarnish, he was in his undergarments scrubbing chaos off his body with freezing well-water."

"You did that?"

"I just made sure he couldn't ever get near chaos again."

Two of the troopers who have been inching closer abruptly turn away and edge back toward the fire. Brede shakes his head.

Dorrin starts to lose his grasp on both the saddle-bags and the heavy leather-covered object, and he fumbles with all that he carries.

"You need a hand?"

"Take the big one. It's yours, anyway."

Brede reaches for the leather, then grabs, as he realizes the weight. "What . . .? This is heavy."

"It's as light as I could make it. That's the problem."

Brede pulls back a corner of the leather to see the black metal, then motions toward the left end of the long building. Dorrin follows the gesture toward a small room with an oblong table and half a dozen armless chairs. Brede closes the door to the small room and sets the shield on the table.

Dorrin takes one of the armless chairs, turns it sideways, and sits.

Brede lifts the shield. Then he sets it down and adjusts the straps before trying to use it. "It's not too bad, but it's really not quite big enough."

"I can make them bigger, but they're heavier. There has to be a certain concentration of the black iron for it to throw off white fire. There's probably some trick to it that I don't know, but I thought I'd make one for you to try out."

"I'll see." Brede nods. "You look like you have something else."

Dorrin points to the saddlebags. "I think I might have something like a magic knife."

Brede raises his eyebrows. "I thought you couldn't deal with edged weapons."

"I can't. I have trouble even carving meat for more than myself." Dorrin opens the bag and extracts what he has brought.

"What is it?" Brede frowns.

"This is really a model." Dorrin explains, as he stretches the wire taut between the two black bars. "You can wedge the black iron bars—I could make them as handles—in trees or behind boulders."

Seeing Brede's confused expression, Dorrin takes out the dried cheese and sets it on the table, then stretches out the wire and forces the bars apart.

Thump . . . The wire slices through the cheese, and both halves bounce on the table.

Dorrin hands one half to Brede. "Try to cut it with your belt knife."

"No, thank you." The strike leader fingers the hard cheese. "How would this help?"

"You told me that the levies will have to use the roads. This wire is strong enough—I'm sure—to cut through a man or a horse that rides into it. Because it's black and order-based, it's hard to see, especially in the rain or at dusk."

Brede winces. "I don't know. There's something . . . almost evil . . . about something like this."

"You don't know?" Dorrin snorts. "You complain that you want weapons, and I do what I can, and you're upset because it's nasty. Darkness! Any weapon is nasty. That's why I get sick when I use a staff.

"You want nasty? What about the Whites? They tortured Liedral with whippings and beatings—and visions of me. They did it to plant an image of her using a knife on me, and she did. They're twisting minds—"

"The trader took a knife to you?" Brede studies Dorrin.

"The slash is just about healed." Dorrin shrugs. "Anyway, they're twisting minds, and you're worried about whether their levies get chopped in half by your strong right arm or by my cheese-slicer."

"Cheese-slicer?"

"That's where I got the idea."

Brede smiles wryly. "I'd hate to think what you'd be like if you didn't have some restraints."

"It would make life easier." Dorrin takes a deep breath. "How many of these can you use?"

Brede reaches for his purse and empties two golds on the table. "As many as I can buy. No . . . don't give me that business about food. If you won't use the coin personally, buy more iron to make your cheese slicers. But don't give them to anyone but me or Kadara. And don't tell anyone else."

Dorrin understands. The more it seems like unknown magic, the better.

CIX

COLD RAIN DRIZZLES across the panes of the closed tower window. A small fire in the hearth warms the room.

The thin wizard concentrates on the glass on the small table. The oil lamp in the wall sconce flickers. Perspiration has beaded his forehead for a time before the white mists in the mirror finally part.

The red-headed smith sits on one side of a rude table; the brown-haired woman sits on the other. They talk, and the smith frowns. The woman cries. A serving woman sets a platter on the table, but neither looks up.

"Light!" mutters the White Wizard, as the mists close over the scene in the glass. He walks to the desk where a map of Spidlar is unrolled.

Diev is a goodly distance from Fenard, Elparta, or even Kleth, and there are few ways to get there easily except by the main roads—or by the sea. "The Northern Ocean?" He shakes his head. "Traders are still strong on the water."

His eyes study the map once more before he takes the weights off the corners and rolls it up. The winter has been long, but spring is arriving, even in Spidlar.

III.

TRADER AND ENGINEER

CX

THE THREE MOUNTS gallop around the last switchback. One is riderless. One White guard wavers in the saddle, crossbow bolt through his shoulder. He mumbles as they rein up before the White Wizard.

"You see how they reacted," the unhurt guard snaps.

Jeslek's eyes blaze. "Idiot! What did you say?"

"Just what you told me. Offered them amnesty if they opened the gates. Big fellow told us Axalt had stood for a millennium and would stand after we were dead. Then he turned the crossbowmen on us."

One of the guards in the retinue surrounding the two wizards finally grabs the reins of the riderless mount, while two others ease the wounded trooper from the saddle. The second wizard, red-headed and female, smiles as she watches the fires of chaos build around the High Wizard.

"They probably had us in their sights from the beginning. There's no way to approach the walls without being totally exposed."

The High Wizard nods. "We don't need to approach the walls." He laughs. "So mighty Axalt has stood for a millennium. We shall see about that."

He dismounts and walks toward the canyon wall. His senses penetrate deep beneath the rocks. Shortly, the road shivers underfoot, once, twice.

The wounded trooper moans from the wagon where he lies. Two other guards glance from each other toward the white mist that surrounds the High Wizard.

The road shivers again.

"So . . . mighty Axalt."

Beyond the switchback, which lies less than fifty cubits from the Fairhaven force, beyond the point where the canyon widens, the ancient stones of Axalt's walls climb a hundred cubits. The iron-bound gate is closed, and the squads of soldiers in gray-quilted uniforms have their crossbows trained upon the narrow gap through which the Fairhaven soldiers must come. The stone sentry box outside the wall remains vacant.

"Just wait," calls the broad-shouldered guard captain. "It has been such a long time since you were able to practice on real targets. But now you can use your bolts on the White guards. If they even dare approach again."

The boulders and solid rock underneath the walls shiver—once, twice.

Nerliat's eyebrows lift.

The wall shakes, and one soldier loses his balance and sprawls on the stones behind the parapet. The walls rock, and stone cracks like thunder.

A thin spout of hot gas lances upward through the crumbling wall, sulfurous, followed by steam and boiling water.

The crashing rocks, the steam, and the falling walls and avalanches from the west rim of the Easthorns all drown out the brief screams of human flesh.

By sunset, all that remains is a steaming, boulder-strewn depression blocking the mountain road between Certis and Spidlar.

A small party of white-clad individuals rides quietly eastward. No one speaks to the two White Wizards. No one speaks, except for the wounded guard, who moans with each turn and switchback.

CXI

"THIS ISN'T SMITHING," grumbles Vaos, as he carries a basket full of mixed weeds and grass downhill.

"No," agrees Dorrin cheerfully. "But it is coin. Do you want to have me fire up the forge and work on the scrap pile?"

Vaos groans. "That's not much better than being a farmer."

"Smithing's not easy work." Dorrin turns the soil along the row, leaving small depressions for the herb seedlings he has nursed through the late winter and cold spring. He hopes they will grow quickly and provide Liedral with another trading good when the last of the ice floes clears the Northern Ocean.

" . . . not smithing . . ." Vaos dumps the greenery into the compost pile.

Dorrin stoops and plants, stoops and plants, taking seedling after seedling from the crude flats and patting the soil around each. "You can start bringing the buckets of water over here."

"I didn't want to be a light-busted farmer . . ."

"Neither did I," Dorrin responds, "but I like eating, and so do you."

"Doing the iron scrap might be easier . . ."

"We'll do that later, when it's dark."

"Darkness . . . you never rest, master Dorrin."

"That's for when I'm too tired to do anything else."

Vaos slowly picks up the buckets and trudges to the pipe faucet Dorrin has added to the water line to the house. "At least, I don't have to climb up from the pond."

"After you water all these—and don't wash them

out, or you'll work all night on the scrap with me—clean up and meet me in the smithy."

"Yes, ser."

Dorrin follows Vaos to the crude faucet. It leaks, and he has been forced to put stones down, and a trench to the garden to carry away the thin dribble of water, but at least it reduces some work. When it gets cold, he will have to remove it, and bury the piping more deeply so that the line does not freeze the way it did on the colder days of the last winter.

After Vaos fills his buckets and heads toward the seedlings, Dorrin washes off with the cold water and shakes the excess off his hands before drying them on a towel that is really a rag. "Don't forget to wash up," he calls.

"Yes, ser."

Grinning at the resignation in the youth's voice, Dorrin walks across the slowly greening grass on the west side of the house toward the door to the smithy. Once in the smithy, he dons the leather apron and then begins to bring up the fire, setting in the charcoal.

Asavah wants a plow fixed. The share has been worn down and rusted, the point ripped off by a buried rock. Although Dorrin does not usually do plows, Asavah's help with the foundation and framing of the house saved Dorrin many days, and Jisle's chief hand needs the plow for planting—now.

Dorrin sets out the fullers and the hammers, studying the scraps he has already begun to gather and the rod stock. Finally, he pulls out a partial plate left from the shield-making and sets it on the anvil.

Vaos trudges into the smithy, still shaking the water off his hands. He looks at the plate on the anvil and grins. "I get to do some striking?"

"We're replacing the share point on Asavah's plow. Actually, it's Jisle's plow, but I owe Asavah." Dorrin shrugs. "Then I need to make some more wire for Brede." He points to the bellows lever.

"Do those wire things work?" Vaos pulls the lever to build the forge fire.

"Kadara says they do." Dorrin takes the heaviest tongs and sets the iron in the forge. "They won't do enough, but I hope they help."

"Can you forge something else?"

"Forging isn't the problem. Finding what to forge is." The smith readjusts the position of the heavy iron in the fire.

CXII

"THERE THEY ARE!" yells the first squad leader.

A squad of Spidlarian troopers, apparently upon seeing the green banners of Certis, rein up, quickly re-form, and retreat back down the road to Elparta.

The Certan strike leader studies the depression between the two hills, but sees little but meadows barely turning green. A rock wall, tumbled in places, runs along the left side of the road that angles along the highest point in the depression between the two ridges before turning due north again.

Near the lowest point of the road, just before it widens into a wagon turnout, on the side opposite the stone wall are two gnarled trees bearing pink blossoms.

The Certan officer studies the road and the trees, but there is no cover in the lower area, and the Spid-larians have already disappeared.

"Let's get the bastard traders!"

The first two squads, maintaining their order, spur their mounts into a quick trot. The strike leader nudges his mount after the lead squad.

Despite the attempt at order, by the time the first squad is nearing the wagon turnout several riders are moving faster than a mere trot.

Abruptly, the leading trooper flails in midair, and his body seems to separate into a top and a bottom half separated by a bloody mist. Two other troopers twist off their mounts, and a horse crumples under another rider.

Suddenly the depression is filled with bodies and horses.

Then the arrows begin to fall, and they fall like death upon the congealed mass on the road.

The strike leader and half a squad struggle back uphill in time to watch the Spidlarians return, led by a blond giant.

When two Spidlarian squads detach themselves from their completed massacre and start up the hill, with a handful of mounted bowmen, the strike leader digs his spurs into his mount's flanks, and the handful of Certan troopers flee for the camp beyond the border.

CXIII

DORRIN SETS THE kettle-piston on the forge bricks and feeds charcoal around the banked coals. He adjusts the air nozzle and gently pumps the bellows's lever. Then he adds the water to the kettle and flicks the clamps in place over the fill plate. Finally, he eases the kettle into place on the adaptor to the hanging iron he has added to the forge. Once the device is clamped in place, Dorrin eases the angled iron over the forge fire and increases his pumping of the bellows.

Before long, the thin trail of steam from around the fill clamps betrays the increasing pressure within the kettle, but neither the piston rod nor the wheeldriver attached to it move. Dorrin uses the narrow-edged pickup tongs to move the piston. He wipes his steaming forehead as the piston chugs through two cycles and stalls again.

"Darkness!" He swings the kettle off the forge. The intake valve has jammed—again. Theoretically, the valve should be easier to make in a larger size, but he cannot afford the materials to experiment in large sizes.

As he waits for the kettle to cool, his senses study the piston and valve assembly. It should work, but it does not. He wipes his forehead once more. Even though all the doors to the smithy are open, the air is so still that it seems to weigh down everything.

He turns, certain a figure stands by the small slack tank, but the smithy remains empty. He studies the valve on the kettle device, finally nodding as he considers changing the angle of the tubing.

Outside he hears the sound of a wagon and a horse.

"There! Easy, big fellow . . ."

Dorrin grins at the sound of Vaos's voice. The boy still loves the horses. With a last look at the kettle device, the smith turns and walks toward the yard and whoever has arrived.

Vaos holds the harness while the gray-haired man in the heavy blue sweater and blue trousers climbs off the wagon. Merga and Liedral stand on the small porch outside the kitchen. Frisa hangs on the railing, looking at the horse. Then she stands and grasps her mother's hand.

"Master Dorrin?" The gray-haired man bows as the smith approaches.

"Hasten, is it time for annual dues or something?"

"Well . . . master Dorrin, it is about money, or services." The gray-haired man bows again.

"Come on inside." He looks at Merga. "Do we have anything to drink?"

"Not really, ser. Not except water." Merga frowns. "It would take a while, but I could brew some herb tea."

"Water would be fine," Hasten affirms, using a soiled square of off-white cloth to blot dust and sweat from his forehead. "Even though it's been a late summer, it's hot now." He picks up a thick leather folder and heads toward the steps.

Dorrin nods to Vaos to water the horse. Vaos smiles.

"Can I help?" asks Frisa, as Vaos ties the horse to the stone post and lifts the bucket.

Merga looks from the horse to Vaos, then says. "You be careful, girl."

"You, too, Vaos," Dorrin adds.

A smile flits across Liedral's face, but vanishes as Dorrin turns toward her, and the two men climb the steps to the porch and the kitchen.

Almost as soon as both men are seated, Merga serves two mugs of cold water. Dorrin motions to Liedral, who has remained in the doorway, wearing a loose brown tunic and trousers. Her hair has been cut short.

"Hasten, this is trader Liedral. Liedral will be the one trading some of what I forge and grow."

Merga looks out toward the yard, then scuttles out.

Hasten inclines his head to Liedral, ignoring Merga's hasty departure, although the eyes question the slim figure. "Pleased to meet you, trader. Where might you be from?"

"Liedral is originally from Jellico, but now has stored some goods here."

Hasten frowns.

"I'm assuming that Liedral's fees to the Guild, as a traveling trader, would be similar to mine," Dorrin adds.

"Ah ... well ... I do suppose you could act as the sponsor, although it is rare for an ... artisan smith ... to sponsor a trader." Hasten coughs. "And that is partly why I am here."

"Coins?" prompts Dorrin.

"You know, of course, that the Whites have persuaded Certis and Gallos to raise levies against us." Hasten coughs again. "The Council is ... frankly ... hardpressed."

"How much?"

Hasten swallows. "Ah ... double ... roughly. A silver for you, and it would be two for the trader."

Dorrin sighs. "I think we might be able to manage it—this year. Darkness knows if this continues ..." Even the hint that he might not be able to manage the dues creates a dull throbbing in his skull. He shakes his head.

"I know, master Dorrin. I know." Hasten looks to Liedral. "But we don't charge near what the Whites require."

Liedral smiles crookedly. "The Whites do extract a high price."

" ... and our ships can no longer travel the Gulf or the Eastern Ocean. The White fleet ..." The Guild functionary looks at the tabletop, then lifts the mug and takes a swallow of the cold water. "The Council may have to call levies and services, yet."

"Services?" Dorrin takes a sip of his water.

"Military goods—supplies, that sort of thing. For you, some forging that the troops can use, harnesses or wagon brackets, perhaps caltrops."

"You either provide services or carry a pike?"

Hasten nods. "It may not come to that."

"It will," Dorrin says wearily. "It will." He pauses. "Let me get the coins, and you write out whatever papers we get."

Hasten opens the folder and extracts several

squares, a quill, and a small bottle, which he uncorks carefully, and into which he dips the quill.

Dorrin walks back into the storeroom, closing the door. He lifts a rack containing a few toys to reveal the iron-bound strongbox, from which he takes the three silvers. He replaces the strongbox, the rack, and the toys.

When he returns to the kitchen, Hasten is still scratching on the parchment squares. "A terrible time it is . . . terrible . . ." Hasten takes a sip of water, then wipes his forehead, and a drop of water or sweat splats on the table, narrowly missing the parchment and the wet ink upon it.

When the receipts are finished, the functionary stands. "A pleasure doing business with you, master Dorrin, and you also . . . trader Liedral."

Liedral inclines her head.

"A pleasure, Hasten," Dorrin says, leading the way back to the yard.

Merga is blotting Frisa with an old dry rag, trying to wipe mud off bare legs, and shaking her head. "I cannot leave you alone . . . not a moment, and you are in the mud."

Dorrin tries not to grin.

"You did not give her too much, young ser?" Hasten asks Vaos.

"No, ser. Just a little, a bit at a time, just as she wouldn't take to colic. Then a bit more."

"Good fellow."

Vaos hands the reins to Hasten after the functionary climbs onto the wagon seat.

Dorrin marvels at Hasten's clothing. A woolen sweater in summer yet, and the perspiration scarcely fazes him. After the Guild man is safely on his road to further collections, Dorrin steps back into the kitchen for more water before returning to the smithy.

Merga has commandeered a bucket of cold water

and is liberally applying it to her daughter's muddy feet and legs. "You will sit here on the porch until your legs are dry!"

"Yes, mummy."

Liedral waits by the table. "Why did you pay the dues for me? I can't pay you back. Darkness, I can't even hold you!" Liedral's voice cracks.

"You still need to be a trader," Dorrin says lightly, though it is an effort to keep his voice cheerful. He still wishes he could hold her. Instead, he stands up.

"What would I trade?"

Dorrin raises his eyebrows. "There's plenty to trade." He walks to the door of the storeroom, where he uses a striker to light the small lamp inside the room. "Come on."

"I didn't have that much, even if you brought it all." Liedral follows him to the storeroom.

"I've been busy."

"I thought you were selling it to local factors."

"I did sell some to Willum, but the White raiders killed him. And I do work for Jasolt, and some of the others, but they can't sell much, especially now." Dorrin gestures toward the racks. "Here are some of the small toys. These are decorative latches. When I made the latches for the doors I made a few extra. And . . ." He laughs. "Here are some more cheese-cutters."

Liedral looks in the racks, eyes widening. "You're building up all this to trade. This is worth more than any three loads I've ever carried. Why?"

"To get more coin. I need it to feed everyone. And," he adds as the deception starts his head throbbing, "to be able to build my first engine."

"You must really want to build it." Liedral's eyes scan the bins and racks. "How did you afford all the iron?"

"A lot of it came from scrap. I charge a little less

for my repairs if people bring scrap. Most smiths will take it, but they just pile it up. We both work on it, but I'm having Vaos learn how to turn it into rough stock."

Liedral glances at the bins and racks again. "This is worth a lot."

"I hope so. Can you sell it?"

"If I can get it to Suthya."

Dorrin nods. Getting in and out of Spidlar may indeed be the hardest task. He inclines his head toward the door back into the kitchen. With a last look at the goods, Liedral heads back to the kitchen. Dorrin blows out the small lamp and racks it, then closes the door.

"You did all that work just for more coin so that you can afford to build your engine. Why do you want to build the engine? What good will it do? How will it help anyone?" Liedral draws herself a mug of cool water and sits on the edge of a chair, wincing as she lowers herself.

"Are you still sore?"

"It's not bad . . . About the ship engine?"

Dorrin ponders. "I'm not sure I have a good answer. I've been thinking about using it to power a ship. It works on the models."

"What's wrong with the ships now?"

Dorrin looks from his chair to hers, then out and down at the pond, where dragonflies hover in the late afternoon, skimming across the water. "They can only go as fast as the wind, and where the wind lets them."

"That's an excuse, not a reason."

"No. How many ships get stuck in contrary winds?"

"Some . . ." the trader admits.

Dorrin smiles, and she shakes her head.

CXIV

"What happened?"

"The levies chased the Spidlarians ... I don't know—except that the first two riders were sliced almost in half, and no one was around. No one ..."

Jeslek's hand slams into the field table. "No one? Or no one that they could see?"

"Did you stop to see what happened?" Anya's voice is calm.

"Yes ... ser ..." stumbles the Certan officer. "Well ... not exactly. The lead horses and riders were sliced apart with invisible swords. That got everyone clogged together on the road. Then archers popped up out of hidden pits. Before things got untangled ... we lost almost three whole squads."

"Invisible swords?" asks Jeslek.

"That's what it looked like. Byler's body was sliced into two pieces. Like a blood sausage."

Anya swallows and looks down at the small portable table before her.

"Were there walls or anything tall beside the roads?"

"No, ser. Not that I recall ... Maybe one scrubby tree on one side, but this was in those rolling plains, not near Elparta or the woods." The officer scuffs his boots on the dirt floor of the tent. "Begging your pardon, ser, but ... I mean ... it's hard to fight magic."

"I understand," Jeslek says slowly. "We'll do something, but I'll need to look at the situation." His head inclines to the glass on the table, and he frowns. White mists swirl in the mirror.

The officer's eyes follow the wizard's, widening as a

scene of an empty road appears, then disappears into the mists.

"You may go," Jeslek suggests softly.

"Thank you, ser."

Anya's eyes take in the broad shoulders of the officer. She watches the back of the sweat-stained green tunic as he marches stiffly back downhill.

"Another clever tactic," Jeslek snorts. "I'm sure there's no real magic to it."

"Does it really matter, dead High Wizard?" asks Anya lazily, a cold edge to her voice.

"Of course not. But why . . . ?" He looks back at the mirror.

"Why what?"

Jeslek clears his throat. "There are a number of 'whys' . . . why women equate appearance with ability, why so many soldiers fail to think, why people who plot always think they won't be discovered . . ." He laughs softly, and the mists swirl in the glass.

CXV

THE CART HORSE snorts, and the pack horse echoes the sound as Liedral climbs into the heavily padded seat.

Dorrin takes Liedral's gloved hand and squeezes it. "Be careful."

"I will. There shouldn't be a problem. The ship's Suthyan, and so far the Whites have avoided taking on either Suthya or Sarronnyn. The longer I wait, the more dangerous it will be. Besides"—her voice almost cracks—"what am I supposed to do? Sit here and damn them for what they did to us?"

"It's better."

"A little, but I can't just sit here. There's no trading going on in Spidlar, and now's the time to make coins."

"That's not why you're going."

"No. I'm going because I can't sit here and look at you loving me. I need some time to think without worrying about you, and you need to get on with your engine and helping Brede and Kadara."

"When is she leaving?" Frisa's high voice carries across the yard from the pen where Merga is feeding Gilda, Zilda's first kid, which Reisa has insisted belongs to Dorrin.

"See?" Liedral says lightly. "She knows I should be going."

"You'll be back by fall?"

"Before then, I hope. That depends on ships, weather, and how well a lot of this ironmongery sells."

"It isn't—" He has to laugh as he sees the glint in her eye.

"You still take things too seriously, love. At least you'll get to sleep in a comfortable bed." Liedral lifts the reins, and Dorrin squeezes her hand a last time.

He watches until the cart disappears down the road to lower Diev and the three small piers where the Suthyan coaster is tied. Then he turns toward the herb garden, where Rylla is already selecting fresh astra and brinn. The healer waits for him as he walks past his stable and along the ridge line toward the herb garden that he has expanded each year.

"I'd be thinking we need more this winter," she says. "Even with the larger gardens. You won't be able to feed all those who do not have enough."

"There will be enough food," the smith says. "Everyone is planting. But we will need the healing herbs."

Rylla nods. "Some will not be a-coming home. Glad I am that Rolta is a seafarer."

"Everyone is talking about the need for levies, but . . ."

"They cannot ask for them until after the planting is finished." Rylla looks across the gardens. "Still, there is more here than an army would need, and you dried much of last year's herbs."

"I sent some with Liedral."

A smile creases the older woman's lips. "You'd be a fool if you had not. Let's get on with it. Are you ready for warts and burns?"

Dorrin sighs.

CXVI

"DIG, DAMN IT!" snaps the squad leader.

"We're not frigging farm hands," complains the trooper with the shovel.

"No, you'll be a dead trooper if you don't keep digging."

"This isn't fighting . . ." mumbles another trooper, but he keeps digging at the low point in the road.

The squad leader looks to her right, her short red hair glistening in the sun that has barely cleared the plains to the east. Uphill, three others labor at another trench. Two others have concealed the heavy road stones that they have pried out of position under brush and turf.

"Why are we doing this?"

"To kill the damned Certans," answers the squad leader. "They still like to use the roads, the idiots."

The two troopers with shovels look from the hard-eyed woman with the twin blades toward the rising sun. " . . . not sure which is worse . . ."

She ignores the comment, watching and listening as the hole that will fill with water deepens. Watching and listening as the archers on the slope above dig in.

CXVII

DORRIN CONTINUES TO watch the iron until it reaches the orange-red just beyond cherry red before lifting it onto the anvil. There he painstakingly fullers the metal into the octagonal end necessary to fit the gear. His face is sweat-streaked, his eyes burning from the sweat before he lays aside the hammer. The delicate work is harder, much harder, than hammering out braces or log peaveys. Especially when he must add order as he shapes. The engine work, as always, has taken longer than he would have wished.

Then he reheats the two pieces, carefully scarfing them before welding them together with deft blows from the hammer, and setting them on the bricks next to the forge to anneal.

After wiping his face with the back of his forearm, he steps out into the still afternoon, squinting against the sun, walking toward the kitchen for some cold water. Once he gets a drink, he needs to find his errant striker, although he suspects Vaos is in the barn, currying Meriwhen or the broken-down bay that Merga uses to go to market. Even after his limited healing efforts, Dorrin has doubts about how long the bay will last.

Every time he turns, he must add more to his establishment. He waits a moment in the shade of the house, looking down across the grass toward the pond, and the narrow mud flats that show the lack of summer rainfall. Turning toward the west, he wonders how Liedral fares, but senses nothing amiss. At least, he feels no pains, nor the agonies of their last parting. Still, she has been gone more than half a season, and he has heard nothing, not that he would expect anything with the few ships that reach Diev or Spidlaria. The news of the fall of Axalt has not helped, either. He would not have believed that the White Wizards would so cavalierly turn a city into crushed rock, yet Brede and Kadara must fight that evil . . . all too often.

He looks into the heat of the day for a time longer. Then, after wiping his sweating forehead, he walks around the porch and up into the kitchen, looking for his mug, but Merga has already filled it, and hands it to him.

"We'll be having a mutton soup, ser."

"That sounds fine . . . Mutton?"

"Asavah liked the plowshare, and the extra nails you sent."

"I only had a handful . . ."

"Might it be all right if your friend Pergun joined us?"

Dorrin tries not to shake his head. "That would be fine." He drains the cup. "But it will be a while."

"The soup will not be ready until later." Merga smiles.

Dorrin understands. Pergun will not finish at the mill for a time, either.

Vaos is in the stable, currying Meriwhen and talking to the mare. "You're such a pretty girl . . ."

"Stop the sweet talk, striker. We've got some work to do for Froos."

"Those heavy wagon pins?" Vaos groans.

"They pay the bills. Then we need to work on some of the scrap. I need to make more of those gadgets for Brede. And Jisle ordered some log peaveys."

"Jisle's a farmer."

"They're going to cut some timber from the woodlot for the Council. That's their service call." Dorrin pauses. "We have to do more nails—the square-ended spikes. Two kegs' worth."

"It's going to be late tonight, pretty girl," Vaos tells the mare.

Meriwhen whickers, and Dorrin nods.

CXVIII

"HAVE YOU DISCOVERED how this is happening?" Jeslek's voice is calm.

"Yes . . . ser . . ." stumbles the Certan officer. "We found a black oak post on each side of the road, wedged in place, and there were black wires."

"And, of course, they set up some decoy, and all of your troops ride after them full speed and run into the wires?" Acid drips from Anya's words.

The Certan officer looks down at the mud-smudged carpet. Then he looks up. "They weren't obvious decoys. One time it was a small squad. Another time it was a pair of traders with fat packs. Another time—"

"Spare us," Jeslek says tiredly. "Do you have any evidence of this? Something that will help us track it down?"

"Might I see it?" Anya asks.

"Yes, ser." The officer extends a small coil of wires wrapped around a small iron bar toward the red-headed wizard.

Anya puts out a gloved hand. Even so, a faint acrid odor rises from the leather as the black wire touches it. "Order-based . . ." Her lips twist. "It smells like Recluce again."

"You may go," Jeslek orders the officer.

"Yes, ser." The officer releases his breath slowly, stiffly turns, and leaves the tent.

"And you still think that Recluce won't help

Spidlar?" asks the square-bearded Fydel. "Who made that . . . thing?"

"You know as well as I do—that renegade smith. The one whose letters you so conveniently held for a season or so before letting me see them."

"Are you accusing—"

White fire shrouds Fydel.

"Don't tempt me, Fydel. I'm tired of all of the second-guessing and scheming and plotting that you all think I'm too dense to see."

"You're not exactly infallible, dear Jeslek." Anya's voice is honey-coated. "Clearly, your trap with the smith failed. Unless there is more than one Recluce-trained smith in Spidlar."

"I don't see why this slows everything down so much," says Fydel.

"Because," Jeslek responds with deliberate slowness, "it is hard to travel over meadows, woods, and hills. The levies prefer the metaled roads where wagons, food, and horses don't get bogged down. There aren't that many roads from Fenard into Spidlar, and they are narrow. The Spidlarians use that to pick off our troops unit by unit." The thin wizard takes a deep breath. "If it's not black iron wires, it's water traps in stone-paved roads. Before long, as we near Elparta, they'll probably destroy the bridges over the streams. That will slow our advance even more."

Anya and Fydel look at each other.

"I know, I know." Jeslek shakes his head. "You're probably asking why we don't use the river to send troops to Elparta, and then cut off their forces? Because," he answers his own question, "Elparta is heavily fortified along the river, for just that reason. We can't use the river until after we take Elparta. Unfortunately, we can't take it until we can get there, and the streams are too small this far inland."

"The levies are getting unhappy. They've been fighting all summer, and we're no more than a hundred kays into Spidlar. You took control here, great wizard. What are you going to do?" Fydel makes a deep ironic bow.

"If that is what you want," the High Wizard states, "then, whatever it takes, we'll have Elparta before winter."

"You said we'd have all of Spidlar before winter, and that was *last* fall," Anya notes coolly.

"You must admit," Fydel adds, "that it is difficult to explain how a great White Wizard can destroy a city like Axalt utterly, and yet not get his forces across a bunch of rolling plains."

"You both know the difference."

"I don't think so, dear Jeslek," Anya says.

"Fine. We will have Elparta." Jeslek gestures at the two. "Go off and plot somewhere else."

Both the redhead and the bearded wizard stand up.

Anya smiles at Jeslek. "Remember, you did suggest it."

"I know," Jeslek says calmly. "You are anyway, and it would be amusing if it weren't so pathetic." He watches for a moment as the two walk across the camp side by side. "Idiots . . ."

He looks toward the fire of the setting sun, thinking of the fires he must summon. "Idiots!"

CXIX

To THE SOUTH of the hill, pillars of black and gray smoke swirl into the gray sky, marking small farms and isolated cots that continue to burn.

The Spidlarian group leader stands in his stirrups for a moment to survey the forces moving along the road. Before the green banners of Certis and the purple banners of Gallos walk two hundred men, women, and children, flanked by Gallosian lancers. As the Spidlarian officer watches, a man ducks and scrambles down a ditch beside the stone-paved road, squirming through the mud, out of sight of the Gallosian lancers flanking the plodding peasants.

A White Wizard rides partway into the peasants and lifts a hand. White fire lances into the ditch. A scream fades, and an acrid odor rises on the wind carrying the smell of fear northward on the road from Fenard to Elparta.

The White Wizard looks toward the hilltop where the blond man watches. A firebolt flies northward, but the cavalry officer has spurred his mount below the ridge line and toward the troopers who wait on the far side of the hill, on the road that the combined army marches across.

"That bad?" asks Kadara as Brede reins in.

"Worse. There are at least two thousand of them, and they're using villagers as a shield, walking them in front of the troops." He points toward the city that lies less than five kays up the road. "They've given up on taking it. Instead they'll destroy it. Like Axalt."

"We could get some with archers," offers another squad leader.

Brede shakes his head. "If you get close enough to hit the levies, you'll be close enough to get fried by the wizards. We've forty bodies left. They've got fifty times that, and there's no cover once they reach the crest."

He gestures, and the three squads ride toward the gray walls of Elparta.

Kadara rides beside Brede. "You thought they'd do something like this."

"Yes." He coughs, clears his throat. "It had to happen. When they couldn't take over Gallos with smaller units, they created mountains and fired the grasslands. They won't raise more mountains, but the rest will come."

"They'll take Elparta—and then?"

They'll take the river towns and split the country, then follow each road. They'll just burn anything that resists."

Kadara shudders.

"It's a wonderful choice. If Spidlar doesn't resist, the wizards take over and burn those who resist. If Spidlar resists, they destroy everything."

"We could leave."

Brede snorts. "Where? People from Recluce haven't been welcome in either Sarronnyn and Suthya for generations, and those are about the only places where the ships can go now—unless you want to spend a year at sea going around the continent and across the western ocean to Hamor."

"A year at sea—that doesn't sound too bad." She looks behind him at the pillars of smoke and fire.

"Probably not. Do we have the golds to purchase passage?"

Kadara takes a deep breath. "It's never easy, is it?"

CXX

"MASTER DORRIN?" VAOS'S voice penetrates the smithy.

He turns the tongs to ensure an even heating of the metal. "Yes?"

"Liedral's back."

"I'm coming."

"I'll tell her, ser."

"No, you won't. You clean up the smithy." Dorrin

sets the tongs on the fire bricks, ignoring the clatter, runs to the front of the smithy, then walks into the fall coolness.

"But . . ." Vaos's protest is lost as Dorrin leaves.

"You do look like a smith." Liedral stands by the cart, grinning.

He steps forward to take her hand, wishing he could hold her.

She hugs him, but she steps back. "I'm better, and I'm learning."

They stand, looking at each other.

"You have a few more muscles, I think," she finally says.

"Ser . . ." Vaos says, tentatively, "I could stable and curry the horses."

"Ah . . . yes. That would be . . . wouldn't it?" He looks at Liedral.

She nods solemnly.

"She's back! Liedral's back!" Frisa's squeal carries from the garden where she and Merga have been harvesting the long yellow gourds.

Dorrin takes the cart reins from Liedral's hand and gives them to Vaos, who has still followed him outside. Liedral turns and hands Dorrin a small chest from the closed compartment under the cart seat. They walk across the fall-dampened ground toward the porch steps, and Dorrin wipes his boots while untying his leather apron. He opens the door, waits for Liedral to step inside, and hands her the chest before hanging his apron on the peg.

"We finally have some early cider." Dorrin retrieves a jug from the icy water of the cold box and wipes the dampness away.

Liedral sets the iron-bound wooden chest on the table, which shivers with the *thunk* that accompanies it. She sits on one bench. Deep circles ring her eyes, and her clothes are loose. "It was a long trip."

"Would you rather wash up?"

"I'm hungry."

"And of course you are," snaps Merga from the doorway. "The smith, begging your pardon, master Dorrin, is thinking about drinks when you need solid food. We have some bread I baked this morning, and there's some brick cheese, with some apples from Rylla's trees."

Dorrin pours two mugs of cider and sets one before Liedral.

"Did you go on the big ships all the way across the Northern Ocean?" demands Frisa as she leaves the kitchen door open.

"Close the door, Frisa," her mother orders.

"Is the trader back?" asks yet another voice from the porch. Pergun peers through the half-open door.

Liedral begins to laugh. Dorrin coughs, trying not to choke as he stifles laughter.

"I don't see what's funny," says Frisa solemnly.

Merga cuts three thick slabs of bread and hurriedly puts the knife away before using one of Dorrin's cheese cutters on the yellow brick. Then she sets the platter before Liedral.

Frisa takes two apples and offers them to the trader. "These are the best ones."

"Thank you." Liedral takes the one from Frisa's left hand.

"You take this one, master Dorrin," the girl insists.

"Now ... Frisa, we need to finish with the squash," Merga says firmly, but she smiles as she speaks.

"But, mummy ... I wanted to hear about her trip ..."

"Later," Merga insists. "You, too, Pergun. You can help us."

Dorrin and Liedral smile as footsteps trail off the porch, and voices drift from the garden.

" ... never cared much for squash ..."

" . . . you never had squash the way I fix it, you picky mill hand . . ."

" . . . this one's really big, mummy . . ."

Dorrin takes a long swallow of the cider. "How are you?"

"I'm better. I told you. Tired . . . hungry. And I'm glad to be back. Even if things aren't going well."

"I've had to make nails, brackets for wall barricades, even ship spikes."

"Ship spikes?"

"That was so the harbor smiths could do things like caltrops and stimuli. Pretty soon, I'll have to do caltrops, or get Yarrl to do them for me."

"Caltrops?"

"Pointed iron stars to get in horses' hoofs, sometimes enough to destroy the animal or the rider."

"Ugghhh . . . are we down to that?"

"Yes. I think so," Dorrin says tiredly.

"The trade rumors are that the wizards and their levies have reached Elparta. Have you heard from Brede or Kadara?"

"No." Dorrin shakes his head. "They've been gone since early summer. He's sent a messenger or two for some things I've forged for him."

"Your magic . . . cheese-cutters?"

"You, too." Dorrin finishes the mug. "You know, it's really amazing." He sets the mug on the table with a thump. "People seem to think it's perfectly decent to forge a blade that's light enough, sharp enough, and strong enough to cut through mail and turn a man or woman into dead meat. But you figure out how to do the same thing with wire and steel, and everyone shudders. Dead is dead."

Liedral frowns. "I didn't mean that."

"Sorry. I guess I felt that because Kadara and Brede felt that way. Even Vaos gets this sick look on his face."

"It was sort of my doing," she says slowly.

"Don't feel guilty. The people who tortured you are the ones—"

"No... they're not. The wizards always escape. Some poor soldier gets killed. I'm not blaming you, but usually the dukes and viscounts and prefects all escape their wars. Everyone else has to pay."

Dorrin reflects—even in his own life, that has been true. His attempts to keep Frisa and Merga from being beaten resulted in Gerhalm's suicide. The Whites' attempts to manipulate him have resulted in pain for Liedral and Jarnish. Being involved with him has cost Kadara something, perhaps her life, for he has not heard from either Brede or Kadara in nearly a season, and not even a messenger for the past five eight-days. He swallows.

"I didn't mean you."

"I'm not so sure I'm not the same as they are."

"No... you're not." Liedral reaches across the table and squeezes his hand.

The silence draws out, punctuated by chatter from the garden.

"I did a little better than I thought," Liedral says slowly. "In the trading, I mean." She opens the chest, from which spill silvers and golds. "I did much better. You're very well off, Dorrin."

"We're well off. You took all the risks. At least half belongs to you."

"We'll talk about that later." Liedral tilts the chest and eases the coins inside. "Do you have a safe place?" She looks toward the storeroom.

Dorrin stands, lifting the small and heavy chest. "Let me show you."

She follows him into the storeroom, where he shows her how the false rack works and sets her chest by his smaller and far lighter one. Then he replaces the rack and closes the storeroom door.

Liedral reseats herself and continues through her second slice of bread and cheese before speaking again. "I was hungry." She finishes her cider, and Dorrin refills the mug. "You were right about the brinn. The Councillor's healer paid two golds for one of the bags. So did another of the healers. He wanted to know where I got it. How did you know?"

"I didn't, for sure, but it's hard to grow, even for me, and I can grow most herbs. Brinn only grows east of Brista, unless you use order to help. So I thought it might bring a lot more than the more common ones, and it's good against the flood flux."

"I must have gotten twenty golds for the herbs." She takes another sip of cider. "Even the simple toys went for more, but that's because a lot of your competition has been cut off."

"Things from Recluce?" Dorrin asks.

"The only goods from Recluce are coming the long way—along the Great Canal of Hamor to the Great East Highway through the Kryada Mountains and then down to the ports of Western Hamor. Fairhaven has changed all the trading patterns. They all flow from east to west." Liedral coughs gently. "That raises the prices a lot for anything from Recluce . . . if it even gets to Sarronnyn or Suthya."

Dorrin finally straightens in his chair and looks directly at Liedral. "I missed you."

"I missed you, too." She lets out a long deep breath. "Things are better . . . not so many nightmares. But I think it will take a long time." Liedral brushes at a lock of hair that is too short to stay in place. "It's not fair to you."

Dorrin looks down at his own mug. "I'll wait."

"That's easy to say now. How will you feel in a year?"

"We'll see in a year." He forces a grin. "And we'll

be busy ... very busy." He clears his throat. "I've gotten more done on the engine."

"Are you still going to use it on a ship?"

"How would you like to have your own ship for trading?"

"Ships come in two varieties—those that make you rich and those that are more trouble than they're worth. Most are the second kind, I suspect."

"Then it will keep us busy." He extends a hand halfway across the table.

She takes his fingers, squeezes them, and holds them lightly.

" ... I'm hungry ..." Frisa's shrill complaint penetrates the kitchen.

" ... we're almost finished ..."

" ... but my tummy hurts now ..."

Liedral shakes her head. "I think it's time to let Merga back into the kitchen. I'm going to take a real bath, and you probably need to work on your engine if you really intend to put it on a ship." She stops. "Won't you have to build a ship?"

"Build it, or buy it," Dorrin concedes.

"There are a lot of golds in the chest ... but I doubt there are enough to buy even a small ship."

"Then I'll see what it will take to build one."

Liedral stands. "I meant it about the bath. You do still have that old metal tub, don't you?"

Dorrin nods. "But I rigged a shower off the smithy. I use that, mostly. It's cold."

Liedral shivers. "Not for me, thank you." She walks to the door and waves to Merga.

Dorrin goes to reclaim the tub from the corner of the smithy, even as Frisa skips toward the kitchen.

CXXI

STEAM RISES FROM the water, boiling as it rushes downstream toward and then past the walls of Elparta. Smoke thicker than winter fogs cloaks the hills, and tongues of flames dance across the now blackened grasslands to the south of the city.

Under the green-edged white flag, the three messengers approach the southern gate. A man in a blue cloak waits for them, his short white beard hastily trimmed. A smudge of soot or dirt mars his left temple.

"A request of the city . . ." begins the messenger in the middle, his sonorous voice almost droning.

"Forget the fancy language," replies the older man in blue. "What do the wizards want?"

" . . . from the honorable Jeslek, and the commanders Grestalk and Xeinon," continues the messenger, "beseeching that the citizens of Elparta, in the interests of justice and mercy, lay down their arms and pay homage to the greater hegemony of Candar . . ."

The man in blue takes a deep breath and waits.

" . . . that the river gates be destroyed and the water piers be open to all . . . that the battlements be cast down . . . that unmarried women be made available as consorts for . . . that all followers of the Black heresy, including the officers of the Spidlarian Guard who have committed atrocities and used evil magical tools against the hegemony, be turned over to the honorable Jeslek . . . that reparations from the granaries of the city be made to the forces of the hegemony . . . that all able horses are to be turned over to the representatives of the hegemony for proper redistribution . . . that all members of the so-called Council of Traders be returned to the Candarian Guild for proper disciplinary action ..."

The man in blue holds up his one good hand. The other rests in a sling. "If I understand the thought behind the fancy words, we must make the city totally defenseless. After that, our daughters get to be whores for your troops; all the good officers are to be executed, all the traders slaughtered, and all the horses and all food for winter taken."

"Not so ..." protests the messenger. "These are honorable terms, especially given the depredations committed upon all Candar, the unfairness in trading, and the slaughter of defenseless traders."

"How long do we have to consider these terms?" asks the man in blue.

"Until sunset."

The Elpartan emissary glances at the midafternoon sun. "Very generous."

"Oh, extremely generous is the honorable Jeslek."

"You will have an answer by sunset." The man in blue limps back toward the walls.

The emissaries in white turn and walk back toward the mass of soldiers and horses who wait on the plain overlooking the river and stretching toward the small city.

CXXII

DORRIN LIFTS THE iron back into the forge, using his right hand on the bellows lever. In time he removes the piece and places it in the end curve in the swage block. Using the block is harder than using a hammer-driven swage, but is the only way he can shape the iron single-handedly. Whether the swaging is harder

or the mental concentration to avoid suffusing the raw
metal with order is more difficult, he is not sure, only
that he is sweating from more than the heat of the
smithy when he is through.

With a sigh, he lays aside his work, a stubby length
of metal hammered into an octagon at one end and
welded to a blank circle of iron at the other. Then he
sets down the hammer and walks out to the stone-
walled water tap to wash off his face and get a drink
of cool water.

Outside, he lowers the bucket under the dripping
tap and turns it, letting the bucket fill with icy water.
He begins to rinse away the grime and other residues
from the smithy. The shower would be quicker, but he
does not feel up to total immersion in icy water.

He wishes that his efforts to build the engine have
not taken so long, but with each idea, each discovery,
something else is required. The situation is getting
more and more critical, but how can he and Liedral—
or anyone—return to Recluce any time soon? Should
he be thinking more about leaving Spidlar? But where
would he go? As a Black healer and a man, he will
not be terribly welcome beyond the Westhorns.
Assuming that Recluce would have him back—which
is rather unlikely, as he is still building an engine—to
get there he would have to circle the world—and that
is a disturbing thought.

He looks up from the water tap to the house. Merga
and Rylla have dried and stored everything from the
gardens, and he has dried herbs, and even driven
the wagon borrowed from Yarrl halfway to Kleth to
bring back barrels of apples and pearapples for both
families. He shakes his head at the thought of his
household as a family.

How long the Spidlarian Council will retain its tenu-
ous rule in the face of the inexorable advance of the
White Wizards is also a question. According to rumors,

the Spidlarian Guard has already lost more than two of every three squads, and now must rely on levies. It is the first time levies have been required in Spidlar in centuries. The "requests" for smithing services are also growing with each eight-day.

Even the seas are not free from the heavy hand of Fairhaven. From what Liedral has heard, the vessels of Fairhaven have still cut off most of the trading ships to and from Land's End, and the price of spices has begun to rise even in the marketplace of Diev.

Dorrin shakes his hands dry in the cool fall air, cooler already than would be the case on Recluce. He looks at the wheelbarrow. When Vaos returns from the market with Liedral, Dorrin will have him bring in more charcoal from the bin behind the small stable.

Charcoal is getting dearer, perhaps because the Certans and Gallosians have pushed into the lower wooded hills west of Elparta where the charcoal burners have operated. Would coal be usable for the smithy? That, at least, can be gotten locally, and it would be ideal for fueling the steam engine he has envisioned. Still . . . where could he find hundreds of stones' worth of coal? And how could he pay for it? Besides, he has no ship—not yet.

"Master Dorrin . . .?"

He looks at Merga. "Yes, Merga?"

"Have you eaten since breakfast?"

"No . . ."

"A starving smith does not work well. You're always forgetting to eat. I have set out some bread and preserves and some cheese."

Everyone is always trying to make sure he does what he is supposed to. He follows the small woman up the wide wooden steps. Once on the porch, he views the yard and the ridge leading toward Rylla's. For now, there are few complaints of sickness, but the harvest has been good, although some of the ground vegetables are still in the fields, and not all the grains have fully headed because of the cold spring that made early planting impossible.

He checks the road, but sees no sign of Liedral and her cart—or Vaos. He steps into the kitchen. Merga has already laid out a dinner for him, and Frisa has finished half of what is on her plate.

"Master Dorrin . . . could you make me a toy?"

"I gave you the windmill." Dorrin slathers the preserves on the bread.

"I meant . . . a special kind of toy?"

"Frisa . . ." Merga says.

Dorrin holds his hand up. He wants to hear what the girl has to say. "What kind of special toy? A doll or something?"

"Dolls are stupid. I wanted something like an iron wagon, one like the kind that brings your iron."

"I can't make a horse for it."

"That's all right." Frisa gulps the last of the cider from her mug.

Dorrin grins at the patronizing tone, and chews through the half-warm bread. He is still eating the last morsels of his dinner when he hears Liedral's cart and heads for the door. As he steps onto the porch, Merga calls after him, "I'll set out some dinner for them."

Vaos is unhitching the horse, and Liedral is carrying a basket of potatoes to the porch.

"How did it go?" Dorrin lugs another basket.

"There's plenty of root crops, but not much flour yet, and it's still dear. No fruit except for local things, and no spices."

"We don't need spices."

"I know. It shows that there's nothing coming in, though."

"Sorry. I wasn't thinking like that. You are the trader."

"Don't forget it." Liedral smiles.

Dorrin sets down the potatoes and squeezes her shoulder. She brushes his cheek with her lips, then turns back to the wagon.

"You got a lot of potatoes."

"Merga said to get a lot of them if they were cheap. They were the only thing cheap. I dropped some off for Reisa, and she sent a mutton leg. She also said that you could have three bales of hay, but you ought to pick them up today because it looks like rain before long."

"Can we have it tonight?" Vaos walks back from the barn to the house.

"Tomorrow," affirms Merga from the porch. "And for that, you can take these down to the root cellar."

"Oh . . ." Vaos looks at Dorrin. "Do I have to, master Dorrin?"

"No," Dorrin says. "Not until after your dinner."

"Yes, ser."

Dorrin looks to the low clouds in the north. "I hope the rain holds off until more of the grains head."

"Vaos can help me with the hay, if you can do without him for a while."

"I'll need him for a bit after he eats, probably until midafternoon."

"We can do it after that."

Dorrin touches her shoulder. "You need to eat, and, if you and Vaos are going to get the hay, I need to get back to the forge."

"All right." Liedral touches his shoulder for an instant.

Dorrin heads around the porch to the smithy, to rebuild the fire and to finish working on one of the engine gears.

"What's this?" Vaos walks in after his meal and points to the metal on the side of the hearth.

"That will be a gear," responds Dorrin absently.

"Out of iron? How will you make the teeth regular?"

"A lot of work with a template, sort of like a hot set. A cutter won't work on black iron."

"That must be real special. Can I help?" Vaos bounces on the balls of his feet.

Dorrin looks at his striker's already splitting boots and shakes his head, then wipes the sweat off his forehead with his forearm. He will have to send Vaos to the bootmaker within the eight-day. If it is not expenditures for iron and copper, it is expenditures for food or clothes or something.

"We've got to do another batch of spikes for the Council."

"Oh . . ." Vaos wilts. "Spikes? Will you use the rod stock?"

"We'll use the scrap. I know it's more work, but they're not paying for this. Get those rusted brackets at the end of the pile there."

"Yes, ser."

Dorrin levers the bracket into the forge with the heavy tongs and waits until the metal heats enough to cut it. Then he brings it to the anvil and lifts the hammer, thankful at least that his muscles no longer ache all day, only in the late afternoon. With his slender frame, he will never have the massive biceps of a smith like Yarrl.

. . . clung . . .

Vaos says nothing as the hammer comes down on the iron, cutting the bracket into two workable sections.

Dorrin nods at the piece on the floor. "Take the tongs there and set it aside for later." As he talks he returns the half in the tongs to the fire.

"A little more on the bellows. Then, while I work this into shape, you need to break up the charcoal and bring in a couple of barrows full. We've got a lot of spikes to do, and I want to work on the condenser case."

"Condenser case?"

"Part of the steam engine."

Vaos puts the cut section of the bracket against the forge where Dorrin can reach it when the time comes, then racks the tongs. "I was going to help Liedral with the hay."

"You still like the horses?"

Vaos looks at the hard-packed floor.

"Never mind. After you bring in the charcoal, you can go with Liedral to get the hay. You did carry the potatoes down to the root cellar."

"Yes, ser. Merga made sure I put them in the right places." Vaos pauses. "You're buying a lot more food this year, master Dorrin."

"This winter may be even worse than last."

"Do you think the White Wizards will come here?"

"Eventually . . . maybe sooner." Dorrin pulls the iron from the forge. "Get the middle sledge. There . . ."

Clung . . .

The sounds of iron work preclude further conversation.

CXXIII

"MOVE, DAMN IT!" screams Kadara at a gray-haired woman with twice her weight upon her shoulders, as she stumbles into two other women, equally laden. The woman looks up dumbly as the redhead reaches down from her saddle and yanks the woman upright. "Move, if you want to live!"

On the other side of the gate, another guard in blue stretches from his saddle and slams a figure in the crowd with the flat of his sword. The thief drops the chest and runs, while a heavy, bald, and bearded old man staggers onward toward the open northern gate, and the downriver road to Kleth. The wiry trooper glances at the red-headed squad leader until he catches her eye. Then he gestures toward the road.

Kadara studies the thinning crowd and the long line of figures trudging northward toward the clouds rolling up the river valley from the distant Northern Ocean. Then she yells, "Green squad! Green squad!"

The six troopers ease their mounts through the jostling crowd.

"Please ... take me ..." A pale and thin young woman reaches and grabs for Vorban's saddle. "Don't leave me here! Please! I'll do anything." The trooper reaches back and touches her shoulder, then reaches farther, but the girl does not protest, instead tries to swing up behind the trooper.

"Vorban!" snaps Kadara. "Either carry her or leave her."

The trooper lifts the woman behind him.

" ... scheming bitch! Harlot ...!" Mutters run through the crowd, even as the fleeing Elpartans spread on the far side of the causeway, some plodding through the mud and grass to avoid bumping into others.

Most carry more than they will be able to manage on the long walk to Kleth, and some items—a stool here; a box there, ripped open by some later refugee— already line the stone-paved road. Those lucky enough to have had mounts or wagons are visible on the ridge line ahead.

Kadara and her squad form a tight-knit wedge as they trot toward the first bridge below the city, where they will re-form with the other squads.

"'Ware horses! 'Ware horses!"

"Why couldn't you save us?" screams a white-haired woman.

"Greedy guards! Saving their own skins . . ."

Kadara glances over at Vorban, and her blade flashes, then turns and smacks the shoulder of the fair-skinned woman. A knife drops to the stone below, but the clink is lost in the hubbub.

Vorban looks up.

"Take your purse back," Kadara snaps.

The young woman smiles, and says, "I'll throw it."

"You do, and you're dead!" snaps Kadara to the woman.

The woman hands the purse to Vorban.

"Get down!" commands Kadara.

The woman sneers. Kadara's blade flashes, turning and leaving a red welt across the thief's temple—even as a dull clunk sounds and the young woman's fingers loosen on Vorban's jacket.

"Dump her!"

Vorban sets the dazed figure on the road. She staggers to the side and sits in the muddy grass. The trooper slips his purse into his tunic.

Brede and the other two squads wait at the bridge. The blond officer turns toward the west, where the sun touches the rim of the low hills that lead up to the more distant Westhorns. "Let's get across!"

Three troopers swing out into the road, and halt the pedestrians.

"Armed bastards . . ."

" . . . own the roads . . ."

The rest of the squads cross the swirling and steaming waters, trying not to breathe deeply of the odors of boiled fish and sewage.

Brede calls a halt several hundred rods beyond the bridge, on a flat rise where the low walls of Elparta can barely be seen.

"Why we stopping?"

"Hold!" snaps Brede. "Watch Elparta. Just watch!"

Even as he speaks, the ground shivers, then shudders. Firebolts play across the distant walls.

Another shudder rolls across the plains, and a handful of horses whinny and whicker.

Several older refugees stagger and sprawl on the road or the grass, then try to regain their footing before another quake shakes them back onto the ground.

A trooper's mount skitters, staggering as if one leg had given way.

With yet another shudder, the ground heaves. To the south, the walls of Elparta shiver, and the stones begin to tumble. Fires play across the city, and the pall of smoke begins to increase.

With each successive temblor, more stones fall from the walls, some into the river, others into the city. But in the end, the walls are rubble, and a column of greasy smoke pours into the sky.

"Anything left?" rasps Vorban.

"The center parts, away from the walls and the river, don't look too bad," hazards Kadara.

"Just enough for their winter quarters," Brede says dourly. He looks northward, toward Kleth. "Let's go."

They ride past stumbling men and women, past crying children, past discarded packs of clothes, past old men and women panting in the muddy grass, past a troupe of brightly painted women who shriek obscenities, and past a dead, white-muzzled mule . . .

None of the troopers speaks as they ride north, girding themselves against the occasional ground shock that persists.

CXXIV

TIME—THERE IS never enough. Dorrin rubs his shoulder, and sets down the mug on the kitchen wash table. The sky is gray, but no rain falls.

He wishes Hasten had not come with the Guild demand for caltrops—not that it was at all unexpected. He still worries about Kadara and Brede, but with the chaos to the south no one has heard who survived the fall of Elparta.

Instinctively, he would know if Kadara had fallen . . . but where are they?

He thinks again about forging caltrops and shakes his head. All he can do is ask Yarrl for a trade . . . or pay the older smith. He crosses the kitchen and slumps into the chair at the end of the table, knowing that he should either return to the smithy or ride over to see Yarrl about the caltrops. Instead, he tries to massage his shoulder with his left hand.

"Are you stiff?" asks Liedral, lifting her eyes from the ledgers spread across the other end of the kitchen table.

He shakes his head. "Not really."

"That means you are." She rises from her chair and edges behind him with the faintest of limps. Her fingers knead into his shoulders.

"Ah . . ."

"Not stiff? Really?"

"You lift hammers all the time, and sometimes you'll get stiff."

"You're upset about the Guild order?"

"Of course. Caltrops are edged weapons, even if they're designed to be used against horses. They want three score within a couple of eight-days. I really should go to see Yarrl . . . see if I can trade with him, or pay him."

"You could afford to pay him. You're on your way to being a wealthy man." Liedral continues to work out the knots in his shoulders.

"You're the one who's making it possible." He tries to relax under her fingers, enjoying the quiet before Merga and Frisa return.

"How about us?"

"All right. I'll take that. I just wish . . ." He wishes that he could hold her for more than a few instants fully clothed—but even that is an improvement.

"So do I, but talking to Rylla helps."

Dorrin should spend more time with the older woman, or in the smithy.

"You need to go."

"Why do you say that?"

"You've got that expression. You need to get back to work." As Liedral shakes her head, the dark hair fluffs away from her face for a moment. "And you still worry about your friends."

"What can I do? I'm not a soldier. Darkness, I feel like I can't even get everything done around here."

"If it helps . . . I did arrange for regular shipments of the brinn to Suthya. Old Ruziosi likes the idea, and he hates the Bristans. That's worth twenty golds a consignment. Will that help?"

"All I have to do is grow it."

"You have three years' worth in the cellars. Your first consignment is due at Vyrnil's—he's their agent here—in two eight-days." Liedral sits back in front of the ledgers.

"You do work wonders."

"Too bad we have to rely on their ships."

"I'm working on that," Dorrin says. "It's all because

of something you said." Dorrin takes a last bite of the bread, crusty and not all that fresh.

Liedral holds the heavy mug as though it were a crystal goblet, then sets it upon the wooden table. Dorrin admires the grace of the gesture.

"Something I said?"

"We've talked about this before. About the importance of speed in trading, and going where and when other people couldn't. And I wondered about ships. They have to go where the wind goes. Well, fans make the air move, and I asked why they couldn't make the water move."

Liedral's heavy eyebrows knit, but she does not speak.

"Well . . . if you paddle a boat, you sort of move the water, and that moves the boat. It's really not that simple, but it works. So I thought about a machine that would move paddles, but that seemed really too complicated, and you'd have to build a huge wheel to hold all those paddles." Dorrin grins. "Anyway, that's why I was building the toy boats."

"You've been working on those, according to Reisa, since the day you arrived in Diev—or almost."

"It takes time. The engine is mostly built."

"I still can't see why it would be better than a well-built sloop or brig."

"Trust me . . . even if I can't explain exactly why." Dorrin stands. "I guess I will go talk to Yarrl."

Liedral smiles. "Don't take too long. It looks like rain."

"I don't mind a little rain."

As he saddles Meriwhen, he can sense the wind rising, but Yarrl's is only a short ride, and Meriwhen needs the exercise.

Vaos waves from the herb garden, where he is helping Merga and Rylla cut the last herbs for drying. Dorrin waves back, then turns the mare downhill.

The light rain gusts around the smith, but, by the time Dorrin reins up in Yarrl's yard, the falling water slices in almost like knives.

Reisa steps onto the porch. "Put her in the barn." Her voice barely carries above the howling of the wind and the splatting of the cold rain.

Dorrin rides over to the barn, dismounts, and leads Meriwhen inside. The third stall is still vacant, and he ties the mare there. As he steps away from the stall, a white form butts him in the leg. He stops to scratch the nanny between the ears. "How are you, girl?"

Zilda looks up almost placidly, then tries to nibble on his trousers. Dorrin shakes free, and the goat attempts to follow, until the chain brings her up short.

"Still at it . . ." He closes the barn door and hurries through the rain and across the muddy yard to the smithy. He should have paid more attention to the weather, but the Council summons delivered by Hasten has bothered him.

Reisa stands inside the smithy. "This came up so sudden. Wizards' doing, you think?"

"No. Just a nasty storm. It feels normal, anyway." He casts a feeler at the low clouds, but the storm winds are clean and cold.

"How's Liedral?"

"Fine. She was more tired than she realized, but she's resting up."

"Yarrl's working on his services. The Council extended it beyond Guild members." As Reisa gestures toward the glow of the smithy, Dorrin looks at her left arm, and the bruises. He lifts his hand, as if to touch her arm, but she starts to back away, then laughs, harshly. "You are a healer." She lets him touch the bruises, and infuse some order, although they are nothing more than bruises.

"Left-handed?" he asks. "You and Petra?"

"What else can we do? You heard about Elparta?"

Dorrin nods. "But they'll winter there."

"And come next spring?" Reisa asks.

"They'll use the river to take Kleth and Spidlaria."

The wind shakes the smithy roof.

"You're here to see Yarrl?"

"Yes. I wanted to ask if I could trade some services."

"You don't do blades or sharp things, do you?"

Dorrin looks at the damp clay underfoot. "How did you know?"

Reisa chuckles. "You're a healer, and you use a staff. Go talk to Yarrl. I've got some bread in the oven."

Dorrin steps into the circle of light cast by the forge, watching. Rek controls the bellows lever as Yarrl works a length of iron perhaps a span long and half as thick. With even strokes, Yarrl points each end, then reheats the iron in the forge. Deftly, he retrieves the piece and splits each end on the hardie. After another return to the forge, each split end is bent at forty-five degrees. The result looks like a four-pointed iron star.

After he sets the star on the forge bricks, alongside at least half a dozen others, Yarrl lowers the tongs and hammers, and nods to the youngster on the bellows rod. "That's enough, Rek. Go get yourself a drink of water."

"Yes, ser." Glancing from Dorrin to Yarrl, Rek heads for the open door.

"He's a good boy, Dorrin."

"I'm glad." Dorrin nods toward the metal stars. "Those your services?"

"Caltrops. For cavalry. Scatter them on a road, especially one that's got a muddy surface, and you chew up a lot of horses' hoofs."

"Cruel weapon," Dorrin says. No matter how the caltrop is thrown, one pointed end will always face up, ready to impale anything that steps or falls upon it. "Do you think the Whites will attack this winter?"

"No one's saying. Does your red-headed friend know?"

"Kadara? I haven't seen them. I hope they survived the fall of Elparta. We all knew this was coming a long time ago."

"After the Whites brought the mountains down on Axalt . . ."

Dorrin recalls the guard captain friend of Liedral's, so certain that Spidlar would fall first. "A Council request?" He points to the caltrops.

"More like a Council order. All the smiths have to provide five score every two eight-days for the next season."

"I know," Dorrin says dryly. "I have a small problem. I can't make them."

"Course you can. Easier even than butt hinges . . ."

"I'm a healer, remember?"

"Oh . . . darkness . . ."

"Exactly. I wanted to know if I could trade some other services for my quota or pay you. Vaos isn't far enough along to do them quickly."

"He still likes the horses?"

Dorrin grins.

"Told you so. Rek likes the metal, bad leg or no. Well . . ." muses Yarrl. "I promised Fentor an iron moldboard plowshare. Scratch job—you supply the iron and do it, and I'll do—how many are you supposed to do?"

"I'm considered an artisan, because of the toys—so my share is three score over the next two eight-days."

"Do you have plate for the share?" asks the older smith.

"Yes. I've some left from another job."

"All right. I'll give you some rod stock. You have

the plow done in ten days, and I'll have the caltrops and the stock for you."

"I can use Liedral's cart to bring it down." Dorrin inclines his head. "Thank you."

"It's not a problem, young fellow." Yarrl looks toward the door. "Rek! Let's be at it."

"Yes, ser." The boy limps up to the bellows lever. "Good day, master Dorrin."

"Good day, Rek."

Yarrl swings the stock into the forge for another caltrop.

Dorrin nods to the smith again, and steps from the smithy into the gusting wind and icy rain.

"Dorrin!" Petra gestures for him to come into the kitchen.

After knocking the mud from his boots and wiping them as dry as he can on the tattered mat, he steps into the warmth of the kitchen.

"You need to take this," Reisa explains as Petra hands him a battered basket covered with a waxed canvas. "There are a few things that your trader lady should enjoy."

"But . . ." Dorrin protests.

"Just do it."

All stop talking as a gust shakes the house, and a long cracking sound rips through the moaning of the wind. The house shakes again with a dull thud. Dorrin rushes to the door to see that the center tree of the three that border the field has snapped halfway up and fallen into the field.

Reisa looks through the rain-whipped afternoon at the jagged stump. "This is one of the worst I've seen. I hope no one was caught offshore in it."

"I'm glad I wasn't," Dorrin affirms, as he takes hold of the basket.

"You aren't going?" asks Petra.

"I'll be all right." He touches her arm and then

dashes for the barn. The ride back will be wet, but he does not want to leave Liedral and the others alone in such a storm—not that he can probably make any real difference, but that is the way he feels.

CXXV

"YOU LIKE WORKING for Hemmil?" Dorrin rummages through the scrap bin for the red oak for his toys. More and more the wood is getting harder for him than the iron—or the iron work is getting easier, more likely.

"Hemmil's fair enough," answers the dark-haired journeyman with a shrug. "But the mill's going to Volkir, and . . . well, Hemmil's fair."

"Couldn't you start your own mill? Last week I heard Hemmil say that he couldn't deliver some timbers for at least three eight-days."

Pergun smiles tightly. "I could run a mill, Dorrin. Tell me how I can afford to buy one."

"What about building one?" Dorrin adds another short length of oak to the pile he has set aside.

"What about starving until it's finished? How can I afford the steel for the saw blades or the stonework for a millrace or land with enough water?"

The simplest questions have complex answers. "I wonder . . ."

"Finish up. Hemmil's looking this way." Pergun pauses. "You wonder what?"

"Do you always want to be a mill worker?"

"What else do I know?" Pergun pauses. "Merga's a nice girl."

"She's a woman with a daughter." Dorrin laughs. "And you do visit a lot."

"Do you mind?"

"Hardly. So long as you're good to her."

"Dare I be otherwise with you around?" Pergun looks toward the front of the building.

"Am I...?" Dorrin lifts the wood into the carrying straps. "This is all. How much, do you think?"

"I'd let you have it for a copper, but—"

"Hemmil would charge at least three," finishes Dorrin with a laugh. "How about two coppers?"

"What are you going to do with this?"

"Same as before. Make some toys." Dorrin offers two coins.

"Quiller doesn't mind?" Pergun takes the coins.

"I'm very careful not to make anything like what he does."

"Pergun! Finish up there. We need to change the blade." The millmaster's voice echoes between the rows of rough-sawn boards and timbers.

Dorrin's brows remain knitted in thought as he carries the wood out into the yard where Meriwhen is tied. The mare's breath is a cloud of steam in the fall drizzle. Meriwhen skitters as he loads the wood into the saddle baskets.

"Easy, lady. Easy." He should have asked for Liedral's cart, but he enjoys riding Meriwhen, and he never gets much wood for toys.

Wheeee ...

He pats her neck and shoulder firmly. "Easy..." Then he mounts and rides through the continuing light rain toward the road.

Rivulets of icy water leave the stone pavement more like a paved river than a road, and Meriwhen tries to edge toward the warmer mud and grass. Dorrin edges her toward the crown of the road.

Along the highway lie trees toppled by the storm of days earlier, and Dorrin has heard that a schooner lies beached off Cape Devalin. A schooner?

Whheeeee . . .

"Easy, lady. Easy . . ."

Whhheeeee . . .

"Enough!" Dorrin snaps, still thinking about the beached ship.

Guiding the mare onto the rutted road that leads to Rylla's cottage, and to his own house and workshop, he wonders if he and Liedral can ever regain what they once had—or how long it will take.

Ahead, he can see the smoke from the chimney. The house will be warm, against a chill that promises, once again, a long and cold winter, and a summer that will be filled with blood.

CXXVI

SITTING JUST SHOREWARD of the center pier, the Port Council building is two stories high, and less than forty cubits broad. The unpainted plank siding has faded into gray, despite the years of oiling.

Dorrin wraps the heavy brown cloak about him, brushes the unseasonably early light snow out of his eyebrows, and opens the heavy oak door. After closing it, he knocks the sides of his boots with the black staff to remove the slush. The sole light comes from a dim single oil lamp in a tarnished brass bracket dangling from a support timber. The once-white plaster has dimmed to yellowed gray. Both doors on the lower floor are closed, the one on the left with the port master's sign and the one on the right with the customs seal of the Spidlarian Council.

Dorrin climbs the worn and hollowed steps to the upper floor, where he finds an open doorway.

A clerk on a stool looks up. "Might I help you, healer? The portmaster's office is below."

"Thank you, but I was looking for ser Gylert."

"Might I tell him the matter at hand?"

"A matter of commerce. My name is Dorrin."

The clerk slides off the stool and inclines his head. "My pardon, ser. I will tell him." The man's dark and greasy hair, bound at his neck with an ornate copper clasp, swirls as he slips inside the rear office that overlooks the piers.

The front office contains a small iron stove, two desks with stools for clerks, and two shoulder-high red oak chests with iron-bound doors and locks. The other desk is dusty.

The clerk returns with another bow. "Ser Gylert would be most pleased to see you, ser."

"Thank you," Dorrin responds gravely. He steps inside the second door, closing it behind him.

"Good day, master Dorrin." Gylert, lean, balding, and muscular, stands behind a narrow writing desk in the corner of the room, angled to allow the shipper to view the piers through the three sliding windows. Two are shuttered against the wind and cold fall rains, and now snow, but the center window has no exterior shutters. A hanging dual-chimneyed lamp illuminates the office, also leaving the faint scent of soot and oil.

"Good day to you, ser Gylert."

Gylert motions to the wooden armchair beside the writing desk.

"You told Kinsall you wished to discuss a matter of commerce?"

"I did. I understand that since the crew of the ship that grounded off the cape perished, the shipper's council is acting as the salvage agent."

"That is correct. Once the weather clears, we'll be offloading what we can, and clearing the canvas and fixtures."

"Honsard will provide the wagons?"

Gylert nodded. "You wish to bid on the goods?"

"No." Dorrin smiles. "I was wondering about the masts and hull."

"For iron scrap? There won't be much of that."

"For a number of purposes."

"Hmmmm . . ."

"According to . . . a few . . . most don't think the ship's worth the effort to refloat. That means she's scrap lumber."

"I wouldn't say that, exactly."

"Do you have the right to convey title?"

Gylert frowns. "Are you thinking you would enter the shipping business?"

Dorrin holds up a hand. "Not to carry any cargoes that you would carry. That schooner's too small for most bulk cargoes, and not all that speedy."

"Spice runs?"

"That's possible. I promised Liedral . . ."

"The young trader from Jellico?"

"I owe a debt."

Gylert nods. "Some would say otherwise, but you have been honest and fair. Not that honesty's any great virtue, and we all know that the *Harthagay* is not a long-legged vessel. Perhaps a hundred golds."

Dorrin forces a smile. "It would take me more than that to refit her, assuming I could get her off that sand. Besides I'd be helping the port."

"Are you certain you have no trading background?"

"Thirty golds," counters Dorrin.

"You don't want a ship. You want firewood at that price."

Dorrin sighs, loudly. "Twenty for the rights to salvage her, and until next summer to get her off the sand. *If* I get her to port, another twenty when she arrives, and ten more before she leaves again."

Gylert frowns, then glances out the window.

"Dessero says she can't be broken clear of the strand," Dorrin adds. "If that's so, the council gets twenty golds and will regain salvage rights."

"Unlike Dessero, I'm not convinced that you cannot work something out. Honsard swears you can do miracles. The man's terrified of you, you know."

"Me?" Dorrin doesn't have to counterfeit surprise.

Gylert smiles. "Well . . . why not? We all gain if you can do it."

"If you would have your clerk write up the papers . . ."

"You read Temple, don't you?" Gylert asks with a wry smile.

"Yes," Dorrin admits.

"I thought I'd ask, not that I doubted it. About the twenty . . . before we get to the agreement stage . . ."

Dorrin sets the purse on the desk, and counts out twenty golds.

"How many did you bring?"

"Twenty-five," admits Dorrin involuntarily.

"There is this five-gold processing fee . . ."

Dorrin opens his mouth to protest before he catches the glint in Gylert's eye. Instead he shakes his head.

CXXVII

HONSARD BOWS TO Dorrin. "Good day, healer."

"Good day, ser." Dorrin gestures toward the sea. "Could you tell me who might be in charge of the ship?"

"Varden is acting for the Traders' Council. He's a thin man, wearing a purple slash on his jacket. He has a black mustache. He was down on the wreck."

Honsard glances from Dorrin to Liedral, then back at the wagon. "Keep them bags on center, Noskos!"

Honsard turns to Dorrin, almost apologetically. "Got to get these back to the port 'fore it warms. Hard to carry heavy loads through the mud, and the flour and grain would spoil—what hasn't already."

"Good hauling," Dorrin says.

Low bushes and stubby pines cover both the bluff and the sloping ground beyond, which drops off toward the Northern Ocean. The underbrush and trees block any view of the beach itself.

"He's afraid of you," Liedral says. "Why?"

"I healed his son."

They walk down from the coast road, following the muddy track churned in the slope by the dozen or so men struggling up through the low brush and between the sea-swept low pines. The rest of the hillside retains a dusting of snow under the gray sky. As the various barrels are carried past them, Liedral studies each. Dorrin studies Liedral.

"What do they tell you?"

"Your ship's not all that watertight."

"I can do something about that, given a little time."

"I sometimes think you feel you can do something about everything." She laughs, and one of the laborers grins—until he sees Dorrin's face.

The *Harthagay*'s stem rests firmly on the sand, although the stern almost seems to float free in the low chop coming straight in. Even in the chill air, the odor of uprooted kelp and seaweed seeps across the beach, and gulls and other sea birds dive at the line of detritus that marks the high-water line of the storm that grounded the schooner.

Varden stands in the hard-packed sand by the planks that serve as a gangway, watching the barrels being rolled down the planks. "Easy . . . there!" He turns to the newcomers. "This is Council salvage."

"I know. I'm Dorrin. I assume ser Gylert—"

"You're the one. Well . . . be a day or so before we've got her off-loaded. That's if another storm doesn't rise, and if Honsard's wagons don't get trapped in the road mud. Too bad the coast road up there's not stone, like the main highway."

"Do you mind if I look over the ship?"

"Darkness, no! Suppose you qualify as the owner, much as anyone does, leastwise." Varden twists the black handlebar mustache. "Easy! Them barrels'll break if they run together. One at a time!"

Dorrin waits until the barrels are coming down smoothly. "The agreement was that the front and back winches were to remain."

"Aye, and they will." Varden grins. "It be in my interest that they do. Gylert bet me ten you couldn't get her off—at ten to one." The Council man looks toward the gangway. "Light! Don't be banging them together!"

Dorrin scrambles up the rope ladder that has clearly been added by the salvage crew. Liedral follows.

What canvas that remains is in tatters. A section of the port railing between the bowsprit and midships is missing, and the lighter color of the decking indicates to Dorrin that the removal was recent.

They circle around the open hatch from which the salvage crew hoists barrels in a leather sling. The man controlling the rope and pulley arrangement nods curtly.

Dorrin steps onto the low poop deck and checks the wheel, which, surprisingly, rotates easily. Further examination reveals that cables to the rudder have snapped, either the result of the grounding . . . or its cause. Dorrin has no way of telling which, only that the problem must be remedied before the *Harthagay* is pulled off the strand.

"What do you think?" he asks Liedral.

"You have some work to do. Not to get her ready to float clear—she's not that firm—but to turn her into something. She's been neglected for a long time."

Keee . . . aaa . . . keee . . . aaaa . . .

He looks to the gray of the sea and the circling gulls who take turns landing and pecking at the weeds and storm-tossed offal on the sand. "It will be a busy winter."

"I do not look forward to spring." Liedral takes his hand for a moment before releasing it.

"I don't either, but spring will come, like it or not."

Keee . . . aaaa . . . keee . . . aaaa . . .

The gulls circle as the barrels rumble across the deck and down the heavy planks onto the sand.

CXXVIII

A SINGLE TROOPER, bearing two swords, rides into the yard, brushing snow from a winter cap. The rider heads for the lighted window behind the porch.

Liedral opens the door.

"Liedral?"

"Kadara! Are you all right? Where's Brede?"

"He's fine. No, he's not. He's tired. He's not a marshal, but there's no one else. He couldn't come. So he sent me." The redhead dismounts.

A dull clanging resounds from the smithy.

"He's still at it? Does he always work this late?"

"I think everyone from Reluce must." A touch of bitterness edges Liedral's voice. "If it isn't Council services, it's goods to sell. If it isn't goods to sell, it's engine parts." Liedral brushes snow from her uncovered hair. "I'm sorry. Let's put your horse in the stable. I'll get you hot cider . . . and whatever else we can offer."

The two women walk toward the stable.

"Is he still working on that darkness-damned engine?"

"Yes. He's even found a ship to put it on—if he can salvage it. He's arranged for space in the shipwright's yard, and he stays up all night calculating how to put his engine into that old hulk."

"I don't know." Kadara's voice is hoarse, and she coughs. "Maybe . . . well, come next spring or summer, owning a ship might be damned good."

Liedral opens the barn door and gropes for the lantern and the attached striker. "It's small, but at least it's out of the weather."

Kadara looks around the small barn. "Most places I've slept lately make this look like a palace. It's even dry."

"I know. It was good to come back to."

"At first, I thought he had it easy. He never makes anything easy, does he?" Kadara ties the reins to an iron ring on the wall near Meriwhen's stall. "Hello there, girl." She coughs again. "It's hard, being a trooper. Oh . . . I don't know what I'm saying. I'm so damned tired."

Liedral touches her shoulder. "You need something warm."

"Brede needs more magic knives . . . something for the rivers . . . anything that Dorrin can think up . . ." Kadara slips as she steps out of the barn onto the packed wet snow that comes down almost as thick as rain. She puts a hand out to the barn wall.

Liedral blows out the lamp and rehangs it before closing the barn door. Meriwhen whinnies as the barn door comes shut with a dull thump.

"Have to go back to Kleth before too long." Kadara straightens. "Darkness, I'm tired."

"Is that where Brede is?"

"That's where all the Guards are. That's where the Whites and their damned levies will be come summer." Kadara's feet are heavy on the porch steps, and her motions are slow as she stamps and brushes her boots.

"Now . . . you can't get things too hot . . ." Merga explains as she peeks at the bread in the oven. " . . . shouldn't be too long . . ."

Frisa sits on the stool watching her mother.

"Frisa . . .?" Liedral asks. "Would you tell Master Dorrin that his friend Kadara is here?"

"Go ahead, but mind your footing, and take my jacket off the peg there, child," Merga cautions.

Kadara slumps into the chair.

"Won't be a moment before the cider's warm," Merga explains as Liedral removes five mugs from the cupboard and sets them out on the table.

"I'll get some cheese from the cellar." Liedral slips out the door to wrestle with the root cellar door next to the porch.

"You just stay there," suggests Merga.

Kadara looks blankly at the table, then slowly removes her leather cold-cap, revealing short and limp red hair.

Liedral returns shortly, carrying a square block of cheese wrapped in wax, which she sets on the serving table. She looks toward the cutlery box.

Merga follows her eyes. "I'll take care of that, mistress."

"I'm not the mistress . . ." Liedral shakes her head.

Kadara's grin makes a caricature of her drawn face.

The door opens, and snow and a light wind follow Frisa into the kitchen.

"Wipe your feet, girl!" snaps Merga.

"They'll be here soon as master Dorrin banks the fire and splashes the grime off his face and hands." Frisa looks around the kitchen. "That's what he said."

"Your feet, girl."

Frisa stamps back to the porch and wipes her feet before returning and closing the door. She stands on tiptoes to replace the jacket on the peg.

When the door opens again, Dorrin steps into the kitchen, followed by Vaos. The lamp in the wall bracket flickers with the gust of wind that flows around it, then steadies as Dorrin closes the door.

"Kadara!" He touches her shoulder lightly.

Merga is pouring warm cider into the mug at the redhead's elbow, then goes on to fill all the mugs. "Bread's almost ready. I'll be a-cutting the cheese now."

The smith seats himself at the end between Liedral and Kadara. Vaos slips into the place almost at the end of the table, nearest the corner where Frisa perches on her stool.

Merga sets the plate of cheese slices in the center of the wooden table. Vaos immediately reaches and takes two. Dorrin looks at the boy, and Vaos hands one slice to Frisa.

"You look tired," Dorrin says into the silence.

"Darkness-tired, Dorrin. Been a light-fired long year." Kadara coughs, covering her mouth. "Brede sent me. Couldn't come himself. They made him marshal. Don't call him that, but it amounts to that."

"What does he need?"

"Anything ... everything. More of those magic knives ... something that will work on the rivers next spring ... something you can't see that kills people. Brede thought of mines—using gunpowder—but you can't get close enough to the levies with those damned wizards to light the fuses. Same problem as guns—they see anything that looks like a gun, and, poof! There goes the powder and anyone who's near."

The smith touches his mug.

"Just don't have enough arms and trained people."

She coughs again, then takes some cheese and slowly begins to eat.

Vaos reaches for the cheese again, and Dorrin glares at him.

"Just one," the smith says. "You had a full supper." He knows Vaos is well-fed, but Kadara is thin and drawn.

"But he's hungry," Frisa says.

"He's always hungry."

"When did you get back to Kleth?" asks Liedral.

Kadara swallows before answering. "Yesterday. We had to find space and arrange for reshoeing about half the mounts. I took a spare horse. Not mine. Used to be Josal's, until they got him." She absently takes another piece of cheese.

Dorrin waits until she finishes it. "What happened at Elparta? No one seemed to know how it all happened—just that it did."

"They decided that Spidlar was too hard to conquer. Much easier to destroy." Kadara clears her throat.

Dorrin motions for Merga to sit down at the table. The dark-haired woman shakes her head and points toward the oven.

"They burned everyone who opposed them. Everyone who even looked like they supported order. They boiled the river and shook the earth until the walls fell. Then they killed every man and woman left in the city—except they used the women first. The damned fools—we told them to leave, and a lot did, but not enough." Kadara's voice is even, level, and colder than the snow that falls outside the kitchen. The steam from the hot cider in her mug drifts past her chin, past the worn braid on her officer's jacket.

By the stove, Merga makes the sign of the one-god believers, then glances toward the corner where Frisa sits on the stool.

"Your magic knives and Brede's tactics killed

several hundred of them. Slowed down their advance. Also got them madder than light." Kadara coughs, a racking cough.

"Let me get you something for that," Dorrin says.

The redhead sips from the mug. "Hot cider helps. Almost forget things here."

Dorrin enters the storeroom and finds the packet he wants, carrying it back to the kitchen, where he crushes some of the leaves, then eases them into another mug. He spoons out a dollop of rare honey— Frisa watches with open eyes—and pours hot cider into the mug, stirring the mixture. "Here."

Kadara swigs down the mixture in one gulp. "Uggggh . . ."

The eyes of the little girl in the corner open even wider.

"Best get it over, girl," Kadara says. "Don't ever let the men see you weak." She sets aside the medicinal cup and takes several more sips of the hot cider. "Brede made the wizards mad. Don't like not getting their way. Come spring, they'll burn their way north."

Liedral glances toward Merga, who is lifting bread from the oven. The aroma wafts toward the table.

"Still hard to believe," Kadara says. "Warm house, good food."

Dorrin stands behind her, and touches her wrists, trying to let a little order flow into her tired frame.

"Feels better." She shakes his hands off and lifts her cider.

Dorrin eases into his chair and waits. Behind him, Merga slices a loaf of bread, muttering, "Really too hot . . ." She sets the three others on the cutting table to cool.

"I take it the cheese-cutting things didn't work too well at the end."

"No. They just walked villagers in front of them—

slowly. Took their time. Ran horse troops alongside the roads with archers."

Merga sets the sliced bread in front of Kadara. Vaos looks from the platter to Merga and then to Dorrin. Dorrin shakes his head.

"Let him have a piece," Kadara says. "Life's too short." She leans forward and puts her head on the table, then slowly sits up.

Vaos puts down his hand.

"You're staying tonight," Liedral says firmly. "You need the rest and the food." She stands up and steps behind Kadara's chair. "She can sleep in the main room, on the cushions."

"Sleep on the floor," mumbles the trooper.

Liedral guides her toward the main room, which was designed to be a parlor someday but which contains little but cushions and two old chairs.

Vaos reaches for the bread once Liedral and Kadara leave the kitchen.

Dorrin carries his cider to the kitchen door, opening it and looking out. The heavy snow continues to fall, and there is already no trace of Kadara's tracks to the house.

Only the faintest glimmer of light penetrates from Rylla's house.

Dorrin closes the door and swallows the last of his cider. What can he possibly build for Brede? How will it make any difference? He carries his mug to the wash tub and sets it in the lukewarm water.

Outside, the snow keeps falling.

CXXIX

DORRIN AND VAOS slowly fuller the heavy stock into a square bar, strong enough, Dorrin hopes, to hold the greater length of black wires. He nods at Vaos to strike again after he turns the stock. When he sets the second piece on the back of the forge to anneal, Kadara steps past the slack tank.

"I need to go." While Kadara's face is pale, some of the darkness beneath her eyes has lightened.

Dorrin walks with her toward the smithy door and the welcome cool outside. They stand by the porch, where a warmer breeze blows in from the south, a wind warm enough that, under the midmorning sun, the snow has melted into a layer of slush barely covering the toes of Dorrin's boots.

"You were up early, Liedral said." Kadara looks toward the barn.

"I'm working on something for the rivers. The Whites can't walk people ahead of boats, but the wires have to be heavier, and so do the stocks. That will make them harder to carry." Dorrin sighs. "Maybe that won't matter. I'll work on some way to use gunpowder, but that will take some doing."

"Brede has confidence in you. He says you have all winter." Her laugh carries a bitter undertone. "And don't abandon your ship . . . we may need it."

"I've begun to think about that." His eyes turn across the slush-covered yard toward Liedral, who is leading Kadara's mount from the barn. "Still, it's only one, and, come spring, the Whites may have dozens offshore."

"Perhaps you'd better get it refitted earlier." The redhead coughs and covers her mouth.

"If I don't figure out how to help Brede, we won't have that long."

"How long before you have those river slicers?"

"I can have a few within the eight-day. Why?"

"It might be nice to have them in case the White Wizards don't wait until spring." She coughs again.

"They'll have to do something before there's ice on the river."

Kadara takes the horse's reins from Liedral.

"You shouldn't be riding."

"I've ridden with worse. So have most of my squad."

"He's been fed and curried." Liedral strokes the neck of the bay. "There are supplies in the saddlebags: dried apples and cheese, and some crushed astra for that cough. And a loaf of good bread. Give some to Brede."

"If there's any left." Kadara smiles.

"Even you can't eat all of what we packed," responds Liedral.

Kadara swings easily into the saddle.

"I'll bring what I have in an eight-day or so," Dorrin says.

"Send a messenger. It's a long trip if we're not there."

Dorrin looks at Kadara.

"Sorry. There aren't any spare horses, are there?"

He shakes his head. "The Council left us alone, but they took one of Yarrl's, and all but the plow horses from Jisle. If you're not there, or Brede isn't . . . then what would you suggest?"

"Ask for Brede. If he's not there, he'll leave instructions. That's probably the best we can do."

"Tell Brede we're thinking about him," Liedral offers.

"I will." Kadara touches the reins, and the bay eases

across the yard, each step squashing through the slush and mud.

Dorrin reaches out and takes Liedral's hand as they watch Kadara ride down the ridge drive toward the main road. He squeezes her fingers lightly, and is rewarded with a tightening of her fingers around his. As he stands there, her lips brush his cheek, but only for an instant. He turns to her, catching the tears in her eyes.

"It's so hard, sometimes," she says. "So unfair."

"Yes." Dorrin has thought that, especially over the last year. Chaos seems to triumph over order, and those, like Liedral or Kadara or Brede, who try to hold back chaos seem to suffer more than those who accept it.

"She looks so tired," Liedral continues.

"She is tired, and it will get worse."

"You look tired, too."

"That's going to get worse also." Dorrin forces a laugh.

"But why? Why do bad things keep happening to good people?"

"I don't know. I only know that I have to do the best I can." He takes a deep breath. "And it's not half the price that Brede and Kadara are paying, and they don't even want to stay here in Spidlar."

Liedral squeezes his fingers a last time before letting go. "I'm sorry. You need to be held. So do I."

"Shall we try?" Again, Dorrin tries to make his voice light.

For a long moment, they embrace, standing in the slush and mud.

CXXX

"You've spent nearly a full year, Jeslek, dear," says Anya coolly, "and you have exactly one small city. Not the most promising of campaigns."

Jeslek matches her smile, looking out the tower window. "It's nice to be back in Fairhaven."

"So you can check up on everyone, I suppose."

"Do you really think I care about all the little plots? I'm more interested in you." He glances toward the table set for two.

"What about your renegade smith? Or your Recluce-trained warriors? Don't you need to worry about them more than about the Council?"

Jeslek gestures, and the mists of the screeing glass part to reveal the red-headed smith, working with a large wheel in his smithy, aided by a youth.

"What's he doing?" asks Anya.

"Drawing wire, it looks like. Much good it will do him."

"Maybe he has some other use for it."

"Perhaps. But it doesn't matter. We've still only lost a few hundred levies, and perhaps four or five score cavalry—and none of the White company. I'd rather take some time, and fewer casualties."

"You are so rational it makes me sick."

"Does it now?" He steps toward her, reaching for the clasps to her gown. "Does it now?"

CXXXI

AFTER GLANCING AT the clouds overhead, Dorrin rolls the last barrel down the path toward the *Harthagay*. The dull rumble of thunder echoes off the flat gray of the northern sea. A jagged flash illuminates whitecaps beyond Cape Devalin, barely visible in the moments after dawn. The fine cold mist of the winter sea rain bites at his face, mixing with the sweat from his forehead.

He pauses at the edge of the narrow beach, looking down at the old schooner. His eyes flicker to the three hummocks beyond the sand where the Guild buried the bodies that had washed onto the sand—what little had been left by various scavengers.

With a deep breath, he resumes easing the barrel down to the ship. Each movement is gentle, and his senses almost caress the barrel, looking for the signs of chaos that will send him scrambling for cover.

The sands are hard and flat shoreward of the ship, but he eases the barrel halfway across the sands, then stops. Leaving the barrel upright, he walks to the ship.

The *Harthagay*, according to Liedral, had scarcely been the most seaworthy of vessels even before her grounding, but most of her problems had rested with her captain, the young and presumably dead Jarlsin.

Dorrin runs a hand along the clinker-planked side, letting his senses check the wood again. The hull remains sound, and even the mainmast is intact. The winds have left only shreds of the canvas, and Dorrin had been forced to cut away the pieces of the dangling lower crossbeam. The winter current has shifted the sand so that the *Harthagay's* stern half floats in three cubits of water. The low waves lap two-thirds of the way to the stem, which remains hard on the dune that now lies less than ten cubits from the high water mark.

More than an eight-day of work has cleared the beach and built what amounts to a channel behind the stern. Now he must loosen the stem—hoping his calculations are correct.

Dorrin walks to the barrel and takes his pry-bar, levering off the top and extracting the first wax-dipped basket. He walks toward the low dune where the shovel waits.

He digs two cubits into the sand before he places the basket and lights the fuse with the striker. Then he runs, throwing himself behind the hull.

Crumpppp!! Sand flies with the noise.

Dorrin returns and surveys the hole in the sand, deciding that he could have dug somewhat deeper. He checks the hull. Outside of a thin coating of sand driven into the varnish, no damage appears.

He digs again until he is ready to go for another basket, which he places within the hole, and lights, repeating his dash around the stem.

Another explosive charge, and the hole under the stem fills with water.

Dorrin begins on the northern side. After the first charge, his too-shallow sand pit is filled with water, and he is forced to use the baskets with the long wax-coated fuses.

Four more explosions and the *Harthagay* settles onto an even keel, rocking in a long pool of cold water.

Next comes more work—work and faith. He straps the bladder around his waist and steps into the boat that dips ominously under his weight, and the weight of the small toothed anchor. Slowly he rows seaward, watching the line uncoil, until there remain but a dozen cubits. After inching his way toward the stern, he levers the anchor overboard. The boat lifts in the water, rocking him backward and jamming a davit into his back.

"Darkness . . ."

He rows slowly back to the *Harthagay*. Even under his leather gloves he can feel blisters forming. Rowing is not the same as smithing, not exactly.

After tying the boat to the ship, he walks to the stern and the waiting winch. Slowly he turns the handle. The schooner rocks, grinds on the sand, and edges seaward perhaps a cubit. Dorrin cranks again, but the ship remains motionless. Soon he is cranking easily, but only to retrieve the anchor and to start over.

Before long, he is back in the boat rowing seaward again, to the north, where perhaps the bottom will offer more to hold the anchor.

At least the sea is almost flat in the late morning as he rows back and climbs back aboard. He pauses and takes a deep drink from his water bottle, sitting on the poop deck, his feet on the ladder to the main deck.

Once more, he takes the winch and turns—slowly. The cable tightens. He cranks again. The cable creaks. He edges another quarter turn, and the *Harthagay* shivers. Another turn, and another, and the schooner shivers backward toward the sea.

When the stem is even with the former shoreline, Dorrin takes another quick sip from the water bottle before increasing his efforts.

By midday, the schooner floats free, anchored, but with less than three cubits of water under her keel.

Dorrin takes the first rocket and puts it in the circular trough, then clicks the striker.

Quickly, but deliberately, he ducks behind the mast of the *Harthagay*.

The green flare explodes—as designed—a good hundred cubits above the sea toward lower Diev.

Dorrin waits, then takes another signal rocket, and repeats the process.

He finishes the water bottle, and eats a wedge of cheese and a half a loaf of old bread.

Three gulls wheel about the bare mainmast of the ship, then dive toward the chop of the sea. Dorrin scans the horizon for Liedral and the *Mocked Hare*, but no canvas appears from the south. He turns toward the north, finally, and there, bearing in on the *Harthagay*, is the Suthyan coaster, easily twice the size of the sloop.

Dorrin waves the green flag and watches until the coaster dips her flag.

Then he triggers the striker and touches the fuse. The rocket carries the line, but veers in front of the coaster, plowing into the water.

The *Mocked Hare* trims into the wind, and a seaman with a hooked pole leans down, jabbing at the line in the water. After three attempts, the man snags the line.

Gently, Dorrin pays out the heavier line, and then the cable.

Once the cable is taut, he uses the axe and cuts the anchor line.

The *Harthagay* swings about, and the cable squeaks as it takes the schooner's full weight. Dorrin wonders if the cable will hold.

The schooner rolls and turns slowly in an arc after the *Mocked Hare*. According to Kusman, skipper of the *Hare*, all he must do is keep the rudder straight until they near the breakwater for lower Diev. Dorrin hopes so.

When the *Mocked Hare* sheds sail outside the breakwater, the captain dips his ensign again. Shortly, a boat and four sailors bounce across the chop, guided by the cable. The four tie the boat to the *Harthagay*, and climb aboard.

"You're a clever man, master Dorrin. Not a soul thought you'd bring her off." Kusman checks the ropes from the wheel to the rudder, and motions another man to take the helm from Dorrin.

Dorrin flushes. "I almost didn't, and may not yet. She's taking a little water." He releases the wheel.

"Light! If it's only a little, you're doing a demon-damned sight better than Jarlsin did. Say his crew pumped half the day." Kusman studies the harbor. "Have to winch her in, but that's no problem." Then he grins. "That's where your problems begin. Owning a ship is nothing but headaches."

CXXXII

MERIWHEN'S HOOFS CRUNCH through the ice-crusted snow that covers the stone pavement. Dorrin glances at the thin plume of smoke rising from the Red Lion. All the windows, save the one closest the front door, are shuttered. The Red Lion is open, unlike the Tank-ard, which once hosted the troopers, until the previous summer, when all squads were rushed southward to protect the river road against the Certan incursions.

The cold damp wind from the Northern Ocean rattles the shuttered windows of the Red Lion, and Dorrin fumbles the top button of his jacket closed.

Wheeennn . . . Even the heavy-coated mare protests.

"Easy, girl." Dorrin pats her neck as they turn down toward the shipwright's. He touches the black staff he feels he must now carry everywhere, then looks down the near-deserted street.

A man in a heavy herder's jacket is pounding the knocker of a doorway, and two young men, their breath like steam, are wrestling a barrel out of the cooper's shop. Nothing else moves except the overhead clouds. Like the previous winter, only a handful of chimneys show smoke against the gray sky.

Dorrin looks north toward the ocean, where the clouds are lower and blowing southward, promising more snow, more cold. Meriwhen tosses her head.

All the piers in the harbor are empty, the warehouses shuttered tight.

At the shipwright's, where the *Harthagay* rests on blocks beside the foot of the western breakwater, Dorrin ties Meriwhen inside the open shed. There a fishing boat or some craft under construction normally rests, but the blocks are empty. Then he takes the leather case and walks toward the building beside the schooner.

The shipwright opens the door. "Only could be you in this weather."

Dorrin unfastens his jacket and spreads the drawings he takes from the leather case across the drafting table, weighting them on the corners with worn brick fragments.

He points toward the top drawing, his eyes flicking to Tyrel. "I'd like a platform, braced like this, right here. Ladders . . ."

The shipwright swings the lantern bracket over the drafting table, ignoring the faint black smoke and the acrid odor of the not-quite-pure lamp oil, and studies the drawings. "That platform's heavy. You need something that strong?"

"It might have to support a hundred stone of iron."

"You need something that strong, maybe even a cross-brace set here." The shipwright looks up. "That'll play demon-light with your aft cargo hold, and how will you get there?" Tyrel walks over to the fireplace and eases a small log onto the coals. "Another ass-freezing winter. Like the frigging wizards ordered it."

Dorrin looks at the drawing. "What do you suggest?"

Tyrel recenters the log with a poker. He returns to the drawing, worrying his lower lip with a pair of buck teeth. "I can move this aft another couple of cubits . . ."

Dorrin frowns. That will make the angle from the engine to the shaft even steeper, when he has been trying to minimize the angle, but he will save some weight by using a shorter shaft. "All right, but that means these braces for the shaft have to be changed."

"We can do that." Tyrel gestures toward the door. "What else we going to do? Once you get her in the water again, you'll need guards."

"I know."

"What about sealing this shaft of yours? It's well under water . . ."

Dorrin looks over the drawings again, while the lamp sputters for a moment and releases a thin line of black smoke before settling back into an even yellow light.

Outside the long shedlike building, the wind whistles, and light snow drifts under the eaves and falls toward the timbered floor like white dust.

CXXXIII

AFTER SPRINKLING DRIED willow bark and astra into the mortar, Dorrin takes the pestle and begins to grind the mixture into a finer powder.

Rylla, adding a touch of syrup to crushed brinn, clears her throat. "You really don't have to be here, you know."

"I suppose not." He looks to the small south window, one of the few unshuttered. Outside, granular snow skids across the crusty white surface. Even though the window is small, Dorrin squints against the glare.

"Merga says you're still trying to build an engine for your ship."

"The engine's mostly built, but I need to finish the boiler and get the pieces down to the shipyard." He continues to grind, although the best he will do with the willow bark is to create very small, striplike pieces.

"Boilers, engines—they're all magic." Rylla spoons her mixture into a small cup, then adds steaming cider and stirs. "And your lady?"

"Things are better ... but ..." He shrugs. "I wish there were a quicker way than just being loving and patient."

"Did you build that engine in a season, or learn how to?" Rylla's voice is somewhere between sharp and amused.

"Of course not. It doesn't make things any easier." He funnels the mixture into a bag, which he carefully ties and carries into the main room.

A stocky woman bundled in faded woolens stands by the armless chair where a thin and pale youth slumps. Dorrin can feel the boy's fever, and has already strengthened his system with some slight addition of order. He hands the bag to the mother. "Add two pinches of this to a cup of something hot at breakfast and supper. It will help keep the fever down."

"Thank you, healer. He's better for a time when he sees you, but it doesn't seem to last."

"I do what I can."

She presses a copper upon him. He does not refuse, for he will pass it to Rylla. Dorrin closes the door behind them and watches as Rylla brings the small cup to a white-haired woman.

"You need to drink this, Gerd."

"It's vile stuff, Rylla. Vile . . . smells like the river where the fisherman leave their offal, maybe worse."

"I've sweetened it with syrup and cider."

Gerd lifts the cup and sets it down. "It smells vile."

"You want to die of the flux, go ahead," Rylla snaps. "I just wish you hadn't wasted my good herbs."

"I'll drink it, but I don't have to like it." She lifts the cup and swallows. "Uuughhhhh . . ."

Dorrin understands. While brinn is effective against the flux, its bitterness is legend, even buried in sweetened cider.

"You'll feel better afore long, Gerd." Rylla hands her a tiny folded square of cloth. "Put this in something hot tonight. Drink it all."

"Do I have to?"

"No. You can have your guts run out the jakes on you until you're so weak you can't walk here."

"You're a hard healer, Rylla."

Rylla snorts.

At last, the thin figure wraps her cloak around her and totters out into the cold white glare. Rylla closes the door and turns to Dorrin. "You don't need to be here," she repeats. "Scat! Get on your jacket and be on your way to that smithy. All you do here is humor an old woman."

"I need to be here, and it's not humoring you. What I'm doing for Brede is creating death. This helps a little."

"That's the way of the world. Fighting death with death." The healer shakes her head. "But we're done for now, and you best be going."

"I keep trying to find a better way . . ."

"Aye . . . and that's a problem, too."

Dorrin pulls on his coat and waits.

"New ways aren't always better."

"You sound like my father."

"Ha!" Rylla cackles. "Old ways aren't always better,

neither. People pick a way, be it old or new, and then they want to do it that way. Takes a strong soul to accept the best of both the old and the new." She cackles again, then motions toward the door. "Scat. We can't tell if your engine thing will be good or bad, leastways, not until you finish it, and you won't be finishing it jawing with an old healer."

Dorrin is still grinning when he reaches the smithy. Perhaps he can add Rylla's words to his growing penned thoughts on order and chaos.

CXXXIV

THE SQUARE-BEARDED WIZARD studies the unfolded parchment on the table. Beside it lie fragments of blue wax from the seal that had closed it.

Whistling outside the window, the wind still cannot drown out the clink of masons' trowels and stones. The candles in the three-branched candelabra flicker with the gusts that find their way around the ill-fitting window.

The White Wizard walks to the cloudy glass of the window. Below, conscripted villagers toil with the stones of the walls, slowly dragging them back into position for the masons. Dark clouds overhead promise snow or rain, but neither yet falls.

Finally, the more slender wizard, hunched in a heavy white wool cloak, speaks. "What are they offering?"

"Just about everything to save their necks." Fydel laughs. "They'll turn over any of the 'unfaithful'; effectively disband the Guards by reducing them to a handful of squads; open the roads to our traders."

"Why aren't you taking their offer?" asks Cerryl.

"You assume too much."

Cerryl laughs softly. "I'm assuming nothing. You won't take the Spidlarian Council's offer. I'd just like to know why."

"Isn't it obvious? Why hand it to Jeslek? He's back in Fairhaven, enjoying fires, good food, and a few other pleasures." A wide grin reveals large white teeth. "Who knows? We might get a better offer before spring."

"We won't. What you're hoping is that Jeslek will have to face some mighty Black. But that won't happen. Do you really think that Recluce will send more warriors or wizards to Spidlar?"

"No." Fydel smiles. "But there's no reason to make it easy for Jeslek, is there? No real reason to hand him an easy victory after he's muddled through a year of doing nothing, is there?"

"What about the levies? Why kill them off unnecessarily?"

"You're too soft, Cerryl. What are a few hundred peasants one way or the other?"

Cerryl shakes his head, but says nothing.

The wind whistles, and the sound of stone work echoes through the window, and the candles flicker in the late afternoon.

IV.

ORDER-FORGER

CXXXV

From the room next door, Dorrin hears Liedral's breathing, and he wishes he were lying with her. While they can now hug each other, or exchange brief kisses, the internal scars from her torture have only faded, not disappeared. Outside, the low wail of the wind reminds him that winter is not yet over, even though the days are getting longer once more.

Dorrin slowly sets the paper back in the box, and leans back for a moment in the chair, reflecting on order. His father, his mother, Lortren—they all equate order with good. Yet Dorrin himself has used order to create destruction. Is destruction of those who would impose chaos by force good?

In an ideal sense, probably not. But pure order almost invariably loses to pure chaos. Yet even Creslin used order to create destruction to stop the Whites.

Is it wrong to use ordered metal to destroy or stop the spread of chaos? He frowns. If all destruction is evil, then, could not those who oppose order claim that the use of force to oppose chaos is also evil?

If use of destruction is good for some purposes, then cannot any means be justified by a good enough end? He shakes his head. Logic will not solve his problems there, for he can certainly think up good excuses for anything.

Still, his father has said that there is always an order-based way to solve a problem. He smiles grimly. Supposedly, the White Wizards can enchant someone's eyes so they see what is not there. In some way, that is what they did to Liedral—made her see false images of him.

Conversely, could he not use order to show true images? But what good would that do? Yet ... he cannot tell a lie, but as a child—and even as an adult— it has not been as uncomfortable to tell part of the truth.

He looks at the lamp, then at the small mirror on the chest. He stands and places the lamp before the mirror, then stands behind the lamp. If the lamp were not there, the mirror would only show him—and that would be part of the truth.

He concentrates on somehow letting the image of himself flow around the lamp, as if it were not there. For an instant the room is plunged into darkness—so dark that he cannot see, and he can always see in the dark. He can sense where things are, but not see. Between surprise and speculation, he loses his concentration, and the room fills with soft lamplight again.

He laughs softly. Of course, if the lamp were not there, neither would the light to see by be, and the room would be dark. But since the lamp did not move, did he merely imagine the darkness? Or did he somehow remove the image of the lamp and its light?

His forehead is damp, and he has a slight headache. With a deep breath he finishes putting away his scribblings.

Outside, the wind still moans. Next door, Liedral turns uneasily in sleep, and somewhere in Kleth, Kadara and Brede prepare for the spring invasion of the Whites. Dorrin turns back the quilt on the narrow bed that has replaced his pallet—once he realizes that Liedral's recovery will be slow. Then he blows out the lamp.

CXXXVI

"FORCE LEADER BREDE, is it not true that, unless the Certan and Gallosian forces are stopped before Kleth, they will take over all of Spidlar?"

Brede looks across the table at the white-haired man in the royal-blue velvet. "Yes, Councilman. They intend to take all of Spidlar."

"Do they not intend to destroy all traders in Spidlar?"

"I cannot read their minds, ser."

"Let me put it another way, Force Leader. So far, have they allowed any traders or anyone else who opposes chaos to live?"

"Not within Spidlar."

The Councilman spreads his velvet-covered arms. "Then we must stop them before they advance farther."

The two other members of the Council, one on each side of the Councilman, each also in the blue velvet, nod.

Brede inclines his head respectfully to the Council. "What do you suggest? And how would you recommend we accomplish this effort? You have managed to gather perhaps three hundred half-trained cavalry and two thousand levy troops. The Whites have twice that many garrisoned in Elparta, and have posted levies for the spring for another five thousand. They also have a company of White Wizards who throw thunderbolts."

"We leave the details of such to you, Force Leader. But you must stop them before Kleth."

"Might I ask if you have tried to negotiate with

them?" Brede asks. The Council room is suddenly hot and stuffy.

"We have sent intermediaries," concedes the Councilman.

"And?"

"It was suggested that until either victory or stalemate developed, negotiations would be premature."

"Then, could I presume that you are ordering an all-out effort to hold Kleth, regardless of cost or losses?"

"We leave the military details to you, Force Leader. But if Kleth falls . . ." The Councilman shrugs. His cold eyes center on Brede.

CXXXVII

"THEY'VE BUILT SOME fortifications around the southern side." Dorrin leans in the saddle toward Liedral. In the rear of her cart are eight sets of slicers adapted for use on the river. His other works of destruction are still in progress, but the spring melt has come sooner this year, and Brede will need the river slicers soon, once the runoff dies down.

"Will that do any good, really?" Liedral fingers her bow.

"Against a White Wizard who can raise mountains and topple walls?" Dorrin's laugh is hard. "Not if they get close to the city."

The day is bright, even with the white puffy clouds that dot the sky, and the wind blows warm out of the south. The road mud is only damp, rather than ankle-deep. The road itself is empty, save for Dorrin and Liedral, and flattened, bearing the imprint of many feet, all headed from Kleth.

Four soldiers stand by a rough hut meant to guard the western approach.

"Where you bound?" asks the stocky man in an ill-fitting breastplate.

Dorrin studies the ironwork for an instant, dismissing it. "I have some equipment ordered by Brede. We're delivering it to him."

"Aye, and you've also got fine wines for us all, no doubt," cracks a soldier with a goatee.

Dorrin rests his hand on the dark staff. "I don't think he would be too happy if he didn't get what he ordered."

"Sure, and you've traveled this road from far Diev just to deliver a small cart?"

The staff is in Dorrin's hands, and then at the guard's throat, almost like black lightning. "My name is Dorrin. I am Brede's smith, and you will let us pass. If you wish, you may escort us to him."

"Dorrin . . . oh . . . shit . . ." mumbles the man in the rear. "This here's the Black smith . . ."

The front guard swallows. "Ah . . . Fredo will escort you, master smith."

"Thanks for nothing . . ."

Dorrin leaves the staff ready until the cart is rolling toward Kleth.

"The red-headed cat told Ralth you might be a-coming, but he never believed her," Fredo chatters. "But I told him that mighty as the great Brede is, he can't be doing it all without some help . . . and terrible as Kadara of the blades is, she's not enough, either . . ."

Liedral rolls her eyes and looks at Dorrin.

"They say that the High Wizard of all of the Whites is leading the hordes. Must want to trample us poor folks pretty bad, but I don't see as why. After all, Spidlar's a pretty thin country, leastwise compared to Certis or Gallos, and all we have are animals and traders. Course sometimes it's hard to tell which is

which"—Fredo laughs, and continues—"but our traders, leastwise, leave us be and mostly don't raise levies
or try to fatten their purses through taxes..."

More than half the houses in Kleth are deserted,
some obviously so, with shutters fastened tight and
planks covering unshuttered windows. Others are just
empty, and a few have gaping doors and emptied
interiors.

On the main road, a single store is open, more of a
food stall than a market, and around it gather a handful of levies and blue-liveried cavalry. A handful look
at the cart, watching as Dorrin and Liedral pass. After
another three kays, they reach the houses on the southern side of Kleth that serve as barracks and headquarters.

"There be the headquarters place, where all the
squad and section leaders meet." Fredo gestures
toward a larger house, with a split-slate roof and moss-
tinged brick walls.

The smell of the stables wafts over them from the
building behind the headquarters house, and Dorrin
coughs. Idly, he wonders what that much manure
would do for his herb gardens in the clayey soil of
Diev. Liedral halts the cart in front of the doorway
with a blue-coated sentry. After dismounting, Dorrin
hands Meriwhen's reins to the trader and steps up to
the blue-coated sentry. "My name is Dorrin. If you
would convey to Brede that—"

"I'll be telling him immediately, master Dorrin. If
you would just wait here."

Fredo shakes his head. "If Ralth could see this...
the headquarters guards treating the smith like a
Guildmaster or a Councillor..."

"He is a Guildmaster," Liedral whispers. "Everyone
in Diev bows to him, and he hates it."

"He hates it? A Guildmaster who dislikes respect,
but o' course it wouldn't be respect, would it, him

being so young? It'd be fear, and no man with any self-respect wants to be feared, less he's a bully, and your smith seems like a decent enough sort."

"He's more than decent. This sort of work is hard on him." She stops as Dorrin returns and takes the mare's reins, absently patting her on the neck.

A squad leader Dorrin has not met follows the sentry out, and Brede follows the squad leader. "Dorrin!"

"Brede. I have some of what I promised." Dorrin gestures to the cart.

"Cirras will show you to the armory, where you can unload. Then he'll help you stable your horses, and we'll talk."

"Kadara?" asks Liedral.

"She's on patrol." Brede looks back to the building. "I'll see you in just a bit."

"That would be fine." Dorrin senses the many demands on Brede's time.

"If you would follow me," begins Cirras.

The armory is a barn behind the headquarters. Dorrin studies the forge and the slack tanks, including one containing an oily solution. The anvil has a larger horn than his and a wider variety of stakes for the hardie hole.

In addition to the armorer, there appear to be two strikers, and several boys. One is bringing in charcoal, another handling the bellows, and another one powdering some sort of ashes, presumably for a flux paste. The armorer sets aside the hammer and lifts the iron that will be a helmet off the stake form, placing it on the fire bricks, before he steps to the doorway.

"There are some weapons that go in the locked room," Cirras tells the lanky armorer. "Made by master Dorrin for Force Leader Brede."

Dorrin dismounts, but does not move to enter the armory.

The armorer nods to Cirras and steps around him. "Master Dorrin, I'm Welka, the Guard armorer here."

"I'm glad to meet you."

"I wanted to meet you . . . especially after I saw the stocks of those . . . devices . . ."

Dorrin looks down for a moment, then back up. "I'm not . . . not totally pleased about making weapons, you know?"

The armorer smiles wryly. "I can sense that. It's good for us that you're not. That shield you made Brede? What was it?"

"Black iron."

"I thought as much. Too bad. That's not something that can be taught, is it?"

"Not unless you can handle order."

As they talk, Cirras and two armorer's aides unload the eight canvas-wrapped packages and carry them through the iron-bound door into a back room whose mismatched timbers reflect hasty construction.

"Well . . . you do good work, master Dorrin. Right now, I wish you could handle edged weapons, but I've only met a couple of order smiths, and they couldn't either. You seem somewhat . . . more . . . adaptable . . ."

"Much more adaptability may be my undoing," Dorrin blurts.

"I won't ask what's in the canvas."

"It's probably better that way." Dorrin looks at Liedral and the empty cart. "I guess."

"Why are you doing this?" asks Welka. "If I might presume?"

"I owe Brede and Kadara . . . and I owe Spidlar for accepting me, and I feel bound to oppose chaos."

"You take your debts seriously."

"Very seriously," adds Liedral quietly.

Welka nods to Dorrin. "Good to meet you, master

Dorrin." He steps back toward the forge and the half-turned helmet.

"Darkness . . ." mumbles Fredo. "Special he is, your master Dorrin, when the master armorer pays his respects."

"The stable is this way," suggests Cirras.

After unsaddling Meriwhen and unharnessing the cart horse, and sending Fredo back to his duties, the three walk across the packed clay of the yard to the building where they had met Brede. Cirras takes them past the sentry, and into a small anteroom with chairs.

"I'll tell Force Leader Brede you're here."

After the young officer leaves, Liedral grins at Dorrin from her armless wooden chair. "You are very important, master smith Dorrin."

"I'm not that much of a master smith, just one who can twist his soul farther than most." The chair creaks as Dorrin shifts his weight and looks toward the closed door.

"You really dislike building weapons, don't you?"

"Yes. But I don't see any alternatives now. Force is all that seems to hold chaos at bay. I don't like that."

Outside, the hoofs of another squad of cavalry echo against the closed window, as the troopers head out toward the field.

"Force or violence?" asks Liedral.

Dorrin smiles. "You're right. Force doesn't seem to be enough. It's the violence I don't like."

"The world is filled with violence."

"Recluce isn't."

"Do you think they sent you away to find that out?"

"It could be," Dorrin says slowly, "but I think it was more because of my fixation on building machines."

The door opens with a low creak, and Brede stands there. "I'm sorry it took so long." He brushes the blond hair off his forehead and gestures toward the room behind him. It contains little more than a round table, a half dozen chairs, and an open cabinet with shelves stacked with various maps.

Brede waits until Dorrin and Liedral seat themselves. "What did you create this time?"

"A variation on the cheese cutters. These are designed to use on the river. I did eight sets, but the way the spring arrived, I decided I didn't have time for any more."

"The runoff is already dropping to normal flow." Brede rubs his forehead. Finally, he looks at Dorrin. "I need your help."

"How?"

"I want you to go with Kadara and set up your devices. I'm trying to organize things here."

"Things are that bad?" interrupts Liedral.

"Yes. The Council has told me to defend Kleth at all costs. There are no alternatives."

"That's so they can buy their way out if you can't stop the Whites," Liedral says. "Dorrin's not exactly a warrior."

"I know. Kadara can take care of that—"

"But you want me to see the Whites, and you think that I might be able to figure out something else if I see them in action. Is that it?"

"Yes." Brede's eyes meet Dorrin's.

Dorrin looks at the scratched wood of the table, then at Brede. "All right. I don't see that I can do less, but I need to get back to the engine."

"I'm just asking you to set them up the first time."

"I understand." What Dorrin also understands is that he is on the way to being at least a part-time combat engineer, an occupation not exactly suited to someone who tends to get blinding and incapacitating headaches in the commission of violence.

CXXXVIII

DORRIN'S BOOTS SKID as he steps onto the slippery ice in the shade of a boulder. "Darkness..." He catches himself on the rock, thankful for his gloves. A long scratch in the leather hints at what could have happened to his hand. To his left the river swirls, strongly, but without the turbulence of eight-days earlier, the major runoff time past.

Upstream, Dorrin knows, float the flatboats and barges of the Certan and Kyphran levies. The Gallosians will be plodding northward along the road.

Dorrin calculates, then waves to the figures across the narrow section of the river. Here the river is as narrow as it gets, a little more than three rods of smooth-flowing water.

"Is this about right?" asks Kadara. An archer stands by her elbow.

"If we put the first set up there"—Dorrin points upriver to a larger boulder—"and these here, and the third set down there... there's a chance, at least. I'll set them at different heights."

The archer lifts her bow and releases the shaft that carries the light line across the river.

Dorrin carefully scrambles upriver to the boulder he pointed out. There he takes the midweight sledge from the makeshift belt sheath and the first of the black-iron stocks from his pack.

In time, the first stock stands firm, invisible black wires running a cubit or so above the water to another stock on the eastern side of the river.

They repeat the process twice more before a rider trots up. "The barges are coming, squad leader."

"Take cover!" Kadara snaps. She gestures to the depression behind a stump. Dorrin eases into the space.

"Are you sure you want to stay?" she asks.

"No. But unless I get a better idea of how you fight, how can I design things?" He wishes he were not there. He is not a fighter, not a hero, and not even the staff behind him offers much comfort. His head begins to ache.

The handful of archers hide in their concealed pits, and the horse troopers ride downstream.

"More archers would help..." he whispers to Kadara.

"Do you know how long—Never mind, we just don't have that many."

Dorrin understands. After two years, Vaos is barely a striker. Then again, Vaos also loves horses.

The dark water, the empty dark water, flows between the apparently deserted banks of the river. Because the area is mainly used for grazing, few trees grace the banks. Dorrin and Kadara wait.

The river flows.

Around the gentle curve plows a dark-hulled barge, followed by two others. On the first barge, bearing the green banners of Certis, are archers, and perhaps a score of foot levies. The second barge carries archers and levies under a gold banner, presumably of Kyphros, while the third bears both banners and levies. There are no white banners.

Holding his breath, Dorrin waits as the lead barge nears the upstream wires, wires that should cut like knives.

Cut they do, as the first three archers are swept, bloody and screaming, into the dark water, but their weight momentarily drags the low wires down, where they catch on the barge's hull.

With the screaming, the Spidlarian archers rise from

their pits and loose a volley at the barge. Archers from the second barge lift their bows.

Dorrin winces, ducking behind the stump, realizing that nothing is going quite as planned. Kadara releases one arrow, then another. Bodies fall from the lead barge, almost in slow, slow motion, as the barge struggles against the order-reinforced wires.

Sensing the fraying of the wire beyond the power of order to hold, Dorrin shouts, "Down!"

Kadara remains upright, nocking yet another arrow and aiming toward the barges. Beside her, Vorban also releases his arrows.

Dorrin stands, and lunges, knocking the redhead to the muddy ground.

"Bastard! You—"

"Stay down!" snaps the smith, as he rolls and yanks Vorban's feet from beneath him. "Stay down!" The wiry man scrambles away from Dorrin.

Thwannnnngggg . . .

Like the invisible knives they are, the three wires part nearly simultaneously, and like giant iron whips, slice through water and back toward the second barge, which has nearly caught up to the slowed first barge. The black iron knives lash four archers into the water, then continue in their backlash.

"Aeeeeiiii . . ."

As the recoil from the black iron wire slices Vorban into two asymmetrical sections, flames burn through Dorrin's skull, and he sinks to the ground, arrows of pain slamming through his eyes. He shudders as silently as possible as his mind and skull are slashed by the unseen white whip.

When he finally straightens, Kadara has fired several more arrows into the barges. Levies dive from the first barge as it passes under the higher second set of wires, and three standing officers are sliced apart.

The rudderman of the third barge, seeing the

disaster ahead, has managed to ground his vessel on the eastern side of the river, upriver and across the water from the bulk of Kadara's squad.

The archers on the second barge flatten themselves on the deck, as do some of the levies. The second wires slice through those who do not. Another handful of arrows rains on those lying prostrate.

The first barge runs under the last wires, which clear the decks and then catch on the tiller post raised by the rudderman.

"Down!" snaps Dorrin, although he must force the words past the heavy hammering within his brain.

"Down! Now!" screams Kadara as she flattens herself.

The arrows from the Spidlarians cease as the third wires part explosively, gutting first the rudderman who caught them with the braced and raised tillerpost, and sweeping back across the second barge.

The tillerman on the second barge ducks, but some of the incautious levies who thought the first wires were the only wires are slashed by the recoiling wire whip.

After the wires pass, the tillerman on the second barge manages to swing the heavy craft shoreward, this time toward the western shore, where it grinds to a halt, less than a handful of rods from Kadara's squad.

Of the nearly two score men originally upon the barge, less than ten stagger shoreward. None make it more than a dozen steps from the barge.

The empty first barge wanders downstream, grinding over sand and gravel, but not quite catching.

The levies from the third barge, however, remain untouched, and form up on the far side of the river, using the barge as partial cover.

Dorrin looks at the bodies, and parts of bodies, bobbing in the water. He swallows hard, and puts his fingers across his forehead, trying to rub the pain away.

"Let's go!" Kadara stoops to recover Vorban's sword, belt, and purse, then continues downstream, exhorting her squad. They carry four bodies, including Vorban's, downstream and out to the dusty trail flanking the river. The main stone-paved highway runs a kay east of the river.

Dorrin follows, trying to stand up against the pain behind his eyes. Kadara has eight troopers from the dozen who had waited. He clears his throat and spits the bile onto the riverbank.

"No way to get to them and really not much in the way of arrows left," Kadara explains. "We'll regroup farther downstream."

A trooper looks wide-eyed at Dorrin, then back at the carnage in and out of the water. He looks at the black staff and the heavy sledge and slowly shakes his head.

Dorrin wishes he could shake his head, but with the pain of the trip-hammers behind his eyes, he is having trouble walking, let alone thinking. As they walk northward, Dorrin can hear hoofbeats as horses are brought to them.

With the mounts comes Brede. He looks down at Dorrin and the brownish specks on his boots.

Dorrin mounts Meriwhen. "The river slicers worked this time. They probably won't again."

"Why not?"

"All they have to do is put an iron post out front to catch the wires, and have everyone lie flat. A few will still get killed, but nothing like this." Dorrin spits out the residue in his mouth onto the road.

Brede raises his eyebrows and turns to Kadara.

"We wiped out the first two. The third grounded on the far shore and saved the levies. We didn't have any more arrows and were out-numbered about five or six to one. Where they grounded we couldn't get to them. We lost four—Vorban was one of them—to Dorrin's gadget when the wires snapped. He warned us, but Vorban didn't listen."

"He never did." Brede turns his mount back in the direction of Kleth. "We'll try your gadgets again, as soon as possible. There's a chance they won't rerig the barges immediately." He urges his horse toward the main body.

"Is it always like this?" Dorrin asks Kadara, as she waits for the bodies to be tied to the dead troopers' horses.

"Hardly." Kadara's laugh is harsh. "This was a victory, if you can call it that. Sometimes we lose, especially if they have White Wizards with them. They don't like the water much."

Dorrin ponders, still rubbing his forehead. He and Kadara have wiped out nearly four score of the enemy, with a handful of losses. "Why can't we get those other levies?"

"We would, if they were on this side of the river. We didn't leave anyone on that side. Too much danger of getting trapped between the road and the river with all their levies."

Dorrin does not understand.

"Look, Dorrin. To wipe out the three score levies left there would take every archer we've got on this side of the river, and Brede can't afford to get them this far away from our main body. He's been hoping to make it so costly that they'll get tired."

"They won't," Dorrin says.

"No. I know they won't. So does Brede. But the more we can wound or kill without heavy losses on our part before we have to fight a real battle, the better our chances."

"We need to set the wires up and find the next place, but this time, let's try it just before the narrow point." Dorrin looks at the canvas-wrapped bundles behind him.

"You think they'll be expecting it the same way as before?"

"I hope so."

"So do I."

As they ride downstream, Dorrin does not look toward the river and what may float in it, concentrating on what he must do to assemble and test his steam engine, and knowing he is a coward to think about a way of escape.

CXXXIX

DORRIN SADDLES MERIWHEN, reflecting on the previous day's efforts on the river. The second time, the traps were not nearly so effective, and Kadara's squad lost another five people, killing only a score of Certan levies. Even after an uneasy night's sleep, he still carries a headache into the dawn. Even more unfortunately, the whole White force has used the river to move another five kays closer to Kleth.

Liedral waits with her cart outside the stable when Dorrin leads Meriwhen into the spring drizzle. The quiver is propped beside her, and her bow is strung, but both are covered with oilcloth against the rain. He walks the mare up beside the wagon where Liedral stands and gives her a quick hug.

"Brede wants you to stay?" Liedral slips out of his embrace.

"Probably. But I can't do any more for him here, and I'm trying to develop some gunpowder bombs that he can use."

"That's dangerous. What happens if the Whites find out that you're working on it?" Liedral shudders.

"That depends. If they're close enough to fire it, I'm

dead. But from what I recall from the old books and what I've figured out, they have to be almost in sight of you. Theoretically, I suppose, if I could figure out something that didn't explode until all the parts— Anyway, I can't. But I've got another idea, and I'll bring it back here for Brede."

He sniffs. Even in the predawn light, the faint smell of fire permeates Kleth, carried northward in advance of the Whites and their horde, although it may be two eight-days or more before they reach the second river city, since they are systematically destroying all holdings on each side of the river.

Slowly, Dorrin swings into the saddle, wishing he could do more, and simultaneously wishing he didn't have to worry about the conflict between Fairhaven and Spidlar. Liedral flicks the reins and leads the way past the armory and toward the street that will lead to the west road to Diev.

"There he goes, the demon smith . . . swear it's him, the one who turned the river into a slaughter-house . . ." The words echo across the predawn light.

"Wizards always hurry out . . ." Metal clinks dully against metal.

"From what I heard, that one will probably come back with more troubles, just like a tin copper . . ."

"Syriol says he's killed a score of men with that staff . . ."

"Who's the other one?"

"Some trader . . . Some say he saved him from the wizards . . . others say the trader fled Jellico . . ."

" . . . think the wizard likes men . . ."

"Let him like what he wants . . . just leave us alone . . ."

Liedral's countenance is impassive, and Dorrin lets the words drift by in the chill air. Before long they have passed onto the churned and packed mud of the road that will lead them home—if any place can be considered home in the face of the White assault.

They see no one during the first twenty kays, just footprints, hoof prints, and an occasional wagon track, but the wagon tracks were laid down earlier and have been overlaid with later imprints.

When they stop by a creek crossed by a narrow stone bridge, Dorrin leads Meriwhen down to the water, but is careful not to let her drink too heavily at first. He fills a bucket from the cart and brings it back to the road.

"Thank you," says Liedral. She holds the cart horse's reins to ensure that the gelding does not try to drink all the cold water instantly. "Are we trying to ride straight through?"

"Maybe not straight through, but only short breaks. This road is going to get more and more dangerous."

"And you plan to come back?"

"Brede and Kadara need me."

"What about us? What about your engine?"

Dorrin takes a deep breath. "I still don't have the engine quite completed, and we need to get the parts to the ship."

"Are you going to rename it? *Harthagay* doesn't seem exactly . . . I don't know . . . it doesn't sound like you."

"Probably. I don't know what, yet. Until the engine's in place, all we have is a hull." He leads Meriwhen back down to the creek for more water.

Liedral watches, checking the road ahead—still empty. She opens the pack and removes the cheese, and the cheese slicer. When Dorrin returns, she offers him several slices and a chunk of bread. They eat silently.

Finally, Dorrin asks. "Are you ready?"

She nods.

Late afternoon comes before they find other travelers.

Through the drizzle that is beginning to fall, a group of figures struggles through the mud that covers the road. A half-dozen adults and nearly as many children slog through the dark mud. The children slip often on the downhill slope. Liedral drives the cart as much on the shoulder as on the road as they near the group.

As Dorrin watches, two of the men slip to the side of the road and let the others plod onward.

"You see that?" Liedral asks.

"Yes. Just keep driving. I'm going to try something." Dorrin concentrates, slowly wraps the light around him, easing Meriwhen closer to the cart.

The short and stocky man bears a curved blade that has no sheath, while the tall man brandishes a cudgel.

As he lifts the cudgel, the tall man steps forward, within three paces of the slowly moving cart. "We'd have that cart. We need it far more than ye."

"That may be," Liedral says coolly, "but it's not yours." She has the bow in her hands, and the arrow ready.

"You use that bow, pretty boy, and the rest will pull you down," blusters the tall man.

"Now . . . be a good boy—"

Dorrin eases Meriwhen closer, then drops his concealment and strikes.

Crack . . . The cudgel drops into the mud from the force of the staff. The tall man holds a dangling wrist with his other hand. His eyes gape as he sees the dark figure on horseback. "Darkness . . ."

"You could call it that," Dorrin snaps, reeling in his saddle, eyes burning and head aching.

The short man steps forward, and Dorrin forces back the burning in his eyes as he parries the awkwardly swinging blade, then thrusts to disarm the second traveler.

Neither Liedral nor Dorrin has to do more, as the entire group of refugees scrambles out of the road. Dorrin rubs his forehead, trying to massage away the results of his violence with the staff.

"Where did you learn that trick?"

"I've been practicing. It's hard, though. I can't see. So I sort of have to feel where I am, and I'm not all that good at it." He continues to watch the refugees, but none of them even look at the cart and horseman. A woman in gray tatters tries to bind the broken wrist of the tall man.

Dorrin's head continues to pound—but what else could he have done? Force—always force. Is force the only thing anyone in Candar respects?

Wheee . . . eeeee . . .

Dorrin pats Meriwhen on the neck. "Easy, girl."

"How much longer?"

Dorrin tries to calculate, despite the headache. "Too long."

"How long is too long?" Liedral asks dryly. "That doesn't say much."

"You've traveled this road more than I have. How long do you think?"

"With this mud . . . we'll be lucky if we can make it in another day."

"That's too long," Dorrin says.

"I think you're right."

Neither looks back as they plod through the drizzle and the mud.

CXL

DORRIN STRUGGLES OUT to Yarrl's wagon with another section of black iron, easing it onto the bed. The wagon creaks under the weight.

Vaos stands in the mud by the wagon, wiping his forehead in the still air. "Need any more, master Dorrin?"

"That's all for this trip. Should only take one more." Dorrin glances toward the north. So far the spring sky is clear. His eyes shift to the herb garden he has not touched. There is only so much he can do, and, if by some miracle Brede should halt the White hordes, they have more than enough herbs for the year. Besides, the perennials will continue without his help.

Frisa stands on the porch, scratching between Gilda's ears. The goat is chained to the corner post. "Can I ride with you, master Dorrin?"

"Not this time, Frisa." Dorrin closes the tailgate and climbs onto the wagon seat.

"You come inside and get your jacket, you imp," calls Merga from the kitchen.

Dorrin grins and flicks the reins. Slowly, slowly, the wagon groans its way out of the yard and downhill toward the stone-paved road. As he turns onto the road, he must swing wide to avoid a group of men and women who trudge toward Diev. In the group are three children.

None even look at the wagon as they put one foot in front of the other, one in front of the other. Their clothes, well-made, are still filthy from the mud of the road, and they all, even the children, bear good-sized packs.

Dorrin looks back up the Kleth road, squinting, and sending his perceptions. There are others walking his way. He concentrates on the road, guiding the wagon down toward lower Diev, even as his thoughts center on the refugees. If Brede cannot hold Kleth, there will be more, many more.

The wagon rumbles past the Red Lion, with its windows unshuttered and open, and past the Tankard, which is also open and serving.

Dorrin smiles wryly. For now, the war is providing business for Kyril and also for the Tankard's owner. For now.

"A copper, good ser . . . a copper, for the sake of the good darkness . . ." Beyond the Tankard, a stooped woman with two children at her ankles cries for his coins. He carries few coins, and he cannot help all those who beg.

Only a single small ship—a sloop with tall masts—is berthed at the piers. Fast and small, clearly a smuggler. A well-made wooden carriage sits at the foot of the pier. Dorrin turns the wagon toward Tyrel's.

On the hillside to the west of the shipwright's are several ragged tents, and a thin and bearded man watches as the wagon rolls into the yard and up to the blocked *Harthagay*. Dorrin pulls on the reins, and the brake, and the wagon creaks to a halt.

The ship's name will have to change, but names are not his highest concern right now.

Liedral waits, her hand on the blade she has begun to carry once more. Dorrin looks at the staff by his feet.

"Any problems?" she asks.

"No. But more refugees are beginning to walk the road from Kleth. Did you see the smuggler in the harbor?"

"It's Drein. He'll go anywhere if the coins are high enough."

"Someone with a carriage was talking passage, I think."

"There will be more." Liedral looks toward the yard where the *Harthagay* still rests on blocks out of the water. "Once she's in the water, you'll need guards." She gestures toward the hillside. "People are going to be getting more and more desperate."

"The way things are going, if Brede can't stop the Whites, we probably should think about moving everyone down here, and my smithy stuff. At least within the next eight-day. Do you want to talk to Tyrel about it while I get the last load? Or should I?"

Liedral smiles. "I already have. He'd actually feel better if you did. He's banking on you to get him out of here."

"I think everyone is."

"How many can you take?"

"A score, maybe. I don't know. I haven't finished assembling the engine. I don't know if it works. I still have to finish Brede's damnable devices, and now I have to think about moving everything out of the house and smithy." Dorrin climbs off the wagon and begins to lead the mismatched team through the gate and up alongside the ship.

"You don't like what you've done for Brede?"

"Darkness, no. You know that. Forging things to kill people? Or to stop them from killing more people? What an awful choice." He ties the horses to the post.

"That's life." Liedral smiles a tight smile. "I didn't think you cared much for the Whites."

"I don't. But so far, I don't think anything I've forged has killed any Whites—just soldiers, just their tools."

"We all make a choice of what we serve."

"And I thought making caltrops was bad." He shudders, then takes a deep breath and lets down the tailgate. "It doesn't make sense. I still can't really handle an edged weapon, but I can forge something that's worse."

"Could you make another pair of those slicers?"

Dorrin thinks, then shudders. "It would be hard. I don't know."

"There's your answer."

He looks puzzled for a minute. "You mean, in a way, I have to learn what's destructive?"

"You have to teach your feelings through experience. Isn't that how we all learn?"

Dorrin frowns as he eases the curved iron that will protect the condenser from the wagon.

Tyrel and his apprentice step into the sunlight. "Don't work so hard, master Dorrin. We'll use the hoist and swing this stuff up."

Dorrin sets down the iron and waits.

Liedral grins at him. After a moment, he grins back.

CXLI

WITH THE HEAVY tongs, Dorrin turns the plate and nods to Vaos. The striker brings down the hammer as they begin to fuller the iron into a sheet not much thicker than three or four sheets of parchment.

After several reheatings in the forge, the plate reaches the right thickness. Then Dorrin takes the bench shears and trims it, uses the flatter to rough-smooth the edges before setting it on the bricks to anneal. They begin work on the next plate.

"How many . . . of these?" pants Vaos.

"Thirty-six," Dorrin says.

"What are they for?"

"You don't want to know." The smith neither wants to explain, nor to dwell on the specifics of what they are forging. That he must forge something so destructive because he can find no other solutions is bad enough. Equally important, if Vaos does not know what they are forging, he cannot reveal it.

Vaos rolls his eyes and lifts the hammer. Dorrin slips the hot iron onto the anvil and nods.

By midday, both are soaked with sweat, even though the late spring day is cool. As he sets aside the tongs, Dorrin looks at the stack of thin iron plates. Welding and forging them into black iron boxes will be neither quick nor easy. Should he just punch and rivet the sections together? Will it make that much difference? Rivets will do. He sets the tongs in the rack. "Time for something to eat . . . and drink."

Vaos slowly racks the sledge, then rubs one shoulder blade and then the other. "We doing more after dinner?"

"It's fine work, no more heavy fullering until tomorrow. We still haven't finished all the plates."

The two walk out into the breeze, cool despite the bright and cloudless green-blue sky.

"Don't forget to wash up," Dorrin says.

"Yes, ser."

"Mistress Liedral rode over to see Reisa. That's what she said," announces Frisa as Dorrin passes the porch.

"Did she say what she was doing?" asks the smith.

"No."

"Did she take the cart?"

"She rode like you do. She even had a sword."

Dorrin pauses. Liedral has always preferred the bow. Sword? Reisa? Is Reisa doing her best to train Liedral and perhaps Petra?

He splashes cold water from the new tap across his face. Despite his precautions, the old tap had frozen and snapped, leaving a large pool of water in the middle of the yard once the ice thawed. The new tap is no better than the old, but he did not want to spend the time to design and forge something better—not while he is trying to split his time between the smithy, where he must spend some time on paying work, such as it is, and on Brede's infernal devices, and the shipyard, where he is trying to assemble his engine. He is already paying two men whom Pergun and Asavah recommended to help Tyrel guard the shipwright's yard.

"Oooffff..." Dorrin wobbles from his squatting position, almost sprawling onto the damp stones around the water tap. He turns and looks at the small white goat. The chain is just long enough to reach from the bottom post of the porch stairs to the water tap.

The smith sighs, then scratches Gilda between the ears. "Goats ... there's always some goat around." He stands up and dries his hands, moving aside to let Vaos use the water.

Then he walks across the ridge to the herb garden. His boots still sink into the soft soil. Despite his resolve not to plant or tend, already the brinn is flourishing, blue-green shoots branching out, and so is the astra.

The soft cool wind ruffles his hair, and he stoops. His fingers brush the herbs, infusing a touch more order into the weaker ones. He smiles as he straightens and heads back to his house for supper.

And after the midday meal ... after that, he must ride to Tyrel's to finish installing the steam engine on the newly renamed *Black Diamond*. The engine will work, of that he is convinced, but how well it will work is another question. Are the tolerances in the twin cylinders good enough? Are the rods strong enough?

He pushes away the questions he cannot answer until he begins to test the engine, stops by the water tap and scratches Gilda once more before he climbs the steps to the kitchen.

Over the Northern Ocean, the clouds gather.

CXLII

"THE TRADERS HAVE told their field commander, the young one from Recluce, to hold Kleth," Jeslek announces quietly. The tent billows overhead.

Fydel nods. Anya smiles brightly, and Cerryl smiles politely, with a deferential nod to the High Wizard.

"Where is Sterol?" asks Anya.

"In Fairhaven, I presume, which is fine with me. We really don't need another set of schemers." The High Wizard pauses. "Your refusal of terms from the Council was brilliant, Fydel, even if you didn't mean it that way."

"I'm so glad you found it so." Fydel smiles.

"It forced them to decide on an early defense, in order to plan their escape if it failed. Traders would always rather run than fight. This Brede of theirs is better than they deserve, young as he is, and they'll squander his talent—and him. It's a pity."

"You intend to spare him?" asks Anya, her tone almost idle.

"Demon-light, no. After what he's done to the levies . . . politically, that's not wise."

"What about your elusive smith? Hasn't he cost you even more than their commander?" Anya adds, "Drawing wire . . . much good it will do . . ."

"It cost us less than four score levies to get through his river traps, and we control the river all the way to Kleth. Brede is more dangerous."

"He's only a soldier, no matter how good," reflects Cerryl. "Your smith may have more tricks planned."

"Perhaps... but they will not save Spidlar." Jeslek smiles again.

CXLIII

DORRIN STEPS ACROSS the plank to the *Black Diamond*. On the hillside above the shipwright's, a half-dozen makeshift tents now flutter in the breeze. The smith surveys them before turning aft and descending the ladder to the engine. On each side of the compartment are coal bins, each with a chute that opens by the firebox door.

Tyrel stands by the engine. "Will it work?"

"I hope it works well enough." Dorrin bends and runs his fingers across the beams that support the engine platform. Then he opens the small hatch that provides access to the shaft. The water level in the bilges has not increased. The greased seals are holding, but will they hold when the shaft is rotating? He hopes so, but there are so many things he has not tested other than on models.

He closes the hatch and returns to the engine. There he lights the shavings, then slowly adds a shovel of the finer coal. After pacing until the fire catches, he adds another shovel of coal. He lets his senses check the heat in the water-filled cylinders through the top of the cylindrical firebox, trying to sense whether the tubes remain watertight. So far, so good.

"What now?" asks Tyrel.

"More coal, and more steam."

Dorrin waits for a time, then adds more coal. After

that he steps back to the big clutch, making sure that the screw shaft is not engaged.

Fwwuuuphhh . . . fwuppp . . . The engine begins to turn over.

Dorrin studies the black iron rods as they work, then checks the steam spill valve, opening it to watch the white vapor stream into the sky. Next comes the condenser. Already, it seems too hot. How hot is too hot? Then he checks the piping and twists a valve. How many other problems will he find? The condenser cools immediately, and he moves along to the side of the forward cylinder, listening closely for hisses or gurgles or anything unusual.

Fwwwuuuppphhh . . . fwupp . . . fwuppp . . . The engine and the flywheel pick up more speed, settling into a smooth rhythm.

Tyrel looks at the swiftly stroking rods, the planetary gear, and the flywheel. He is white. "Darkness . . ."

"You're right," Dorrin says calmly. "It's based on order." He opens the firebox door to shovel in more coal. Checking the condenser, he finds a trickle of water oozing from the bottom. More leakage.

"You're grinning, young fellow!" bellows Tyrel above the engine noise.

Dorrin is grinning, despite the leaking condenser. He climbs up to the deck and studies the harbor. Another smuggler is tied up at the far pier—a black-hulled bark. Two armed guards stand at the base of the gangway, and several wagons are lined up on the pier.

After checking the hawsers, Dorrin climbs back down to the engine room, where he shovels more coal into the firebox. Then he closes the iron door and steps to the side, where he eases the clutch into position.

Clunk . . .

He winces at the force on the gears, black iron or

not, as the shaft begins to rotate. A rough humming rises, vibrating the deck underfoot.

Dorrin opens the hatch behind the engine to check the shaft. Grease oozes from both the support collar and the hull seals. The vibration increases as the engine builds up power, then seems to level off. Dorrin sends his perceptions along the shaft, trying to sense any roughness. Although he is uncertain, he feels the shaft collar needs to be raised. He darts back to the deck and scurries aft to check the screw, and the water boiling up past the rudder. The lines tighten, and the *Black Diamond* strains at the hawsers that hold her to the flimsy pier.

Creaakkkkk . . . creeakkkk . . .

"Master Dorrin! She'll pull loose the wharf! Do something!"

Dorrin hurries back to the engine, forcing himself to go down the ladder deliberately. The heat in the engine space is nearly overpowering, and his clothes are drenched. When he reaches the clutch lever, he pulls on it. The lever does not move, even as the power to the screw continues. Dorrin again jockeys the clutch to release the gears, but the mechanism seems frozen.

"Master Dorrin! Do something!"

Dorrin walks to the side of the engine, yanking the steam release wide open.

WHHHHHEEEEEEEEEEeeeeeeeeee . . . The scream of escaping steam roaring up the tube into the atmosphere is deafening, and Dorrin wants to plug his ears. Instead, he twists another valve to reduce the water flow to the firebox. Immediately, he can sense the temperature of the tubes rising, and he reopens the water flow valve.

Clearly, he needs some sort of emergency bypass—or a better clutch—or both. He tries to move the clutch again, but it remains locked.

Still, the loss of the screaming steam reduces the power and the engine and screw slow. But it is a long time—nearly twilight—before the screw comes to an absolute stop, even though the immediate loss of power is enough to keep from threatening the wharf.

As they wait for the firebox to cool, Tyrel looks across at Dorrin. "You really got something here, young fellow."

"I hope so." Dorrin wipes his forehead. He remains hot and sweaty, despite the bucket of water brought on board by one of Tyrel's apprentices. He takes another dipper full, then splashes some across his forehead.

"Never would have believed it, excepting that everyone says you do good work." Tyrel coughs. "Told my boys that if they said a word to anyone I'd flog 'em, unless you turned 'em into toads first."

"You're making me into a monster."

"Better a live monster than having every tradesman in Diev down here the day the Whites march up the Kleth road."

"You think it's going to be that bad?"

"Worse," grumps the shipwright. "Most every merchant in Diev moved their hulls out of here early last winter—right after Elparta fell. Lot of 'em kicked themselves for letting you have the *Harthagay*—the *Diamond*, I mean. But they figured no one else could get her off the sand."

"It wasn't that hard. I read about the way it could be done when I was a boy. The Bristans do it a lot."

"How many people read? Reading's an order-based study, isn't it?"

Dorrin has never thought about that, but reading is the use of ordered symbols to convey meaning. But the chaos wizards read—he is certain of that. Again, it seems as though chaos must use order.

Another thought crosses Dorrin's mind. "Can we get some canvas? If anything happens to the engine . . ."

"I'm ahead of you, master Dorrin. You let me help you run this little ship, and bring my yard boys, and you can use anything I've got."

"Done." Dorrin doesn't even have to think. Without Tyrel, he will have no ship. "Let's go look at that clutch."

With the pressure off the gears, the clutch disengages easily. Dorrin studies the gears. "Darkness . . ."

The angle of the teeth on the gears and the tension created once the shaft starts to turn effectively create a lock. He frowns. Redesigning the clutch is definitely necessary, as is a better steam bypass system.

Tyrel watches as Dorrin moves to the condenser system. The puddle of warm water on the deck testifies to the leak. Dorrin pulls the wrench from his belt, thankful he had enough foresight to make all the bolts with the same-sized heads, and begins to remove the cover.

Once he opens the cover, he has to laugh. The problem is clearly one of condensation, and that means another set of tubes and some adjustments. Can he use the external condensate as a partial replacement of the fresh water lost from the system? Again, he nods as he loosely refastens the cover.

Even in the growing darkness, Dorrin is again sweating by the time he climbs back to the deck. After wiping his forehead, he glances at the hillside. Only a single tent remains. At least there are some benefits to a malfunction—it reduced the interest in the *Black Diamond*.

CXLIV

DORRIN LOOKS AT the black box. Then he shrugs, looking at the three holes in the road, each roughly three rods apart. He hopes the different-length fuses will burn as he has calculated. And that the wooden rods will support the smaller paving stones. And that the stones are wide enough so that one of the Certan or Gallosian horses or levies will step on them.

The two troopers wait as he sets the first thin-walled, black iron box in place, and then places the nails in position around the plunger cylinder.

"What are those for?" asks the heavy-set and sandy-haired trooper.

"To tear horses and people apart," Dorrin says quietly.

To the west, across the green of the meadows and south toward Elparta, a low cloud of dust and fires spreads on either side of the White horde. The air is clear, and the sun sparkles in the blue-green sky of spring. A chorus of *terwhits* echoes from beyond the stone wall bordering the south side of the road.

The trooper swallows.

Dorrin positions the wooden dowels that support and balance the hollowed stone. "For darkness's sake," he cautions the troopers, "don't step on that stone. You won't leave enough raw meat for a stew." He wipes his dripping forehead before he sets the stone in place.

The other trooper gulps.

Dorrin wipes his forehead. How has he gotten into the position of designing demon-devices? And installing them, when a misstep will shred him into small bits of meat?

He finishes with the first one. "Hand me the broom." Carefully, gently, he brushes dust across the stones until the whole area looks—he hopes—untraveled since the last rain.

Then he does the same with the second box, and the third.

His arms and hands are shaking by the time he finishes, and the sweat rolls down his forehead, even though a cool breeze blows from the Westhorns across the sloping plains. His head pounds with a dull aching.

Brede's troops have already cleared the herders and the few farmers, insisting all leave, and retelling the tales of Elparta. Few have needed much encouragement after learning that the Whites are marching downriver.

"Are you done?"

Dorrin looks up to see Kadara, accompanied by a trooper holding Meriwhen's reins. He wipes his forehead. "I've done what I can. I hope it works ... I think."

Kadara frowns as Dorrin slips the broom into the lanceholder next to his staff.

"Each time I design something to kill, the Whites do something worse."

"I don't think they can do much more than burn everything and torture and kill anyone who resists," Kadara says dryly. "We need to get out of here. Keep your horses on the grass until we get to the curve up there."

Dorrin follows her directions, looking back over his shoulder to gauge the progress of the White horde.

"Why aren't there any outriders?" asks the heavy trooper.

"Because we've always killed them all," answers Kadara. "That's why this just might work. This time, we didn't leave them villagers or herders to march in front of the army. So they'll be slow and crowded. I hope."

"What now?" Dorrin asks.

"We wait up on the knoll beyond the curve, right where they can see us. Brede says that way, they won't be quite so suspicious, at least not as suspicious as if they reach an open stretch of road, and see no one."

A handful of riders wearing blue trots across the meadows to the southwest, out from behind a low hill.

"They just fired some arrows and tried to lure out some outriders," Kadara tells Dorrin. "Brede wants them to think that we're still trying to harass them as well as we can."

"Darkness-damned fine commander, Brede is," mumbles the thinner trooper.

Dorrin rides and watches. The blue-clad riders approach from the west, slowing as they near the curve in the road.

"You're a darkness-better rider." Kadara reins up on the knoll overlooking the road.

"I've had practice."

Leading the long advance, that train of riders and foot soldiers that stretches two kays back toward Elparta, are two squads of cavalry under the purple banners of Gallos. Behind the vanguard, separated by less than a dozen rods, are the first Gallosian levies. Behind the first set of levies, a half-hundred rods back, are the shimmering banners of the White Wizards.

As the wizards pass, the grasses blacken and shrivel, with fires started by firebolts that strike the far edges of the meadows bordering the road. The effect is to leave a green ribbon winding through blackened and sooty fields and meadows.

"Why doesn't the wind carry the fires toward the road?" asks the heavy trooper.

"It will," Dorrin says, "but not until later. That's why they throw the firebolts so far out."

The second group of Spidlarian riders reins up beside the four who wait. One horse is riderless.

"They got Ertel. I hope this works." The woman trooper looks at Kadara, then at Dorrin. "This your Black mage?"

"I'm a smith, mostly."

The woman turns to Kadara, dismissing Dorrin. "How long?"

Kadara glances at Dorrin.

"I tried to set it so that it would blow around the first wizards."

"Those are the young ones. Their High Wizard—his name's Jeslek—is way back . . . way back."

"I couldn't make the fuses any longer." '

"Well . . . better some wizards than none."

" . . . darkness, yes . . ."

" . . . pot any wizard in a storm . . ."

Dorrin finds himself holding his breath as the vanguard oozes slowly uphill and onto the level stretch where his devices rest.

He watches. Has one horse stumbled? Did the plunger work?

The vanguard passes over the mined section, and the first group of levies clears the area.

"Darkness! When will something happen?" mumbles the heavy trooper.

"A little longer . . ." Dorrin says, hoping . . . not knowing what he hopes, for he has used order to create great potential for chaos. And yet, what can he do? The people of Spidlar do not deserve to be killed or burned because they oppose chaos.

The purple banners advance, as do the white ones. The vanguard slows as the mounted troopers near the curve in the road, as they see the Spidlarian Guards on the knoll. Behind them, the column slows, and begins to bunch up.

CRRRRRuuummmmmpppp!!!! Earth, stones, bodies, blood . . . undefined shreds spray skyward.

CRRRRRuuummmmmppppp!!!! A second gout of colored soil, stones, and flesh erupts into the sky.

CRRRRRuuummmmmppppp!!!! By the third gout of gore, Dorrin is blind from the pain that has seared through him, barely able to hang on to Meriwhen.

None of the troopers speaks.

The first line of white banners is no more, nor is the second group of levies, nor the third. From pits below the knoll, perhaps a score of archers appear, and begin to fire upon the vanguard and the remaining Gallosian levies. The vanguard circles, then charges the knoll.

By the time Dorrin can breathe and straighten up in the saddle, only two mounted Gallosian troopers remain, and they ride back toward the Gallosian levies—fully half of whom are either lying on or around the road, or wounded. The remaining Gallosian levies scramble rearward, toward the green banners of Certis.

"Too bad we can't follow up," Kadara says.

Dorrin rubs his forehead, seeing the carnage intermittently, between flashes of white and black that seem to cycle behind his eyes. His breath is ragged, his thoughts scattered.

"Not enough troops. We've got maybe two thousand trained people left. They've got twice that down there—or they did."

"Got a couple hundred, maybe more."

The woman trooper who had earlier dismissed Dorrin looks at him slowly. "Darkness help us if they had you."

"It helps, but it's not enough." Kadara shakes her head. "Let's go." She looks at Dorrin. "Can you do something like that again—but different?"

"Maybe once more," he admits. "But not for a time. It will have to be in a forest, or something. They'll watch the stones now." He urges Meriwhen to keep up with the redhead. "I only have three more devices. They're hard to make." He says little more because he does not want to reveal where the devices are, not so close to the Whites, not when he has finally struck at the Wizards themselves. The black flashes that momentarily blind him continue less frequently, but the pounding headache does not subside, and he squints against the light that has become almost too bright for him to see.

"Can't someone else make them?" asks the hard-voiced woman trooper.

"It takes a Black smith who's an engineer and a healer," Kadara says wearily. "Do you know any others?"

CXLV

A BREEZE CARRIES though the room where a handful of tables and benches seems lost in the center. The walls are planks nailed to heavy beams, and occasionally, shafts of hay sift through the low ceiling from the former hayloft above. Two squads of troopers lie on bedrolls in one end of the barn.

Dorrin chews on bread and cheese that Kadara had rounded up from somewhere, trying to ignore his headache, the searing light that still blasts through his skull intermittently, and his growling stomach.

While the second set of mines was not quite as spectacular as the first, the explosions were great enough that Kadara's squad had to load him on Meriwhen. He does not remember much about the ride

back to Kleth. How much more success he can take is
another question. All he wants is to return to Diev.
Clearly, warfare is not for him.

"As soon as I'm feeling a little better, I'll be
leaving."

"Dorrin, you can't travel that road again. You just
can't," snaps Kadara. "The White Wizards would send
three or four squads after you now."

Dorrin slowly eats the bread and cheese. What
Kadara says makes sense, too much sense. But no one
in Diev knows he will be staying. "Will your armorer
mind if I work here?"

"You're the only hope we may have, and you worry
about that?"

"I didn't bring any tools."

"I wouldn't worry about that, either. Welka won't
mind. Besides, Brede needs you now. He'd have my
head if we let you go unprotected—and we really don't
have any way to protect you."

If he is the last hope of Kleth, the city is doomed.
In the time before the White horde arrives, he can
forge perhaps another dozen devices similar to those
he used on the road. If they are well-placed, if the
Whites do not notice them, if they work as designed,
if Brede can round up enough raw materials to make
the gunpowder, or find some . . . if, if, if . . .

He rubs his forehead. Even contemplating what he
must build intensifies the headache that never seems
to leave him now. Darkness knows what will happen
if his linked mines work as designed. He takes a last
bite of the bread and cheese and sips the thin beer—
Kadara says that the water is not safe to drink, and
he doesn't want to search for potable water.

"Aren't you eating?" Dorrin asks Kadara.

"I'm not hungry right now." A faint look of distaste
crosses her face. "Do you want any more?"

"No. This was fine." His headache has subsided to

a faint throbbing, and only occasionally do the flashes of blackness flicker before his eyes. Why is Kadara not hungry? Is she healthy? "Are you all right?" he asks, extending a hand to touch her wrist.

"I'm fine." She jerks away her hand, but not before Dorrin has a sense of her problem. "I'm sorry, Dorrin. This isn't easy now. We're outnumbered, and the Council won't let us retreat."

"They're still insisting?"

"Of course. You think they want to risk their skins? That's what we're paid for."

"Don't they understand?"

"No. They still think that somehow they can buy off the Whites."

The door to the yard opens, and Brede steps inside, accompanied by the faint odor of horse manure. His blue tunic looks like he has slept in it for an eight-day, and his normally smooth-shaven face is covered with blond stubble.

Kadara gives a half-salute, half-wave. "Hail, great commander."

"Hail, great squad leader." Brede's grin fades too quickly as he steps toward the table.

Dorrin takes another sip of beer, and finishes the bread in his hand.

"Kadara," asks Brede, "can your people check out whether the Whites are sending outriders toward the road to Diev? Rydner is checking on the old Axalt road."

"Now?"

"You don't have to go. You could send some of your squad."

Kadara snorts. "You want it done right, don't you?" She gets up from the bench on the other side of the table. "How far?"

"If you can't see any evidence within ten kays, there

won't be anything. They aren't about to try the Kylen Hills."

"I wish they would." Kadara turns to Dorrin. "You need to get busy."

"I know."

"Good luck, Kadara," Brede says gently.

She walks toward the bedrolled troopers at the far end. "Stow your bedrolls, and saddle up. Scout run to the south. I'll see you in the yard."

Brede slides onto the bench beside Dorrin, watching as Kadara leaves the barn by the end door, heading for the stable that remains a stable. His eyes remain on the closed door through which she has left.

Outside of a few groans, there are no complaints from the troopers who struggle up in the wake of Kadara's orders.

Dorrin slides the half-full pitcher of beer to Brede, and the chipped mug. "You look like you need this."

"Thank you." Brede refills the mug and swallows about half of it in one gulp, but his eyes drift back in the direction of the stable he cannot see. After a moment, he leans forward, but he does not say anything, instead wetting his lips.

"Kadara?" prompts Dorrin.

Brede nods.

Dorrin understands Brede's silence, even though a part of him finds it amusing that the always-eloquent Brede is having trouble speaking his mind. "She's a little touchy."

"Isn't she always?" Brede asks with a laugh that dies too soon.

"Do you want me to guess?" Dorrin tries not to sound sharp, but his head still throbs, and he feels sore all over.

"You know, don't you?"

"That she's carrying your child? But not until just before you arrived."

"Did she tell you?"

"Of course not." Dorrin forces a grin. "She may not even know that I know. She jerked away from me when I touched her arm."

"It wasn't a good idea. Not now."

Dorrin disagrees, at least in a way, since Brede has been told to hold Kleth at any cost. "Was it her doing?"

"She told me..." Brede looks around the near-empty room and lowers his voice. "... that if I were going to be a demon-damned hero I should at least leave her something."

The smith nods slowly. Will it make any difference? Will any of them leave the battlefield for Kleth alive? "She feels strongly. How do you feel?"

"I love her. It doesn't always show, and I just can't leave these people. I'm not talking about the traders. I mean the troops, and the farmers—people like your Yarrl and Reisa and Petra." Brede refills the mug, rubs his neck and shoulders, and then his eyes. "If... if... anything happens... and you're there..."

"I think you're more likely to survive this than me."

"That's demon crap. Will you take care of her?" Brede's eyes bore into Dorrin.

"If I'm there... yes." Dorrin looks at the table, feeling guilty because he still wants to finish and sea-test the *Black Diamond*, guilty because he has doubts about the usefulness of throwing himself into a battle when his success may blind him—possibly forever. "What does the battle look like?"

"Not good. They've added another five thousand levies from Hydlen. We'll do what we can. But with everything I can drag together, we're talking perhaps thirty-five hundred troops—and you."

"I appreciate the flattery," Dorrin says dryly, rubbing his forehead. "How long do I have to work this magic?"

"The way they're advancing—maybe ten days."

"Is there any way I can tell Liedral where I am?"

"I don't think you'll have to." Brede shakes his head. "I had Tylkar—he was the one raising the last levy in Diev—request that she come back with the levies. They should be here tomorrow."

"Wasn't that a little presumptuous?"

"Darkness, yes. But I'd use whatever I could to keep you here. This isn't a game, Dorrin. A lot of people are going to die."

The smith swallows. In Brede's and Kadara's terms, he never really had a choice about staying. He could have left—they couldn't hold him—except for Liedral. "You're a bastard."

"I had to learn that." Brede coughs. "Welka's expecting you. You've also got the small room in the headquarters next to mine. That's the least I can do now, and little enough." He laughs harshly as he stands.

Dorrin watches as the tall blond commander strides out of the converted barn. Then he stands up. He needs to find the armorer and begin forging destruction.

CXLVI

THE SPIDLARIAN FORCES comprise an entrenched circle on the hillside. The road from Elparta to Kleth angles up the slope from southwest to southeast. To the east lie the bluffs overlooking the river, and to the west, the hill slopes downward into the Devow Marsh, which stretches westward a good four kays. Beyond the marsh are the Kylen Hills, rugged and filled with pot-holes and crumbling sandstone ledges.

Dorrin peers over the earthworks at the banners on the lower and opposing hill—the crimson of Hydlen, the purple of Gallos, the green of Certis, the gold of Kyphros, and, of course, the crimson-edged white of Fairhaven. He looks uphill, hoping that Liedral will stay with the rear guard, wishing that she had stayed in Kleth itself.

The sky is covered with high thin clouds that give a gray cast to the morning. A light breeze out of the south, barely lifting the banners of the White forces, carries the odor of burned fields uphill.

A thin wavering horn sounds from the chaos forces.

Dorrin's eyes flicker from the earthen barriers to the troops arrayed across the low valley. After a second blast from the horn, fire gouts from the area of the white banners, flaring toward the Spidlarian hillside, spreading until it impacts. Only a handful of screams follows the fire, demonstrating the effectiveness of the earthworks against the direct impact of the wizards' fire. Several thin lines of greasy black smoke spiral into the sky. A second line of fire follows the first, with even less impact.

Then the ground shakes.

The blue-clad riders stand by their blindfolded mounts, waiting for the shaking to end, calming the nervous animals.

Dorrin grins. So far, Brede has anticipated the wizards' tactics.

A semi-hush falls across the hills, and Dorrin waits. Then the purple banners surge uphill toward the lower front line of timbered trenches where the outlines of Spidlarian pikes and halberds wait. Only a handful of troops are there, and they should be scuttling back up the trench to higher ground.

Behind his own higher timbered wall, Dorrin holds his breath, his perceptions trying to check the situation, hoping that the last troops will be up the trench before he must act.

The Gallosian troops crash over the first line, and pour into the trenchworks, splitting to follow the trenches to the higher emplacements. Dorrin swallows and pulls the line buried in the wooden casing that sticks out of the side of the shallow pit. Once the line is taut, and his senses tell him that the striker has lit, he pulls the second line, the one that removes the supports from one section of the casing. Then he climbs out of the pit and begins to refill the area around the flattened wooden casing.

"Now!" he snaps to the two men beside him. "Shovel."

They shovel as if the demons of light were after them, and before the fuse lit by the striker has reached the buried charges.

The purple banners continue to push uphill, nearly halfway to the higher emplacements. Arrows—not many, but enough—fly toward the first ranks, trying to slow them.

Dorrin gnaws on his lower lip, hoping his advice to Brede—pulling back the troops and leaving wooden weapons decoys—will be borne out. He sits down, fearing what is about to happen, both to the advancing troops, and to him. The banners follow the troops near the trenches, with attendant shouts, as the Gallosians sense victory, despite the handfuls of arrows that rain down upon their uphill charge.

CRUUUMPPPPPP!!!! The hillside erupts, and even the clay-filled pit under Dorrin wells up, throwing him against the wall and plastering him with clay.

"Light," screams one soldier.

The other gurgles for a moment. Dorrin tries not to claw out his eyes from the pain and from seeing the splinters of wood protruding from the man's abdomen and throat.

His own shoulder burns, and he blinks at the wooden barb that has ripped through his jacket and tunic. His senses tell him that the wound is flesh only, and he slowly works out the wood, fumbling with the dressing in the small pack he has carried, before finally wedging one in place.

Only then does he look downhill at the mass of churned earth that has covered almost all of the charging Gallosians. The wave of whiteness from the devastation strikes him, and he slumps to the bottom of the trench under his own darkness, darkness propelled with a white agony that slams at his skull.

"Where is he . . .?"

Words pass by, as he lies there, vaguely aware of Spidlarian troopers easing their way downhill toward his observation trench, or what is left of it. How long he has lain there, he does not know, only that his head pounds.

"Light! Look at this mess."

"Ugggghhhh . . ." Someone retches.

"This one looks like a pincushion." The voice is cool.

"Where's Dorrin?"

At the sound of Liedral's voice, Dorrin tries to open his eyes, but the blackness remains, despite the diffused warmth of the midmorning sun that tries to penetrate the high clouds. Slowly, his fingers touch his fluttering eyelids. His eyes are open, but he cannot see.

"One of them's alive. His hand moved."

"That's the smith."

Dorrin coughs, bringing up a mixture of bile and what tastes like clay. With Liedral's help, he sits up. His head pounds. When it does not pound, a fire burns within his skull. She eases some cider down his throat.

Finally, he coughs again. "What . . . happened? After the explosion?"

"Nothing," Liedral says. "What was left of the Gallosians withdrew to their positions."

"Probably not a score of their two thousand left," adds one of the troopers accompanying Liedral.

Dorrin swallows. "Two thousand?"

"See why the Force Leader wanted us to help him?" demands another voice in the darkness.

Dorrin tries to reach out with his senses and gain an impression of those around him. With effort, he gains the blurred image of Liedral and three other troopers.

"What's the matter?" Liedral asks. "You aren't looking at me."

"I can't see you," he admits. "I can't see anything."

"Shit!" exclaims one of the troopers.

"I need to get him out of here," Liedral says.

"We'll help. Leastwise, he got rid of those damned Gallosians."

Dorrin staggers along the trench, partly leaning on Liedral, losing track of the direction in which they are heading. Even before they have reached the hilltop, the effort leaves Dorrin shaking. Each step seems to intensify the pain in his head.

In the distance, he can hear screams, horses, and shouts. He tries to take another step, but the darkness is too heavy, and pounds him into the damp soil.

CXLVII

"DARKNESS WITH THIS measured approach!" snaps Jeslek.

"It was your idea," observes Anya.

"So? I can be wrong." Jeslek looks across to the

hillside that resembles an instantly churned and plowed field.

"You can? I never would have guessed it." Anya's voice is bitter.

"Fydel," orders Jeslek, "have all the levies march over the mined ground there."

"What?"

"The one thing we know is that they can't have planted more of those devices where they already exploded. And we don't want them to retreat and mine another section of hill or field."

Even Fydel nods at the logic.

"Everything that damned smith has done requires advance preparation. We can't give him any more chances. Order the charge. Pour everything into that point. And keep the troops moving."

"Yes, Jeslek."

"I mean it. Keep them moving."

As Jeslek turns to survey the battlefield, Anya and Fydel exchange glances. They nod.

Then Fydel hurries toward the field commander's tent.

CXLVIII

THE SOUNDS OF metal on metal rumble in the distance, and the ground trembles under him. Muffled curses, yells, grunts, and other assorted sounds creep toward him, but the sharp, knife-edged whiteness that throbs and slashes within his forehead continues to dominate his consciousness.

He swallows, and feels something cool against his lips. "Drink this, Dorrin . . . please."

The voice is gentle, and he sips slowly. Is it his

imagination, or is the pain in his head receding slightly?

"Dorrin?"

He recognizes Brede's voice.

"He's blind," Liedral says. "Are you satisfied?"

"Satisfied?"

"You can't expect a Black smith to create so much destruction and not suffer, can you? Even your great Creslin was blind most of his life."

Brede sighs loudly enough for Dorrin to hear. "I'm sorry." He half turns. "You troopers need to get back to your units. The Whites are pressing the attack." His voice is lower when he turns back to Liedral and Dorrin. "What do you expect from me? We're out-numbered ten to one, and I probably won't leave the field."

Liedral swallows. "I'm sorry."

"Don't be. We all end up doing what we have to. Get Dorrin back to Diev. Go around Kleth."

"I can ride," Dorrin snaps. "I've got some perception. Not much, but enough."

"You're not riding. The cart can carry two. And you need to rest."

"Keep him in hand, Liedral." A silence follows before Brede speaks again. "I've got to go. Good luck." Dorrin gains the sense of a sad smile. "You did more than anyone, Dorrin. Darkness be with you. Don't wait too long." Brede turns back toward a chorus of voices clamoring for his attention.

"Where are you putting the old pikes?"

"Can Hydre's troopers crack the flank . . ."

"What about the Certan heavy foot . . ."

Dorrin tries to sit up, but the white knives within his skull burn more brightly, and are relieved by the darkness.

When he wakes again, the ground still shivers, and

the sounds of metal on metal are closer, and the screams more piercing.

"Dorrin, you have to get up . . . I can't carry you."

Slowly, slowly, he sits up.

"Here's some water." Liedral presses the water to his lips, and he drinks.

The water, now lukewarm, helps, and the throbbing in his skull recedes to heavy dull aching.

"Can you stand up? Just lean on me." Liedral's voice is insistent.

The smith stands, and his legs hold.

"Come on." Liedral tugs Dorrin's arm, and they head downhill away from the sounds of battle. She stops. "You're still bleeding a little."

"Took a wooden dart or something in the arm. It's all right."

"Are you sure?"

"As these things go. I'm more worried about seeing. My engine isn't finished."

"Your engine? You're thinking about your engine at a time like this?" Liedral's voice rises.

"Do you want me to think about the destruction I've already created?" His words slur, perhaps because of the effort it takes to speak.

"I'm sorry. But I'm not."

Dorrin moves away from her and onto the flatter meadowland, sensing Meriwhen, and his staff in the lanceholder ahead. He stumbles, but catches himself and struggles on through the damp ground. Behind them, horses approach.

Dorrin tries to cast out his perceptions, but the white knives stab inside his skull, and he waits, hoping the cavalry are Spidlarians.

"There's the smith-healer—and the trader," calls a voice.

"You the one called Liedral?" asks another voice.

"Yes." Liedral's voice is cautious. "Oh . . . darkness . . ."

Dorrin catches the anguish in her tone. "What is it?"

Liedral does not answer, but she stops and looks toward the horses.

"Can you take care of the squad leader?"

"Of course, my cart's up there. Can you put her in it?"

"Kadara?" rasps Dorrin.

"She's . . . wounded . . . unconscious . . ."

Dorrin forces himself to the cart, just touching Liedral for guidance.

"Let me arrange this . . . put her there . . ."

"We've got to get back. They're coming up the side . . . Owe her this, but the Force Leader needs us."

"Go!" snaps Liedral. She turns toward the stake that holds the harness and leads, and Meriwhen's reins.

Dorrin reaches out and touches the unconscious figure. Kadara breathes, but shallowly. He pushes back his own pain, trying to sense her injuries: the fractured collar bone, the deep slash across the upper arm, and some sort of bruise-gash above her ear.

"Dorrin . . . you can't . . ."

"Not much," he grunts. "Bleeding's stopped. Need to get out of here."

He turns toward where he senses the mare. "Meriwhen . . . girl?"

Whheeee . . .

"I'm here, girl." He steps across the uneven ground and pats the mare's neck, feeling for the reins. Liedral lets go, and Dorrin takes them. "I'll ride."

"You can't."

"I can. I have to."

"You're impossible."

Dorrin feels his way into the saddle.

"You can't ride."

"I can follow you." Dorrin waits for Liedral. His fingers grip the black staff, and for a moment, but only a moment, the mud-tramped meadow stretches before him, and there is no pounding in his skull, only the burning in his shoulder. Just as quickly, the vision is gone, and the hammers of his headache return. He takes a deep breath, hoping that concentrating on order will return his vision, at least before too long.

"You're a stubborn man." After fastening the tail-board of the cart, Liedral climbs onto the cart seat.

"You should be glad for that, woman."

"How is your arm?"

"The bleeding's mostly stopped. How's Kadara?" Dorrin lets Meriwhen follow the cart along the rutted tracks that lead to the main road.

"She's pale, but she's breathing."

The cart lurches onward, and Kadara moans. Dorrin purses his lips tightly, and follows.

"Who's there?"

"It's the smith—the Black one . . . he's wounded," answers a voice next to the picket post.

"No one's supposed to be going back that way."

"You want to tangle with him?" asks a third voice.

Dorrin concentrates on following Liedral as the cart bounces through the meadow and onto the road. Each effort to sense where they travel intensifies the pain, and he tries just to follow the cart, letting Liedral and Meriwhen lead him along.

CXLIX

"HERE COME THE Certan bastards," mumbles Cirras.

"Just hold the first two lines," Brede commands. "They'll bring up the Kyphrans before long."

As Brede watches from the slit in his earthworks, the green banners fall, cut down by the blue-clad Spidlarians, who, once the Certan levies drop, and the remainder scatter, scurry back into their earthworks so quickly that only a few fall to the fireballs of the White Wizards. Brede nods. So far, so good. His men have remembered the danger of the wizards' fireballs. He glances toward the other squad leader, Rydner.

Rydner nods. "Ready, Commander."

Two messengers stand behind the squad leaders. Each carries a black iron shield. Brede looks back through the slit in the earthworks, wishing he had more of Dorrin's demon-devices, but hoping that Dorrin has been able to save Kadara, and their child.

Another trumpet sounds from the far side of the valley, wavering but insistent, in the midafternoon sun.

"They aren't going to wait us out. That's for sure," observes Cirras.

"After that?" asks Brede wryly, pointing to the churned earth on the hillside below.

Even before the trumpet dies away, the golden banners begin the march uphill toward the upper Spidlarian earthworks. Despite the arching fall of arrows, the Kyphran levies reach—and pass—the lowest of the three lines.

"Bring in Bylla's levies," Brede decides.

"That will leave the right side weak."

"It may, but they're not attacking the right. Not yet."

Cirras nods at one messenger, and the two scuttle away through the trench. Shortly, Cirras returns. "They're moving over."

Brede watches as the gold banners stall at the second line of trenches. The arrows redouble for an instant. The blond man turns to Cirras. "Get your squad ready. They'll bring some horse up the right and try to sweep across. Try to wait until the last moment, and close as fast as you can. That should make it harder for them to use the fireballs."

Cirras nods. "Yes, ser."

As he leaves, Brede adds, "I'll be behind you in a bit."

Rydner frowns, chews on his lip.

Cirras straightens, and Brede takes a quiet and deep breath, his eyes flicking from Cirras back to the hillside below as the Gallosian horse charges his right flank, that side of the hill slightly less steep than the center or the left. A handful of the White horsemen falls to arrows, but the flight of arrows ceases as the wizards' fireballs pepper the trenches protecting the archers. While few archers are seared, neither can the others see clearly enough to aim while remaining beneath the protection of the earthen berm.

"When should we—" begins Rydner.

"Not yet. Not until they close. You go down to them, and not a handful of you would make it."

The Gallosian cavalry turns the end of the earthworks below and to Brede's right and begins to cut down the levies from above and behind. Like a squall cloud, two squads of Spidlarian cavalry slam into the Gallosian horse from behind.

Brede races through the trenches, down to the archers, long blade in hand. "Now! Hit the gold banners! There!"

The archers emerge from the earth; the bows tighten; and the wave of shafts topples scores more of the Kyphran levies.

Brede hurries along the trenchworks toward the right upper level, trying to keep his head low, ignoring seared bodies, or blue figures transfixed with arrows.

Firebolts flash after him, even as he drops into a trench. "Move! Toward the center."

"But—" The serjeant sees the blade and the fire in

Brede's eyes. "Nyta, Jort . . . toward the center. Move, you slizzards!"

Brede circles back through the trenches, back up to where Rydner and his squad wait. He swings into the saddle, leading them toward the right side of the hilltop. He gestures to Rydner. "Now!"

"Yes, ser." Rydner leans forward, blade out, and the troopers follow downhill.

They collide with less than a handful of Gallosian horse. Brede's sword flashes twice, and two men fall.

"Archers!" Brede's voice booms out, and the handful of archers remaining looses shafts at the score of Kyphran levies still assaulting the middle earthworks.

As the archers loose their shafts, the fireballs return. Screams and black oily smoke twist uphill. The firebolts fall across both Cirras's and Rydner's squads as the remaining troopers and their mounts scramble back uphill to join Brede's small force behind the earth-banked wall. The few archers still alive duck into the earthworks.

Brede holds up his blade. "Wait until they reach the top. Then close as quickly as possible." He catches Cirras's eyes.

Cirras nods grimly. Rydner wipes his blade with a rag he stuffs back into his belt.

The trumpet sounds once more, and another wave of mounted troops surges uphill toward the Spidlarian forces. The Hydlen levies pour after the mix of Kyphrans and Gallosians, and all hack their way through the few remaining Spidlarians.

The White cavalry, now a mixture of forces from Certis, Gallos, and Hydlen, churns up the right flank unopposed except for a few scattered arrows. Three White troopers fall, but the attack does not falter.

Brede watches, then nods. "Now!"

The blond officer spurs his mount from behind the concealed revetment, slashing through the White forces, his sword flickering like lightning. Three men fall to that lethal blade before the Whites realize Brede and his force are even among them.

"Magic . . .!"

"The blond demon . . ."

Troopers scattering from Brede fall to the blades of others, and the White forces break, clattering and scrambling away.

"Back!" snaps Brede, ducking instinctively even before the firebolt singes his hair and turns the officer behind him—Rydner—into a torch.

"Poor bastard . . ." mutters Brede under his breath.

The force behind the makeshift revetment numbers less than a full squad. Brede eases his mount up to the wood-backed earthen berm. He stretches in the saddle to peer over the top, glancing to the left side of the field, where the levies from Hydlen have turned the flank and are beginning to circle back, and then to the hillside below where the White cavalry has begun to re-form.

"Archers!"

Only a handful of shafts wavers toward the White cavalry, and the archers are silenced by a line of fire that blankets their trench. The Hydlen levies march grimly back toward the Spidlarians, completing the encircling movement.

Brede looks at the thin line of foot that his squad could break through, then turns to the hillside below.

Another trumpet sounds, and the White horse begins the charge.

Again, Brede waits until the enemy troopers are almost to the hilltop before he drops his sword. The Spidlarian forces surge forth, and again, Brede's blade flashes like the lightning of high summer, smashing through nearly three lines of White cavalry, scattering them.

"To the hill!" the blond officer commands, ducking

as another firebolt seeks him; but less than a handful of cavalry in blue remains to follow him.

The half-score archers left in the uppermost of the earthworks begin to target the remaining White horsemen, picking them off one by one, until fireballs rain across the hillside. Then the Kyphran foot marches toward the crest of the hill. Amid groans, screams, and dust, they clear the last earthworks that protect the archers.

Brede turns his mount, sees a Kyphran footman spear an archer, and swings downhill. Cirras and the other four follow, slashing down another score of levies.

Brede straightens in the saddle as the firebolts fall, lifting his sword yet again, his eyes flicking to the north and west, toward the road to Diev, before the firebolt burns through him. Even so, as the flames consume him, he hurls his blade through a last footman. His smile is bitter.

It is nearly twilight as the last of the White forces gain the hilltop. There are no Spidlarians left as the White banners, hanging limply, precede the wizards past the charred heaps littering the hillside.

The red-headed wizard's eyes linger on one blackened corpse fractionally before she follows Jeslek to the clearing.

"We cannot afford another battle such as this," states the field commander, wiping his forehead. "We have lost more than half our force."

"Two-thirds," suggests a voice from behind the commander.

"You won't have any more battles at all," Jeslek says. "Only a few skirmishes on the way to Spidlaria. They have no troops at all left."

"I hope to the light you are correct."

"I am," snaps Jeslek. "We move to take the whole river valley first. Leave a small force here to guard the road to Diev. Once we secure Spidlaria, we'll take Diev."

"As you wish."

Anya and Fydel exchange glances. Cerryl's face is politely impassive.

CL

THE CART CREAKS. Meriwhen whickers. Kadara moans. Dorrin rubs his forehead, wondering in his darkness how much distance they have covered.

"Drink a little . . . please . . ." Liedral wets Kadara's lips. "Dorrin, she's hot, and she can't drink."

Dorrin guides Meriwhen next to the wagon, and dismounts slowly. "Could I have a sip?"

"Oh . . . here."

After he drinks, Dorrin touches his staff, trying to hold on to the cool blackness, the cool sense of order. Then his fingertips brush Kadara's forehead, and he tries to transfer some of that order to her.

" . . . ooo . . . aaaa . . ."

Despite the moans, Kadara does not rouse, nor can she drink.

"How far have we come?" Dorrin asks.

"Perhaps a quarter of the way—just beyond the turnoff for the charcoal camp. We'll have to stop before long. It's getting dark, and I can't see like you can at night."

"Like I could," he corrects.

Liedral rustles in the cart, and finally hands something to Dorrin. "Bread and cheese."

He chews slowly, evenly, listening to the rustle of the leaves, the occasional *terwhits* and chirps.

"Ready?" Liedral finally asks.

"Oh, yes." Still almost in a daze, he climbs back on Meriwhen.

Again, the cart creaks. Meriwhen snuffles. Kadara moans. Dorrin rubs his forehead, wondering in his black prison how much more distance they have covered.

The feeling of darkness grows as they struggle along the packed and rutted road that is now empty, until Liedral finally reins up at a wider spot in the road, with a clearing and a gap in the tumbled stone wall wide enough for the cart.

"I can't go any longer."

"Fine," Dorrin mumbles, half-asleep in the saddle.

"Neither can you."

Mechanically, Dorrin follows Liedral's directions.

"Tie up Meriwhen to the stake."

Dorrin does, fumbling with the leathers.

"Can you unsaddle her?"

Dorrin fumbles the girths loose by feel and unsaddles the mare, patting her flanks as he does.

"Can you sense enough to help me move Kadara?"

He holds the surprisingly thin and fevered body of the redhead while Liedral arranges blankets.

"Set her down here."

He does, wincing. "Oooo . . ."

"Oh, I'm sorry. Does your shoulder hurt?"

"Not too much." Not so much as Kadara does, or even as his head, although there is no physical damage within his skull.

"You need to eat and drink this."

He mechanically chews more stale and crusty bread and warm cheese, drinking water from the jug Liedral has filled from somewhere.

Before long, he lies down under the shelter of the uptilted cart, with Liedral on his left, Kadara on the other side of Liedral. He sleeps for a time, then wakes—although it is still dark, he senses.

Dorrin smiles at Liedral's light snoring, barely audible above the sounds of the insects in the trees bordering this stretch of the road. Most of the trees, Dorrin recalls, date from the climate change brought about by the great Creslin, when the former upland farms and meadows did not get enough spring and summer rain.

The throbbing in his skull has subsided some, but he remains sightless.

"Oh ... no ... darkness, no! Brede ... don't leave me ..." Kadara's words are half whimpered, half murmured. "Don't ... oh ... bastards ... white bastards ..."

Liedral wakes with a start, then turns and touches Kadara. "Easy, easy. You're all right."

"Where ... who?"

"Liedral ... Dorrin and I are here."

"Brede ... where is he?"

"He's still in Kleth," Liedral says quickly. She eases out from between the two injured forms. "Let me get you some water."

" ... never leave there ... darkness ... arm hurts ..."

"It will take a while to heal," Dorrin adds.

" ... took four of the bastards ... head hurts ... Brede ... miss you ..."

"Drink this," Liedral says.

Dorrin sits up. "Can you get my small pack? There's some astra in it."

"Why didn't you think about that—Sorry."

"It's hard to think when white knives are slashing through your skull."

"I said I was sorry."

"It's all right." Dorrin takes the pack and fumbles for the packets, identifying them by shape, scent, and sense. "Put this one in place of the dressing on her arm. Can you?"

"I'll need to light this candle."

Dorrin waits until Liedral takes the first dressing, then searches for the crushed astra.

"Oh! Light! . . . hurts," moans Kadara.

"Anything else?" asks Liedral. Her voice is curt.

"Is there any way to get this in her?"

"I'll try."

A clinking and other rustling sounds follow. Dorrin can sense that Liedral is working with some utensils.

"Open your mouth, please . . . Kadara."

" . . . so bitter . . . like poison . . . You aren't hurting me, are you?"

"I'm not hurting you. This will make you feel better."

" . . . so bitter . . . what . . . ?"

"It's astra mixed with beragin," Dorrin explains calmly.

Liedral continues to rattle things for a time, before returning and stretching out between Dorrin and Kadara again.

Dorrin reaches out and squeezes her hand. "Thank you."

She squeezes his in return. "Go to sleep."

In time, he does, not to wake until the chirpings of the dawn birds seep into his awareness. He still cannot see, but his headache has subsided into a duller ache. Liedral is already up, moving quietly, watering the horses.

Dorrin slips out from under the cart, careful not to touch it or the braces that hold it in position.

"There's still some bread and cheese," Liedral offers.

"Thank you." Dorrin takes the chunk of bread and the slab of cheese that she has sliced, then sits on the stone wall by the road. "Still using the cheese slicer?"

"It's a lot more comfortable. I still shiver when I look at a knife." Liedral sits beside him. "It's pretty this morning."

"I'm sorry."

"It wasn't your fault." Liedral's fingers touch his cheek.

"I wish I could believe that. They went after you because you loved me."

"I still love you, you impossible man." She reaches out and squeezes his wrist. "I wish you could see the trees on the hill. They look like shining silver in the light, with the dew on the leaves."

"So do I."

They eat silently.

"Kadara's still sleeping. Is that good?"

"If we can keep getting her to drink, and get more of the medicine in her. She needs liquids."

"Do you want any more bread or cheese?"

"Is there enough?"

"Merga sent me off with as much as she could get together. We still have four loaves left—stale, but we won't go too hungry before we get back."

Dorrin eats another half loaf of bread and more cheese. While he is finishing, Liedral gets up, and his thoughts turn back to order again.

While some believe in order as a god, almost, order has to be more mechanical than that. Otherwise, how could good people be punished for the means they use? He sips from the jug. Or do the means compromise the ends? Always?

He thinks of Fairhaven. The city, despite the rule of those who espouse chaos, is orderly, and there is little crime. There seems to be less poverty than in Spidlar. But is that because Fairhaven has become wealthy from its conquests?

"Dorrin, if we want to get back to Diev without being . . . caught by . . ."

Dorrin understands. Who knows who will be on the road behind them before long? He slowly makes his way into the woods for certain necessities. By the time he returns, Liedral is kneeling, spooning more of the astra and beragin into Kadara's mouth.

" . . . uuugggg . . ." Kadara swallows and coughs, but most of the mixture goes down, and Liedral eases water into her mouth.

While Liedral ministers to Kadara, Dorrin manages to saddle Meriwhen by himself, although he pinches one finger in the girth buckle in the process. He mutters grumpily under his breath at his clumsiness, but continues finishing saddling the mare.

For just an instant, when he touches the black wood of his staff, he can see—the grass is damp with dew, and the trees dark green in the early dawn light. Then the blackness drops across his eyes. He turns toward Meriwhen so Liedral will not see the tears of frustration that ooze from his eyes.

Order! Why is order so unfair? Pure order seems unable to stop chaos, and whenever he tries to focus order against chaos, he is punished, just as the Whites and the traders of Spidlar have together, in a way, punished Brede because of his talent and reliance on the tools of order.

He tries to reason as he places the staff in the lanceholder. Is it because death is the ultimate form of chaos, the destruction of human order, so to speak? Certainly, despite the complaints by his family and Lortren, he has not suffered for his use of order to make his models or his machines. Nor has he been punished much for making his devices of destruction— only for using them.

"Can you help me get Kadara into the cart?"

Dorrin wipes his face with the back of his sleeve and turns toward the cart. His shoulder barely twinges as he lifts Kadara.

" . . . hurts . . . don't leave me . . ."

"You're with us," Dorrin says softly, trying to keep his voice level, trying to keep the frustration and anger from showing. His senses tell him that she is slightly better, but she is still fevered and weak, and it will be a long time, if ever, before she regains full use of her right arm.

Terwhit . . . terwhit. Despite the cheerful tone of the bird in the low oak trees, Dorrin is not encouraged.

CLI

THE CART CREAKS as Liedral turns at the hillcrest overlooking the river valley. "Everything looks all right."

"We still haven't run into any other travelers." Dorrin can extend his senses to some degree now, without headaches, but he still cannot see, except every once in a while when he touches his staff. Even that vision is neither predictable nor more than fleeting.

"You wouldn't expect any. People were leaving Kleth when I came back with that troop of cavalry and the last levy."

"I'm glad you had an escort."

"So was I. There were some rough souls on the road."

Dorrin touches the staff again, but he receives no glimpse of the sunlit expanse of the valley that lies between them and Diev. "How is Kadara?"

"Not much different. Sometimes, she seems awake, but mostly she sleeps."

"For now, that's probably better." Dorrin eases Meriwhen up beside Liedral as the road widens.

"For now . . ." Liedral says quietly. She looks behind her and lowers her voice. "What do you think about Brede?"

Dorrin shakes his head, hoping Liedral is looking at him.

"That's what I think, too."

Neither wants to confirm in words what both know must be true. The Whites will not allow anyone to survive, particularly a man from Recluce who has cost them so many troops. They continue silently until they near the turnoff from the main road that leads to Dorrin's cottage.

" . . . there yet . . . ?" asks Kadara.

"We're almost home." Liedral turns slightly and bends toward the rear of the cart where the injured woman lies. "Oh . . ."

"What is it?" Dorrin asks.

"Darkness . . ." mutters Liedral.

"What did you see?" asks Dorrin.

"Rylla's cottage—it's burned down. But your barn and the cottage are all right. There's a barricade of sorts around the yard . . . and some people. It looks like Pergun and another older man, and Reisa. She's wearing a blade." Liedral turns the cart off the main road and up the ridge drive.

Dorrin wishes he could see, but follows the cart until they are past the barricade and in the yard.

"It's master Dorrin! And Liedral! They're back!" Frisa's voice echoes across the yard and past the barricade.

"Master Dorrin . . ." Pergun begins.

Dorrin turns in the direction of his voice. "Yes?"

"What's wrong with you? You're not exactly looking square at me."

"He's blind," Liedral says quietly. "And Kadara's in the wagon here. She's badly wounded. We need to carry her inside."

"Put her in the bed I was using," Dorrin suggests.

"Blind? Blind . . . ? Was it the Whites? The evil bastards!"

"No. I did it myself." Dorrin dismounts and leads

Meriwhen toward the barn, letting his senses guide him.

"Is he daft?" Pergun turns to Liedral.

"Can I help?" Reisa's voice carries to Dorrin.

"He's not daft." Liedral descends from the cart. "He's an ordersmith who forced himself to create devices to kill more than a thousand people."

"A thousand?"

"More or less. It wasn't enough. Between Brede and Dorrin, I suspect that the Whites lost more than half their army. That would have left more than five thousand under arms."

Dorrin ignores the conversation as he opens the barn door. The scent of horses is strong, and Dorrin stops when he is just inside, trying to sense how many there are. Five, he thinks, two tied in the far corner in what seems to be makeshift stalls. He leads Meriwhen to her stall, slowly unsaddling her, racking the saddle, setting the staff aside, and beginning to curry the mare in slow and even strokes.

"You can't stay here." Reisa stands by the stall. "They'll burn the whole countryside to get you."

"Me? A humble smith?"

"You and Yarrl." Reisa snorts. "Do you ever think you can escape what you are? What about your ship? It's still floating. Yarrl saw it from the hill on the way here."

"Yarrl's here?"

"Of course. It made sense. Your place is easier to defend. We loaded most of his smithy into the big wagon, except the anvil. No one can get that quickly anyway. Pergun wanted to be here, because of Merga, and when the troopers took Liedral, we decided . . ."

"You didn't have to . . . I'm grateful, and thankful . . ."

"Dorrin, there's a lot you never had to do. You didn't have to heal Honsard's son. Shameful—that man. You didn't have to take Merga in. Or heal all those people who couldn't pay. Or refuse to take any of Yarrl's customers. Or expand Rylla's herb garden and share what you got with her." Reisa coughs. "So . . . for once, let someone help you. Darkness knows, you need it right now, you stiff-necked and proud . . ."

Dorrin puts aside the brush and fumbles with the barrel to dig out some grain for Meriwhen. Reisa holds the top and hands him the iron scoop, one of the miscellaneous items he has forged along the way and almost forgotten. The iron is cool to his fingers, almost healing.

"You need to rest."

After Dorrin dumps two scoops of grain into the manger box and closes the stall on Meriwhen, he slumps onto a bale of hay and leans back against the stall wall. "Where are you all sleeping?"

"Pergun . . ."

"I can figure that out. I meant . . ."

"We took the liberty of using the front room. There's space there, and we did bring mattresses."

"That's fine." Dorrin takes a deep breath, realizing that he is more tired than he thought as his eyes close.

CLII

DORRIN WANDERS THROUGH the cold smithy, his fingers brushing the forge, his tool rack, wondering when, or if, he will regain his sight. He has not realized, truly understood, how much of his smithing required vision. Why is he being punished? Or why is he punishing himself? For not having the ability to stop chaos without destruction? For trying to help good people?

"Darkness!" His eyes burn in frustration. Within days, the Whites will be back on the road to Diev, unless, miraculously, Spidlaria holds out. He snorts. With what? Less than a few hundred soldiers and mounted horse escaped the carnage at Kleth.

He walks to the smithy door and out into the sunlight, listening to the sounds of the wooden wands that Yarrl has produced for blade practice. Even Rek, with his foot twisted beyond Dorrin's poor ability to heal, has insisted on learning.

"Keep your guard up!"

Dorrin grins, imagining how intimidating Reisa once must have been. The grin fades. He is helpless with chaos about to pour out of the south. He supposes he should go to see the *Black Diamond*, but what good will seeing his ship do? Pergun and Yarrl have both assured him that it is fine, and that Tyrel is working on the rigging. Dorrin still needs to forge the replacement sections of the clutch and build the recirculating collector for the condenser, and he can forge neither while blind.

He pauses. Yarrl could forge the collector and tubing, but the additional slip plates need to be forged from black iron, and Yarrl has never forged in black iron. Still ... once Dorrin worked with Hegl ... and there isn't much time left.

"Are ye still moping, still feeling sorry for yourself?" Rylla's rasping voice intrudes.

"Not too sorry. More like planning ... how to fix the ship."

"How about planning to fix you?" The healer sits on a stool on the porch.

"And just how would I do that?"

"Well ... I'm no great master Black healer ... but were I one, I just might wander over to the herb garden and meditate ..." Rylla laughs.

"Meditate?"

"What ails ye isn't in your body. It's in your soul."

Dorrin shrugs. Order has a basis in growing things. Why not? He turns his steps toward the ridge and the garden that lies outside the barricade of hastily felled trees and brush.

"Vaos! You can't handle that heavy a blade with just your wrist." The voice is Yarrl's, not Reisa's.

"You can," adds Reisa, "but no one here besides you could."

"Hush, woman."

Dorrin can sense both Vaos and Rek, Pergun, Liedral and even Merga, all with wands in their hands. Will it do any good? What can they learn in an eight-day or so? Enough to hold off conscripted levies?

He trudges up the gentle incline toward the garden. The early summer day is cool, with a northern breeze, and bright sun falling on his face. Dorrin sits carefully on the ground between the rows of astra and the brinn. His fingers brush across the brinn, drinking in the coolness that flows within the stalks and leaves.

Meditate? Upon what? The nature of order. What is order? Why can those who follow order be punished—even if they seek a good end? Is it just because their actions increase chaos? Does that mean that order represents merely a set of laws? Or that no goal, no matter how good, can justify use of order to create great chaos?

He takes a deep breath, and a second, trying to relax.

Chaos breaks things apart—people, armies, cities . . .

The once-and-still healer frowns. Is it order when two people are bound together, be it through friendship or love? Then love cannot exist in true chaos. In a way, that follows. Men who truly love women normally do not hurt them. True friends do not knowingly hurt each other. Pain is usually a result of chaos of some sort—a disruption of bodily order for some reason or another.

Dorrin tries to drink in the herbs around him, but the nibbling whitish-red of root-rot in the brinn gnaws at him, disrupting his concentration. He turns to trying to strengthen the plants against the rot, projecting what little sense of order he can find within himself into the brinn.

"Master Dorrin? Why are you sitting in the garden? Can I sit here?"

Dorrin has to smile. "Yes, Frisa. Try to sit between the plants, not on them."

Frisa plumps herself down by Dorrin's right knee. "I like your garden."

"So do I."

"Why don't plants go places?"

"They don't have legs," Dorrin answers slowly. "And it's very hard to move without legs."

"Fish move. They don't have legs."

"They live in the water, and their tails and fins are like legs. Even water plants don't have fins or tails that move."

"I'm glad I'm not a plant. I like to go places," Frisa announces. "Can we go on your ship some time?"

"Where would you like to go?"

"Some place where people are happy. I want Mommy and Pergun to be happy. Then I'll be happy all the time."

Dorrin represses a sigh. "It's not always like that."

"I know *that*. You want Mommy to be happy, don't you?"

"Yes."

"Then you'll take her and Pergun on your ship, won't you?"

Dorrin laughs softly. "If I can make the ship go, they can come."

"Good! You always make things work." Frisa skips to her feet. "Can I tell Mommy?"

"Only if you tell her that I'll try to take everyone."

"Mommy will be happy. So will Pergun." Frisa skips down the ridge toward the brush barricade and the house and barn . . . and the weapons practice.

Dorrin rubs his chin. Reisa had been a blade, but why has he never considered Yarrl as one? Because the smith never mentioned weapons?

His fingers touch the brinn again, as he lifts his head toward the house and the slope leading to the pond, his ears picking up Frisa's announcement.

"Master Dorrin says he'll take everyone on his ship. If he can make it work. But he'll make it work. He always does."

Dorrin laughs softly, and just as softly, the blackness melts, and he looks out on the morning, drinking in the short grass waving in the breeze, the puffy clouds over the foothills to the Westhorns, just holding a vision he knows may depart at any instant.

Finally, he stands and begins to walk downslope to the house, still taking in the brightness of the day. Not until he sees the strain on Yarrl's face, and the newly-forged shortsword at the smith's hip, does the blackness return.

CLIII

Dorrin steps across the yard toward the barricade where Liedral and Pergun stand. Pergun wears the blade Yarrl made for him, and Liedral's bow lies on a makeshift stand.

Both watch the road below, where, at the moment, despite the growing twilight, another handful of herders, or farmers, trudges not toward Diev, but uphill toward the road leading to a narrow trail into the Westhorns. They have found no ships in Diev—except for the occasional smuggler.

Even the *Black Diamond* is not at Tyrel's pier, but anchored three or four rods offshore, at Tyrel's insistence. Few boats of any size remain in Diev.

Liedral points eastward toward a pillar of smoke. "That's a day away for us, probably three the way the Whites are moving."

Dorrin fingers his chin. "We need to finish loading the *Black Diamond*."

"Is it ready?"

"No. But we're close."

"Begging your pardon, master Dorrin," Pergun says respectfully, "but could you tell me why we've waited so long?" His hand strays to the scab on his forearm, the result of an encounter with a desperate farmer who climbed the barricade.

Dorrin looks to the three mounds on the hill before he answers.

"Because the White ships are off the coast, and unless I can get the engine working right, we don't have much chance of escaping them."

"With all their fireballs, do we have any chance? Why can't you make fireballs?"

"The engine should make it possible for us to go where they can't. A White Wizard has to get close to use a fireball. But you're right. We'll load up everything that's left tonight and leave at dawn for the shipwright's. Yarrl and Reisa and Vaos took some things down yesterday when no one was around."

"Why are the Whites taking so long? It's been more than an eight-day since they took Kleth."

"They're taking control of every town and hamlet. That's why it's been so slow, thank darkness. Their leader is very methodical." Dorrin shivers. His senses have shown him exactly how methodical. The route of the White horde is etched across Spidlar in fire and written on the land in ashes. "You'll tether the geese, later?"

"Aye, and we will," affirms Pergun as Dorrin walks back down to the house.

Merga is fussing in the kitchen, slicing cold mutton and checking something in the oven. By the table are two rough boxes, into which she has been packing the contents of the cupboards. "I stopped to fix a bite for Kadara. The rest of you will just have to slice off what you want."

"That's fine. I need to check her arm. Then I'll be going back to the smithy."

Merga does not answer, but looks to her daughter. "Frisa, see if you can find those two little pots in the bottom cupboard and set them on the table."

"Yes, mommy. Do you want the tops?"

"Child, what would I do with pots without tops? Without tops, indeed!"

Dorrin slips into the storeroom, now mostly empty, since Liedral has packed the contents into the cart, and digs out another dressing from his pack, carrying it back to the room where Kadara lies. "I need to check that arm."

Kadara does not speak, instead turning her head toward the wall as Dorrin changes the dressing. The stitches are rough, but stitching is not something he has practiced much, and, in time, he can use his healing skills to remove any scarring.

He checks the edges of the slash, but they are firm, with none of the signs of infection, and no red-white of chaos within the wound. Then he checks the bruise-cut above her ear. Through his ministrations, Kadara clamps her lips, uttering not a sound.

Finally, he steps back.

"Why did you save me? Why didn't you just leave me?"

"For what? For the Whites to burn you into charred meat?" Dorrin's patience is wearing thin.

"Brede would still be alive if you'd stayed with us. You could have stopped more of them if you'd only tried. And he could have used a healer." Kadara's voice is colder than the water that flows into the holding tank in the kitchen. She tries to reach for the mug by the bed, the narrow bed that Dorrin had been using, but her right arm just trembles. "And maybe I'd still be able to use my arm."

"In time, you will," Dorrin adds quietly.

"What good is a one-armed blade? Or a one-armed mother?" She shakes her head, and the short ragged hair lifts away from the still-scabbed scar above her left ear.

Scccffff ... Dorrin glances up as Merga eases through the open doorway from the hallway, a plate in her hand. "You need be getting back to work, Dorrin. I've some dinner here for her."

"Yes, Dorrin. You need to be getting back to work. After all, your work was more important than stopping the White bastards . . ."

Dorrin refuses to argue, even though he knows that he personally has doubtless killed more souls than anyone on the Spidlarian side. "Had I stayed, the only thing I would have done is get killed, or get someone else killed." His head still aches intermittently. At times he cannot see, for the blindness still comes and goes.

"Then what good are you? Where were you when Brede needed you?"

"I did what I could," Dorrin answers. "I'm not a fighting man. Call me a coward, if you will."

"You aren't a coward, Dorrin. You just never found

anything worth fighting for. Not me, not Liedral, not Recluce . . ."

"What do you call the mess I created at Kleth?"

"That was engineered destruction, not fighting—"

"Here's your supper," interrupts Merga gently.

"Why should I eat?"

"Because of your son." Merga says.

"Who won't have a father . . ."

Dorrin does not answer as he steps into the hall. He glances at the back bedroom. A faint smile creases his lips. Under the press of people, at least he and Liedral are sharing the same bed—in a way. Although there is a definite wall down the middle, the arrangement is an improvement. Sometimes, at least, he can reach out and touch her gently.

He walks back to the kitchen, where he stops, glancing at the steam rising from the kettle. The steam, again, reminds him of the painfully built engine that he can only hope will work.

But what good is he, Kadara has asked. Brede is dead, the victim of the concentrated forces of the wizards, and Dorrin is alive, alive because he was so pain-scarred and blinded that he could barely ride.

Slowly, he walks from the kitchen out onto the porch and down into the yard and around the cottage to the smithy. Overhead, the heavy gray clouds mass. He rubs his forehead. What can he do to stop the oncoming Whites? Certainly, killing large numbers of relatively innocent troopers and levies will not stop the horde. In the few eight-days remaining, can he devise a way to stop the White Wizards—or some of them?

Under the gray skies, light rain continues to fall.

Inside the smithy, the warmth of the forge is comforting, as is the sound of hammers. Yarrl has not only built the new condenser, but improved the design considerably, and his touch with the grindstone, with the physical efforts of Rek and Vaos, has resulted in a much truer finish on the clutch parts that are not black iron.

"I've been thinking, Dorrin..." Yarrl sets the hammer on the anvil.

The younger smith grins. "What else could I have done easier?"

"Not easier... and we can't do it now, but if you build another ship, Froos showed me an idea for holding a shaft in place. You take two rings, one smaller than the other, and flange the edges, sort of, and put metal balls between the two, and lubricate the balls with grease. Now if you made it out of black iron, and collared the inner ring to the shaft..."

Dorrin nods. "How would we get the balls to be round? They'd have to be really round."

"Make them big."

Dorrin thinks. "Why use balls? How about something shaped like a barrel or a pail? We could make them out of rod stock, and fuller the ends smaller, and turn them like a grindstone or a lathe."

"That might work better." Yarrl wipes his forehead. "I roughed out those sections of the clutch the way you drew it with the charcoal, except I made the angle on the teeth different, because it seemed like they'd bind." He steps toward the forge and gestures with the hammer.

Dorrin tries not to smile, or to kick himself. Had he enlisted Yarrl's help earlier, he could have avoided darkness knows how many problems.

The clutch pieces gleam on the firebricks.

"You polished them?"

"A little." Yarrl yawns, and Dorrin notes the circles under his eyes.

"You're tired."

"Time enough to rest later. The boys and I need to pack the tools and these parts into the wagon. Morning's coming all too soon."

Morning, and the Whites.

Dorrin reflects upon the pillar of black smoke, upon the question of fireballs. How is a fireball that different from fireworks? Could he build something that throws a firework of sorts in a thin black iron tube?

He picks up the hammer, and absently uses the smaller tongs to pull out a small irregular piece of plate. A tube with a handle, and a cylinder with a small open end. If he made the small end long and narrow, then expanded the front end? He shrugs.

"Look out, Vaos," cautions Yarrl. "He's got that look."

Dorrin slips the iron into the forge. The night may be long, but he will have time to rest later, if there is a later.

CLIV

IN THE GRAYNESS before dawn, Dorrin turns in his saddle and looks at the cottage, and the barn, the barricade of brush—and at the charred timbers that remain of Rylla's cottage. Even the herb garden is flat, with all the herbs cut, bagged, and stacked on Liedral's cart. He studies the southeast, seeing the lines of smoke where the Whites camp at the edge of the valley.

Liedral's cart leads the way, with Reisa and Dorrin riding before her. Vaos sits beside Liedral, his fingers on a blade that Dorrin hopes the youth will not have to use. Kadara is propped up in part of the cart, sharing it with the remainder of Dorrin's and Liedral's trading goods and herbs.

The wagon follows, with Petra holding the reins, and Merga beside her. They also wear blades. Yarrl and

Pergun ride just behind the wagon, which, in addition to the last of the smithy tools, three small barrels, and a grinder, carries Rylla, Frisa, and Rek. The healer talks gently to the girl and Yarrl's apprentice.

Dorrin's fingers brush the staff, and perversely, the blackness drops across his eyes once more. He takes a deep breath, and sits straight in the saddle, letting his fingers caress the staff for a moment. Then he thinks about herbs, and the bitter strength of the brinn.

"Reisa," Dorrin says quietly.

"Yes."

"I'm having a little trouble seeing, right now."

"Well, you don't need to for a while, do you? The road's clear ahead."

Dorrin rides silently, letting Meriwhen keep pace with Reisa's mount.

"Will anyone be out this early?" Vaos's voice carries to Dorrin.

"We hope not," answers Liedral, "but in these times, nothing is certain."

"What will happen to Diev?"

"I don't know. There's not much left of Kleth. It was razed and burned. But the Council fled Spidlaria and left the city open, according to travelers. The Whites killed just the people who tried to fight or who were tied to the blue guards or to the traders. So far they've left most people there alone."

"So why are so many people running away?" asks Vaos.

"It's not certain what the Whites will do. They can do great cruelty, but they also can be merciful and sometimes even do good. They keep the peace in their cities, and there is little violence. They have already started rebuilding Elparta. They are terribly cruel to their enemies and those who oppose them."

"That's why we have to leave?"

"Yes. Dorrin and Kadara and Reisa and Yarrl and

I have all opposed the Whites—Dorrin perhaps most of all."

"They'd kill us because we worked for him?"

"Yes."

Vaos tightens his fingers on the hilt of his blade.

Dorrin rides silently, trying to concentrate on the orderly things in his life—the herbs, the healing, the smithing, and Liedral. As they pass the turnoff to Honsard's cartery, the blackness lifts. Dorrin breathes more easily. Petra glances toward the deserted buildings, and Dorrin follows her glance. So does Reisa.

"Sometimes the wicked prosper," she says.

"Too often, it seems." He adds, "It's better this early."

"So far." Reisa's words are measured. "You all right now?"

"For now."

They ride up a gentle rise that is the last hill before the River Weyel and the bridge to Diev. Dorrin's stomach tightens.

A small group of men, and several women, armed with cudgels and pitchforks has gathered by the bridge. In the field to the east of the road wait the children and several older women.

"Trouble," observes Reisa unnecessarily.

"I'd rather not fight." Dorrin rubs his forehead, then his shoulders.

The rudely armed men and women turn toward Dorrin and those who follow him. They lift cudgels and pitchforks.

"They got food! Horses!"

"Damned traders! Make 'em pay."

" . . . too proud to accept the Whites . . ."

Reisa wraps the reins around her right forearm and puts her left hand on the hilt of her blade. "Do you have any ideas how to avoid a fight?"

"Let me try something." Dorrin urges Meriwhen in

front of Reisa and rides down the gentle slope toward the peasants.

" . . . get the bastard . . ."

" . . . uppity coin-counter . . ."

When he is perhaps two rods from the group, seeing no bows and hoping there are none, he reins up.

"We would appreciate passage." Scarcely eloquent, Dorrin knows, but no words will suffice in any case.

"Oh . . . he would appreciate passage, would he?"

"Not without some hefty tariffs . . . and some trade from the ladies . . ."

Dorrin waits for a moment, then lifts the staff, letting its blackness spill forth. Then he wraps the light around himself and Meriwhen.

" . . . he's gone . . ."

" . . . frigging wizard . . ."

Dorrin guides Meriwhen forward, focuses on the iron of a pitchfork, then thrusts with the staff.

" . . . ooofff . . ."

Leaning forward, he begins an effort to clear a path through the mob.

" . . . get him!"

" . . . how? Can't . . ."

A thunder of hoofbeats follows him, and he can sense two others on horses sweeping toward him.

" . . . run!"

"Stand fast . . ."

"*You* stand fast!"

" . . . not worth it . . ."

Dorrin drops his shield as he reaches the bridge, reappearing in the sight of the others as Reisa and Yarrl join him. But the peasants have scattered. One man cradles an arm, eyes blazing. He spits toward the road. Several others glare as the cart and wagon cross into Diev, but none move back toward the road. Dorrin's head throbs, but he can see, for the moment.

"For someone who's not a wizard, you do a fair imitation," states Reisa.

"I am a wizard of sorts," admits Dorrin, "just a poor one, just like I'm a poor healer and a poor smith."

"Not a poor smith, just a young one." Yarrl edges his mount off the road. The smith is so at home in the saddle, and the blade seems so much a part of him, that Dorrin wonders how he failed to see how dangerous an adversary Yarrl could be.

As soon as the wagon crosses the bridge, Dorrin and Reisa follow, then ride on the shoulder of the pavement to return to the front of the entourage.

"Was the smith once a blade?" asks Vaos as Dorrin passes.

"He hasn't said," Dorrin responds. "I'd guess so, but that's his business, not mine."

The streets of Diev are empty, and the shutters are tightly fastened on all the structures. Even the Red Lion is locked and shuttered, and the Tankard's front doors are boarded tight.

The wheels of the cart and the wagon echo through the scarcely post-dawn shadows of the streets of lower Diev as they make their way to and past the piers. A barricade of planks and barrels bars the way to Tyrel's.

"Holloa!" calls Dorrin. "Tyrel?"

A shutter opens from the single window facing the street. "Oh . . . it's past time—hoped you'd be here yesterday. Afraid you got into trouble with the mobs." The shutter slams shut.

The tattered tents are gone from the hillside beyond the shipwright's.

"Open that section. Make it quick. Bully-boys could be back any time. Move it, Styl!" Tyrel's voice sounds hoarse, but a section of planks is lifted away. Liedral guides the cart through. Petra follows with the wagon.

The planks are dragged back into place after Pergun awkwardly rides through. The cart and wagon roll toward the pier, where the *Black Diamond* is once more tied.

"Master Dorrin." Tyrel bows as Dorrin dismounts. "We got enough coal to fill those bins. Don't ask me how."

"I won't. How long will it take to load up all of this and the rest of the gear in the shed?"

"Maybe till midafternoon."

"We need to make those repairs on the engine." Behind Tyrel, Dorrin sees Rylla leading her charges toward the ship. Dorrin represses a grin as he sees that she has also ensured that they carry their bags.

"I'd be doing it quick, were I you."

"We'll try."

Dorrin finds Yarrl, who is tying his horse to a rail beside unused boat blocks inside the nearly empty structure. "Can you help me get those clutch pieces and the condenser on board and in place? We're running out of time. The others can handle the loading, I think."

"Good idea."

Dorrin finds Tyrel again, and commandeers his apprentices. "We need all of these pieces from the wagon on the deck above the engine."

"Sure as you're not going to tear it apart?"

Dorrin sighs. "We'll see about the condenser. But the bypass tubing and valve and the clutch replacements have to be done. We won't clear the harbor otherwise." He nods at Yarrl. "I'll be back in a bit."

"I'll take care of it," the older smith says.

Dorrin studies the half-finished stalls amidships, then looks at Pergun, who is carrying a barrel of grain from the shed. "Can you get those finished by midafternoon? We don't have much time."

Pergun scratches his head. "I can get 'em usable— not finished good."

"Do what you can, and load the horses. Probably

blindfold them. Leave one stall for Meriwhen. The Whites are at the edge of the upper valley on the road from Kleth." Dorrin rubs his forehead. "Tyrel's people are going to load most everything except for a few smithing tools."

"More of your wizardry?"

"I have a score or two to settle, and I think I know how."

"I don't like it when you look like that, master Dorrin." Pergun shivers.

Dorrin frowns. How does he look when he thinks about applying his efforts to the White Wizard—is his name Jeslek?—who tortured Liedral.

He walks back across the plank and down to the shipwright's shed, to the corner where the tub and the barrels are. There, he begins to measure. He would prefer to add water and make a cake he could grind, but he doubts that he has the time to dry the mixture. All he can do is ensure that the powders are well mixed before he pours them into his crude rocket shells and fuses them. He fills all three shells, ignoring the figure who stands in the shadows while he finishes.

"Going to be a hero, like Reisa?" asks Yarrl once Dorrin has finished.

"No. I am going out to do a job, hopefully as quietly and silently as possible."

"That's better. Not much, but better. Need help?"

"I need it, but I think it will work better if I do it alone. I couldn't shield anyone else." He slips the small rockets into one set of saddle-bags and the compact launcher into the other. "How did you do on the clutch?"

"Think it's right. Replacing the tubing and the condenser was easy."

Dorrin shakes his head. Things would have been so much easier had he asked Yarrl for help.

"You'll learn," says Yarrl. "Take a look."

Dorrin walks back across the shipwright's yard and across the plank, skirting around Liedral and Petra, who are wrestling bags of herbs and other goods onto the ship. When he gets to the engine, he finds the work accomplished perhaps better than he could have.

"I should have let you do it from the beginning." Dorrin's tone is rueful.

"I wouldn't have thought it up," Yarrl admits. "Once you see it, it ought to work, but . . ." He shrugs.

Dorrin looks at the late midmorning sun. "Darkness! I need to be going."

"Good luck."

The smith and sometime engineer and infrequent healer waits until the plank is clear before walking back into the shed to find Meriwhen.

Is what he plans wise? Hardly. Does he have a chance of success? A slim one. Does he have any choice? Not after what Brede and Kadara and Liedral have given.

He walks Meriwhen outside, tying the mare to a thin pole by the bollard closest to the barricade. Then he waits until Liedral nears the wagon and steps forward.

Liedral's eyes take in the saddled mare, the staff, and her shoulders slump. "What can you do now? Haven't you given enough? Do you want to be blind the rest of your life, like Creslin?"

He puts his arms around her. "I won't be blind if this works, not for long, anyway."

"No, you'll be dead." Liedral steps back, not bothering to wipe the tears from her cheeks.

"I owe too many people." He gestures toward the *Black Diamond*. "Too many lives paid for her."

"Who else—?"

His fingers touch her lips. "Yarrl can duplicate what I've done, if need be. I have to pay my debts."

"Men. You'll pay your debts and leave me alone."

Now Dorrin's shoulders are the ones that slump. "I have to do this."

"I know." Her lips brush his cheek. "I don't have to like it."

They embrace again, but separate. Almost on cue, Tyrel and Yarrl appear.

"If I don't make it back before the Whites do, I won't. Take the ship to Recluce, and try to get them to accept it. If they won't, I'd suggest Hamor."

"That be a demonish long trip without you, ser," observes Tyrel.

"I'll try to make it."

"Don't try. Just take care of your job. We'll wait." Yarrl's voice is gruff.

The three swing back the planks as Dorrin rides southward through the echoing empty streets once more. He hears nothing in either upper or lower Diev, although lines of smoke have appeared from a few chimneys, signifying that at least some hardy souls have arisen and are cooking—or something.

When he nears the bridge, he again struggles with the bending of the light around both Meriwhen and himself, but the patterns weave together, and, in time, he rides invisible in the early summer air that wafts past him, bearing faint hints of burning from the south.

He cannot see, not in any conventional sense, but he can sense the world around him, from the muted blackness of the objects in his saddlebags to the solidity of his staff. Ahead he can sense the white fog that seeps over the hills to the southeast.

The peasants or displaced farmers or herders who disputed their passage have gone on from the bridge, and Dorrin rides across as quietly as possible, even though he knows Meriwhen's hoofs click on the stones. No one appears, and he continues onward, up past Honsard's, past his own dwelling, until he can sense the rolling mist of white. He pauses in a shallow depression between two hills.

Three men, one stumbling, with blood splashed across his face, the other two running downhill toward the hill Dorrin has just descended, pass him as he nears the unseen heat of fire and chaos. But nothing pursues them.

For the moment, as he hoped and sensed, the White horde has paused for a mid-day break. Not much more than a short and a long hill separate him from the soldiers and the white-bannered tent on the crest.

In the depression between hills before him, there are several buildings, crushed meadows, and no people. There he dismounts and ties Meriwhen to a shrub behind an empty shed on the deserted herder's holding. The herders who lived in the hut have since left, for one reason or another, although the smell of sheep lingers.

Dorrin takes a deep breath, wondering again what he has to prove, why he could not simply board the *Diamond* and leave.

His mouth frames a smile that neither his eyes nor thoughts reflect as he recalls Kadara's words. "You aren't a coward, Dorrin. You just never found anything worth fighting for. Not me, not Liedral, not Recluce . . ."

So what is he fighting for? Recluce will not like his machines any more than the White Wizards will.

His hands tighten around the simple tube mounted on the hand grip, around the black iron shell packed with fireworks powder. He places another shell in his pouch and closes the saddlebag. He leaves his staff in the lanceholder, and begins the climb up the first hill. He is still breathing easily after descending beside the road and climbing the second hill. He tries to keep his steps quiet as his feet carry him sideways along the side of the hill and through the vanguard of the White forces. Still cloaked in bended light, unseen, he steps around soldiers, many of whom, could he but see their eyes, would look blankly into the distance that is chaos, even as they would lift their swords to remove his head from the body beneath.

Click . . . click . . .

He pauses as he senses the concentration of chaos no more than a dozen rods before him on the hilltop. He steps forward, and hearing the sounds of his boots upon the hard-packed mud and gravel, edges onto the trampled grass and weeds beside the road, still moving forward until he pauses outside the light fabric of the single tent pitched amid the White forces. He listens, standing almost within an arm's length of the White Command . . .

" . . . get ready to head out . . . not too far until we reach that homestead. Don't fire it. The High Wizard wants to study it first—the one with the brush barricade around it and the charred cottage in front."

Dorrin smiles at the thought of the White soldiers so highly valuing his establishment. After a few moments, his senses point him toward the swirl of white mounting nearly to the clouds that must be the wizard who embodies chaos incarnate. While there are other swirls of white, they are dwarfed by the sullen red-tinged whiteness that is Jeslek.

Slowly, he edges into the high-ceilinged tent, still amazed that he has gotten so close.

" . . . look over there . . ."

" . . . concealment . . .!"

Dorrin drops the shield and points his device at the white-haired man who jabs a finger in his direction.

WHHHsssttt! The firebolt singes Dorrin's ear as he releases the striker, and the black steel rocket ignites.

Crack . . . thump . . . whummmmmmPPPP-TTTTTTT . . .

EEEEEEEEIIIIIIIIIiiii! As the black order-forged

steel of the rocket shell and the red-tinged white meet, an incandescence sears through the tent, rending the walls and scattering the wizards and soldiers around the target like so many children's toys swept aside by a householder's broom.

Thurrrrummmmmmmmmmm . . . thuruummmmm . . .

Dorrin staggers against a tent pole, momentarily forgotten as the winds buffet the tent, and the thunder-claps shake the hillside.

"Jeslek! Jeslek!"

With the methodical nature he has cultivated, Dorrin forces himself to reknit his cloak of bended light even as he crawls across the fallen tent wall and through the lashing hail and rain that has appeared nearly instantaneously with the destruction of the white vortex of force that has to have been the master chaos wizard.

The sometime smith, sometime healer continues to crawl through the lashing winds, ice, and water for a time. Then, he stands and staggers downhill toward the west, dropping the illusion that has become too hard to maintain as he weaves toward the shed where he hopes Meriwhen waits. Inside, he is as cold as the occasional ice that pelts him, for he has no illusions about what he has done. He has built a tool of destruc-tion, unloosed it from hiding, and exterminated a pest. And he has done so out of personal revenge, with no real hope of saving Spidlar or Diev.

He shakes his head as he unties the black and tries to mount, failing the first time because his legs are shaking. He tries again, using the strength in his arms to pull himself up. His head throbs, and occasional arrows of pain lash his skull.

No glorious battles . . . no honor in besting a skilled foe. No, Dorrin knows he is no warrior, no hero. He is a coward who has built a tool for killing at a distance, even if the killing were the most necessary thing of all.

With a sigh that is almost a shudder, he turns Meriwhen around on the road, urging her onward, knowing that the White soldiers will still overrun Diev, that all of Candar east of the Westhorns will belong to Fairhaven.

At the bridge where they had met the armed peasants, he pauses, noting absently that there is no sign of them, nor of anyone else. Should he toss the black iron tube into the swirling water that rises under the sheets of rain pouring from the all-too-suddenly dark gray skies? He shakes his head. More order-knit destruction may yet be necessary.

Once he crosses the bridge the rain falls away, as if it were confined to the area around the White horde, and the smell of burning is stronger, as if other fires have been lit.

They have. The Tankard is in flames. On the street dance what appear to be the same folk who had menaced him at the bridge. A row of barrels sits on the stones, and on the first sits a man with an arm bound in rags. Others use the Tankard's mugs and dip beer from the barrels, their tops rudely smashed open. Dorrin guides Meriwhen down another street.

" . . . I saw him! The Black wizard . . ."

Dorrin urges Meriwhen into a trot, but no one follows, and he slows to a walk, casting his senses out as he nears the piers. But the piers remain empty, desolate. He looks seaward, seeing two ships flying white, circling beyond the breakwater—waiting.

The road before Tyrel's is not empty. Half a hundred people stand around the burning shed.

" . . . frigging bastards . . ."

"Find the arrows . . ."

"Get a boat! We'll make them take us!"

Dorrin recasts his cloak of light and walks Meriwhen

down an alley he hopes leads to the other end of the channel. At the end of the alley, he turns back toward the water, where, for a moment, he releases his concealment.

The *Black Diamond* floats perhaps two rods off the pier.

A half-dozen Spidlarian soldiers stand on the main deck of the *Diamond*. Another dozen seem trapped between the mob and the water.

Dorrin sees Kadara, hair mussed, face bruised, ropes cruelly wound around her splinted and shattered arm. Rylla carries Frisa, and the child cries. He continues to look for silky short brown hair and broad shoulders.

On the poop four others stand side to side—blades out—Yarrl, Reisa, Petra, and Liedral. Below them stand the soldiers. From what Dorrin can tell, Tyrel, or someone, has closed the hatch to the engine. A faint wisp of steam rises from the stack.

Dorrin takes a deep breath and studies the positions of the soldiers. An officer is arguing with Yarrl.

"Get this thing going . . ."

"I don't know how. Only Master Dorrin knows how . . ." Yarrl keeps looking toward the shore.

Dorrin sighs, then urges Meriwhen forward at a gallop. They hit the water with a surge, and Dorrin uses every bit of effort to wrap the light around himself, even as Meriwhen swims toward the ship.

" . . . just a frigging horse . . ."

" . . . even it doesn't want to be left to the Whites . . ."

Dorrin's eyes burn as he stands in the stirrups and, one-handed, draws himself onto the narrow brace for the rudder. His desperate leap momentarily pushes Meriwhen deeper into the water. He clutches his staff with the other hand and struggles upward until he can lurch over the railing.

His eyes continue to burn as he listens to Meriwhen

churn aimlessly around the stern, but he forces himself onward, still shielded, still blind, until he is on the main deck.

He steps behind the rearmost soldier and lifts the staff. His staff lifts and falls, as does the soldier—as does Dorrin's cloaking from sight. Two soldiers whirl, and Dorrin strikes, once . . . twice.

The second time, he misses. The soldier does not, and a pain like white fire rips across his arm.

The soldier does not lift his sword again, cleft as he is almost in two by Yarrl's blade.

Seven bodies lie on the deck, one of them Pergun's. Dorrin clutches his arm, realizing that blood is also dripping into his eyes.

Rylla rips away his shirt, and begins to sprinkle powdered astra into the slash. "Sit down!" she snaps.

"Got to get clear."

"They can handle that."

As the *Black Diamond* bobs on the choppy water, the soldiers on the pier, dancing back from the mob, begin to jump into the channel.

"Take us . . . we'll pay you . . ."

" . . . anything . . ."

Yarrl has persuaded Tyrel to open the engine space hatch, and the two men talk as Rylla continues to bind Dorrin's arm. Yarrl steps down, and Tyrel hurries aft to the helm.

Dorrin grins in relief as he hears the *fwwuuuphhh . . . fwuppp . . .* of the engine as it begins to turn over. He senses the faint vibration of the black iron rods as they work.

Fwwwuuuppphhh . . . fwupp . . . fwuppp . . . The engine and the fly-wheel pick up more speed, settling into an even smoother rhythm than on the trials.

"You be taking it easy . . ." warns Rylla, as Dorrin totters toward the engine space. He stands in the hatchway and looks down at Yarrl.

"We were all hoping you'd make it." Yarrl continues to shovel coal into the firebox.

"We need the screw turning before we ground."

"You take . . . care . . . of that . . ." puffs Yarrl.

Dorrin slowly eases the clutch into place, then lets out his breath as the piston and flywheel continue to pick up speed. As the *Black Diamond* eases seaward, he continues to watch until the pressure is well above the minimum operating level.

Then he wipes his forehead and struggles back on deck. Pergun lies on the deck, but on his back, and he breathes shallowly. Rylla looks up at Dorrin helplessly. So does Merga.

Dorrin takes another deep breath, then kneels, hands gently touching the forehead, reaching out with all the skill and strength he has left, chasing the encroaching whiteness away, pushing back the influx of chaos. But the deck swims before him, the rough planks rising against his chin, and he falls into the darkness.

CLV

THE RED-HAIRED WIZARD finishes binding her arm, then stoops and lifts the gold amulet from the pile of dust and clothes on the trampled and burned grass. Stepping around the body of a White guard, she dangles it toward the bearded White Wizard with the gash across his forehead.

"Would you like it, Fydel?"

"Darkness, no! Give it to Sterol."

She turns to Cerryl. "Would you—"

"It's past time for games, Anya. Sterol should have the amulet returned to him. Especially now."

"Don't tell me that you two brave and strong White brethren are afraid of a poor black smith and healer who must stoop to stealth and murder?"

Fydel looks away.

Cerryl does not, instead meeting Anya's eyes. "He was rather effective, wouldn't you say?" His arm takes in the pile of dust that had been Jeslek, the two bodies, and the missing side of the tent ringed with charred patches. "There were three of them—just three, according to Jeslek. Between them, they've destroyed more than half our forces, a half-dozen of the White brethren, and the High Wizard. Just what would happen if they had decided to send a few more—perhaps older and more experienced order-masters and Black warriors?" Cerryl's smile is crooked. "For such reasons, I would prefer to defer to one of great experience, such as Sterol."

"Do we wait for him—to finish this rabble?" snaps Anya.

"No. I think we can proceed—slowly."

"You are always so cautious, Cerryl," Anya says brightly.

"When one cannot rely on sheer force of chaos, dear lady," the smooth-faced White Wizard replies slowly, "one must needs be cautious."

"Bah . . . let's get the troops moving." Fydel blots the blood from his forehead and steps through the space where the tent wall was. Then he pauses and points toward the remaining two bodies. Fire flares, and only ashes remain.

Anya and Cerryl raise their eyebrows simultaneously.

CLVI

DORRIN WAKES TO find his head in Liedral's lap. She is blotting away the dried and not-so-dried blood with a cool and damp cloth and sprinkling the crushed and powdered astra into the gash on his forehead. The powder burns, and his head aches, not to mention his shoulder.

For some reason, he thinks of Meriwhen and his eyes fill. He hopes the mare made it to shore. He shudders, and Liedral squeezes his shoulders.

"It's all right."

"No. It's not." He sits up and takes the cloth from her. So many others, even the mare who has carried and brought him through so much, have paid for his desires and dreams of building his engines.

His shoulders slump. Brede is dead. Liedral was tortured, Kadara left alone and pregnant. Rylla's cottage lies in ashes, with the old healer uprooted. Thousands of relatively innocent soldiers lie dead. Kleth has been razed and burned, and Elparta half-destroyed. Why?

Because order threw him out and he has set himself out to oppose chaos? Or just because he is stubborn? He recalls Fairhaven—clean, peaceful, even orderly. Just because he cannot tolerate chaos ... is that any reason to create disaster?

He takes a deep breath and squares his shoulders, ignoring the throbbing in his head and arm. Now is not the time to philosophize, but to seek safety for those on board. He looks across the deck and up onto the poop deck to Tyrel at the wheel, then to the sea to the north.

The *Black Diamond* is merely holding position inside the breakwater. Two, perhaps three, kays offshore are the two schooners that bear the white and crimson ensigns of Fairhaven.

Dorrin starts to stand, and Liedral helps him to his feet.

"Don't be so hard on yourself," she murmurs.

He touches her hand and walks across the gently rolling deck to the short ladder up to the poop and the helm.

"We need to get out of here," Dorrin says to Tyrel.

"How? Where they're lying, with that wind out of the east-north-east, they can cut us off either way we go. Under full sail, they're faster than we are, even with your engine, I think."

"Which direction can't they go?" Dorrin rubs his forehead, where the dull hammer of a smith beats still within his skull.

"They can go where they want to. They're White Wizards."

"I don't need old jokes. Can they go upwind?"

"They'd have to tack."

"All right. How close to the shore will they dare to come?"

"With this wind?" Tyrel looks to the sky, and the clouds on the edge of the northern horizon. "Not a lot closer than they are now."

"Fine. We'll just head east right along the coast."

"But . . ." Tyrel shakes his head. "It's hard to remember that we can go where we want to." He pauses. "If your engine fails, we'll go aground."

"I understand. But if we go farther offshore, they'll be able to get close enough to fry us with their wizards' fire." Dorrin limps forward toward the hatch to the engine compartment, where, as Yarrl watches, he shuts off the bypass and channels the engine's power all to the screw.

The *Black Diamond* surges past the breakwater, sails still furled to her spars as Tyrel slowly swings the converted schooner onto an eastward course paralleling the coast.

Dorrin wobbles across the deck to where Pergun lies on a pallet under a makeshift awning. The dark-haired man's breathing is even, and his eyes are closed. Merga lifts a damp cloth from his forehead, even as the tears dry on her face. Dorrin bends and touches Pergun's forehead again, offering what little additional order he can spare.

"Thank you, master Dorrin."

"Please don't thank me now. Thank me if we make it to safe haven." Dorrin moves to the railing, watching the choppy green water, letting the wood carry some of his weight.

Kadara, her arm bound into a sling, joins him. "You could have done that for Brede."

"If you will recall, I wasn't in much shape to do anything."

"Mule crap! You were off babying yourself again. Here you are, two minor flesh wounds, and you can barely walk."

Dorrin turns to the redhead. "You have to think what you think, and nothing I say has ever affected that. But I don't think strength is measured by how well one bears physical pain or how many people you cut down with a sharp blade. Brede understood that.

"You've still got a son you'll have to raise. He's born of Recluce parents, and he just might not take to a blade. Will you lose him because you'll insist on making him into something he isn't—like my parents did?"

"You should talk. You don't care what anyone thinks. All you care about is your damned engines."

Dorrin keeps his eyes level on Kadara. "You're right. I know what I am."

This time Kadara looks down at the railing and the water beyond.

Dorrin steps back as Liedral motions to him.

"You were hard on her," observes Liedral. "You were harder on yourself."

"Truth is sometimes hard."

"Do you like it when someone applies hard truth to you?"

"Of course not." He grins. "Except when you do it." Then he looks northward once more. The easternmost White schooner, probably twice the size of the *Diamond*, has begun to turn, running crosswind. After watching the ship for a time, Dorrin climbs back up to the helm to talk to Tyrel.

"He's going to try and cut for the Cape there—Cape Devalin—where we'll have to go farther seaward."

"Would more speed help?"

"Aye, for if we can clear the Cape 'fore him, he'll be forced into the teeth of the wind."

Dorrin totters away from the helm and down the ladder to the main deck.

Near the bow, Rylla points to the beaches, with an arm around Frisa. Vaos is attempting to reposition a board on the amidships stalls, and talks to the horses. Dorrin swallows as he sees the empty stall once more, wipes his eyes and continues back toward the engine compartment.

Yarrl sets down the shovel and wipes his forehead. "Hotter than a forge, this beast you built. And wetter. But this boy likes it."

From one corner, Rek watches the engine, trying to puzzle its workings.

"Too wet," Yarrl says.

Water seeps from several tubes, and the deck is soaked. Dorrin tries to trace the leaks. One is in the seawater line that provides cold water to the condenser shell. Another is around the exit valve of the first cylinder. From what he can tell, nothing will break, split, or fail—not immediately.

"We need to fire up more."

"Will it take it?"

"For a while."

"You're the engineer," Yarrl says with a crooked grin, opening the firebox door again and lifting the shovel.

Slowly, slowly the connecting rods begin to pick up speed, and the heat from the boiler builds, and more water spills across the heavy-timbered half-deck that holds the engine. A dull vibration builds, and Dorrin spills steam, fractionally, until the engine returns to a stable rhythm, faster than before, but not what, he thinks, the engine might be capable of with work and time. Unfortunately, he has had neither.

After stepping back on deck, Dorrin checks the White schooner, then hurries to Tyrel, who is talking to Styl.

" . . . pails of water . . . any sand left?"

"We put some on." The lanky bearded man jabs a fist toward the approaching schooner. "Don't know as it will work if they got a hot White."

"We'll do what we can."

"Aye, ser." Styl vaults gracefully onto the main deck.

"Used to be a mate for Gossag. Good man," Tyrel says.

"How are we doing?"

"Going to be close. Looks like we're going to hit off the Cape at about the same time."

Dorrin studies the full-sailed vessel. "Will our canvas burn if a fireball hits?"

"Probably not if we keep it furled. See, they get you one way or another. It's hard to fire ship's wood with a flame; needs something like burning canvas, pitch, to set it going. But . . . you furl your sails, and you go dead in the water, and they board or flame the crew standing off a bit."

"If everyone's below, and the sails are furled tight, we could get pretty close."

"Aye . . ."

"I'll get everyone below." Dorrin climbs down the ladder to where Merga ministers to Pergun. "Can you and Petra get him below?"

"It's cooler here, master Dorrin."

Dorrin points to the oncoming schooner. "They're going to attack. You can bring him up later."

Merga looks at the fevered man.

"He'll die here. They'll flame the deck." Dorrin takes down the blanket that has served as a shade for the former mill hand, folding it quickly and setting it on the deck. "Get this below also."

He begins to search for his staff, both with his eyes and senses, and finally reclaims it from a corner in the empty stall where Meriwhen should have been. He steps out of the stalls, carrying the staff, toward the bow. Kadara sits propped against the forward side of the one fully completed stall, in the shade. She looks up warily.

"You need to get below. There's a White ship coming."

"I can fight."

"I think we can get by without fighting. If they board, you'll need to fight, but I'd rather avoid this fight."

"Wouldn't you always?"

"Yes." He steps around her toward the bow and Rylla and Frisa, where he repeats his warning, and asks Rylla to pass it on to Vaos. Looking to the helm, he sees Tyrel gesturing and motioning below. Styl and the two other men finally leave the poop deck, but not until they have lashed an open-topped barrel, filled with seawater and a bucket, to the railing closest to the helm.

Liedral? Where is she?

He finds her in the mess space with Reisa and Petra. Reisa is directing Liedral in sharpening an ancient pike. All three are fully armed.

"We may not need that ... I hope." He repeats his warning, and then climbs topside, where he goes to the engine space.

"The Whites are getting close. I'm going to close this halfway."

"Leave it open. We'll die from the heat," Yarrl yells over the sound of the engine.

Dorrin looks from the oncoming schooner to the engine compartment. "Then stay low on the deck here."

Yarrl nods and glances at Rek, even as he throws another shovelful of coal into the firebox. "You hear that, boy?"

"Yes, ser."

Dorrin climbs back to the helm, almost dragging the staff.

The White ship is perhaps a dozen cables from the *Black Diamond*, close enough that Dorrin can make out the name—*White Storm*.

"Let me take this," Dorrin insists, looking over his shoulder at the approaching *White Storm*.

"I'm a better helmsman, master Dorrin," Tyrel insists.

"I know. I need you alive. You don't want to get fried, do you?"

"I was a-hoping you could protect us both."

"I'll be lucky to protect myself," Dorrin admits.

Tyrel looks nervously to the starboard, toward the breakers that seem all too close. "Don't get any nearer to shore ... and if ... when you get abreast of the cut in the beach there, just before the tip of the cape, you need to bring her seaward another dozen rods at least."

"Let me loop this here." Tyrel makes two quick rope loops to secure Dorrin's staff to the side of the wheel cage.

"Thank you. I'll need it." Dorrin takes the wheel, swallowing. Why is he getting into positions like this?

"Thought you might." Tyrel eases down onto the main deck, where he stands by the hatch into the poop. Other than the man Dorrin regards as the ship's captain, the decks are now clear.

The *White Storm* seems to slash through the water, and the bearing between the two ships seems almost constant, the distance steadily decreasing. Dorrin watches the approach. Is the *Black Diamond* gaining ever so slightly?

A swirl of wind carries coal cinders into his face, and he blinks. The stack should be taller, and that would also increase the boiler draft. But again, he has not had the time to work all the details out. It is a miracle of sorts that the engine works so well.

More cinders fly in his face. He looks at the stack, sensing a vibration in the deck, realizing that Yarrl is forcing more power into the engine.

The *Black Diamond* continues to gain on the angled approach of the *White Storm*. Dorrin is now actually looking slightly back.

More cinders fly toward Dorrin. Why now?

He grins. They're nearing the Cape and the time when the White ship will face a straight headwind. Dorrin sobers and swallows as he sees the cleft in the beach appear to starboard. Now he must turn the *Diamond* seaward, cutting the distance between the two ships. He eases the wheel, but the turn is gentle—too gentle.

He turns the wheel more, and the *Black Diamond* angles closer to the White schooner, close enough that

Dorrin can see a white-garbed figure standing just aft of the bow. The White Wizard raises an arm and white fire flashes southward.

PHssstttt . . .

The fireball sails by the upper spars.

"Turn her back, master Dorrin!" yells Tyrel.

Dorrin tries to bring the *Black Diamond* back onto a more eastern course now that the ship has regained its separation.

PIIIIIIsstttt . . .

Another fireball flies past, lower, and close enough that Dorrin can feel the heat and the chaos as he wrestles with the wheel. As he straightens the helm on what he hopes is the proper course line, Dorrin grabs for his staff with one hand, yanking it upward as another flash of fire flames toward the *Black Diamond*.

Phhhssst . . . platttt!!! Fire sprays around Dorrin and the staff he has raised barely in time, but the ship heels because Dorrin has lost the wheel. He grabs for the spokes, and pain sears through his hand, although, somehow, he halts the bow from falling off into the breakers and brings the ship back toward course line.

He looks over his shoulder, and raises the staff one-handed against another fireball.

Shhhh . . . platt . . . Chaos-fire splatters around him, blown back by the wind.

Suddenly, it seems, the *Black Diamond* begins to pull away from the *White Storm* as if the White ship were standing still.

Another firebolt flies, but lands in the green sea behind the *Diamond*. Dorrin turns the helm slightly more seaward, hoping he has not already run too close to the breakers and the sandbars and rocks over which they break.

His head aches; his shoulder throbs, and now his thumb seems broken or . . . something, as he shifts the staff to the injured left hand and tries to wrestle the ship onto the course he feels is safe.

Yet another fireball falls astern.

"Master Dorrin, let me take her!"

Dorrin nods, and Tyrel scrambles for the helm, frantically turning the ship more to sea.

The sometime healer and smith holds the staff loosely facing aft, watching as the *White Storm*, sails almost flat, struggles to find the wind before being carried onto the cape. The *Black Diamond* chugs onward.

Dorrin finally walks forward to the engine space. "Let her go slower," he yells.

Yarrl wipes his forehead and closes the firebox door, slumping against a cross-brace.

Dorrin listens. A series of vibrations he does not like have crept into the engine ... or the shaft. He limps aft to the helm once more.

"Can we run on sail later?" he asks.

"Aye ... if we can get enough to sea."

"I'm going to let the others come on deck."

Tyrel laughs and jabs a hand back toward the cape. "He'll not be coming after us for a time. White bastards ..." He spits downwind.

Dorrin sits down on the deck, too tired to move, but the word has passed, because Liedral arrives carrying a basket.

"You need to eat."

Dorrin does not protest.

"What did you do to your hand?"

"Lost an argument with the wheel."

"Dorrin ..." Liedral shakes her head, and her short hair flies out. "You eat, and I'll get Rylla."

He eats, one-handed, while Tyrel sings a vaguely obscene song, tunelessly, and Styl and the other two begin to rig for sail.

CLVII

"RAZE THE CITY." Sterol looks down at the twisted links in his hand and the blackened amulet.

"The whole city? Those who were left surrendered and accepted the banner of Fairhaven." The eyes of the red-haired female wizard widen.

"I don't care about the people. Let them go where they will. No city strikes down a High Wizard and remains to mock Fairhaven. I want all the crops and livestock taken. Then sow every other field with salt and fire, and level every structure. Destroy the breakwater and fill the port with stone."

"I did not realize you so loved Jeslek."

"I hated the man. That's scarcely the point, is it?" Sterol's voice is almost silky. "Do you want the world thinking that leaders should be targets in warfare?"

"I understand. Do you wish a reward published for the Black . . . wizard?"

"Light, no. Do I have to spell out everything for you? We post a reward, and those idiots on Recluce might take him back. This way, everyone around him has to look over their shoulder."

"Wasn't that Jenred's idea with Creslin?"

"Hardly. Jenred forgot that those he drove out had no alternatives. Do you think those sniveling cowards on Recluce are going to take in someone who is using machines, black steel, and order to create horrible destruction?"

"What if he forces them—"

"With what? He has one magical ship and a handful of followers."

CLVIII

PURE ORDER CANNOT nourish life, for living requires growth, and the process of growth is the constant struggle to bring order out of chaos.

When a fire destroys the great forests of the Westhorns, immediately order replenishes itself with scores of seedlings and bushes striving to recover the hillsides.

When a stone wall is built, the forces of frost and heat continually tumble the stones. So too is it with a house, once the constant order of the hearthholder is removed.

The function of order is to support that life which can order chaos; and without chaos to be ordered, there can be no purpose to life.

The function of chaos is to destroy order. Without order, no structure can exist—no man nor woman, no plant, not even an earth upon which to walk. Thus, the total triumph of chaos is its defeat.

What can be said of order and chaos, then? Since the world was, is, and will be, neither order nor chaos may triumph. Therefore, in the world as a whole there must be equal measures of each, and that Balance will be maintained; for, if it is not, there shall be either no world or no life.

And upon this world are the lands and the seas.

People call the sea chaos, but the sea contains a deeper order within the ever-changing waves and depths, and the seas wash upon the beaches and retreat, and that changes not.

Likewise people call the land orderly, for it changes seldom, yet beneath that surface order is great disorder, filled with the fires and chaos of the demons.

A people of the sea must be of order, for order must contain the surface chaos of the oceans and harmonize with the deeper order under the waves.

Likewise, a people of chaos can only exist upon the land, for the sea will rend them unto nothing.

> *The Basis of Order*
> *Fragment attributed to Section II*

CLIX

THE BLACK DIAMOND is tied at the end bollard on the smallest pier inside the breakwater at Land's End, and smoke and steam trickle into the air as the firebox cools. A barrel, perhaps two, remains of the coal.

Four Black guards stand beyond the foot of the plank, although two large barrels of fresh water have been set by the plank for the use of the crew and passengers of the ship.

"Now what, Master Dorrin?" asks Tyrel.

"We wait," Dorrin says tiredly. He tries to wipe his forehead, but the splint on his thumb makes the gesture difficult. At least, his shoulder is on the way to healing, and the white-fired headaches are less frequent.

"Not for long." Liedral points toward the harbormaster's flag, below which several individuals in black alight from an open carriage.

One is a tall and thin Black wizard. Dorrin takes a deep breath.

"Oh ... shit ..." Kadara's curse carries from the bow on the light wind.

Dorrin shares her feelings, but he waits as the

black-clad group walks down the pier. Liedral stands beside him, grasping his hand.

The tall wizard gestures to the guards. One salutes, and all four walk back toward the harbor and, eventually, to the old keep on the hillside. The wizard turns to the ship, looking directly at Dorrin. "For now, you all have the freedom of Recluce. We would prefer you remain near Land's End, but that is your choice." The tall wizard smiles gently. "In view of your various ... ordeals, we offer the two guesthouses beyond the inn to you, and the guest apartment in the old inn to Dorrin and his ... consort." Oran gestures toward the middle of the ship. "You may also avail yourself of the stables."

"That's very generous," Dorrin says. "The last few eight-days have been rather hard. If you could persuade a master healer to attend to Pergun for us, I would appreciate it. He received a head injury. I may have stopped the worst of the damage, but ... more needs to be done."

" ... fine, mast' Dorr ..." Pergun leans on the railing, Merga by his side, but he still clips and slurs his words.

"We would be pleased to see what might be done." Oran answers smoothly.

Merga drops her hand from her mouth, and clutches Frisa in one hand.

"Later, after dinner, we would like to meet with you." Oran's eyes meet his son's. Dorrin nods, but does not look away. After a time, Oran does.

Even after the pier clears, after Tyrel, his crew, Pergun, Merga, and Frisa have made for the guesthouse, Dorrin stands by the gangway.

"Dorrin ...?" Liedral sits on the clean-scrubbed planks by the mainmast with Reisa, Yarrl, and Petra. Kadara sits next to them, but back, as if she is not quite a part of the group.

Dorrin grins as he walks toward them, for they look like a council of war. The grin drops. It is a war of sorts. He sits on the hard planks next to Liedral, enjoying the afternoon sea breeze.

"You haven't said much about what we can do," Liedral begins.

"I haven't really thought it through. Originally, I just wanted to build an engine and then the ship and stay in Spidlar. I can't say that Recluce will take us— me, anyway—back. They don't like machines . . ."

"But they've suffered from the trade cutoff," Liedral says. "Your kind of ship—you proved it could be valuable. Wouldn't they be interested?"

"No." The cold voice is Kadara's. "They'll die before they'll change their precious beliefs."

"Who says they have to?" offers Reisa. "We'll build the ships and protect them. They don't have to change. They could just let us alone."

"You'll still"—Kadara searches for words—"contaminate them."

"They can't be that cold," protests Petra.

"Maybe not," Dorrin says. "What if we build an enclave on the south end of Recluce? There's a small inlet and cove there. The plateau behind it is fertile; it's just too far from Land's End for Recluce to have settled yet. I mean, there are a few holders, but they're the kind that wouldn't mind."

"Dorrin," Liedral says, "don't give that to them. Trade for it."

Dorrin understands. Still . . . "I don't know if I can."

"Makes sense to me," affirms Yarrl.

"We'll stand behind you," Reisa adds.

Kadara shakes her head.

"Well . . ." Dorrin draws out the words. "We might as well avail ourselves of the facilities." He does not add "while we can," though the thought occurs.

Before long, the six descend the plank, all carrying

bags or packs. Long shadows from the hills west of the harbor almost touch the pier.

Dorrin glances back at the deserted ship. At least Recluce is a place where one has no worries about theft. He laughs, suspecting that Fairhaven itself is the one other place where theft is rare, if not unheard of.

He has closed all the doors and hatches on the *Black Diamond*, and checked and pumped the bilges. The leaks around the shaft remain small, but the ship will still have to be pumped periodically, at least until he can design and build a better seal.

"Cleanest harbor I've seen," observes Yarrl.

The stone pier is swept, and all the joints between stones are tightly mortared. Even the wind whipping in off the Eastern Ocean smells fresh. The roofs of Land's End form an orderly mosaic on the hillside, and above them rise the stones of the old keep, under the replica of the Founders' original ensign—the crossed rose and blade. The current banner of Recluce the starker black ryall on a white background—flies from the staff before the single-storied harbormaster's building between the two piers.

"Where's this inn?"

"To the left of the harbormaster's. Up that lane. The two-storied building is the inn. Then come the stables where Styl and Intar put the horses. The guesthouses are on the hill to the left of the stables." Dorrin squeezes Liedral's hand.

Outside the inn, a youth in clean brown leathers, wearing a black armband with a white ryall, jumps up as they approach.

"Master Dorrin." He bows. "If you and your consort would enter the inn, Mistress Barla will escort you to your quarters. I will show the others to their guesthouse. The bells will announce the evening meal in the inn."

"Is there room?" snaps Kadara.

The youth bows. "Each guesthouse has four separate bedrooms, magistra, and more than adequate water and showers for everyone."

" . . . heard they believed in a lot of washing here . . ." mumbles Yarrl.

"Do you good," Reisa replies.

Dorrin opens the inn door for Liedral, clumsily, with his splinted right hand. The thumb twinges as he bumps it against the iron latch.

"Greetings," offers the silver-haired older woman who rises from a small desk. "You are master Dorrin and trader Liedral?"

"Yes."

"I'm Barla. Let me show you to your quarters."

A stone staircase to the left of the door circles the open foyer and brings them to the second-story landing, where there is a single door with a brass handle. A corridor stretches the length of the inn, but their guide halts by the door and opens it.

"These are your rooms. You also have a washroom beyond the bath. If you wish to bathe, I would suggest a little haste, because it will not be long before dinner." She smiles an apparently genuine smile.

"Thank you," Dorrin says.

"Enjoy your rooms," Barla turns.

"Rooms?" asks Liedral, stepping through the door. "Oh . . ."

Dorrin closes the door behind him. They stand at one end of a sitting room that opens to a small balcony with a pair of carved wooden armchairs. In the sitting room are a table, with four matching armless chairs, a half-filled bookcase, and two large wooden armchairs before the fireplace, in which a fire has been laid.

Liedral steps into the second room, containing a triple-width bed with a large but simple red oak headboard, a dressing table, and two matching wardrobes. Beyond the bedroom is a bathroom, with a shower, but no tub, and a doorway that presumably leads to the washroom mentioned by Barla. The coverlet is a repeating design of green and gray, without lace, and the bed has real sheets.

"I suspect your bargaining position is better than you think," Liedral says dryly.

"You can have the first shower," Dorrin says.

"Shower? Are they all freezing like yours was?"

"Oh . . . That was just mine. Let's see if this one is warm or cold." Dorrin steps into the bathroom. There are two other doors. He opens one, to a simple jakes, and closes it, then peers into the ceramic-tiled shower, turning the single handle and feeling the water, before turning it off, and wiping his hand on one of the large towels hung on separate pegs.

"Lukewarm," he announces. "Sunwarmed from a roof cistern. You take off your clothes—"

"Very funny. I could understand that much."

"—and stand under the water. There's some soap there, and you wash. If you don't like cool water, you just get wet and turn the water off, and lather up, and then turn it on to rinse off."

"I'll take the first shower," Liedral announces, dropping her pack on the floor. "I haven't been clean in days."

"I'll be on the balcony. Let me know when you're done." Dorrin carries his pack into the bedroom and pulls out his clothes. He only has three outfits, and the one he is wearing and the smithing clothes are filthy. He leaves those in a pile on the smooth stone floor, and folds his few clean underclothes and good brown outfit, setting them on a shelf in the wardrobe. He pauses and draws in the faint scent of the trilia oil used to treat the wood. Then he tucks the battered pack into the bottom of the wardrobe, and walks through the sitting room and onto the balcony, where he sits facing the harbor.

A light breeze ruffles his hair, bringing the tang of seawater. To the north, a scattering of clouds hugs the ocean horizon. Dark green water, with but a tinge of white, ebbs and flows against the dark stone of the harbor breakwater, while the harbor waters bear only the faintest of swells.

The *Black Diamond* sits alone at the pier, the only time Dorrin can recall the harbor so empty. Where are the Recluce ships? Must they spend their time at sea now that all trade with eastern Candar is blocked?

Watching a gull sweep down toward the *Diamond*, as if hoping for a meal, sweeping and rising, sweeping and rising, he loses track of time, and his eyes close.

"Dorrin . . ."

He starts in the chair. Liedral, towel wrapped around her, stands in the open doorway behind him. "I think I heard a bell of some sort."

"I didn't hear anything."

"You're tired."

He rises and stretches, but his eyes go from the damp brown hair to the uncovered shoulders above the towel to the unclothed legs beneath the towel.

"I don't think I'm ready for that, yet."

"I know."

Liedral leans toward him and brushes his lips with hers. Dorrin steps closer and embraces her for a long moment before letting go.

"I need a shower." He steps around her and does not look back. It will only hurt. Damn Jeslek! Damn all the Whites!

Before he showers, he washes the dirty clothes and hangs them out in the washroom next to those Liedral has already washed. Then he takes off the splint before getting into the ceramic stall.

The shower water remains lukewarm, but Dorrin enjoys it, shaving, and scrubbing himself thoroughly twice. He doubts that he has been so clean in seasons, and he has missed such luxuries. Is this just to tempt him to renounce his engine and what it stands for? He turns off the water.

The second set of bells rings. He dries and dresses quickly and rejoins Liedral on the balcony, where she watches the shadows lengthen across the small harbor.

"It is peaceful... orderly... here. I can see now why your cottage was the same way. How could anyone raised here not be that way?"

"There are some who find it boring."

"Did you?"

Dorrin shakes his head. "I just wanted to build my engines."

"Was that just because they decreed the engines were wrong?"

"It's not that simple. But we need to go down for supper, I mean, it's dinner here."

They walk through the quarters and out onto the landing.

"No locks. Just bolts for privacy. That says a lot right there."

"It does. Now... about the engines. To make one work, you need to burn coal at high temperatures and turn water into steam. When coal burns that hot you have chaos. Also, steam is a form of controlled chaos." Dorrin guides Liedral from the foot of the staircase to the right and the public room. "That's not the only problem. Engines take a lot of iron and a lot of coal. That could create a lot of slag rock and a lot of ashes and mine leavings, and all those create problems, possible chaos, with the streams and the land."

They stop inside the public room. Tyrel raises an arm. "They must like you, master Dorrin. They have great beer, and they know how to cook fish." His rough voice carries across the high-ceilinged room.

"Master Dorrin, I have a big bed all to myself. And

it's soft." Frisa's excitement brings a smile to Dorrin's face.

He bends down as he stops by the table where Merga, Pergun, Rylla, and Frisa sit. "I'm glad, Frisa."

"A healer named Rebekah is going to see Pergun tomorrow," Merga says.

"Keep tongull a-gettin' mess up," slurs Pergun.

"And mommy said that we might get to have a house like where we're staying. Will we, master Dorrin?"

"I don't know yet, Frisa."

"You'll get us a house. I know you will."

Dorrin tries not to wince at Frisa's faith, instead patting her shoulder. Merga just smiles, and Pergun watches as a serving woman sets a plate down.

"Your table seems to be there." Liedral points to the only table set for two.

As they sit, Yarrl, Reisa, Petra, and Kadara enter and take places at a square table for four. The tables are polished red oak, smooth, and the cutlery seems to be of pewter, with cloudy-blue glass tumblers on the table.

"Would you like wine, beer, or redberry?" asks the older, but dark-haired serving woman who has delivered the meal to those at Merga's table.

"Wine, I think," says Liedral.

"Redberry for you, ser?"

Dorrin nods, and the woman leaves.

"How did she know?"

"I guess it shows."

"What? That you work in order? Why does that affect what you drink?"

"Very few Blacks can handle any form of alcohol. It's really a subtle form of chaos, I guess."

"I'm glad I'm not that orderly."

Even as Liedral speaks, the serving woman has returned with two pitchers. "Here you are. Dinner tonight is whitefish, with fried quilla on the side, and we do have honeycakes as a sweet." She is gone with the last of her words.

"She's quick."

"Advantages of order, I think."

"You're nervous, aren't you?" Liedral sips the wine. "This is good."

"It should be. There are advantages to order." Dorrin sips the redberry slowly. "And yes, I am nervous. Wouldn't you be if your father—the man who threw you off Recluce—was one of the Council that would decide your fate?"

"I suppose so. But isn't he just one of them?"

"It doesn't help to have one of three against you before you start."

"Why is he against you?"

"I suppose because I didn't accept his word unquestioningly. He was right sometimes, but I didn't even want to give him that because he'd never admit when I might be right."

"Can you afford that now?"

"No." Dorrin laughs. "But that doesn't make it easy."

The fish dishes arrive. "I'll bring the honeycakes later."

"How can they have honeycakes with a trade embargo? Honey is expensive."

"Not here. It's a trade item. Honeybees thrive on order. So do crops and flowers."

Liedral shakes her head, then cuts a slice of fish and lifts it to her mouth. Dorrin swallows, realizing that his mouth is watering and his stomach growling. He can't remember when he last had a meal other than bread and cheese and fruit or roots—or cold mutton. For a time, they eat silently. Except for those at Tyrel's table, so does everyone else in the room.

"No wonder everyone hates Recluce," Liedral says finally.

Dorrin raises his eyebrows, afraid to open his mouth. The quilla is still as crunchy as he remembers. Now it only grows in the highest southern hills, although old tales mention when it was once common.

"Orderly, calm, rich—and with good food."

"I put a higher value on running water."

"I noticed that before I got here. And I thought you were so clever with the running water in your house." Liedral sips the wine.

"I was. I was clever enough to figure out how to install it. You know, just dreaming about something or knowing it can be done is the easy part. Doing it is what's hard." Dorrin savors the redberry, glad to have it again, then eats the last slice of the delicate whitefish.

Their plates disappear, to be replaced with smaller light brown dishes, each containing a large honeycake.

"Such luxury . . ." murmurs Liedral.

"Such temptation," snorts Dorrin as he picks up the cake, sniffing the aroma of fresh-baked pastry and warm honey and carna nuts.

"You're so cynical."

"Perhaps." He bites off half the pastry.

"You think they're actually tempting you?"

Dorrin slowly chews and swallows. "More like reminding me."

Liedral, her mouth full, nods in turn, then swallows. "How good order truly is?"

"Something like that. They're also putting on a show for everyone else."

"So you'll think about the fate of the others?"

"Of course."

"Maybe it's more like a bribe? Maybe, just maybe, they need you."

"You really think so?"

Liedral makes a motion with her hand to indicate her mouth is full.

"And you clearly like the bribe?" Dorrin grins.

"I intend to enjoy it fully."

The serving woman passes, and Dorrin raises a hand. "How much for the supper?" He reaches for the leather purse at his belt.

"Nothing, ser. The Council is paying for your stay." The serving woman smiles, and refills the glass tumbler.

"That makes it very expensive," Dorrin remarks to Liedral.

"Perhaps," Liedral says. "On the other hand, maybe other members of the Council are less against you and your machines than your father."

"You may have something there." Dorrin rubs his chin. "So long as it were just me, they'd defer to him . . . but if it affects all Recluce . . ."

"Keep that in mind." Liedral looks toward the door where three figures in black stand. "Here they come."

Dorrin stands and waits until the three are near. "I'd like you to meet Liedral. She's the trader to whom you and I owe my success in building the *Black Diamond.*"

Liedral has also risen. She inclines her head and half-bows.

"Dorrin, Liedral, Magistra Ellna, and Magister Videlt," Oran says. The two other Councillors both incline their heads to the couple.

Dorrin inclines his head in return.

"I am honored to meet you," Liedral offers. "I was just leaving—"

"We would also be pleased if you would join the discussion," offers Oran. "Your views would be helpful." He nods to a large table in the corner.

As the group walks toward the table, Merga's and

Rylla's eyes follow, and Dorrin can catch the whisper from the old healer.

" . . . them's the real mighty of the world . . ."

Pergun eats slowly with Merga and Frisa, while Tyrel eats with several of his crew, their fare spiced more with frequent refills from tall bottles of a green brandy. Dorrin sees the brandy bottles and shudders. The green brandy of Recluce is powerful. Besides the three Council members, none of the tables holds anyone who was not on the *Black Diamond*.

Once the five have seated themselves, Oran begins. "We understand that you and Brede and Kadara made a valiant effort to save Spidlar."

Valiant—that is one word, Dorrin thinks. How about doomed, stupid, and bloody? "We did make an effort," he concedes. "At times, I doubt that it was wise."

All three Blacks look at the table. Finally, Oran looks up. "You feel that building your engine was unwise?"

"No. Building the engine, I still believe, was necessary and wise. Using what I learned to try to defend Spidlar was unwise."

"Would you like to explain that?" asks the magistra, her eyes even darker than her black tunic and trousers.

"The Whites don't do much harm to most people. They do maintain better order than would exist without them. They have good roads, clean cities, and not much crime or theft. But they're caught in a trap. Their power rests on chaos, but to maintain their power they also need order. Too much order would destroy their power; so will too much chaos."

Videlt nods; Oran watches; Ellna puts both hands on the table.

"That's really beside the point," Dorrin says. "I'm sorry about wandering, but my mind isn't as clear as it should be. Anyway, by introducing better tactics and some combat engineering, all we succeeded in doing was killing a lot of innocent, or relatively innocent, people, a handful of White Wizards, and ensuring that a lot of people will go hungry this winter. We forced the traders to relocate, which will improve the trading abilities in places like Sarronnyn and Suthya and which will hurt eastern Candar." His eyes turn on the three. "Part of this is your fault."

Oran's mouth opens, but the black-haired Ellna extends a hand. "Let him finish." She looks again at Dorrin. "Go on."

Dorrin clears his suddenly dry throat. "You pushed me out, and the Whites didn't like what I was starting to do. Blacks—especially not male Blacks—aren't welcome west of the Westhorns. So . . . I tried to defend Spidlar. A lot of people died, and where am I? Back here, being judged again. I don't claim to be wise. But that sort of foresight is supposed to be what a Council is for."

"There is that." Videlt's hand strays to his short-trimmed and dark brown beard, a beard darker than his lank light brown hair.

"You have shown that the White blockade can be broken," says Ellna.

"But only with Dorrin's ship," interjects Liedral. "That won't encourage either the Bristans or the Hamorians."

"In any case," says Dorrin, trying to steer the conversation back where he wants it, "because we share this responsibility, I think we should try to work out something that will benefit everyone." He smiles grimly. "Unless you've already made a decision."

"The Council hasn't come to a final decision. We felt we ought to talk to you."

Dorrin wipes his forehead, tanned from nearly an eight-day at sea, wrestling with sails and a ship never designed for open ocean or an engine. Despite his shower, he still feels grimy, almost as if still smeared with the black of the coal. "It seems that you think I might offer some sort of answer, but you still don't feel I quite belong, and you don't know what to do."

"That's close enough," Ellna says. "Why do *you* think you might offer us an answer?"

"Without something like my ship, Fairhaven will choke Recluce again. Or at the very least, isolate you. Is that what you want?"

"The Council has been concerned . . ." begins Oran.

"We're more than concerned," Ellna says. "But we also don't want to destroy what Recluce is based upon for mere survival. That's what the Blacks in eastern Candar did in the time of Creslin. They accepted more and more domination of the chaos wizards for the sake of civil peace and good roads. We don't want to build machines or devices that lead us down the same path."

"Any high-energy machine must embody chaotic energy by definition," adds Oran.

"Life embodies some chaotic energy—by definition," says Dorrin. "The question is whether order or chaos dominates." Is he being wise in being so forthright? Can he be otherwise?

"You really haven't answered the question," observes Videlt.

"I can tell you what I think," Dorrin says. "And you can tell me what you think. But what any of us thinks isn't the issue. My engine is mostly of black iron, and you can sense its roots in order."

"Chaos can use order . . ."

"How about this? You let me build my smithy and shipworks at Southpoint. There's nothing there."

"There's no harbor. How?"

"There's one small inlet. That's enough for now for the *Black Diamond*. Later, we can expand it."

The color leaches from the tall wizard's face. "We can't accept potential chaos on Recluce itself."

"Stop jumping to conclusions. Machines and chemicals aren't chaos. I can't deal with chaos either, and you know it."

"You've changed."

"Probably not enough."

"Oran," interrupts Ellna gently, "have you considered a trial period? Let Dorrin build his works, and then let us evaluate them. We could gain, and at the least he would have a respite."

"How long?" asks Videlt.

"At least two years," Liedral says.

Dorrin is glad she has spoken. He would have asked for less, because he feels that he must have a new ship ready long before two years.

"Isn't that a bit . . . extended?" asks Videlt.

"It is if things go well," Dorrin admits. "But matters often don't where the Whites are concerned. Also, we have to build facilities . . ."

"I suspect there would be some willing to offer their help," says Oran dryly.

"Perhaps," Dorrin responds. "In that case, you can evaluate earlier."

"That seems fair," Ellna interjects. "It is in our interests."

"Oh?" says Oran.

"He's building another port, Oran. How can that hurt us? You've often pointed out how the winter seas make Land's End unsuitable."

The taller wizard nods—reluctantly. His lips pucker as if he has swallowed a pickled pearapple.

"There's one other thing," Dorrin says. "I need iron—enough to build another ship."

"Another one?" Oran's voice is tart.

"I didn't build this one," Dorrin explains. "It was a grounded hull, and I put an engine on it. If you want to evaluate my works, I should have the chance to build one ship the way I think it should be built."

"That seems fair to me," says Ellna. "It fits the idea of a trial."

"Surely, you don't expect us to pay—"

"I think I have enough to pay for at least some of the iron," Dorrin says, "thanks to Liedral. We have some more trading goods which we can factor here."

"Hmmm . . ."

"We'd have to sell some to whatever Bristans or Hamorians put in here."

"There aren't many," says Videlt with a twist to his lips. "But we'll give you a Council letter. You'll need that for the iron, you know."

"No," Dorrin smiles, "I didn't know that. I can't say I'm surprised. What about coal?"

"That's not under Council seal, and you'll have to make your own arrangements there."

"How soon can we begin?" Dorrin is tired, and feels the evening is dragging on, even though they have not talked that long.

"You will have the Council letter for the iron in the morning, and it will cover not only the iron, but convey a suggestion that your . . . project is in our interests." Ellna's smile is more than perfunctory, but not much.

Dorrin yawns. "I'm sorry, but . . ."

"We understand." Ellna rises, and the other two Blacks follow.

Oran catches his son's eyes, and Dorrin understands the tall wizard would like a few words privately.

Dorrin waits until Liedral has touched his hand, kissed him lightly on the cheek, and climbed the stairs. Ellna and Videlt have already left the inn.

"I'd like to think you've changed, son," Oran says gently.

"I haven't changed the way you'd like," Dorrin says heavily. "And I think that might be why you're losing to the White Wizards."

"Creslin destroyed Jenred, and you destroyed Jeslek."

Dorrin shakes his head. "You *still* don't understand. Jeslek was a chaos focus. That was why he could raise mountains. I destroyed the focus, but the forces remain. There will be another Jeslek ... with great powers, and another, so long as Recluce embodies order."

"You're being too mechanical. The higher order considerations . . ."

"That's animal crap," snorts the engineer. "Creslin sold his soul to found Recluce—or at least his sight for a good part of his life. The order you already have created Jeslek—I didn't. And you're worried about a few order-based machines on one end of the isle. The Whites sure as the demons didn't like order-based machines."

"Don't you see? That's exactly why we can't afford more concentrated order."

"Do you want me to take my ship and my ideas to Brista—or Hamor? Is that what you have in mind?"

"We agreed to a trial . . ."

"I know. But I want a real trial, not just a few years so that Recluce can get back on its feet and throw me out again."

"We'll keep our word."

Dorrin does not shake his head, however much he wants to. "I know you will. So will I."

"Good night, son." Oran raises his hand in almost a benediction before turning.

Dorrin waits until his father has left before he walks up the stone stairs. He smiles when he enters the bedroom. Liedral is asleep on one side of the bed, facing the door, the lamp still lit. He undresses silently, blows out the lamp, and slips into the cool sheets, permitting himself only a single gentle squeeze of her bare shoulder.

" . . . night . . ." she murmurs. " . . . love . . ."

"Good night," he whispers.

CLX

"How DID YOU incompetents ever let this happen?" Sterol's voice is low.

The three White Wizards look at the table with the mirror, then back to the High Wizard. Finally, Fydel speaks. "He built a ship that can run into the teeth of the wind. The *White Storm* went aground trying to catch him."

Cerryl nods in agreement, stepping back from the others ever so slightly.

"Why didn't they at least fire his ship?"

"They weren't carrying canvas. He'd stripped the topside, and this engine thing somehow pushed or pulled them away. They skirted the sandbars all along the coast until they got to the Gulf, where the winds changed. Then they lifted sail, and with the engine and sails, no one could catch up."

"Wait an instant. You said they didn't have sails."

"The sails were furled," explains Anya. Her voice is cold, cutting. "This engine of his is as hot as chaos and bound in black iron."

"How does it work?"

"We don't know, exactly."

"Wonderful. Just marvelous. We now have a renegade Black Wizard who can build an engine that nullifies our whole blockade of Recluce, and his ship is sitting at Land's End." Sterol sighs. "Well . . . you three and Jeslek did it. You'll have to live with it."

Anya raises her eyebrows.

"Really, Anya. Are you that dense? Have we ever

had any success against Recluce proper?" The High Wizard smiles coldly. "You three incompetents can leave. You had better hope that the Blacks on Recluce hold the price of asylum on their fair isle as no more Black engines."

"Or . . .?" asks Anya.

"I told you. Now, please go away." Sterol fingers the gold amulet. After the door closes, he wipes his forehead with a white cloth from his pocket and looks toward the mirror. Then he wipes his forehead again.

CLXI

DORRIN AND KADARA ride down the Great Highway, side by side, with Liedral and the cart following.

"I never thought I'd get home." The redhead holds the reins in her left hand, her right still in the sling across her abdomen.

Dorrin glances to his left, down into the fertile plains around the Feyn River, and the waving green stalks of grain. "It is home, and it's not."

Shortly, if he understands the directions, they must turn uphill and take the winding road toward the one iron mine and smelter that exist on Recluce.

The solid gray kaystone is clear enough. Two arrows appear. The one points straight ahead and states *Feyn—5*. The other points to the right, along a narrower, but still stone-paved, road, and reads *Iron Works—4*.

They turn uphill, following the gently inclined road with the wide turns.

"This is a side road and better than some highways in Candar," says Liedral above the creaking of the cart.

"It's designed for the iron wagons."

"The road to Froos's place didn't look like this."

There are definite advantages to order. Thinking about the doubt on his father's face, Dorrin decides there are also definite disadvantages.

The iron works is a complex of five stone buildings set on a terrace cut from the hillside roughly two hundred cubits below the top of the ridge lines. Smoke filters from the top of several beehive-shaped structures—the blast furnaces. A slightly inclined stone-walled road runs from what appears to be the mine entrance to the top of the blast furnaces. Lower yet are two shorter buildings from which an earthshaking and dull hammering issues. Between the two buildings runs a millrace with an overshot waterwheel.

Dorrin reins up in front of the smallest building, the one away from the furnaces and the hammering and slitting mills. "Do you want to come in?" he asks Kadara.

"No." She draws the single blade she wears and begins to work through the exercises with her left hand.

Liedral ties the cart and follows Dorrin.

A gray-haired man looks up from the table where he studies what appear to be drawings of the mine shafts. He steps forward. "I'm Korbow. How might I be helping you?"

"Dorrin. I'm a smith with a special Council project." Dorrin takes out the letter with the seal and presents it to the lean older man.

Korbow slowly reads through the letter, scratching his head as he goes. Finally, he looks up. "You want how much iron?"

While Dorrin would like a ship built entirely of black iron and steel, he knows that it is not feasible, not yet, since he would need well over ten thousand stone of iron, and he cannot possibly calculate the cross-beams, and even the structure he would need. So he gives his estimate for what it will take to plate the oak and fir ship he has in mind.

"Something like two thousand stone."

The mine chief shakes his head. "Maybe a thousand stone in two seasons, and that would run close to two hundred golds." He looks at the letter Dorrin has presented. "Must be a terrible-like problem for the Council to be so interested."

Liedral raises her eyebrows.

The engineer clears his throat. He has perhaps a hundred golds, another thirty golds' worth of goods, and the *Black Diamond.* "What about a season and a half?"

"For a thousand? We'd have a problem with the slitting mills there, running it through."

"What if I took most of it in plate, half a span thick?"

"Might make it easier, but those plates weigh almost seven stone each, and they're just two cubits by three."

Dorrin laughs. "That's about the right size."

"Shouldn't that lower the price?" suggests Liedral.

Korbow grins. "Aye."

"By about half," adds Liedral.

Korbow's grin fades somewhat. "I don't know that it would be that much."

"You're delivering to one customer, and that's easier," persists Liedral.

"Aye." The iron works man coughs into a huge hand.

"And the Council thinks it's a good idea."

"That they say." Korbow shakes his head. "We do this, and I need to run out extra stock for my regulars first. What are you building, something out of all iron?"

"Not quite."

"It's also a long haul to Land's End."

"I'd want it at Southpoint."

"There's nothing there."

"Not yet, but there will be."

"What about my regulars?" Korbow asks again.

"You take care of them first." Dorrin will not be in a position to use the iron for at least four eight-days, in any case.

"Be three-four eight-days."

"Eighty golds for the thousand," Liedral says.

Korbow's face turns sour. "You drive hard, trader."

Dorrin calculates, then decides. "I'll offer more than coin . . . if you'll trust me. I'm working on a new kind of ship that doesn't rely on just the wind. I don't know as you'd need it . . . but once the second one is built, you can look and see if there are devices we build that you can use."

"So . . . you're the one with the magic ship?"

"It's not magic. It has an engine powered by steam."

"The Council won't allow that ashore, not even here."

"I know. But what about gears, clutches, other things? I might be able to make a better pump."

"Pumps . . . that's another thing. They'd rather I go deeper than farther north on the seam, but I can't do that without better drainage." Korbow purses his lips. "I'll take your eighty—and a pump or something that will help." He grins. "I know you Black types. If I leave it to you to be fair, I won't get cheated."

Dorrin grins back. Liedral shakes her head.

"You have to send someone to come with the wagon, the first time, anyways. We'll say four eight-days from now?"

Dorrin nods.

"Now . . . not that I wouldn't trust a man supported by the Council, you understand . . ."

"But you want a token of faith?"

"Your faith, I'm sure, is good. But what if you fail,

and I have to cart back all that plate and reslit it smaller?"

"Say ten golds? Toward the iron, but forfeit if we fail?"

Korbow frowns.

"Each time," Dorrin adds. "I give you another ten when you deliver the first load."

"Fair's fair."

Dorrin counts out the ten golds, not wanting even to think about how much more his project will cost.

"In four eight-days in your location by Southpoint, and you send a messenger to guide my wagon."

They shake hands.

"You're stronger than you look. Might be a smith at that." The iron works chief smiles again. "Now . . . I need to figure out how to squeeze and brace the lower seam . . ."

Dorrin inclines his head. "Our thanks."

After they leave, and find Kadara still practicing outside, almost in rhythm to the dull hammering from the hillside above, Liedral turns to Dorrin. "He would have taken eighty."

"I know. But he's happy now, and . . . if I get him a better pump or something, he just might help more in the future. I don't want to build just one ship."

"You really think they'll let you?"

"I don't think they have any choice. Has any ship ported since we did?"

"I see what you mean."

"They really don't want the world to ignore Recluce, and that's what's happening." While he can tell himself that, Dorrin's thoughts still come back to the doubtful look on his father's face, and his recollections of even more adamant opposition to engines of iron.

CLXII

To the left of Great Highway, grass stretches perhaps a kay, then ends abruptly at the cliffs that drop sheerly to the Eastern Ocean below. To the right, the grass stretches nearly three kays, sloping downward to a lower set of more ragged bluffs overlooking the Gulf of Candar.

Winding through the grass, and marked by occasional scrub oaks, is a narrow stream, no more than a few cubits wide. On either side of the road, the plains grass grows almost stirrup-high. The muted wash of the sea and the twitter of insects are the only sounds besides the impact of hoofs on stone and the creaking of Liedral's cart.

"I can't believe this road," says Liedral. "It's magnificent, and there's nothing here."

"Supposedly, it was Creslin's last project. He liked stonework a lot, and he insisted that there should be a Great Highway from one end of Recluce to the other." Dorrin studies the nearly straight road ahead, looking for the point where it will drop through the rocky hills to the more marshy land at the tip of the isle. "It does stop about a half kay from the inlet. Back then, no one could see the point in driving it through a saltwater marsh."

"That was only because he died before they finished the Highway," adds Kadara sourly. "Otherwise, we'd have a road and a stone pier there."

"I'm beginning to see why everyone here is so driven," Liedral says. "Trying to live up to the accomplishments of the greatest hero in history is a bit much."

"He wasn't that great," Kadara points out. "He put Megaera through the demon's hell itself, and then followed her to redeem himself. They almost didn't survive their daughter's birth."

Dorrin is silent, reflecting on what Kadara has said. Must every great accomplishment require a price not only from the doers, but from those around them? Do the payments of soul and blood ever end?

"What happened to the daughter?" asks Liedral.

"She lived and had children. Ask Dorrin."

"Dorrin?"

"Supposedly, her name was Dylyss, after Creslin's mother, although some insist it was Lyse, after his dead sister. She had three children." Dorrin reins up at the top of the slope down to Southpoint and waits for Kadara and Liedral. "There." The Highway angles right for nearly a kay to a wide sweeping turn that carries the road back nearly directly below them for another turn. From the second turn, the stone road arrows straight for a marshy area bisected by a narrow inlet. Twice the stream, spanned with well-crafted stone bridges, wanders under the road. While the stream runs into the marsh, the road stops at the edge of the marshy area. From the sides of the marsh rises slightly higher grassy land that circles the marsh and almost touches the inlet where the thin line of water meets the ocean.

"Not very prepossessing."

"It has possibilities," Dorrin says. "I can blast out some of the marshy area and widen the inlet. The ground north of the marsh is solid, and the rocks can be cut and order-hardened into solid black stones for building."

"You are an optimist," Kadara responds.

"I did build an engine." Dorrin urges the gelding forward and down the dusty stones of the seldom-used highway.

Liedral and Kadara exchange glances as they follow Dorrin downhill. With the lower elevation comes dampness, and various bugs, including flies, which Liedral fans away one-handed.

At the end of the Great Highway, Liedral pulls up the cart. "What next?"

"I'd like to ride around the marsh."

"I can't take the cart, you know."

"Tether it. Basla can carry us both for that little bit."

Dorrin dismounts and uses his small sledge, taken from Liedral's cart, to pound in the iron tether stake. Then, while she secures the cart, he unharnesses the cart horse and leads both animals to the edge of the stream. Their hoofs and his boots sink into the swampy ground, and, as they drink, he flails at the flies. Kadara just rides her mount to the stream and lets the mare seek the water herself.

When Dorrin walks back, Liedral takes the harness leads from him and ties them to the tether stake. He mounts, but slips his foot from the stirrup to allow her a step up. Then he helps her into place behind the low saddle. "We'll have to go slowly, I think."

"You think? This isn't the most comfortable position I've ever been in."

Dorrin, feeling her arm around his waist, grins.

"And stop grinning."

"How do you know I'm grinning?"

"You just feel like it."

"She knows you, Dorrin," calls Kadara from behind them.

"It's firmer here." Dorrin guides the black gelding around the left side of the marsh, still enjoying the feel of Liedral's arm around his waist. So long as he follows the shorter grass, the horse has no problem with footing.

As they near the end of the vegetation and the soft

sound of the ocean on sand and rock increases, he realizes that the area of grass has widened into a rough oblong that sits almost two cubits higher than the grassy path they have taken.

"Let's get down. I want to look at this." He helps Liedral down and then dismounts, prodding the grass and scuffing away the shallow layer of dirt until he reaches stone—flat stone. "Someone used this as a harbor or outpost before."

"It has to have been a long time ago."

"Longer than that, and what difference does it make?" asks Kadara.

"Not much, except that the inlet might be deeper than we thought." He pauses. "On the other hand, if it was all man-made—"

"It might be shallower?"

Dorrin walks toward the point where a pile of stone rises even above the grasses. He looks across the inlet to a similar pile of stone and nods. "We'll need to widen this, probably not for the *Diamond*, but the next one."

"The next one?" asks Kadara. "They'll let you build another one?"

"They already agreed." Dorrin looks back around the small marsh, certainly no more than five hundred cubits from end to end, less than half that wide. "I need to get busy figuring out where to put things and what we'll need where. Promised Tyrel I'd be back before long with some idea of supplies."

Once more, Liedral and Kadara exchange glances. This time, Liedral shrugs.

Dorrin turns from his study of the ocean, and swings up into the saddle. "There's some sort of channel beyond the points, and it's still pretty deep. You can tell by how smooth the water is—almost like someone put an underwater breakwater there." He extends a hand to Liedral. " . . . a lot to do here . . . not much time . . ."

They ride back toward the cart under the midafternoon sun, the cool breeze sliding in off the Gulf of Candar and toward the Eastern Ocean beyond.

CLXIII

DORRIN NODS TO Vaos, and the youth lifts the white flag with the crimson crossbars. Dorrin kneels and flicks the striker. As the fuse burns, he and Vaos race along the planks and drop behind the low embankment.

CRRRuuummmppp! Earth, sand, vegetation, and water erupt from the edge of the marsh.

Dorrin rises and surveys the mess, watching the water from the hillside stream slowly carry some of the debris seaward. So far his efforts have succeeded in widening the inlet into a channel nearly sixty cubits wide and almost twenty deep.

Still, the *Black Diamond* is anchored offshore in the momentarily quiet water on the Gulf side of the point, waiting until the blasting is complete.

Behind him beyond the end of the road, a pile of stones is slowly growing, already almost enough for the footings for the first pier.

He turns and squints into the midmorning sunlight. Another wagon rolls down the road from the last turn.

"Who's that?" asks Vaos.

"I don't know. Let's go see." The two walk toward the end of the road. Northward, on the hillside, below the tents, are foundations for five buildings where Pergun, his lisping and slurring almost gone, toils with the stones and soil until the timber Dorrin has ordered arrives.

"Looks like timber," Vaos comments.

"They said it wouldn't be here for another two or three days."

"Maybe they're early."

Dorrin doubts that, but anything is possible, he supposes. He lengthens his stride toward the faint dust raised by the approaching wagon. The carter, a slender figure with graying hair, reaches the road end before Dorrin does and stands by the team.

Dorrin swallows as he recognizes Hegl. The smith waits by the wagon laden with heavy timbers. "You brought her back, Dorrin. I owe you."

"No." Dorrin shakes his head, thinking of Kadara's injuries, her anger, and her losses.

Hegl smiles, a bitter smile. "I know my daughter. I talked to her. She'll never tell you, but I know." His face clears. "Besides, I like the idea of building a Black seaport and a real ship like what you started. And I like the idea of you getting the last word on your father. Makes me small, I know, but in some ways, I am small." The old smith gestures to the wagon. "These are for a temporary wharf. They're just pine, but you'll need that until you can quarry the right kind of stone. Julka's bringing another wagon with smithy tools and firebricks. That'll take longer, probably a couple of days."

Dorrin has trouble keeping his mouth from dropping open.

"There'll be others, too. Some of us want to see some changes." Hegl grins. "Like your mother."

"Dorrin! Those the timbers we need?"

"So where do you want them?" asks Hegl. "You got work to do, and I need to rustle up some more stuff."

Dorrin calculates. The ground is too soft for the

heavy wagon. "Right there. I'm just about through cleaning out the channel, so we can put the footings down."

"I'm just an old smith, boy. But, remember, you need to make this a big port, so don't think small, like me." He gives Dorrin another grin and his face sobers. "I owe you more than you know. Weidra never thought she'd see Kadara again, let alone see grandchildren."

Vaos stands back, his eyes darting from one smith to the other.

Dorrin wants to scream that it wasn't his doing. He holds back, instead only demurring. "Kadara did it all. The only thing I did was build a ship."

"The only thing . . . nonsense. Now let's get on with these timbers."

Dorrin knows what he is, and he is not the hero figure that some are making him out to be. Belatedly, he points to Vaos. "Hegl, this is Vaos, my apprentice. Vaos, Hegl was the smith who made it all possible."

Hegl flushes. "Nonsense, I say . . . stuff and nonsense." He looks at Vaos. "You're strong enough for the shorter crossbeams. Pitch in."

Vaos smiles and steps toward the wagon.

Idly, as he lifts a timber, Dorrin wonders if Creslin ran into the same problem. Then he shakes his head. Even mentally comparing himself to Creslin is sheer gall. He cannot control storms, nor can he wield a blade, nor has he founded a kingdom and the basis of order. All he has done is build one ship and get a whole lot of people killed—scarcely the basis for greatness.

He lifts down another timber.

CLXIV

STEROL GLARES AT the mirror, and the vision of the ship at the pier, and the buildings on the hillside. "How you ever let this happen, Anya . . ." The White Wizard gestures and the swirling mists refill the mirror.

"The question is whether they keep him." Anya brushes her long red hair back over her shoulder, seating herself in a chair placed to catch the afternoon breeze from the open window. "What happens next?"

"It would appear they're staying on Recluce. The chief Councillor *might* still send them off to Hamor, but it doesn't look that way."

"Chief Councillors have been known to be overridden . . ."

"Veiled hints don't become you, Anya. Every High Wizard has to worry about being replaced. Perhaps you should take the post to learn about it."

"Me? A mere woman? No, thank you."

Sterol coughs and rubs his forehead. "If their Council allows him to stay, it might cause actual chaos on Recluce."

"You're dreaming. I saw that young smith, or whatever he is. He's so Black that even Jeslek's fire wouldn't touch him." Anya shivers at the recollection. "Whatever he does, he won't create chaos."

"He certainly did in Spidlar," reminds Sterol.

Anya frowns. Her eyes flicker from the bed in the corner to the door, and she forces a slow deep breath.

CLXV

"How do you like the fish?" asks Merga.

"Good . . ." mumbles Pergun from one side of the long table.

Beside him, in a row, are Frisa, Rek, and Vaos. Frisa stares at the fish, much as Dorrin does, while the two youths eat without tasting. Across the table, Rylla grins, but half her fish is already gone.

"I'm beginning to feel like a fish," Dorrin says in a low voice to Liedral, who sits to his right. He looks at the fish on the plate, one of a mismatched set scrambled together by his brother Kyl, then out the as-yet-unglazed window. Above him rises a roof, with exposed beams, but no ceilings.

All five of the buildings at Southpoint share the same state—mostly finished walls and roofs, but minimal interior work, except for the shipwright shed and the smithy.

The basic frame for the second ship is taking shape, and already Dorrin and Tyrel have had words, and Dorrin has been forced to compromise yet again, although the compromises have not changed the look of the ship from the model he developed, mainly for Tyrel.

"Begging yer pardon, master Dorrin . . . begging yer pardon . . . you cannot put that much iron on that small a ship . . . not if you want her to cross the Gulf . . ."

" . . . that bad. Are you listening? Dorrin?"

"Sorry," he apologizes.

Liedral gives him a rueful grin. "Even when you are here, you're not. It's a good thing I'm going back to Land's End for a while."

"Oh . . . yes." Now he remembers that she will be waiting for a Hamorian ship that seems likely to put in on the way back from Renklaar. "What do you think will sell best?"

"I don't know, but I'd guess the toys. If you could spare a little time to make a few more for the next ship, whenever it might come in, I think it would be well worth the time."

"Listen to the trader," suggests Yarrl from the other end of the table.

Reisa and Petra grin. Even a faint smile crosses Kadara's lips, followed by a disconcerted expression as she covers her mouth with the back of her hand. A hand strays to her slowly growing abdomen before she catches herself and cuts another piece of the dark fish.

Rylla follows the gesture. "You need all that fish, mistress Kadara."

Kadara groans.

Fish tastes like fish to Dorrin, and the meat at Southpoint has been generally fish supplemented with some mutton. On good days, there are crunchy quilla roots, or perhaps dried pearapples. Although there is adequate food on Recluce, the blockade has limited imported food to items that can be dried or salted, since most must come from Brista or far Hamor.

Even past midsummer, it is too early for the fresh pearapples, or for the few apples nursed along in secluded orchards, or for the greenberries or redberries that cling to the higher cliffs, but ripen late.

There is some flour, barley bread, and mutton, and fish. There are adequate spices, but Dorrin feels that he has already tasted every spice possible on mutton, and no spice changes a fish from a fish—not any that he has tasted.

Still, he should not complain about the fish, not when much of it is basically a gift from Kyl. His brother has only come to Southpoint once, and then only to bring in a huge basket of fish from his boat. All the other times, his crew or someone else has delivered the fish, almost like a peace offering or a thank you. But why? They had never fought, not beyond boyish squabbles, and what has Dorrin done to merit thanks from Kyl?

Thinking about the fish will not get it eaten or Dorrin back to the smithy. He cuts a large slice and stuffs it in his mouth, trying not to think about it. Then he takes a drink of water. Water is about all they have for beverages. Redberry is out of season, and, with the constant drain of his coins for supplies, Dorrin cannot buy spirits, nor has there been time to set up a brewery, or a distillery, let alone do the brewing.

He takes another bite of the fish and of the boiled seaweed, which tastes even worse. Kadara was right: he had been well-off in Spidlar, and he misses those small luxuries.

"Could you wait a day?" he asks Liedral. "I could work on some toys and things. There are a couple of things that I could do this afternoon and tomorrow— like the simple boats and the crank-fan."

"If I leave early the next morning . . ."

"At least, you're listening some of the time," says Yarrl.

Dorrin knows he isn't always listening, but he is trying to juggle so much, and more and more he feels like everything is chaotic, out of control.

Still . . . the improved new boiler sections are almost done, and the shaft gearing will take days, if not an eight-day. He takes another bite of fish and seaweed, and follows it with the last of the stale biscuits on his plate, and more water.

"Master Dorrin eats his seaweed," Merga explains to Frisa. "It's good for you."

Both Vaos and Frisa look unconvinced as they stare at the brown tendrils on their plates.

"Tomorrow, we'll have quilla. It's soaking now," Merga adds.

"That's not much better," mumbles Rek.

Reisa, looking up from a clean plate, only shakes her head. Dorrin will appreciate the quilla more than seaweed, but the choice is between something crunchy and tasteless and something that tastes like oily sawdust. He finishes his water.

After lunch—Dorrin finds it hard to adjust to "lunch" as opposed to dinner as the midday meal—the smith marches back to the smithy and, after packing the forge fire, and starting Rek on a gentle rhythm with the bellows, pulls out a section of three-span-wide plate.

"What would you like me to do?" asks Yarrl.

"Can you finish the steam drum without me?"

"Mostly. Least until we get to the last weld. That's going to take us both if you want it to hold."

"Let me know. I really need to do these boats."

"I know, Dorrin. Coin speaks." Yarrl pauses. "You know, some of those holders want some wagon work. They don't like traveling all the way to Feyn for that smith there."

"Do it." Dorrin measures on the workbench before lifting the tongs. "If they want it tomorrow, start taking it. We can work on the ship later, if we have to, but . . . you need coin. You can't live forever on what you brought."

"It's not that bad. You know, Reisa's charging the holder youth for blade training. Not much, but it helps."

"Everything helps." Dorrin swings the iron into the forge. "Pick it up a little, Rek. Vaos, you'll need the small sledge. We're going to fuller this down to not much more than sheet."

Vaos slips the bottom fuller onto Dorrin's anvil.

"You take over the bellows for a while. Yarrl's going to need Rek for that boiler section."

"Yes, ser." Vaos's voice is resigned to the assignment of the drudge work, and that, Dorrin reflects, is normal. His eyes stray to the large grindstone that will be necessary to polish and shine the propeller for the *Black Diamond*. The metal surface must be as smooth as possible, Dorrin senses. He shakes his head. He needs to get on with making goods for coin, not wool gathering over the new ship when he is not working on it.

Both smiths move iron from opposite sides of the forge, and their hammers lift . . . and fall . . . lift and fall.

CLXVI

DORRIN WIPES HIS forehead, wondering when Liedral will be back from Land's End, and how successful she has been with the Nordlan brig, and with his toys and gadgets. Darkness knows, they need the coins. He lifts the hammer again, and again, until the iron has cooled below the cherry red he needs. With the tongs he thrusts it back into the bricks.

On the other side of the forge, Yarrl works on replacing the curved claw side of a peavey for a holder. His hammer is almost musical on the iron.

"You're working like the demons of light are after you." Rek's face glistens under the sheen of sweat as he pumps the bellows.

"More like the Black Mages of Recluce." Dorrin retrieves the block of iron, deftly eases it onto the anvil with the tongs. He never knew building a new engine would take twice as many parts, it seems, as the old one.

"But they're your people."

"Things are never that simple." Dorrin nods to Vaos. The striker brings down the hammer on the swage— once, twice.. Dorrin returns the iron to the forge, heated here by coal, which requires more work with the bellows by Rek, and occasional sprinkling of the coals with a water can—another item Dorrin had to quickly forge. Dorrin returns the iron to the anvil and nods to Vaos again, for another series of blows. He taps the anvil to signify that the striking on this piece is done. When Vaos lifts the small sledge, Dorrin sets the short and rough valve casing on the fire bricks.

"No one is my people. Not at the moment. They're more afraid of me than the White Wizards. The White Wizards can only starve them to death."

"That's . . . a funny thing . . . to say," pants Rek.

"Slow down for now." Dorrin pulls another flat plate from the stack on his work table, built of a few of the timbers delivered by Hegl. In between engine parts, he must continue to work on the black iron tubing, hoping that it will not be needed, and knowing that it will.

Frisa slips in through the open door, her hair fluffing away from her head. She studies the iron annealing on the firebricks. "Is that something special, master Dorrin?"

"Is it?" asks Rek.

"It's for a special purpose." Dorrin's head throbs as he realizes the evasion he has voiced.

"Mommy told me to tell you that master Kyl is walking up from the pier."

Dorrin sets the iron back on the bench. "Take a break, and get some water, Rek, before you burn up. Vaos, stay here in case Yarrl needs you." Then the smith walks through the doorway of the space that is

part smithy, part engine works, and part something
else and looks down the hillside to the pier where the
Black Diamond is tied. In front of the converted sloop
is a smaller vessel, with two lower masts and nets
drying across the main deck.

A stocky figure marches up the gravel pathway from
the Great Highway. Dorrin raises his hand. The other
grins, raising his own hand.

Dorrin walks over to the porch. "Merga, do we have
anything to drink?"

"Water and cool tea."

Dorrin grimaces and waits as Kyl crosses the last
few rods between them. "I didn't think we'd see you
for a while."

"I didn't think so, either, but the winds aren't right,
and it's easier than fighting them. Sort of nice to have
a port down here, even if getting in is tricky under
sail."

"All we have is water and cool tea."

"Water's fine."

As if she has heard, Merga arrives with two
tumblers.

"Let's go up on the porch." Dorrin leads the way
to the bench. Some time he hopes they will have chairs,
but the new ship comes before chairs, and the only
two they have are the two at each end of the long
kitchen table.

Dorrin sits and takes a deep swallow of the water.
At least it is cold, and he is glad he did divert some
of the stream for running water in the house. At least
he could buy piping rather than having to forge it.

"Still can't get over how you've changed." Wispy
hair straggles across the tanned forehead of the stocky
man.

"So have you." Dorrin surveys Kyl, taking in the
weathered clothes and sun-bleached eyes. "Was it
hard?"

"Getting them to let me go to sea? No . . . not after your letters."

"I hoped . . . but I was never good with words—not like Brede."

"What happened to him?"

"He was good enough to be made marshal of Spidlar. The Whites got him when they crushed his forces at Kleth."

"Was that when you got injured and blinded?"

Dorrin nods.

"What about Kadara?"

"She was almost killed early in the battle. Liedral brought us both back. How I'm not sure. I just managed to hang on . . . my horse." He swallows hard, thinking of Meriwhen, still picturing her in the water behind the *Black Diamond*.

"I didn't mean about Kadara being wounded. You once were . . ."

Dorrin grins. "I was. I wanted her for a time. Then I found Liedral, and I recognized the difference. Kadara's always been in love with Brede. I finally realized that Kadara was indeed more of a sister than a lover. We've adjusted, although she was bitter for a time, and will be, because I couldn't save Brede. I hope that will pass and that I can become some sort of an uncle to her son when he's born. That would be fine." He lifts himself off the bench. "I need your help."

"With father?"

"No. He won't listen to either one of us. As a matter of fact, he still has trouble listening to common sense. Sometimes, anyway." Dorrin strides past his brother and into the part of the high-roofed building that is the metal fabricating area.

Kyl follows, a puzzled expression on his face.

Dorrin stops by the newly built and already battered workbench, lifting the black model of the new ship. "Look."

"It's low, not much freeboard, deep keel."

"You need that to carry the black iron plating." Dorrin turns to a black box nearly four cubits long, which he opens. Inside is a black metal tube with a shoulder rest and a handgrip. "This is just as important."

"What is it?"

"A rocket launcher. Here." Dorrin hands his brother a shell. "It's filled with explosive powder."

"Won't the White Wizards just set it on fire?"

"It would be hard for any except the greatest ones. The casing is thin black steel. Take it."

Kyl holds the projectile, then sets it on the bench. "Why?"

"I'd like you to tell mother about it. You might also explain that I don't intend to be driven off Recluce."

"You wouldn't!"

Dorrin's eyes are like black steel as he looks at his brother. "I intend to save Recluce. And my ships are the only way that will work right now. But Oran insists that everything will be all right so long as we maintain the old order, and he's working on Ellna and Videlt to change their minds. I can't build a ship and politic." He ignores the headache that reminds him that he is doing just that as he speaks to his brother.

"I think you're doing just that." Kyl smiles, and hands back the shell.

"You're right. Do you have any better ideas?"

"Forget about the weapons. They already know you can do something awful. It's better if I just talk about your feeling responsible for all these people and worried that father will let his fears mess up everything." The younger man gestures toward the sun-framed smithy door. "Already, you must have thirty people here from elsewhere on Recluce. It will grow. Darkness, I'd like to live here."

"I haven't counted. I'm glad we had some tents.

You're welcome, though I don't know as we're the best market for your catch."

Kyl laughs. "You will be. You don't need force. All you need is time."

Dorrin has been using force too much, and Kyl is right. But will the Whites and the Council give him time? "You're right. But I worry."

"You can always use force, Dorrin," Kyl says. "Remember, your letters worked—after mother read them."

"I trust your judgment." Dorrin points downhill. "Do you want to see the plans for the new ship?"

"I saw the keel and frame on the way up. It looks like the model, keel and all—demon-damned deep."

"I'll show you the plans. Just wait here." He ducks into the house and walks into the large room in the far corner that contains but a chest, a table and a stool, and a big bed—the only kind he and Liedral can still share—and pulls the drawing from under the chunk of iron that serves as a paperweight.

Kyl smiles as Dorrin sits down and smooths out the paper on the part of the bench between them. "Here."

"It's low," Kyl repeats. "No masts and not as much freeboard as a schooner."

"It's a warship. Nothing more."

"It looks nasty." Kyl gives a shiver. "Do you have a name yet?"

"Not yet. Black something, I suppose."

"You ought to call it something appropriate, like *Black Smith* or *Black Blade*."

I don't know. It's not a smith or a blade."

"*Black Hammer*, then."

Dorrin purses his lips. "Maybe. That sounds better than anything I've thought up. We'll see." He begins to roll the sheet up to keep it from blowing in the breeze. "You know, I've never thanked you for the fish . . . or for being one of the few that weren't always after me."

Kyl glances at the rough stone of the porch floor. "You always were there for me. I never could do anything for you. Now I can."

Dorrin looks at his brother. "I'm glad."

"So am I." Kyl stands and looks at the whitecaps beginning to form on the ocean beyond the inlet. "I need to catch the winds or my crew won't forgive me." He clasps Dorrin roughly for an instant. "I'll see you when I can."

Dorrin watches as his brother hurries toward the fishing boat tied in front of the *Black Diamond*. Then he carries the tumblers into the kitchen and sets them on the wash table.

Unfortunately, he will still need the rockets. He has no doubts that the White Wizards will try something.

CLXVII

DORRIN SITS ON the porch bench, hoping Liedral will join him before he heads down to the shipwright's.

Gee—ahhh . . . A gull circles and dives toward the inlet that is becoming a harbor under Reisa's direction. The stone walls now stretch a good two hundred cubits on each side of the temporary wooden pier, and she is beginning to build a permanent stone pier. With the recent immigrants from as far north on Recluce as Land's End, Reisa has assembled a formidable work crew.

Dorrin stands and opens the kitchen door just as Liedral emerges. "I was looking for you."

"I thought you were going down to Tyrel's."

"I am." Dorrin gestures to the bench.

"I have to get things ready to leave. They say a Bristan trader will be in next eight-day." Liedral sits on the bench, and Dorrin settles next to her. He puts an arm around her and squeezes, but only for a time, until he can sense the tension rising in her. More than a year has passed, and they still cannot hold each other for long before the discomfort that was once screaming agony begins to bubble up in Liedral.

"I'm sorry," she says.

"So am I." He stands, then bends and kisses her cheek. His eyes burn as he goes down the steps. Once he turns back to look uphill, but Liedral has gone inside, getting ready to head out to the warehouse, he supposes.

The late summer sun warms Dorrin as he pauses by the latest structure, a small, squarish, one-story armory—black, like all the other stone buildings. At least he had enough sense to lay out a plan that sets plenty of open space between buildings for the town that seems to be growing.

Silently, he watches as Kadara stretches and forces her right arm to full extension, then lifts the small weight once, then again, then again. Not only can he see the streaking on the redhead's face, but he can feel the agony and discomfort of her exercise. The discomfort arises from her swelling abdomen, and the weight of her son, and the agony comes from rebuilding that slashed and sundered arm.

He has added his own order to that struggle, silently, without thanks, but without Kadara's opposition, either. She suffers him to help heal her.

Dorrin blots his forehead with his sleeve in the stillness. While it is well before midmorning, the stillness promises a warm fall day, and the sea beyond the point is almost glassy, the green-blue sky carrying the faint haze that foretells searing heat later.

Through the heat, the clinking of hammer and stone rises, and the hammering of spikes and nails.

He shifts his glance to Reisa, who also exercises, but with an iron wand twice the weight of a real blade, to Petra, and to several others who have joined the blade squad that Reisa and Kadara have formed—including Quenta, a former farm youth from Feyn who has begged for their training, and others whose names he has never known.

Beyond the armory are the foundations of yet another building—a barracks for the new Black Guard of the port town to replace the tents that Quenta and the others are now using. Dorrin smiles. Pergun has become the de facto director of building. All the buildings are "his"—his armory, his warehouse, his barracks.

Already, Dorrin can sense that the community created out of necessity is developing its own character—and drawing others from the isle in the process. So far, all of them have been orderly in character, but Dorrin has no illusions that it will remain that way. Will he have to follow the exile precedent of the Council?

He shivers, then turns and resumes quick steps downhill to the shipwright's, where, no doubt, Tyrel will be grousing about some new detail.

Even before his booted feet carry him inside the shed and toward the blocks where the ship rests, Tyrel has found him.

"Master Dorrin . . . you sure the new engine won't go over four hundred stone?"

"It should be less than that—two hundred and fifty or less, but we still have to consider the water tanks, and the coal bins . . ."

"The bunkers are both fore and aft and braced different." Tyrel points toward the slideways into the channel. "Those ... are ye sure they'll support this little monster?"

"They should." Dorrin hopes the calculations he has checked and rechecked are accurate.

"Do ye have a name yet for the monster?"

"Why are you always calling it a monster?"

Both look at the near-completed hull, seventy cubits long, perhaps twenty-five wide, with the deep keel that has required both higher graving blocks and a deep trench beneath, not to mention use of explosives and the *Black Diamond* to dredge the inlet deeper.

"It's a black monster. All ye designed it for was destruction. Hasn't got cargo space for much. Just room for troops and coal and weapons and an engine."

"You told me I couldn't build anything bigger ... and I can't afford more. Darkness ... I can't afford this."

Tyrel looks up. "You're getting a mite of help, young fellow."

"I'm getting help." More than he probably deserves, but his coins are running out, and neither the ship nor the engine is close to completion. He pauses. "Let's call it the *Black Hammer*."

"*Black Hammer* it is. Fitting enough for a smith, leastwise." Tyrel coughs. "We need to look at the collar for the main shaft bearing."

Dorrin takes a deep breath. Every time he and Tyrel discuss the ship—the *Black Hammer* now—he has another half-dozen smithing items to redo or develop or add to his list.

The two men climb the ladder and edge across the beams that will support the engine deck.

"If you brace that the way you drew it, and there's any vibration in that shaft, you'll be a-tearing that right out." Tyrel points to the problem.

Even without trying to calculate, Dorrin can sense that the shipwright is correct. "What do you suggest?"

"Run a set of false beams right inside the hull, next to the structural ones. They'd be held in place by weight, but if the shaft vibrates, you see, it won't separate the hull from the beams."

"How much extra weight?"

"With the iron you're putting on, you won't notice it. Maybe fifteen stone."

Fifteen stone is fifteen stone. Where can he shave off another fifteen stone? He must keep the ship as light as he can for the speed. Tyrel doesn't really consider speed, only structural soundness.

"Do it. I'll have to find where else I can cut weight."

The tapping and clinking of the rest of the shipwrights are underscored by the sound of a heavy wagon pulling up beside the big shed.

Dorrin looks down through the beams, recognizing both Hegl and the healer beside him. "Excuse me, Tyrel." He climbs across the unfinished beam work and down the ladder. Why has his mother made the long ride to Southpoint? Is something wrong with his father? Has the Council changed its mind, and is she warning him?

The wagon is laden with a variety of items, ranging from a cradle to a barrel of ship spikes and hull bolts.

Rebekah waves to Dorrin with a smile, but has stepped away from the wagon to allow the unloading to proceed. "Go ahead and unload, Dorrin."

Dorrin turns to the wagon.

"I'll be leaving these with Tyrel," says Hegl as he lowers the tailgate and lifts the barrel of bolts.

Styl appears behind Hegl and grasps the barrel of spikes. "Never say the smiths don't bring what ye need when ye need it." He offers everyone a gap-toothed smile as he carts off the heavy barrel.

Dorrin unloads two shipwright's adzes with spur heads, and looks at the cooper's adz beside it. "This for them, too?"

"Tyrel said he'd have to make some special barrels for this monster of yours."

"It's got a name now. Kyl's idea, mostly. The *Black Hammer*."

"*Black Hammer*, eh? You going to hammer the Whites?" Hegl sets aside several shovels and two pick-axes. "These be for the one-armed lady." He picks up a narrow hoe. "And this for the old healer and her garden. Light as a feather."

"You didn't have to do this."

"Of course I didn't. Haven't had this much satisfaction in a long time. I just grinned at your father every time I put something on the wagon."

Dorrin looks at his mother, but she is smiling. So he unloads a half-barrel of smaller deck spikes. Intar carts the barrel off into the shed.

"That's it for here," Hegl announces. "I'm up to the big house next to unload Kadara's goods. Hop on."

Dorrin offers a hand to his mother, as she climbs back onto the wagon seat. Then he vaults into the back.

When they reach the point on the road nearest the house, Hegl sets the brake and blocks the wheels. Except for Merga and Frisa, the house proper is empty, although Yarrl's hammer rings from the smithy.

"Where is Kadara?" asks Hegl.

"Down where the armory will be, I'd guess." Dorrin points to where several figures are digging out a foundation.

"We're here. Let's unload."

Hegl and Dorrin carry the furniture into Kadara's room—a bed, a mattress, the cradle, and a small dresser.

"Next trip I'll bring the rest." Hegl closes the tail-board and wipes his forehead. "Think the one-armed lady'd mind if I gave the pick and shovels to Kadara for now?"

"Darkness, no!" laughs Dorrin. "Half the time they work together anyway."

"I'll be heading down there."

"You're welcome for lunch," Dorrin insists.

"Aye, and I'll be there—after I unload."

Dorrin and Rebekah watch from the porch as the wagon rumbles back down to the armory site.

"Why did you come?" Dorrin asks as relative quiet settles over the porch.

"Kyl tells me that I might be able to help."

"You did. I can't thank you enough for what you did for Pergun." Dorrin shifts from one foot to the other, looking down on the slight and red-haired figure, who seems ageless.

"You still do it . . . hopping around when I look at you. You'd think I'd set you on a bed of red ants." Rebekah smiles fondly at her son. "I was talking about Liedral."

"There isn't anything physically wrong." Dorrin gestures to the bench, and she sits down. He sits at the other end, straddling it to face her.

"I figured that. But . . . I do have some experience." Her voice is wry.

"I'll readily grant that." Dorrin laughs ruefully. "If you want to see Liedral, she's down at the warehouse."

"I saw her on the way in—just from the wagon. I wanted to talk to you first. If you're willing for me . . ."

"I'm willing for anything. Rylla's tried everything she can think of. So have I."

Rebekah nods. "I need to know exactly what the Whites did."

"I don't know exactly. From what she can remember and the cuts and welts, they . . . whipped, tortured her . . . and planted false memories of my doing it to her. She knows the memories are false, but that doesn't seem to help much. The idea was to get her to kill me."

Rebekah's voice is steady as she asks, "Was she raped?"

"No. At least there was no blood and no memory."

The healer sighs. "That's something ... I think ... although that would have been hard on a White."

"What do you have in mind?"

"I'd like to talk it over with Liedral first. It has to be her decision, son. I don't see why she wouldn't agree, but ... it is her body and her choice."

Dorrin frowns. She sounds as if she has something fearsome in mind.

"Oh ... it's nothing fearful. It's rather simple, certainly physically painless, even possibly pleasurable ... but it will take a long time. You have to keep in mind that Liedral must be totally in control, and you listen to her, and especially not to your male instincts."

"I understand."

"I doubt that. Not fully." Rebekah smiles.

Dorrin blushes.

"Tell me about the progress with your ship."

Dorrin looks down at the porch floor.

"Darkness, I'm not your father, and I am old enough to make my own mind up, as I hope you would have understood a long time ago."

The young engineer represses a grin at the asperity in his mother's voice. Some things don't change. "Well ... we've decided on a name, the *Black Hammer*. It really came from Kyl in a way ..."

CLXVIII

"THE COUNCIL WANTS to know what you intend to do." Anya's eyes drop to the blank mirror upon the table.

Sterol gestures, and the white mists vanish. A view

appears in the glass, so solid that it might have been painted there, a view of a black ship moored at a pier in the narrow inlet, with five black stone buildings on the hillside above. "Look. Have you ever seen anything so clear?"

"No."

"I haven't either. What aspect of the Balance created that monster, I don't know . . ."

"The Council is worried. They want you to do something."

"Fine! What am I supposed to do? Send a fleet out against Recluce? What good will it do?" Sterol snorts and looks at the image in the mirror on the table. "The old Black ones won't respond. Should we attack the island? Do you know what black iron swords do to our White guards? Do you want one of those things he built blowing you into shreds? Like the great Jeslek?"

"The Blacks are divided," says Anya quietly. "They want this Dorrin to disappear as much as we do."

"That may be, but how does that explain all the people helping build this new town? He didn't carry them all on that little ship. And they're all still Blacks. That means he isn't creating any chaos on Recluce, the demons know why . . ." Sterol rubs his forehead.

"Why can't you send a fleet? Recluce doesn't have even a half-score of warships, if that. They don't like fighting. And most of those ships are spread across the oceans."

Sterol rubs his forehead again, then touches the amulet that rests against his chest. "Haven't you heard a word I've said?"

"The Council wants some action, Sterol." Anya's voice is sharp.

The High Wizard lifts the amulet. "Here. You take it. Be my guest."

The redhead looks at the amulet, then at Sterol. "I won't be tricked like Jeslek."

"Either shut up or take the amulet," Sterol snaps.

Anya's hand lifts, then drops. Finally, she sighs. "Someone has to do something."

"Why?"

"Do you intend to do nothing while this... oddity... builds so much order into black iron that Recluce will dominate the Eastern Ocean forever?"

"I don't see that much of a threat. He can't live forever."

Anya laughs, harshly. "You know those were Jenred the Traitor's exact words? Creslin didn't live forever, but he lived long enough that you—the High Wizard of Fairhaven—are afraid to take any direct action against Recluce. Will you be the one who's remembered for letting Recluce dominate all of Candar?"

"No." Sterol chuckles, bitterly, and lays the amulet on the table beside the mirror. The image of Southpoint vanishes. "You want action. Take the amulet—or give it to someone else."

"I'm asking you, Sterol."

"And I'm refusing."

She nods toward the door, and three guards appear, all bearing chains. Behind them stand three White Wizards.

"How predictable, dear Anya. You would all chain me rather than act yourselves."

The redhead's eyes burn; her fingers tighten on the white bronze dagger.

Fire, white flames, and swirling mists fill the room. The mirror upon the table explodes, and two of the guards shrivel into dust on the white-powdered stones.

As the remaining white smoke subsides, Anya picks up the amulet, glancing down at the pile of white dust that lies within the white robes and white boots. She turns to one of the remaining wizards and extends the amulet. "Here. You earned it, Cerryl."

Cerryl looks at her sadly. "No. You earned it, but I'll wear it for you." His eyes flicker to the white powder on the stone, which vanishes as he watches.

"Good. We need to plan the attack on Recluce."

"As you wish." He gestures. The sole guard, the other wizard, and Anya step outside the tower room. Anya closes the door behind her.

CLXIX

DORRIN CLOSES THE bedroom door and turns to Liedral.

"You don't have to do this." Liedral's eyes meet his.

"What do I have to lose?"

"Your patience, your mind, your self-esteem..." She forces a laugh.

"What do I do?" Dorrin looks at the smoothed plank floors that need oiling or some sort of finish, then at the bed, almost stark in the light of the single lamp.

"Lie down on your stomach."

"On the bed?"

"No. On the floor." Liedral snorts. "Of course on the bed. I may be difficult, but I'm not that cruel. Besides, I don't want to be responsible for the splinters."

Dorrin eases off his boots and lies on the bed, fully clothed, face-down. "Now what?" His voice is muffled.

"You just lie there and let me rub and massage your back. According to your mother, I need to reestablish physical closeness and an instinctive understanding that you won't hurt me."

"But—"

"I know. But . . . will trying this hurt?"

Dorrin feels like shrugging, but does not. She is right. Nothing else has worked. He takes a slow deep breath and releases it, conscious of the faint perfume from the coverlet that reminds him of Liedral and the physical closeness they once shared. His eyes burn, but he keeps his face averted as her strong fingers knead the muscles in his shoulders and upper back.

"You've put on more muscle."

"There, anyway, it's muscle."

Despite the knot in his stomach, her fingers are strong, and soothe the strain in his shoulders and neck. His breath becomes more even.

"How do you feel?" he asks.

"Hush . . . I'm working." Despite the amused tone to her voice, there is also an edge.

Dorrin turns his head more to avoid breathing through the feather mattress that seems determined to cover his nostrils. "Ahhh . . . chwwww." He rubs his nose and resettles himself so he breathes fewer stray bits of down.

The intermittent wind carries bits of conversations to them.

" . . . thought black stone . . . be depressing, but it's not . . ."

" . . . amazing the difference . . ."

" . . . you think master Dorrin's a wizard, a real wizard?"

Liedral proceeds quietly and methodically for some time, and Dorrin enjoys the relaxation.

"My fingers are tired." Liedral shakes her hands and leans back.

"You've been doing it for a long time." As Dorrin shifts his weight on the soft mattress and turns over to see her, Liedral wobbles on her knees. He reaches and catches her, momentarily holding her close.

"Ah . . . that's not . . ."

Dorrin lets go as if she were molten iron.

"I didn't mean . . ." Liedral shakes her head, lets her lips touch his cheek.

Dorrin sits up, leaving a slight space between them.

"Now . . . you do the same thing."

He grins.

"Exactly the same thing. No additions."

Rather than kneeling, Dorrin sits at an angle and begins with her shoulder blades.

"You can knead just a little harder. I'm not made of porcelain."

He applies a touch more pressure.

"That feels good."

Dorrin continues to work down her back, eventually going slightly below her lower back.

"That's a little low and a little familiar . . ." Again, the humorous tone has an edge, almost of fear, and Dorrin moves his fingers upward to her lower back, where he returns to kneading out the kinks.

"That feels so good."

In time, he, too, must stop, for his fingers are almost numb. As he shakes them out, Liedral sits up.

"What happens next?"

"Wait and see." She flashes a smile that fades quickly.

This time Dorrin understands. If she tells him, then she may not feel she has control, and it is all too clear she needs that feeling of control.

"I understand." He squeezes her arm and stands up.

She blows out the lamp, and slips out of her clothes in the dark, and into the long shift. Dorrin, as always, refrains from looking anywhere near her, although he feels himself breathing more quickly, and forces himself to take deeper and slower breaths.

They lie there, side by side, hands flat, only the edges brushing. A cool evening breeze flutters in through the open window, as do gnats and infrequent mosquitoes.

Dorrin almost wishes for the distraction of a mosquito, something that he could crush, but in the late summer, or the early fall—he is not sure of the seasons at Southpoint, which seem milder than at Extina, and certainly milder than in Spidlar—even mosquitoes have become rarer.

While Dorrin has been blind, often for nearly an eight-day, while he has been wounded, while he suffers agonizing headaches for his misuse of order, others have suffered far more. Although he is convinced, and his rough calculations bear him out, that the Balance is mechanical, and nothing more, he sighs softly in the darkness. Is the world just a mechanism? Why do the beliefs and strivings of those who hold order count for even less than those who would use chaos, the destructive force?

Even among those who seek order, why do so many reject difference, such as his engine, merely because it is different? Why will they not look at the order beneath?

The breeze across his face brings no answer, nor did he expect that it would. Liedral snores lightly, and shivers. Dorrin draws the coverlet over her. His eyes rest blankly on the rough-dressed ceiling beams as the wind moans, and the distant surf whispers against the base of the cliffs.

CLXX

THE COLD FALL wind whistles down off the brown grasses of the southern plateau and whips dust off the Great Highway, past the laboring wagon heaped with the last load of iron plate for the *Black Hammer*.

As the wind gusts around the large house, it rattles the newly installed windows, almost as if testing them.

On the wide front porch, Liedral wraps the cloak around her more tightly. Dorrin's arm drops away from her. Why? Why did Jeslek have to pick such a nasty torture? He sighs. Torture is by definition nasty.

"What are you thinking?" she asks.

"Cruel thoughts about cruel people."

"Being angry at the Whites doesn't help much." Her voice is soft, and a warm hand touches him. "I love you, you know."

"I love you."

"You must." Her short laugh is both sad and harsh at once.

The cool wind fluffs her hair into his, and he puts his arm back around her for a time. Before long he must head back down to the shipwright's.

"You're testing the new engine today?"

"Just the engine. We still haven't finished the gearing for the shaft, and Yarrl's had troubles with the shaft bearings."

"For something that was supposed to make traveling by ship simpler, it sounds more complicated."

"It's always—" Dorrin breaks off.

"What is it?"

He laughs. "I was thinking. In a way, Oran was both wrong and right. In the natural order of things, you harness the wind with your sails and you go where you can with the wind. Then, if you get more complicated sails and rigging you can tack and go crosswind and sometimes upwind. With my engine, which is made possible by order, you can go against the natural order. When you think about it, natural order isn't always orderly. Storms are a mixture of order and chaos, and they cause the winds. So he was right that what I'm doing is against natural order, but he's wrong in assuming that all things natural are orderly. I need to write that down and add it to the book."

"That book about order you've been working on ever since I've known you?" Liedral shivers again as the wind gusts around them. "It's cold out here."

Dorrin nods.

"Why don't you give it to him—your father?"

"I'd really need it copied."

"Petra and I can do it. I've been teaching her to write Temple, and it would be a good exercise."

Dorrin glances downhill, toward the gray waters of the small harbor, with the stone pier that holds the *Black Diamond* and the *Gatherer*—Kyl's fishing boat. Reisa has ensured that the new pier is long enough to berth four ships the size of the new *Black Hammer*. Pergun has salvaged the timbers from the temporary wharf and is using them to build a second warehouse.

Liedral stands. "I need to get down to the warehouse. If you can, don't forget about the cheese cutters and one of those windmill toys . . . if you can."

"I'll see after we test the engine." He gives her a hug, and her arms go around him for a while—proof, he supposes, that the exercises between them have helped. But building everything, from affection to ships, takes so long.

Her lips touch his, and the kiss is real, if short. He grins as she steps back.

"See?" asks Liedral.

"I do see." After she steps into the house to get her manifest for the next trading ship, Dorrin begins the short walk down to Tyrel's.

Tyrel has already slid the *Black Hammer* halfway down the graving ways to the water in order to ensure that the funnel is clear of the shed.

The hull is complete, and Dorrin admires the smooth curves once again, letting his fingers drift over the varnished black oak and even across his own work.

The thin black iron plates above the waterline seem to meld into the lower beams. While copper sheathing would improve the hull, there are neither the coins nor the time necessary to install it. Even though the White Wizards of Fairhaven have been quiet, even though the Council has said nothing, Dorrin has no doubts that he will soon have to respond to both.

He walks to the stern, where only the housing for the shaft and the screw need to be completed. On the blocks beside the hull rests the black iron screw, the largest single piece of work Dorrin and Yarrl have ever done. The polishing alone took almost three days and a special hoist.

"Friggin' big chunk of metal, master Dorrin," offers Styl, pausing to set down a set of shorter beams that are braces for the main deckhouse or the pilot house above. "Lot bigger than the screw on the *Diamond*."

"More power at a lower shaft speed, I hope," Dorrin answers.

"You know . . . master Dorrin . . ." Styl coughs.

"Yes?" Dorrin says cheerfully.

"I was wondering . . . I mean about the black iron. Folks know that iron binds magic . . . Guess it's always been that way . . . I was wondering if you could tell me why. It must do something, the way you plated this here *Hammer*."

Dorrin's eyes slide along the ship, visualizing her as complete, with the angled and black-plated sides to the deckhouse and the pilot house and the big funnel aft of both, tall enough to add significantly to the draft and power of the engine. The *Hammer* has no masts, only two covered wells where low temporary masts can be set in the event of engine failure, for Dorrin has designed her only for use in defending Recluce or in the Gulf of Candar. He has neither time nor coins to build a more ambitious vessel, and to carry and steep even a single large mast will add too much weight.

"Iron and magic," Dorrin begins, belatedly realizing that his thoughts have wandered from Styl's question. "Have you ever watched the iron when a smith works? What does it look like?"

"It gets hot, sort of reddish."

"Cherry red. That's because the iron absorbs all that heat—call it the power of the coals. Well, magic is like heat. It's a power, and just like iron can hold the heat of the forge, it can hold and bind the heat of magic. Black iron does it even better. That's why some of the magisters carry black iron shields. The troopers on the *Black Hammer* will, too."

"Hmmmm . . ." ponders Styl. "Sounds right, least-wise to me. That a secret among the wizards?"

Dorrin frowns. The conclusion is his, but outside of his own writing in his book, he has never seen it in ink anywhere else. "It might be. I had to figure it out. No one told me, if that's what you mean."

Styl nods, almost ponderously. "Thank ye, master Dorrin. Best I be getting these up to Tyrel afore he starts bellowing."

"Don't let me stop you. Tell him I'll be up there in a bit." Dorrin continues to check the hull before walking up the ramp onto the main deck.

A new assistant Dorrin does not know passes by with another set of braces, and Styl grunts as he lifts his load. The two move toward the deckhouse structure.

Dorrin has to climb down a temporary ladder into the engine compartment because the walls and the permanent ladder cannot be installed until the shaft and main thrust bearings are in place. Right now, the power train stops at the big flywheel, but the engine is complete, and Yarrl has fired up the boiler at low temperatures several times to help temper the firebrick.

The low temperature runs also disclosed tubing

leaks and, unfortunately, the need to rework both cylinders' steam inlet valves.

Wondering what will happen on this higher-pressure test, Dorrin checks the water level in the tank and inspects the firebox. Then he whittles shavings into a pile, which he lights with the striker from his pouch. As the wood fragments catch, he runs his fingers across the boiler and then the engine. It feels solid.

A shovelful of fragmented coal goes into the firebox.

"You starting already?" asks Yarrl from the deck above.

"I just began lighting her off. I didn't think you'd mind, since it will be a while before we have enough pressure."

"Why would I mind? It's your engine." Yarrl climbs down beside Dorrin. "At times ... it's hard to believe ..."

Dorrin feels the same way; and yet, the engine feels right—so black and so solid. How could his father ever believe it was a creation of chaos? He smiles crookedly. Then again, that has been the problem with Recluce itself. Its very order requires a greater amount of chaos in opposition.

Does that mean each engine will create more chaos in the world? Dorrin's smile fades. The ship is necessary—but can the world stand many of them?

"What are you thinking about?" asks Yarrl.

"Order and chaos," Dorrin says absently, looking up to see Tyrel's crew gathering on the deck to watch. He reaches for the shovel, and Yarrl opens the firebox door. Another shovel of coal goes through the open iron door.

Shortly, Dorrin adds another, and yet another. The boiler creaks as the heat increases, and the plume of smoke from the funnel thickens.

Dorrin checks the bypasses, waiting for the pressure to build more. Finally, he looks at Yarrl. "Let's hope."

He twists one valve and then another, and steam hisses within the carefully crafted tubes toward the cylinders.

As the operating steam pressure builds, even above the chunking/sliding sound of the rods and the wisps of steam escaping from the packing of the cylinder rods, a fainter hiss begins to build.

Dorrin cocks his head, trying to listen, trying to sense the source of the new hiss.

"Looks good!" Yarrl bellows above the combination of muted boiler roar, moving pistons, and steam.

Dorrin walks back to the heavy flywheel—the extra weight was Yarrl's idea for smoothing the power delivery to the shaft gears. The gears stand separated from the flywheel because the last conversion gear has to be completed. Then, if Dorrin and Yarrl can get the new bearing system to work, the shaft can be installed and the propeller attached. Then the *Black Hammer* can be floated.

For a long time, the younger engineer studies the flywheel, thinking about a better design for the next engine. He shakes his head. He needs to finish one engine at a time.

The faint hissing is not so faint when Dorrin steps back toward the steam section of the engine.

"Do you know what it is? The hissing?" asks Yarrl, bending close to Dorrin's ear and not quite bellowing.

Dorrin shakes his head, then begins to trace the steam flow from the boiler tubes to the steam drum and to the cylinders, and from the cylinders to the main condenser. He stops. Air is entering the condenser, dropping the vacuum pressure and the engine's efficiency, and causing the hissing.

Getting down on the deck on his knees he studies the cover plate, finally straightening up and looking at Yarrl. "There's a little gap in the plate, almost too small to see. Maybe it got chipped somehow when we installed it. We'll need to do something about it. It's costing us power."

"Always something."

Dorrin shakes his head. There is always something going wrong. This is the fourth test, and each has revealed another problem. He throttles up the steam pressure another notch, but the power rods still run smoothly.

Dorrin and Yarrl watch and study, until midmorning, when Dorrin begins cooling the engine, slowing it back down, and finally venting off enough pressure to stop the cylinders.

Taking the heavy cloth and tongs, he can finally remove the condenser cover plate and store it in a canvas bag to carry back to the smithy/engineering shop.

"It can cool down from here on its own," Dorrin tells Tyrel. "I need to replace the condenser cover, maybe rebuild it. Then we'll finish the last gear and the bearings."

"How long?" asks Tyrel.

"Another eight-day," Dorrin guesses.

"We should have the deckhouse framing finished before that, and we'll need the plates for it."

"I know." The plates from the iron works are too soft and too thick, and even with the rough triphammer Yarrl has rigged off Dorrin's small millrace, reforging each is time-consuming.

Dorrin walks uphill slowly. The condenser cover is heavy.

"Let me carry it for a while."

The younger man hands over the canvas case. "What about the bearings?"

"They bind too much, even when there's almost no weight on them. You install them like that and the whole shaft will vibrate."

The two walk into the smithy, where Rek is using

the small anvil to forge nails. Vaos is using the large anvil for spikes. There are never enough nails or spikes, it seems.

"Let's see the bearings." Dorrin takes the canvas sack and puts it on the corner of his bench. The bearing problem comes first.

Yarrl hands one of the cylindrical bearings to Dorrin. "They bind here on the edges. You can see where the metal's scratched."

Dorrin runs his fingers across the cylinder. The center section is smooth, but he can feel the abrasion, even on the hard steel, at the edges. Setting the bearing, its diameter not much smaller than the large rod stock from which it was forged, on the smooth iron plate Dorrin uses to check the parts for evenness, he places another plate on top of the bearing, and gradually exerts as much force as he can, gently rolling the bearing back and forth, trying to sense where the pressures fall.

From beside the slack tanks, Vaos and Rek watch. Vaos scratches his head, but the younger brother suddenly grins.

Finally, Dorrin straightens and wipes the dampness from his forehead with the back of his sleeve. "Let's trying grinding bevels on the ends."

"I thought of that. Won't that make them wobble in the track?"

"Maybe . . . but what if we slanted the holding flange just a bit? The tangs on the ends will help."

"Might be worth it."

Dorrin takes a deep breath and pulls off his tunic. "Let's get the big stone moving, Vaos."

"Yes, ser."

Dorrin takes down the bearing tongs he built, with the attached screw clamps to hold the tang ends against the grinding pressure.

"I can't help with that. You've got a finer touch,"

Yarrl says. "I'm going back to that last blank on the gears."

"Good." Dorrin takes the first of the bearings. It will be another long day, and after that he must still redesign and reforge the pressure cover for the condenser. Then, once the gear and bearings are finished, they will have to test the system for vibration again. And probably again after that. Sometimes, he wonders if the ship will ever be completed.

At least, he can take a short break for lunch, and at least Liedral will be there, before she goes back to Land's End again.

He sighs, remembering the three uncompleted cheese-cutters, real cheese-cutters, for which he must still draw the wire before she goes.

CLXXI

DORRIN TIES BASLA to the iron ring on the stone post, half turning to glance at the Black Holding, where the Council usually meets. Then he turns toward the well-kept stone walk, still damp from the morning rain. The yellow flowers in the plantings beside the walk still bloom, but they will fade within the eight-day, for fall is indeed upon Recluce.

He steps toward the house, carrying the folder with him. While he does not look forward to the meeting, it is something he must do.

Rebekah opens the door even before Dorrin reaches the stoop. "I hoped you would come before long." She smiles and gives him a quick hug before stepping back. "How is Liedral?"

"We're doing better." Dorrin knows what she really means by the question. "I'm following her suggestions, and I'm glad you spent the time. Sometimes, it's hard. The touching exercises..." He almost winces. "But they seem to work. It's so hard to think of what we had and lost... and it wasn't even our doing."

Rebekah nods sympathetically. "Would you like some redberry?"

"Please." He has not had redberry since early summer at the inn.

"What's in the folder?" His mother inclines her head quizzically.

"Something for father."

"He's in the library. The porch is a little chilly. I'll join you before long.

Dorrin understands this as well. He wanders down the hall and into the library. "Hello."

The thin wizard sets down the book on the reading table. "Dorrin. Sit down." He gestures to the other chair, clearly moved from the kitchen into the study in anticipation of Dorrin's arrival.

"Thank you." Dorrin takes the chair, setting the heavy folder in his lap, then meets his father's eyes. For only the second time since Dorrin can remember, Oran looks away from his son.

"What do you want?" asks the older man.

"I'd like you to stop trying to persuade everyone that what I'm doing is wrong and tied to chaos. I'm not a little boy anymore, and you're not always right. Neither am I," he adds, thinking about Diev, and Kleth, and Liedral and Kadara, and even Meriwhen.

"I love you, Dorrin, and you're my son. But this business with black iron and machines is wrong. Do you want me to say it's right when I don't think it is?"

"I'd like you to think about the reasons why you feel it's wrong." Dorrin pauses. "Creslin did things which were not exactly perfectly in line with pure order, but had he done otherwise, neither you nor I would be here."

"You've done much, Dorrin, but you're not a Creslin."

"No. I know that, but the lessons are the same. I intend to preserve Recluce. Intentionally or not, you intend to commit suicide, because you've never really understood order."

"Understood order? You've never stood on the storms, or held the sky, and you know about order?"

Dorrin lifts the bound sheets beside him. "I had these copied for you. One of the things I found out in Candar is that nothing in your library explained the basis of order, just the constraints. So I did my best."

"Oh . . . it must be interesting, applying your engineering logic to order. Tell me, do you prove that your steam engine is a creation of the Angels of Heaven and founded on order?" Oran smiles crookedly.

"Hardly. This is much more basic." Dorrin tries not to sigh. "If that's the way you want it, keep trying to persuade the Council to send me off to some darkness-forsaken corner of the globe."

"I don't want to send you off, son. I just want you to return to the way of order."

"I have returned to the way of order."

The tall wizard's mouth opens, then closes, but he listens as Dorrin continues.

"I've had some time to think, and I've had to work things out for myself, and I had some help. You seem to have forgotten two things. First, I did stop Jeslek. And second, I'm still Black. There's not one flicker of chaos around me, and you know it. And that doesn't lie."

"Being honestly mistaken is not the same as being right."

"Perhaps not, but I've watched Southpoint, and the people there. We're building something that is solid and order-based. You ought to give it a chance."

"For what? To corrupt generations of order?"

"Perhaps there is a third way," offers Rebekah. She has a tray with two glasses on it and offers it to Dorrin.

Dorrin takes the redberry and inclines his head to the healer. "Yes, mother?"

"Perhaps the Council could leave Southpoint and the defense of Recluce to you, and to any who would join you. That would give us each time to consider how to work out what you have discovered. That would also allow use of Dorrin's work without the dangers of the corruption you fear, Oran."

"How do you know this would work?" mutters the air wizard.

"I don't," Dorrin says, "but isn't it better than handing Recluce over to the Whites, or leaving you isolated and stagnating while Fairhaven grows and dominates the world."

"He has a point, Oran. The Council has raised the same questions."

"But machines?"

Dorrin nods and lifts the manuscript. "If you would read this . . ."

Oran makes a gesture to push them both away. "All right . . . I'll read the fool thing and think about it. That's all you can expect."

Dorrin takes a sip of the redberry, enjoying the taste despite the circumstances.

"I'd like to read it also," says Rebekah.

Oran takes the second glass of redberry, and swallows. After a moment, he says, "Tell me about this trader lady."

Dorrin finishes his glass, looking at it as if he cannot believe he drank it all.

"I can send a large jug back with you." Rebekah laughs.

"Her name is Liedral. She's a trader, originally from Jellico . . . helped us away from Fairhaven . . . factored some of my toys . . ."

"Was she a White trader?"

"... free trader... the Whites tried to put her family out of business..."

Late afternoon comes before Dorrin finishes his narrative. He looks out at the darkening clouds. "I really need to go."

Rebekah stands from the padded stool she has brought into the study. "I'll get that redberry, and there's also a whole cold fowl you can take, and even a leg of mutton—not that it's that much for that establishment of yours. And you keep some of that redberry for yourself."

Dorrin grins. Even Oran grins.

After watering and feeding Basla, he makes three trips from the kitchen out to load his mount before he finally rides southward once more. He whistles as he rides along the High Road, back toward the *Black Hammer*, back toward Liedral.

CLXXII

THE HEALER LOOKS back away from the damp gray stones that lead to the High Road, and her eyes dwell briefly on the Black Holding while a faint smile plays across her lips. She turns to the tall man. "Have you looked at your son, Oran? Really looked?"

"He's the same old Dorrin. He's obsessed with those demon-damned contraptions of his."

"He's not the same Dorrin."

"He is still obsessed with those machines."

"No." Rebekah's voice is hard, almost as cold as black iron as she turns to her husband. "He is so steeped in order, so Black, that where he stands is like a pillar anchored deep into the earth. Oran, he makes you look shallow. Don't let yourself act shallow. Why can't you take pride in your son?"

"You're certain?"

"Don't listen to me. Just look for yourself."

The tall man licks his lips, shivering at the cold certainty in his guts and in her words. "What of Recluce, then?"

"I doubt that much will change, dear. The really great ones don't come along that often."

"But his machines . . ."

"Oran . . . have you really considered your own question? The one about how to hold back chaos without turning the world upside down? The White ones cannot stand up to black iron."

"But . . . machines . . .?"

"Trust in the Balance, dear."

The tall wizard shakes his head, but the gesture is not all negative, and the slender woman takes his hand and squeezes, as they walk out from the front stoop around to the terrace off their kitchen to watch the shadows of the bluff lengthen across the Eastern Ocean.

CLXXIII

"ALMOST A SEASON has passed, and you have made no moves against the Blacks, or against the renegade smith who cost us so dearly." Anya's voice is level as she looks across the table at Cerryl.

"What would you suggest?" Cerryl's tone is mild, inquisitive. He looks toward the tower window that is but ajar, observing the painted wooden rose that does not move with the cool breeze that passes it.

"You cannot let such acts go unpunished, you know."

"We razed Diev, and neither the city nor the harbor remains. Kleth is no more, and Spidlaria does whatever we wish—willingly. We have added another half-dozen ships to the trade blockade of Recluce." The High Wizard smiles politely. "I take it you believe that more should be done?"

"You are so unfailingly polite and attentive, Cerryl. It's one of your charms."

"I am so glad you find it so. Are you suggesting that an expedition against Southpoint is in order? A fleet, perhaps a firing of the new city?"

"It is so refreshing not to have to outline the details. Sterol was so dense about it."

"I know." Cerryl's voice is dry. "Would you like me to propose this in the next meeting and appoint you to develop the plan, under my direction, of course?"

Anya leans forward and touches his cheek. "You are so understanding, Cerryl. So understanding."

"We do try, Anya. We do try."

CLXXIV

"EASY . . . EASY . . ." CALLS Tyrel.

The *Black Hammer* shivers on the greased blocks, edging along the stone-braced and heavy timbers toward the gray-green waters of the harbor. Dorrin wipes the cold mist from his face and tries not to hold his breath as his ship ever-so-slowly slides seaward, watching the propeller housing as it barely clears a slight hump in the inclined ramp, hoping that Tyrel has calculated accurately and that neither the rudder nor the shaft will be bent.

"She's lovely," admits Reisa, standing on the far side of Yarrl from Dorrin. "Lovely like a well-turned blade."

"Not much for a trader," adds Liedral.

"And you sure couldn't fish with her. Scare off everything for kays," laughs Kyl.

"All right." Dorrin continues to watch as the *Hammer* slides into the harbor water. A spray rises from the stern and a low rippling wave spreads across the calm water.

A low cheer rises from the score of workers and others who have lined the pier to watch the launching.

Dorrin wipes the chill mist from his face again, then steps toward the pier, checking the waterline. He grins as he sees that two lines of oak planks below the black iron are exposed above the water, just as he had calculated. That will change when the plating on the pilot house and deckhouse are completed, and the coal and water bins are filled.

He peers at the stern and tries to sense whether the shaft has grounded, but there is no mud boiling up, nor tangles of vegetation, nor any bending in the rudder brackets. Tyrel and Reisa complained at his insistence on deepening the harbor more beyond the graving ways, but they had done so.

Styl has already attached the bow line to the windlass mounted on the pier. The shipwright begins to crank, and the *Hammer*'s bow turns as the ship is drawn into position next to the pier. Tyrel stands by the three men holding the stern line, ready to tighten it around the other bollard.

Dorrin waits until the ship is pulled alongside the pier. Then he jumps and clambers over the side, not waiting for the gangway, and scrambles down the engine compartment ladder and through the second hatch into the narrow space that holds the shaft. He lights the wall lamp and detaches it from its bracket, carrying it deeper into the ship and toward the stern, where he inspects the housing where the shaft penetrates the hull.

From what he can see, there are no immediate leaks. He looks at the small pump in the bilges and the narrow steam line that runs to it. Dorrin grins. A hand-powered version forged mainly by Hegl has already been delivered to the iron works for Korbow.

Dorrin lifts the lamp, and begins to check the hull. According to Tyrel, some leakage is likely, but for the moment, the engineer sees none. He climbs out of the bilges and back forward and up to the engine compartment.

"There ye be." Tyrel peers from the deck down.

"The shaft looks sound, and I don't see any leaks."

"We got no leaks tomorrow, and I'll be happy. No leaks right after she hits water doesn't mean much."

Dorrin agrees, but he will take what he can. He climbs back up onto the deck, where Liedral, Reisa, and Yarrl are waiting.

"Gives me the shivers," Yarrl admits.

"What? The rain?" asks Reisa, with a half-smile.

"You know what I mean, woman."

Dorrin knows. While the *Hammer* is solid and order-based, the ship has the directness and deadliness of a fine blade.

Liedral has walked to the bow, where her fingers caress the smooth lines of the railings and their supports, all crafted without unnecessary projections.

She turns, extends a hand. He takes it and steps up beside her, and they look westward, out over the gray waters of the channel and toward the black-green waters of the Gulf, toward the blackening clouds in the west.

"It's going to storm," Dorrin says.

"It won't be much, not compared to the storm you've built here."

"You think I should have called her the *Black
Storm*?"

"No. The *Black Hammer* is right. You are a smith,
perhaps the greatest ever."

Dorrin laughs, harshly. "Both Hegl and Yarrl know
more than I'll ever learn about smithing."

"You know what I mean. Yarrl told you that he
understands what you do. He just can't see it until you
do it. Maybe I should have called you the greatest
engineer ever."

"What am I? A magic engineer?"

Liedral squeezes his fingertips. They stand watching
the dark storm on the horizon as the shipwright's crew
begins to carry the last black iron plates aboard to be
installed, as the cold drizzle drops around them, and
as the whitecaps begin to form out in the Gulf of
Candar.

CLXXV

"Oh ... I got a fair amount of coin." Liedral opens
the small chest on the bedroom table that doubles as
her desk and Dorrin's drafting platform.

"I'd say so." Standing just behind the trader, Dorrin
takes in the heap of silvers and golds in the chest. He
squeezes her shoulders. "So what was the problem?"

"They'd buy but not sell. I couldn't get any of the
cordage Tyrel wanted, nor any commitment for copper.
According to Henshur, no one's ever had trouble getting copper from Nordlans before." Liedral closes the
chest.

"I missed you." Still standing behind her, Dorrin
puts his arms around her waist and his cheek against
hers.

"I missed you." Liedral turns in his arms. Her lips demand his, and for a time they remain locked together.

"Dinner's ready! Master Dorrin and Mistress Liedral! Dinner's ready." Frisa's high voice penetrates the closed door.

Liedral lifts her lips. "I know it's been a long time, but . . . please . . . just keep trusting me . . ."

His lips brush hers. "I will . . . I do . . ." He wipes away a tear, and finds her hand wiping his cheek.

"Dinner!"

Dorrin starts to respond, but has to clear his throat. "We're coming."

"Not yet," comments Liedral wryly. "But we will get there."

Dorrin blushes. Liedral straightens her tunic and steps around Dorrin to open the door.

Everyone else is at the long table, except for Merga and Frisa. Frisa sets two baskets of fresh-baked bread on the table—one at each end.

"Smells good," Yarrl announces.

Dorrin sits in the chair at the head of the table, while Liedral slips next to him on the bench to his left.

"Be lifting your rafters tomorrow, Reisa," Pergun announces.

"It's about time," Reisa says. "I expect you might even get the roof finished before midwinter."

"Aye, but that depends on the stonecutters. I need more of the slate tiles."

Merga sets a large casserole on the table.

"What is it?"

"Fish stew."

"Fish, always fish," mutters Vaos from the middle of the bench.

Dorrin agrees silently.

"Fish be good for you," snaps Rylla. "Better than

starving in Spidlar. Or worse, and don't ye forget it, you ungrateful scamp." She spoils the effect by not being able to hide a small smile.

"I got some greenberry from the holders." Merga holds up the pitcher. "You like some, master Dorrin?"

"If you please." Although the drink is bitter, Dorrin prefers it to the watery beer or water that are the alternatives. He ladles out the stew onto his plate, noting various sliced and chopped creatures, as well as seaweed and quilla roots. At least it is nourishing, and the spices will help—he hopes. The bread is also good, but Merga has always baked good bread.

"Whose dwelling comes after Yarrl's?" asks Rek.

"I'd say it was Mistress Kadara's, and Rylla will be with her, I understand." Pergun still speaks with his mouth full, and breadcrumbs spray onto the table.

"Stop talking when you're eating," reminds Merga, settling next to him.

"Somebody's got to look after that child she's carrying," Rylla mumbles.

Kadara chuckles. "You'd think it was your grandson about to be born."

"Only one I'd like as to see."

"You're not that old," prompts Vaos.

"Never said as I was old." Rylla gestures around the table. "You see any other children coming around this place?"

Merga blushes and looks at the table. Petra raises her eyebrows and looks toward Dorrin and Liedral.

"You never can tell," Dorrin temporizes.

"So ... maybe you'll prove me wrong," the old healer says, "but with his mother a blade, and her own family an isle-length away, her son's going to need another grandmother." Rylla breaks off a chunk of bread and dips it into the stew on her plate.

"Could I have some more greenberry?" asks Rek.

"Stop washing your food down," admonishes Reisa.

"I wish we had something besides fish and mutton."

"I baked some pearapple pies for later," Merga adds. "But you don't get any, lad, unless you eat your stew."

"Master Dorrin?" protests Rek, looking at the heap of fish on his plate.

"I have to agree with Merga."

"You're mean," Liedral teases.

Dorrin recovers the bread, and finds he has the end crust.

"When will your ship be going to sea, master Dorrin?" asks Frisa. "Can I have a ride on the new one?"

"Not this time, young woman." Dorrin realizes he has too much in his mouth and swallows, but not before Liedral glances sharply at him. "I think we'll be taking her out into the Gulf in about an eight-day." If the gear train works as it is supposed to, if the thrust bearing mounts can stand up to the vibrations, if ...

He takes a sip of the bitter greenberry, and then another mouthful of fish. His next ship will be a big steam trader. He has been well-off; he is not well-off, at least not in food, and he prefers the former.

"You best eat that stew," Rylla warns Kadara.

Liedral rolls her eyes, and Dorrin waits for the pear-apple pie.

CLXXVI

AT THE STURDY stone pier are tied a small schooner with sails apparently furled and a black pipe protruding from the main deck, a small two-masted fishing boat, and another ship, jet black, without masts, but with a slant-sided deckhouse, an open cylinder behind it, and smooth curved hull lines. Workers attach black metal to the rear of the deckhouse.

The three White Wizards study the scene in the mirror.

"What in darkness is it?" asks Fydel.

"Do we really want to find out?" Cerryl's voice is sardonic.

"Cerryl dear, you are so cautious. Look at the hillside. Those are tents beyond the houses. Clearly, this . . . settlement is scarcely begun."

Fydel raises his eyebrows. "The stone buildings appear rather solid, Anya."

"You . . . men! If you can call yourselves that. We need to stop this before the Black Council gets fully behind this . . . renegade. Right now, all he has is two small ships and a fishing boat, and a few buildings. We wait much longer, and it gets that much harder."

"Anya, the southern fleet is already gathering in the Great North Bay. Within the next two eight-days, depending on the winds, it will be ready to set forth— exactly according to your plans." Cerryl offers the redhead a broad smile. "What else would you have us do?"

"You are too accommodating, Cerryl." Anya's voice is smooth. "But I appreciate your thoughtfulness. I do trust that the fleet's departure will be as you have projected, and that there will be sufficient troop support to level this Black settlement."

"You wish to prove to the Blacks that we can strike even upon their beloved isle?"

"It would aid our effort, would it not?" asks the red-headed wizard.

"If you so believe, then I bow to your wisdom." Cerryl inclines his head. "I will ensure that the fleet leaves as you have planned."

"Thank you." Anya steps back, and inclines her head. "By your leave, Highest of High Wizards?"

"Of course." Cerryl inclines his head in return, watching as she leaves.

Fydel waits impassively until the door shuts. "You push her too much, Cerryl. With all her supporters, she could have your head tomorrow."

"Perhaps. But would you want this position?"

Fydel shakes his head.

CLXXVII

THE CLEAR MORNING light of early winter cascades across the harbor, and steam seems to rise from the water. On the hillside above, white rime begins to melt off the rooftops. Hoofs sound on the extension of the High Road that now extends all the way to the black stones of the wharf.

Dorrin turns from his study of the needle-shaped *Black Hammer*. At least in comparison to the *Black Diamond*, the *Hammer* is longer and narrower, with a correspondingly narrower but deeper keel. And the *Hammer* not only looks black, from the iron and lorkin finish, but feels black.

The engineer watches as the post carriage clicks past the small building serving as Reisa's office as harbormaster. While Reisa insists that she is only a disabled blade, Dorrin knows better, having watched as she has rebuilt a marshy inlet into a real, if small, harbor, and as she has begun to extend the break-waters to allow for operation in more stormy seas.

Dorrin frowns momentarily, for the post carriage normally stops to deliver letters at the harbormaster's. He waits until the carriage pulls up, the door opens, and three figures step out—Oran, Ellna, and Videlt.

He bows. "I had not expected you."

"We had not expected to be here." Ellna's normally musical voice is hoarse. "But we thought that we should see your progress."

"This is our progress." Dorrin gestures toward the *Black Diamond*.

"Frankly," states the squarish Videlt, "I am more impressed by the buildings and the harbor and the organization than a single ship."

So is Dorrin, but he would prefer the Council come to that conclusion without his words. "Since you are here, would you like to see the ship?"

"We might as well." Oran's voice is sour. "Would you show us?"

"This ship is not much larger than the first. Is it that much more capable?" asks Videlt.

"It is a warship," Dorrin states flatly, leading the way up the gangway. "There's nothing that is easily flamed."

"Could we see your engine?"

Dorrin leads the way to the engine compartment, climbing down the ladder first. "This is the fire box, and the coal is shoveled from the bins here . . ."

The three Council members are silent as he explains the steam generation, flow, the reciprocating nature of the cylinders and the gearing to the shaft and the propeller.

"No chaos . . . not now," mumbles Videlt.

"You won't find any traces, either." Dorrin watches his father's face go blank, knowing Oran strains to find any sense of the whitish-red of chaos.

Oran blinks and straightens up. "Has your ship been sea-tested?"

"Twice. She can outrun Kyl's craft, especially in rougher seas or in light winds." Dorrin nods toward the ladder, then follows the three back onto the main deck.

Ellna touches the plate on the deckhouse. "Did you forge all the black iron?"

"No. I had help from Yarrl and others."

"You forged it, then, so far as adding the order component."

"Put that way, I suppose so. But I could not have done it by myself."

"Commendable modesty," offers Videlt.

Dorrin follows the three past the funnel to the stern, where Videlt looks down into the gray-green of the harbor.

"Not a big rudder."

"If it's behind the screw, we don't need as big a rudder. The flow of water past it increases its effect."

"It seems to be a very solid ship, Dorrin," offers Oran.

"We hope so."

"We don't have that much time, and I would like to see some of the buildings. What is the long one there?" asks Ellna.

"That's Liedral's warehouse, where we keep our trading goods. She has an office there also. Actually, she will when we can make furniture for it."

"Is it full?"

"Hardly." Dorrin laughs. "It's mostly empty now, but she thinks that's what we'll need within a year."

The three Councillors exchange glances.

"Dorrin," begins Ellna, "you may not have a year."

"The Whites are coming?"

"How did you know?"

The engineer shrugs. "I didn't know for certain. I had the feeling that they would. That's why we pushed so hard on completing the *Hammer*. That's why we don't have furniture, why we keep eating fish and quilla and tough mutton, why all my coins have gone into iron and lumber and fittings."

He starts back to the gangway and leads the three

forward to the gangway, where he pauses to survey the ship. Booted feet click on the order-strengthened black oak of the deck.

From the top of the pilot house, Styl and two assistants who have appeared from somewhere on the isle look down silently. When the Council members look away, Styl clenches a fist and lifts it in a gesture of triumph.

Dorrin represses a grin and walks down to the pier. After the others join him, he asks, "What else do you want to see?"

"You don't want to know about the Whites?" Ellna's voice is curious.

"Magistra, if you wish to tell me, you will. If you do not, no effort of mine could make you."

"Like Creslin . . ." mumbles Videlt.

Dorrin waits.

"The White fleet is gathered in the Great North Bay off Lydiar. We expect that they will set sail within the next eight-day." Ellna coughs to clear her throat.

"How do you plan to defend Recluce?" Dorrin asks.

"As we always have. They will have to land, and we do not believe that could be successful anywhere near Land's End."

"And at sea?" Dorrin pursues.

Videlt adds. "There's not much we can do. We've not that many ships, and only two are within days of Recluce. We have to send a pair on every trading voyage these days, and we have no copper or tin on Recluce. Nor cobalt for the glass works, nor . . ."

"We're on our own, then?"

"How would you plan to stop a White force?" asks Oran.

"I'd try to stop them at sea, first."

"With what? I did not see a ram on your ship, and one ship cannot match a fleet in troops."

"We have a small boarding force—and some black steel rockets."

"Rockets? Those firetubes?" Videlt frowns.

Dorrin nods.

"Barbaric weapons."

"No more barbaric than the White Wizards' fire-bolts."

"Some of them are designed to go through a hull," Dorrin adds.

Ellna winces.

"I'm not pleased, either, magistra, but if we must fight, we must be prepared to fight to win." Dorrin wonders if he will ever be able to avoid volunteering disturbing information. Will the existence of his ship dissuade the White Wizards? That he doubts. Can his ship turn back an entire fleet? Not without more rockets ... and a great deal of luck—or unless the Whites can be persuaded to turn back themselves.

"We will leave such decisions in your hands," Videlt adds smoothly, brushing back the long brown hair off his forehead. "I, for one, would like to wander around your ... town ... by myself."

"Whatever you wish."

Ellna looks to Videlt, then Oran. "We'll meet back at the harbormaster's before noon. That's when the post coach is scheduled to leave." She turns and begins to walk toward the empty warehouse.

Videlt walks along the harbor wall, as if he will circle the eastern side, leaving Dorrin and Oran standing on the pier.

After a long moment, Oran asks, "What are you going to call your town?"

"We really haven't discussed it. We just refer to it as Southpoint."

"That's really the whole end of the isle."

"Do you have any suggestions?" Dorrin inquires.

"How about Nylan, after Ryba's first smith?"

"I don't have a problem with that, but I'd like to ask a few others, like Yarrl and Liedral and Reisa. Besides, names haven't been a real priority."

"I know. Kyl said you had your ship half-built before you ever got around to naming it."

"I guess I'm more interested in the results than the name."

"I know that, too." Oran's voice no longer contains its earlier edge and sourness. "Let's walk to your place. Tell me about the town . . . and the people."

The two men start inland, passing the harbormaster's building.

"That's for the harbormaster, Reisa. She's a former blade, from Southwind—"

"The one-handed woman?"

"Yes. She's also been training our troopers."

"You have armed troopers?"

"Not a lot. Roughly two squads, so far. She heads one, and Kadara heads the other—or did, and will, later."

They turn to two other buildings spread apart and across from the armory and training grounds.

"This is Yorda's. He's a cooper and basket maker—from up beyond Feyn, I think. And this"—Dorrin points—"belongs to Alerk. He's a wool factor. I asked him why he wanted to build a place here when most of the herders and sheep were at the other end of the isle. He said that he wanted to be where the trade would be." The younger man laughs. "He's also got a larger place at Land's End."

They pass a small house, where roofers are setting tiles. Pergun pauses from giving instructions and waves, then resumes his discussion.

"That's Pergun. He was a mill hand in Diev, but he's the one who's done most of the building. He helped me build my place in Diev."

Oran watches as a horse-crane levers a timber frame

up and into stone-framed foundation holes. "I don't recall seeing that used before."

"Something I worked out in Diev when I couldn't afford much help to raise the walls."

Farther uphill, they stop before another modest home, this one with turned soil, some in the shadows with traces of frost upon it, edged in neat stone borders, with a stone walk leading to a narrow porch. The front windows are shuttered, awaiting glazing, but side windows are glassed and the shutters drawn back. A thin line of white smoke rises from the chimney.

"This is Kadara's. Rylla, the older healer, lives with her. Usually, we still all eat together most of the time. That way, people have more time to get things done."

Halfway up the hill, the air wizard turns and looks out onto the cold green Eastern Ocean. "You have a good view here."

"Yes." Dorrin wishes they had more time to enjoy it.

The two walk to Dorrin's, toward the door of the smithy, from where the sound of hammers and the whir of the grindstone filter into the cool air.

Dorrin gestures, and Oran steps inside. Yarrl is busy with the big anvil and what appear to be wagon braces or iron straps. Vaos employs the smaller anvil and hammers out nails. He nods at Dorrin, but does not stop.

Rek alternates between the bellows and the grindstone, where he is finishing edges on blades for wood planes.

Dorrin waits until Oran nods, and they step back into the cold sunlight outside the smithy and under the empty porch. The thin line of white from the chimney that serves the stove tells Dorrin that Merga is baking. Then, with the crowd she feeds, Merga is always baking.

"You've done a great deal here." Oran looks down at his son. "The coach is waiting, and I should be going. Take care, Dorrin." The tall man steps away from the door to the workshop and smithy, then walks briskly downhill.

Dorrin watches, conscious that Liedral has stepped onto the porch.

"What did they want? To make our life harder?"

Dorrin takes the stairs and gathers her in his arms. "No. They came to warn us. The Whites are moving a fleet against us. They think it will leave the Great North Bay in the next few days."

"Will they help us?" Liedral eases out of his arms.

"They can't." Dorrin snorts. "All but two of their ships are out trying to get the goods no one will bring here voluntarily."

"Two ships? That's all?"

"I don't think Recluce has ever had more than a dozen in my lifetime. Who would bother them? Who wouldn't take gold or buy the needed goods or spices?"

"That's stupid." Liedral glances westward, out at the sun-sparkled waves of the Gulf. "What will you do? Don't tell me. You're going to be a hero."

"Do I have any choice?"

"No." Her hands take his. "What are you going to do next?"

"Build more rockets. Have you and Rylla gather more of the ingredients for powder. Make sure we have enough black iron shields for the boarding force. What else can I do?"

"I'll tell Reisa. Rylla will have to stay with Kadara. Her labor won't be easy, even with the help you've already provided. Rylla says she's nearly ready to have that baby." She kisses him lightly. "You might as well get started."

He might as well. He returns the kiss, more lingeringly before he lets go of her, and takes a deep breath.

"I'll gather the sulfur and saltpeter . . . and what else

I can round up. The holders north of here said they
would have some, and there's a little in the big warehouse." She heads for the shed at the end of the house
which serves as the temporary stable.

Dorrin strides back into the smithy. "Vaos!"

"Yes, ser!"

"We'll be working late—for near an eight-day."
Dorrin studies the plate he has—more plate than he
will have powder, he suspects.

CLXXVIII

"You will direct the fleet, Fydel." Anya smiles win-
ningly.

The wizard with the square-cut brown beard frowns,
looking from the High Wizard to Anya. "You want
me to go against that demon ship?"

"It's only one ship, and you'll have a dozen well-
armed war schooners. Besides, you don't even have to
land. Just use your skills to fire the town."

"What if the . . . whatever he is . . . comes after us?"

"You sink his ship," Cerryl says quietly. "I recall
your telling the Council that would be possible were
you in charge. You're the wizard in charge."

"Fine. I'll need some assistants."

"Pick whom you need."

Fydel purses his lips, then inclines his head. "By
your leave?"

"Of course."

After Fydel has departed and the door has been
closed, Cerryl massages his forehead and looks out the
window into the rain pelting Fairhaven. "Damned rain,
always gives me a headache."

The red-headed woman sits, legs crossed, before the

table. The circular mirror that lies upon the white oak is blank. She smiles.

"You really don't care if we win, do you?" asks Cerryl.

"What ever gave you that idea?"

"Everyone who supported you has been given a position on those fleets. That's a page from Hartor's book."

"You've read a great deal of history. It makes you much more appealing."

The High Wizard fingers the amulet once worn by a High Wizard named Hartor, and more recently by Sterol. "If they win, they owe you—"

"They owe you, High Wizard."

"That is so thoughtful of you." Cerryl inclines his head to Anya. "Humor me, if you please, and listen. You owe me that, at least."

Anya smiles faintly, but only with her mouth.

"If we somehow destroy or humiliate this Black builder of magic ships, then all your supporters will be indebted. If this unknown Black proves as great as, say, Creslin, then no one is left to challenge you. And," Cerryl adds wryly, "like Hartor, no one will want this position for at least a decade, or until their memories grow somewhat fainter. You are rather astute, Anya dear." He pauses. "Of course, if they fail, but return, then I will follow Sterol."

"Then why did you accept my proposition?" Anya asks.

"Why not? All life is a gamble. Besides, like Sterol, I suspect attacking Recluce is doomed to failure."

"You admit that, and yet will send out those fleets?"

"I could be wrong." Cerryl smiles.

"So you could." Anya returns the smile, stands, and steps toward him, lips parted.

CLXXIX

BOTH THE HAMMER and the anvil horn blur in the lamp-light. Dorrin racks the hammer and sets the curved sheet that will be a rocket casing on the forge bricks. He rubs his forehead.

"You all right, master Dorrin?" asks Rek.

"Just tired. Can you sweep up and bank down the coals?"

"Yes, ser."

Dorrin trudges out toward the stone-walled shower that is as similar to the one he grew up with as he could make it—or have the masons make it, more properly. All he provided was the shower head and the valves.

After checking to make sure there is a towel in the covered box set in the wall, he strips, frowning at his own stench, and turns on the water.

"Ooo . . ." The water is not lukewarm, or cool, but frigid. As soon as he is wet, the water goes off, and he lathers up with the soap Liedral brought back from her last trip to Land's End. Then he rinses, shivering. He has to repeat the process once more before he feels clean.

After drying, he steps from the shower into the back hall and tiptoes, clothes in hand, towel around his waist, into the bedroom.

"How are you?" Liedral is reading from his manu-script, the table and lamp pulled close to her side of the bed and the coverlet almost to her neck.

"Cold . . . tired . . ." He sets his clothes on the rack in the corner. They need to be washed, but he will worry about that later. Then he rummages in the wardrobe for some underdrawers, which he exchanges for the towel.

"I can't believe how well you thought this out," Liedral says, reaching over and replacing the pages in the wooden box.

Dorrin sees her shoulders are bare and looks away. "Thought you read it when you and Petra copied it."

"I only read what I copied, and I really didn't have time to think about it."

He slides into his side of the bed. The sheet and coverlet are cool, but not so cold as the air or the shower were.

"You smell clean."

"Mmmm..." Dorrin has not realized how tired he is until he lies back.

"Tired?"

"Yes. I was making casings for a few more of the heavy rockets."

"When will you take the *Black Hammer* out?"

"Tomorrow, I'd guess. Maybe the next day. Not until we see them. Not much sense in wasting time or coal." He leans back on the thin pillow.

"I need something..."

He half turns toward her.

"Hold me... please." She slips into his arms. She wears no shift, and her skin is warm against his.

"Don't think... Is this... wise? I mean..." Wanting her, he still worries, wonders... Will the memories surface?

"Very wise ... almost ... too late ..." Her hands reach his damp hair and draw his face to hers.

In time, her hands reach lower, and her lips warm his, then caress his cheeks, burning away the tears that flow from his eyes, even as his hands stroke her back and brush along the smooth skin of her thighs.

They move together, slowly... warmly.

The lamp flickers in the faint breeze, and the top page in the wooden box flutters.

When they separate, her lips nibble his left ear. "I missed you."

"Darkness ... I missed you. I love you."

"You can keep holding me ... please." Her arms wind around him yet again, and her lips are warm and soft on his.

Dorrin's arms tighten around her, holding her even as he wonders what has changed after so long. He draws in the scent of her, of fine soft hair, and his lips brush her cheek before their lips meet again.

CLXXX

THE WAGON CREAKS up to the pier, opposite the *Black Diamond*, and Dorrin hops down onto the stones, taking out the wagon blocks and setting them on each side of the iron tires.

He lowers the tailboard. In the rough crate are another dozen rockets—the heavy kind, as Dorrin thinks of them, that will penetrate ship hulls.

Kyl is the first to reach the wagon. "More of the rockets?"

"The heavy kind."

Tyrel appears. "There's a sail just at the horizon."

"Do we know whose sail?"

"Not yet."

Dorrin rubs his forehead. His head aches even in anticipation of using the damned rockets. "All right. Light off a small fire in the firebox, just enough that we maintain a little steam."

Tyrel nods. "Yarrl coming?"

"No. If something happens, I'd like someone left who could build another ship."

"Makes sense." The shipwright and captain of the *Black Hammer* frowns. "You're not planning on losing, I hope?"

"Hardly."

With the sound of hoofs on stone Dorrin looks up. Liedral rides toward the pier, leading a riderless Basla. In the lanceholder is his black staff.

"Rylla needs you."

"But . . ." Kyl looks puzzled.

"Kadara?"

Liedral nods.

"If it is the White fleet, and it looks like they're getting within say . . . less than ten kays, blow the whistle." Dorrin looks at Tyrel. "With Basla, I can be back here quickly. Kyl, you know where the rockets go, and I'm counting on you." As he speaks, Dorrin mounts, looking at Liedral, whose eyes seem red-rimmed. He reaches across the gap between horses and squeezes her hand, but loses touch as she turns the brown and starts back uphill.

There is no hitching post outside the small dwelling, and Dorrin ties Basla to the timber supporting the railing on the left side of the porch steps. Liedral ties her mount to the right side.

Merga is in the small kitchen, and two large pots on the small square stove—Yarrl's doing—contain boiling water. On the cutting table is a jar of astra.

Dorrin stops and pours astra into a bowl. "Merga, would you crush this as fine as you can? Use a clean spoon or something."

"Yes, ser."

Dorrin follows Liedral to the bedroom.

"Oh . . . oooohhh . . ." Kadara's moans are low, almost wrenching.

Rylla looks up. "Be back in just an instant, love."

She motions to Liedral, who slips onto the stool beside the laboring mother.

"I'll stay with you," Liedral promises.

Rylla shuts the bedroom door, and edges down the hall. "I can tell . . . the baby's too big, and the cord's not right."

"You want me to see what I can do?"

"O' course I'd be sending for you just to watch, wouldn't I?"

"You're as crabby as ever." Dorrin's quick smile fades as he opens the door and edges next to the bed.

" . . . that you, Brede?"

"It's Dorrin. I just want to help." His fingers rest ever so lightly on her tightening abdomen, and he waits for the contraction to pass.

"Dorrin . . . it hurts . . . hurts more than Kleth . . . Darkness . . . it hurts . . ."

Rylla is right. He wipes his forehead on the back of his sleeve, wishing he had more experience, or that his mother were near. Wishing will not help, and he concentrates, first on the child, and the cord that sustains him, infusing more strength, more order there, and on somehow loosening, making the birth canal that fraction wider.

Rylla nods, as if she approves. Liedral has retreated to the doorway, and Dorrin wipes the sweat off his forehead by rubbing it against his shoulder, still concentrating on sustaining the child as Kadara's contractions push him closer and closer to the world.

" . . . have to push . . . push . ." groans Kadara, red hair so damp with sweat that it is plastered against her skull like a battle helm.

"You can do it," insists Rylla. "Another push . . . now . . ."

" . . . hurts . . . have to . . . ooohhh . . ."

Dorrin shifts his position, moving toward Kadara's shoulders, his fingers still lightly upon her bare abdominal skin, somehow feeling like an intruder, even as he fights for the mother and child.

"Brede! . . . Oh . . . darkness . . . hurts . . ."

"Push again . . . now . . . dearie. Now!" Rylla insists.

Kadara grunts. Dorrin concentrates, and, in the doorway, Liedral bites her lip.

"There . . . he's coming . . . another push . . ."

Dorrin tries not to swallow at the mess and the darkish blood that arrive with the infant, instead working to stem the bits of chaos that try to gravitate toward Kadara.

The boy seems strong and healthy, even as Rylla untangles him from the cord. She shakes her head minutely, looks at the boy, and then at Dorrin. "Aye . . . he's a healthy one, Kadara. A healthy one. Now . . . push . . . push again . . ."

Kadara grunts, and Dorrin waits until she has expelled the afterbirth.

"Rylla, be very liberal with the astra and the boiled water in cleaning her up. I had Merga crush it, and it should be boiled into the water."

"Bitter stuff . . . but good against wound chaos."

"She probably ought to be washed with it every day until she heals."

The old healer nods.

Dorrin eases away from Kadara, his fingers touching her forehead before he goes. "You need to rest . . ."

"You were here . . . for Brede . . . this time." Kadara's eyes droop, but from tiredness. She struggles to keep them open, looking at the reddish-pink child at her breast. " . . . harder than Kleth . . . He's beautiful . . ."

Liedral smiles from the doorway, waiting.

As Kadara slips toward sleep, Dorrin touches her arm again, trying to infuse her exhausted form with a touch more strength, a touch more order.

Rylla looks at him. "She'll be fine now. You need to be seeing to your ship."

The *Black Hammer*—Dorrin nods and steps away.

"Darkness . . . with . . . you . . ." whispers Kadara.

Dorrin looks back from the doorway, but Kadara is asleep. He walks slowly to the front porch, Liedral beside him, and they step into the cold bright day. Below, the *Black Hammer* waits, a thin line of steam rising from the funnel into the clear winter sky.

Liedral turns and takes his hands. "Thank you."

"For what?"

"For waiting, for putting life above destruction, for just being you." She puts her arms around him and brings their lips together. "And for last night." Her eyes are still red.

"You're worried."

She nods. "Kadara was right. We don't have forever. Lers—"

"Lers?"

"Lers, that's what Brede asked her to call his son. Lers is all she has of him, and she loved him."

"You're afraid that will happen?"

"Dorrin . . . how many times can you go out against the Whites? And if you do come back, will you be able to see? Or think? I remember what you looked like after Kleth. Kadara doesn't, but you were in worse shape that she was in a lot of ways."

"It wasn't that bad."

"Dorrin, I love you, and I want you back. But what we want doesn't often count. Sometimes . . . when you're fighting your own demons, it's hard to realize . . ." She breaks off and clings to him. "I want something of you . . ."

He clings to her, and their tears mingle.

The low steam whistle from the *Black Hammer* echoes uphill, and Basla whinnies.

"You need to go."

The whistle sounds again, and Dorrin looks west-ward, into the Gulf, out toward the white triangles on the water that mark the White fleet.

Their lips touch, and part, before Dorrin runs from the porch, untying the reins and swinging into the black's saddle. He blots his cheeks with his sleeve as he rides downhill toward the waiting black ship, the fingers of his right hand straying to the staff, even as the twinges of the headache warn him.

CLXXXI

DORRIN PASSES A half-dozen houses in various stages of construction on the flat at the base of the hill, all of the black stone that results from ordering the softer and more brittle blue stone that underlies the dark clay. Half of the houses have dark slate roofs. He returns the wave of a stoneworker as he guides Basla onto the end of the High Road that leads to the pier. The air smells fresh, still crisp, in the bright and cool sunlight, except for the faint odor of burning coal.

To the east, he sees several sails, impossibly white against the waters of the Gulf. Then he is at the pier, where he hands the reins to one of Tyrel's assistants he has never properly met. "Please tie her in the shed."

He glances back uphill and waves, hoping Liedral is there, watching, before he turns. "How many ships are there?" he asks as he hurries up the gangway, his staff in one hand.

"Lift it!" snaps Kyl, and the line-handlers pull the railed plank away from the ship, and then hurry to the singled-up lines that hold the black warship to the pier. "More than a score, according to Selvar." Kyl frowns. "He says that it's hard to tell because about half the ships have white wizards on board, and they're using wizardry to hide themselves. If you just look with your eyes, it seems like a handful, maybe seven or eight, but they can't hide their wakes."

Dorrin hurries toward the engine compartment, where Tyrel is shoveling coal into the firebox. Beside him is Styl, watching closely.

"If you would—" begins the captain.

"Go." Dorrin studies the crude pointer indicator. "We've got enough steam to head out."

Kyl waits for Tyrel to climb up the ladder before descending. Dorrin shovels another heap of coal into the box, then motions to Styl. "Once this gets to here"—he points to the indicator—"just keep the fire where it is."

"Yes, ser. Master Tyrel and master Yarrl had me practice on the last run."

Dorrin shakes his head. Styl had been right there, and here he is repeating his own instructions.

Kyl steps onto the engine deck. "What are you going to do?"

"We're going to persuade them to go home and leave Recluce alone."

Kyl looks from Dorrin to Styl and back to the engineer. "You are serious, aren't you?"

"Yes. I'm no Creslin. And besides, it wouldn't do any good."

Kyl and Styl exchange glances, then look at Dorrin. "What wouldn't?"

"Destroying their whole fleet. Anyway, we don't have enough rockets for that." Dorrin begins turning the valves to feed the steam to the cylinders, and the sound and heat rise in the engine compartment. He continues to listen, and to adjust the flows until he feels the engine is running smoothly. Then he eases the clutch, and the shaft begins to turn, with the vibration of the water churning behind the ship rising.

Dorrin checks the firebox and throws two quick shovels inside, then closes it and hands the shovel to Styl. "Keep shoveling until the steam pressure's up. You know what to do."

"Yes, ser."

Dorrin climbs the ladder and makes his way to the pilot house, with Kyl close behind. By the time he reaches the helm, Tyrel already has the *Black Hammer* into the channel and outbound.

For a time, Dorrin watches as the *Hammer* glides through the protected waters of Reisa's extended breakwaters. The pitching begins as the ship hits the rougher waters of the Gulf.

"Where to?" asks Tyrel.

"Take us straight toward the flagship."

"Which one?"

"Sorry. See the shimmer behind the schooner with the blue banner? Head there."

Tyrel turns the wheel. "Still can't believe this. No worry about the wind. You just go where you want."

Like heavy butterflies in the wind, the White ships move with the wind, while the *Hammer*—a solid quarrel of order—plunges outward.

The schooner downwind of the flagship veers to port as the wizard on board senses the blackness of the *Hammer*.

Dorrin realizes he is holding his breath and releases it, as the *Hammer* eases alongside the big schooner bearing the name *White Serpent*.

"Ease back. Match her speed." Dorrin wipes his forehead, once, then again.

The *Serpent* begins to tack, and Dorrin nods, grinning. Tyrel grins in return as the *Hammer* follows the *Serpent* into the waves. Dorrin grasps the pilot house's inside rail. He motions to Kyl. "Light off one rocket. Aim at the bowsprit."

"Firing first rocket." Kyl drops through the hatch and down to the deckhouse where the rocket tubes are located.

The black iron missile streaks toward the *Serpent*. The flare and the explosion are almost simultaneous, and are followed by the pattering of debris on the forward shield.

The *Serpent*'s bow swings port, and the big schooner wallows as the forward jib and the forward section of the bowsprit sag into the Gulf waters.

"Circle around to the other side." Dorrin wipes his forehead. The longer before his weapons injure or kill someone, the better.

Whhhstttt . . .

A fireball streams past the black iron of the pilot house. Then a second one, and a third. Tyrel winces as the third sprays across the metal.

By now the *Serpent* lies nearly dead in the water, main sail half lowered, and fluttering in the light breeze, as several men hack at the wrecked bowsprit and sail that drag into each swell.

"Kyl, can you destroy the rudder with another rocket?"

"We can try." Kyl turns. "Fire another one. Right aft and below that poop porthole there."

Three black iron missiles later, the rudder hangs uselessly, and the *Serpent* begins to list ever so slightly to starboard.

Occasional fireballs flash past the *Hammer*, from both the *Serpent* and the surrounding ships, as the small ironclad continues to circle the larger schooner.

A seaman pants up into the pilot house. "Styl says that the shaft's running hot, Master Dorrin."

Tyrel looks from the helm to Dorrin. "Told you we'd have trouble with those bearings."

The bearings work better than grease seals, but they do not work well enough. Dorrin can only hope the shaft will last for a while. "How hot?"

"Need to shut down and grease her 'fore long, Styl says."

Dorrin looks at Reisa. "Send up the boarding crew. Tyrel, bring her around to the starboard side of the *Serpent*."

"They'll fry you, Dorrin!" protests Kyl, standing halfway up the ladder into the pilot house.

"That's what the shields are for." That's also what he is for, he thinks. "If we can't hold the deck, start firing rockets."

"The angle's lousy. We can only hit a couple of places."

"Fine. Put several large holes in the hull, right at the water line."

Dorrin grabs the staff, and nods to Reisa, who stands below in the space below the ladder to the main deck. The ten men and women in black, with the black blades and matching shields, wait behind the hatch door.

"We're right opposite her gangway point."

"Go ahead and grapple."

The hooks go out, cast from beneath the turtleshells on the *Hammer*'s deck. Dorrin watches as the forward grapple bounces off twice. The third cast is successful, and the *Serpent* and the *Hammer* are locked together with the rope/chains that cannot be burned.

"You take care of the shaft, Tyrel, and we'll take care of the wizard. Bowmen!"

The iron shutters on the side of the pilot house roll open half a cubit in three places. Behind each opening stands an archer, each with a quiver of black iron and lorkin arrows.

The shafts immediately clear the deck area opposite the *Hammer*.

"Boarders away!"

Quenta swarms up and onto the *Serpent*'s deck, swinging his shield forward as he bounces over the railing. The first fireball sprays around him, followed by several arrows.

"Archers! The poop deck!"

The black arrows fly aft, and the white arrows cease.

Reisa, Petra, and two others reach the deck, and Dorrin scrambles up. Even before he is steady on the white oak planks, Quenta and another black trooper lock shields before him.

Dorrin probes, his senses out, for the feeling of concentrated chaos, his staff automatically pointing toward the higher poop deck.

"Get the Black bastards!" Nearly a score of White armed men charge from the forecastle toward the handful of Blacks.

The black arrows drop five before the defenders reach Dorrin's party.

Dorrin's staff drops another, and the black blades begin their work.

"Aeeeiii . . ." One White guard's arm flames from the bite of Reisa's blade.

Two firebolts flash toward the Black forces, but Dorrin turns his staff and thoughts, and they flare harmlessly onto the deck as the infighting intensifies.

Quenta slashes and drops one White guard, but loses his blade as the white sword of a third man slices his biceps. He swings the shield on his left arm to block the next slash.

Petra's blade drops that White guard, and Dorrin steps farther left, using the staff to disarm and drop another guard. He ignores the twinges beyond his eyes.

A screaming black arrow knocks down yet another attacker.

Out of the corner of his eye, Dorrin can sense a black figure—and another—go down before the

Whites are felled or have thrown down their blades, the second falling as fire blazes past his ear. He lifts his staff and deflects another fireball, and a third, searching for the White Wizard. Dorrin finds the man in white standing to the left edge of the poop deck, shielded by the overhang from the archers on board the *Hammer*.

The three remaining White crewmen hold their hands up. One White archer lies propped against the port railing of the *Serpent*, his body almost level with Dorrin's eyes because of the schooner's list.

Dorrin steps toward the wizard.

Another fireball flies toward the engineer, but he lifts the staff and the heat flares away from him as he takes another step aft.

"Stop, you Black worm. I'll destroy the entire ship."

Dorrin takes another step and stops. "Why?" He casts his senses out, circling the white flame that is the chaos wizard, a man with a square beard.

"Why not? You're out to destroy me."

"You're not exactly here on a mission of peacefulness," Dorrin points out, strengthening the wall of order around the wizard.

"What are you—" Before the wizard finishes his sentence, another fireball flares toward Dorrin, who lifts the black staff and lets it absorb the energy.

A second fireball flashes, and a third. The third is far weaker, and dies even before it can reach the staff

Dorrin walks steadily across the planks toward the bearded figure in the white cloak.

A bit of flame erupts from the wizard's fingers, then dies.

Dorrin extends the staff, almost gently, cracking the wizard, now aged and creaking, across the wrists, and then the neck. A dead body pitches headfirst onto the deck.

Dorrin turns.

The White crewmen all kneel, as if in reverence, pleading. Dorrin ignores them, instead dropping to the prone figure on the deck and rolling her gently over. His fingers feel clumsy as he fumbles out the dressings and the powdered astra from the pouch at his belt, as he simultaneously tries to hold order within Petra's wiry body.

The thrust is deep, but her heart and lungs are safe, and he can use order to bind the slash together, thank darkness, once he spreads the powdered astra into the wound, although the pool of blood on the white deck tells the real danger. Dorrin's eyes burn as he works, Reisa standing over him like a one-armed avenging angel.

Finally, he straightens up, and nods to Reisa. "We'll need something stiff to carry her on."

"How . . . will she . . ." Reisa's voice is like frozen iron, blocking all feeling.

"She's lost a lot of blood, but I think I stopped it in time."

Styl vaults over the side of the white ship, carrying a canvas stretcher one-handed as if it were a toy, and Dorrin looks at the young man, at the rage and the tears, and then at Reisa, realizing that, once again, he has been so tied up in his own world that he has not seen the loves and pain of others.

"She be all right . . . master Dorrin?"

Dorrin eases Petra onto the stretcher. "I hope so . . ."

"White bastards . . ."

They carry the injured woman back to the *Black Hammer*, though it takes four of Reisa's troopers, including Quenta, to ease the stretcher between the grappled ships.

Dorrin slowly reenters the deckhouse and climbs to the pilot house.

"Hadn't you better take care of that shoulder?" Tyrel asks.

Dorrin looks stupidly at the gash in his shoulder, its throbbing lost in the anguish of Petra and Reisa, and his own headache. "Oh . . ." He uses the last of the astra, and Tyrel helps him bind it.

"The shaft fixed?"

"For a time. You need to figure out something better, though."

Dorrin sighs. He is always trying to figure out something better. Cast off."

Tyrel raises his eyebrows. "Release grapples."

When the *Hammer* stands well clear of the *Serpent*, Kyl turns to Dorrin. "Do you want us to fire her?"

"No. Not unless we have to."

Dorrin turns his attention to the remainder of the fleet. More than ten ships have already turned back westward, their sails tiny white triangles upon the horizon.

Another handful, each bearing a wizard, circles just beyond the *Hammer* and the *Serpent*.

"Head for that one." Dorrin jabs at the largest, a bark with a high freeboard.

Once again, the fireballs splash off the black iron as the *Hammer* plows toward the bark, disregarding the wind.

"Run up a parley flag."

The white banner with the blue stripe flutters upon a short jackstaff aft of the pilot house. Shortly, a similar banner flies from the bark bearing the nameplate *White-fire*.

When the *Hammer* is abeam the bark, Dorrin opens one of the iron shutters and calls out to the man at the railing. "I'd like you to take a message back to the High Wizard." Dorrin manages a half-bow, one hand on the iron shutter.

The captain yells back, between the hissing of swells

and spray. "That's not for me to say, Master. I can only ask the White one."

"I know that." Dorrin nods, and drops a waxed pouch containing a heavy parchment and a brief message, the first of three Dorrin had Liedral prepare almost an eight-day earlier, into a basket. The young seaman attaches the basket to a long-handled pole and extends it across the gap between the ships until an equally young seaman on the bark can take the pouch. The dark pouch is passed to the ship's captain and then carried aft.

"Stand off, or whatever you call it," Dorrin orders.

The wizard on the *Whitefire* has only one response to the request—another barrage of fireballs.

"Idiots!" snaps Dorrin, turning to Kyl.

"A set of the nasty ones?" asks his brother.

Dorrin nods, and winces at the headache that strikes behind his eyes.

"Fire rockets."

Five rockets depart the *Hammer*, each landing with a gout of flame upon the wooden-hulled *Whitefire*, a flame that clings and spreads until the Fairhaven ship is a torch upon the water.

Shortly, the *Hammer* chugs up beside a third Fairhaven ship to pass across another pouch.

Dorrin closes his eyes, not that it matters, because, between the blindness and the headache, he can no longer see.

This time, when the *Hammer* stands off to wait for the response, there are no fireballs, only a double dip of the parley flag.

Kyl puts the second pouch in the basket for the master of the *Pride of the Easthorns*. The master even leaves the parley flag in place as his ship heels and turns westward. The other three ships carrying wizards follow.

Dorrin wipes his forehead and turns in Tyrel's

general direction. "Let's head back. No sense in wasting coal."

"I think we have enough to spare." Tyrel laughs.

"I wish you'd burned them all." Reisa stands at his elbow, and her low voice blazes.

"It won't heal Petra."

"I know. And it was her choice. But I still hate the bastards."

"And I ... I do like seeing..." Dorrin's shoulders sag. He should be strong, like Creslin, and to light with the consequences, but he enjoys looking at Liedral, at the sea. Even now, he worries whether, this time, his sight will return. The pounding in his skull is not so pronounced as when he destroyed the Gallosian levies outside Kleth, but it seems that each use of order for destruction requires less impact to create head-wrenching pain and blindness—blindness that has been temporary so far.

"I know." Reisa touches his shoulder, and he can feel her pain, the sources past and distant, and present and near. "Letting them make their own choices and knowing they did doesn't always help. Someday, you'll understand that better."

Dorrin already understands that. How many have suffered so far for his dreams? He does not remind Reisa of that. Instead, he says, "The world, and the Balance, don't care much for what we feel. That doesn't mean I don't feel."

Reisa drops her hand. "That's why you're a great wizard ... and why so many will offer themselves up for you. Somehow, along the way, you learned to keep your feelings and your dreams without betraying either." Reisa slips away and down the ladder to check on Petra once again. Dorrin grasps the railing to balance himself against the rolling as Tyrel brings the *Hammer* about on the last course line into harbor.

"What now, Master Dorrin?" asks the captain conversationally.

"We build a better version of the *Hammer*. And a Black city. What else?"

"Darkness help us if'n you'd been White," mumbles the captain.

Dorrin turns his sightless eyes eastward toward the hillside above Nylan, wondering how Liedral is, and whether he should have allowed her to come.

CLXXXII

DORRIN PAUSES AT the door, then knocks. Beside him, Liedral is silent.

"Master Dorrin, come in." Rylla stands back from the doorway.

"I just wanted to see how Kadara and Lers were. I had to leave in a bit of a hurry."

"I know. Rushing off to teach those Whites a lesson. We saw it all from the porch—the ship you fired, and the rest of them scuttling away across the Gulf."

"Even Kadara?" asks Liedral.

"I wouldn't let her. But she must have made me tell her three times what happened."

Dorrin rubs his forehead and gingerly feels his way into the house. He can sense Rylla's hand going to her mouth. "You're not . . ."

"Hush . . . not a word," he says. "Not a word." His fingers lightly hold Liedral's hand as she guides him to the bedroom. He stands just inside the door.

Kadara lies in the bed with her sleeping son cradled next to her. "Rylla told me Lers wouldn't have lived if you hadn't been here . . . and that you risked losing the battle to save him."

Dorrin drops his head. "I can't say that. We had time."

"You have to be honest, don't you? No matter what it costs?"

"Yes. Mostly, at least."

"I suppose that's why you have to calculate every-thing—probably even ... never mind. I know you don't, but still ... it's hard."

Sensing her anger and the deep and endless pain, Dorrin touches her shoulder. "The Balance, and the world, don't care much for what we feel. But I still feel, and it still hurts."

Kadara's fingers curl gently around the infant. "That's why you're a great one ... and why Brede is dead, and why everyone looks up to you. You can hold on to order without losing your feelings."

"You give me too much credit. I just ... tried to do ... what I had to." Dorrin's head continues to throb, and his knees feel weak.

"You're tired, aren't you?" Kadara asks.

"Yes."

"So am I. Take him home, Liedral. And ... Dorrin ..."

Dorrin looks toward her, sightlessly.

" ... thank you for my son. Brede would thank you too ... and I hope it won't be too long before you can see again."

Dorrin can't help grinning.

" ... can't fool me ... Take him home and make him sleep, Liedral."

"Get well, Kadara," answers the engineer gruffly as he leaves.

Liedral edges him into the hallway. They step onto the front porch, and she says, "You've given too many people too much. Kadara was right. You need some rest."

"What about you?"

Liedral laughs, a sound that is edgy, bell-like, and happy, all in one. "I have you . . . and more. I was more fortunate than Kadara. I think we'll have a daughter."

"How do you know? I can't even tell."

"It doesn't matter. We will have a daughter." She kisses him full upon the lips, warmly and without reservation. "We need to get you fed and rested. You really shouldn't have stopped to see Kadara."

"I had to."

"I know."

The late afternoon wind whips around them with a chill that borders on frost. They have covered perhaps two hundred cubits toward their home when Liedral takes a deep breath. "Oh, darkness!"

Dorrin can sense just that, although he still can see nothing except occasional white flares of light. "What is it?"

"Your damned father! He can't even let you rest."

Dorrin gathers himself together. "Let's get on with it."

They walk through the shadows Dorrin cannot see and into the house.

"The Black wizard is in the kitchen," Frisa announces. "He says he's your father. Is he? I didn't know your father was a big wizard."

"He's my father." Dorrin walks into the kitchen.

Before he can speak, Liedral steps almost in front of him. "Merga, get something hot, and some bread and cheese for Dorrin before he collapses. Dorrin, you sit down now. Right here." She pulls out the chair at the end of the table and guides him into it.

"Would you rather I come back?" Oran says mildly.

"No. I just need something to eat. It's been quite a day."

"Here's the bread, ser."

Dorrin manages to break off a corner and begins to chew.

Liedral, sitting on the end of the bench to his left, uses the cheese slicer on the yellow brick cheese, then hands Dorrin a slab. Only then does she turn to Oran. "Would you like some?"

"No . . . that's fine."

After he has chewed and swallowed the first chunk of bread and cheese, and sipped some hot cider, Dorrin can feel the shakiness in his knees begin to subside, and the throbbing in his head decreases. He rubs his forehead. "Why did you come?"

"To see how you would handle the Whites, and then to talk to you. Your ship was very effective, it seems."

Dorrin raises his head, still letting the warm vapor from the mug seep around his face. "That's true. Tyrel really didn't need me. He and Kyl could have burned every ship in the Fairhaven fleet." A sharpening of the throbbing in his head causes him to revise his statement. "Not at once. They would have needed to return for more rockets. But I'd guess around ten ships like the *Black Hammer* will be more than adequate to ensure that no one ever restricts trade with us again."

"Why can't they build ships like that?"

"Because you need black iron, and they can't handle order. It takes order-hardened iron to make the shields and the rockets. You put powder in anything but black iron, and any chaos wizard can touch it off." Dorrin shrugs. "I suspect that the Nordlans and Hamorians will be able to put lower-pressure steam engines on their sailing ships. In fact, I'll even give them the design."

"What?"

"We'll trade for the design. We'll still need more trade with the eastern continents. Liedral's working up what we need."

"Is that wise?"

"Why not? I doubt that we could keep it a secret for long. Why not take credit for it? They'll have to use regular iron, and with the chaos of the heat, it's really not suited for anything but ocean ships at low pressure. A good schooner could still sail rings around them, but the engines would be handy for calms and getting in and out of ports."

"Are you sure?"

Dorrin sighs, not caring if his father hears the exasperation. "I tried not using black iron. You can't get enough containment and pressure for a high-power engine—at least I can't—without a lot of black iron. If you use a lot of regular iron, the engine gets too heavy, and it doesn't generate much power. If it's light enough to get the power, it's only a couple of days before things start cracking and breaking. Maybe on some other world—or the planets of the Angels—but not here, not with the force of chaos and the Balance."

"Why did you let most of the Fairhaven fleet return home?"

"You should have figured that out. If I destroyed half a dozen chaos wizards at once, the Balance would want to concentrate that chaos in one focus. Candar doesn't need another Jeslek. Besides, sending them back to Candar is bound to disorganize chaos there even more." Dorrin laughs. "Disorganized chaos— what an absurdity."

"You've made everything a matter of calculations and numbers, haven't you? There's no art . . ."

"There never was," Dorrin snaps. "The Balance is mathematical in nature, not some god of the ancient Angels. That's why you'll still win."

For the first time, Oran is silent, and Dorrin can feel the confusion.

"Look . . . Every bit of order that's placed in black iron, every bit of order concentrated in a steam-powered ship or a black iron rocket means that there has to be an equal amount of chaos somewhere. Chaos can be concentrated through wizardry. Generally, order can't except through machines and black iron. No matter what I feel, Recluce can't afford order machines—only those necessary for her defense. Building machines into every hamlet in Recluce would only guarantee greater chaos in Fairhaven, perhaps enough to raise hundreds of Jesleks."

"What . . . how can . . ."

"The Black Order of Engineers stays in the Black City of Nylan. You and the Brotherhood just keep doing what you're doing. Except . . ." Dorrin pauses. "Anyone who wants to come to Nylan and whom we accept can stay."

Oran looks at the floor, the smooth-planked, evenly matched, near-perfect flooring. Then he focuses on the red-headed engineer at the other end of the table. "How will you do that?"

"A wall should do the trick. The symbolism is what will make it effective. But a tall wall of ordered black stone separating the peninsula and Nylan from the rest of Recluce will make it real enough for most, and for those who don't accept it . . . well, Nylan is where they belong . . . or Candar."

"So you'll just take all the rebels?"

"I'm not a Temple priest." Dorrin snorts. "You made a simple mistake, my dear father. You never understood the difference between rebelling against something and wanting to create something. Even so, you were right."

Oran waits.

"Steel and ideas have to be tempered and quenched." Dorrin shrugs. "Why should I change what works?"

Oran clears his throat. "You know, son, you're a bigger man than I ever was."

"Nonsense." Dorrin flushes. "I just did what had to be done."

Oran nods. "How did you know just what had to be

done? How many people know what has to be done and still don't act?" The tall wizard steps forward and around the table, setting his hands on the shoulders of the shorter engineer for a moment before releasing his son.

Dorrin's eyes burn, and he cannot speak, not just because of his father's approval, but because of all those others who have helped pay the price, and who will continue to pay—like Kadara, and Petra, and Quenta, and the dead Black trooper whose name he does not even know.

"Your lady trader is right, son. You are one of the great ones, even though no one will ever list your name with Ryba's or even with Creslin's or Megaera's. In that, I suspect, you are most fortunate."

Liedral, who has remained silent, takes Dorrin's left hand, squeezes it. "A live engineer is more fortunate than a dead hero."

Dorrin squeezes her hand in return as his father, the tall black wizard, bows deeply. "You need rest, I think. But come to see us when you can. You are welcome anywhere on Recluce. The Council would have decided that without me, but I'm glad I can agree with them." His narrow face breaks into a smile as his hand sweeps around the room. "But we all know this is your home. You are, after all, the magic engineer." Then he bows and is gone.

"It is home, isn't it?" Dorrin swallows.

Liedral squeezes his hand and lets go. "You knew that a long time ago." She grins at him. "You magic engineer."

CLXXXIII

THE SWIRLS IN the mirror depict perhaps a dozen ships bearing the red thunderbolt banner straggling back into the Great North Bay. Cerryl raises a finger, and the image vanishes from the mirror. "Now what?"

"You send out another fleet, this time one that will follow orders," Anya says lazily from the reclining chair. Her eyes focus on the high gray clouds visible through the tower window slit beyond the table. On one side of the table sits a deep basin of cold water.

"Sterol was right," Cerryl adds, his voice conversational as he looks at the box on the small table, a box containing a gold-painted amulet.

"Don't tell me you're going to let that nobody on Recluce humiliate us?" Anya's voice takes a harder tone.

"There is a Balance, and we can accept it, or fight it. Everyone who has fought it has lost. The trick is to make it work for you."

"You sound like you're weaseling out, Cerryl. We can't have that." Anya sits up straight in the chair, but does not rise to her feet.

"Why don't you listen, for a moment? It won't hurt."

"I'm listening." The words are cold, yet white flames lurk beneath her eyes.

"This smith-wizard builds machines. Those machines must contain chaos-fired steam or water. That means they embody great, great order. If he builds many of his machines, he increases the amount of chaos in the world. That would increase our power more greatly than his, because his order would be locked in those machines."

"So you would encourage him to build those machines? To attack and destroy our ships? That would certainly increase chaos. How much good it would do us is another question." Anya rises like a pillar of white flame.

"He won't do that." Cerryl gestures at the now-blank mirror. "He could have destroyed the entire fleet with his little black ship. He didn't. He's certainly no weak-willed Black idiot either. Weak-willed idiots don't fight head-on. He destroyed Jeslek and Fydel one on one—Fydel with a staff, not even that ironclad chaos of his." He steps over to the larger dining table and slips off the amulet he wears, setting it on the table, his back to Anya. He opens the box and removes the painted amulet, concealing a wince as the metal burns his hands. "Besides, you saw his ship. Even if we could board it, what could anyone do? Our White Guards couldn't even touch half of it with all that black iron."

Anya steps toward Cerryl's back. "It's too bad you'll follow Sterol, Cerryl dear."

"I don't think so." Cerryl lifts the amulet and turns. "But, here, you wear it. You always wanted to." With a quick gesture, he drops the gold-painted iron links around her neck.

Anya lifts her hands, then screams as a circle of flame burns away the gold paint and the white cloth beneath it. Her hands reach for the hot iron, but Cerryl grasps her wrists and nods toward the door.

"I'm not quite as dense as I look, dear Anya. And while I'm not as powerful as you, or Sterol, I do occasionally think."

The three guards who hurry across the white stone floor bear chains of heavy and cold iron.

"You need me!" the redhead screams as the additional heavy iron chains slip around her.

"Indeed we do. You will make a perfect example

for future would-be schemers. You will look ravishing once your image is captured for display. Most fetching." Cerryl smiles and inclines his head to the guards. "Good day, Anya." He plunges his hands into the basin of cold water, taking a deep breath as the water cools his burns.

CLXXXIV

LIEDRAL UNWINDS THE black string, letting it drop on the light-green grass of early spring. Dorrin follows with the heavy stakes and the black steel hammer. With short strokes, he pounds in each stake and fastens the string.

In time, they reach the dusty stone road in the middle of the peninsula. Dorrin hammers in another stake on the eastern side of the road, then takes his belt knife and cuts the string, tying it tightly to the stake. After crossing the road he pounds in another stake and ties the string to it. They proceed westward until they stand on the rocky headland overlooking the western shore. Dorrin hammers in a last stake and turns to watch the dark green of the Gulf waters, to drink in the whitecaps that break on the gray stones below.

Liedral stands beside him. After a time, his arm goes around her broad shoulders, and he squeezes.

"Will the string be enough?" She removes the broad-brimmed hat and brushes back the light brown hair.

"It's only a symbol. That's where the wall goes that we promised the Council. All our people will live on our side, except for trade or visits to family—and all machines, ships, and the artifacts Oran has worried about for so long will stay behind the walls. Nylan, the Black City of the order-smiths."

"I prefer the magic engineers." She shakes her head. "I know, I know. We don't want to say much about the deplorable machines. You've said enough about that."

"It's not because the Council deplores them. I agree with them, because too much order in machines can only lead to greater chaos."

"You think it will?"

"With people like us in the world?" Dorrin grins. "Of course. But not for a long time. Then it will be someone else's problem." He kisses her cheek. "In the meantime, we'll look for other problems."

"Problems?" asks Liedral putting her arms around his neck.

"Problems," he answers before her lips cover his, as the gentle rounding swell of her body against his defines the next problem.

THE ORDER WAR

L.E. Modesitt, Jr.

The magnificent fourth novel in the saga of Recluce

The deadly White Wizards of Fairhaven, wielding the
forces of chaos, have completed their great highway
through the Westhorns and now threaten the ancient
matriarchy of Sarronnyn, the last bastion of order
in Candar. The ruler of Sarronnyn appeals to
the Black order wizards of Recluce for help.

Justen - a young Black Engineer in the city of
Nylan - joins the relief force. Despite their success
in destroying more than half the White armies,
Sarronnyn falls to the White Wizards, and Justen
is chased into the most inhospitable desert in
Candar. These trials are but the beginning, for
the White Wizards have all Candar in their grasp.
Justen must fight both Recluce and Fairhaven, as well
as use the highest powers of order and forbidden
technology to harness chaos itself, in his efforts
to halt the conquest of the chaos wizards.

AN ORBIT BOOK
FANTASY

MAIL ORDER - BOOKS BY POST

All Orbit books are available through mail order or from your local bookshop or newsagent.

☐	The Magic of Recluce	L.E. Modesitt, Jr.	£5.99
☐	The Towers of the Sunset	L.E. Modesitt, Jr.	£5.99
☐	The Order War	L.E. Modesitt, Jr.	£15.99
☐	The Eye of the World	Robert Jordan	£5.99
☐	The Great Hunt	Robert Jordan	£5.99
☐	The Dragon Reborn	Robert Jordan	£5.99
☐	The Shadow Rising	Robert Jordan	£5.99
☐	The Fires of Heaven	Robert Jordan	£5.99
☐	Lord of Chaos	Robert Jordan	£6.99

Please send cheque, eurocheque, or postal order (sterling only), or complete details for Access/Visa/Mastercard:

☐☐☐☐☐☐☐☐☐☐☐☐☐☐☐☐☐☐

Expiry Date: _____ Signature: _____
UK Customers: Add £0.75 per book for post and packing.
Overseas Customers: Add £1.00 per book for post and packing.

All orders to:
Little, Brown
Special Sales Department
Brettenham House
Lancaster Place
London WC2E 7EN

ORBIT

or fax 0171 911 8100

Name: _____
Address: _____
_____
_____

Please allow 28 days for delivery.
Prices and availability are subject to change without notice.
Please tick box if you do not wish to receive any
additional information.   ☐